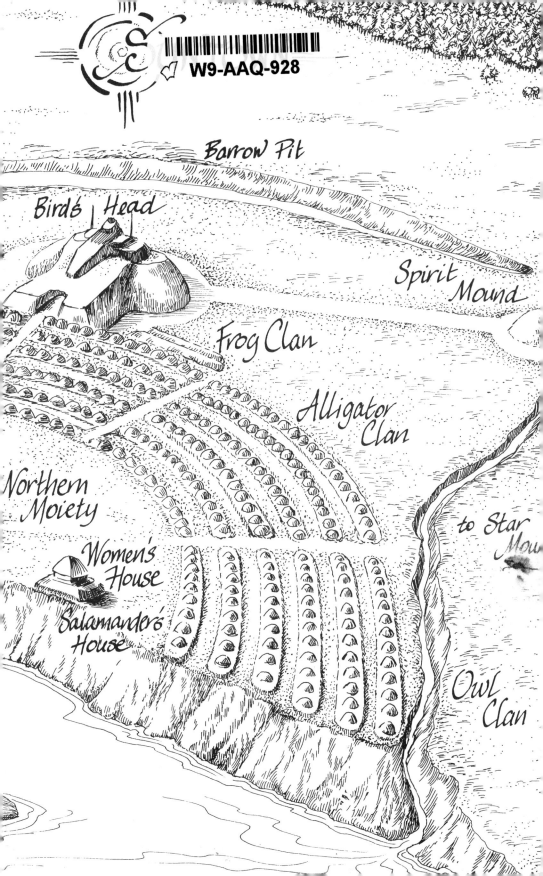

Barrow Pit

Bird's Head

Spirit Mound

Frog Clan

Alligator Clan

Northern Moiety

to Star Mou

Women's House

Salamander's House

Owl Clan

People
of the Owl

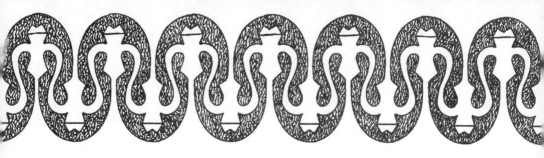

People
of the Owl

A Novel of Prehistoric North America

Kathleen O'Neal Gear
and
W. Michael Gear

A Tom Doherty Associates Book
New York

F
GEA

This is a work of fiction. All the characters and events portrayed in this novel are either fictitious or are used fictitiously.

PEOPLE OF THE OWL

Copyright © 2003 by Kathleen O'Neal Gear and W. Michael Gear

This book is printed on acid-free paper.

Book design by Michael Collica

Maps by Ellisa Mitchell

A Forge Book
Published by Tom Doherty Associates, LLC
175 Fifth Avenue
New York, NY 10010

www.tor.com

Forge® is a registered trademark of Tom Doherty Associates, LLC.

Library of Congress Cataloging-in-Publication Data

Gear, Kathleen O'Neal.
    People of the owl : a novel of prehistoric North America / Kathleen O'Neal Gear and W. Michael Gear.—1st ed.
        p.   cm.—(The first North Americans series)
    "A Tom Doherty Associates book."
    ISBN 0-312-87741-2 (acid-free paper)
    1. Indians of North America—Fiction.   2. Poverty Point culture—Fiction. 3. Prehistoric peoples—Fiction.   4. North America—Fiction.   5. Shamans—Fiction.   I. Gear, W. Michael.   II. Title.

PS3557.E18P485 2003
813'.54—dc21

                                                                    2003040019

First Edition: June 2003

Printed in the United States of America

0   9   8   7   6   5   4   3   2   1

To

Tom Espenschied, Ellen Pyle, Bob Williams,
Larry Yoder, Nancy Lindbloom,
Ev Ferris, Rebecca Wik,
Mark Janus,
and Bill Farriker

With deep appreciation for your work
on our behalf through the years

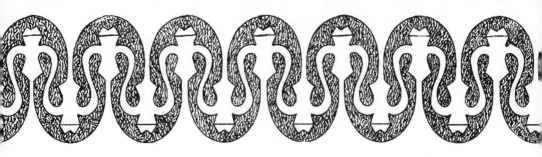

Acknowledgments

This book was inspired by Dennis Labatt during our visits to the Poverty Point site. Every North American archaeological site should have such a dedicated and enthusiastic supervisor. We would like to thank Robert Connolly, Lisa Wright, Linda York, and Kay Corley for their assistance during our visits and for their cooperation in providing Poverty Point Objects (cooking clays) for our ongoing research in prehistoric starch, phytolith, and pollen analysis at Poverty Point.

We would especially like to acknowledge the work of Dr. Jon L. Gibson, who has dedicated so much of his life to the interpretation of Poverty Point's archaeology.

Once more we would like to thank our longtime friend and colleague, Dr. Linda Scott Cummings, for her endless enthusiasm and pioneering ethnobotanical research. Working with us, she has recovered the first starches, pollens, and phytoliths from Poverty Point cooking clays. Now, when we say they were cooking foods like yellow lotus and little barley in the earth ovens, we can prove it. Thanks, Linda.

Special thanks to Barbara and Anders Lock of Viking Technology for their hard work maintaining our website at www.gear-gear.com.

Finally, the Holiday Inn of the Waters in Thermopolis, Wyoming, still makes the best buffalo jalapeno cheeseburger in the world. We thank them for maintaining our "office away from the office."

Land of the
Wolf People

Great East River

NORTH

Father Water

Wash'ta
People

Yellow Mud
Camp

Suntown

Ground Cherry
Camp
Diving Eagle
Lake
Panther's
Bones

Twin Circle
Camp

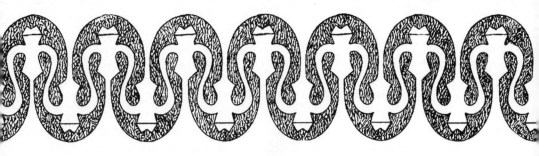

Nonfiction Foreword

Ask any American to name the oldest city in the United States and he might tell you St. Augustine, Florida (A.D. 1565). Among an enlightened few, the name Old Oraibi (A.D. 1240), in the Hopi Mesas, might pop up. But, with apologies to both of these places, we wish to point out that North America's oldest city was not located in Florida—or even in the Southwest—nor was it built around St. Louis, or in the fertile valleys of Ohio. Rather, to find it, you must journey to northeastern Louisiana, just outside of the small town of Epps. There, under the superb management of the state of Louisiana, you can still walk the stunning earthworks of Poverty Point, North America's first true city.

While earthen mound construction begins over six thousand years ago in North America, Poverty Point was inhabited between 3,750 and 3,350 years before present. From radiocarbon dates, most of Poverty Point's incredible earthworks were created during the last century of occupation. At its height, a permanent population of several thousand people lived on Poverty Point's curving ridges. They traded for goods as far north as Wisconsin and Ohio. Materials were imported to Poverty Point across nearly fifteen hundred miles of Archaic wilderness.

The site itself is huge. From Lower Jackson Mound on the south to Motley Mound on the north is a little over five miles. The main earthworks cover more than four hundred acres and may contain as much as *one million cubic yards* of earth that was dug out of the ground and packed on human backs to build this leviathan. In sheer size it would remain unmatched for another fifteen hundred years.

We agree with Jon Gibson that Poverty Point is a grand-scale projection of the human mind onto the landscape. Its form was not accidental or random, but a reflection of a shared vision of their physical as well as spiritual world, their kinship systems, and creation mythology.

A note on kinship: Non-Western societies organize their social structure in many different ways. What we see reflected in Poverty Point's architecture suggests two moieties, or social divisions, that contain three clans each. We have utilized a matrilineal matrilocal kinship system since that was present throughout the south.

Our reconstruction of prehistoric cosmology in *People of the Owl* must remain tentative; but we have looked for constants in South and Central Eastern Woodland mythology and oral tradition. We discarded elements that reflect later Mississippian (*People of the River*) agricultural traits. What is left is a shared tripartite belief in the surface of the earth, the sky above, and the underworld.

We have used real places as a setting for the story. Poverty Point is Sun Town. The Panther's Bones is set at the Caney Mounds (16CT5) in Catahoula County. When Saw Back is exiled, it is to the Jaketown site in Mississippi. Twin Circles references the Clairborne Site near the mouth of the Pearl River in southern Mississippi. While we did not extensively explore distant Poverty Point settlements in *People of the Owl*, sites containing Poverty Point's distinctive artifacts have been found as far away as the Florida Gulf Coast.

So, what explains this spectacular thirty-five-hundred-year-old cultural florescence? These people were hunter-gatherers. Intensive corn agriculture wouldn't catch on for another two thousand years. The answer seems to lie in the richness of the Lower Mississippi Valley and its yearly floods. The people at Poverty Point ate everything that walked, crawled, swam, burrowed, and grew in their benevolent food-rich environment. In short, the Lower Mississippi Valley provided the surplus in resources that allowed remarkable cultural achievements.

In coming years, we hope to learn a great deal more. As of this writing, one-half of one percent of the site has been excavated. In our own research with Linda Scott Cummings on Poverty Point Objects—PPOs—or cooking clays, we have recovered the first starches, phytoliths, and pollen residue from the food they cooked in their earth ovens thirty-five hundred years ago. As more research is tackled, our view of this complex site is going to change substantially. It will be important research. We believe that Poverty Point was to North America what the Fertile Crescent was to Europe: *the place that generated and disseminated cultural concepts that would influence subsequent cultures across the eastern woodlands.*

Information on the site is as close as your computer: poverty-point@crt.la.us. Jon Gibson's excellent read, *The Ancient Mounds of Poverty Point,* is available from University Press of Florida. For an overview of the whole of North American archaeology, we recommend Brian Fagan's *Ancient North America* published by Thames and Hudson. At the end of *People of the Owl* you will find a selected bibliography. Finally, we urge you to visit the Poverty Point State Commemorative Area in person. Until you experience the wonder of it yourself, you will never fully understand the magic.

People
of the Owl

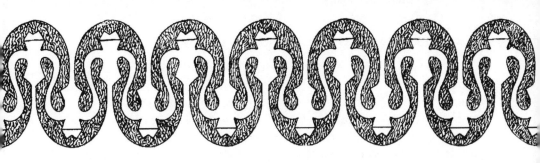

Preface

Arnold Beauregard liked to think of himself as a modern-day cowboy. His family had first come to Louisiana in the 1720s. To this day his mother insisted to anyone who would listen that, yes, Beauregard was French, but that their ancestry was Creole. True French aristocracy rather than that Johnny-come-lately Cajun riffraff that had begun trickling into Louisiana in the 1760s.

Fact was, the clinging fingers of the past still pulled at old Louisiana families. But for Arnold, the lure was the Old West, not antebellum plantation life. In his dreams he was a cattle baron, not a cotton king.

The SUV, a Toyota Land Cruiser, could be seen waiting just past the gate as he turned into the farm lane off Route 577. He pulled up and stopped his brand-new white Chevy one-ton duly behind the Toyota before shutting off its big diesel engine.

Picking up his cell, he punched the office number and, at the secretary's voice, said, "Julie, I'm at the Hoferberg place. Those archaeologists are already here. I'll have my cell on if anything comes up."

A genuine straw Stetson was perched atop his black crew cut. The left breast pocket of his Wrangler snap shirt outlined an obligatory can of Copenhagen. A tooled-leather belt snugged his waist while six-hundred-buck Lucchese razor-tips peeked out from under his creased boot-cut jeans.

Yep. One hundred percent cowboy.

The irony, of course, was that his business was farming, not ranching. Not the actual sweating-in-the-sun-and-driving-the-tractor kind of farming, mind you, but administration.

He stepped out of the Chevy and walked toward the people climbing out of the Toyota. His first thought was to glance at his watch. If this didn't take too long, he could check on fertilization and field prep over at the Badger Unit this side of Alsatia and be back to Delphi in time for lunch.

"Mr. Beauregard?" A tall thin man called from the Toyota's driver's side. He wore bifocals and looked about fifty, with a neatly trimmed beard and brown cotton pants. To his right stood a blond woman, medium height, perhaps thirty, in jeans, long-sleeved shift, and hiking boots. She had a pensive expression—and eyes way too intelligent to be in a face that pretty. Next to her was a grungy-looking kid, maybe twenty-five, with long bushy brown hair pulled back in a frizzy ponytail. He had on a checked shirt, baggy cloth pants, and running shoes that had to have been stolen off a bum on Bourbon Street.

"Call me Arnold," he answered, extending a hand. "You're from the university, right?"

"Dr. Emmet Anson," the bearded man said as he shook.

"I'm Patty Umbaugh," the pretty blonde said. "I'm with the state. Department of Culture, Recreation, and Tourism."

He smiled thinly. The state? What the hell did they have to do with this?

"Rick Penzler," the longhair told him, giving him a cool, some-what arrogant look.

"My pleasure," Arnold answered evenly, turning this attention to Anson. "Dr. Anson, you asked for a meeting concerning the Hoferberg property. Said it had something to do with some dead Indians?"

Anson nodded. "That's right. A couple of years back we did some work on the mounds out back there." He pointed down past the house and barn toward the bayou. "Mrs. Hoferberg had talked about taking steps to protect and preserve the site. She had mentioned that when the time came to sell the property, that we might be able to come to some sort of agreement."

Arnold stuck his thumbs in his belt, saying, "I see." That bought him time while he considered. "Well, I don't know anything about any site here. The thing is, the bank foreclosed on the Hoferberg farm, Dr. Anson. Our dealings have all been through the bank when we acquired title to this property Any questions relating to that would have to be directed to Otis, our attorney."

"Yes, we know," Patty Umbaugh said seriously. "The reason we called this meeting was to see if we could come to some agreement—with your corporation, of course—concerning the archaeology."

Arnold gave her his winning cowboy smile. "Well, that would depend, I suppose. We'll be happy to hear what you have to say."

From the look Penzler was giving him, you would have thought Arnold had wrapped tape sticky-side-out on his fingers when the collection plate went by of a Sunday morning.

"Why don't we drive down and show you what we're talking about," Anson suggested. "It's kind of boggy down there." He glanced at the shining Chevrolet. "Want a ride?"

"This won't take long, will it?"

"Half an hour?" Anson asked, raising a hopeful eyebrow.

"Let me get my cell phone."

He stepped back to his truck, unplugged his cell, and stuffed it into his shirt pocket. By the time he walked up to the passenger door, Umbaugh and Penzler had climbed into the back. Anson was at the wheel and turned the key as Arnold slammed the passenger door.

"What do you do, Mr. Beauregard? For BARB, I mean?" Anson asked as they started down the tree-lined lane.

"I'm the operations supervisor. That means I drive from farm to farm, seeing to it that the local managers are doing their jobs and that everything is running smoothly. I act as the corporation's eyes and ears in the field. Rambling troubleshooter and problem solver." He chuckled as he pulled out his Copenhagen and took a dip. "I guess you'd say that I'm the feller that makes the machine run."

"What does BARB stand for?" Prenzler asked flatly. "What does it do?"

At the tone in Prenzler's voice, Arnold fought the urge to crane his neck and spit snoose on the kid's filthy shoes. "It's short for Brasseaux, Anderson, Roberts, and Beauregard. We're the board. We buy up bankrupt family farms in northern Louisiana and southern Arkansas, recondition the soil, and make them pay. Our equipment is stored and serviced at our shop several miles east of Monroe. In all, BARB runs more than six hundred thousand acres of agricultural property."

He smiled down, admiring his expensive boots. If truth be told, neither BARB nor Arnold even owned a cow. Still, he never missed a rodeo, and his daughter, Mindy, had a beautiful barrel horse that she kept in the stable at their elegant house north of Monroe.

"Take this place." Arnold flipped his index finger around in a circle. "We'll have a crew in here next week to take out these trees."

He waved expansively at the lines of stately oaks that shaded the lane.

"Take out the trees?" Penzler asked incredulously.

"And these buildings." Arnold nodded at the white frame house and shabby-looking barn as they drove into the yard. They stood empty now, looking forlorn. "Our crew will salvage what we can from the structures, anything we can sell for scrap. Then we'll bulldoze the rest."

"Why?" Umbaugh asked, concern in her voice. She was looking longingly at the old red barn, its huge door open to expose an empty gloom.

"Miss, uh, Patty did you say? You gotta understand. This house and barn, these trees, shucks, even this lane we're driving on, isn't in production. The margin in American agriculture is about as thin as a 'skeeter's peter. It's because in this country we have the cheapest and best food in the whole world. At the same time, urban sprawl and development is taking millions of acres a year out of production. At BARB we grow food, and we're good enough at it that we can still make money."

"Six hundred *thousand* acres?" Penzler asked hostilely as Anson passed the barn and followed a two track between two large fallow fields. A quarter mile ahead, trees rose in a gray thicket, barely starting to bud in the late-March warmth.

Arnold couldn't stand it. He turned, letting his gaze bore into the squirrelly kid's cold blue eyes. "You might ask Mrs. Hoferberg how much she made on this place these last few years. This farm has just over a thousand acres of good land under cultivation. Mrs. Hoferberg was sixth-generation—going clear back to the civil war. Hell, her great-great-great-granddad waved to U. S. god-damned Grant when he went by on his way to Vicksburg. The family farm just can't cut it in a global economy."

"So you plow it all up?" Penzler asked.

"Productivity drives the country," Anson said easily. "Myself, I'm not so sure I wouldn't rather just go back to the good old days. Fish, hunt, raise a few cows, and grow a garden. Life would be so much simpler."

"Suits me," Anson said easily as he skirted the fallow field.

"You hunt, huh?" Arnold glanced at the bookish-looking Anson.

The professor smiled. "Hey, I grew up in Melville, down on the Atchafalaya. When I wasn't running a trotline I was after ducks or rabbits with my old 20 gauge. Went to Harvard on scholarship, so I had to lose the accent."

Arnold nodded. "What got you into archaeology?"

"Hunting and fishing," Anson said with amusement. "I wanted to know how people made food before John Deere and Cargill."

Anson followed an overgrown track into the trees, dropped down through a marshy area, and up over a hump of dirt. Pulling to a stop, he looked around and shut off the engine. "This is it."

Arnold opened the door and stepped out. Overhead, branches wove a gray maze against the cloud-speckled March sky. Irregular humps in the land could be seen. It reminded him of a brown, leaf-covered golf course. "What am I supposed to be seeing here?"

Umbaugh stepped up beside him, pointing to the contours of land. "This is a Poverty Point period mound site. It dates to about thirty-five hundred years ago."

"Poverty Point?" Arnold cocked his head and spit some of the Copenhagen floaters onto the damp leaves. "Like the state park down the road a piece?"

"That's right. Have you been there? Seen the museum and earth-works?"

"Naw. I just drive through. It's old Indian stuff, isn't it? You seen one pile of dirt, you've seen them all. I mean, hey, they ain't coming back."

He could sense Penzler's blood beginning to foam.

Anson walked around the front of the Toyota. "Personally, I wish they would. I've got a half a lifetime's full of questions to ask."

"Like what?" Arnold followed Anson up onto the low embankment of earth and looked around. For all the world, it looked to him like old levees and meander bottoms.

Anson had a curious gleam behind his bifocals. "The pyramids were new when these people built the first city in North America. You're in agriculture, you can understand the problem, Mr. Beauregard. How do you build a city like Poverty Point, organize the labor to move over one million cubic yards of earth, and do it without agriculture?"

"What do you mean, without agriculture? You gotta have agriculture. Tell me how you're gonna be Bill Gates and invent computers when you're out for half a day hunting and fishing for each meal."

"Tell me indeed," Anson agreed. "But they did it. Right here in northern Louisiana, they created a miracle." He turned, waving his arm in a circle. "Everything started here. It's Egypt and Babylon. Moses and Ramses. I can feel it in my bones."

"God, here he goes again," Penzler muttered, walking off a stone's throw to study the low mounds.

When he was out of earshot, Arnold asked, "Why is he here?"

Anson's lips bent in amusement. "He's finishing his Ph.D. on

Poverty Point trade relationships. He's got this idea of interlocking clan territories regulated by the redistribution of resources." Seeing Arnold's look of incomprehension, he added. "Like groups of relatives that trade back and forth to keep the family together. That sort of thing, but on a larger scale."

"What was that bit about Egypt and Moses? What's that got to do with Louisiana?"

"It's the same period of time." Anson pointed at the low earthworks. "Sure, these people didn't build huge cities of stone. They didn't leave us records of their leaders, or their laws. But they did something that the Egyptians, the Babylonians, the Hittites, and all of their Old World contemporaries didn't."

"What was that?"

"Back before the first Pharaoh even thought of a pyramid, the people at Poverty Point put together a cross-continental trading system. But their most important gift to the future was an idea."

"Or so you think," Patty Umbaugh chided. Glancing at Arnold, she said. "We've barely scratched the surface here. We haven't even investigated a tenth of a percent of the archaeological sites in Louisiana. If Dr. Anson is right, we're sitting on a wealth of revelations about these people."

Arnold cocked his jaw, considered, and asked point-blank. "What is your interest in our farm. So far as I know, this site is on private property."

Umbaugh nodded. "Yes, Mr. Beauregard, it is. Louisiana has over seven hundred mound sites that we know about. Hundreds more that we don't. Perhaps thousands have been destroyed by field leveling, and others have been hauled away over the years for highway fill, causeways, and levees. We would like to work with you in the preservation of this site. We have programs—"

"Yeah, yeah, I know about government 'programs.' It sounds so good. 'We're from the government, we're here to help you.' Next time you turn around, you're in noncompliance with some damn thing. That, or some EPA or OSHA asshole is poking his nose up your bohungus to certify your fertilizer, or check the green cards on the hired help, or the frogs are being born with too many legs, or some damned thing."

"I know, but our program—"

"With all due respect, Ms. Umbaugh"—he gave her the ingratiating smile again—"we would like to politely refuse your help."

"Well," she said with a sigh, "thank you for at least letting me come and see the site. I'll leave you a card, and if you ever have any questions—"

"Yeah, right, I'll call."

Anson turned, head tilted. "Mr. Beauregard, I can sure understand your attitude about the government."

"You can?"

Anson nodded. "Out of fear of the government, some of the most important mounds in the state have been bulldozed by worried landowners."

"They must have snapped those guys' butts right into court before they could grab their hats."

"It was private property," Anson replied laconically. "Just like your farm here. I'd hope that we've all learned our lesson. You see, the reason we're here is that you are the legal owner of this site. We want to let you know what you have here, and why it is important."

"What's it worth?" he asked absently, squinting at the mounds of dirt. Just at rough guess, he figured it at about ten thousand cubic yards.

"Worth?" Anson shrugged. "In dollars, not much. But when it comes to information—to the questions we can answer—it's priceless. This is a satellite site, an outlier tied to the Poverty Point site a little ways up Bayou Macon." He pointed to the thicket of trees that dropped off toward the muddy bayou no more than fifty yards beyond the brush.

Patty Umbaugh said, "We have a registry of sites—"

"Nope!" Arnold shook his head categorically. "First you register it, then every tourist in the damned world wants to trespass on your property to see it, and some government bureaucrat wants to tell you how to run it." He waved a finger. "The answer is no. Period."

She looked pissed, but he had to hand it to her, she did a good job of covering.

Anson rubbed his jaw. "If you don't want to work with the state to preserve the site, that's fine. Would you mind, however, if we brought field schools, students, up from time to time to dig here? Everything that we find belongs to you, of course. You can keep the artifacts here, or at your corporate headquarters, or we would be happy to curate them at the university."

Arnold rolled his lip over his chew, and slowly shook his head. "I don't think so, Dr. Anson. First off, there's liability to think about. What if one of your students fell and broke his neck, or some such thing? Or they snuck in at night to dig for arrowheads? And third, sure, BARB might own this site free and clear now, but who's to say what's gonna happen in the future? I heard tell of folks got taken to court over down by Lake Charles by some Injun group over a burial ground. We don't need those kinds of headaches."

Anson looked as if he were about to throw up. "But, you will preserve the site, right?"

Arnold smiled. Hell, cowboys and Indians never did get along together. "Yeah, well, we'll take it under consideration. Like I said, either we're efficient, or, well, just like your Indians. Extinct."

Arnold squinted in the midday sun. The soft Gulf breeze blew up from the southwest. It sent puffy clouds sailing across the sky and brought the promise of afternoon rains. The big yellow Caterpillar growled and roared as it dropped the rippers and rolled a sweetgum stump out of the damp black soil. The roots popped and snapped like firecrackers.

The Hoferberg farm was unrecognizable now. The old oak trees that had shaded the lane had been cut down and sold for lumber. The house and barn, the foundation, the cisterns, and outbuildings had been flattened or plucked up with the backhoe and trucked off. Where the trees had somberly guarded the archaeological site, now an unrestricted view of the Bayou Macon could be seen; only the cane brakes under the slope of Macon Ridge remained standing.

Arnold had made a special effort to be here for the leveling. He'd never seen an archaeological site until Dr. Anson brought him here. And he sure as hell had never seen one scraped flat before. So he was curious. As the Cat cut great swaths through the mounds, he walked along with his cup of black coffee—because real cowboys drank it that way—in his hand. He spat his Copenhagen every now and then, and looked at the black dirt.

Most of Macon Ridge was a tan-brown loess, a silt blown clear down from the last glaciers up north. But the dirt in and around the mounds was crankcase-dripping black. Every now and again he had picked up one of the oddly shaped clay balls—finding them the perfect weight to fling out into the bayou—and wondered what the Indians had used them for.

Little flat flakes of stone came up, and yes, he had even found a gray-stone arrowhead a while back. He had wanted to find an arrowhead just as much as he wanted to see Indian bones come rolling out of the ground, but the rich loamy soil seemed against him on that one. All in all, there wasn't much exciting to see. So how, then, could that Dr. Anson have spouted all that nonsense about ideas, and trade, and all the rest?

Out by the highway the big John Deere 9000s, brought in on

flatbeds, were already starting their runs. By noon tomorrow, the whole of Hoferberg farm would be disked, harrowed, fertilized, and ready for the trucks bringing the seed drills.

Arnold shook his head, disappointed at the bulldozing. He had expected something a bit more entertaining than featureless black dirt rolling under the blade. He looked again at the gray-stone arrowhead—a big thing, as long as his finger—and slipped it into his pocket as he turned to walk back to his truck. Glancing at his watch, he could still meet Harvey Snodgrass at the Delphi café and show off his arrowhead.

He was watching his razor-toed cowboy boots as they pressed into the damp black earth. The light brown polish looked so clean and fresh against the dirt. That's when the gleam caught his eye. He bent, reaching down past some of the endless, oddly shaped clay balls, and picked up a little red stone.

With his thumb, he cleaned the clinging dirt away and stared in surprise. It was a carving. A little red potbellied stone owl. Something about it reminded him of a barred owl.

Arnold was more than a little intimate with barred owls, having shot his first one when he was fifteen. Not content just to leave it lay, he'd dragged it home to show off to his friends. Someone called the warden. But for quick work with a shovel, they'd have caught him with that owl. It had been closer than a 'skeeter's peter.

Turning the little red owl, he could almost believe that the craftsman who'd made it had carved a mask on the face. A masked owl? What did that mean?

Thing was, he couldn't call up that Dr. Anson and ask. It wasn't as if they'd parted on good company.

"Sorry," he told the little owl. "Reckon your home had to go. Trees got to go down and crops got to go in. People can't live without farming. It's the future, little guy."

He opened the door on his shiny new pickup, and paused, studying the little owl one last time before he put it in his pocket. "It's not like your Indians are coming back."

Thunder roared so close it was deafening. Arnold jerked his head up to stare at the sky.

The lightning bolt flashed white-blue, the *clap-bang!* startling the soul half out of José Rodriguez's body where he sat at the Caterpillar's controls.

"*¡Madre de dios!*"

With the afterimage of the flash still burning behind his eyes, José leaped from his idling Cat, and ran. He reached Arnold within moments. Rolling him over, José got his second fright for the day. The lightning bolt had done horrible things to Arnold's head.

"Blessed Mother," he whispered, and backed away.

José glanced at the tiny red owl that lay in the soil inches from Arnold's fingers. It glinted in the storm light like a glaring eye.

José crossed himself, then he stumbled for the open driver's door of Arnold's pickup. The cell phone was fried. He had to get to a phone. Fast! As he cranked the wheel and sped away, the rear tires pressed the little red owl back into the rich black soil.

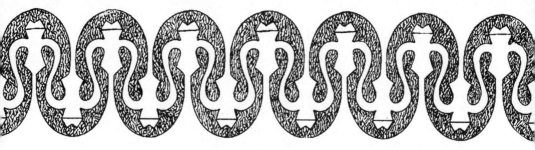

Prologue

From the shadowed mouth of her cave, old Heron stared out past the Tree of Life. Another in the endless cycles passed as the winter broke and the old Dance started again.

In the far north, the strengthening spring sun released moisture from the winter-banked snows. At the same time, warm winds blew glistening silver bands of rain up from the gulf to fall on the awakening forests. Freshets added their contribution to the flood as it swelled, rippling like flexed muscles along the great rivers that fed the Father Water.

The waters flowed, draining the continent, swirling and breaching the banks, cutting crevasses through the levees. In places it rerouted the wide span, changing its course, dissecting backswamps and meanders. Where it rushed, soils were scoured and old glacial gravels were lifted and carried along, pattering like hail along the worn channel. In other places the water slowed, dropping its load of fine silt. It was ancient—this dance of movement and renewal—the majestic pumping heartbeat of the continent.

As it neared the gulf, the great river slowed and spread its bounty over the wide, tree-choked floodplain. There, hemmed by a ridge of glacial dust on the west and ancient eroded hills to the east, the waters disgorged their final rich bounty of silt and sand before filtering down to the crystal blue gulf.

Limpid brown water inundated the backswamps, rising around the trees. Silt settled slowly. It swirled when churned by silver-sided chad, suckers, and long gar; aquatic insects burrowed through its brown blanket. Crawfish hunted those still depths, picking through the muck with delicate claws—alert for the ever-prowling catfish, heron, or bass. Cypress and tupelo swelled, their leaves lush, while prop roots sucked nutrients from the renewed mud. The flood was life, rebirth.

The old woman sharpened her gaze. She tilted her head, hearing the faint voice rising and falling. "Yes, I hear you. Where are you, boy?"

Extending her hand, she could feel tendrils of Power being gathered, manipulated.

"The Brothers," she whispered. "They're at it again. Always fighting."

They were old adversaries, those two. Day and night, order and chaos, they remained inextricably bound yet opposed, creations from the dawn of time. In this place, for this latest duel, they had taken the form of birds: one white, a silent hunter of the night breezes; the other black, a raucous creature of the sun-drenched sky.

She could feel the tension between them rolling out of the future. A lonely boy's voice called out, caught at the point where their lines of Power collided.

Another of their endless contests was approaching, borne across the still evening waters on four slim canoes. How would it end this time?

One

Dark clouds slipped soundlessly across the sky as night fell. The faintest glow could be made out in the periodic breaks between the flooded trees. The lead canoe sailed silently forward, driven by the fatigued strokes of two young men. Unease reflected in the youths' dark eyes. Behind them brown water rippled in the expanding V of their wake. It licked at the trunks of bitter pecan and water oak, then lapped against pioneer stands of sweetgum, hackberry, and ash that rose above the backswamp.

In the dusky shadows, three more slim vessels followed, the occupants silently paddling their craft. On occasion they glanced warily about at the hanging beards of moss, at the silvered webs spun by hand-sized yellow spiders, and at the clinging mass of vines. Occasionally a copperhead draped from a water-crested branch.

"White Bird, are you sure you know where you are going?" a young paddler called from the second boat. He spoke in the language of the river—a Trade pidgin that had grown over generations.

"I know these backswamps as surely as you know the twists and turns of your forests back home, Hazel Fire. Trust me." White Bird blinked his eyes where he sat in the rear of the lead canoe, his back pressed hard against the matting that cushioned the concave stern. He had hoped to be home by nightfall. Ahead of him, Yellow Spider's paddle moved mechanically, his arms as tired and loose-jointed as White Bird's own.

"I don't blame them for being nervous." Yellow Spider scratched

at a chigger bite on his calf. "It is a frightening thing, being cast loose in so much water, never knowing which way you are going. Remember how we felt in their country?"

Twelve long moons had passed since they had struck north, following the winding course of the Father Water, keeping to the backwaters, avoiding the river's current as they battled their way upstream. By the fall equinox they had landed their canoe in the far northern country of the Wolf People.

Trade was old, but it was mostly conducted between peoples, or by solitary Traders in canoes who traveled the rivers. The key was the river system that linked the huge continental interior. Copper from the great northern lakes, special chert from Flint Ridge in the northeast, soapstone from the eastern mountains, and hematite from the northwest were but a few of the exotic Trade items prized by the Sun People. But goods moved slowly and in a trickle. The farther a person traveled from the source, the more valuable the Trade was. The farther a Trader traveled, the less likely he would have the items he started with. The Power of Trade was that items be Traded at each stop.

White Bird and Yellow Spider had tried a different tack. They had carefully avoided the River Peoples, often traveling by night, on their journey northward. Upon their arrival, with their Trade intact, they elected to spend the winter. That meant freezing and shivering in the Wolf People's thatch-sided huts while snow twirled out of the cold gray skies, and frigid winds moaned through the naked trees. In that time they had traded judiciously, offering their beautifully dyed textiles, their basswood rope and cordage, small sections of alligator hide, and necklaces made of the beast's teeth and claws. They had pitched in with the hunting, packing firewood, and generally making themselves useful. Both had struggled to learn as much of the language as they could. As honored guests, each had been provided with a young woman, and by the time of their departure, their wives had begun to swell with children.

"These women," the chief had told them, "they do not wish to go south and live with strangers. Their families, clans, and people are here. They will be here when you come back."

Their Trade had been wildly successful. So much so that the piles of goods stacked in their small hut would have overflowed their single canoe. In the end it had taken all of White Bird's guile, the promise of immense wealth, and the gift of half of his profits, to talk three additional canoes into accompanying them south.

With the breaking of the river ice, White Bird, Yellow Spider, and the Wolf Traders had loaded their canoes and slipped them into the frigid current. The descent of the river had taken but two moons, a third the time needed to paddle upstream. Nor had the journey been as dangerous, their travel time through potentially hostile country being shorter, their numbers larger and more threatening to potential raiders.

As they neared the end of the long voyage, their narrow craft were stacked gunwale high with fabric sacks that contained the winter's Trade: chipped stone blanks, copper beads, thin sections of ground slate, polished greenstone celts, and adzes. In addition they had large winter hides from buffalo, elk, and a highly prized hide from the great silver bear. Smaller prime hides came from beaver, northern bobcat, mink, and marten. One hide, traded from the far north, came from something called a carcajou—an animal they had never seen—but the fur was black, lustrous, and soft. Other pouches contained herbs and medicinal plants: wild licorice for sore throats; alum root for diarrhea; gayfeather for heart and urinary problems; puccoon for wounds, menstrual problems, and to stay awake; mint for tea, the relief of gas, and stomach problems; yucca root for joint soreness and a laxative; and coneflower for toothaches.

But in White Bird's mind the most important thing he carried was the fabric sack of goosefoot seeds that rested between his feet. That was the journey's greatest prize. And for that, he would gamble everything. What would the People do for a man who offered them the future?

"I thought we would be there by now," Yellow Spider muttered, banking his paddle long enough to roll his muscular shoulders.

"The cut across from the crevasse is longer than you remember." White Bird smiled. "Besides, if you will recall, we were fresh and excited when we left here last spring."

"And the backswamp is deeper," Yellow Spider added. "Look at this." He gestured at the high water ringing the trees. "Fishing must be more difficult this spring with such deep water. People will be adding on to their nets. We should have gone northwest for ironstone. Given the depth of the water and the size of the nets needed to fish these currents, net sinkers will be in demand."

"We did fine." White Bird tapped the sack of goosefoot seed with his foot. "Besides, had we gone northwest, the mountain people wouldn't have provided their women. Not like those Wolf People." He paused thoughtfully as he stroked with his paddle. "I, for one, will miss Lark. She kept the robes more than warm."

As Yellow Spider picked up his paddle, White Bird rested his across the gunwales and rolled his weary shoulders. Fatigue ran from his fingers, up his arms, and into the middle of his back. His belly had run empty long ago, as though nothing but hunger lay behind the corded muscles. An image of Lark flashed in his head. He remembered the sparkle in her eyes that first night when she had crawled into his bed. If he closed his eyes, he could almost feel her hands tracing the swell of his chest and the ripple of muscle that led down past his navel. Her gasp of delight as she reached down to grip his manhood lingered in his ears.

"Yes," he whispered into the stillness of the swamp, "I shall miss you, Lark." In his nineteen turning of seasons he had never had a full-time woman before. The notion that she had been waiting every time he returned to their cozy home had grown on him. She was a strange one, true, raised as she was by a different people with different gods and peculiar beliefs, but she had been pretty, devoted to him, and always there. Rot take it, a man could get used to living like that.

"I wouldn't worry," Yellow Spider said smugly as he ducked a clump of hanging moss. "Your mother probably has a whole string of women lined up for you. Not only are you worthy—as our return will prove—but you're in line to replace your uncle." He hesitated tactfully. "If you haven't already."

"Uncle Cloud Heron will be fine. Owl help me if he isn't."

Yellow Spider laughed. "Oh, stop it. You'll be a better Speaker for the clan than anyone I know. You have a way about you, White Bird. A calm assurance that no one else has. People can't help but like you. Look at how we did up north. Look at the return we got. How are you going to explain that you gave half of your Trade to these barbarians?"

"Watch your tongue." White Bird shot a quick look back over his shoulder. "You never know if any of them have been learning our language. Lark and Robin were learning it quickly enough."

"I was just thinking how much I miss that Robin." Yellow Spider sighed. "Somehow I think the clan is going to marry me off quick as a snap. Who knows whom they'll pick for me." He paused. "Unlike you. Or are you sorry that Lark isn't in your canoe instead of me?"

"Come on, Cousin. Think! Lark and Robin belong up there. That's where their families are. They'd be strangers here, cast loose without kin of any kind. And, you're right. The clan will have you married to at least one other woman, perhaps two, within the turning of seasons."

Yellow Spider lowered his voice. "Do you think Spring Cypress is a woman yet?"

White Bird shrugged. "If she is, she may be married already."

Did his voice cloak the sudden sense of worry? She'd begun her fourteenth summer when he and Yellow Spider had left for the north. But for a late menstruation, she'd have been married—most girls were by that age.

"I talked to Spring Cypress before I left. It was a risk we had to take. Even if she passed her moon, her uncle, Speaker Clay Fat, could have been persuaded to wait."

"Or not, as the case may be."

"Are you always so gloomy?"

"No, I'm just connected to this world. You, my cousin, live in another. Take those seeds you're so enamored of. Goosefoot is goosefoot. We have our own. Why invest in someone else's?"

"Because these seeds are twice as big as ours."

"If they'll even grow here." Yellow Spider smashed a mosquito that managed to penetrate the grease he'd smeared on his skin. "The dirt's different."

"Dirt's dirt."

"Shows what you know. And the seasons are different. It doesn't get as cold here. Maybe those seeds are just like ours and . . . and it's the cold that makes them get that big?"

"Trust me."

Yellow Spider nodded in the shadowy half-light that penetrated the canopy of trees and filtered through the hanging moss and vines. "To be sure, Cousin. I've trusted you this far, and look where it has gotten me. I am coming home with the most successful Trading venture ever. Not just a canoeful of goods, but four! We own the world, Cousin!"

White Bird smiled into the increasing darkness. They did indeed own the world. No matter that the Wolf Traders considered half of their canoes' contents to be theirs, the fact was, it would all end up being spread among the clans. The credit would be his. People would listen to him. His influence would maintain his clan's position, and if anything, add to Owl Clan's prestige. The seeds at his feet were the next step in changing the people, making them greater than they had ever been.

Suffused with the glow of success, he barely heard the whisper of wings in the darkness as an owl circled above, charting their progress.

Two

Jaguar Hide had come to his name from the spotted yellow hide he continually wore. He had been but a spare youth, running for his life, when he'd fled to the south. In a leaky canoe he had traveled along the coast, avoiding the grease-smeared tribesmen who lurked in the salt marshes. After being plagued by mosquitoes and salt-cracked skin for several moons he had found safety in the tropical forests. There, attached to a small band of tribesmen—refugees like himself—he had lived for four long turning of seasons, learning their various languages and living hand to mouth.

The day he had tracked the great spotted cat had changed his Power, changed his life. That morning he'd followed the cat's tracks, seeing where the pugs pressed so delicately into the mud. The forest had swallowed him as though to digest him in a universe of green. Water had dripped from the palmetto and mahogany.

He and the jaguar had seen each other at the same moment. In that instant of locked eyes, he had seen his death—and refused to meet it. As he extended his arm to cast, the jaguar leaped. The dart nocked in his atlatl might have been an extension of his Dream Soul so straight did it fly. He was still staring into those hard yellow eyes as the fletched dart drove half of its length into the great cat.

The animal's flying impact sent him rolling across the forest litter, but the cat's attention had centered on the stinging length of wood protruding from the base of its throat. The first swipe of its paws had snapped the shaft. Thereafter, the frantic clawing did nothing more than tear the splintered shaft sideways in the wound. Great gouts of blood pumped with each of the cat's heartbeats.

When the jaguar finally flopped onto its side in the trail, their gazes remained joined. The cat's strength drained with each bloody exhalation. To the end, the claws extended and retracted, as though in the cat's brain, it was rending the man's flesh. He watched the pupils enlarge as the cat's raspy breathing slowed. He was still staring, partially panicked by fear, when the animal's Dream Soul was exhaled through those blood-caked nostrils and, having nowhere else to go, entered his own body.

Later that night, in a rain-drenched camp, he had squatted under a palmetto lean-to and eaten the cat's meat. He could remember the blue haze of rain-slashed smoke. He could still smell it, and taste the sweet meat in his mouth. Jaguar's Power had penetrated his heart and wound its way around his souls.

The frightened youth he had been was eaten that night—consumed by the jaguar's Power. The next morning he had stridden forth a different man, and begun the long journey north, alternately canoeing and portaging the sandbars that blocked the salt marshes. He had returned to his people, and with the Power of the jaguar in his blood, he had destroyed his old enemies, taken five wives, and closed his fingers around his people until they all fit within his callused grasp.

That had been tens of seasons ago. No longer young, he looked up at the soot-stained roof of the cramped house he now crouched in. Spiderwebs, like bits of moss, wavered in the heat waves rising from the low-banked fire. Before him on a cane mat lay his nephew, young Bowfin, wounded and dying as evil spirits ate his guts out. The boy's sister, Anhinga, crouched beside him, and the mother, Jaguar Hide's sister, Yellow Dye, balanced on her feet, her chin on her knees as she sobbed softy.

In his mind's eye, Jaguar Hide could see himself: Gray hair had been pulled into a tight bun on the back of his head and pinned with a stingray spine. His old jaguar hide, once so bright yellow, now lay hairless over his shoulder, the smeared skin tattered in places, shiny from wear in others. The turning of seasons had treated the hide no better than they had him.

A fabric loincloth sported the design of a spotted cat on the front and rear flaps where they hung from the waist thong. His brown skin, weathered from sun, cold, and storm, was puckered here and there with scars. It had lost its supple elasticity and turned flaky, grainy with age and loose on his wiry muscles. He still had his bones, big and blocky, a frame that had once given him a rare strength among men. The muscles, however, had faded with the turning of seasons until now he was but a gnarly shadow of himself.

He knotted his bony fist; if he were young again, he would show them. He would pay them back for this.

"Elder?" the young man on the mat croaked. Dried blood mottled his sweat-shiny skin. He raised a trembling hand. Jaguar Hide took it in his own, feeling how cold it was, how weak. He forced himself to ignore the rising stench that came from the wound and curled around his head.

"Save your breath, Bowfin. You need to regain your strength, then we will go back and teach that filth a thing or two about invading our territory."

The young man swallowed hard, his eyes shining in the firelight. Jaguar Hide watched as the pupils expanded ever wider, knowing that gray darkness was flooding the warrior's vision. Holding his dying nephew's cold hand, Jaguar Hide could sense the life going out of him. He felt Bowfin's heart slow, weaken, skip, and stop. With the shallow breathing at the end, the vile odor was no longer pumped from his punctured gut. Jaguar Hide's skin prickled as the young man's Life Soul slipped out through his open mouth and rose. He could imagine it as it drifted to the door, caressed Yellow Dye where she sat at the opening in the thatch, and slipped out into the darkness above the hut.

"He's dead." Jaguar Hide placed young Bowfin's hand on his still chest. Yellow Dye bit off a sob as she fled through the low doorway into the night, where her son's Life Soul now hovered like a bat.

"Uncle?" Anhinga knelt next to him, staring curiously at Bowfin's vacant eyes. The boy lay naked, his body bathed in firelight. The wound in his belly gaped open under the rib cage. "Can't the Serpent save him? Call his souls back to the body? He has already tried to suck out the evil the Sun People shot into him, but . . ." She pointed at the clotted blood on the boy's side.

Jaguar Hide had watched as the Serpent, the old medicine Dreamer, had punctured the boy's skin with a sharp chert flake. Then the white-haired elder had bent down, using a clay tube to suck at the blood in an effort to draw the evil from the body. No amount of piercing and sucking or smoking with medicine herbs had stilled the fever or the ever-stronger stench rising from the wound.

"Sometimes, Niece, nothing can be done."

They had come here from the big settlement—a circular complex of clan houses and seven mounds called the Panther's Bones—to the western margins of their territory in response to reports that the Sun People were raiding again. They constantly tried to sneak into Swamp Panther territory and quarry the valuable deposits of sandstone in the western ridges. Jaguar Hide's arrival at Raccoon Camp had coincided with young Bowfin being wounded by the skulking raiders.

"I don't agree, Uncle." She was glaring at him, eyes hard.

"I meant about Bowfin." He leaned back on his haunches and studied her. Firelight shot gold through her long black hair and accented the hollows of her cheeks. She had a straight nose and perfect mouth. The past fifteen winters had shaped the little girl he had once known into a most attractive woman. She was fully budded now, with high breasts, a slim waist, and rounded hips leading into long sleek legs. He understood the fire in her eyes, felt it himself as he looked at the dead warrior.

"It is *our* land. He was *my* brother!" Anhinga whispered passionately, her fist clenched. "Why do they come here?"

"For the stone," he answered simply. "Stealing it is far more exciting . . . and a great deal cheaper than dealing with us."

Bowfin made a gurgling sound. As the dead man's gut hissed, clots of black blood, white pus, and intestinal juice leaked out. Anhinga clamped her nose with her fingers. Jaguar Hide could see the crystal shine of tears as they crept past her eyelids. The shaking of her shoulders betrayed her an instant before the first sobs broke her lips.

Jaguar Hide ignored the stench. "He was just defending our territory. Remember that, girl. Remember what you see here."

"Bowfin?" Anhinga cried as she turned away.

Jaguar Hide watched the girl's muscles tense as she fought to control grief. She was twisting the knotted fringes of her short skirt, her beautiful face tortured.

He stood slowly, reached down, and pulled her to her feet. "We have tried to keep them away. It would seem as though their gods favor them, for they grow as numerous as the trees. Now they are building their huge earthworks, as if they are to become gods themselves."

Through a grief-tightened throat, she choked out, "They are malignant spirits, Uncle. I would destroy them if I could."

He studied her speculatively. The wound in her souls was raw and bleeding. Pain had mixed with anger, seething, burning, consuming. *My, such passion for a woman just coming into her own.*

"One day," she continued, "I will become our leader, and when

I do I will take war to the Sun People and destroy them."

This brought a crooked smile to Jaguar's old lips. "Do you think I didn't try just that?"

"But this time—"

"You will be defeated, just as I was."

"He was my brother." She pointed at Bowfin's corpse, ignoring the fact that his Dream Soul was still watching her from those wide, glassy eyes. "Uncle, we cannot allow this to happen. Not anymore. This is a disgrace! To Bowfin, to our clan, to you and me. All of us!"

"Yes. It is. But the Sun People cannot be defeated by war."

"Then how?" she demanded. "You tell me, and by the Panther's blood, I will destroy them!"

"Will you, girl?" The amused smile remained on his lips. He fought the urge to laugh aloud as she ducked under the low doorway and stomped off into the night.

Your mother is going to have her hands full controlling you. She was very different than her older brother, Striped Dart. She had never had the relationship with him that she'd had with the personable Bowfin. If any of Yellow Dye's children had to die, too bad it couldn't have been Striped Dart. When he heard about little Bowfin, he would posture, stomp, and curse, and do nothing. The fires of life hadn't hardened him like it had others.

So, what are you going to do, old man? What will become of your people when you die and your nephew takes over?

In the darkness, he glimpsed the midnight-colored crow that circled on silent wings above him.

The clamor gave Mud Puppy his first hint that something was happening. He lay quietly on the cane mat, a small ceramic jar cupped upside down in his hand. The glow from the central hearth illuminated the inside of his house with a reddish hue, the light so dim that the cricket's natural wariness should be lulled. The beast had been chirping under the split-cane floor matting. Rather than tear it up, it was much better to let the fire die down and coax the cricket into stepping out. Then he'd catch it.

Mud Puppy turned his head, listening to the calls on the still night. Excited, yes; panicked, no. Therefore, whatever it was, he would eventually hear about it. Everything came with time.

That attitude drove his mother to distraction. She was Wing

Heart, the Clan Elder, or leader—the most important woman in the world. It wasn't that he wanted to disappoint her, he just didn't act the way she wanted him to. He couldn't. That simple reality made her half-frantic with frustration. He suspected that she loved him in spite of the way he was.

"Just once can't you be like your brother? White Bird is the kind of man our clan needs! And you, boy, what will you be? Just a thorn in his side? He is going to be a great leader, the best our clan has ever had, and you, you will be like a net sinker tied around his throat. Forever dragging him down."

He wouldn't be, of course. White Bird had his way, that was all. And yes, if he returned alive from the journey upriver, he would be a great man, a born leader for their clan. Owl knew, Uncle Cloud Heron was just hanging to life, the pain in his bones debilitating no matter how many times he sweated or that the old Serpent and his acolyte, Bobcat, sucked bits of evil out of his body with their copper lancets and stone sucking tubes.

Mud Puppy hunched his fifteen-winters-old body. People said he was skinny, just bones wrapped around an insatiable curiosity. He was short for his age, too. Shaggy black hair tumbled over his eyes as he grasped the ceramic cup in his hand. The cricket began singing its shrill music. How could such a little creature make such a noise? It pierced the ears like a lancet, almost painful.

He barely heard the continuing commotion outside. Someone shouted. Voices called in answer as a party trotted past his house, coming in from one of the outer ridges. "They're back," one of the voices called. "At last, they're back!"

Back? Mud Puppy frowned in the red-tinged gloom. Perhaps the party that had gone down to steal sandstone from the Swamp Panthers? Over the turning of seasons they had become ever more stingy about their precious sandstone. The trouble was that the Sun People depended on the hard sandstone for so much of their manufacturing. When people weren't packing baskets of earth for the mounds, or Singing and celebrating, they were making things. Making plummets, gorgets, celts, and adzes required hard gritty sandstone. It was used for all kinds of things, even smoothing wood and grinding pigments. Lately it seemed like every expedition to the Swamp Panthers' country, two days' journey to the south, ended in a fight. Surely, there had to be a better way.

The cricket darted a finger length out from the mat, its body a black blot against the charcoal-stained dirt of the floor.

Mud Puppy waited, still as could be. The gray cup filled his hand, his arm poised. He would have to be fast, like a striking snake, lest his little target escape. Did his muscles have it in themselves? Could he do it?

Wait. Let Cricket relax. He is on his guard now, freshly removed from cover.

Mud Puppy didn't breathe, wondering how long it would take for Cricket to drop his guard. Long moments passed as Mud Puppy closed his ears to the continued calling and laughter outside. He blinked his eyes when Cricket's black body blurred into the shadowed earth and seemed to lose its shape.

At last the little beast began its high-pitched screeching.

Mud Puppy nerved himself and clapped the cup down over the cricket, the move so violent it was a wonder the fiber-tempered pottery didn't shatter.

"Got you!"

Now, how did he turn the cup over without allowing the cricket to escape? For a moment he puzzled on that and, in the end, rose from his bed and crossed the room to the net bag that held basswood leaves. Reaching in, he removed one of the big leaves and returned to his cup. He took a moment to toss a couple of hickory sticks onto the fire and waited for the flames to cast yellow light over the inside of his mother's house.

He glanced around at the wattle-covered walls and the wood-framed thatch ceiling overhead. Seeing nothing helpful there, he considered the soapstone bowls, the loom with its half-finished cloth, and the stacked pottery, then returned his attention to the cup, upside down on the dirt that separated the cane matting from the fire pit.

He stooped and carefully slid the leaf under the cup. Only when it extended past the other side did he lift both leaf and cup, slowly turn them over, and smile.

"Got you!" The swell of triumph expanded under his heart. "Now, tomorrow, when the sun is bright, I'm going to see how you can make such a loud noise, little fellow."

Feet beat a cadence toward the doorway, and Mud Puppy looked up as Little Needle came huffing and puffing to duck his head into the doorway. Despite being thirteen, Little Needle—of all the children—was Mud Puppy's only good friend. He had a face like the bottom of a pot with a pug nose pinched out of it; his most prominent feature was a set of large dark eyes that had a moony look. "Are your ears plugged, or what?"

"My ears are fine." Mud Puppy held up his leaf-capped cup with pride. "I just caught a cricket!"

"Why do I put up with you?" Little Needle shook his head, a look

of disbelief on his round brown face. The black tangle of his unkempt hair had tumbled into his eyes, and he took a swipe at it
with a grimy hand. "Your brother's back! He's alive. After all this
time . . . and despite the people who bet he was dead. And you
won't believe it, but he's brought *four* canoe loads of Trade. Four!
Can you imagine?"

Mud Puppy nodded, a thrill shooting through him. "I know."

"You know?" Little Needle's brow furrowed. "He just got here,
fool. You couldn't have known."

"Maybe," Mud Puppy retreated, using one hand to tap his chest.
"But I'd have known here if he was dead."

"Uh-huh." Little Needle's frown deepened. "I suppose one of
your pets"—he indicated the jar—"came to tell you."

Mud Puppy's expression fell. "I can't say. I promised."

Little Needle studied him thoughtfully. "At times, my friend, I'm
almost tempted to believe you. It's scary, some of the things you
know. Like Soft Moss being hit by lightning that time. You said it
was going to happen."

"You didn't tell anybody, did you?" Mud Puppy felt his souls
twisting with sudden anxiety. He hadn't meant to tell Little Needle,
but there were times that his souls just cried out to share some of
the things Masked Owl told him. He didn't. He wouldn't. Not even
to Little Needle, whom he trusted completely. Masked Owl was too
precious to him.

"It is the price you must pay for now." Masked Owl's Dream words
echoed in his memory. *"Be worthy of me."*

"Well? Are you coming or not?" Little Needle was dancing from
foot to foot. "Barbarians came with him! Six of them! They call
them Wolf People, but they just look like real people, except different. You know, in their hair and what they wear. But then White
Bird and your cousin, Yellow Spider, are dressed like them, too."

Mud Puppy looked around, wondering where to put his cricket.
"All right, I'll come."

"How can you be so unconcerned?" Little Needle almost
shouted it.

"Because my cricket might escape!"

"Sometimes I think everyone is right, you're nothing more than
an idiot!" With that Little Needle turned and sprinted off into the
darkness.

"He just doesn't understand, does he?" Mud Puppy asked the
trapped cricket as he set the cup down and laid a piece of polished
slate over the leaf to keep his catch in place. Then he turned and
ducked out into the warm spring night.

The Serpent

I watch the boy with my eyes squinted.

This evening, for the first time, I think maybe he's not the half-wit people say he is.

There is a very old story my people tell in their lodges on cold winter's nights—about a bridge guarded by animals. You see, we believe that there is a narrow log bridge that spans a deep canyon on the trail to the Land of the Dead. That bridge is guarded by the animals each person has known in his life. If the person treated those animals well, cared for them, and helped them, then the animals will be happy to see him and will guide him safely across the bridge to where his ancestors wait in the Land of the Dead. But if the person treated the animals badly, if he shouted at them or hurt them, they will chase him across the bridge, tearing at his heels with sharp teeth, or stinging him, or clawing his head with their talons, until he loses his balance and falls into a rushing river of darkness and is lost forever.

As I study the boy, I wonder.

He listens very attentively to everything alive, and often to things like windblown leaves that I'm fairly certain are dead.

But I could be wrong.

Innocence is the opposite of Truth, isn't it? That's what I've always thought. But perhaps it's just the price, and maybe that price is too high.

The thought makes me smile.

Perhaps if I sought my solace in innocence rather than Truth, I would see what the boy sees.

I vow to watch him more closely.

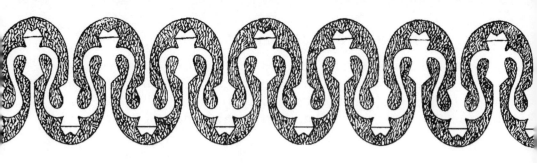

Three

The scar tissue that crisscrossed Mud Stalker's mangled right arm ached and itched. That boded no good. Mud Stalker, Speaker for the Snapping Turtle Clan, son of Clan Elder Back Scratch, ran idle fingers over the ridges of hard tissue. He had been but a youth when an alligator clamped itself on his arm and began thrashing the water into bloody froth. He had been insane with pain and panic, half-drowned and vomiting water, when Red Finger had beaten the alligator off with an oar and pulled him from the red-stained water. It had nearly killed him, infection eating at his flesh, fever burning his souls from his body. It had taken several turnings of seasons to recover—and crippled his arm for life.

As the itchy feeling increased, he scowled, thinking it a sign. It was bad enough that White Bird had returned. It was worse that so many people were coming down to the canoe landing to see his late-night arrival. Mud Stalker stood between the beached canoes at the water's edge and watched the people trooping to the landing. They carried cane torches down the slick incline from the high terrace above the lake; the yellow flames bobbed with each step. In the inky night the light might have been a Dream creature that flowed down the packed silt embankment.

Mud Stalker turned his head, staring out at the silent black waters where the canoes waited. Four of them, solid craft, floated less than a stone's cast from the shore. They reminded him of fingers stretching out of the night, monstrous and black. The canoe's occupants were standing, their feet balanced on the narrow gunwales. Over the babble of excited people, Mud Stalker could hear the grunting and clucking sound of the barbarians' tongue as they talked. What could have possessed White Bird to bring them down from the north?

"Are you sure we cannot land?" one of the foreigners asked in Trade pidgin.

"Not until we are given permission." That was Yellow Spider, another youth from the Owl Clan. Unlike White Bird's family, Yellow Spider's had declared him dead just after the Winter Solstice.

Mud Stalker turned his attention to where White Bird stood in the rear of the canoe. Even across the distance, he could see the young man's teeth shining as he smiled, cupped hands to his mouth, and called, "What news?"

"Things are well," Clay Fat, the Rattlesnake Clan Speaker returned. His round stomach stuck out like a pot, his navel a protruding knob. "We have sent for your mother."

"And my uncle?" White Bird asked cautiously across the water.

Yes, there it was. The dilemma they all faced. Cloud Heron was little more than a breathing corpse. He could die at any moment. Why hadn't he had the grace to do so before this foolish youth floated back from the dead?

"Not so well," Clay Fat replied. "Your return has come at a very opportune moment for your clan."

That, Mud Stalker thought, was just the problem. He turned, aware that his cousin, Red Finger, had stridden up. The old man held a flickering cane torch in his bony hand. He raised it high to look out over the black water at the canoes riding so peacefully.

"So, it is true? White Bird is back?" Red Finger kept his voice low, fully aware of the continuing flood of people who were descending to the landing.

Mud Stalker lifted a foot and planted it on the gunwale of a beached canoe. "He is back." He tried to keep his voice from communicating his displeasure. "Back, indeed—and with three up-country canoes full of barbarians. Not only is he not dead—as we had hoped—but he returns at just the right moment. With canoes packed full of Trade."

"Look at them," Red Finger muttered, as more people crowded the shore and raised their cane torches to stare across the water. In the yellow light they could better see the new arrivals. "If those piled bundles are Trade, and for as low as those canoes ride in the water, he has brought back great wealth."

Yes, if he has, his status will soar. Aloud, Mud Stalker said, "Let us wait and see, Cousin."

"Why, in the name of the Sky Beings, couldn't he be long dead with worms crawling in and out of his skull?" Red Finger growled under his breath, looking around. "Where's Wing Heart? I would have thought she would have been one of the first people down here. Is she missing the opportunity to prance up and down while telling of Owl Clan's Power, courage, and skill?"

"Oh, she'll be here." Mud Stalker wet his lips. "But only when the timing is right. As always, she will want to make a grand entrance."

"Wretched bitch. What I'd give to—"

"Patience, old friend. A great many things may yet go wrong for our young hero."

"White Bird!" The shrill yell carried over the growing babble of voices. Mud Stalker turned in time to see Spring Cypress running down the slope, pushing through the growing throng of people. Having passed fifteen summers, she was a tall girl, thin and lithe. Her dress consisted of a virgin's skirt loosely woven from bass-bark thread. It had been tied in the back with two beaded tassels. Cord fringe that attached to the hem dangled down past her knees. Each had been tipped with a stone bead so that it clattered and swayed with her steps. Born of the Rattlesnake Clan, Spring Cypress was Elder Graywood Snake's granddaughter. The girl had pinned her hair for White Bird long ago. As the seasons passed, and rumors circulated that her young swain had died upriver, she had grown despondent. Now, despite the fact that she carried no torch, she seemed to glow. But that might just have been the reflection of the light on her oiled skin.

"Spring Cypress?" White Bird craned his head, the canoe bobbing at his action. Despite the youth's exceptional balance, a careless move could capsize the boat.

"Yes! It's me! They said you were dead!" She was jumping up and down on charged legs, her immature breasts bouncing in time to the necklace on her chest. The weighted fringes jerked and jangled on her skirt.

"Dead?" White Bird threw his head back and laughed. "Anything but! I'm more full of life now that I've come home."

"What have you brought?" someone called.

"Where have you been?" cried another.

"What took you so long?"

"White Bird, who are these people with you?"

"Yellow Spider? What did they do? Marry you off to one of their grease-smelling hags up there?"

"How was the river? Is the water high?"

A thousand questions came boiling out of the crowd, each trying to outshout the others.

Mud Stalker struggled to hear the answers White Bird and Yellow Spider hollered back, but the roar of voices drowned them out. Instead, he turned his attention to the six young barbarians who stood uneasily on their canoes, watching with wide eyes. He couldn't make out much about them, other than their hair was pinned to the backs of their heads in tight buns. They were muscular, naked to the waist, where hide breechcloths had been secured by thick white cords. Someone, probably White Bird and Yellow Spider, had given them grease and taught them how to smear it over their bodies to thwart the plagues of mosquitoes and biting flies that filled the swamps.

"Hides, tool stone, copper, buffalo meat and medicines, a great many things . . ." White Bird's words carried through a lull in the conversation.

"Here comes Wing Heart!" Red Finger pointed up the hill.

The Owl Clan Elder was picking her way down the slope, two of her clan's people, Water Petal and Bluefin, bearing torches to light her way. The yellow light reflected from her silver-streaked hair as if it had previously caught the sun's rays and was now releasing them into the night. She wore a bearskin mantle pinned atop the left shoulder with a deer-bone skewer. Her right shoulder and breast were bare. Despite the late hour and the unexpected call, she wore a finely woven cloth kirtle. Spotless and white it swayed with each step she took. The preceding turning of seasons had been hard on her. Speaker Cloud Heron, her brother, had been slowly failing, his mind and health draining away like upland floodwaters. When White Bird had not returned last fall, she had taken it stoically, calmly stating that her son was detained. But the months had passed, and winter had dragged on, one grim gray day after another passing as her clan's influence ebbed.

Now, here she came, looking to all the world as if it were just another day and not the salvation of her authority and prestige. The crisis of clan leadership had been delayed yet again, perhaps forever.

"You'd think she planned this from the very beginning," Red Finger hissed irritably. Then he paused. "You don't think she did, do you? Do you think that rascal son of hers has been hiding out in the swamp for months? Did she do this just to keep us off-balance? To make us show our hands?"

"What about these barbarians?" Mud Stalker twitched his lips in their direction. "Did she hide them in the swamps, too? And all the Trade things that I overhead White Bird say he brought? She might be a Powerful old hag, but she and White Bird didn't just conjure Trade and barbarians from the mud and swamp moss. No, Cousin, he went north. Just as he said. We had better plan on how we are going to deal with that."

"He was always a Powerful boy. Had a way about him." Red Finger tapped his chin thoughtfully.

"We must take other steps, Cousin."

Red Finger shot a sidelong glance at him, his eyes shadowed black in the torchlight. "Are you thinking what I think you are?"

"Perhaps. Let us be patient. We are descended from Snapping Turtle, Cousin. Like him, we must be prudent, silent, and crafty. Snapping Turtle always lies where you least expect to find him. He is a master of camouflage and stealth." A pause. "And his bite can snap a man's bones in two."

Red Finger's expression hardened. "We must be very *very* careful."

The dark soil underfoot had turned treacherous. Evening mist had fallen, then hundreds of feet had churned it. The last thing Wing Heart would allow herself to do was to slip and take a tumble—not with half the town watching her. All of the terrible months of mixed hope, grief, and despair culminated here, now, at this moment and place: White Bird was home! She must use every sliver of advantage and opportunity.

Moccasin Leaf had been nipping at her heels, ready to slip Half Thorn into the Speaker's position. Just that morning she had been contemplating whether any hope remained. The question had been: Would it be better to declare her son dead before her brother died, or after? Points could be made for either decision, but in the end it had been her Dream Soul rather than her Life Soul that had won out. She simply couldn't stand to make a public admission of what she had come to believe in private. To do so would be too final, too void of even her thinly frayed hopes.

Then out of the darkness had come the word that White Bird had arrived. She was told that even as the runner spoke, her son was waiting in his canoe at the landing. She could hardly believe that he had brought not just himself and Yellow Spider, but three more canoes full of Trade paddled by barbarians!

She picked her way carefully in the flickering torchlight borne by her cousins. No trace of the rushing ecstasy in her heart betrayed itself on her stern face. She kept the fingers of her left hand tightly knotted in the silky bearskin she'd pinned over her shoulder. Aware that all eyes had turned her direction, she held her head high. That was it, let them all see. Owl Clan would remain the preeminent clan in Sun Town.

She cast a quick glance around as the land leveled. Of course Mud Stalker had beaten her here. Snapping Turtle Clan had been poised to move on her. She could practically see him choking on his disappointment as he fingered the scars on his ruined forearm. Too bad the alligator hadn't taken the rest of him along with his stripped fingers and skin.

To the left, amidst a knot of his kinspeople, Thunder Tail, Speaker of the Eagle Clan, stood with crossed arms, his face like a mask. She inclined her head politely in his direction, thrilled by the smoldering emotion in his eyes. *You would love to cut my throat, wouldn't you, old lover?*

To the rear, just back from the beached canoes, old Cane Frog stood. The Frog Clan Elder's left eye gleamed like a white stone in the firelight; the empty socket of her missing right eye made a black hole in her face. She was propped up by her daughter, Three Moss. As always, Three Moss was whispering in the old blind woman's ears, acting as her eyes. Several of the Frog Clan's young hunters had gathered behind her, as if for moral support. Their gazes darted back and forth like a school of shiners in shallow water. The two plotters, Hanging Branch and Takes Food, hovered to one side, whispering to each other. But Frog Clan, for all their bluster and strutting, had never really been in contention for leadership of the Council. Cane Frog hadn't the wits, and given Three Moss's dull head, the future didn't bode well for them either. Frog Clan would only be trouble if they aligned themselves with a rival.

Then she saw Deep Hunter. He stood back from the rest, illuminated by a single torch. His sister, Colored Paint, was the Alligator Clan Elder. Colored Paint had recently named her brother Speaker after the death of their uncle. Deep Hunter had his arms crossed, the thick muscles bunched and shining in the firelight. She met his dark eyes, seeing a hard gleam that didn't match his formal smile. Deep Hunter didn't look happy. No, indeed, she thought he looked like a man who had just suffered a disturbing upset. Throughout this last turning of seasons, Deep Hunter—with Colored Paint's approval—had promised Owl Clan their support. Deep Hunter would do anything to keep Mud Stalker and Alligator Clan in a subservient and obligatory position. Even if it meant supporting Wing Heart and Owl Clan.

Why do I feel that I've been betrayed? She nodded a greeting to Deep Hunter and bent her lips into a facile smile—just in case she needed to keep the fiction alive.

Eagle Clan's Elder, Stone Talon, perched on her wooden crutches, her gnarly hands gripping the smooth wood of the polished branches that kept her crooked legs from collapsing. Toothless, her face looked like a desiccated gourd; Stone Talon worked her gums and wrinkled her fleshy nose as though smelling something foul. Her faded vision seemed to be wavering, as though searching for something. A group of her young hunters—no doubt the ones who had borne her down to the landing—looked as if it was all they could do to keep from crowding at the water's edge and shouting questions at White Bird.

Deep Hunter strode down to face his sister. Gesturing for emphasis, he asked Colored Paint a question, then turned at the answer to frown out at the water where the canoes floated. Deep Hunter was a brash man, given to impulse. He had no halfway in his souls, but being a hothead and unpredictable made him dangerous in his own right.

Yes, they were all worried. That brought Wing Heart a twist of amusement she wouldn't have felt earlier in the day. Cloud Heron wasn't even dead yet, and they had already buried him? Had the fools considered Owl Clan to be defanged? Without any Power at all? She allowed herself to smile with an oily satisfaction. After a turning of seasons filled with worry and fear, her heart felt as though it might burst. This moment was worth savoring. She let the glory of victory fill her, felt it throbbing in her nerves, pulsing in her veins. She might have been a youth again, charged with the sheer joy of being alive.

People parted for her as she neared the shore. In the halo of torchlight, she walked imperiously between the hulls of beached canoes and out into the murky black water. Slippery, clinging mud slipped between her toes. Water lapped against her ankles like a lover's tongue.

The surface lay smooth and glassy before her, blackness lit by dancing yellow ribbons of light that reflected from the rings thrown by the bobbing canoes. Slim arrows of the night, the craft drifted at the edge of the torchlight: four of them, just as had been reported. She gave a cursory inspection to the barbarians, not that they mattered much, and turned her attention to the tall young man who balanced so perfectly on the stern of the canoe floating off to the right.

What a hero he made! Firelight reflected off the grease that he had smeared over his rippling skin, accenting the swell of his thick muscles. He stood like one of the warriors in the stories about the first days. A foreign-looking breechcloth hung from the leather belt at his slim hips; a bright yellow wolf's face was painted on the front flap. His hair, too, was in a bun pinned up at the side like the barbarians wore theirs. She could see his white teeth as he smiled in her direction.

"Are you well, my son?"

"I am *very* well, Mother."

She didn't react to the satisfaction in his voice. "And you, Yellow Spider? Are you well?"

"I am, Elder. Thank you. And my family?"

"They, too, are well. I shall send a runner immediately. Your mother and your brothers and sisters are out at Turtle Shell Camp. They will rejoice to hear of your arrival." Her voice turned dry. "It seems that they have worked most assiduously to placate your angry and lost ghost."

Across the distance she could see Yellow Spider take a deep breath. "I am sorry for that, Clan Elder. I can only hope that my return, with the Trade we bring, will reimburse the clan for any hardships my funeral might have incurred."

Scattered laughter broke out at that. It brought a smile to her thin lips. She had always liked Yellow Spider, had approved of his offer to accompany White Bird upriver. "I would imagine so, Yellow Spider. We can only wish that all deaths would reward us as well as yours appears to have."

"How is my uncle?" White Bird called.

"My brother, the Speaker, is not well, White Bird. Your absence has caused us some concern. Others worried, but I knew that you would not have prolonged your absence were it not that you were acting in the People's greatest interest."

White Bird, in a demonstration of his supreme balance, bowed low at the waist, the canoe barely rocking. "Indeed, Mother, were there any other way, I would have returned last fall. I apologize for leaving you without my help, but my responsibility to the People must be of more importance than my personal desires."

Well spoken, boy.

"And who are the people you have brought in these loaded canoes?"

White Bird was standing straight now, his canoe having drifted sideways as he looked over the torchlit crowd on the bank. "I would present my companions, they are Wolf People, from the far north. Yellow Spider and I, hearing of remarkable Trade up beyond the confluence of the three great rivers, made the decision to change our plans. Rather than simply barter for a load of Trade in the Blue Heron lands, we risked the way north. Many hostile peoples guard the river between the Blue Heron lands and the land of the Wolf People. By means of craft and guile, Yellow Spider and I passed those wild tribes. By the fall equinox we had reached the land of the Wolf People. There, Chief Acorn Cup, father of my friend, Hazel Fire"—he pointed to the young barbarian in the stern of the next canoe—"welcomed us into his village. He was a most gracious host. At Acorn Cup's insistence, we stayed the winter. And such a winter . . . you have never seen snow so deep! Or felt such a biting cold that almost splintered a man's bones!"

Wryly, she thought, *Chief Acorn Cup, good host that he was, no doubt left something warm, willing, and female in your bed to keep icicles from forming on your manhood.*

"Acorn Cup was right in warning us not to travel, so I spared my Trade, passing out a little at a time as the winter passed. And as you can see"—he made a grandiose gesture that rocked his canoe—"we have brought a great many things for the People as a result."

"Then our wait was well worth the time you spent far away." Wing Heart nodded slowly for the benefit of the gathered people.

Addressing the crowd, White Bird raised his voice. "Yellow Spider and I, at great risk to our lives, have brought four canoes piled high with Trade. What we have is a gift from the Owl Clan to the people. We provide these things freely and with an open heart. Owl Clan asks but two things: We ask that you provide for the needy among the clans first. He who is hunting with a blunt dart must receive the first of the stone points we have brought. He whose children are shivering in the cold must first receive the fine furs until all are warm. Those inflicted by spirits and evils shall partake of the medicine herbs we have brought. We ask that only after the needy are taken care of, will the rest of you take your pick of the remaining Trade."

"And the second thing?" Clay Fat called.

White Bird pointed at the barbarians. "These brave men have risked their lives to help me bring this Trade to the people. Owl Clan asks that you treat them as our honored guests. That you bestow upon them gifts to take back to their distant homeland. We ask that you provide every courtesy to them, as they have provided to us. They come from a different place and have different customs. When we lived in their village, they did not mock us when we made errors in their ways. And, my people, believe me, we made some very silly mistakes! They are not stupid, though through ignorance of our ways they may act like it. We simply ask that you do not mock them because they do not know our customs."

"These things shall be as you wish," Clay Fat cried happily. "Tell your friends that Rattlesnake Clan offers our homes and hospitality to these Wolf People."

Wing Heart lifted her chin slightly, thankful once again that Rattlesnake Clan remained loyal to her.

"What are your orders, Clan Elder?" White Bird called ritually.

"You are to camp on the Turtle's Back. There, you will be attended to. You are to cleanse yourselves before entering the sacred enclosure of Sun Town. You are to divest yourself of evil thoughts, of pettiness, and spite. You are to submit to the Serpent and his attendants when he comes to prepare you. When you are ready, we shall receive you and your Trade."

"It is as you order, Elder." White Bird bowed again, then settled himself easily into the canoe's stern. In what Wing Heart assumed was the language of the barbarians, he said something, and the rest of his companions lowered themselves into their boats. Paddles were collected, and the canoes turned to stroke off into the night, following White Bird's wake.

Wing Heart remained as she was, tall, head up, watching her son paddle away. There, just beyond the glow of the torches, he would land on Turtle's Back, a low island that broke the lake surface. Traditionally, Traders camped there, allowing themselves to be cleansed of any evil taint that they might have picked up, or that might be hovering close to their goods. The People couldn't be too careful. Surrounded as they were by jealous and spiteful peoples, curses and spells constantly flew in their direction—especially from the Swamp Panthers to the south. Despite the Power of their town, malignant evils continued to invade them. No matter that the earthen bands protected their central ground, and that spirits couldn't cross the water boundary of the lake that stretched east of the village, people still came down sick, and wounds festered, even when rapidly and efficiently treated by the Serpent.

After what Wing Heart deemed as a proper amount of time, she turned, slogging out of the mud and onto the crusted shore. Passing between the canoes, she stopped. People began drifting back up the slope, talking animatedly in the light of their torches. Cane Frog's young hunters lifted her and bore her away on their shoulders, while

Three Moss, trotting along behind, muttered in low tones.

"Mother?" the voice caught her by surprise.

She glanced down, seeing Mud Puppy standing there, his thatch of hair unkempt, preoccupation behind his large watery eyes. A cup was in his right hand, a flat piece of slate held over it with his left. "Where have you been?"

"I was catching a cricket."

A cricket! He was catching a cricket? Fifteen summers old, but he might have been ten, given the way he acted most of the time. She shook her head, biting off the harsh comment that leaped to her lips. Not here, someone would overhear, and Power take it, though everyone knew her son to be an idiot she needn't go out of her way to prove them right.

"White Bird is back?" he asked plaintively.

"Yes, yes, your brother is back. Now, go away. I have things to do. Much must be arranged."

She pushed past him, starting up toward the trail as Clay Fat stepped in beside her. He was a ball of a man, chubby of face, with a wide mouth. His belly preceded him like a canoe's prow. In his four tens of winters he had alternately been an irritant under her skin or a blessing, depending upon the circumstances.

"I see that Mud Puppy actually managed to show up. What happened? No spider dangling from the ceiling to distract him?" Clay Fat smiled; some of his kinspeople close enough to hear chuckled. Even Wing Heart's torchbearers smiled as they walked behind her, their burning cane torches held high.

"It was a cricket this time, can you imagine? What is it about that boy? I'd swear, his souls aren't anchored to his scrawny little body. He'd rather hide out in the forest staring into a pool of water for hands of time than learn or do anything useful."

"He has become a very capable stone carver for someone so young," Clay Fat pointed out. "Children his age can't usually sit still to make it through a meal, yet Mud Puppy can finish intricate carvings."

"Carvings will not make him useful when it comes to running a clan." She lifted her arms and let them drop. "As much as I feel cursed by Mud Puppy, White Bird more than makes up for him. Old friend, a weight is lifted from my souls. My son has returned. You cannot know how relieved my heart is."

Clay Fat's smile widened. "I cannot tell you how happy I am that White Bird has returned." He jerked a thumb back at Mud Puppy, who was talking to one of his scrawny friends. "Some people have begun to worry about him. There is talk that he has Dreams. That he sees things. Did you know that the Serpent has been watching him?"

"Mud Puppy? Why would the Serpent be watching him? He's harmless. Witless. And as to his Dreams"—she made a face—"you can tell people to relax. I have more faith in Power than to believe it would be interested in a skinny half-wit like him." She paused, then added pointedly, "He's Thumper's yield, you know."

"Yes. Curious isn't it? He's so different. Matings are such puzzling things."

She raised an eyebrow, shooting him a glance from the corner of her eye.

"Now that White Bird is back," Clay Fat mused, "Spring Cypress has just passed her first menstruation. She is a young woman now, and I know she favors White Bird."

Wing Heart knew for a fact that Spring Cypress had passed her first menstruation last winter out at Sweet Root Camp—where she would have remained had Clay Fat and Graywood Snake not decided that White Bird was dead. In lieu of that decision they had brought her back to Sun Town to troll her through Frog and Alligator Clans to see what young man snapped at her allure. Gorgeous nubile thing that she was, and Rattlesnake, having the influence that they did, she had had more than her share of young males swarming after her. Either of those clans would have been more than happy to send one of their sons to her house.

"We shall see," Wing Heart replied casually. Did she dare contemplate another alliance with Rattlesnake Clan? Or, given the potentials of White Bird's exploding popularity, would she be better served marrying the boy to one of the other clans?

"You could do worse, you know," Clay Fat continued. "And, well, until tonight, a great many people were worried."

"As was I," she relented.

"They thought you might name Mud Puppy as Speaker!" Clay Fat laughed, his rotund belly wiggling.

"Mud Puppy as Speaker . . ." At that moment she caught sight of old Mud Stalker. He was walking in the shadows off to the side, his ruined right arm cradled in his left. Beside him, Deep Hunter was talking, his hands moving to emphasize his words. The one person Deep Hunter hated more than Mud Stalker was the Swamp Panther cutthroat, Jaguar Hide. So, why were they talking now? *What venom are you concocting, old man? How do you intend to inject it into my flesh?*

The thought of it sent a cold shiver down her spine.

When she looked back toward the night-veiled lake, she could see nothing. No fire had yet been built on the Turtle's Back.

Instead, oddly, she noticed Mud Puppy where he stood at the water's edge, a solitary figure, totally absorbed by his cup.

Mud Puppy? Speaker for the clan? I'd lose my souls before I'd allow that to happen.

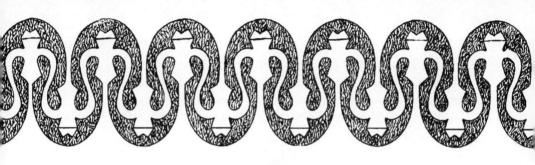

Four

That night as Mud Puppy lay deep in sleep, a soft gulf breeze blew up from the south. It carried the tendrils of rising smoke northward, away from the curved lines of houses that dotted the concentric ridges of Sun Town. The darkness lay thick, light from Father Moon and the myriads of stars blotted by the mass of clouds that alternately drizzled rain on the land.

As the Dream slipped its hazy fingers around Mud Puppy's souls, Owl wings sailed silently through the falling tendrils of misty rain and over the arched ridges of Sun Town. The great bird circled slowly above a single dwelling on the eastern end of the first ridge.

The oval-shaped house had been built of saplings driven into the ground, woven together with vines, and plastered with clay. Sheaves of grass formed a thick thatch that was bound to the cane roof stringers by wraps of stout cord. The tight thatch shed the rain, letting it drip just beyond the clay walls to pool in the rich soil.

The door was an oblong hole in the wall covered with a hemp-fabric hanging just thick enough to block most of the chill. Around the top, and along the overhang of thatch, smoke drifted out, carrying with it the odor of hickory and maple.

Inside, a cane-pole bench that served as seating and bedding had been built into the wall circumference. The woman slept fitfully on the western side, her aging body covered with a fine deerskin blanket. The boy, in his bed on the eastern side, lay lost in dreams, his body covered with a worn fabric. He had curled on his right side, the rounded angles of his face visible in the reddish glow cast by the coals in the central hearth. His eyes flicked and wiggled under tightly closed lids.

The Dream knotted itself in Mud Puppy's souls, wrapping around them, spinning and cavorting.

He sat at the top of a high mound, the ground warm under his buttocks and thighs. He reached down and raked the earth into his hands. Holding it to his nose, he sniffed the pungent musk, drawing it into his body and souls. After it became one with him, he pinched the dark silty soil into shapes with his fingers. The moist earth seemed to flow as though of its own accord, forming at his very thoughts, the image perfectly rendered by his supple brown fingers.

First he sculpted the body, rotund, with a protruding belly. Then he shaped a round head, his thumbs curving up and around the face to reveal a hooked beak between two broadly recessed eyes. With thumb and forefinger he pinched out the ears, pointed and high. Using a fingernail he circled the large eyes—and when he lifted his hand, they blinked at him, bright yellow with gleaming black pupils.

Along either side of the rotund body he shaped the wings, outlining the feathers with his nails. From the bottom of the torso he pulled out the feet, his thumbnail tracing the individual toes and talons.

"You have done well," the mud sculpture told him. "But you have to learn to fly before you can learn to Dance."

Mud Puppy stared at the owl, aware that it was changing, that its beak had turned yellow, feathers softening around the ears, but the face, he realized, looked fake. *A mask! He's wearing a mask!* "You are Masked Owl!"

"Yes, I am." Masked Owl chuckled at that. "And what is a mask, boy?"

"A covering."

"Is it?"

"Of course. Just like at the ceremonies when the deer dancers come in. It's to make them look like deer."

Masked Owl cocked his head. "In so many ways you remind me of Bad Belly."

"Who?"

"A young man I once knew, one carried away by the world. Like you, he saw wonder in everything. It comes of an innocence of the soul. I cannot tell you how precious that is."

"What happened to him?"

"Oh, he became a hero in spite of himself."

"He didn't want to be?"

Owl's head tilted again. "Have you ever been a hero?"

"No." Mud Puppy frowned down at his dirty hands. "But my brother is."

Masked Owl considered this. "Then you do not know what it costs to be a hero. The price is high, as your brother is about to find out."

"Is he—"

"Why are you called Mud Puppy?"

"I—I had one. A mud puppy, I mean." He looked down at his hands again. As he picked the silt from his fingers, he rolled it into worms. In the sway of the Dream, they began to wiggle and burrow into the rounded top of the mound upon which they sat. Below him the world seemed to inhale and breathe, the trees, water, soil, and grass alive and vibrant with color.

"What finally happened to your mud puppy?"

"I kept it in a ceramic pot filled with water. I petted it and went out every day and caught it insects."

"And?"

"It changed. It became a beautiful salamander. It went from an ugly brown color to the most incredible reddish orange. Like sunset in the clouds, with black spots all over it. Its eyes were bright yellow, like yours, but smaller."

"That's the Power of Salamander." Masked Owl's haunting yellow eyes bored into Mud Puppy's as if seeing inside to his Life Soul. "People don't understand how magical Salamander is. They ignore him for the most part."

"It's because he's close to the Monsters Below."

"He is, but that's not why people ignore him."

"It's not?"

"No." Masked Owl hesitated. "People usually see the world as a reflection of themselves. Pride, arrogance, and status preoccupy them. Let me ask, would your brother rather have Falcon or Salamander for a Spirit Helper?"

"Falcon," Mud Puppy replied without hesitation.

"And you? Which would you chose?"

Mud Puppy jabbed his fingers into the dirt. "My mother says I'll never have a Spirit Helper. She says that I'm too stupid."

"But if you could have a Spirit Helper?"

Mud Puppy glanced shyly at the owl. "I don't know much about them, but Spirit Helpers pick the people they go to, don't they? So

I guess I'd want a Spirit Helper that wanted me. If it was Salamander, that would be all right. Everyone wants Falcon. Maybe it would make Salamander happy if someone wanted him." He paused. "Do Spirit Helpers worry about things like that? About whether people want them or not?"

"Yes, Mud Puppy, they do. And now let me tell you something that most people don't know. Falcon is indeed powerful, and many people want him for a Spirit Helper, but he has a weakness. He is very fragile. His bones are hollow. His body breaks very easily. He can't stand any sort of poison because his system is so delicate it will kill him."

"And Salamander?"

"Ah, Salamander is anything but delicate. He can survive floods, drought, fires, and frost. Not only can he live underwater, but atop the ground, too. His flesh is poisonous to his enemies such as Wolf and Raccoon. Best of all, he stays out of sight most of the time. While the great beasts rip and tear each other's flesh, Salamander lies under the stones and Dreams the Dance."

"The Dance?"

"Ah, yes, the Dance." Masked Owl twirled around, his wings rising in a splendid arc. "To Dance the One. As I am doing now."

"You are?"

"Indeed."

"Can I learn your Dance? I'm not as stupid as people think I am. I learned the Circle Dance last winter at solstice when we Danced Mother Sun back into the sky."

Masked Owl stopped, and those huge black pupils seemed to expand in the yellow eyes behind the mask. They grew, larger and larger, and as they did, Mud Puppy's soul seemed to shrink.

"Would you like to Dance, Mud Puppy?"

"Very much."

He felt rather than saw Masked Owl's smile. "I am glad to hear that." Then came sadness. "But I can't teach you yet."

"You can't?"

"No."

Mud Puppy pursed his lips, a terrible grief that he didn't quite understand lying deep in his breast. Instead he said, "That's all right."

Masked Owl's eyes swelled again, engulfing the world around them. Like pools of darkness, they ebbed and flowed, pulsing with the rhythm of the universe. "You are a good person, Mud Puppy. It pains me to ask, but will you do some things for me before I teach you the Dance?"

"Yes. If I can. But Mother says I'm not very good at doing important things. I heard her tell Uncle Cloud Heron that I can't even be trusted to carry a cup of water through a rainstorm. You should know that before you ask. And I'm small for my age. Mother says I can't keep my mind on important things. Most of my friends are working hard to become men. They hunt and fish and learn to be warriors."

"Why don't you?"

"I'm not good at those things. I try, but somehow . . ."

"Yes?"

"I like finding out secrets."

"Secrets?"

Mud Puppy grinned. "Yes, like why Cricket can make such a loud noise. Or how a caterpillar can become a moth in a cocoon. Have you ever looked into a cocoon after the moth leaves? There aren't any caterpillar parts left inside. So, where does a moth come from? And, if you cut a caterpillar open, it's all full of juice. It sure doesn't have a moth hidden in there anywhere. I know. I used a stick and stirred the gooey stuff to find out."

Masked Owl's eyes seemed to shrink, enough that Mud Puppy could see that Masked Owl had thrown his head back. His laughter shook the world and left the clouds trembling. When he stopped, he said, "Mud Puppy, you are a special boy. It has been a long time since I have found such an honest and humble soul."

Mud Puppy winced, turning his attention back to his hands, picked mostly clean of mud now. All of the worms he'd made had burrowed into the ground. "I'm sorry."

"Sorry?"

"Yes. Sorry that I'm all those things. You might want to ask my brother. He's just come back from the north. Everyone is proud of him. If I can't do what you need, he might be able to."

Masked Owl was studying him with those terrible eyes. "What if I said I wanted you?"

"I will do my best," Mud Puppy asserted. "Especially if you will teach me your Dance. Maybe if I do well, and try very hard, I could get a Spirit Helper? Maybe even one that was Powerful like Salamander?" He frowned; then an image of his mother's face formed.

"What's wrong?"

"Would Salamander mind if I didn't tell my mother?"

"Why wouldn't you tell her?"

"She wouldn't like it if she found out that Salamander was my Spirit Helper."

"Why not?"

"She wouldn't understand."

Masked Owl chuckled again. "No, I suppose not. And you, you really wouldn't mind if Salamander was your Spirit Helper?"

"No!" Mud Puppy cried, abashed. "I would be so grateful."

Masked Owl laughed again. "I shall talk to Salamander. I shall also accept your promise of lending me help. You should know, however, that it will be a terrible trial. What I will ask will take both perseverance and cunning. It will mean that you must stay true to your beliefs and never lose faith in yourself, no matter what other people are saying. If you are not clever and committed, it could cost you your life."

Mud Puppy swallowed hard; for the first time fear began to squirm around in his gut. It prickled through him, raising beads of sweat from his skin and making his heart pound.

Masked Owl noted this and nodded. "Ah, good, you understand."

"I will get a Spirit Helper and learn your Dance?"

"If you do not fail me, yes."

"I . . ." the words couldn't quite form in his throat. *Do I really want to do this? Can I do it? Will I fail? And what if I do? What if I can't do what he asks?*

"Then I will be most disappointed, Mud Puppy." Masked Owl cocked his head. "I do not know if you can do the things I'm asking. Others have failed me in the past. I cannot resist your free will."

Mud Puppy's soul twisted like old fabric as he said, "I will do my best."

"Do you promise on your souls?"

"I do."

"Then, come, let us fly." Masked Owl leaped from the mound top, spiraling in the air. Looking back, he called, "Raise your arms and jump!"

Mud Puppy, his heart trembling in fear, raised his arms and spread his fingers, willing to try, even if Masked Owl laughed when his flailing arms dropped him back to Earth.

It was to his surprise, then, that he rose, carried by the powerful beat of his arms. He flew! His arms flattened into strong wings that silently caressed the night air. He could see the land, as though in muted daylight, colors oddly drained into a bluish gray cast.

Among the clouds he soared and spiraled. Lightning flashed silently around him, flickering from the spotted feathers on his broad wings. Thunder Beings darted and hid among the clouds, showing their faces, only to vanish again, the memory of their grins left behind in the patterns of cloud and wind.

The sound of the birds brought Hazel Fire awake. He blinked, yawned, and sat up, his elkhide robe falling from his shoulders. Fatigue still hung in his muscles, the night's rest hardly a payment on the debt he owed his body for the constant days of ceaseless paddling. But they had made it! He was here, just outside the legendary Sun Town. A place that Traders spoke of with awe-hushed voices. He and his friends were going to see this storied place with their own eyes, the first of their kind to do so. It was the stuff of legends.

The canoes were drawn up on the muddy shore just below his feet. He could see their bundled contents; everything glistened silver with beads of dew. A drop spattered on his head, and he looked up at the overhanging branches of the sweetgum tree. The star-shaped leaves hung listlessly in the still air.

Droplets, like little diamonds, shimmered on his elkhide as he laid it aside and stood. The effect was magical. A low mist lay over the silver-gray water. It drifted past the trees, curled around the sleeping bodies of his companions, and seemed to slither around the patches of hanging moss that clung to the branches. A fish jumped in the lake, rings widening in lazy circles.

Hazel Fire walked down to the water and relieved himself. For the moment he was limited to looking across the opaque surface of the lake that separated him from the mythical Sun People's town. What little he could see of it was perched atop a gray cliff that rose to the height of four men above the distant shore. Several buildings—tall things with thatched roofs—looked ghostly in the silvered mist. One perched on a mound to the north. Another stood atop a mound to the south, just above where the bluff sloped to a canoe landing. Barely visible, the mist shrouded it again with a closing wall of white. Had it really been there?

Memories came back of their arrival last night, of the procession of torches that had wound down to the canoe landing. Tens of ten at least, so many they had cast a warm yellow light over the landing the likes of which Hazel Fire had never seen. The clamor of the voices had been fit to shake the waters and raise the dead. In that magical moment, the torchlit column of people, like a serpent of light spilling onto the shore, had been dazzling in its spectacle. White Bird and Yellow Spider had called back and forth with the horde for what seemed an eternity, and Hazel Fire had suddenly wished he'd taken more time to learn this odd language. It sounded like turkeys squawking to him. Something impossible to wrap the human tongue around.

"Where are we? Is this real?" Snow Water had asked in awe from his canoe.

"I've never seen so many people," Jackdaw had replied warily.

"Those are only a few of the tens of tens of tens who live in Sun Town," Yellow Spider had assured them from his bobbing canoe.

"Are we going to land?" Gray Fox had asked. "My legs feel like wood."

"For the moment," White Bird had replied, "we will make camp there, on that island. We call it the Turtle's Back. Being surrounded as it is by Morning Lake, it is protected as well as protection from evil spirits and hostile ghosts." He had pointed, and the torchlight had been such that Hazel Fire had seen the black hump of earth like some monster lurking in the calm water.

"Who would have thought?" Hazel Fire wondered aloud to himself as he replayed the events of the night before. Until he died the sight of all those cane torches burning in the night would be lodged in his head.

"Thought what?" White Bird asked in heavily accented Trade pidgin. His head poked up from the painted buffalo hide he had slept under.

"That I'd really be here." Hazel Fire turned and gestured back at the town, now hidden behind the mist like an eclipsed vision. "Is it really as you said? I mean now that we're here, are we going to be disappointed? Are we going to find out that everything you told us is, well, shall we say, something of a story? A bit of imagination?"

White Bird laughed, a twinkle in his eyes. "No, my friend." The young man threw back his painted hide and stood, stretching. Once again Hazel Fire admired his muscular body and the character reflected in that handsome face. Something about those shining black eyes made a man instinctively trust White Bird. No wonder Lark had fallen so deeply in love. Despite what Hazel Fire's father, Acorn Cup, might have told White Bird, it had taken all of his Hickory Clan's influence to keep Lark from running off to this magical southern land.

White Bird stepped down to stand beside Hazel Fire. "If anything, Sun Town is grander than I have told you." White Bird placed a reassuring hand on his shoulder. "I've been gone a complete turning of the seasons, my friend. I wager a great deal more has been built in that time. It will almost be as new to me as it will be to you."

"When do I get to see this mythical place? Three days? It will take a whole three days?"

White Bird's smile remained infectious. "If all goes well."

"Why so long?" Hazel Fire raised an eyebrow.

"We have come a long way." White Bird pointed northward with his right hand. "Across many lands. We have been exposed to a great many evils. Spirits can attach themselves to us, or to our Trade. You know this. So before we enter the city's protection we must drive them off, cleanse our souls."

"Cleanse how?" He crossed his arms. "Some magician isn't going to steal my souls, is he?"

White Bird laughed, his white teeth shining. "I sincerely hope not. I'm as fond of my souls as you are of yours. No. I know you, know all of you. We have shared too many trials, Hazel Fire. All of us have done something marvelous. No one has ever brought so much Trade to Sun Town at once, or from so far away. There is Power in that, good friend. Instead of six days, they will cleanse us in three."

"Six? Three? What is the difference?"

"Three." White Bird held up three fingers, touching each fingertip as he talked. "The worlds of Creation: Sky, Earth, and Underworld. Sky is the domain of Father Moon and Mother Sun, the place of sunlight, clouds, and birds. Earth is the surface where we live and the trees grow and the water flows. Third is the Underworld, home of the fish, the roots, moles, and badgers, the place where all things originated. We are born of the underworlds, raised into the light to walk the land, and doomed to forever Dream of flying through the Sky."

"Hmm." Hazel Fire rubbed his chin. "Among my people . . ."

"Yes, the Magicians can leave their bodies and fly. Here, too, though we call them the Serpents. You'll meet one soon enough."

"He won't try and steal my Power?" Hazel Fire reached for the small leather pouch that hung from his neck.

"Your umbilical cord is safe." White Bird referred to the dried loop of tissue that all Wolf People carried with them from birth to death. And woe unto he who through flood, fire, or accident lost his. The stories among the Wolf People told of sudden insanity, debilitating illness, and often a wasting death that came within days. It had been a matter of no little awe to Lark that White Bird and Yellow Spider could live, thrive in fact, without one.

"And yours." Hazel Fire pointed to the necklace that draped around White Bird's neck. "I always wondered about those tokens, but thought it rude to ask. I noticed that your necklace never left your neck. Is it magic?"

White Bird reached up, fingering the small stone fetishes hung there. Though some were cubes, others were sections of slate incised with geometric designs, but his fingers went to the little fat-bellied owl carved out of a bloodred stone. "Perhaps it is magic. A protection of sorts. My little brother, Mud Puppy, made this. Can you imagine? He carved each of the pieces, and him barely past ten and four winters when I saw him last."

"I look forward to meeting him." Hazel Fire saw the sudden reserve in White Bird's eyes. "Is that a problem?"

"Hmm? Oh, no. He's just strange, that's all. A different child. Always has been." The Trader's eyes had focused on something in the distance beyond the fog.

"I suppose, Husband of my sister, that you are normal for your kind? You who braved everything to travel so far north in search of this magical Trade of yours?"

White Bird smiled. "I would like to think I am normal, but no, I suppose I Dream too much."

"I could Dream of that young woman who ran down to wave at you last night." Hazel Fire tried to look unconcerned. "A sister of yours, perhaps? Someone you could introduce me to?"

"Sorry." White Bird had caught his subtle meaning. "She's Rattlesnake Clan. There's a chance I might end up married to her. She won't be Lark, but . . ."

"She'll be here," Hazel Fire supplied with a shrug. "That is the way of things. Though I wouldn't mind you coming home to be a permanent husband to Lark."

White Bird kept his eyes on the shimmering wall of mist that hid Sun Town. "You don't know how tempting that might be. I have no idea of the situation here. I could tell by my mother's actions last night. By the way she stood. The clans are at it again."

"And how is that? I would learn what I'm stepping into before it's on my moccasin."

White Bird's preoccupation seemed to vanish. "Oh, you'll be fine. They'll treat you right. It's in the nature of the gifting. You helped to bring the Trade. For that the clans will make you most welcome. Fear not. Just turn your Trade over with a smile, and they will shower you with gifts. Enough to more than fill your canoe before you must head north."

"This giving interests me."

"Giving, Trade if you will, is what binds us together. We are a people of parts and pieces. It goes back to the beginning, to the Creation. It is said that in those times we fought with each other, constantly at war. And then, one day, a magical Masked Owl, one of the Sky Beings from the Creation, came spiraling down to tell us that there was a better way."

Hazel Fire nodded. "Go on."

"We have two moieties." White Bird squatted, using his finger to draw a circle in the charcoal-black mud. This he divided into two sections. "Everything we do is meant to achieve balance. My moiety consists of Owl Clan, Alligator Clan, and Frog Clan. Sky, Earth, and Underworld. We are the night side, that of the north." He divided one-half of the circle into three to denote the clans. "On the other side is the world of day, or the south. The clans are Eagle, Rattlesnake, and Snapping Turtle. Again, Air, Earth and Underworld. Eagles live in the air. Rattlesnakes crawl across the ground and snapping turtles live in the mud underwater." He divided the southern half of the circle into three sections.

"But that's a total of six clans."

"You're right. Six is the number of directions that make up the world. Your people have four sacred directions: north, south, east, and west. My people believe them to be sacred, too, but we add up and down for a total of six directions. In our stories the clans came together here, at the center of the world, from each of the different directions. My people, my clans, my city, all reflect the world. Opposites crossed, night and day, north and south, east and west, up and down. Everything must be brought together to keep Creation intact. We constantly strive to do that, and gifting is how we accomplish such a seemingly hopeless task. The greatest challenge is to hold the world together. Forces, people, are always trying to split it apart. We have to work constantly to bind it back together."

"You told me once that your clan will just give all of these things away to people in other clans." Hazel Fire was frowning. "You won't take anything back from them? Nothing in Trade? No reciprocity?"

"Oh, we'll get our value back," White Bird assured. "We just won't get it in things. Our return comes from the influence our Clan Elder and Speaker have in the Council. We don't collect large amounts of things because that would create envy. People who covet what other people have turn wicked, their souls are the perfect home for evil. But if you give necessary things to the needy, they cannot feel slighted. In turn, when you need, they will provide. We have a very complicated system of give-and-take. It works, it keeps us together, and we keep the Creator happy."

"But I know you were worried when we arrived last night. You and Yellow Spider were unsure about your homecoming."

White Bird nodded absently. "I didn't say that we do not compete with each other. It would have been very different had another clan gained ascendancy. My arrival could have proved, well, shall we say, uncomfortable, for Alligator or Snapping Turtle Clan had they become dominant."

"What about your uncle?" Hazel Fire watched the interplay of emotions on White Bird's handsome face. "You were worried that he might have died while you were gone."

"He wasn't well when I left last spring." White Bird pursed his lips for a moment. "It was a gamble that Yellow Spider and I made. My mother is Clan Elder, her brother, my uncle, is Speaker for the clan when in Council. I told you, Power is passed through the mother in my people. When my uncle dies, my mother, as Elder, has the right to nominate another Speaker. I hope to be that Speaker."

"Then what is the problem? Why can't she just put your name forward?"

White Bird thumped his chest. "I'm young. Not even married."

"You are to Lark. And, if I don't miss my guess, the father of her child."

"On my soul, take no offense from this, but she isn't here, and none of my people recognize her clan. Formally, among the clans, she wouldn't be recognized as a real wife."

Hazel Fire nodded. "No offense is taken. So, let's say you marry that pretty young thing I Dreamed about all night. Marry her and be Speaker."

"Not that easy." White Bird waved a cautionary finger. "Most men live all of their lives before they are nominated to be Speaker. It's different for a wet-nosed boy like they consider me to be. That's why Yellow Spider and I had to go so far north. That's why we needed so much Trade. That's why I had to risk so much. I had to do something spectacular, Hazel Fire. I may not have gone farther than any of our people have gone before, but I brought more Trade back from that distance than anyone else has."

"For that alone they should name you Speaker." Hazel Fire made a gesture with his fingers. "But what about your uncle? What if he would have been dead?"

"Mother would have had to nominate another Speaker. I'm the

only one left in her lineage. She had no sisters, just brothers. And Cloud Heron is the last of her brothers who is alive."

"What about Cloud Heron's children? Why don't they qualify?"

"You forget, we trace descent through the woman. Uncle Cloud Heron's children belong to his wife. Her name was Laced Fern, and she is a member of the Eagle Clan. So all of Cloud Heron's children belong to the . . . ?" He cocked his head, an eyebrow raised to provoke the answer.

"The children are all Eagle Clan," Hazel Fire supplied. "I understand." He pressed his fingertips together. "Is it so bad for your lineage to lose the Speaker? Couldn't some other clansman serve just as well?"

White Bird shrugged as he dug some of the silty mud from his drawing. Black and slick it stuck to his fingers. "Perhaps. This is difficult to explain, but neither my mother nor I wish to see another take over leadership of the clan. It has been in our lineage for three generations. I am the last. After me, it will go elsewhere because my children will belong to my wife's clan."

"Not the ones from Lark, if you'll recall."

"But Lark is a long way from here."

"Yes, yes, I know, and your people probably consider her to be some kind of wild animal or something."

"I never said that."

"You didn't have to." Hazel Fire laughed. "That's how my people would think of that pretty Spring Cypress if I carried her home; why wouldn't it be the other way around?" In a more serious voice, he said, "Besides, there's your little brother. What's his name?"

White Bird made a face as he rolled the black silt into a small round ball. "We call him Mud Puppy."

"Like a dog covered with mud?"

"No, a mud puppy is our name for immature brown salamanders. You know, before they are mature, when they still have those star-shaped gills sticking out behind their heads." White Bird rubbed the silt ball between his hands. "Perhaps he'll grow out of this stage he's in, just like a mud puppy grows into a salamander."

"He's how old?"

"Just ten and five winters now." He reached up to finger the fetishes on his necklace. "Mud Puppy as Speaker, now there's a thought for amusement. They would destroy him."

"Destroy?" Hazel Fire cocked his head. "What about all that talk about harmony?"

White Bird gave him a sober look, his dark eyes haunted. In a low voice, he said, "Why do you think we work so hard at it? Prominence of the clans is everything to us. We give things to place people in our debt. Owing something to someone else holds us together like water holds this mud." He lifted the silt ball. "Without gift giving and the obligation it implies, we are nothing. Barbarians. We need Trade to overcome our real nature. Without it, we would be at each other's throats. I swear, within a generation, we would destroy ourselves."

As he said that, he extended his hand, holding the silt ball between his fingers as he placed it into the water. Hazel Fire watched as the lapping waves melted the ball into goo.

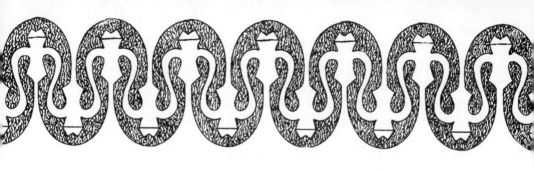

Five

Mud Puppy sat on a cane mat in the sunlight on the eastern side of his mother's house. Images from the Dream the night before burned through him, replaying between his souls with such clarity that he might have just seen them spun out of the misty morning sunlight. A shiver ran down his bones. He could sense the lingering Power that emanated from Masked Owl. It had been so real!

Frown lines ate into his forehead when he stared down at the cricket. As long as his thumb from knuckle to nail tip, its shell gleamed midnight black in the cup bottom. The antennae were waving in sinuous arcs. But, despite his vigilance, the cricket refused to surrender its secret. Crickets and Sky Beings—they both eluded him.

"What have you got there?" Mother's words caught him by surprise. He looked up, seeing her standing beside him, her arms braced on her hips, face shadowed. The morning sun blazed like white fire in her silvered hair. She had left it down this morning, and it hung over her shoulders. Her white skirt was belted about her hips, leaving her top bare. Mud Puppy could see the line of tattoos, like a chain that circled her sagging breasts and merged to make a double row that ran down the midline of her stomach to surround her navel.

"It's a cricket," he replied in a low voice, wary and unsure. He never knew how she was going to react.

"A cricket?" Wing Heart seemed distracted, her face reflecting no emotion. "What are you doing with it?"

He swallowed hard, knowing better than to lie to her. "I told you about it last night. A cricket is such a small animal. I was trying to see why it makes such a great noise. I've been waiting patiently for cricket to sing, then I will discover his secret. You told me that patience was the footprint of greatness." He hoped that would win him a little goodwill. It pleased her to have him repeat her teachings. "When cricket sings, I'll rip off the bass leaf and see how he makes his noise."

She chewed on the corner of her lip for a moment, then reached out with one hand. "Give it to me."

Reluctantly, he extended the little gray ceramic cup with its bass-leaf cover. She took it, removed the leaf, and stared down into the cup. "A cricket."

"Yes, Mother."

"Do you understand that your brother has returned? Did you see him last night? Are you aware of what he's done?"

"I was at the landing last night. Me and Little Needle—"

"Ah, Little Needle. I'd wager that but for Little Needle you wouldn't have had the slightest notion that anything was afoot, would you?"

He didn't answer, lowering his gaze to the dark-stained earth at his feet. A bit of red chert gleamed in the sunlight, an old perforator; someone had broken the tip off and discarded it. It seemed to wink maliciously at him.

"What am I going to do with you?" Mother asked plaintively. "I swear by Mother Sun, I could almost believe that Back Scratch and Mud Stalker knew in advance that you would come of it when they sent Thumper to my bed. I could almost believe that they paid the Serpent to cast a spell on the man's testicles. Thumper's not a dolt, and neither am I, so how did our union produce you?"

Mud Puppy winced, his heart hurting at the tone in her voice. He kept his eyes focused on the bit of gleaming red chert so out of place in the black dirt. Was it trying to talk to him? Was that why it was winking so?

"All you do is waste time." Wing Heart lifted her arms in supplication. "Do you not understand how close we came to disaster? It is not enough that your uncle's Dream Soul has fled? What if he had lost his Life Soul as well? What if White Bird hadn't come back in triumph?" She squatted, lifting his chin with one hand to glare into his eyes. "Do you understand that we are the last in our line to dominate the Council? Do you understand that if we lose that, we are nothing? That we will be just like everyone else?"

"Is that so bad?" he whispered.

"Is that so bad?" she mimicked his voice. "Very well, I'll explain it to you *one . . . more . . . time.*" She paused as if searching for the right words. "As you live your life, Mud Puppy, you will want things. Perhaps it will be a certain woman, though Mother Sun knows, I should be so lucky given your proclivities. When that happens, you must have the position, the prominence among others, and the outstanding *obligation* to be granted that desire. You like to quote my lessons back to me, very well, quote this one: With obligation comes prestige. With prestige comes authority. With authority comes gratification."

He nodded, hating the eye-to-eye contact she maintained. That burning look made his souls squirm around each other.

"Everything we do is based on obligation." Her words were like burning coals. "All that I have achieved, I have achieved through binding others to me through their debt. I didn't achieve my position by studying crickets, or carving little stone figures, but by playing one clan off of the other. By knowing my enemies, and making them beholden unto me. That, my misguided son, is the secret to survival. It is by adhering to such a strategy that, in the long run, we will keep Owl Clan in the center of our world."

"I understand." Why did she dominate him like a hawk did a mouse? His ears burned with humiliation. "With obligation comes prestige. With prestige comes authority. With authority comes gratification."

"Very good." She stood then, a frown lining her sun-browned forehead as she studied him. Without a thought, she flipped the cricket from the cup and tossed the empty vessel back to him. "I don't seem to make any impression when I tell you these things." Her eyes drifted to the distance, searching the west. A sudden smile crossed her thin lips. "I want you to know that you have driven me to desperation. I am going to teach you a lesson once and for all."

Mud Puppy swallowed hard. Mother's lessons were never easy.

She narrowed her eyes, a finger on her chin as she thought. "Yes, just as soon as the Serpent can free himself from his duties. It may take a couple of days, but I am going to have him take you up the Bird's Head—and leave you!"

He blinked, trying to understand. No one frightened him like the Serpent did.

She continued, "I want you to spend the night alone up there, Mud Puppy. All by yourself. Just you and the darkness. And if you don't come down changed, I'm going to send you up there again and again until the spirits of the Dead finally get you."

He shot a quick glance westward to where the looming pile of earth rose like a small mountain above the plaza flat. "Can I take Little Needle—"

"Alone!"

"But, if I get afraid—"

"*Alone!* When you get scared—*and I want you trembling to your bones*—you will stay and overcome your fear. No son of mine has the luxury of fear. Do you think your brother was afraid when he went upriver? Do you think he let fear stop him from taking the most dangerous of risks? No. And one day he's going to need you, need your courage and your loyalty to back him." Her voice hardened. "*And you will be there for him, or I will haunt you to your dying day.*"

She turned, striding purposefully away down the side of the earthen ridge upon which they lived. Her back was straight, her silver-streaked hair swaying with each regal step.

"But I get afraid in the dark," he whispered, turning his eyes to the southwest, past the house where his uncle lay dying, past the line of clan houses and across the plaza. As if embraced by the curve of the raised earth, the tall mound stood, and just below the top, he could make out the little thatched ramada. Terrible things happened up there. Gods came down and whispered things into people's ears. Lightning frequently blasted that high summit. From those heights, it was said that a man could see into the Land of the Dead. Worse, that the Dead could look back and see you. That's why nobody but the most Powerful of hunters and warriors, and old Serpent and his students, ever spent the night up there.

"*You'll lose your souls,*" a tiny voice said.

Mud Puppy looked down at the broken fragment of red chert between his feet. He reached down and plucked it up, watching the sunlight shine off the smooth stone. "Then you'll lose yours with them," he answered, "because I'm taking you with me. Whatever happens to me will happen to you."

The swampland around the Panther's Bones had been inundated for two moons now. Sultry brown waters lapped at the water oak, sweetgum, tupelo, and bald cypress. Long wraiths of hanging moss dangled from the branches. Birds perched amidst the lush green leaves, disturbed only rarely as squirrels scrambled from tree to tree in search of ripening fruits. Fish leaped with hollow splashes that barely dented the whirring of the insects and the rising birdsong. Far out in the swamp, a bull alligator roared his desire for a mate.

At the sound, Jaguar Hide turned his head, holding his paddle high. Was it worth turning, going after the big bull? As he considered, his canoe drifted forward, a V-shaped wake disturbing the smooth surface and rocking bits of flotsam and tacky white foam.

"I would rather go home, Uncle," Anhinga said from the bow, her paddle resting on the gunwales. "I have a feeling."

Jaguar Hide cocked his head, asking, "Yes? A feeling? Of what?"

"Of something changing."

He watched the back of her head. She had been silent most of the day, moody since they had departed from the western uplands. Twice he had observed the shaking of her shoulders as sobs possessed her. The grief had been a palpable thing, like a swarm of mosquitoes that shimmered around her.

"Things change, girl. That is the way of the world." He lowered his voice. "But I can see that this is something more. Tell me."

He watched the slight lowering of her head. Dappled sunlight sent shafts of yellow through the green leaves above to speckle her gleaming black hair. "Bowfin's Dream Soul met mine the night he died. He was so anguished to be dead. It was so unfair. I am angry, Uncle. His death has changed my life. I have learned to hate."

Jaguar Hide considered her, noting how her back arched. The set of her head. Gods, she looked just as his sister Yellow Dye had at her age. "Indeed?"

She remained silent, so he extended his paddle, sending the canoe forward as he guided it between the trees. Here and there they had to duck as low branches blocked the way.

"Whenever I close my eyes I see him lying there, sweat running off of his skin in rivers . . . his eyes glazed with fear and pain," she whispered. "The smell haunts me, Uncle. It clings to my souls. I can imagine what he felt . . . how it was to have his guts eaten out like that. It must have burned, like a fire being pulled through his belly on a splintered pole." She shook her head. "He could smell himself. Smell that awful stink coming out of his ripped guts. How did he stand it? Knowing it was his own?"

"Niece, you can stand many things when you have no other choice." Jaguar Hide winced at the pain her voice. "It is how the Panther made the world. Look around you." He gestured at the brown-water swamp they paddled through. "Everywhere you look, you will see life dancing with death. Does the alligator cast a single tear for the fawn he drags down to death? Does the egret weep for the minnow she spears out of the calm waters? Do you cry at the sight of fish gasping and flopping in the netting of a mud set when it is pulled aboard a canoe? Do these sweetgum trees mourn for the saplings they suffocate with their spreading branches? No, girl. When a hanging spider catches a beautiful butterfly in its web, it eats it with a smile. That is the lesson you should learn. Life is a desperate hunt. As you grin gleefully over your victim's body, remember that tomorrow someone else will be grinning over yours." He hesitated, letting that sink in, then asked: "Do you understand, Anhinga?"

She nodded.

Once again he waited, allowing her time. To his right, a line of yellow-dotted gourd floats indicated that Old Blue Hand had set a gill net.

"It just seems so unfair. This was Bowfin, my little brother. He was just a boy, Uncle. I took care of him. We played together, laughed and cried together. They *murdered* him."

He paddled steadily as she broke down into tears. He had wondered how long it would take for the reality of her brother's death to settle over her souls like a net. Sometimes the young didn't understand, and Anhinga had been lucky, life had protected her for the most part. She had never suffered such a rapid and painful loss.

Their relations with the Sun People were always tenuous. Sometimes they traded, but with the most guarded of interactions. Fact was, Jaguar Hide's Panther People had little need for anyone else. The Creator had given his chosen people the finest place in the world to live. Here, in spring, as the floods filled the great river to the east, the waters actually reversed, changed direction, flowing backward into the lakes and watercourses. In the rejuvenated waters fish thrived. The highlands in the western portion of their territory contained sands, gravels, and their fine panther sandstone: a white, coarse-grained slab that was perfect for smoothing wood and grinding stone. The Creator had made a perfect place for his people. Here they wanted for nothing.

Not at all like what he had done for the Sun People to the north. Perched on their silt ridge, they had no source of stone for cutting, no sandstone for grinding, no sand to temper their pottery. The only riches the Sun People had been given were fish and plants. So they came here when they needed sandstone, to Jaguar Hide's land, and tried to trade, or more usually, to steal stone. It was when they were caught that young men like Bowfin paid the price.

His heart twisted at the pain and grief in Anhinga's broken sobs. How many times in his life had he heard the wailing and sobbing of relatives grieving for a loved one? How many lives had been taken from them by a brutal stone-headed dart? If the Creator had meant for the Sun People to have sandstone, he would have given it to them.

I will do something about this. This time, I will find a way to pay them back.

He knotted his souls around the problem as he continued to paddle through the muggy swamp. At their approach a turtle flipped off a cypress knee, a line of bubbles marking its descent into the murky depths.

Anhinga sniffed hard and straightened. "On my brother's soul," she whispered fiercely, "I will do whatever it takes to make them pay."

"Anything?" he asked casually.

"Anything," she insisted doggedly, picking up her paddle and driving it into the brown swamp water.

An idea was forming in his mind. Something that he hadn't tried. It would take more thought once he had returned home to the Panther's Bones.

The watering of his mouth came as White Bird's brief warning before he bent double and threw up the bitter-tasting brew. Again and again his stomach pumped, heaving violently as it emptied itself of what remained of a boiled fish breakfast.

The sun burned down on his bare back, its heat adding to the sweat that beaded his flesh. It wasn't enough that he and his companions had spent the night alternately sweating in the small domed lodge and bathing in the brackish waters of the lake, but the Serpent had showed up several hours before dawn and begun brewing his concoctions.

The Serpent had begun by Singing, painting his face, and shaking a gourd rattle as he circled the area. With great care he laid a fire of red cedar. Then he placed tinder in the center and used twigs to place a hot coal atop it. Bending low, puffing his cheeks and blowing, he coaxed the fire to life.

On this he placed a soapstone bowl propped with clay balls so the fire could lap around the stone vessel's sides. From his belt pouch he extracted yaupon leaves and dropped them into the heating bowl. As he did, he called to the four directions: to the east, the south, the west, and north. With a round stone he crushed the leaves, bruising them to release their color. Using a hickory stick painted crimson, he stirred the leaves as they slowly reddened and curled. When appropriately roasted, he employed a bison-horn dipper to carry water from the lake and one after another filled the pot until a yellow froth formed on the boiling liquid. The Serpent stirred it with his red stick, satisfied to see that the roiling liquid had blackened beneath the foam. Reaching into his pouch again, he extracted a section of snakemaster root and, with a white chert knife, shaved slices into the brew. Then as the steam rose, he began to dance his way around them, thrusting the rattle this way and that.

"Why is he doing that?" Gray Fox asked nervously.

"To announce to any evils that he is coming to drive them off," White Bird had explained. "It is hoped that by so stating, the harmful spirits and malicious ghosts will simply leave, making his work easier. This way he can turn all of his attention to the few stubborn and recalcitrant spirits who remain. It gives him a chance to identify the ones that wish to challenge his Power as a spirit warrior."

"I wouldn't challenge him . . . alive or dead," Jackdaw muttered in his own language. "Isn't he just the ugliest old man you've ever seen?"

Hazel Fire and the others had laughed at that, and White Bird couldn't find it in himself to disagree. The Serpent had passed more than five tens of winters. His hair had gone white and thin. Now it waved about his head like a wreath of water grass in a changing current. The old man's face might have been trod upon, so flat was it. The nose looked as if it had been mashed into his features, the sharp brown eyes staring out of thick folds of flesh. Skin hung like dead bark from the Serpent's frame, and through the wrinkles one could see patterns of snake tattoos that had faded into blue-black smears. He looked more like a walking skeleton, his ribs sticking out, the knobby joints of his knees thicker than his thin thighs.

Not even a finger of time had passed from the moment they had drunk the Serpent's concoction before the first of them had bent double and thrown up.

White Bird's stomach wrenched again. He cramped with the dry heaves.

"We're poisoned!" Hazel Fire cried between gasps. The Wolf Traders were clustered around, some on hands and knees as they wretched and groaned.

"No!" White Bird made a face at the vile taste in his mouth. "Trust me. This is good for us. It's driving any illness or sorcery out of our bodies. I swear, you're not poisoned. It's just . . ." His stomach knotted, and he doubled up again as his gut tried to turn him inside out.

When the spell passed, he rolled over to seat himself on the damp soil. A shadow blocked the sun as the Serpent bent, mumbling to himself as he inspected the goo White Bird had deposited on the ground. The old man used a blue-painted stick to prod the watery mess.

"I see," the old man muttered. "A chill was headed for your bones, young man. Good thing we got it out."

"How do you know that?" White Bird placed a hand to his aching stomach and gasped for breath.

The Serpent cocked a faded brown eyebrow, the action rearranging the mass of wrinkles. He lifted the blue stick, gaze locked on a thread of silvery mucus that glinted in the sunlight. "You think this is easy? You think just anybody can read what's hidden in vomit? It takes many turnings of seasons to learn these things. And very hard study. The signs of sorcery, not to mention the imbalance of the souls, are difficult even for the trained eye to detect. The spirits alone know what tricks foreign sorcerers would use to kill you."

White Bird blinked, hesitating lest talking lead to another bout of retching. Finally, he said, "What about the others?"

The Serpent had turned and begun to jab his stick into the spattered remains of Jackdaw's breakfast. "This boy was going to have a pain in his leg soon, but it's out now. Haw!" The old man jabbed repeatedly at the vomit as if he were tormenting some unseen thing.

Jackdaw leaped back, crying, "What? What's he doing?"

"You're all right," White Bird told him in his own language. "He just saved you from a pain in your leg."

Unsure, Jackdaw backed away as the old man continued to chant and jab. "I'd have been happier with a lame leg. My stomach feels like it's been turned inside out."

"Mine, too," Cat's Paw moaned. Like his friend, he scuttled back as the Serpent turned to the place where he'd thrown up and began jabbing at it and uttering terrible cries.

One by one he attacked their vomit, and finally raised himself straight, his face lifted to the bright morning sun. "Mother Sun, I have seen the things carried by these people. I have exposed the blackness to your light." He lifted his arms, the stick held high. "Help me now as I purify this place. Burn away the sickness and evil. I brandish your daughter in the cleansing." With that he swirled about in an elaborate circle. "Take this evil—and *purify* it!" The old shaman dramatically threw the blue stick into the fire, where cedar flames greedily devoured it.

"Why a blue stick?" Cat's Paw asked.

"Blue is the color of the west, of death and failure. It is the color of ending, just as the sky darkens at night after Mother Sun slips away into the world below." He pointed up at the sun. "In the beginning time, just after the Sky Beings came to Earth, they ensured that Mother Sun would light the world and the creatures that lived here. Fire came from Mother Sun, sent to the Earth in a bolt of lightning. With it Mother Sun ensured that the Earth could always be cleansed of darkness and disease and sorcery and corruption."

"What now?" Hazel Fire asked warily as he wiped a hand across his mouth.

"We're going to build fires where we threw up. It's all got to be burned." White Bird pointed to the stack of firewood under the thatched shed at the base of the sweetgum tree.

"Is there much more of this?" Snow Water was on all fours, staring hostilely at the old man. "I'm starting to wonder if it's worth it. I might just take my chances canoeing home alone."

"Trust me, it's worth it. One more day," White Bird promised. "And it's easy by comparison."

"It better be." Hazel Fire shook his head. "Or I'm slipping away in the middle of the night, too."

"It's important that we undergo this," White Bird replied gently. "For the safety of Sun Town. We don't fear the enemies that we know, only the ones we can't see. I ask you to trust me. I told you about the cleansing."

"You did," Cat's Paw admitted. "I just didn't really appreciate what it was going to be like."

"Just wait," Hazel Fire promised, "and see what we do to you next time you come upriver."

White Bird made it halfway to the woodpile before his gut caught him by surprise and sent him into convulsions. Maybe his friends were right about slipping away. But deep in the spot between his souls, he knew the correctness of a proper cleansing.

The Serpent

True leaders, it seems to me, are born in betrayal.

My first teacher was a very old woman, a Clan Elder. When I became the Serpent, she told me that she believed we are born at the foot of the log bridge that leads to the Land of the Dead, and that the instant we slip from our mother's canoe, if we truly listen, we will hear the animals we have known in our lives calling to us.

The boy is smiling to himself.

I watch him.

Does he know?

At his tender age, can he possibly understand that a person has to be shoved off the bridge by the one he trusts most before he can look up, see no one standing above to help him, and grasp that being alone is not the curse, it is the task?

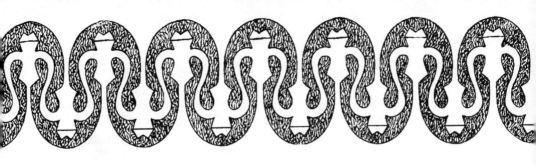

Six

Wing Heart sat in the afternoon shade of the thatched ramada beside her house. With a facility that came from many seasons of practice she used her thigh and one hand to spin basswood fibers into cordage. She had stripped the fibers from the tree's bark by first soaking, then pounding it with a stone-headed mallet. That loosened the fibers so that they could be pulled free, then combed, and assembled into the flaxen pile on her right. As she spun the fibers she looped the finished cord into a coil to her left.

Her house stood at the eastern end of the first northern ridge. From her ramada she could look out over the wind-patterned waters of Morning Lake. Waves lapped at the bank four body lengths below the sheer drop-off. Three glossy white herons sailed soundlessly southward, their wide wings catching the updraft along the bank before her.

Looking out onto the lake, her view included the Turtle's Back: a low hump of earth topped by three sweetgum trees and trampled grass. She could make out the Serpent's thin figure as he walked from one young man to another, tapping each of them lightly on the shoulders with an eagle-feather wand.

White Bird sat with his back to the gum tree's trunk. If his posture was any indication, he looked absolutely miserable. It brought a smile to her lips. That was the point, wasn't it? The people didn't want evil spirits from distant places being carried into their midst. By making the host body uncomfortable, those same malicious forces would drift away in search of a more pleasant body to inhabit while they worked their dark and sorcerous deeds.

"Bless you, my son," she said with satisfaction, her gaze lingering on the four long canoes that had been pulled onto the small island's muddy shores. Even from her vantage point she could see the piled packs and reflect on the salvation it meant for her lineage and Owl Clan in general.

She added more fibers from the pile to her right, twisting them into the center of the cord. Fibers had to be added as others were exhausted so that the cordage remained uniform in strength and thickness. The manufacture of cordage was important to her people. Not only did it bind things together like houses, drying racks, and roof thatch, but it was the essential ingredient in their fishnets and small-game snares. From it they braided strong ropes. On their looms it became a coarse fabric for burden bags and storage containers. Cordage allowed them to measure out the uniform earthworks that defined the limits of Sun Town and the holdings of the clans. Cordage was always in demand for Trade, as were the fine fabrics they wove and the wooden products they carved. Small loops of cord even provided for days of entertainment as the children played the finger-string game, creating patterns and designs as they plucked the loop back and forth from hand to hand.

She saw Clay Fat as he approached, walking across the open plaza from the line of houses dotting the ridges to the southeast. Rattlesnake Clan had its holdings there. The moment she saw him she knew he was coming to see her. No doubt the single unifying feeling among the members of Rattlesnake Clan was relief. White Bird had arrived despite their dire predictions. Their political situation, especially their relationship to Owl Clan, had been not only justified but was about to be solidified.

Whereas last week her very existence might have been suspect—given the lack of attention she had been receiving—her circumstances had changed with White Bird's arrival. One after another she had been entertaining Clan Elders and Speakers. Indeed, the world might have flipped from end to end since her son's flotilla had nosed into Sun Town's placid Morning Lake. Even old Back Scratch, the Snapping Turtle Clan Elder, had been forced to swallow her pride and toddle her creaking bones across the plaza to make pleasant talk. Sweet Root, her daughter, had accompanied her, slinking like the predatory cat she was. One day—and not so far away—Sweet Root would inherit her clan's mantle. Spirits help them all.

Back Scratch kept a lid on most of Mud Stalker's poison. Sweet

Root, however, wouldn't have the sense to keep her brother on a short string. She had always been in awe of him, and after her mother's death she would be a cunning and willing accomplice, ready and anxious to add her own machinations to those of her bitter, alligator-bitten brother.

As the day had passed Wing Heart had entertained them all. Smiling, gracious, she had played the game with all the skill that her turnings of seasons and innate ability had given her. Calling on her clan she had provided smoked fish and bread made from smilax root. A stone bowl continued to steam by the fire, sweetening the air with the pungent odor of black drink. The foamy tea made from holly leaves was normally reserved for special occasions. Having a pot of it on hand provided that extra bit of elegance to reinforce the notion that Owl Clan remained preeminent.

Wing Heart watched as Clay Fat continued amiably on his way across the plaza. His belly protruded over his loincloth, his knobby navel like the stem on a brown melon. A half-lazy smile traced Clay Fat's thick lips, his expression dreamy, as if he had not a care in the world.

Wing Heart considered him. Clay Fat wasn't an acutely smart man. Rather he was wedded to stability the way a fisherman enjoyed a deep-keeled canoe. He liked balance and was happiest when he knew exactly what was coming with the next sunrise. The passing of the last six moons—in the shadow of Speaker Cloud Heron's impending death—had been hard on Clay Fat's nerves. The uncertainty over young White Bird's whereabouts upriver—let alone whether or not he was still alive—had been excruciating. Now, with the world set back to rights, he looked much like a fat toad full of bugs.

She owed him. Of them all, he had stood by her, steadfastly believing her promise that her son would return from the north, and that when he did, it would be with a stunning coup that would assure Owl Clan's hegemony.

No, Clay Fat might not be the brightest of the Clan Speakers. Had he been someone other than himself, he would have taken that opportunity to try to propel Rattlesnake Clan into leadership. At least she, or any of the other Clan Elders, would have struck like a hungry snake when she sensed the slightest vulnerability in her rivals.

But is he so dumb? Wing Heart turned the notion over in her mind, trying to see it from Clay Fat's perspective. Was it not better to place Rattlesnake Clan in a perpetual secondary role rather than risk falling into even more pressing debt to the others?

"Greetings, Wing Heart," Clay Fat called, waving as he trooped across the muddy shallows of the borrow pit and climbed the earthen ridge upon which the Owl Clan houses were built. As Clan Elder, Wing Heart had the most prestigious location, on the eastern edge of the berm overlooking Morning Lake. Here she could greet the sunrise, and best of all, monitor the comings and goings at the Turtle's Back.

"A pleasant day to you, Speaker. How is your Elder, Graywood Snake, today?"

"She is well, Wing Heart. She sends her fondest greetings." He strode up, breath coming in labored gasps. She could see the sweat beginning to bead on his swollen brown skin. "I must say, things are happening. So much talk."

"Talk?" She pointed to the cane mat across from her. "Sit, old friend. Enjoy the shade. Would you like a cup of black drink? As you can see, the bowl is still steaming."

"Bless you, but no. It's too hot," he muttered. "Here we are but a half-moon past spring equinox and it already feels like midsummer." He grunted as he eased himself onto the matting. "Is it me, or are the passing summers getting hotter and hotter?"

"It is you," she told him, her fingers spinning the cord along her thigh. "The summers are no hotter. It's just that your belly gets larger and larger. It holds your heat in like a giant cooking clay."

He laughed at that, slapping a callused hand against his stomach.

"So, there is talk you say? Anything of interest or are they just scrambling to cover themselves, saying, 'Oh, I knew all along that White Bird would return!'"

He shot her a knowing glance, his dark brown eyes measuring. "Hardly. Envy and venom are whispered behind the hand while smiles and nectar drape public speech. At least that's the way of the leaders' lineages. For those who have no stake in the squabbles among the Council's leaders, interest centers on what lies hidden under those packs in White Bird's canoes. Most people, as you well know, Wing Heart, could care less who holds the ropes to the fish traps so long as they can share in the catch."

"Runners have gone out?"

He nodded, reaching down to finger the end of the cane matting he sat on. "People are beginning to trickle in from the outlying camps. Everyone is expecting a feast and dancing, and an excuse to get together and gossip. For the people who are in need, it is a chance to refit, to replace what is broken or worn-out." He glanced out across the lake, fixing his gaze on the Turtle's Back and the figures that hunched out there in a line next to the sweat lodge. "Is everything all right?"

"My son is going through a nasty cleansing. For a while yesterday he couldn't stop throwing up. I believe that the Serpent is being particularly thorough this time. He wasn't happy about a three-day cleansing. At White Bird's suggestion, I requested it rather force-fully. It seems that his Wolf companions, as he calls them, are leery about what it will do to the health of their barbarian souls."

"Their souls? Why? Is there something wrong with them?"

"Put it like this: Would you trust some Serpent you didn't know to cleanse your souls? Say, perhaps, some Wolf Serpent whose ways you couldn't differentiate from witchcraft? A strange Serpent from way up north? One who did things you didn't understand? Sang strange songs, made you bare your souls to him?"

"I would be more than a little frightened."

"So are these Wolf Traders," Wing Heart added. "The last thing I need is for them to bolt in the middle of the night and take those loaded canoes with them."

"There's risk in that."

"There's risk in everything."

"What if someone takes sick? What if after they've been rushed through cleansing, something goes wrong? People will say that you didn't take enough precautions."

"I'll take my chances."

He nodded, that slight smile returning to his lips. "Well, there is already talk."

"Talk? We're back to talk?" Which of course was what he'd come to tell her in the first place.

"My cousin, Fork Tail, and his party returned from his trip down south last night. He has several nice pieces of that white Panther sandstone. Not as many as he would have liked to have, but enough to still make the trip profitable. It will allow Rattlesnake Clan a chance to offer something at the same time you have to rid yourself of all those canoe loads of exotics."

"Good for you." She noticed the reserve behind his bland eyes. "But . . . ?"

Clay Fat shrugged. "There were complications. He couldn't load his canoe with all the stone he wanted. It seems that some of the Swamp Panthers ambushed him. In the fight that followed he wounded at least one of them. A youth."

"Kill him?"

"He doesn't know. Apparently the dart was sticking out of the boy's belly when he ran away. As to how serious it was, Fork Tail couldn't tell."

"These things happen." Wing Heart spliced more fibers into her cord and continued spinning it along her thigh. "If we're lucky, the kid just got nicked. Were others involved?"

"Apparently a party of youths."

"So there's no chance the boy might have gone off and died before anyone found out?"

Clay Fat gave her a shake of his head for an answer. "You had better circulate the word to Owl Clan that the Swamp Panthers will probably retaliate. My clan is already spreading the word through the lineages to the camps in the south."

"Is that all the bad news you've got?"

"Of course not." His thin lips widened in a smile. "You should know that Mud Stalker is nearly foaming at the mouth. He and Back Scratch were in the process of tightening their grip on leadership in the Council until your son paddled into the middle of their plans. He had come to think you were toothless, and all he needed to worry about was Deep Hunter. Then White Bird floats into Morning Lake with his barbarian friends, and Mud Stalker's world is upside-down. It's all that Mud Stalker can do to keep from popping the veins in his head."

"Cane Frog wasn't happy either. She and Deep Hunter would have been overjoyed to wrest control of the Northern Moiety away from me, let alone take a chance on gaining leadership of the Council."

Clay Fat was watching her through his expressionless brown eyes. "Very well, Wing Heart, you've pulled the proverbial hare out of the hollow log yet again. What about the endless tomorrows? You have two sons, the last of your lineage. White Bird has a great future ahead of him, but you can't risk him on another venture like this one. Somewhere, sometime, some barbarian is going to kill him, or his canoe is going to be swamped in a spring flood, or he's going to catch some foreign disease and die. Beyond the protection of our city, the world is a dangerous place. Tens of tens of things could happen. Somewhere out in those distant places something will eventually get him."

She nodded, aware of just how frightened she had been of exactly that.

"And it's not like you have a lot of choices." Clay Fat tilted his head back to stare up at the thatch overhead. "Mud Puppy is your only other child."

"Would to Mother Sun I had had a daughter out of that mating with Thumper. I could marry her to some daring young man and send him upriver. If he didn't come back, I could marry her again, and again, and again, until one of them got it right and brought me back another four canoes of Trade."

"You wouldn't even need that," he told her. "You would have an heir. A daughter to carry your line on into the future."

"Correct."

After a pause, he added, "You could always name Mud Puppy Speaker. Then it wouldn't matter if White Bird didn't come back." He laughed one of those deep belly laughs.

"You find that funny, do you?"

He straightened his face; the attempt failed in the slightest to mask his amusement. "He's young. He might change. You know, grow out of it."

She arched an eyebrow. "Mud Puppy, grow out of it?"

"Boys do. When they step into the world of men they can't help but change."

Snakes! He's almost a man now, but you'd never know it. "He thinks differently than any boy I ever knew. I'm at my wit's end. Water Petal has him in the sweat lodge. I've made an appointment to have the Serpent take him up to spend the night atop the Bird's Head. Maybe that will scare some sense into his witless noggin. He's completely hopeless! His brother returns, the most important event in the lineage in how many winters, and he's looking at a cricket in a jar!"

Clay Fat nodded, his head oddly cocked. "In the last few moons I have come to discover how important leadership of the Council is to you, Wing Heart. Tell me, if it came right down to it, would you declare him Speaker?"

"Perhaps if I'd been hit in the head too hard, or if lightning struck me."

"I've stood with you through the last moons, Wing Heart. Stood with you when many urged me to look elsewhere for obligations. Your clan and mine have made a good alliance through the endless turnings of the seasons."

"What are you getting at?"

"All jesting aside, I need to know something."

"Very well." She had ceased spinning her cord. "What is that thing, old friend?"

"What would you do to retain Owl Clan's hegemony? What would you do to keep your leadership?"

She felt trapped in his wary brown-eyed stare. The universe might have narrowed to the two of them. "I'd do anything, Clay Fat. I've lived all of my life preparing for the leadership. I *don't* want to give that up. I *won't* give it up."

"Then you'd do anything to keep it?"

She nodded, wondering what this was going to cost her, wondering where it had come from. What did he suspect? Worse, what did he know?

"Anything," she reaffirmed.

He contemplated her in silence, his eyes prying into her souls, as though to see what she really meant. In the end, he sighed, relaxing, his smooth smile returning. "Then you will understand when I tell you that I . . . my clan cannot allow Spring Cypress to marry White Bird. Your son will insist. You must refuse."

Mind racing, she asked, "Why?"

Clay Fat's expression had turned bland again. "I almost made a terrible mistake, Wing Heart. But for the return of your son, I could have lost a great deal and found myself and my clan in the same position as Frog Clan is in today. At the bottom, mucking about in the silt for scraps. Obliged to everyone. I will support you, do what I must to maintain your leadership, but I want you to understand that I am going to strengthen the position of my lineage."

"And who were you thinking of?"

"Copperhead."

"Mud Stalker's cousin? He's twice her age." Her mind wrapped around the implications of Rattlesnake Clan brokering an alliance with Snapping Turtle Clan.

"Copperhead is freshly widowed."

"He used to beat Red Gourd when she was his wife. Some people think he killed her."

"That was never proven by her clan." Clay Fat seemed nonplussed.

Her voice dropped. "You'd do that to Spring Cypress?"

The corners of his mouth twitched. "Let's just say there is a compelling reason, shall we?"

"What does Graywood Snake say about this?"

"The Rattlesnake Clan Elder understands and agrees."

She studied him thoughtfully. *So, you, too, had abandoned me. White Bird's return caught you off guard, didn't it? Now I catch you scrambling to reclaim your balance.*

As if he could read her thoughts, he said, "Make this thing easy for me, and I shall give you my obligation for the future." He paused. "Besides, it might not be so bad, having an ear close to Mud Stalker. As you well know, Elder, the future is a very uncertain place."

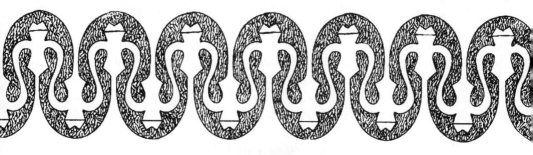

Seven

No son of mine has the luxury of fear. The words echoed around in Mud Puppy's head as he followed the Serpent up the long steep slope of the Bird's Head. Having almost completed White Bird's cleansing, the old Serpent had finally come for Mud Puppy.

The old man wore a simple fabric breechcloth bound to his waist by a cord. From it hung several small leather sacks that held who knew what kind of magic potions. A patchwork cloak made of muskrat hides draped the old man's shoulders. He might have been a walking skeleton, thin muscles hanging from his old bones. Mud Puppy couldn't help but notice how the old man's knees and feet seemed so big in comparison with his skinny legs. In all, the Serpent was the most frightening man Mud Puppy had ever known.

His entire body tingled, partly from fear, partly from the ordeal he had endured in the sweat lodge purifying himself for the coming night's trial. The endless hands of time he had spent alternately roasting and dripping sweat in rivers, versus those few moments when Cousin Water Petal tipped a pot of cool water over his head, had left him feeling oddly weak, though rejuvenated.

"I don't know what your mother's after, boy," Water Petal had told him ominously. "She's been over to the island"—she referred to the Turtle's Back—"talking to the Serpent. Something you did set her off. What was it this time? Did you leave a worm in her water cup? Or did she catch you with your butt up in the air, peeking under leaves when you should have been doing chores?"

"It was my cricket," he had started to explain, but Water Petal had silenced him by pouring another bowl of chilly water over his head. She had just passed two tens of winters, and should have given birth to three or four children by this time; her abdomen now bulged with her first. Those sharp black eyes of hers intimated that she would rather be anywhere than helping Mud Puppy with his ritual cleansing. A sentiment he shared. But when the Clan Elder ordered, people obeyed, especially those in the lineage.

Despite a deep-seated fear in his belly, he and the Serpent finished the long climb. The Bird's Head, a huge mound of earth, dominated and guarded the western edge of Sun Town. It rose as if to scrape the sky. So high, so huge was it that from the peak Mud Puppy could see the entire world. He could look down on the tops of trees. People looked like mites as they inched along below him.

The old man wheezed, one hand to his chest as the wind whipped his filmy white hair. A faint flush had darkened the wrinkled mass of his platter-flat face; but thoughtful eyes hid deep behind the folds of his skin. His gaze drilled through Mud Puppy like a perforator on a stick.

Mud Puppy fought to still his sudden fear, shamed by the loose gurgle in his bowels. A desire grew in his souls to turn around and run down that long slope on charged legs. Anything to get away from this inspired and terrible place.

His heart began to pound as they topped the highest point. The world spread out before him to the west. The vista made his bare feet curl, toes biting into the crumbly clay soil. They were so high here that when he looked upward he half expected to see the clouds rubbing against the Sky dome. The feeling gave him the giddy sense of seeing the world as a bird must, everything below him, so far below. He might have been Masked Owl himself.

"In the beginning"—the Serpent raised his hand, pointing at the tree-covered western horizon—"at the Creation, the Sky was cracked off from the Earth. That is a most important event. Do you know why the Great Mystery did that?"

Mud Puppy swallowed hard. Would the Serpent give him that same disgusted look that Mother did? He shook his head in a hesitant no.

"Take a moment and consider," the Serpent told him mildly.

Mud Puppy tried to avoid those hard black eyes. He let his gaze wander, his mind half-locked with the terror of his situation. He had never stood at the top of the Bird's Head. The enormity of the high mound staggered him. How had his people ever managed to build such a mass of earth, basket by basket, one turning of the seasons after another? Could such a miracle really be of human manufacture? Had hands really built this monument to the gods? It had to be the highest point in the world—though the Traders said that other mountains, far to the northwest, were higher.

Along the western base of the great mound he could see the narrow pond that filled the mighty trench his people had dug into the ground. It glinted silver, like a gleaming worm stretched across the greensward. It was said that monsters lurked under that deep water. Had his people unwittingly opened a door to the Underworld in their effort to erect this huge mountain of earth?

"That's not where the answer lies," the Serpent murmured, as if reading his thoughts.

Mud Puppy reached down to pull nervously at the frayed flap of his breechcloth. *It was the clay.* The thought just popped into his head. His people needed the sticky gray clay. No mound of earth the size of the Bird's Head could be raised out of the rich brown silt that covered the ridge. The deeply buried clay was necessary to give the huge earthwork stability. Without it, the silt would soften and flow in the rains, slumping and sagging, until the Bird's Head sank right back into the ground from which it came.

The picture formed in his head: a digging stick being driven down into the hard gray clay and leaving a scar, just one of a number of similar scars in the side of the excavation pit. Like jagged alligator teeth had gnawed the soil away.

"Why did the Great Mystery rip the Sky away from the Earth?" the Serpent's voice reminded.

Mud Puppy raised his head to stare at the glowing clouds, backlit by the dying sun as they scurried northward. Here, so high above the Earth, the southern wind tugged at him as it rushed up from the gulf, the smell of forest, swamp, damp earth, and spring flowers carried on its warm caress.

"Because the Great Mystery didn't like it that way?" Mud Puppy guessed.

"And why would that be?" The Serpent bent down, his eyes prying away at Mud Puppy's.

"Because a question is always hidden inside another question," Mud Puppy whispered, and instantly winced, afraid that the Serpent would hiss and strike—lash his frightened souls right out of his terrified body.

Instead, the terrible black eyes softened. The old man nodded, which made the wattles on his neck shake. "You are smarter than your brother was when he was your age." The Serpent arched a grizzled eyebrow. "Yes, there is always another question inside a question. But for the moment, I need an answer for this one. And, boy, I do not expect you to give me the answer right now. Indeed, I expect you to think about it, to study it. The answer isn't what you would expect. Certainly not one to be given off the tip of your tongue like an insult or a compliment. Think, boy. Consider it long and hard."

The old man abruptly turned, faced the east, and used one knobby hand to spin Mud Puppy around so that he looked out over Sun Town. The effect took his breath away. In the growing twilight the arcs of concentric ridges spread out to the left and right in a huge curve. Houses, like warts, might have been marching away along the length of the ridges. The immensity of it—coupled with the perfect symmetry of those nested curves sculpted so artistically onto the plain—left him awed.

As he looked down the long eastern slope the Bird's Head fell away from his toes in a broad ramp that widened as it fanned out like the spread tail feathers of a great hawk. At the base of the tail the huge clan grounds created a gigantic half oval transected along its midline by the steep bluff running north–south above Morning Lake.

Two large poles, one for the Northern Moiety, one for the Southern Moiety, marked the geometric centers of the offset circles. The six rows of ridges were in turn interrupted by breaks that separated the clans. In the north, Mud Puppy's Owl Clan occupied the easternmost ridges, Alligator Clan lay in the middle, and the Frog Clan's ridges ran right to the base of the Bird's Head on the west. A use-beaten avenue that ran due east–west through the town separated the moieties' plazas north from south. The westernmost ridges on the south belonged to Rattlesnake Clan. Another gap on the southwest separated them from Eagle Clan.

Unique to Eagle Clan's territory, a narrow earthen causeway led straight as a stretched cord for three dart casts beyond the city to the southwest. There the Dying Sun Mound rose above the plain in a flat-topped oval. Yet another gap separated the Eagle and Snapping Turtle Clans. The latter occupied the far southern course of the ridges.

Two small mounds lay within the plaza area. The Mother Mound was situated at the edge of the eastern drop-off. A two-tiered earthwork, its flattened southern side supported the Women's House: the large menstrual lodge where women resided during their moontied cycles. The fact that a woman's cycle was tied to the moon had provoked considerable speculation. The moon, after all, was a masculine being. But then, without male involvement, a woman was incapable of bearing children. In the end, the location of the Mother Mound had been chosen by sighting from the center of Sun Town to the northernmost point where the moon rose on the eastern horizon at the end of its eighteen-and-one-half-turning-of-seasons migration across the sky.

On the south lay the Father Mound, with its gaudily painted wooden-and-thatch Men's House. The rites of war, of the hunt, and Trade were conducted there. Mud Puppy had never seen the inside of the Men's House. Boys weren't allowed. But someday, when he was admitted into manhood, he would. Terrifying stories circulated among boys of his age, tales of the curious ceremonies and bloody initiations that occurred behind those secretive walls. Similar to its maternal opposite to the north, Father Mound had an odd relationship to Mother Sun. When sighting southeast, the Father Mound was in line of sight of the point on the horizon where the sun rose on the shortest day of the turning of seasons—another oddity, but one that made sense when placed in context of the People's struggle to achieve unity and harmony. Opposites crossed, brought into balance, that was the central spiritual force that bound the People together.

Mud Puppy could see it in the form and beauty of Sun Town. The disparate moieties, the constantly bickering clans, north and south, east and west, sun and moon. Sun Town unified them all in the form of the great Sky Being, Bird Man. He had sailed down from the Sky World on fiery wings to shape the Earth after the Creation.

From above, Sun Town looked like a huge bird, its wings curved protectively around the clan grounds. The Power of the place seemed to pulse in the evening.

And there, out in the purple water, he could see the Turtle's Back, where his brother should be taking the last of his sweat baths and preparing for the final night of purification.

"Look at what you see, boy," the Serpent told him. "No other place on Earth is like this. We live at the center of the world. The gods and spirits know this; they are reminded each time they look down. It was here, on this spot, that Bird Man first touched the Earth after the Creation."

"It is huge," Mud Puppy said in awe as he looked north across the fields and patches of trees to the distant Star Mound. From here it looked like a bump rising above the tree line. Star Mound provided protection from the terrifying Powers of the North, the way

Bird's Head protected the People from the dangers of the West. Winter came rolling out of the north, dark and cold, while in the West, death lurked, and Mother Sun died.

Two smaller mounds had been built, one to the north, the other to the south on a line that transected the Bird's Head. The conical Spirit Mound three dart casts due north was where the people offered gifts at sunset on the summer solstice. She would need them to sustain her in her southern flight as she perpetually fled Father Moon's infidelity.

The flat mound at the end of the earthen causeway three dart casts to the south was called Dying Sun Mound. It was there, on the winter solstice, that people implored Mother Sun to begin her journey northward across the Sky.

"From where you now stand you can look straight south across the Dying Sun Mound." The Serpent pointed at a pole that rose from the shoulder of the Bird's Head. "Each day, at midday, that pole marks Mother Sun's journey across the Sky. On winter solstice, the tip of the shadow falls right here, where your feet now stand, marking the shortest day of the winter." Then the Serpent turned north. "And at night, you look straight north to the Great North Star, around which the Sky World turns." He pointed at a second pole. "By standing here, and bending slightly, you can see that star night after night, season after season. It is because the North, for all of its terrors, is a place of stability unlike the realm of Mother Sun. She and Father Moon are forever advancing and retreating across the sky, he pursuing, she fleeing. Forever mindful of the time he betrayed her bed by locking hips with another woman."

"You said the Sky World turns?" Mud Puppy blurted in surprise. His terror had begun to recede replaced by fascination with the things the Serpent was telling him.

"Indeed it does. If you sit here on a cloudless night, boy, you can watch the stars slowly spin around the North Star. You must be very still and patient and mark the paths of the stars as they circle the heavens. They move so slowly. No one can tell you why. It is only one of the many mysteries." The Serpent smiled wistfully. "But that is not what I have come to teach you today. No, I just tell you this to tease you, to stimulate your curiosity. There are more mysteries, but they are for the future, boy. Instead I want you to look down at Sun Town and tell me what you see."

Mud Puppy turned back toward the dusk-heavy town. Cooking fires had begun to sparkle on the concentric ridges. The south wind carried blue tendrils of smoke northward across the ridges and toward Star Mound. Was it imagination, or could he smell the burning hickory and maple from this great height?

"I see Sun Town." The thought struck him again that it resembled a huge bird, its wings outspread. Power rose around him, slipping along his skin with a feathery touch. "I've never seen it from up here before. It's so different."

"Yes, it is. There is a reason for that. You see the One. The unity. That is the miracle of this place, boy. The Power of Sun Town—of the moieties, the clans, and the lineages—is that we are all so many pieces. Just like a body, made of bone, muscle, blood, and organs. Each piece separate under the skin. Sun Town is our body, the whole of the People, living, breathing, *being* . . . but it is more than that. It is our world. The directions: East, South, West, North, Up and Down. Our mounds rising to the Sky, our borrow pits sinking into the Earth. All the pieces of the world come together here. This place is the reconciliation of the world. What you see around you is the harmony of all the parts of Creation working together."

"You said that we are at the center of the world."

"Ah," the Serpent replied, his old toothless mouth agape, "now you begin to understand. I am an old man, but the wonder I see in your eyes still fills me when I stand up here. All those tens of winters have flowed past like the Father Water, and still I look and marvel at who and what we are. It is here, of all the places on Earth, that the One is knit together."

"The One?"

The old man's eyes had turned dreamy. "The One, the Dance, the terrible disruptive harmony."

Mud Puppy shivered, hearing the words of Masked Owl reverberating from his dreams. *The One! The Dance!* A tingle of excitement ran through him.

The Serpent waved a callused hand out to encompass the curving lines of houses below them. "They don't see it, don't feel it, don't Dance it in their souls. No, boy, they stand at the center of the world, bathed in a pitch-black brightness, and study the mud between their toes. They scheme, dicker, bargain, and plot to gain prestige or authority—and forget the miracle of who they are."

The venom in the old man's words shocked Mud Puppy. He couldn't help but think of his mother, the Clan Elder, and her constant preoccupation with the demands of keeping clan and lineage preeminent.

"You are different, boy," the Serpent whispered. "No matter what they do to you, remember that. If you ever doubt, climb up here and look down. See with the eyes of your souls and listen to the deafening silence. They will try to take the harmony away from you, to weight your feet down until you cannot follow the Dance."

"I don't understand."

The old man glanced at him, his thin form silhouetted against the scudding charcoal clouds. The wind sent its fingers rippling through the frail white hair and tugged at the old man's sash. Despite the growing darkness, the Serpent's eyes were aglow. "*He* came to me in a Dream. *He* told me your mother would come, that she would give me this chance."

He? He, who? The old man's words made no sense. Fingers of sudden worry stroked at Mud Puppy's souls. He turned his eyes back to the darkening lake and the dimple created by the Turtle's Back. A flickering fire had sprung to life there. "I would have thought you would be out with my brother. It's his last night of purification."

The Serpent muttered something under his breath, sighed, and finally said, "Tell me about how people first came into this world."

Mud Puppy squinted as the wind batted his straight black hair against his forehead. "It was after the Creator split the Sky from the Earth. Everything was water. The Sky Beings looked down from above the dome of the Sky and saw water everywhere. It was Water Beetle who finally flew from the Sky on his wings, dived into the water, and swam to the bottom of the ocean. There, he found mud and brought it up to the surface. Time after time he dived down and brought up mud. That's why to this day Water Beetle's children dive to the depths. They are still making the Earth a bit at a time."

"Yes, that's right. What happened then?"

"The mud was soft and wet and sticky, and the Sky Beings who flew to Earth couldn't land lest they sink into the mud. That was when Bird Man soared across the world, and with each beat of his wings, he pushed the land down or pulled it up. From that, mountains were formed. In the low places, Brother Snake crawled out of the Underworld and slithered down to become the river." Mud Puppy looked out to the east, where he knew the great Father Water flowed beyond the flooded sweetgum swamps.

"And the animals?"

"They were fashioned out of dirt, molded into their shapes and sizes by the Sky Beings and the Earth Monsters. Wolf was the one who dug into a giant earthen mound and fashioned the dirt he dug out into the shape of First Man and First Woman. He breathed his soul into them and led them out into Mother Sun's light."

"That's right. So tell me, Mud Puppy, having looked down on

Sun Town, do you understand why we raise soil into giant mounds?"

"It is to remind us that we are of the Earth."

"What purpose does that serve?"

"I don't know."

"It is to remind us of *what* we are, where we came from. Our bodies come not from the Sky, but from the soil itself. It is our souls that are of the Sky, breathed into us by Wolf just after the Creation. Very well, you have just told me the story of First Man and First Woman. How did the other people come into being?"

Mud Puppy frowned. "They were born of the Hero Twins, the two sons of First Man and First Woman. One, Light Boy, was born of the joining of First Man and First Woman when they lay together. He passed from her womb into air and light. The second twin, Dark Boy, was born of blood and water."

"Very good. Can you tell me how that happened?"

"First Woman had her regular bleeding while she was bathing in the river. The blood draining from her womb mixed with the river water and the dark twin was conceived. It was Raven who plucked him from the water as he floated past. That's why women are not to enter the water during their bleeding. Instead, they must secret themselves in the Women's House." He pointed at the Mother Mound now barely visible at the eastern edge of the plaza.

"You are here"—the Serpent gestured at the mound top—"to reflect on that story, boy. You are here, at the highest point of the Bird's Head. Symbolic of the place where people were brought out into the light. But your mother wants you to learn another lesson up here."

"She does?"

The Serpent chuckled, the sound like the clattering of cane slats. "Oh, indeed. But I'm not sure if she understands what you are—or the Truth that you will learn here." He filled his lungs, the ribs sticking out on his thin chest as he looked up at the cloud-choked sky. "Remember this, boy: You cannot know the light until you have been blinded by the darkness. Just like this place, opposites crossed. She has never understood that."

"I don't think I do, either."

"Your mother, boy." He knotted a fist of gnarly bone. "She doesn't understand what's coming. She has lost the harmony, never set her feet to the Dance. They are going to destroy her."

"Who is?"

"She is caught between the Twins. Strong, yes, that she is. But the mighty Wing Heart is brittle inside. Her souls hang in the balance." His voice had gone far away, worried by the wind. "The lightning is coming." A pause. Then he clapped his hands together, shouting, *"Bang!"*

Mud Puppy jumped in spite of himself, his heart racing again. The fear that had ebbed with the magic of the place came rushing back to strangle the breath in his lungs.

The Serpent gave Mud Puppy a sad look. The intensity of those dark eyes sent worry pumping through Mud Puppy's veins with each beat of his heart.

"Take this, boy. Eat it." The old man reached into his pouch. When he withdrew his hand it clutched some shriveled thing.

"What is it?"

"The future, boy." The Serpent extended his hand as if it held something dangerous. "If you're strong enough."

Mud Puppy felt it drop onto his palm, surprised by the lightness. It had the feel of desiccated bark. He lifted it to his nose, smelling must and dust.

"Eat it," the old man said. "*He* told me to give it to you."

"Who?"

"Eat!"

Mud Puppy placed the bit of desiccated plant matter on his tongue. Dry and flaky it crumbled under his teeth. The taste made him think of rotting logs and leaf mold.

"What did you make me eat?"

The old man smiled sourly. "You ate a tunnel, boy. A hole. Through it you will pass into other worlds. See other places and talk with other beings. But I must warn you: Do not leave this place. Most of all, do not let loose of your souls. Do you hear me?"

"Let loose of my souls? How can I do that?"

"You will know, boy. *He* told me to make you do this. It was *his* will, not mine."

"Who is he?"

"What did I tell you not to do?"

"Not to leave this place and not to let my souls loose."

"That is correct. I will add one more thing. You must be brave, boy. Braver than you have ever been before. If you are not, if you surrender to fear, *he* will eat you alive. When that happens, you will die here, Mud Puppy."

Mud Puppy blinked, bits of soggy mold still floating around his tongue. "I don't know if I can be brave."

The Serpent pulled his shawl up over his shoulder, hitched it, and pointed to the thatch-covered ramada just down from the summit. "If it rains, you can go there." His sharp eyes searched the scudding clouds that had darkened overhead. "But otherwise I want you sitting here. At the highest spot. It will be dark tonight. *Very, dark.*"

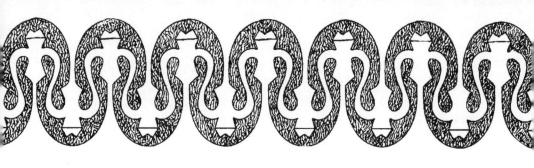

Eight

Firelight flickered in yellow phantoms on the inside of the house walls and cast a shadow outline of Speaker Cloud Heron's dead body. It gave the wattle and daub a golden sheen, accenting the cracks that had appeared in fine tracery through the fire-hardened clay. Overhead, the ceiling was a latticework of soot-stained cane poles and bundles of thatch. Net bags hung from the larger poles, the contents bathed by the rising smoke. Such was the gift of fire. Not only did it heat, light, cook, and purify, but its smoke preserved, kept roots, dried fish, nuts, and thinly sliced meat from molding in the damp climate of Sun Town.

The dead Speaker lay on the raised bench built against the wall. Poles set in the ground supported the framework that was in turn lashed together to support a split-cane bed. A thick layer of hanging moss rested atop the cane, and a tanned buffalo hide atop the moss. All in all, it made for a comfortable and dry bed just high enough off the floor to stay warm in the winter but low enough that in summer the haze of smoke kept the hordes of humming mosquitoes at bay and allowed the sleeper some peace in his repose.

Not that Cloud Heron, Speaker of the Owl Clan, would ever need to worry about mosquitoes again.

Wing Heart bit her lip as she studied her brother's body in the firelight. That he had lasted this long was a miracle. Now, after months of watching his muscular body waste into this frail husk of a man, her strained emotions only allowed her a soul-weary sigh. It was over. For that, and for her son's return, she could be grateful.

"How is he?" Water Petal asked as she ducked through the low doorway. Her thick black hair was parted in the middle, indicating her marital status, and hung straight to her collarbones. She wore a brightly striped fabric shawl over her shoulders, its ends fringed. Her kirtle had been tied around her waist with a silky hemp cord, its girth relaxed now that her pregnancy was apparent.

Wing Heart added another piece of hickory to the crackling fire. "The Speaker is dead."

Water Petal exhaled slowly, eyes raised involuntarily, as if she could see his Life Soul floating up in the smoky rafters. "He was a great leader, a man who never flinched in his duty."

"Even in death," Wing Heart whispered. "He waited until my son returned before surrendering his souls. When will we see another like him?"

"When your son assumes the mantle of Speaker," Water Petal said firmly, eyes glittering with resolve. "Who in the other lineages could compare? Name anyone else in the clan—and surely not Half Thorn, no matter what Moccasin Leaf might say about him."

Wing Heart stared absently at her dead brother's face. The flesh had shrunk around it as though sucked down across the skull by the withering souls inside. His empty eyes lay deep in the hollow pits of his skull, the lips drawn back to expose peglike teeth. Sallow skin outlined the bones of his shoulders and chest. This man whom she had shared so much of her life with, whom she had loved with all of her heart . . . by the Sky Beings, how could Cloud Heron have faded into this wreck of bone and loosely stretched skin?

"Do you wish to be alone, Elder?" Water Petal asked. "To speak with his souls while they are still near?"

Wing Heart vented a weary sigh. "He has heard everything I have to say to him, Cousin. Over and over and over again until I'm sure he's weary of it." *As I am weary of saying it.*

Snakes take it, had she grown so caustic and cynical? She could imagine Cloud Heron in another time, giving her that measuring stare. His brow had risen to a half cock, questioning her as only he could.

Her throat tightened at the sudden welling emptiness inside.

"Elder?"

"I'd rather have cut off my leg," Wing Heart whispered, barely aware of the tear that burned its way past her tightly clamped eyelids and traced down her cheek.

"I understand, Elder."

"No. You don't, Cousin." She knotted her fists in her lap. "For ten and two winters now, my brother and I led the Council. For three tens and nine winters we have lived the same life, breathed each other's air, shared each other's thoughts, and bound our souls together. He was me. I was him. We were one. Like no two people I have ever known."

"That was what made you great."

Wing Heart nodded, hating the grief that rose as relentlessly as the spring floods; brutal and inevitable, she could feel it pooling around her lungs and heart, lapping at her ribs.

"How shall I continue?" she asked of the air. "Brother, what can I do? How can I do it? Without you, it seems . . ." Empty. So very empty.

"Your son is ready to step in at your side." Water Petal sounded so sure of herself.

"My son is not my brother." Her fists knotted, crumpling her white kirtle with its pattern of knots. "But he will do." She bit back the urge to sob. "As I have trained him to."

"Elder?" Hesitation was in Water Petal's voice. "Would you like me to care for the Speaker? He must be cleaned, his clothes burned. The corpse must be prepared for the pyre."

"Not yet."

"As you wish, Elder."

Wing Heart ground the heels of her palms into her eyes, twisting them as if to scrub her traitorous tears from her head. *I thought I had myself under control. I have been so calm, so prepared, and now that he's truly gone, I am broken like an old doll. Why didn't I know this was coming? Why didn't I understand I would hurt so badly? Why didn't you tell me, Brother?*

"Would you like me to make the ritual announcement, Elder?" Water Petal's voice remained so eerily reasonable.

"No, Cousin. Thank you. That is my job."

A long silence passed as Wing Heart sat in numb misery, flashes of memory tormenting her with images of Cloud Heron, of the times they had shared triumph and pain. How did one pack a lifetime of memories, as if into a clay pot, and just tuck them away?

Brother, after a turning of seasons of watching you die, why is it now beginning to hurt?

"Elder, someone should at least let White Bird know that his uncle is dead. He should know before the others. It will give him time to prepare."

"Yes." *Tomorrow, yes, tomorrow I will be able to think again.* She waited hesitantly, struggling to hear Cloud Heron's response to that, but the clinging silence of grief washed about her.

"And Mud Puppy?" Water Petal asked as she rose and crouched in the doorway.

"What about him?" Wing Heart asked, slightly off guard at the change of subject.

"Should I tell him?" A pause. "He's up on the Bird's Head. The Serpent left him up there at dark."

Wing Heart shook her head, trying to clear the dampness from her eyes. She blinked in the firelight, gaze drawn inexorably to Cloud Heron's death-strained rictus. "No. Forget him. He's a worthless half-wit. It's the future, Water Petal. That's what I have to deal with. The future."

This is not a good idea," Cooter said from the darkness in the front of the canoe. He stroked his paddle in the rhythmic cadence they had adopted.

Anhinga glared where she sat in the back behind the others. She hadn't anticipated the night being this dark. They canoed northward in an inky blackness that was truly unsettling. On occasion someone hissed as unseen moss flicked across his face or over his head.

"You would think you had never been out at night," Anhinga managed through clenched jaws. Truth to tell, she was a little unnerved herself. Was it lunacy and madness to strike out like this with her young companions, to sneak north through the swamps in darkness?

"But for the wind, we'd be lost," Spider Fire reminded. Overhead the south wind continued to roar and twist its way through the backswamp forest. With that at their backs they couldn't get lost. And it helped to keep the humming hordes of mosquitoes down. They had greased their bodies, but the bloodthirsty insects still swarmed.

"I don't worry about getting lost," Mist Finger muttered. "I do worry about smacking headlong into a tree, capsizing, and drowning out here in the darkness."

"Not me," Right Talon declared uneasily. "It's the stuff we keep sliding under. I don't know when it's hanging moss or when it's a water moccasin dropping down to bite me in the face."

"Thanks," Slit Nose grumbled from his place in front of Anhinga. "That's *just* what I needed to hear! Panther's blood, I'd just about let myself forget about the snakes, and then you let your lips flap."

"Some brave warriors," Anhinga cried. "Should we turn around and go back? Is that what you want? My brother's ghost is wandering about, unavenged because my uncle will do nothing!"

"Out here, in the darkness, where spirits can drift in with the mist and kill us, I'm not inclined to argue," Cooter replied from his position up front. She could barely see his shoulders moving, or did she just imagine them as he stroked with his pointed paddle?

"He was your friend," she reminded hotly. "You were there. You saw it."

"I did," Cooter said. "It was all I could do to escape. There was only the two of us against ten of them, their bodies slick with grease. We caught them levering our sandstone from the side of the hill. When Bowfin shouted at them they turned . . . didn't even hesitate, and cast darts at us. Luck must have guided the hand of the first, for his dart sailed true. I still don't know how Bowfin could have missed seeing it. He should have been able to dodge out of the way."

"But he didn't," Anhinga told them. "I was there when he died. No one should die like that, their guts stinking with foreign rot while their blood runs brown in their veins and fever robs them of their wits."

"I was lucky enough to run." Cooter's vigorous paddling mirrored the anger in his voice. "It was stupid of us to make ourselves known. It would have been better if we'd just sneaked away, called for more warriors."

"That's wrong!" Anhinga felt the anger stir in her breast. "It's *our* land! It's *our* stone! They have no right in our country, treating it as if it were theirs!"

They paddled in silence for a while, accompanied by the sounds of the swamp, splashing fish, the lonely call of the nightjar and the chirring of insects. Overhead the wind continued to slash at the spring green trees, rustling the leaves and creaking the branches.

Spider Fire finally said, "You're right, it's our territory, given to us by the Creator, but they have been raiding our land since the beginning of time. I will help you end this once and for all."

"Will you?" Mist Finger asked wryly.

She had been glad when Mist Finger volunteered to accompany her. For the past several moons she had been alternately delighted and annoyed by the way he kept creeping into her thoughts. At odd times of the day, she'd remember his smile, or the way the muscles rippled in his back. The sparkle in his eyes seemed to have fixed itself between her souls.

"Branch!" Cooter sang out. "Duck, everyone."

The canoe rocked as they bent their heads low to drift under a low-hanging branch. Anhinga felt trailing bits of spiderweb dust her face, crackling and tearing as the canoe's momentum carried them past. She reached up and wiped it away, hoping the angry spider wasn't trapped in her hair. The thought of those eight milling legs tangling in her black locks made her scalp tingle.

Slit Nose broke the silence. "That doesn't mean it's acceptable. Anhinga's right. It's got to stop sometime. It might just as well be now."

Mist Finger laughed, the sound musical in the windblown night. "You don't think it's been tried? How many of our ancestors, no matter what the clan, have died fighting with the Sun People? How many stories can you recall? You know, the ones about great-uncle so-and-so, or cousin what's-his-name who was killed in a raid on the Sun People, or who, like Bowfin, was skewered by a dart, or smacked in the head with a war club. Is there any clan, any lineage that you can name that doesn't have a story? In all that time, all those generations going back to the Creation, don't you think that others have tried to teach them a lesson?"

"Does this have a point?" Spider Fire asked.

"Of course," Mist Finger answered easily. "The point is that nothing is going to change. Our war is eternal. No one is going to win."

"Then why are you here?" Anhinga asked, anger festering at the bottom of her throat.

"I'm here for you." Mist Finger's voice carried an unsettling undercurrent. "As are the rest of us. Bowfin was our friend and your kinsman. We would indeed see his ghost given a little peace."

"But you don't think this is going to do any good?" Anhinga tried to stifle her irritation.

"In the long run, no." Mist Finger sounded so sure of himself.

"But you came anyway?"

"Of course." Where did that reasonable tone come from? He might have been discussing the relative merit of fishnets rather than a raid against the Sun People. "Like my companions, Anhinga, I am here for you. As I said."

For me? "I don't understand."

"Then I shall lay it out for you like a string of beads." Humor laced Mist Finger's voice. "Though I doubt my friends will admit to it out loud. We are here to prove ourselves to you. Oh, to be sure, we wouldn't mind killing a couple of Sun People in the process. Bowfin was a good friend. We share your anger over his death. But, most of all, when this is over, each of us wants you to think well of us, to admire our courage and skill."

Her thoughts stumbled. "What are you talking about? Prove yourselves?"

"Shut up, Mist Finger," Spider Fire growled unhappily.

His admonition brought another laugh from Mist Finger, who added, "Anhinga? Are you not planning on marrying soon? And when you do, which of your suitors would you choose? Some simpleminded fisherman who worried more over the set of his gill nets, or one of the five dashing young warriors in this canoe?"

"Be quiet, Mist Finger," Slit Nose muttered.

Anhinga started, considering his words, ever more unsettled by them. "Why are you telling me this?"

Mist Finger calmly replied, "So that my companions here know that they have no chance."

Chuckles and guffaws broke out from the others while Anhinga felt her face redden. Snakes take him, he'd embarrassed her, and in the middle of this most important strike against the Sun People.

"Well," she told him hotly, "if and *when* I marry, it won't be to you, Mist Finger! And for now, it would do all of you good to think about what we're doing. This isn't about courting. It's about revenge."

"Nice work, Mist Finger." Right Talon couldn't keep the gloating out of his voice. "That's one person less the rest of us have to worry about."

The canoe rocked as someone in the darkness ahead of her slapped a paddle on the water, spraying the front of the boat where Mist Finger sat. Laughter followed.

"Stop that!" Anhinga ordered. "You want to know who I'll marry? Very well, I'll marry the man who kills the most Sun People." There, that ought to set them straight.

"Is that a promise?" Slit Nose asked.

"It is. My uncle might be willing to remain at the Panther's Bones and talk about revenge," she told him. "I intend on doing something about it. If I do nothing else in my life, I will see to it that the Sun People finally pay for the wrongs they have committed against us. On that, I give my promise. By the life of my souls, and before Panther Above, I swear I will harm them as they have never been harmed before."

"No matter what?" Right Talon asked.

"No matter what," she insisted hotly. "So there. If you've come to impress me, do it by killing Sun People."

Out in the blackness of the swamp, the hollow hoot of the great horned owl sent a shiver down her soul. It was as if the death bird heard, and had taken her vow.

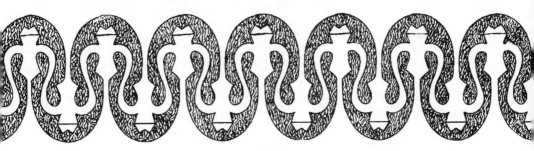

Nine

Lightning flashed in the night. The wind continued to gust up from the south. Atop the Bird's Head, Mud Puppy pulled his ragged shawl about his shoulders and huddled in the wind-whipped darkness. He had removed the little red chert flake from his belt pouch and clutched it tightly in his right fist while he rubbed his temples with nervous fingers.

Sick. I feel sick. His stomach had knotted around the bits of mushroom that he had swallowed. Now it cramped and squirmed, while the tickle at the back of his throat tightened and saliva seeped loosely around his tongue.

Please, I don't want to . . . The urge barely gave him warning as his stomach pumped. Time after time, Mud Puppy's body bucked as he heaved up his meager supper; and then came slime until finally a bitter and painful rasping was all his wracked body could produce.

Coughing, he gasped for breath. When had he fallen onto his side? Cool dirt pressed against his fevered cheek. Hawking, he tried to spit the burning bile from his windpipe. Vomit ate painfully into the back of his nose. Tears dripped in liquid misery from his eyes, coursing across the bridge of his nose and slipping insolently down the side of his face.

Had he ever felt this miserable? When he blinked his eyes, odd streaks of color—smeared yellow, sparkling purple, smudges of blue and green—belied the blackness of the night. His body seemed to pulse, his flesh curiously distant from his stumbling thoughts.

Waves, timed to the beat of his heart, rocked him. Yes, floating, as if on undulating darkness. He had felt this way in water. Water. The notion possessed him, and for a moment he forgot where he lay, so high on the Bird's Head.

"Hold on to your souls," he reminded himself, and when he swallowed, his body turned itself inside out.

What is happening to me? The words scampered around his tortured brain, echoing with an odd hollowness.

"Are you afraid?" The voice startled him.

"Who spoke?"

"I did."

"Where are you?"

"In your hand."

Mud Puppy tried to swallow the bitterness in his throat again and felt his flesh rippling like saturated mud. Raising his hand, he opened it, staring at his palm, nothing more than a smear in the darkness. The flake! That tiny little bit of stone that had winked at him in the sunlight.

"You can talk?"

"Only to those who dare listen."

Mud Puppy blinked his eyes, his body seeming to swell and float. Bits of colored light, like streamers, continued to flicker across his vision. "Do you see them?"

"See what?" the flake asked.

"The lights." Mud Puppy told him in amazement. "Colors, like bits of rainbow broken loose and wavering."

"You're seeing through the mushroom's eyes," the flake said.

"How?"

"The world is a magical place. An old place, one in which so many things have become hidden. The simple has become ever more complex. Creatures come and go along with the land, growing and shrinking, mountains rising and being worn away. Shapes shift. Forms flow."

"How do you know these things?"

"I am old, boy. So old you cannot imagine. Carried across this world from my familiar soil, I am left here, separated from the rest of myself."

"Do you grieve?"

"Do you?"

"Yes."

"Then I do, too."

"I don't understand."

"Neither do I."

Mud Puppy frowned at the thin bit of stone, running his finger over the smooth chert. "What are you?"

"Whatever you make of me. I was alone until you picked me up. As long as you hold me, I shall be whatever you want me to be."

Was it the flake of stone talking? Or the voice of the mushroom echoing around his souls? Mud Puppy blinked, his souls twining about and floating in his chest. Did it matter? The flake's answer was oddly reassuring: "*I shall be whatever you want me to be.*"

The first spatters of rain pattered his skin. The impact of the drops went right through him, as though he were pierced by a cast dart. He forced himself to sit up, dazed, failing to understand as the raindrops thumped and hammered on his head. Each drop sent echoes of its impact through his skull, like rings on a pond. Eternity stretched as he lost himself in the sensations. The water trickling down his cold skin was alive. He could sense its living essence, silver and fluid.

Cold. Have I ever been this cold? Dumbly he ran his hands down his arms, squishing the water from his skin. He could feel himself, feel the blood being pushed around inside him as he tightened his grip on his arm. His body seemed to glow despite the cold.

A gust of wind pushed at him and relaxed. Wind, a thing of the sky.

I flew! The memory of the Dream floated out of the recesses and re-formed within his souls. Yes, hadn't that been magical? His souls turned hollow with the sensation of dropping, weightless, from a great height. Were those really Owl's wings that had carried him?

"They were indeed," a deep voice told him from the night.

He blinked, lashes wet and cold on his face. "Flake?"

"No." A pause. "Do you remember me? Do you remember the promise you made?"

"Masked Owl?" In the flickering glow of distant lightning, Mud Puppy saw him. The giant owl perched on the grass-thatched ramada. Those huge eyes seemed to gleam in the night.

"Are you seeking the One, Mud Puppy?"

"The One?"

"The One Life. It comes after the Dance."

"Which you will teach me?"

"Someday." Masked Owl agreed. "But first, I want you to talk to your uncle. He is here with a message for you."

"My uncle?" Mud Puppy frowned. "Cloud Heron? Is that whom you mean?"

Lightning flashed again, this time to display Cloud Heron, his body lit by a pale shimmer. To Mud Puppy's surprise he stood several hands above the earth, floating as though it were the most normal of activities.

"Hello, boy." Cloud Heron cocked his head; his eyes looked as if they'd been painted with charcoal.

"You look well, Uncle," Mud Puppy cried happily. "The illness is gone! I'm so happy! Now, everything is right again. You are well, White Bird is home from the north. Mother won't have to worry so much."

"I'm dead, Mud Puppy. What you see is my Life Soul." The words sounded hollow on the storm. "As we speak, my sister is crying beside my body. I came here, to the Bird's Head, because it is the way."

"What way?"

"To the West, Nephew. You know what lies there?"

Mud Puppy suffered a sudden shiver. "The Land of the Dead."

"That's right. And once my Life Soul crosses the boundary, steps off the mound, it can't come back. Not to this place. Spirits can't cross the rings, boy. They can't walk across water or lines of ash. My Life Soul will be gone forever."

Mud Puppy frowned. "I'll miss you."

"Why?" Cloud Heron demanded. "I never liked you."

"That doesn't matter."

The ghost seemed to waver, shifting when the wind blew through him. "You are right. It doesn't matter now. I never understood who you were, what you were. If I had known, I would have taught you more. Treated you differently."

"Taught me more of what?"

"The things you will need to lead. The world will have to teach you. So many will try to kill you, to destroy you, you must be crafty and cunning. You have so much to learn, and no one to teach you."

"You could teach me, Uncle."

"I don't have time now, Nephew. Perhaps my Dream Soul might, if it is ever so inclined. I can't say how it will decide to treat you." The ghost shifted, twisting in the air. "A canoe is coming. From the south, from the Panthers. Five young men. As many as the fingers on your hand. With them is an angry young woman. They are going to raid Ground Cherry Camp. Can you remember that?"

"Ground Cherry Camp," Mud Puppy repeated.

"They will strike at first light on the third day. She must be allowed to escape."

"Who?"

"She will try to kill you, Mud Puppy. She is very devoted, her soul wounded and angry. Don't trust her." The ghost wavered again. "I don't want to go. So much . . . undecided. He's going to die."

"Who, who is going to die?"

"So much greatness. Taken before his time. How wrong I was . . . how very wrong."

"Uncle?"

"Don't fail us, boy . . ."

Only black wind remained. In the distance to the east, white strobed the clouds as lightning flared and died.

"Uncle?" Mud Puppy tried to stand, wobbling on his feet. His senses spun and tricked him. His small body thumped as it dropped onto the mound's sticky wet clay.

"He has taken the leap," Masked Owl said, his eyes glowing like coals in the darkness. "His Life Soul has fled. From here it will begin the journey to the West. Do you remember the promise you made to me?"

"That I will help you, yes." Mud Puppy's vision kept swimming, losing sight of the gleaming owl's eyes. "Are you still wearing your mask?"

"Of course."

"Why?"

"Why does anyone wear a mask?"

"To make them look like someone else."

"Sometimes, but not this time."

"Then why?"

"You must find the answer to that, Mud Puppy."

"Everyone is asking things of me."

"It is your destiny. Do you have another question to ask me?"

From the recesses of his head, the question came: "Why did the Creator separate the Earth from the Sky?"

Masked Owl laughed at that. "You must answer that one on your own, too, boy. But, lest you become totally frustrated, I bear a message for you."

"You do? Is it from Salamander? Would he be my Spirit Helper?" Hope leaped up within him like a fountain of light.

"He is considering it. But, no, the message isn't from him. It is from Cricket."

"Yes?"

"He wanted you to know that he sings with his legs. By rubbing them together. He also said to tell you that there is a lesson in that. The lesson is that you should never judge based upon appearances.

A cricket might be a very small creature, but it can still make a great noise. In all the world only thunder has a louder voice than Cricket. Remember that, Mud Puppy."

"I will."

"You had better rest now. Your body needs time to Dance with brother mushroom. Oh, and about your uncle's message, I would give it to the Serpent. He is the one most likely to understand. And, for the time being—outside of myself—he is your single ally."

Masked Owl vanished as if he had been but a fanciful flight of imagination. Blackness, cold, and a terrible sickness remained.

White Bird could have chosen better weather for his homecoming, but instead of bright sunshine he got a gray drizzle that filtered down in streamers from the cloud-choked skies. Nevertheless, he stood in the rear of his canoe as it slid onto the mucky bank of the landing.

On shore a throng had gathered amidst the clutter of beached canoes. People stood respectfully behind the Serpent, their brightly dyed clothing creating a speckling of color against the gray, dreary day. In dots and clots they stretched up the incline above the landing. An expectant excitement ran through them as they talked anxiously with each other. Most were wearing flats of bark on their heads to shed the persistent drizzle.

Yellow Spider leaped out of the bow as White Bird stepped into the calf-deep waters at the stern. Together they pulled the heavily laden dugout as far as they could onto the bank. The dark silty mud seemed to grip the rounded bottom in a lover's tight embrace. Behind them, the rest of the Wolf Traders landed, dragging their canoes fast against the bank.

White Bird and Yellow Spider straightened, extending their arms to where the Serpent waited several paces beyond them. The old man had a curiously haunted look on his flat, wrinkled face. Water trickled down the faded tattoos on his sagging brown skin. He might have been a standing skeleton, so thin and delicate did he look. Behind him the crowd went silent. White Bird was aware of their eyes, dark, large, and peering at him in anticipation.

"Great Serpent!" White Bird shouted the ritual words into the misty rain. "We are returned from the north with goods for the People!"

"Are you cleansed?" the Serpent called back.

"We are, Great Serpent. By your Power and skill."

"Are your Dreams pure?"

"They are, Great Serpent! My Dreams have been pleasant this last night. My souls, and those of my companions, have been at peace."

"Do you leave anger and disharmony behind you?"

"We do, Great Serpent."

"Then enter this place and be welcome, White Bird and Yellow Spider of the Owl Clan of the Northern Moiety. And enter this place, you Traders of the Wolf People, and be welcome."

"Is that finally it?" Hazel Fire muttered out of the side of his mouth.

"It is, my friend." Yellow Spider answered in the Trader's tongue. "Now come and be dazzled by the greatest city on Earth."

Together they started forward, but the first to break free from the crowd was Spring Cypress. She shot down the bank on bare feet, hair streaming behind her in a dark wave. She threw herself into White Bird's arms, hugging him desperately.

"White Bird! I've missed you so!"

He clasped her to him, feeling her round breasts against his chest, enjoying the sensation of her damp skin against his. She was taller and fuller of body than he remembered. After a winter of experience he could feel the promise in her woman's body. Taut and firm, she conformed to him. Her damp hair smelled of dogwood blossoms. From somewhere hidden in the back of his souls Lark's face flashed, the image unsettling. He pushed it away and clasped Spring Cypress for a moment longer, then stepped back to look at her.

Snakes, she was beautiful, her heart-shaped face dominated by large dark eyes and a slightly upturned nose. She looked so delicate, and her souls were mirrored in her gaze; that longing and excitement was for him. For a moment he struggled with the desperate urge to lift her up and twirl her away from the watching crowd. What a shame that once again he had to be the man his mother demanded of him.

"Where is my mother? I would have thought the Clan Elder would be here to greet me. Is she detained?" he asked, matching her smile with his own.

In that instant Spring Cypress's eyes dropped, her smile fading. "I am sorry, White Bird. Your uncle. Last night."

"Is he . . . ?" He couldn't make himself say the inevitable words.

She nodded. "I just found out. I heard Moccasin Leaf telling the Serpent. Cloud Heron has been sick for so long. It wasn't unexpected."

He closed his eyes, exhaling as he controlled his expression. "I wished to see him one last time." A pang of loss began to grow in his chest. "I had so much to tell him. So many things to ask about."

"What is it?" Yellow Spider asked, disentangling himself from some of his friends. They had charged down the slope ahead of Yellow Spider's sister, Water Petal.

"My uncle," White Bird said. "Last night."

Yellow Spider flinched. "I'm sorry to hear that."

"What happened to him?" Hazel Fire asked, nervous eyes on the crowd that surged down toward them.

"Dead." The word sounded flat in White Bird's throat.

"He's the one you are named after?"

White Bird nodded. Then he forced himself to meet the oncoming crowd. The Serpent, he noticed, had already turned to leave, plodding up the slope on his stick-thin legs. No doubt he was wanted at Mother's. It was his duty to begin the rituals to strip the body of flesh and cleanse the house site.

"Greetings, White Bird." Gnarly old Mud Stalker strode purposefully down and extended his good left hand. His hard brown eyes took in every nuance of White Bird's expression. "It seems we have a day of joy and sorrow, all mixed together."

How did he take that? *What is his real meaning?* "Indeed, Mud Stalker"—White Bird gave the man a facile smile—"it is always a joy to see you. Or were you thinking of something else?"

"I was referring first to your return, and second to the news about Cloud Heron. He was most adept."

He was . . . especially when it came to thwarting you and your clan. "He will be mourned by all."

"At least the alligators didn't get you, White Bird."

"Well, we can't always depend on alligators, can we?" He avoided glancing at the man's mangled right arm. "I have brought a great many gifts for your clan, Speaker. I thought of you constantly while I was upcountry."

"I shall look forward to hearing your tales," Mud Stalker said, touching his forehead in deference. "But I am taking up too much of your time, what with the death and all the responsibilities that now fall on your shoulders." He kept his eyes locked on White Bird's. "My deepest sympathies. If I can be of any service, or if I can advise you on any subject, do call on me." He walked on to greet Yellow Spider.

Clay Fat came next, a jolly smile on his face as he clapped White Bird on the back. Rainwater traced rounded paths over his belly and dripped from his knob of a navel. "Glad to have you home, young man. And even happier to see that welcome you gave Spring Cypress." He winked, the action contorting his round face. But behind it, White Bird could sense the man's nervous tension. "I think she's going to be declared a woman soon!"

"Oh?" White Bird asked, wondering what his mother's old friend was hiding behind his bluff and glowing expression.

Clay Fat lowered his voice. "Well, perhaps we could have done so several moons ago, but we were waiting for a special event." A pause. "Have a word with your mother, young man. I can't think of a better match than the two of you."

So, Mother is against a match with Spring Cypress? Why? What has happened since I have been gone? "I will speak to her as soon as I can." He cast his eyes up the slope of the canoe landing, searching for some sign of the Owl Clan Elder.

"I think she's detained. About your uncle, my deepest sympathies, White Bird. He was a great man." Water ran from Clay Fat's bark hat. It sat crooked on his ball-shaped head so that the runoff trickled onto the curve of his greased shoulder. The drips beaded and slid down his brown skin in silver trails.

"As are you, Speaker. You filled my thoughts the entire time I was upriver."

"Better that you had spent your thoughts on Spring Cypress than me. That would have been a great deal more productive—not to mention more pleasant, eh?"

"We will talk more later, Speaker." White Bird clapped him on the back, passing to face Thunder Tail and Stone Talon from the Eagle Clan as they took their place next in line.

"Greetings, young White Bird." Aged Stone Talon offered her hand, birdlike under thin skin. As she balanced on rattly crutches, the top of her head barely reached the middle of his chest; the old woman seemed to have aged ten tens of turnings of seasons since he had seen her last. Her flesh reminded him of turkey wattle, loose and hanging from her bones. Hair that had been black a summer ago had gone as white as the northern snows. Her back had hunched and curled like a crawfish's tail. But she looked up at him with the same predatory eyes that a robin used when it considered plucking an unlucky worm from the ground. "So, the barbarians and the monsters of the North didn't get you?"

"No, Elder, they did not." Instinct told him that no matter how her body had failed, her wits seemed as sharp as a banded-chert blade. The question was, which way would she cut? And which clan would drip blood when she was finished?

Her son, Thunder Tail, the Eagle Clan Speaker, cleared his throat. He wore a necklace made of split bear mandibles that hung like a breastplate. His weathered face reminded White Bird of a rosehip that had been kept in a pot for too many winters. His tattoos had faded through the turning of seasons, darkening and blurring until, like the patterns in his soul, they were hard to decipher. "Are we to call you Speaker, now?"

"Respectfully, I have no idea. I have just arrived."

"Difficult, isn't it?" Stone Talon gave him a toothless smile that rearranged her shriveled face. The thoughts behind her eyes, however, were anything but pleasant. "Having to face all of this when your souls are freshly plunged into grief." She gestured toward the crowd that still awaited him. "Your uncle was a strong leader. Where will you find his like?"

"There is no one like him," White Bird agreed easily. "My clan's loss is indeed grievous, but it wounds us all. My uncle served all the people. Fortunately, Elder, I have four canoes to help lighten the People's sadness. I have set aside some special presents for the two of you. As soon as I find a moment, be sure that I shall bring them to you personally."

"Clever boy, that one," he heard Stone Talon say as they passed on.

"At last!" Three Moss cried from where she waited impatiently. "Come, Mother. Let us greet White Bird." Three Moss led Elder Cane Frog into White Bird's presence. Her hand rested on her mother's bare shoulder.

He reached out, taking the blind Elder's frail hand and clasping it respectfully. "My souls are pleased to see you, Elder. I'm sure your daughter has told you about the Trade we have returned with."

"She has." Cane Frog smacked her lips, as if something distasteful clung to her pink gums. Her sightless right white eye wiggled and quivered, while dirt encrusted the empty orbit of her missing left. "She also told me you brought barbarians with you?"

"I did, Elder." He laughed lightly. "There was no other way to carry so much Trade. It was that, or sink the canoe."

"Never that," Cane Frog agreed. "You know, I lost my oldest brother that way. Tragic. Such a Speaker he would have been for the clan. Best to be safe out on the water. Yes, always safe."

"I agree, Elder."

"Our hearts are wounded by the news of your uncle." Three Moss was looking at him speculatively. Life had been unfair to her. Plain, thickset, and bland of feature, she didn't have that spark of animation in her flat brown eyes. "We are, however, joyous at your safe return. So many had declared you dead. Most had lost hope."

"Hope should never be given up completely," White Bird told

her evenly. "In my case, I must apologize for making so many people worry. Events, however, dictated that I go farther than I had planned, and once there, that I dedicate myself to the Trade through the winter. But I assure you I longed for home. In fact, I have some special gifts that I have picked out, just for Elder Cane Frog."

"We are obliged to you," Cane Frog rasped. "Your return was propitious, young White Bird. Indeed, most propitious. But then, luck has always favored your clan, hasn't it? You know, it was just a couple of days ago that we were talking—"

"Mother"—Three Moss took the old woman's arm—"come, we can't monopolize White Bird. Others wish to welcome him home. There is still Yellow Spider to see and the barbarians to welcome."

"Yellow Spider? Who is he?" White Bird heard the old woman ask, as Three Moss led her away.

"Brother to Water Petal, of the Owl Clan," Three Moss was hissing as Speaker Deep Hunter led Elder Colored Paint to White Bird.

Deep Hunter, Speaker for the Alligator Clan, was watching Cane Frog as Three Moss stopped her in front of Yellow Spider. He had a curious smile on his lips. By the time he turned to White Bird his expression had grown thoughtful. "So, you are well and healthy. Welcome home, White Bird. After so many declared you dead, it is a joy to know that your souls are safe and returned to those who love and cherish you."

"Thank you for your kind greeting. I regret that I worried so many, Speaker."

"Oh, fear not. It does them good every once in a while to be proven wrong."

"Who, Speaker?"

"The ones who come to think that they know how the world works . . . and that they are the smart ones. It is always such a shock when they find out that they are not as cunning as they thought. It is healthy to be reminded that people, things, or events can come from unexpected quarters to disrupt everything and throw the simplest of plans into confusion." Deep Hunter's thoughtful black eyes were taking White Bird's measure. His long face always had a sad look, but Deep Hunter was never a known quantity. "Stew, as you no doubt know, is tastier when it is stirred every so often."

"I hear the wisdom in your words, Speaker."

"Do you?"

To change the subject, White Bird reached out to take Colored Paint's hand. "Greetings, Elder. I have brought you some special gifts from upriver. You filled my thoughts throughout the winter. So much so, that it gives my souls great joy to see you again."

"It was cold, your winter up north?" Colored Paint asked, her glinting brown eyes on White Bird.

"Yes, Elder."

"I spent a winter up north, you know. Poison and snakes, but that was a long time ago. How many winters? Three tens? Three tens and three? I can't recall. But cold? I tell you, I thought my bones would crack. You don't know the value of a good hot fire until you've been that cold."

"I agree, Elder."

"We not only come to welcome you," Deep Hunter interrupted, "but to offer our respects over your uncle's death." The enigmatic smile remained on his thin lips as he asked, "There is talk that Owl Clan will have a very young Speaker. Have you given that any thought?"

White Bird kept his expression blank. "I have been in seclusion, Speaker. My first responsibility was to the purification of my souls and body. I have no hint as to what my clan might be considering."

Deep Hunter nodded absently.

What was he hiding? White Bird's souls tingled with warning. It was one thing to deal with Mud Stalker. He had always been an enemy, but what motivated Deep Hunter?

The Speaker smiled easily. "Come and see us when you have a chance. After that winter up north the Elder will have a warm fire for you, and I shall make sure our stew has been adequately stirred. We will have a great many things to talk about."

"Thank you, Speaker. And you, Elder Colored Paint, have a pleasant day."

"Going back to the fire," Colored Paint muttered. "Just talking about it has made my bones shiver. A bit of winter lingers inside me. I think it was because I got so cold upriver that time. Hope it doesn't bother you the way it does me."

"I hope not, too, Elder."

Deep Hunter added: "Give your mother my greeting. Send her my respects concerning your uncle. Tell her that we need to speak. Soon." He led Colored Paint down the line to Yellow Spider.

White Bird glanced uneasily at the growing crowd. He wished he could just press his way through them and sprint up the slope to the plaza. From there he could run full tilt north to his mother's house on the first ridge and learn the news.

Time began to drag as he worked his way through the throng. It seemed that the entirety of Sun Town had poured out to greet him. Everyone was curious as to what he had brought, and just as anxious to see the barbarians and to invite them to visit, eat, and tell their tales of the far north. It took but a suggestion from White Bird to the gathered young men, and they surged to the beach and muscled the muddy damp canoes onto their broad shoulders. He smiled at the clans vying for the honor of carrying the Trade up to Owl Clan's territory.

As they started up the slippery slope, people crowded around Hazel Fire and his companions, shouting questions and invitations.

Not that Traders didn't come from distant places, but these were young warriors, not the professional rivermen with wild tales that were meant to awe their audience into a lucrative Trade.

White Bird did enjoy a moment of satisfaction as the crowd surged up the slope from the landing. He was watching the Wolf Traders, noting their expressions the moment that they stepped out onto the expanse of the great southern plaza. They stopped short, stunned at the sight of the huge curving ridges topped with lines of houses. Even with the drizzle that masked the Bird's Head to the west, they stood stunned, speechless at the majesty of Sun Town's earthworks and the geometric perfection with which it was laid out.

"There is no place like this on Earth!" Gray Fox finally gasped. "Do the gods live here?"

"No," Yellow Spider assured him. "They are in the sky above and under the earth beneath your feet, where they should be. No, my friend, you have just entered the center of the world. We are the Sun People, and there are no others like us anywhere."

White Bird led the procession, striding with the same presence and posture he had seen his uncle adopt for formal occasions. Behind him the crowd lined out, a gaudy procession who marched and clapped their hands, Singing and laughing, the canoes bobbing on a buoyancy of shoulders.

He had forgotten the immensity of Sun Town. In respect, he touched his forehead as he crossed the town's center line, the low beaten path in the grass that delineated the Southern Moiety from the Northern. As he entered Owl Clan territory, his heart seemed fit to burst. A swirl of emotions—joy at success, sadness at the news about his uncle, and pride in his clan—swirled within him like mixing floodwaters.

As he came striding up to the first ridge, he stared through the rain, feeling water trickle down his face to soak his already wet breechcloth. "Greetings, Elder Wing Heart," he called as he stopped short of the borrow ditch below his house. "Your son has returned. He has been cleansed and brings Trade for the People."

As if on cue, his mother stepped out from behind the hanging, stately, looking every inch the influential Elder that she was. "Wel-

come home, White Bird. My heart is filled with gladness to see you."
She paused. "More so given the sorrow that has filled us after your
uncle's death."

"I grieve for the Speaker," he answered, voice ringing.

It was at that moment that the Serpent stepped out behind Wing
Heart, his face streaked with charcoal as was appropriate when dealing with the dead. A black face didn't frighten the freshly dead souls.

The crowd had flowed around his party in a semicircle, watching
the greatest of spectacles. He could feel the anticipation, the rising
excitement. People hung on every word, wondering if Wing Heart
would declare him to be the new Speaker. Or would she wait? Did
she have the kind of influence to make such a declaration, knowing
full well that her clan would be forced to support her? Would she
take that kind of risk, knowing that to have to withdraw it later
would amount to a terrible loss of face?

White Bird straightened, his heart hammering with anticipation.
Yellow Spider was standing by his side, spine stiff, shoulders back,
head proud. The four heavy canoes were lined up behind them,
evidence of his ability to provide for the People.

Wing Heart stood as if frozen, staring across the divide created
by the borrow pit. In its boggy bottom, cattail and cane had
sprouted, the first green shoots of spring. Water lilies were coming
back to life, the emerald leaves floating on the black water.

"White Bird," she called out imperiously, "nephew of Cloud
Heron, who was once Speaker of the Owl Clan, I would . . ."

A muttering ripple ran through the western end of the crowd,
people parting as if they were water. White Bird cocked his head at
the interruption and the rising babble of excited talk. Unease tightened in his chest, his muscles charged the way they would for combat. He realized he was breathing hard, as if he'd just run for several
hands of time.

When the crowed parted, it took White Bird a moment to recognize the boy. He looked like a drowned urchin, black hair plastered to his head. Smears of watery soil blotched his cheeks,
shoulders, and scrawny chest. What had originally been a white
breechcloth looked gray, stained with clay and ash. But what af-
fected White Bird the most was the look in those large, haunted
eyes. Power seemed to radiate from them like heat from a glowing
cooking clay.

"Mud Puppy?" the question popped unbidden from White Bird's
lips as the boy walked past, that eerie stare locked on a world beyond
this one.

The boy didn't hesitate but plodded down and splashed through the water and up the ridge toward Wing Heart.

"Mud Puppy?" she barked angrily. "What are you . . ."

But Mud Puppy walked past her, stopping instead before the Serpent. In the sudden silence, White Bird couldn't hear what the boy said, just the mumbling of his low speech.

"That is ridiculous!" Wing Heart blurted.

White Bird couldn't stand it. Snakes take the little imp, he'd just ruined everything! Before he could think, he was striding forward, enough aware to round the eastern edge of the borrow pit instead of slogging through the water so that he could stalk up to his mother's house. No; he wouldn't wring his brother's scrawny neck, not here where the entire world could see, but he'd sure do it as soon as no one was watching.

The Serpent had straightened, his face oddly drawn by a frown. Wing Heart shot a hard hand out to grasp the boy's arm. White Bird could see the muscles in her back tense and knot as she dragged the boy toward the doorway. Her body twisted as she pitched him unceremoniously into the shadowed depths of the house.

"People!" The Serpent raised his hands high. "Word has just come to me that the Swamp Panthers are sending a party to raid us. Five warriors will attack Ground Cherry Camp the day after tomorrow at dawn. Who will go to ward off this threat?"

The announcement stopped White Bird cold. Without looking, he could tell that the crowd hung upon a precipice of indecision. It was instinct that led White Bird to raise his hand, shouting, "I will!" only to wonder what he'd done, and what had happened in this moment that should have been his greatest triumph.

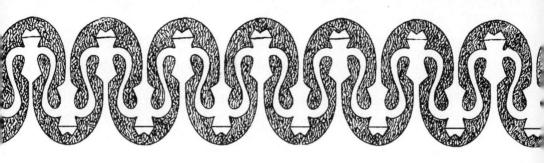

Ten

A low bank of clouds rolled up from the gulf. They drifted across the dense forests, following the valley of the Father Water northward.

In their inky shadow, Many Colored Crow dived and soared, riding the warm southern winds. On wings of night, he flipped and cavorted. High atop its ridge, Sun Town lay tucked away in sleep.

Many Colored Crow had waited for the last of the figures to leave the Men's House. Had waited for the Dancing and Singing to conclude. He had let the young warriors preparing for battle purify themselves with sweat baths and liberal doses of black drink. He had let the dancers gyrate and pirouette as they wore their totem masks of redheaded woodpecker, bobcat, and snapping turtle. He had allowed the Power to flow into the warrior's muscles and enervate their souls. This night it was to his benefit to allow Masked Owl's vision to come true.

As he spiraled down through the humid air, he located the lone house in Snapping Turtle Clan grounds. It stood at the easternmost summit of the first ridge, not a dart's cast from the Men's House.

Inside, Mud Stalker had just fallen into a deep sleep, his body lying on a cane-pole bed against the back wall. The Speaker's gray hair was tousled on a raccoon-skin pillow, his body covered with a tailored fox-hide blanket.

Many Colored Crow settled silently on the thatched roof and surveyed the surroundings. He could see the souls glowing in the night. These poor humans who were falling into the lines of Power being drawn by Masked Owl and himself.

For now, however, he had more urgent matters to attend to. The future had to be prepared just so. Perhaps his brother didn't understand what was coming, how so much was going to be decided here.

You never spent enough time looking into the future, Brother. It is a fault which will cost you this time.

Satisfied, Many Colored Crow spread his wings and began to insert himself into Mud Stalker's Dreams.

Anhinga disliked mist. As dawn broke it lay on the swampy land, cottony and thick, tendrils drifting through the trees and rising off the stale water. It obscured the grayish light that filtered through the trees, blurring her surroundings as she led her small party of young warriors up from their beached canoe. The air oppressed, cool, and damp. Moisture beaded on her hair like pearls and left the weapons—the atlatl and darts she clutched in her right hand—clammy in her grip.

She knew this place, had come here once in the company of her uncle. The Sun People called this Ground Cherry Camp: a clearing where the plants grew in the sandy soil of an abandoned levee a half day's run south of Sun Town. Despite the mist that clung like torn ghosts to every branch and bole, she knew this was the way.

At the landing, several overturned canoes had been propped on sections of rotting log, awaiting their owners' return. A well-beaten path led up through tangled vines that wove an impenetrable web through the mixed sweetgum and oak. Even in the dim light she could see footprints, still clear from the night before, unfaded by the heavy dew that settled on the green world; it beaded on silvered leaves and dripped stolidly onto the damp ground.

Bobbing mayapple leaves danced as she passed, her bare feet water-streaked as she stepped through the ground cover. Buds were just forming, anticipatory to blooming. Overhead a small beast scampered through the parallel rows of lanceolate leaves on a white ash—then identified itself by a fox squirrel's high-pitched chattering.

Snakes take it, had the squirrel given them away? Anhinga raised a hand, and Spider Fire stopped close behind her. The others, too, froze in place. In silence they waited, ears cocked to the gray dawn, but only the calls of the birds, the soft moaning of insects, and the irregular patter of water dripping from the trees could be heard.

"No voices," Slit Nose whispered from the rear. "Maybe there's no one there?"

"Or they are still asleep," Spider Fire added. "It's early."

"Hush." Anhinga glanced nervously at the encompassing fog that pressed down around them. Was it her imagination, or had it thickened, drawn closer?

A shiver played down her spine. She had never liked thick mist like this. Something about the way it rose from the water, as though alive, played eerily with her imagination. That it flowed around everything in its path bespoke a great Power that she had yet to comprehend. In times like this, when death prowled the land, mist could carry ghosts right around a person. She could imagine wraith hands tracing their way along a living person's body, caressing it, slipping thin fingers into a person's nose, mouth, and ears. How could you tell? How would you know that you had been witched? Any evil could be lurking just there, beyond your vision, waiting for you to step into its lair.

"Let's go," Right Talon muttered as he clutched his darts and atlatl. "If anyone is there, they'll be wide-awake by the time we finally arrive."

Mist Finger gently tapped his wooden dart shafts in agreement, but said nothing. Anhinga shot him a sidelong glance, measuring him. After his cavalier words the night they had left, he had been solid, never boastful like the others, and calmly capable when it came to making camp and seeing to the things that needed to be done. During the two days they had been traveling she had found herself admiring him more than once. Smooth muscle rolled under his greased skin. He stood straight, proud. Something in his demeanor made it clear that as he aged, he would become a leader. If only he hadn't been so blunt that night in the canoe.

He just spoke what the others already knew, she reminded herself. Yes, they had come to impress her. Mist Finger's assertion that first night in the canoe simply lifted the veil, placed all of the young men's actions in complete clarity.

So, are you going to marry any one of them? She had begun to look at them through different eyes. They were no longer childhood friends, no longer the easy companions of hunting and fishing expeditions or harmless teasing. The seriousness with which they dedicated themselves to her, to this raid, bespoke of adulthood as she had never before understood it.

As she considered that, she realized her attention had fixed on Mist Finger. He alone didn't fidget, didn't stare anxiously out at the mist-shrouded trees, but met her uneasy gaze with his clear brown eyes. That look reassured, speaking to her without words. He smiled the way he might if he were reading her souls.

"Are we going?" Slit Nose asked, "or would you rather wait for the mayapples and greenbrier to bloom?"

Anhinga strode forward, breaking eye contact with Mist Finger. A curious tingle had formed at the root of her spine, warming her pelvis. She flipped her hair, worn long and braided in anticipation of the day's coming trials. Her other hand tightened on the darts and atlatl in her hand. After all, this wasn't about handsome young men who made her heart leap. It was about war—about revenge and blood. Within moments, provided that Panther Above favored her, they would be killing enemies.

Taking a long stride, she tried to ignore the mist that sifted through the vines and branches. A sweetgum seedpod rolled under her heel as she marched up the trail. How far was it? She tried to remember.

The trail leveled off, winding through the trees. The branches overhead disappeared into a gray haze, hanging moss dangling like daggers. The trees themselves might have been ghosts vanishing into the haze. Ghosts?

Why did everything, no matter her momentary revelation about Mist Finger, return to ghosts? Was it because Bowfin's lost souls prowled these selfsame forests? Did her brother's empty eyes even now peer over her shoulder? Was he confused by her oddly timed attraction for Mist Finger when she should be contemplating the death of his killers?

A stab of guilt made her reorder her thoughts. Was this the right decision? Was it the time to strike? Is that what left her filled with unease? When she glanced up, it was to stare straight into the piercing eyes of a huge barred owl. The bird was perched on a branch, half-obscured by the patchy mist. She could see its scaly feet, the black talons gleaming where they encircled the wood. Those night-speckled feathers were grayed by the dew, slick-looking and shimmering; the bird might have been born of the mist itself. The eyes boring into hers did not seem to be of this world.

Attention riveted, she stumbled over a morning glory vine, and her arms windmilled. But for Cooter's quick reaction, she would have fallen.

"Thanks," she whispered.

"You all right?" he asked, voice hushed.

"Fine." She pointed up at the branch. "That owl . . ." The

branch, half-vanished in a gray wreath of mist, vaguely reappeared, empty, the leaves hanging limp. Surely, had the owl flown, they should have been stirred.

Her party had stopped, staring up curiously. She shook her head. "Nothing," she whispered. "Hurry. Let's get this over with."

Her mind on owls, ghosts, and death, she didn't realize how far they had come. The land opened before she knew it. Thick fog masked the clearing, as she led her young men into it. She crouched. Ground Cherry Camp, that was right here, wasn't it? In the clearing?

As she looked around she could see the characteristic plants rising from the patchy spring grass. The telltale triangular leaves were curled under the weight of the dew, cast in gray by the tiny droplets. The trail they followed continued, winding into the thickening fog.

Turn around and run! The words echoed hollowly between her souls. She could feel it, the wrongness, the sense of impending doom. Had everything gone deathly quiet? Her step faltered. It had been lunacy, bringing these young men here to try and do this thing. Someone would be killed as a result.

But you promised Bowfin. You can't back out now. You are Jaguar Hide's niece. His blood runs in your veins Your heart beats in time with his.

"Anhinga?" Right Talon asked under his breath. She could hear his worry.

"It's all right . . . we're close," she almost mouthed the words. "Just being careful, that's all."

In swirling mist, she saw a house—just the gray shape like a blinked image that vanished as quickly into the murk. In that instant she realized it was all right, that they had arrived in secrecy, that the Sun People were caught unawares.

She motioned them close. "That is the camp. We charge in, kill all we can, and escape. Keep your wits about you. It's easy to get lost in this fog. If we get separated, meet back at the canoe. If anyone gets cut off, he gets left behind."

They all nodded, eyes wolfish and gleaming as they smiled their anticipation. She could see the fear, the anxiety bundled in their tense bodies. This day's events would be sung about and retold for generations at the fires of her people. Reputations that would carry them for the rest of their lives would be forged here, today. She would be proven worthy of her uncle's pride and respect. Perhaps this was even the first step on the long road to eventual clan leadership.

"Let's go!" She gave Mist Finger a quick intimate smile, seeing his eyes warm as he caught her meaning. She promised herself that if they survived this, made it home, she would be spending time with him. Perhaps that was the Spirit World's attempt at justice. Bowfin's death would be compensated by providing her this perfect young man to love.

As she moved forward in a crouch, her nimble fingers fitted a dart into the nock of her atlatl. She had crafted the spear thrower herself. Made of osage orange imported from the northwest, the hard wood had been carefully shaped to fit her small hand. The length of her forearm, the wood was engraved with the design of a panther that could have been creeping its way around the shaft. A red jasper banner stone hung from the center to provide a counterbalance. The hook in the far end that cradled the cane dart butt had been laboriously carved into the wood itself. The handle she gripped was wrapped with panther sinew. Two loops had been fashioned to insert her fingers into to keep them from slipping.

Her darts were made of straight sections of cane a little longer than she was tall, each tipped with a sharp stone point flaked from red-orange chert pebbles recovered from the deposits in the hillsides of her homeland. She herself had grooved the cane shafts midway along their lengths. Into them she had tied split blue heron feathers for fletching to stabilize the long darts in flight. In her hand she carried five of the deadly darts. Three she would drive into some enemy's body. Two she would keep in reserve in case they should have to fight their way out, or should she need them on the way home to kill an alligator or deer for the supper pot.

Her heart had begun to batter her breastbone with an unfamiliar energy. Her whole body felt charged with a bursting intensity. This was the war rush she had heard her elders mention, but never, until this moment, had she experienced it. Nothing she had ever done prepared her for the tingling, the excitement, the heady rush of euphoria, fear, and anticipation.

Panther Above, I am alive! On bunched legs she charged into the camp, desperate for the sight of the enemy. The mist-shrouded huts were all around her now. It would be but a moment before she found a target. Borne as if by a storm surge, she threw her head back and a scream of ecstasy tore from her throat.

A shape emerged from one of the low doorways, but to her dismay, it ducked away into the mist before she could make her cast. "We are the Swamp Panthers! We are here to kill you! Bowfin! My brother! Come and watch us take our revenge!"

She danced on feathery feet, muscles charged, but only the swirling mist and the gray-thatched huts met her anxious gaze. Behind her, Spider Fire, Cooter, and Slit Nose, slowed, circling, darts nocked and back for the cast. They bent low, peering into the fog, searching for someone, anyone to attack.

"I saw one!" Anhinga declared. "He ducked out and ran before I could kill him."

"This accursed mist"—Right Talon gestured with his free hand—"is the work of . . ."

She heard the impact: a hissing slap, as it smacked into Right Talon's left side. She blinked, seeing the blood-shiny stone point where a hand's length of dart protruded from Right Talon's right side. On his left, the shaft still vibrated, driven in up to the fletching. The expression on Right Talon's face reflected a wide-eyed disbelieving confusion. The young man's mouth was open, working, but no sound broke his lips despite a mighty contortion of his chest. He sagged to his knees, darts and atlatl clattering to the ground.

Instinctively, Anhinga was in the act of reaching out to him as a second dart hissed and thumped into Slit Nose's body. He had been agape, frozen in disbelief as he watched Right Talon collapse. The scream that ripped from Slit Nose's lungs would haunt Anhinga's nightmares for the rest of her life.

"We are ambushed!" Mist Finger came to his senses first. "Run! Back to the canoe."

His voice broke Anhinga's panicked trance. She turned, pelting back the way they had come. She flinched as something hissed through the air beside her head. Her eyes caught the briefest flicker of something flashing past before it buried itself in the mist.

Cooter, running at her side, grunted, stumbled, and pitched headlong into the charcoal-stained dirt. She saw him hit, saw his body bounce at the impact and slide. He pawed weakly at the damp soil, a long dart implanted in the middle of his back between his shoulder blades.

Screams of rage and ululations of joy broke out on all sides. Shapes emerged from the mist, charging toward her, darts in their hands. *Warriors!* So many of them! Gripped by terror, she opened her hand, letting her darts and atlatl drop into the grass as she sprinted on Mist Finger's heels headlong back down the dark slash of trail up which she had led them brief moments before. She barely heard the sobbing sound her throat made as fear tightened it.

Spider Fire's voice shrieked from behind her, the sound that of wrenching pain. So violent was it that birds broke from the trees, flapping into the gray haze.

Panther, let me live. Help me. Keep me alive. Breath was tearing at her throat as she pumped her arms, flying through the mist-choked forest. The ground dropped away, and she dashed from foot to foot on the wild descent to the canoe landing, feet sliding on the wet dirt as she scrambled for balance and speed.

Mist Finger, too, had thrown away his darts for speed. She was several body lengths behind him as he slewed to a stop, almost toppling as his bare feet slid in the muck. He had started to bend, reaching for the canoe, when a man rose from behind it.

She watched in horror as Mist Finger raised his arm, barely having time to block the blow as a stone-headed ax snapped both bones in his forearm. Mist Finger screeched in agony as the enemy warrior whipped his ax back and forth, each smacking blow breaking through Mist Finger's pitiful attempts at defense. As she watched, Mist Finger was being beaten into a hunched mass of blood and broken bones.

A wild scream, instinctive, broke from her lips as she threw herself at her enemy. Her fingers were out, ready to scratch him apart.

Instead of the hard impact she expected, the man turned. He looked young, no older than she, a smile on his lips. She could see Mist Finger's spattered blood stippling the young warrior's face, hair, and chest. A dancing fire lit the man's dark eyes as he gracefully pivoted on one foot. Carried forward by her momentum, Anhinga couldn't react as he artfully dodged out of her way. As she flew past, his arm swung, the movement blurred. Yellow flashed—lightning in her brain—as her head rocked with a hollow bang that deafened her.

Her loose body hammered the muddy ground. A shrill ringing in her ears and pain, such terrible pain, filled her. Her brain had been dislocated from her body, as though floating behind her swimming vision. Her eyes blinked of their own volition. She was staring into Mist Finger's face—seeing but not comprehending the blood that ran from his gasping mouth or the blank emptiness behind his eyes. That image cast itself on her souls as she fell away . . . and away . . . Drifting into a soft gray blankness.

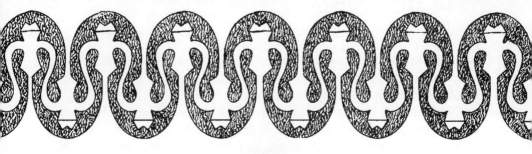

Eleven

The way the Swamp Panthers' slim canoe lanced into the bank filled White Bird with admiration. The wake came from behind, rippling the smooth brown water as it rushed up onto the grimy black shore. People were shouting and waving as they spilled down the long slope from Sun Town to the canoe landing.

White Bird laid his paddle to one side. Ahead of his feet the dead warrior lay limp and beginning to bloat. He had been laid in the canoe bottom, facedown, limbs akimbo. Ahead of the corpse, just behind Yellow Spider, lay the girl, her arms and legs trussed as though she were a captured alligator.

White Bird had studied her all the way back from Ground Cherry Camp. She hadn't regained consciousness; her breathing was labored. The way her head was turned he had been able to see her eyes jerking under the lids, as though she were locked in frantic dreams. Despite the way her face was mashed against the curving side of the canoe, he could see that she was a pretty thing. Thick black hair had been pulled into a braid that now lay curled like a blood-encrusted snake behind her head. The smooth lines of her muscular brown back slimmed into a narrow waist before the full swell of her hips. Her kirtle had been displaced, revealing a rounded curve of buttock above a long and firm thigh. Sleek calves ended in delicate if mud-stained feet. In all, his masculine self had been delightfully distracted by that enticing young body.

And, best of all, she is mine! He had captured her fairly. Not only that, but he had killed an opponent in hand-to-hand combat. Of all of his party, White Bird was the one who had fought toe-to-toe. He glanced happily at the dead warrior lying naked and supine behind the girl's feet. The young warrior's broken arms rested at unnatural angles. A dribble of urine leaked from the limp penis. Bright midday sunlight gleamed on the blackened wounds on his head. The eyes had dried, graying and vacant. A swarm of flies already droned in a wavering column when they weren't crawling across the dead flesh. From where he sat, White Bird could see pale knots of eggs the flies had laid in the dead man's eyes.

White Bird's companions might have killed the others—those who had driven darts into the raiders had been singing ecstatically on the trip and waved their bloody darts when they weren't paddling. He, however, had faced the enemy alone. Power lay in that. His exploits would be talked of among the clans. Pride, like a flood, rose within him as he stepped out of the canoe and helped Yellow Spider pull it onto the shore.

The crowd engulfed him like a wave; people were looking into the canoe, the more adventurous reaching in and prodding the bodies with a foot or hand. The flies rose in an angry buzz.

"Tell us! Tell us!" the cries came. Someone near the rear said, "The boy's vision was true!"

White Bird lifted his hands, stilling the throng. "My people, yes, my brother's vision was true. It was as he said. We found them where he said they would be, at Ground Cherry Camp. This dawn, in a thick mist, we ambushed them. This girl, I have taken on my own."

The other canoes slid onto the beach, warriors laughing as they shipped their paddles and leaped ashore. The victors lifted their bloody darts and shook them as they hooted and pranced in their joy. The trophy corpses were lifted—bloody and leaking fluids—before being borne up the long incline to be displayed on the western side of the Men's House atop the Father Mound.

"White Bird killed one bare-handed and took the girl! He took two!" the story circulated from lip to lip, eyes drifting his way.

Aware of their sudden awe, White Bird acted with the humility expected of a warrior, saying, "I was lucky. That's all. Someone had to cover their escape route. It was the others who laid the trap and broke their attack."

"But it was White Bird's planning," Yellow Spider insisted. He and Eats Wood, a man from Snapping Turtle Clan, reached down to lift the girl from the canoe bottom. "Because of his cunning not one of us was even injured!"

"Carry her correctly," White Bird reminded, fully aware that Eats Wood—who already had an unsavory reputation when it came to young girls—held the captive in such a way that his hand was cupped suggestively around one of her breasts. "You be careful, Eats Wood! Hear? The Snakes alone know, I hit her hard enough to drive the souls loose from her body. I don't want her dead."

"We know how you want her!" old Red Finger barked wryly. "And for that, she doesn't need any souls!"

A round of laughter came in response. White Bird waved it down. "Yes, yes, but let's just get these corpses up to the Men's House, shall we? On the way, please, thank these warriors who have demonstrated their courage and skill. They have placed their lives at risk for your safety. While these were young and inexperienced raiders, they might just as well have been more cunning and dangerous. So treat my companions with the respect they deserve. We are all obligated." In appreciation of the moment, he faced his fellow warriors and touched his forehead in respect. To his surprise, so did the rest of the gathered people.

Water Petal dropped into step beside him as he started up the slope. She wore her kirtle loose around her pregnant belly and a fabric shawl over one shoulder. Behind him, Yellow Spider and Eats Wood bore the unconscious girl. The dead warrior was dragged unceremoniously by his feet; the broken arms and battered head left marks on the damp soil.

"How is Mother?" White Bird kept his voice low, casting a glance to read Water Petal's expression.

Her round face betrayed her concern. "She is grieving, Cousin. All through the last winter she knew that your uncle was failing. The two of them were a team. They built Owl Clan's prestige, indebted the other clans to ours. He might have been dying, but as long as he was alive, she could act as if it were the two of them working in unison. She could go at night, and even though fever was eating him, she could talk her ideas over with him, share her fears as she had since she was a young girl and he a starry-eyed youth." She shook her head. "But now . . . I don't know. It's as if part of her souls died with him."

"When will the funeral be?"

"Since you have returned we will burn his house as soon as you have finished your obligations at the Men's House. Bobcat, the Serpent's apprentice, has cleaned Cloud Heron's bones. Your safe arrival, and in such triumph, will do more than anything to relieve your mother."

He nodded at that. "What about Mud Puppy? Has he . . . I mean, he came out of that odd trance, didn't he?"

Water Petal's frustration showed in her expression. "He has spent most of his time gone, much to your mother's despair. He has been shadowing the Serpent like a hawk, but when the Elder asked, the Serpent said the boy's constant company was agreeable."

He lowered his voice, fully aware of Eats Wood behind him. "Did you hear the talk at the landing?"

In an equally guarded voice, Water Petal said, "I did. But, White Bird, it was as he said, wasn't it? There were five—and the girl?"

He nodded, bothered as he had been since the beginning of this madness. "It was just an accident that I didn't kill her." He glanced back. "But let me tell you, she was a scrappy one. Fit to take me down with her bare hands."

"So, now that you have a wildcat, what will you do with her?"

"Keep her as a slave." He took a deep breath. "A Speaker should have someone to serve him, to cook and keep his house until a suitable marriage can be arranged." He shrugged. "Besides, Spring Cypress can make use of her."

"If she's as scrappy as you say, she'll run."

White Bird nodded. "Before I let her loose I'll cut the tendons behind her ankles. It will slow her down to an awkward walk; but she doesn't need to run in order to cook, or clean, or . . ."

"Or accept your hard manhood?" With that Water Petal laughed. "Under all that blood and mud she looked comely, what I could see of her."

He remembered the rage in her eyes, the terrible desperation as she flew at him, arms outstretched. "Let's say she will be a challenge for me." The knowledge that she hated him would delight him every time he shared her bed.

"Swamp Panther, isn't she?" Water Petal asked.

"Yes." A pause. "How did Mud Puppy know they were coming?"

"Your mother and I have been talking. I think we have an explanation. Some of Clay Fat's cousins killed a boy while they were down digging Panther sandstone. It was probably just a lucky guess on Mud Puppy's part. Of course they would want revenge. Snakes! I should have figured that out on my own."

"By why just these youngsters?" White Bird wondered, idly aware that they were but a few winters younger than he himself. "Jaguar Hide isn't this clumsy."

"No. Keep that in mind, Cousin." Water Petal shot him a warning look. "Tell me, are you keeping her alive just because you want her as a slave? Or do you take Mud Puppy's warning seriously?"

"It was just as he said, Cousin. It might have been a lucky guess, but it was just as he said. There were five young warriors and the girl." It had been luck—not Mud Puppy's prophecy—that he'd managed to smack her unconscious. Since then his interest in her had been enflamed by the charms suggested by her very alluring body.

He concluded, saying, "As to the future of Mud Puppy's vision, we'll see."

"I suppose," Water Petal said into his silence. "Well, when you wear her out, or find yourself married to a willing wife with an appetite of her own, your interest will slacken—as male members always do after they've inserted their seed." She patted her pregnant stomach. "Then you can dispose of her as you will."

He laughed. "How did you come to be such an expert? You're but three winters older than I."

"I've been married for nearly two of those winters," she replied tartly. "My husband, like you, is a young man. Believe me, I have learned about appetites and desire." She lowered her voice, "But your mother may not remember when she was young, filled with a craving for a man's flesh inside her canoe. So we'll share this secret—just the two of us."

He nodded as they crested the rise. The Men's House loomed to the left. The large thatched building dominated the western side of the irregularly flattened mound. Above the centerline atop the roof, carved wooden effigies of Snapping Turtle, Eagle, and Rattlesnake stood against the afternoon sky. The totems of war glared out at the world with painted eyes, beaks, fangs, and talons raised to remind the world that Sun Town's warriors and hunters were to be feared.

Lifting a hand, he placed it on Water Petal's shoulder. "Thank you."

She gave him a knowing glance, a faint smile hiding behind her full lips. "Remember, Cousin, I am here for you. Now, as well as in the future."

He recognized the wariness in his breast for what it was: the realization that the world would never remain as it was today. He met her gaze and nodded, not in commitment, but in acknowledgment. Would she be the one he wanted for Clan Elder after Wing Heart was gone? Could they forge that kind of relationship? The same sort his mother had had with his uncle?

"Where do you want her?" Yellow Spider interrupted his thoughts as they approached the Men's House.

"Lay the dead ones out in a line there." White Bird pointed to the shoulder of the mound. "As to the girl, tie her to the sunset post. Just the way you would a captured alligator."

Yellow Spider nodded as he and Eats Wood carried the girl over. Though she still hung limply in their arms, White Bird was certain that he saw her eyes flicker. Snakes, could she be awake? If so, she must have the self-control of a piece of stone. A blow to the head like that should have been agonizing, and the pain of her hanging head would have felt as if her skull were exploding.

"Tie her carefully!" White Bird added. "I think she is a tricky one. I can't take the time right now to cut her tendons—and I don't want her in a position to wiggle herself free when no one is watching."

"I'll cut her tendons for you," Eats Wood chimed in. He had his hand on her bared breast again, and White Bird could see the girl's brown nipple pinched between his callused fingers.

"No!" White Bird barked, angered by the man's familiarity with the captive. "I want to do it. She's mine, property of Owl Clan. Thank you for your service in bearing her here. I am obliged."

Eats Wood gave him a sour nod, released his hold on her, and allowed her torso to drop soddenly to the ground. The girl's head bounced on the packed silt. White Bird was sure he caught the painful wince before she could hide it. No matter, with Yellow Spider doing the binding, she wasn't going anywhere. For his part, he had the ceremonies and war cleansing to attend to in the Men's House. Even as he turned toward the large thatched building, he could smell the pungent odor of black drink wafting from within.

Mother Sun painted the evening sky with a marvelous display of red-orange, a fire spun through the clouds. The western horizon—glowing like a liquid blaze—outlined the high peak of the Bird's Head in a purple silhouette. So, too, did the marvelous sunset cast the curving ranks of house-topped ridges in perfect profile. The effect could be likened to a series of peg teeth on a giant jaw fixed to snap shut and crunch Wing Heart's very bones.

She sat under the worn ramada on the southern side of Cloud Heron's ominously dark house and watched Thunder Tail, the Speaker of the Eagle Clan, striding away, his long frame like a dancing shadow in the elongated dusk.

"*Perhaps it is time to renew our obligations to Owl Clan,*" he had said. "*We have a long and mutually beneficial history, your clan and mine. With the death of an old Speaker, perhaps it is time for Eagle Clan to marry one of its young women to a new Speaker."*

"*I suppose that you have someone special in mind?*" she had asked. His somber expression had belied nothing as he fingered the bear claws hanging from his necklace. Always a canny player was Thunder Tail.

"*I would have you consider young Green Beetle. She is just a woman, strong, with a smile that would melt your young man's heart.*"

To that she had offered some platitude concerning Green Beetle's charms but remained noncommittal.

Thunder Tail had watched her carefully, searching for some re-action as he added, "*As Speaker for Eagle Clan, I can tell you that we are happy to extend this offer. Elder Stone Talon was most impressed by your young man and his quick wit He is well-spoken and astute. Our Elder enjoyed the gifts of carved stone that he presented to us from upriver. He has prevailed at countering the Swamp Panthers' raid. Our Elder has asked if you would be amenable to considering both Green Beetle and our support for your young man's rapid confirmation to the Council.*"

"*How could you ensure this?*" she had asked in an offhand manner. "*Snapping Turtle Clan might object.*"

He had smiled warily. "*I think I can assure you that Frog Clan would side with us. I assume that you still have Clay Fat's ear, and the Elder, Graywood Snake, would back you. That leaves Snapping Turtle Clan alone to complain. Together we have a five-to-one vote in the Council.*"

There it was. Everything she could have wanted. Her influence and authority were ensured through the foreseeable future. Cloud Heron, may the spirits embrace his souls, would have approved.

Just the thought of him brought a spear of grief to her heart. She couldn't help but glance back at her brother's silent and brooding house. Had it really been six moons ago when she had used her influence to move her brother into the dwelling next door to her own? His wife, Laced Fern, had indicated that she could no longer keep a husband who didn't provide for her children. Not that any great love had been lost between the two of them. Cloud Heron had done his duty, siring four children for her clan. The alignment had been politically dictated at the time. Laced Fern had been Cloud Heron's second wife, a woman ten and four turning of seasons his junior.

Cloud Heron's illness had robbed him of his manhood. Laced Fern, given her age, couldn't be blamed for wanting a younger man, one who could still plant his seed in her womb and contribute his support to Eagle Clan through his hunting and fishing skills. That was, after all, what men were for.

And now Eagle Clan, once ready to strip her of her position and cast her away like a broken clay pot, wished to renew their alliance.

Wing Heart rubbed her shins, her callused hands sliding on the nightshade-scented bear grease she had spread over herself to thwart the humming cloud of mosquitoes. She glanced off across the large plaza to where people still crowded around the Men's House. The Swamp Panthers' corpses had provided great entertainment during the day. Bit by bit they had been cut apart, burned, kicked, urinated upon, and otherwise abused. The camp dogs had gorged themselves on the bits of human flesh that had been scattered far and wide. While their horrified ghosts couldn't cross the mounds, or lines of ash, they could still see what befell their abandoned bodies from the trees just west of the Bird's Head. It was hoped that they would be so appalled that they would return home to haunt the dreams of the living Swamp Panthers. During nightmares they would tell their kinsmen never to repeat such a foolish thing as attempting to raid the Sun People.

But did it ever happen that way? Wing Heart sighed, raising her eyes to stare at the fading light in the clouds. They had darkened now, purpling into a bruised color. As if it were the sunset of her own life, she had grown cynical. She knew the Swamp Panthers, had even traded with their leader, Jaguar Hide. In all of her years she had never heard of an enemy war party being turned back because of pleading ghosts.

Warfare was a thing that people did. That was all. Over the years she had come to the conclusion that abusing the dead was done for the surviving victors' self-satisfaction. It gave them a way to savor the triumph, prolonging the time until they had to return to the ordinary and await the news someday in the inevitable future that some kinsperson of their own was being cut apart and defecated upon in the enemy's village.

"Lost in thought?" a low voice asked from the shadows behind her.

She turned and recognized Mud Stalker as he stepped out from behind her house. "I would have thought you would have been in the middle of the festivities." She indicated the Men's House. "One of your young warriors killed an enemy this morning."

Mud Stalker walked over and lowered himself beside her, his mangled arm cradled in his left hand. "I think such doings are more for the young."

Did he mean that, or was it a way of building a rapport with her? "Were we ever that young?"

He gave her a curious appraisal, the lines of his face deepened by

the shadows. "Once. I think." He chuckled. "I have been told that
your brother is taken care of." He glanced over his shoulder at the
silent house. "I assume the final rites are to be soon?"

She nodded. "As soon as my son is finished with his responsibilities to the People."

Mud Stalker lifted his good hand to chew on his thumbnail. Who
was this new, companionable Mud Stalker? What was he after?

"He will be a great Speaker." Mud Stalker's attention was fixed
across the distance.

"Thank you. I am proud of him myself."

"I salute you, Wing Heart. It is a great coup, a victory well worth
savoring, much more rewarding than what our clanspeople are doing over there."

"I thank you again, Speaker."

He turned hard black eyes on her. His expression, never anything
to contemplate with any pleasure, now appeared strained and
slightly bitter. "Let us be blunt. We are old adversaries, you and I.
Just this once can we speak as two people without the dodging and
darting?"

The old wariness warmed her insides. "Can we?"

He laughed again, sounding genuinely amused. "I'm not sure,
but let us try. I have a question."

"I may or may not have an answer."

"This son of yours, Mud Puppy? Did he really have a vision?"

That caught her by surprise. "The boy has always been peculiar.
Half of the time I'd be forever grateful just to marry him off—even
if it was to someplace like Yellow Mud Camp. He's young, Speaker,
and I don't know if he's going to end up as a great Serpent ten
winters from now, or as a half-wit."

"And the vision?"

"I can only say that he was right about Ground Cherry Camp,
and the Serpent believed him."

"But you don't? Interesting."

"I didn't say that."

"You didn't have to." He continued to stare at the crowd gathered around the Men's House. "What a curious fate Power has
made for you. One son is almost a god—smart, clever, and daring.
Look at him over there. People are already calling him Owl Clan's
new Speaker. Even his rivals admire him. Those who should resent
him are delighted to share their time with him. Two days ago, even
though he should have been locked away in the Men's House in
preparation for the attack, he still managed time to bring me a piece
of copper." He reached into his belt pouch and held up a flat disk

of the metal. "Told me he remembered that I had that necklace of copper beads and that this would make the perfect pendant for it." He turned it in the fading light so that she could see the turtle image engraved in the burnished metal. "It is indeed perfect."

"My son takes his duties to the People very seriously. It is the pleasure of my lineage and clan to make you happy."

Mud Stalker took a deep breath, replacing the heavy copper pendant into his belt pouch. "Thunder Tail was here earlier. I saw him walk away after a long talk with you."

"He was." *Spying on me, are you, old enemy?* "He brought Elder Stone Talon's regards. Apparently her joints are bothering her."

"I heard that Thunder Tail mentioned a potential marriage."

She fought to keep the shadow of a smile from the corners of her mouth. Now she knew where this was going. "He mentioned one of his nieces, a girl named Green Beetle. I've seen her. She was just made a woman two moons ago. She's comely, a bit busty for my tastes, but that just makes milk for babies. I've seen her coming in from the river a time or two. She's the one who likes diving for clams. Most of those pearls that Eagle Clan has been passing around were found by her."

Mud Stalker was silent for the moment, calculating the investment Thunder Tail was making in the offer. Green Beetle, more commonly called Pearl Girl, had been the topic of considerable speculation. Not only was she Stone Talon's first granddaughter, but pretty and charming to boot.

"But I think my son is interested in Spring Cypress," Wing Heart added with a slightly wistful tone. "I may have to look in that direction. We have obligations to Clay Fat and Rattlesnake Clan. If Clay Fat were to ask for White Bird, I'm not sure but that I wouldn't have to give him."

She let that dangle. Snakes, it would break the boy's heart if she promised him to someone besides Spring Cypress. But here, for the moment, she could set a trap.

Mud Stalker tripped it when he said, "Clay Fat and old Graywood Snake can be reasoned with."

"They can?"

"I might have a little influence. You have obligations to Rattlesnake Clan, but they have obligations of their own.

Assuming that White Bird and the girl wouldn't do something so silly as to elope—"

"Never! At least, White Bird wouldn't. As to the girl? Well, whatever lengths she might be tempted to try wouldn't matter. It takes two to elope."

"Indeed." He ran his fingers along the scar tissue that ridged his ruined arm. "Thumper gave you a good child when he was your husband."

"Is that a fact?" she countered crossly. "Did you know that the night of his brother's return, Mud Puppy was engrossed with a cricket?"

"Some would say that was Power speaking through the boy. Rumor has it that he had a great vision up on the Bird's Head in the middle of that storm and that Ground Cherry Camp was only part of it. Even the Serpent is overjoyed to have the boy following him around." Mud Stalker made a tsking sound. "I think the boy's eccentricities are something else."

Like half-wittedness? Is that what you are banking on, that my second son is an idiot?

Mud Stalker slapped his knee with his good hand. "What if I could persuade Clay Fat to look elsewhere for a husband for Spring Cypress?"

"Why should I want that?" *How much is he going to offer?*

Mud Stalker's eyes followed the first of the fireflies that rose over the grass in the plaza. The dancing yellow lights made magic in the gathering gloom as they hovered and whirled. "I might be willing to consider Pine Drop and Night Rain."

"Pine Drop and . . . *both of them.*"

"It's not the first time a man has had two sisters for wives." He sounded so casual about it. "A great deal of prestige could come to a young man who was thought of so highly as to have a clan offer two of its daughters."

She turned the notion over in her mind. Agreeing would cause a major realignment of influence among the clans. It would be a solid bonding with Snapping Turtle Clan, a reciprocal agreement that changed the entire political landscape. "Pine Drop is freshly widowed, isn't she? She was married to that Alligator Clan boy."

"Blue Feather. He died of some lingering illness two moons ago. Nothing she or the Serpent did seemed to shake the evil from the man. It is my belief that White Bird would make her smile again."

"And Night Rain is . . ."

"Her little sister. Sweet Root's youngest."

"Yes, I remember. She was just declared a woman. I saw her in the Women's House last moon. She's a doe-eyed thing in her virgin's dress."

"Both are hard workers. They would make a solid household for a man. It's not like taking two wives from different clans or lineages. They wouldn't be jealous or spiteful of each other. These are sisters.

They already like each other. They wouldn't distract White Bird into tearing his hair out."

With forced aplomb, she said, "I appreciate your kind offer, Mud Stalker. In spite of our past, it intrigues me."

"Let me ask: What if I added nectar to the suggestion?" He was stroking his throat now with the studied indifference of a man who held all the right gaming pieces. "What if I told you I would not only support White Bird for Speaker within the Council, but I would argue, no, insist, that Mud Puppy be confirmed in White Bird's place should anything ever happen to his brother."

It was said so casually, almost in an offhand manner. With difficulty she kept her voice even. "Why would you do that?"

Mud Stalker's head lowered, irritating her that she couldn't see his eyes. "Sometimes, Wing Heart, the best way to win is not to fight. Sometimes a smart person finally realizes that to win tomorrow, he must lose today. For years I have tried to break Owl Clan. This is no secret between us."

"No," she responded flatly. "It isn't."

"The night the warriors prepared to counter the Swamp Panther attack, I had a Dream. A very Powerful and persuasive Dream. Bird Man appeared and told me how the fight would end. He told me that I would know the truth of his words. Very well, I have seen the return of White Bird, seen his Power in Trade and war. He will be Speaker—and a very capable one. Perhaps the most capable of all the Speakers in memory."

"Bird Man told you to make this offer? In a Dream?"

"He did."

"I will still be the Owl Clan Elder."

"Indeed you will," Mud Stalker said grimly. "But you and I both know that it will not be forever."

She finally chuckled, reading his meaning beyond the words. "When I am dead and gone and another is Elder, my son will still be Speaker."

"And he will be Snapping Turtle Clan's friend." Mud Stalker smacked his gums. "To ensure that, I will make you yet another offer. Snapping Turtle Clan will offer to marry Pine Drop and Night Rain to your second son should anything happen to the first."

"They'd go to Mud Puppy?"

"Indeed. If anything should happen to White Bird, Mud Puppy shall inherit his wives." Mud Stalker gave her a challenging grin that the darkness couldn't hide. "Tell me, Clan Elder, can anyone else offer so much? Back Scratch, Red Finger, Sweet Root, Falling Drop, and I have discussed this. My lineage is committed to making this alliance. Your son shall be Speaker. And your second son after him. With their support you shall be the leader of the Council."

"Forgive me, but I still have trouble understanding why."

He chuckled dryly. "Because in six days the world has turned itself upside down. We can't help but believe that the spirits are on Owl Clan's side. Who are we to fight the spirits? For the future of my clan, I will even allow you to maintain leadership of the Council."

She felt like howling in triumph, but not yet. *He knows me too well.* She couldn't help but narrow her eyes against the darkness. "We shall consider, old enemy. First, I have a funeral to conduct. And then, after I dissect this offer you have made, I shall give you my decision."

He inclined his head before standing. "That is fine. In the meantime, as a gesture of our goodwill, we would like to provide a feast in honor of your dead brother. He served the People well."

"We would be obliged."

Mud Stalker waved it off. "It is simply a gift, a gesture of our goodwill."

As he walked away into the night, she couldn't help but wonder: *What kind of trap have you laid for me, old enemy?*

The Serpent

The Truth is in *the error.*
That's the problem.
It is the deep-throated rumble of buffalo calling to each other in the wintertime. The flash of the firefly on pitch-black nights. It is the far-off call of the blue heron on her way to the sunset.
Don't you see?
Meaning is not in words, but in between them.
Do you think the buffalo hears Truth when she is calling out to another buffalo? Or when someone answers her? No. She hears Truth in the space between.
When she is listening.
Just listening.

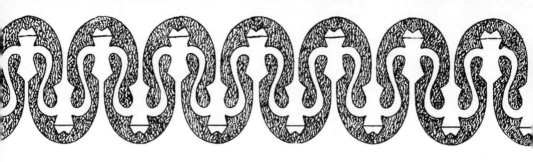

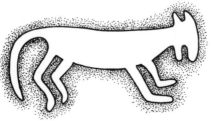

Twelve

Anhinga clenched her teeth, desperate to keep the vomit that burned the back of her throat from passing her clamped lips. Should they see that, it would shame her, as if she were not already more than shamed. Enough of the accursed Sun People had come by to kick her and urinate on her that she could no longer feign unconsciousness. She had surrendered that fiction the first time one of them touched a smoldering stick to her naked side.

She glared around her like a trapped raccoon, snarling and hissing her hatred as her tormentors heaped physical and symbolic abuse upon her. Her legs and arms had been wrapped in tightly bound cords. Even her ability to flop like a beached fish had been curtailed by the rope that tied her to an upright log set into the dark earth. Her skin stung where they had seared it with hot brands. The odors of urine and feces plugged her nose. Most of it had dried. She didn't need their waste spattered upon her to be shamed or broken. They could do nothing to her that she hadn't done to herself.

By craning her neck she could see the remains of her companions. Blood-and-offal-stained earth marked the spot where the bodies had been dismembered. She had watched with horror as little boys gleefully pulled the intestines out of a long slit cut into Mist Finger's abdomen. The horror had been so great that she couldn't help but weep as a young man used a bloody strip of flesh flayed from Cooter's leg to beat her. She'd flinched, more from the feel of Cooter's cold black blood than from the pain.

Her souls numb, she blinked and watched the last of the dancing men. Their bodies flickered in the firelight, greased and shining yellow and black as the flames licked up from a central fire pit. Night had fallen cool and moist; her skin prickled with gooseflesh.

A great shout broke the silence as the men leaped and raised their arms to the night. Then they stood frozen, watching the door where her assailant stepped out into the open. She could see the young man, naked, his muscular body bathed in firelight. The wash of fresh blood might have been painted on the skin of his chest. Her staggering thoughts couldn't quite place it—then she remembered where she had seen the like before: He had been freshly tattooed, the designs pricked into his skin with a copper needle.

Her gut heaved and bile rushed into her mouth. Tattooed: the realization stuck in her head. A victorious warrior celebrating some great accomplishment underwent tattooing to mark the occasion. In this case, her captor was being marked for his actions in capturing her alive and killing Mist Finger face-to-face.

If only I could die! She tensed against the binding cords, finding no looseness. Die, she would, but not yet. Soon though, when they had taken the time to sever the thick tendons that ran behind her heels and finally untied her, then she would take the first opportunity to scavenge a sharp piece of stone and open her veins.

The young men were hooting and dancing, slapping the blood-smeared young man on the back as he passed through their ranks.

"Thank you, my friends," he called out in a fine baritone. "Together we have done great things. We have shared black drink, undertaken the ceremonies to cleanse ourselves of the taint of war, and paid our enemies our highest compliments."

They laughed at that. In the darkness, Anhinga spat the bile from her mouth.

"The middle of the night has come." The young man pointed to the north, a bronzed god in the firelight. "The stars have nearly circled the heavens. Go home, my friends, and sleep. Tomorrow, I am told, my uncle's house will be burned and his Dream Soul set free to find the ghosts of friends long dead."

"And Snapping Turtle Clan will provide a huge feast," the burly warrior on one side called as he shook his fist. Anhinga remembered him—the slimy weasel that had groped her as he carried her up from the canoes. Her nipple, the least of her hurts, was still sore from when he had pinched it.

"Until tomorrow," the war leader cried.

"Tomorrow!" the rest shouted in unison. As they broke up and dispersed into the darkness, she could hear them chanting, "White

Bird, White Bird, White Bird" over and over again.

The blood-streaked White Bird watched them go, a smile on his face as he stood illuminated in yellow firelight. Only when the last of them had stepped out of sight did his expression fall and his shoulders slump. He made a face as he reached up, prodding carefully at the drying blood on his chest. Where the tattoo had been pricked into his skin must have felt like fire.

Walking like an old man, he stopped long enough to stare down at her and say, "Tomorrow . . . I'll cut you then." She almost sighed as he walked past and into the darkness.

Left alone, she finally allowed herself to weep. Tears of rage and grief came welling from the hollow between her souls. One by one she saw the faces of her friends: Cooter, Slit Nose, Right Talon, Spider Fire, and, finally, Mist Finger.

Mist Finger's eyes were sparkling as he looked into hers. If she but glanced over to where his body had been laid, she could still see the bloody arch of his ribs. His hollowed-out pelvis was a dark mound in the shadows. Two of the hungry brown dogs were growling, chewing on the edges of his hipbones as they tugged against each other. In another life, far away in the world of imagination, she would be holding him, sharing her body with him, planning a life with him as her husband.

Sobs choked in her raw throat. All she had left was death.

"Are you all right?" a voice asked softly from the darkness behind her.

She started, fear leaving her shaking as she blinked at the tears that clung to her damp lashes. She jumped at the feel of fingers on her calves, trembling as they moved down to her ankles.

"He didn't cut you," the soft voice continued. "Good. It would be harder if you had been maimed."

"Who . . . who are you?" She struggled to keep her teeth from chattering.

"He said you have to live. He said you have to go back."

"Who . . . who said?"

"He did."

She felt the vibrations as something sawed at the ropes binding her. "What are you doing?" Fear leaped up like a thing alive to sing along her nerves and muscles.

"I'm cutting you free."

Hope like a flame tingled within her.

"He said you had to live. To be free."

"Who? White Bird?"

"No. I can't tell you." It sounded like a boy's voice, and she flopped her head over, staring at the dark form that hunched above her. From the corner of her vision she could just make out his skinny body as he crouched over his work. The sawing was more vigorous, and she could feel cords parting.

"Can you walk?" he asked.

"Yes." But could she? She hadn't been able to feel her arms or legs for hours. And the headache, Snakes! That alone might double her over when she stood up.

"You stink," he said vehemently.

"When they weren't urinating or defecating on me they were pelting me with my friends' guts." How could she say that so matter-of-factly?

"You shouldn't have come here."

"It's your people who shouldn't come to my lands. As long as you come to take our stone and kill us, we will come to kill you!" The last cord around her middle parted, and her arms fell like severed meat to slap onto the ground. Her horror grew when she couldn't move them. *Tell me I'm not paralyzed!*

Had it been the blow to the head? She had heard tales of warriors hit hard on the skull who hadn't been able to move afterward. But then the painful prickling began as circulation ate its way into her upper arms.

She gasped as her legs came free and rolled loosely apart. They, too, might have been wood for all she could feel.

"There," the boy said. "You can go now."

"I can't," she hissed, fear trying to strangle her. "My legs . . . I need a while. Time for them to come alive again."

At this the dark form above her seemed to hesitate. She wiggled sideways enough to see him as he peered owlishly into the dark. The dying fire barely cast a red glow onto his round face. She could see his profile, a stub of nose, thin cheeks, and thatch of black hair. More than a boy, he was less than a man. As he stared around the movements were furtive, frightened.

"Why are you doing this? Are you one of my people? A lost relative taken as a slave? Do you want me to take you home, is that it?"

"No. I'm Owl Clan."

She shook her head, face contorting as blood pouring into her arms began to ache and pulsate. She tried to remain still, the slightest movement shooting fire along her limbs.

"No one can know I did this," the boy continued. "They wouldn't understand. I'm already in enough trouble."

She couldn't stifle a gasp as he reached down and began massaging her leg. "No! That hurts!"

"But it will be gone sooner." He sounded so sure of himself. "We don't have time. He told me to be fast."

"Who?" she gritted through clenched teeth, as his hands ran waves of agony through her legs. She might have been floating on a flood of biting ants.

"He said you had to live," was the simple answer.

Whining, she managed to pull her arms up and blasted her souls numb when she bent her knee. Movement was coming back. No, she wasn't paralyzed. Blessed Panther, she had to get up.

An eternity passed before she could prop herself on all fours, and, one arm around the boy's neck, stagger to her feet.

"Come on," he hissed, as they wobbled off into the darkness. "It's this way."

"What is?"

"The canoe landing. But maybe you could be so kind as to take one of the Snapping Turtle Clan's boats? They don't like us anyway."

"Sure, boy. Anything you want. I owe you."

Mud Puppy stood with his feet sunk in the black mud of the canoe landing and looked out into the darkness. The dugout canoe faded into the night, a dark streak on midnight waters. He could hear the faint gurgle of water as she stroked, droplets tinkling as she raised the paddle.

It didn't make any sense. Why let her go? What could Masked Owl have in mind? She hated them, he had felt it rising off of her like the stench of waste she had been coated with.

A shiver ran down his back as he turned and trudged wearily up the incline above the canoe landing. White Bird would never forgive him if he found out. And Red Finger would slit his throat if he ever learned that Mud Puppy had fingered his canoe for the Panther woman to steal.

What is going on?" Hazel Fire asked, as he and Yellow Spider joined the growing crowd. They stood on the far northeastern corner of the plaza. At their feet the marshy borrow pit separated them from the first ridge. Atop that, Wing Heart and White Bird watched as the Serpent chanted and reached into a small clay bowl of black drink. This he cast from his fingertips onto the walls of the second house in the line that stretched ever westward in the long arc of the Northern Moiety.

"That is the house where Speaker Cloud Heron lived." Yellow Spider's expression betrayed his inner feelings: sorrow, grief, and a curious sort of expectation.

"Ah, yes." Gray Fox came to stand beside them. "He was White Bird's uncle, yes? The one who died just after our arrival?"

"He was my cousin," Yellow Spider replied. "In many ways he was my teacher as well as White Bird's. Snakes, I could tell you some stories. Once, when I was much younger, he caught me handling his atlatl. It was his most sacred possession. He was subtle, our Speaker; instead of beating me to within a hairbreadth of my life he made me eat raw fish guts for a whole moon."

"You *did* that?" Hazel Fire asked incredulously.

"Everyone knew that I had done something terrible. The Speaker never told people what. And you can wager that I never did, either. But it was so humiliating and vile that I never broke one of his rules again."

"I'd have sneaked something cooked when no one was looking," Gray Fox muttered uneasily.

"I wouldn't," Yellow Spider declared. "Trust me, the Speaker would have known. He would have seen it reflected from my souls."

"He was part sorcerer then?" Hazel Fire asked, his eyes focused on the house. Perhaps he thought some smoky spirit was going to rise from the door and cast enchantments around and about.

"No." Yellow Spider rubbed his callused palms together. "He knew people, that's all. Knew their souls. When my punishment was over he treated me as if nothing had ever happened between us. He never even mentioned the event again, and he was most enthusiastic when White Bird suggested that I might go upriver with him."

"Was he much like White Bird?" Gray Fox was watching the increasing numbers of people who walked toward them across the plaza.

"They were much the same," Yellow Spider admitted. "Like White Bird, the Speaker was smart, friendly, and forever thinking two or three steps ahead. Seeing them together you could almost think them twins. That is why so many people are coming to honor his passing. Even the other clans respected the Speaker. He had a way about him."

"And what is the Serpent doing?" Hazel Fire pointed to where he was still casting droplets of black drink from his fingertips.

"That is to feed the soul of the house and the Speaker's Dream Soul. By doing so, it reminds them both that while the site must be cleansed by fire, the People bear them nothing but goodwill. Think of it like this: When people live inside a house they become part of that place. The light is bad, this being sunset, but you can look into the doorway. There, see on the pile of wood? Those are the Speaker's bones. His Dream Soul is hovering there, attached to them."

Hazel Fire swallowed hard, stepping back as if to distance himself from the dead spirit.

"No, don't fear," Yellow Spider said with a chuckle as he reached back and pulled the Wolf Trader forward. "The Speaker was a good and wise man. A person's soul doesn't change just because of death. At least, not unless something terrible was done to kill him. Only then does a soul turn vengeful, just as the living would."

"Why burn his bones?" Gray Fox's brow had lined with worry as he stared uneasily at the low doorway. "Why not bury them as my people do?"

"Fire cleanses," Yellow Spider reminded. "Any evils or bad thoughts that might have gathered at this place will be destroyed or driven off." He pointed to the gaps that separated the sections of concentric ridges. "When the fire starts, any evil that is trapped here can escape out through the gaps. If you walked to the outer ring, you would see that the line of ash has been parted to let any malevolent spirits out. They will flee toward the setting sun, drawn inexorably to the west."

"What happened to his flesh?" Hazel Fire shifted uncomfortably. "Those bones look pretty well cleaned off. He didn't die that long ago. Not long enough to have decomposed like that."

"The Serpent's apprentice, Bobcat, stripped the meat from his bones," Yellow Spider said. "That has to be done soon after death, before the flesh has a chance to draw evil to it. You know what happens to a body after death. Corruption is drawn to it just like ants to fruit nectar. Corruption and the forces that lead to festering are ravenous, forever driven by a fierce and consuming hunger. Since we can't drive them away, it's better simply to take the flesh and carry it outside of Sun Town. Each clan has a place where it leaves corruption and rot. Those locations we mark and no one, unless they, too, are filled with evil, would go there." Yellow Spider shrugged. "Who knows? Maybe as the years pass we'll concentrate so much evil outside the powerful rings of Sun Town that the world will be a better place. Even as far away as your own villages."

"And your Speaker's Dream Soul?" Hazel Fire asked.

"Because of the black drink and the Serpent's requests to his soul, it will stay here, within the safe confines of Sun Town."

"You mean you try to keep his ghost here?" Gray Fox was looking increasingly nervous.

Yellow Spider cocked a disbelieving eyebrow. "Why wouldn't we? Just because the Speaker is dead doesn't mean he isn't still part of the clan. Part of what our earthworks do is keep the spirits of our dead within. This way they can whisper to our Dream Souls at night when we're sleeping."

"I'll never let myself Dream again while I'm sleeping here." Gray Fox touched his breast as if for reassurance.

"I think they speak their own language," Hazel Fire muttered. "At least no ghost has talked to me in my dreams in any language but my own."

Yellow Spider turned his attention to Wing Heart as she stepped to the house, calling, "Brother, hear me. We are cleansing this place now. Thank you for all that you have done for our lineage, our clan, and our people. Stay with us, help us, fight for us from the Land of the Dead. Whisper your wise counsel when we are in need, and intercede on our behalf with the forces of light and darkness. Be well, my brother, for we shall meet your Dream Soul when our earthly bodies fail us."

She turned and walked to a low-smoking fire before reaching out to take a smoldering stick. White Bird stepped forward, his face a mask against the pain in his freshly tattooed chest. He placed his hand around his mother's where she grasped the smoldering stick. Together they touched it to a corner of the thatch. White Bird had to lean forward, blowing the glowing end until the thatch caught and the first flickers of fire began climbing the dry grass.

"I see things inside," Gray Fox said as the fire illuminated the interior of the house. "A man's atlatl, a bundle of darts, and isn't that a pile of folded clothing?"

Yellow Spider whispered, "Good-bye, Speaker. I will see you soon." Then, after a pause, he said in a louder voice, "Those are the Speaker's personal belongings. He cannot take them to the Land of the Dead in their present form. They, too, must be transformed into their spirit selves in order for him to use them in the afterlife."

As they watched, the Serpent cavorted and shook his turtle shell rattle. His reedy voice rose and fell as he Sang in words Yellow Spider couldn't understand. The flames spread through the roofing. Thick white smoke curled through the tightly bound shocks of grass before being whipped up into the sunset sky.

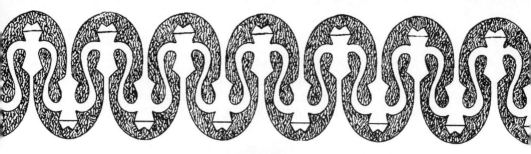

Thirteen

White Bird stepped back, an arm raised to protect himself from the violent heat radiating from his uncle's house. There, just within the doorway, he could see his uncle's bones laid in a careful bundle on the rick of hickory and maple wood. In the midst of the bonfire the skull charred and blackened, grease sizzling as the rounded bone split, steamed, and oozed. The long bones had been tied in a tight bundle that now spilled down into the crackling logs. One by one they popped as the marrow began to boil inside.

White Bird backed up another step to where his mother stood, arms at her sides, a grim expression on her drawn face. He flinched at the heat, amazed that she could stand it, and struggled with the desire to step back even farther to where the crowd had gathered on the other side of the borrow ditch.

"Farewell, Brother," she said in a voice mostly drowned by the fire's roar. Clay began to flake off the walls as the cane-and-pole substructure began to burn. A wreath of black rose in a pillar, bearing the smoke of a dead life to the Sky World. Mother Sun sank below the horizon beyond the Bird's Head, the sky uncharacteristically blue and cloudless.

White Bird might have been able to stand it, but the dull smarting on his chest where the Serpent had tattooed the red pattern of dots became unbearable. The design marked him as a blooded warrior and a leader worthy of respect. He unwillingly took his mother's hand and half dragged her back.

The look she shot him was nearly as frightening as the searing heat. Grief lay behind her eyes, grief so powerful it sucked at his souls. And then, as if he truly saw her for the first time, he cataloged her face: Threads of white streaked her hair where she'd pulled it back and pinned it into a severe bun. Deep wrinkles hatched her hollow cheeks, and her mouth had thinned. When had her angular nose gone to extra flesh? He had never noticed that the smooth skin of her forehead had hardened and lined. Her throat, once so fine, now wattled and bagged like an elderly man's scrotum.

She's so old! He stood stunned, trying to fathom what it all meant. The popping of his uncle's bones, his mother's old age, the pain of his new tattoos. As of that morning the world might have been dislocated, shifted somehow as it floated on the endless seas. From this day onward nothing would ever be the same. His life might have ended and begun anew.

Even the mysterious nighttime escape of his captive seemed somehow of lesser import—though he'd vowed to find the culprit who had sawed her ropes in two. Protestations aside, he was sure it had something to do with Snapping Turtle Clan, and perhaps Eats Wood and his preoccupation with sticking his penis into anything female.

"Are you all right?" he asked as he leaned close to his mother's ear.

For several heartbeats she stared blankly at the fire, then his words seemed to penetrate. She swallowed hard, the loose flesh at her throat working. "Yes. Part of me is in there with him. I am burning, White Bird. My souls are becoming ashes."

"He was a great Speaker for our clan," White Bird replied as he turned his attention back to the flame-engulfed structure. "I am honored to bear his legacy."

"Honored enough to take the responsibilities of the clan over your own desires?"

"Of course." He pointed at the blackened bones now half-hidden in an inky veil of smoke. "He taught me that. My first duty is to my clan."

"Even if it means giving up your own desires for the good of all? Surrendering the needs of your lineage for those of the whole?" Her voice sounded far away, oddly brittle.

"Yes." Must they have this conversation now?

"What would you give up to be Speaker?"

At the serious tone in her voice, he studied her from the corner of his eye, aware that they were surrounded by a huge throng of the people. Tens of tens of tens had come to watch the cleansing of

Speaker Cloud Heron's house, belongings, and remains. For the moment, he and his mother were the center of all attention.

"Whatever I have to," he said in a low voice.

"Spring Cypress?"

The question shocked him. "Why? I love her. She loves me. We want to be together. Why do you think I—"

"For the clan." Her low voice had all the flexibility of a stone bowl. "Or did you mislead me?"

"No, I . . ."

"The clan places its demands above those of its Speaker."

"Yes, but I don't understand what that has to do with my marrying Spring Cypress. Rattlesnake Clan has been our ally for so many years that—"

"Things change, boy. Clay Fat has his own plans for Spring Cypress . . . but that is not your concern. Tell me now, would you marry Spring Cypress, or be Speaker of the Owl Clan? I must know. Time is short, and if you are not interested in serving, I must quickly find another."

He tried to keep from gaping, aware that the Wolf Traders were standing across the borrow ditch with Yellow Spider, several arm's lengths to his left. They kept glancing back and forth between the fire and White Bird. He could see them talking in low tones, trying to understand what they were seeing.

"Mother, I went north—"

"You are talking to your Clan Elder. Whatever your mother wishes is not germane to this conversation. How do you answer your Clan Elder? Will you be Speaker?"

"I would, yes, but to—"

"Even if it means giving up your own desires for those of your clan? Yes, or no?"

"I've planned on marrying Spring Cypress since I was a boy! We've always understood that she and I—"

Her implacable gaze had fixed on the burning house as the thatched roof slumped, sagged, and collapsed. Smoke, sparks, and glowing ash whirled about within the still-standing walls to rise in a curling vortex. Inside the open doorway the inferno obscured the splintered and scalloped bones on the pyre.

"Yes," he muttered, feeling a hollow anger begin to strangle his grief. "As you have known all along."

"No matter the cost?"

"No matter the cost." His heart might have been stone when he added, "Even if it means I cannot have Spring Cypress." How odd? At that moment he could barely remember what Lark's face looked like. Had he left her so long ago? It seemed like a lifetime.

His mother nodded, reaching out to retake his hand and turning him to face the crowd. Raising his hand high over his head, she cried, "People of the Sun, Speaker Cloud Heron is dead. His remains have been cleansed. His Dream Soul will reside with us here forever. As required by our laws, his house and his belongings, the remains of his body, are being cleansed before your eyes. It is in this moment that I, as Elder of the Owl Clan, do raise this young man's hand. Greet White Bird, nephew of Cloud Heron, son of Wing Heart, fathered by Black Lightning of the Eagle Clan. As Clan Elder I place this young man before you for your inspection."

White Bird battled the wheeling sense of confusion, conquered it, and stood tall and straight before them. He wondered what they were seeing. A muscular young man, his chest a painful mass of fresh scabs. A man too young for such a responsibility. This was madness. A Speaker needed to be older, tempered and wise as his uncle had been.

"Hurrah for White Bird!" The shout carried over the crowd. To his surprise, the caller was none other than Mud Stalker.

While he was still reeling from the sight, Spring Cypress caught his attention by bouncing on charged legs. Her whole face beamed with joy and excitement as she clapped her hands for him.

Beside her, Clay Fat's subdued gaze had fixed on the young girl, his look anything but reassured.

What is going on here? White Bird wondered, face neutral against the tight agony in his mutilated chest. Not all of it came from the wounds left by his tattooing, as his mother continued to thrust his hand up toward the deep purple sky. The cheering of the crowd before him did little to ameliorate the heat burning into his back.

From the corner of his eye he noticed Mud Puppy, standing off to one side, his slight form illuminated by the ghastly yellow firelight. A haunted look, one of terror, reflected from his large brown eyes. He was shaking his head, and even across the distance, White Bird could read his lips. They were repeating, "Don't do it!" over and over.

Anhinga let the canoe drift, carried forward by its own momentum. She banked the pointed paddle across the gunwales as the craft curved slightly to the left—a flaw in its shaping during construction. Paddling it, she had constantly had to correct for that peculiarity.

Now, however, she was so exhausted that she didn't have enough energy to feel frustrated.

Around her the swamp pulsed with life: the humming of insects; the piping song of the birds rising and falling in scattered melodies; fish sloshing as they broke the surface for skimming bugs. Heat lay on the water, burned down through gaps in the trees by the relentless sun. Sweat beaded on her aching body.

For a long moment she stared at nothing, blind to the brown water with its bits of yellow-stained foam. Dark sticks from a forgotten forest floor bobbed gently, and the flotsam of bark and leaves lay in dappled shadows. The trees, so rich and green in the light might have been shades cast by another world. She did not see or feel the patches of triangular hanging moss that draped the branches and traced over her skin as she floated past. The dark shape of a water moccasin gliding away from her course didn't register in her stunned mind.

Again and again she relived the nightmare images. All she could see was that last instant when Mist Finger collapsed under the battering of the Sun warrior's stone-headed war club. Heartbeats later that scene faded into fragments of images as she watched her friends being torn apart before the Men's House. The vibrant red of bloody flesh, the odd gray of the intestines, the dark brown of the livers as they were cut loose from under the protective arch of human rib cages, painted her souls.

One instance in particular stood out. She flinched as she watched a blood-streaked warrior toss Cooter's shining liver high. It had risen, flopping loosely, to hang at midpoint and then dive steeply. At impact it had literally exploded into a paste, bits and pieces spattering hither and yon. Who would have thought a man's liver was so delicate?

She stared, sightless to this world, hearing the humming of the mosquitoes and flies as they hovered about her. Even the sweat trickling down her face seemed so far away, intruding from a different world than her own.

Blinking her dry eyes she glanced down and took inventory of herself. They had stripped her naked, of course. Clothing left wounded souls with a final if ever so small place of refuge. They had denied her even that. Blister-covered welts itched and oozed where they had used burning sticks to elicit her screams. A black bruise marked her left breast, where the one called Eats Wood had viciously pinched her nipple. Despite the bath she had taken at first light, she felt dirty, filth-smeared in a way that no amount of scrubbing could ever cleanse. If she reached up, she could feel the swollen lump that stuck out of the left side of her head. That was where the flat of White Bird's stone ax had brought her down. Broken and scabbed skin overlay deeper bruises on her wrists and legs where they had bound her.

In defiance she flexed her feet against the gouged wood on the canoe bottom, thankful that White Bird hadn't had the time to cut the tendons in her heels. Despite her other wounds, she could still walk, still run, instead of hobbling like an old woman on loose-hinged ankles.

Those were the wounds to her body. Try as she might, she could not even catch a glimpse of the wounds to her souls.

As she had paddled through the morning, dream images had flashed in her head: she and Mist Finger in love; their marriage; their first child—his smile as he stared up from moss bedding. She had imagined Mist Finger, grinning at the sight of her as he walked up to their house at the Panther's Bones. Gone, vanished like the morning mist that gave way to a burning midday sun.

Other memories of her and the dead sifted through her disjointed thoughts. She had grown up with them. Like the vines surrounding a tree, she had woven bits and pieces of their lives into her own. Cooter had brought her the first fish he had ever caught. How old had he been? Five summers?

She remembered the accident when Slit Nose had been running full tilt across Water Lily Camp, and fallen to slice his nose open on a discarded stone flake. The scar had never fully healed—and now never would. Until she died she would remember the way one of the Sun People propped his severed head onto the flames of that crackling bonfire. How it had sizzled as his face was blackened and burned, the scarred nose curling into ash while the eyeballs popped like overinflated bladders.

Spider Fire had always been a wit and a tease. Sharp of tongue, a bit irreverent, his puns had often left her incapacitated with laughter. Not more than two winters past, she had held him as he mourned his big brother's untimely death. In a freakish accident, a wind-lashed tree had fallen on him. It was to her that Spider Fire had come for comfort. Then, yesterday, she had seen his muscles carved away and fed to camp dogs until only the blood-streaked bones remained.

Right Talon had been the sober one, the youth of whom no one had expected great things. Instead, he had been carried away by dreams that would never come true. One day he was going to be a great Trader, the next he would become a most holy Serpent. Later that same afternoon he had been sure that a warrior's fame lay ahead of him. Dreams. All Dreams. They had died, locked away behind his sightless eyes, unable to escape past the tongue protruding from his gaping mouth. She could see his disbelieving face, wet and witless as a Sun warrior urinated on it.

The bumping of the canoe jarred her back to the present. She blinked at the swelling knot of pain that grief placed under her tongue. No tears remained to leak past her raw eyes. The canoe had fetched up alongside the trunk of a sweetgum tree. Patterns of green mottled the gray bark where wrist-thick vines twisted their way up into the canopy. A lizard skittered upward, disturbed by her arrival.

Where am I going? How am I ever going to live? The answers eluded her. When she glanced down, no less than a dozen mosquitoes dotted her arms. Their abdomens were dark and swollen, their back legs lifted as they drank deeply of her blood.

She would have to face the families of the dead. How did she explain what had happened to them? How did she put the terror she had observed into words?

One by one she watched the mosquitoes rise and fly off, their blood-swollen bodies heavy on the hot, still air. As they went others landed on airy feet, probing with their spiky snouts until they tapped her veins. Let them. She no longer needed her blood.

She no longer needed anything.

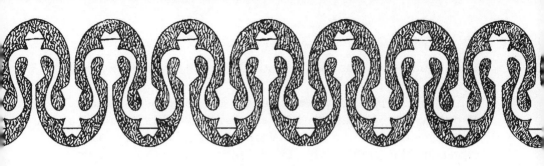

Fourteen

Mud Puppy crouched on the grass and fingered the tasseled ends of the fabric breechcloth his mother had made for him. The knotted hemp fibers rolled roughly under his fingers as he watched the proceedings beneath the roofed Council House ramada. He was but one of the large crowd that had gathered around the circular ramada to watch this historic session. Tens of tens of people ringed the open-sided enclosure, all watching with excitement as a new Speaker was voted on.

The packed crowd reassured Mud Puppy, provided him with the anonymity he desperately desired. Unlike the others who had come to watch, he felt an increasing sense of despair. This was going to doom them all. He couldn't say why he knew that, where it came from. Something that was spun out of forgotten Dreams lay just beyond his ability to grasp.

The Council was a reflection of Sun Town in miniature. Under the northeast portion sat Owl Clan, then Alligator Clan to the north, with Frog Clan in the northwest. In the southwest was Rattlesnake Clan. Eagle Clan sat in the south, and Snapping Turtle Clan in the southeast portion.

The ritual entryway in the east and the exit on the west were left open. A crackling fire burned in a pit at the center of the ring.

Mud Puppy watched with a heavy heart. Masked Owl had come to him in a Dream the night before, telling him exactly how it would come about. But what was the rest? The part that eluded his memory?

Mud Stalker stood by the fire in the center of the Council, his mangled arm covered by a white fabric with an artistic rendering of a snapping turtle woven into the warp and weft. His head was back, expression thoughtful, as he stated, "It has been a long time since such a young man has walked among us. Do we need any more proof of White Bird's abilities? Have we not all seen the wealth that has spread among us from the north over the last couple of days? Do we need to remind ourselves that this young man killed one of the Swamp People's raiders, and took another alive? Have we not heard his thoughtful words, spoken as if from the lips of his departed uncle?" Mud Stalker smiled when he met White Bird's eyes. "It is, therefore, my pleasure, as Speaker of Snapping Turtle Clan, to cast the majority vote in accepting White Bird to this Council."

He stepped forward, offering his left hand to White Bird, saying, "We have often been adversaries, White Bird. Now, with this gesture, I welcome you as my friend, and offer my clan's and this Council's most sincere support."

Don't do this thing, Brother! The words boomed through Mud Puppy's head, but he couldn't make himself stand, couldn't make himself shout them out for the world to hear. Instead, he seemed as impotent as a cooking clay, watching with a kind of mute horror.

White Bird sealed his fate as he rose to take Mud Stalker's hand in both of his, and said, "I thank you, Speaker. I am honored, and will do my best to serve my people and this Council."

Since Mud Stalker held the floor, White Bird reseated himself next to Wing Heart.

Across the distance, Mud Puppy could see his mother's expression—a look of satisfaction that seemed to radiate from the center of her souls. But when he looked deeply into her eyes he saw an unfamiliar bitterness, like a clay pot stressed beyond its limits.

It is short-lived, Mother. Enjoy this day while it lasts. You are lost . . . we are lost.

Mud Stalker raised his good arm high. "Not only does Snapping Turtle Clan vote to accept this new Speaker to the Council, but it is with pleasure that we announce to all that he is promised to marry two sisters from my own lineage."

Mud Puppy watched the surprised looks, curious that only Thunder Tail and Stone Talon appeared surprised.

"They play a devious game," Masked Owl's voice echoed in Mud Puppy's head. *"Like a snake swallowing its own tail, it shall consume them in the end."*

"Tomorrow, White Bird shall be joined with Pine Drop and Night Rain." Mud Stalker raised his good hand, palm up in a gesture of satisfaction. "And in further demonstration of the faith that Snapping Turtle Clan has in Owl Clan's leadership, we make this marriage in perpetuity."

That brought looks of astonishment to everyone's faces except Wing Heart's. Even Clay Fat appeared to be stunned.

"You what?" Cane Frog cried, blinking her one white eye.

"Should anything happen to White Bird," Mud Stalker continued, "the sisters shall go to White Bird's brother. An uninterrupted alliance between our clans."

"You mean . . . they would go to Mud Puppy?" Clay Fat cried incredulously.

"*No!*" Mud Puppy lurched to his feet. In the sudden silence, he was aware of all eyes turning his direction, seeking him out.

In a blind panic, he turned on his heel, almost bowling Little Needle over in his horrified flight. Careening off people, he broke free and sprinted toward the Bird's Head and the dark safety of the summit.

It was all going wrong. This night would lead to a future he wanted to refuse with all of his heart. "Please, Masked Owl? Make it go away! Leave it the way it was. *Please?*"

White Bird stretched, blinking himself awake. Morning light cast a blue shaft through the doorway to illuminate the inside of his mother's house. The central fire still smoldered, smoke rising to collect in a dusky haze that filled the low roof just above his bed. From the angle of the sun entering the door, he knew it was still early. He should have been dead tired. It couldn't have been two hands of time past since he'd crawled into bed, his stomach bloated from the feasts he'd attended. After the breaking of the Council, he and his mother had made the rounds, walking from clan ground to clan ground, shaking hands, eating what was offered, and accepting gifts and accolades wherever they passed.

The worst jolt had come when he finally faced Spring Cypress. The broken look in her eyes had wounded his souls as had nothing he had ever experienced.

"You want this?" she had asked in a quavering voice, her eyes searching his, desperate for any hint of negation.

"I must."

She surprised him with the rapidity in which she pivoted on a heel and raced off into the night. That momentary glimpse of the betrayal she had felt stung the space between his souls.

How do I ever make it up to her? The question rolled around the inside of his head as he studied the smoke-filled rafters. *What are the clans up to?* Even in the glow of his success he could feel the net cast about him, unseen hands ready to draw it tight. His mother's role was apparent enough. Her single purpose in life was to be the Clan Elder. From the time he had been a small boy he had understood that she would do anything, sacrifice anything, to maintain that position. And were she ever to be stripped of that duty? What then?

He shuddered at the thought, then glanced over to where she slept under a thin deerskin robe. Even in the softly filtered morning light her lined face betrayed its age. Her mouth hung open, and he could see missing molars in the back. Deep wrinkles surrounded her sagging breast, and loose skin had folded around her armpits. Tyrant that she was when awake, in sleep she looked pitifully vulnerable.

She couldn't stand it if she weren't Clan Elder. Relieve her of the title, and she would destroy herself rather than accept a lesser role.

For the moment he was unsure what to think about that. It all had been placed on his shoulders—all of her dreams and aspirations—as he had always known it would be.

Am I good enough? Strong enough? Can I meet all these expectations?

"We need to talk." The soft voice caught him by surprise. Startled, he could just make out Mud Puppy's form where it sat in the half darkness behind the shaft of morning light.

"Mud Puppy?"

"Not here."

"But I—"

"Come." Mud Puppy stood, allowing the thin fabric blanket to fall from his skinny shoulders. Without another glance at White Bird, he stepped into the shaft of sunlight and ducked out into the morning.

Swinging his legs over the bed poles, White Bird got to his feet, checked to make sure his breechcloth was hanging straight, and ducked out into the cool dawn. Mud Puppy stood awkwardly several steps from the door, his vacant gaze fixed on the blackened ring of ash that marked Uncle Cloud Heron's house site. Fragments of gray-white bone could still be seen among the smoldering ashes, a reminder that their uncle's Dream Soul was still present, watching.

"What is it? What did you want?" White Bird asked, irritably unnerved by Mud Puppy's manner.

"What are you going to do with that sack of goosefoot seeds you brought from the north?"

The question caught him by surprise. "Plant them. Why?"

"I would ask you the same question, Brother." Mud Puppy slid his haunted eyes toward White Bird. Fear glistened behind the glassy brown depths.

Shaking off misgivings the way he would cold rain water, White Bird stiffened his back. "To grow them, my silly young brother. When I was up in the north I discovered that the Wolf People grow goosefoot. They do it on purpose, not just nurturing stands of the plants the way we do, but they actually plant the best seeds to grow. They take special care of these fields, keeping out the grasshoppers and birds. The end result is that they have made bigger seeds, Brother. The advantage to these bigger seeds is a larger harvest per plant. Unlike leaving Sun Town to travel around to different places . . . uh, Ground Cherry Camp, for example, we can grow these bigger and better plants here, right around Sun Town. If we choose nothing but the best plants to replant, over the years we will have larger and larger harvests. Do you see what I'm after? We won't have to worry so much, or travel so far in the poor years, or when the flood isn't as beneficent as it is this spring. By storing what's left over, bellies won't be so thin during the hard times."

If anything, the haunted look had deepened in Mud Puppy's eyes. "Don't do this thing."

"What do you mean, don't?" White Bird crossed his arms.

"Don't plant the seeds. Make a feast for everyone instead." Mud Puppy's voice sounded as if from far away. "If you feed them to the People, it will be all right."

"What? What will be all right? You're sounding like you've been hit in the head! You expect me to give up on the seeds? Of all the things I brought from the north, Brother, they are the most important! Why do you think I haven't given any away? Why do you think I've ignored them? It's to show people. I'm going to plant them within the next couple of days. When I harvest them from the earth right there"—he pointed at the rich black soil near the bottom of the borrow pit—"I am going to make everyone understand."

"Please don't."

White Bird shook his head. "I swear, you're half-witted. What's wrong with you? Stop being a child. You are ready to become a man, but you act more like a boy than that pesky Little Needle— and he's winters younger than you are."

"Why can't you let this idea go?"

"Because it is better for the People, better for our clan. When they understand, everyone will look up to us."

"He'll kill you." Mud Puppy's voice had dropped to a whisper, his eyes shifting back to the burnt house.

"Who? You can't mean Mud Stalker? He's come over to our side, Brother. We've beaten him. Forced him to make an incredible deal to gain our patronage. He is *obligating* Snapping Turtle Clan to us. Don't you understand what that means? We're the preeminent clan in all the world!"

"If you defy his warning, he'll kill you."

White Bird narrowed his eyes. "Who?"

"Masked Owl."

"Oh, Snakes take us! How can you be so stupid and still be my brother? Today I am marrying Pine Drop and her sister, Night Rain. Name another man of my age to make such a match."

"If you do this, I will be stuck with them. I don't know if I can turn them. They are controlled by their uncle."

"You?" The tone in the boy's voice left him half-hysterical. "You only inherit them if I die!"

"You will," Mud Puppy replied woodenly, "if you don't destroy those seeds."

"Back to the seeds again." White Bird slapped his hands angrily against his legs. "Just why are you so insistent? Do you think they're poisoned, is that what this is about? They're just *seeds!*"

Mud Puppy stared miserably at the few fingers of blue smoke still rising from Uncle Cloud Heron's. "They are the future," he whispered.

"Which is why I'm planting them." A thought crossed White Bird's souls. "Wait a minute. Who put you up to this? Yellow Spider? One of the Wolf Traders? They are the only ones who know the importance of the seeds." He fit the pieces together. "No, they wouldn't have an objection, but if they had told someone else, someone in the other clans who would do anything to keep us from gaining even more influence and position." That could be anyone. He grasped Mud Puppy by the shoulder, spinning him so that he could stare into those large, haunted eyes. "Who, Mud Puppy? Tell me, or I'll whip you to within an inch of your life."

Mud Puppy swallowed hard, his eyes like glistening pools. "*He* did."

"He? He who?"

"Masked Owl. In a Dream."

White Bird shook the boy again, feeling his thin bones slipping under his skin. "Masked Owl . . . in a Dream. You're telling me that because you had a nightmare, I am supposed to give up my seeds? Surrender the future of my people and clan?"

Mud Puppy nodded miserably, flinching at the pain caused by White Bird's strong grip.

Snakes! The fool believes it! "It was a dream, Mud Puppy." He shoved him away. "Go on. Get away from here. I have important things to see to. I'm getting married today. I have new obligations. I'm Speaker now. I can't take up my time with your foolishness." With those words he strode off, needing to relieve himself before he put the rest of his day in order.

The glance he cast back over his shoulder revealed Mud Puppy, fingers absently prodding his shoulder where White Bird had shaken him. His haunted eyes were fixed on the smoking house remains again, and he had his head cocked, as if listening to someone he could barely hear.

Nonsense, all of it.

So, what am I going to do with you? "Mud Puppy you are going to be a burden in my life until the day they burn my bones!"

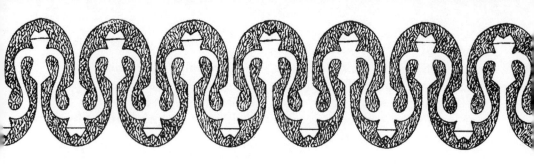

Fifteen

A gentle shower fell as Mud Puppy and Little Needle stood in the crowd and watched White Bird move his possessions into the snug mud-walled house he would share with his new wives. The dwelling lay three houses down on the third ridge in Snapping Turtle's Clan grounds. Unlike the others, it was new: the thatch still tawny, the walls freshly daubed with mud. A darker ring of charcoal-stained soil could be seen where Pine Drop's old house had been burned after her husband, Blue Feather's, death.

The two sisters, Pine Drop and Night Rain, looked like each other. Both were attractive, round-faced, with delicate noses, long glistening black hair, and uneasy white-toothed smiles. As a widow, Pine Drop had dressed in a matron's kirtle. She wore all of her finery, layers of beaded necklaces and colored feathers. In contrast, Night Rain wore a virgin's skirt with knotted fringes. She didn't have as many necklaces, but as Elder Back Scratch's granddaughter, she was still opulently turned out for the occasion. Their skin had been lightly slathered with a rose-scented bear grease. White magnolia flowers were pinned in their hair, and garlands of redbud had been placed around their necks.

Something about the Snapping Turtle Clan Speaker reminded Mud Puppy of a raccoon fishing in a shallow puddle full of crawfish. That smug assurance cast an uneasy shadow on his thoughts. Elder Back Scratch, looking incredibly ancient and frail, stood to one side, eyes gleaming with anticipation. But for what? Mud Puppy could swear that a glint of triumph lay behind Sweet Root's eyes as she watched White Bird take his place before her daughters.

In front of them, Wing Heart held herself erect, her absent eyes on her son as he strode confidently forward. Mud Puppy kept shooting glances at her. Something about his mother worried him. Her posture, the tone of her muscles, that downcast expression, sent unease creeping along his bones.

The women ceremonially greeted White Bird at the doorway of their house. The traditional offerings of baked fish, sweet honeysuckle, and dried wild squash were borne before them on wooden platters. Neither of them looked happy as White Bird lowered his fabric bag of possessions and took the wooden platter in his muscular brown hands. Unlike the women he was calm, in possession of the moment, aware of the gathered crowd and the importance of the event.

"Two wives?" Little Needle asked. "Who has ever heard of such a thing for someone as young as White Bird? You must be very proud."

"He has taken the path," Mud Puppy said sadly. "I cannot call him back."

"You sound as if he's dying instead of becoming the most glorious Speaker in memory," Little Needle muttered. "What's wrong with you? Ever since you went up on the Bird's Head, you've been flighty—like a duck hit too many times in the head. All you do is flap and quack."

"Am I your friend?" Mud Puppy asked suddenly.

"Of course, you silly fool." Little Needle crossed his arms. "But I don't know why. Even though you're older than I am, people still make fun of me for spending time with you."

"I am going to need friends."

"Stop being morose. You'd think you were swimming with rocks around your neck rather than becoming the second most powerful man in your clan. If anything happens to him, those are going to be your wives! I've heard that you will be voted into the Council. It's unheard of. You should be Dreaming about the future, about what to do if anything ever happens to White Bird."

Mud Puppy bit his lip as his brother received the offerings of food and turned, facing the watching people. He raised the wooden plate that bore his first meal as a married man. "By accepting this meal I tie my life with that of Pine Drop and Night Rain, daughters of Sweet Root, who is the daughter of the great Clan Elder, Back Scratch. My clan is now their clan, their clan is now mine. I accept these women as my wives, to share with equally, to comfort and care for."

Pine Drop and Night Rain, hands held demurely before them, cried out in unison, "We accept this man, White Bird, of the Owl Clan, as our husband. In doing this, we bind ourselves to him and to his clan. Let it be known among all people that we are married."

"Let it be known!" Mud Stalker called from where he stood to one side.

"Let it be known!" Wing Heart absently shouted from the other.

"Let it be known!" the gathered people shouted, smiling and slapping each other on the back.

Escape! The sudden desperate urge seized Mud Puppy. He turned and slipped away through the gathered ranks. Ducking behind a house, he made his way down the long curving ridge until the line of houses hid him from view. Cutting across to the steep bank, he let himself down to the water and looked north. From the canoe landing, he could see a slim boat putting out onto the lake. Despite the distance, he recognized that lonely occupant: Spring Cypress. She didn't look happy.

But then, perhaps she, too, could guess what was about to happen.

Jaguar Hide squinted as the morning sunlight burned white atop the mist rising from the still water. He paddled slowly through the boles of trees and out into open water. Across the rippling brown surface he could see a patch of greenery—an ancient and abandoned levee that protruded from the brackish waters. This was the place that old Long Mad, while fishing, had caught a glimpse of the girl. Here amidst the vines and water oaks his people had periodically camped or stopped just long enough to attend to any activities that required dry land.

With relief he passed into the shadow of the trees again and aimed the bow of his dugout canoe toward the shallow bank. As it slid onto the sandy ground, he stepped out and looked around before replacing his paddle with his atlatl and darts. A thousand birds called in the trees, and the faint hum of insects laced the air. The gleaming scales of a small snake shone as the reptile whisked itself into the safety of thicker vegetation. A dragonfly darted past his ear. Muscadine grape hung like thick brown strands of web.

He stepped through the lush matting of spring growth and

sniffed. Ever so faint, he caught the whiff of smoke. On silent feet he wound his way through the moss-patterned boles of trees, ducking vines, spiderwebs, and hanging moss until he found her. She lay in a clearing that consisted of little more than crushed grass, strawberry and chickweed. Her fire pit—a rude hole in the ground—still smoldered. Wood too wet to burn traced lazy spirals of blue smoke into the air.

Though she was asleep, faint whimpering broke her cracked lips. His gaze traveled down her naked body, reading the welts and bruises through the stippling of insect bites. Scabs crisscrossed her skin and her hair was matted with filth.

Are you there, Niece? Or have your souls left this poor body in search of a more pleasant place to live? His heart went hollow, and an empty heaviness sucked at his souls. Blessed Panther, what had she gotten herself into?

He sighed, hunkering down on his knees to probe at the fire. Little help lay there. The wood she'd managed to find had no doubt been soaked through and through. He found chewed frog bones, probably the only food she'd managed to scrounge. A paddle lay beside her, the workmanship unfamiliar to him, though he suspected it was something she'd stumbled across on her errant adventure.

He seated himself and waited, arms across his knees. Perhaps a hand of time passed before she stirred, shifted, and cried out. Whatever nightmare had been winding through her dreams startled her awake. Her eyes flickered and batted, unfocused, before she moaned and twisted on the flattened leaves of her bed.

When she did open her eyes for good they locked on his. He saw her incomprehension, and then fear, shame, and self-loathing reflected as they came tumbling out of her souls. A strangled sob choked in her throat, and she scrambled into a sitting position.

"Old Long Mad thought he saw you out here," Jaguar Hide said amiably. "People have been worried. I have been worried. Your idiot brother, Striped Dart, of course, can't seem to fathom what the trouble might be, for obviously you've just run off to explore the delights that a canoe load of strong young men could introduce you to. Or so he seems to think."

She just stared at him as if he was a corpse freshly risen from the dead.

"Myself," he continued unhurriedly, "I've come to the conclusion that you and your companions fared poorly on your raid against the Sun People. The gods and spirits that oversee war are capricious beasts at best. Snakes, don't I of all people know that?" He cocked his head, pausing. "War is such a chancy thing. When I was young

I had a great deal of good fortune at war. Some would like us to believe that the gods, Sky Beings, and Earth Beings grant us success or 'blind the enemy's eyes' or some such rot."

He chuckled at the notion, hand tracing an easy gesture in the air. "Me, I can tell you that it is just happenstance. Like casting gaming pieces. Sometimes one pattern comes up, sometimes another. I no longer believe in the intervention of spirits, Dreams, or sacrifice." He paused. "In all my years I have come to the conclusion that other ways of harming the enemy must be embraced. Something that doesn't entail chance events."

Her jaw trembled as she hugged her naked flesh and curled in on herself.

"Whatever happened," he continued, "I assume that you blame yourself. I can tell you not to, but you will do as your souls demand. Like your body, they, too, are wounded and need time to heal."

Her glazed eyes were fixed on some terrible vision hidden deep inside her.

"From the bruises on your wrists and ankles I see they captured you. You've taken a bad beating." He couldn't see blood or other evidence that she'd been raped. "How in the name of the Sky Beings did you manage to escape?"

Her frightened eyes widened; her voice seemed locked in her throat. He could see her lungs working, as though her breath couldn't catch up with her heart.

"It is all right," he told her softly and opened his arms. "Come over here. Let me hold you. Together, you and I, we will make this right."

Everything depended on how strong she was, whether she was a survivor or a broken captive. For long moments he waited, his eyes willing strength into her. His arms had grown heavy before she made the slightest movement.

She might have been an old woman, so slowly did she begin. When the tangled flotsam of her emotions finally let loose, she rushed him. He folded her into his arms, and she burst into tears. While sobs knotted her body, he held her, humming gently as he rocked her back and forth.

Mud Puppy was acutely aware of the giant barred owl that watched him with moist brown eyes. The huge bird perched on a branch three arm's lengths above where Mud Puppy's canoe floated on limpid brown water. The flooded backswamp steamed in the hot afternoon, columns of insects wavering as they drifted aimlessly in the still air. The faint hum of their wings echoed over the smooth surface.

Despite the owl, Mud Puppy lay stretched the length of his canoe, chin resting on the bow. He kept his attention focused on the alligator who floated no more than an arm's length away. The big bull had caught Mud Puppy's attention by roaring earlier. After paddling as close as he dared, Mud Puppy had let the canoe drift toward the bull.

Two eyes, like glistening golden brown stones, stared across the glassy surface with pupils in vertical black slits. The nostrils protruded in a rounded hump. Regular lines of scutes made dimples in the water where the big beast's back lay submerged. The bull was old, his muzzle scarred. Mud Puppy guessed that he had to measure twice the length of a tall man. Some would say he was being foolish to drift his canoe so close to a swamp giant like this. Perhaps, but so long as he didn't move, didn't allow his scent to taint the water, he would be all right.

Hello, big fellow. He projected the words with his mind, unwilling to break the spell by speaking. He stared into the single slitted eye facing him. The soul behind that alien eye spoke of eternal patience and age. That same eye might have watched the Creation and absorbed all of the changes that had befallen the Earth since. It was said that Alligator knew of secret things: of poisons and medicines, of ways to breathe underwater, and the workings of debilitating illness and miraculous cures. The greatest secret that Alligator possessed was the knowledge of passages and tunnels that led into the Underworld. Alligator was the messenger. People had seen him slip up to grab people, thrashing them in the water before diving, carrying them down into the murky black depths. All that remained was a trail of bubbles that finally ceased to pop on the opaque surface. They left silence behind.

The bodies were never seen again, but often the souls of those Alligator had taken spoke to the Serpents when they entered trances and traveled to the Underworld. That was how people learned of Alligator's secrets.

As Mud Puppy watched, he noticed minnows flicking along the line of the alligator's jaw. The little fish were nibbling at the scales, tails wiggling as they appeared, then vanished into the murky water. The sight amazed him. A lesson lay in that. Delicate little fish, dancing back and forth, safe in the presence of the most terrifying of beasts. How could they, of all creatures, pass with immunity?

Because they are small, unnoticed, and unimportant. He considered that as he stared into the impenetrable eye. What was he supposed to learn? How did he use a lesson like that?

"Mud Puppy?" an accented voice called, breaking his concentration.

"Shush!" Mud Puppy carefully lifted his chin high enough to answer. "Stay where you are."

The alligator seemed not to have heard. No change of expression could be seen in that black slit of an eye. Not a ripple moved in the still water. Alligator remained oblivious, the little fish playing around his head. Was he Dreaming? Floating and Dreaming, seeing things of Power and magic and joy?

Mud Puppy himself had lain in the warm water, his body buoyed while sunshine beat down in radiant warmth. For him, too, it had been dreamlike, sharing a oneness with the swamp around him. Sound had been dulled, turned inside of him. The faint beating of his heart, his slow breathing, and the water stroking his skin, had left him in a shallow state of bliss. Was that how Alligator lived, his world muted by the pressing warmth of the water?

"Snakes! That's the biggest alligator I've ever seen! What are you doing? Trying to get killed?" the accented voice cried from somewhere behind Mud Puppy.

"Stay back," Mud Puppy replied carefully. "Come no closer. We were just talking, he and I." Reluctantly Mud Puppy gathered himself, inching upward and back. As his silhouette began to emerge over the gunwales, Mud Puppy said, "Go away, Grandfather. I mean you no harm."

With a flip of his tail, the big alligator eased ahead, a faint V drifting back from his nose and eyes. Water rippled along the protruding scutes in his back.

"I don't believe it." The accented voice sounded stunned.

Mud Puppy turned to see Hazel Fire and Two Wolves, the Traders, watching from one of their sturdy canoes. Both had darts nocked in atlatls, ready to cast. Each had a bright expression of wonder in his eyes as their canoe drifted slowly to one side. Mud Puppy looked back in time to see the big alligator drift into a duckweed-filled cove and come to rest, eternally one with the swamp.

"What are you doing out here?" he asked when he looked back. They were still perched, their darts held at the ready.

"We went fishing." Hazel Fire lowered his atlatl and dart, swallowing hard. "We've been out here for hours, just going around in circles. How do you find your way in this mess?" He indicated the endless trees rising from the still water.

"My people just know." Mud Puppy shrugged and pointed. "That way is home."

"That alligator"—Two Wolves indicated the great reptile with his darts—"you talked to him? You speak his language?"

"He was Dreaming," Mud Puppy said. "Seeing between the worlds." Movement caught his eye as a broad-banded water snake slipped from a tupelo root and swam in gentle undulations to a foam-caked pile of flotsam. There it lay quietly, in wait for whatever might chance by. "He was teaching me things." Why he said that, he wasn't sure, but the words might have been a bee sting given the way they jolted the Wolf Traders. Both of the young men looked as if they had been stabbed by an unseen hand.

For a long moment, an uneasy silence passed, and Mud Puppy couldn't force himself to look at them. In the end, he asked quietly. "Please don't tell people I said that."

"We won't," Hazel Fire agreed, and a crooked smile crossed his lips. "If you won't tell anybody we're lost out here."

"It is done." Mud Puppy dipped his paddle and coasted his canoe toward theirs. "To seal our deal, I have something for you." He reached into his small belt pouch and drew out a red jasper carving he had made, the image of a small potbellied owl with a tilted head. "I just finished this. He's a friend of mine. I call him Masked Owl." Mud Puppy reached across and dropped the fetish into Hazel Fire's open hand.

The Trader lifted the little owl, studying it with a practiced eye. "You are very good at carving, Mud Puppy. Look at this! Such fine detail. What is this around the owl's eyes?"

"That's a mask."

"I see." Hazel Fire glanced suspiciously at Mud Puppy, then back at the alligator where it hid in the duckweed. "Along with alligators, do you talk with Masked Owls?"

Mud Puppy considered the question. Did he dare trust these outsiders? Men from a place he could barely conceive of?

"Do not worry," Two Wolves said, reading his unease. "Your brother is our kinsman. Among our people, that binds us. What you tell us, remains among the three of us, and *only* among us." He indicated the gleaming stone owl in Hazel Fire's hand. "Our trust is even bound by a gift. There is Power in that."

"Masked Owl comes to me in my Dreams. He is helping me to find a Spirit Helper. There is a chance that Salamander might come to me."

"Salamander?" Two Wolves asked curiously, but there was no derision behind his question.

"He has special Powers, including the ability to make himself unseen."

Hazel Fire resettled himself in his canoe, laying his atlatl and darts to the side. "Why do I have the suspicion that your brother isn't the only outstanding member of your family?"

"What are you talking about?" Two Wolves asked his friend.

"Mud Puppy, here"—he indicated with a casual hand—"is more than I think most people understand. It was his vision that sent us south to meet the Swamp Panther raiders. Now we find him talking to an alligator and making Power alliances." He held up the Masked Owl charm to emphasize his point. "Yet his own people do not take him seriously."

The talk, along with Hazel Fire's intense scrutiny, made Mud Puppy's gut feel like ants were crawling around his insides.

"Two brothers," Two Wolves mused, "two different strengths. But we are outsiders."

"And perhaps less blinded by our prejudices," Hazel Fire agreed, raising the little carved owl. "Mud Puppy, consider us your friends, no, more than that, your kin."

A sudden idea slipped into Mud Puppy's souls. "Will you do something for me?"

"If it is within our ability, Mud Puppy." Hazel Fire studied the little red owl thoughtfully.

"Tell my brother that he must not plant his seeds."

A wry smile crossed Two Wolves's lips. "I think, married as he is to two new women, he is already planting his seed, young kinsman."

"I don't mean that. I mean the goosefoot seeds he brought down from the north. Tell him not to plant those seeds."

Hazel Fire cocked his head. "Why? He has told us his plan for them. We, ourselves, plant the seeds. Among my people it provides another source of food for the winter. Ask your brother, he ate enough of it last winter to know the advantages."

"It's not me." Mud Puppy hesitated, cringing. Did he dare share this secret?

"If it is not you, then who, Mud Puppy?" Hazel Fire's expression sharpened. "White Bird is a relative through marriage, a member of my family, stranger though he might be. We have shared many things over the last year. His child lives in my sister. If there is some threat to White Bird, I would know of it."

"It came from a Dream," he hedged. "Someone in the Dream told me that my brother would be killed if he planted those seeds. That it is not a thing for my people. Power doesn't want it to happen here."

"Want what to happen here?" Two Wolves looked confused.

"People to grow their own plants." Mud Puppy made a helpless gesture. "I tried to tell White Bird. He thinks I'm being a silly child and won't listen. He has turned blind; his ability to see is overcome by his new status and all the attention people are heaping upon him. He thinks he cannot be defeated."

"Defeated by whom?" Two Wolves asked. "If there is a threat, we will protect him. He has earned our loyalty through his service to us, our clans, and our people, let alone to yours."

"By Power," Mud Puppy said miserably. "Masked Owl has told me that he mustn't plant those seeds. If he does, he will change the world. Masked Owl doesn't want that to happen. He wants us to stay . . ." Mud Puppy clamped his mouth, miserably aware that he'd just said too much.

Hazel Fire's thoughtful eyes had narrowed, his face pensive.

"All this came out of a Dream?" Two Wolves asked incredulously. "Why should White Bird believe your Dream, and not his own?"

Mud Puppy felt a sinking in his chest. He must have been suntouched to have confided in these strangers from the far north.

"Wait," Hazel Fire's low voice intruded. Then he spoke in the Wolf People's tongue, the alien words hammering on Mud Puppy's ears like hail. Whatever it was, it must have been so demeaning they didn't dare talk in a language he would understand.

"Forget I said anything." Mud Puppy picked up his paddle, refusing to meet their eyes. "I shall tell no one that you were lost. The Masked Owl seals that bargain." He turned his canoe. "Come, it is this way home."

"I said, wait." Hazel Fire lifted a hand, those foreign eyes pensive. "You really believe this, don't you?"

Mud Puppy said nothing, but his eyes must have betrayed him, for Hazel Fire said, "We believe you, Mud Puppy." He gestured toward the alligator. "It takes a special person to talk to the likes of him. Your brother has been away from you for over a year. Perhaps he does not understand the changes in his little brother."

"Changes?" Mud Puppy was puzzled.

Hazel Fire smiled. "It took me a while to understand that my little sister had become a woman. It wasn't until I saw your brother's child growing in her womb that I knew. Two Wolves and I, we will speak to your brother. I don't know that we can change his mind, but we are willing to try."

Mud Puppy nodded, a sudden feeling of relief building in his belly. "I thank you. For this, I shall always be in your debt."

"Then we are brothers," Hazel Fire added. "May our bonds strengthen over time despite the distance that will separate us."

"May it be so," Mud Puppy agreed. "Come, let us go. There may not be much time."

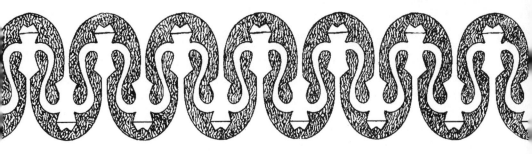

Sixteen

Pine Drop lay on her side, the hard pole of the bed frame under her hips. She could feel the heat from White Bird's body. Her own skin remained damp from the joining that had consummated their marriage. Careful not to wake him, she eased off the bed, squatted, and wiped herself with a handful of dried hanging moss.

She turned, studying the face of her new husband in the half-light cast through the doorway. The stranger slept on her bedding, his muscular left leg raised and braced against the mud-daubed wall. The right arm lay beside him, his left lax on his damp chest. His lungs filled and emptied with a slow regularity; the dancing of his eyes under smooth lids reflected obscured dreams.

How could this have happened? She ran a callused hand down her face, then glanced at Night Rain, where she, too, dozed on the bed adjoining Pine Drop's. Her sister rested on her back, her young breasts flat, a length of cloth covering her hips. She couldn't be sure if Night Rain slept, or just had feigned it during the time Pine Drop had been coupling with White Bird.

White Bird? Her husband? Who was this man? Two days ago she had been a young widow, heartbroken, her souls aching with grief. Today she was married—she and her sister. Together. It might have been a tornado that had uprooted her life.

Just now she had lain with a stranger. In defense she had closed her eyes when he mounted her, wrapped herself in the past, filled her imagination with Blue Feather. In her fantasy, it was Blue

Feather who moved inside her. It was Blue Feather who brought her to ecstasy. As waves of pleasure rolled through her hips, she had tightened her arms around him—not this strange new man.

Time seemed to ebb and flow like stretched cattail dough in Pine Drop's memory. Through the whirl of events, she had glimpses: Blue Feather's body, hot and bright with fever; his eyes, racked by pain, losing focus as she held his hand; those last moments as he gasped for shallow breaths and his souls loosened for the last time. Had it been she who had set fire to the house she had shared for those few moons with Blue Feather? Had it been right on this very spot that she had burned their dwelling down to a ring of charred cinders? She glanced at the tamped ash-laden soil before the doorway. Blue Feather's bones had been there, a tied bundle of them stacked atop a pile of white ash, oak, and hickory wood. He had been of the Alligator Clan. Members of his lineage had come afterward, picking through the bits of charcoal and ash to retrieve the broken and spalled slivers of fire-whitened bone.

Now I am married again. To a man of the Owl Clan, of all things. The hollow ache in her loins for Blue Feather had barely subsided; how could Mud Stalker and Back Scratch think this stranger could fill that place she had shared with Blue Feather?

"Is he asleep?" Night Rain whispered cautiously.

"Yes." Pine Drop glanced at her sister, seeing one eye peering from under a lax brown arm.

"Snakes! Is that what it was all about?" She lowered her arm and swung into a sitting position. "Not like I imagined." She glanced down, her hair falling around her in a tangled black mass. "Not like it sounded when he lay with you."

"I wasn't with him," Pine Drop mouthed words, glancing uneasily at the sleeping man. At the question in her sister's eyes, Pine Drop soundlessly said, "Blue Feather."

"Oh," Night Rain mouthed in return.

Pine Drop reached for her kirtle and gestured. Night Rain dressed silently and followed as Pine Drop ducked out the door. The house was new, built on the ruins of her old structure. It had been on this spot that Blue Feather's dead body had been processed before the ritual cleansing. Now nothing remained of him except his Dream Soul. Had it been prowling around the house, watching this new man as he slid his manhood into her? Had Blue Feather known that she was dreaming of him, that she had willed White Bird's hard member to be his?

Night Rain turned her young face up toward the cloudy sky. A faint misty rain was falling. It speckled the young woman's hair in silver specks. "Remember how we used to talk when we were little? How we swore that one day we would have a household together, that we would marry the same great warrior? That we would live on that way forever? Now, here it is, and it's not like I ever thought it would be."

"No."

"Will I ever enjoy coupling with a man?"

"Perhaps, with time." Pine Drop reached out and placed an arm around her sister's shoulder. "Did he hurt you?"

"No." Pine Drop felt Night Rain's shrug. "It just wasn't what I thought, that's all. I expected lightning, and joy, and some great experience like riding on clouds."

"And instead?"

"It was uncomfortable. He's . . ."

"Big."

"Yes." She glanced sideways at Pine Drop. "I thought it would feel more like a finger."

"I'm sorry."

Night Rain shrugged. "Do you think I'm going to get pregnant?"

"Eventually."

"You didn't. I mean with Blue Feather. And you were married for almost six moons before . . ."

"Yes, well, sometimes it doesn't happen right off in first moons you spend as a woman." She tried to keep the regret out of her voice.

"We have done our duty to our lineage and to our clan." Night Rain smiled sadly. "We are the granddaughters of the Clan Elder. That is all that matters."

How could she say it with such simple faith? "That doesn't mean that we must like it. What has possessed the Elder and the Speaker? We have always been adversaries of Owl Clan, especially that haughty Wing Heart. She acts so superior to everyone else. Did I ever tell you about the time she kicked me out of her path? I was little then, maybe four winters old. She treated me like dirt."

"Now we are married to her son." Night Rain's eyes were on the long lines of houses that surrounded them. Cattails were waving green fronds above the dark water in the borrow ditches that separated the house ridges. "I wanted to marry Saw Back, of the Alligator Clan."

"Well, you had better forget him—and hope that White Bird remains alive," Pine Drop cautioned. "At least he is a Speaker, young though he is. He has war honors that will transfer to our children and clan. He has prestige and status, and from the looks of things, it will only grow greater."

"That is supposed to reassure us?" Night Rain asked hollowly.

"Yes, because the alternative is that if anything happens to White Bird, we go to that witless Mud Puppy! Think about that the next time our husband crawls on top of you and parts your legs."

Night Rain chewed her lip thoughtfully. "What could Grandmother have been thinking? I don't understand this new alliance with Owl Clan. It makes no sense."

Pine Drop sighed, looked furtively back at the doorway to make sure that White Bird hadn't awakened, and whispered, "We are to learn what we can about Wing Heart and help our clan gain ascendancy, silly gosling! The Speaker didn't talk the Elder into marrying us to White Bird to make us happy. We are here to serve the clan, and that, Little Sister, is what we will do."

Night Rain nodded. "I understand, Sister. When it comes to the clan I will do my duty."

The Serpent

My old teacher once told me,
When you are running, just run.
When you are walking, just walk.
When you are standing, just stand.
But never ever wobble.
That's when the Sky Beings see you.

Thick patches of black cloud came sliding up from the gulf, accompanied by low rolling thunder. The moon after equinox was a time for storms. Wing Heart glanced up at rain-swollen heavens as she wondered whether to take down her loom and move it, and the half-finished fabric, into the shelter of her house. Faint teasings of a southerly breeze toyed with her hair and the fine strands of glossy hemp that she played through the warp, knotting the strands on certain threads to create a pattern before pressing it tight with her fine-toothed deer-scapula comb.

As she glanced up at the sky again, she noticed White Bird coming across the plaza, his sack of goosefoot seeds hanging from one hand, a use-hardened digging stick from the other. Hazel Fire stepped out from the Men's House, crossing to intercept him. Across the distance she could see the two men wave in greeting, Hazel Fire breaking into a trot to catch his friend.

A satisfied smile crossed Wing Heart's lips. Her son was married, fresh from his first night in his wives' house. He was the talk of Sun

Town, the culmination of years of her hopes and ambitions. His name was on everyone's lips—which meant her name was close behind, followed, of course, by that of Owl Clan.

Wing Heart filled her lungs, her breast fit to burst with an ecstasy she could scarcely contain. Had it been but two weeks past that she had been wallowing in misery, sure that her noble son was dead, and her only heir was the simple Mud Puppy?

"Hello, Wing Heart," Moccasin Leaf greeted as she stepped around the house wall. She carried a wicker basket in which lay several bass, their mouths gaping, dead eyes staring up at the dark clouds as though in last hope for water.

"Moccasin Leaf." Wing Heart nodded. "Good day to you."

Gray-haired Moccasin Leaf had lived nearly four tens of winters. She had a wrinkled round face with a jaw that sucked up squat against her nose, the teeth being long gone. Aged and frail, her dark eyes had lost none of the quick wit that had so long bedeviled Wing Heart and her lineage. The old woman wore a light brown kirtle today, the shape of an owl woven into the material. She lowered herself, grunting, and placed the wicker basket with the fish on the ground beside Wing Heart.

"I have come to make amends." Moccasin Leaf worked her wide shallow mouth and placed her hands on her withered thighs. "You were right, I was wrong. White Bird has returned, and in the space of days, proven his worth not only to the clan, but to the moiety and our people. No one has been voted into the Council at such a young age. He will be twice the man his uncle was." She paused, looking out to where White Bird had stopped a dart's cast to the south. He and Hazel Fire were involved in some sort of passionate discussion.

"I was just lucky," Wing Heart conceded. "It could very easily have gone the other way. He might have been killed upriver." She paused. "Had he been, I would have declared Half Thorn to be the Speaker."

"As well he should have been," Moccasin Leaf muttered, her eyes on White Bird as he gestured a passionate negation in his conversation with the Wolf Trader. "No matter, the good of the clan has been served. I just came by to tell you that I will support you, and your son. So will the rest of my lineage."

"Half Thorn bears no ill will?"

Moccasin Leaf snorted through her short nose. "What do you think? Leadership of the clan has rested in your lineage for three generations. You have only sons for heirs, and one was missing while the other . . . well . . . Half Thorn was already addressing the

Council in his dreams. People in the other lineages had begun to accord him a greater authority. Now that is gone. Of course he is upset, but it will pass." She gave Wing Heart a sharp look. "It would help if he were consulted on certain matters important to the clan. Especially given the youth of the current Speaker."

The old woman left the hint dangling like bait. Wing Heart considered. On the one hand, she had authority and prestige right now simply to squash her old rival the same way she would a carrion beetle. Perhaps, in another time, she would have. Something stayed her. *Am I grown maudlin? Softened by Cloud Heron's death? Or simply careless in the afterglow of victory?*

"Very well, Moccasin Leaf, I accept your offer of support. The Speaker and I shall be calling on Half Thorn. We look forward to sharing his knowledge and expertise." As if he had any.

She smiled at Moccasin Leaf the way a sister would at the resolution of a petty argument. It was a small price to pay for clan unity. What she and White Bird would spend in time and irritation for the short term would be countered by increased goodwill and the long-term ability to expose Half Thorn for the fool that he was. The man had been too long a fisherman and hunter in the swamp. He had no idea about the complexities of interclan politics or the layers of deception that leaders like Stone Talon, Mud Stalker, and Deep Hunter resorted to. Half Thorn took everyone at their word, thinking in his naïveté that they said what they meant and meant what they said. The idea that a circuitously implied promise might be easily ignored or offered deceitfully had never found even a casual resting place in the man's souls. Even Mud Puppy was smarter than that, or at least, she hoped so.

"Very good." Moccasin Leaf sighed, slapping her thin thighs. "Then we understand each other." She looked out at White Bird, who was gesturing with the digging stick, indicating the sack of goosefoot seeds he held. Resignation lay in the old woman's eyes. "You have a great Power in your lineage. It is as if your blood has been blessed by the Sky Beings. To stand against you is to be like a forest in the path of a hurricane. In the end, only broken trunks and litter are left."

Wing Heart waited long enough to be politic, then said, "I have given my life to the betterment of my clan. Under my lineage's leadership, Owl Clan has risen above the others. All people look to us. All of our lineages, not just mine." Thunder boomed across the sky, and the southern breeze stiffened. "If White Bird succeeds, we all succeed."

Moccasin Leaf tucked a strand of gray hair back where the wind had worried it loose. "Indeed. What you say is true. But know this, Elder: Some of us worry about the risks you take to maintain your prestige. It is said that Water Petal will take your place when you follow your brother to the Spirit World. And if she carries a female child, or bears one in the future, that your lineage will be assured the leadership onward forever."

"That is a matter for the future, Moccasin Leaf. In the time you talk about, neither you nor I will be in a position to influence who is Elder or Speaker. That is for our grandchildren and their grandchildren."

"True. But know this as well: Many are disturbed that in marrying White Bird to the Snapping Turtles you also committed Mud Puppy. You may indeed have found a new ally and blunted other clans' ambitions, but many within our clan think that including Mud Puppy in the bargain went too far."

She smiled. "Mud Stalker insisted. Understand, Moccasin Leaf, in all dealings with the clans, there is an element of risk. Just as you, coming here today, gambled that I, being in a position of strength, would accept your offer of support and fish"—she gestured at the drying bass—"rather than turn you down cold. And it worked out to our mutual benefit. The Speaker and I will do our best to ensure your lineage's position while you support us." Lightning flashed across the sky, followed several seconds later by thunder.

Moccasin Leaf still watched White Bird. The Wolf Trader had turned, looking somewhat upset as he stalked off for the Men's House again. White Bird resumed his course toward the clan grounds, face rigid in anger, the sack of seeds clutched in his strong hand.

The old woman said, "So, what would Mud Stalker gain by placing Mud Puppy in line for the Speaker's position? Why would he insist upon that? He has to know that it would be the decision of Owl Clan to approve him as Speaker. Snapping Turtle Clan cannot tell us who our Speaker must be."

"Exactly. He and his allies are working on many levels," she said thoughtfully, fully aware of her own complicity in the deal. "He has always been a crafty one, Moccasin Leaf, and, finding himself beaten, he has done the best thing he could."

"Which is what? Hope that White Bird dies mysteriously and that he can place Mud Puppy on the Council to humiliate us?"

"That is how it is supposed to look on the surface, but as you and I both know, it wouldn't be the thing to gamble on. No, what appears to be an act of desperation is but the covering to conceal the fact that he is buying time. More than that, he has gained a great deal of prestige, moving to block Rattlesnake and Eagle Clans from strengthening their position with us. Our crafty Mud Stalker now has more room to maneuver, the ability to broker different deals with the clans depending on how the future plays out." She nodded, half to herself. "It was a smart move, daring and rapid, given the sudden turn of events. Our clans come out ahead, the others lose."

"Then he is a very dangerous man." Moccasin Leaf seemed to have forgotten their antagonistic relationship for the moment.

"Yes, very," Wing Heart agreed.

"What is he doing?" Moccasin Leaf indicated White Bird. The young man had stopped at the edge of the borrow ditch, laying his sack down before vigorously punching the digging stick into the damp brown soil. He used his chest, pressing down to drive the stick deep, and then levering the soil to break it.

"He has some idea about those goosefoot seeds. Have you seen them? Larger than the ones we collect around here. White Bird thinks that by growing them, we can tap the plant's Power. That these larger seeds will be produced here."

"Looks like a lot of hard work." Moccasin Leaf shook her head. "Why go to all that effort when the plants grow wild everywhere. For all the work he's going to have to put into it, he could just wait and collect the wild seeds with half the effort. And not only that, when you go around and collect the wild seeds, you find other things: turtles, rabbits, squash, hickory nuts. It looks like foolishness to me."

Wing Heart bit her lip, aware of the darkening clouds. Black stringers of rain could be seen where they whisked down from the closing storm bank in the south. "It may well be. He saw it work among the Wolf Traders to the north and wants to try it here, that's all. He just wishes to see."

"I had better get home," Moccasin Leaf mused, her eyes on the storm front with its flashing lightning.

"Would you help me move my loom inside first?" Wing Heart asked, standing.

The old woman took the other end of the loom. "That boy of yours, I should say, the Speaker, he's going to get wet planting all those seeds of his. From the look on his face, he's determined."

"That is what makes a good Speaker," Wing Heart agreed, casting a glance over her shoulder. White Bird's body bent and swayed as he continued driving the sharp stick into the dirt, breaking the grassy sod, turning the soil. The expression on his face hadn't changed, as if it were a matter of honor that he plant his seeds.

The notion that it was a little silly lodged in Wing Heart's souls, but then young people acted on whims on occasion; Snakes knew, she had as a young woman.

Together, she and Moccasin Leaf maneuvered the loom into the shelter of the house and propped it against the wall beside the doorway. In the shadow of the storm, the interior was dark, inky.

"Thank you for your help," Wing Heart began. A sudden white flash lit the interior, rendering the beds, pots, and fire pit in brilliant contrast to the sharp black shadows. A split heartbeat later, a *bang!* fit to deafen exploded outside. The closeness of the lightning bolt left Wing Heart breathless, half-scared out of her wits.

She glanced at Moccasin Leaf, seeing the old woman's shadowy form, panting, her hand to her heart. "Close one," she gasped.

"Good thing we weren't outside," Moccasin Leaf agreed. "It might have scared the souls out of our bodies."

Wing Heart led the way out into the open. The first large drops of rain came pattering down. She could see people ducking out of houses or peering out from under ramadas. They were owl-eyed, wary, postures half-crouched. Some stared, eyes locked, a look of horror on their faces.

Wing Heart turned, following their gazes. Her thoughts stumbled for a moment, unable to fathom what she was seeing. A faint blue streamer of smoke rose from the lump, rapidly tugged away by the gusty wind. The shape confused her for a moment. A human body didn't smoke like that; it shouldn't be lying so stiff and . . . and . . . Her souls froze. She couldn't move, couldn't think. The word "no" echoed hollowly inside her as if she were but an infinite emptiness.

"Snakes take us," Moccasin Leaf whispered as she stared through the increasing rain at White Bird's smoldering body. The digging stick had splintered; yellow flames flickered on the seed sack beside the body. The rain came in a pounding rush to extinguish it.

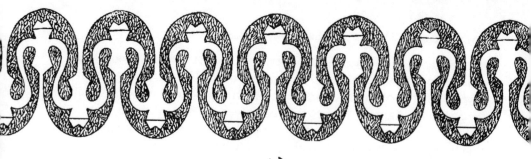

Seventeen

The village called the Panther's Bones lay on a low, flat-topped terrace that rose above the surrounding backwater swamp. Six individual mounds, some of them three times a man's height, overlooked the swamp. The seventh, a single conical mound, guarded the western edge of the village, a lone sentinel against the Land of the Dead and the dangerous souls that hid beyond the horizon. A prominent rise guarded the north, the symbolic place of darkness and cold.

A strong man, skilled with the atlatl, could cast a dart from east to west; it would take him two long casts to span the distance between the Bird Mound at the southern edge of the site and the northern prominence. Within that area, several clans of the Swamp Panthers had built their homes: domelike structures with thatched roofs atop low wattle-and-daub walls.

Jaguar Hide's people lived in a land of plenty. The pine-covered uplands to the west provided them with stone for tools, as well as pinesap to be mixed with bear grease to keep hordes of stinging and biting insects at bay. At the foot of the piney hills lay Water Eagle Lake, a dependable body of water that refilled annually when the spring floods inundated the land. His people wanted for nothing, except, perhaps in bad years like this one, for a little dry land. Relatives had come seeking shelter among clansmen and kin, bringing with them larders of smoked catfish, oven-baked duck, seasoned deer, raccoon, and opossum. Housing was so critical that cane-framed lean-to shelters had been attached to house walls and quickly roofed with palmetto and grass fronds. Under the high bank, row upon row of canoes had been drawn up onto the mud. When they weren't fighting amongst themselves, or squealing in play, a roiling tribe of children and flea-infested dogs was pestering people, snatching morsels of food, and generally being a nuisance.

Jaguar Hide sat in front of his house and watched the last of the storm fading into the northern horizon. Sunlight slanted through the treetops, sparkling in wet leaves. Blue fingers of smoke rose from damp fires in the open, or through the gap between the rafter poles and supporting walls. He could smell fish broiling in the earth ovens. Two women were taking turns pounding cattail roots in a wooden mortar. The rhythmic *thump-thump* of the tall pestles might have been the heartbeat of the village.

He glanced at the dark doorway behind him when he heard his niece stir on the bedding within. How many times had he waited thus? How many times had one of his relatives or friends lain in misery as their bodies or souls struggled to recover from some wound inflicted by the Sun People?

He tried to remember any single turning of the seasons when his people hadn't been mourning some injury. One by one, a seemingly endless litany of faces passed through his souls' memory. So much pain, so much tragedy. All of his life he had tried to harm them, pay them back. His raids, the constant warfare, had done nothing. Sting them too hard, and they struck back, violently, their greater numbers blunting any advantage the Swamp Panthers had in their endless swamps.

If only there was a way to really hurt them!

He heard Anhinga as she flopped on her bed, then groaned. She might have been a grub the way she clung to the darkness inside the house.

"It's a beautiful evening. Why don't you come out and help me eat some of this fish? It is smoked and seasoned with freshly picked mint leaves."

No answer.

"Are you going to lie around in there like a mushroom? Just feeding on the dark?"

Still no answer.

He grunted to himself, knowing full well what her trouble was. His knees cracked as he rose and ducked through the small doorway into the dim interior. She lay on her side, knees up, arms tucked against her breasts. He could see the scabs on her smooth young flesh. Like the old man he was, he settled himself on the bed's pole frame and reached out to stroke her hair. "No one is blaming you, Anhinga. The other clans understand war. They understand that when young men go on raids, sometimes they don't come back."

Her body tensed under his touch, a suffering sound caught in her throat.

"If I could have just one wish, I would have you talk to me again." He gently patted her head. "I would have you tell me what you are carrying between your souls. I would not care what you said, if only you would talk again."

He lost count of his heartbeats as he carefully stroked her long black hair. He had washed it for her, and during the process, she hadn't said a word, enduring, expression vacant as if carved of wood. Her eyes had been fastened on something far away, some terrible memory.

She whispered hollowly, "I want to kill them, all of them. I will dedicate my life to it. I swear."

"Ah, you are set to lead another war party?"

"No," came the weak reply.

"How will you do this thing, then?"

"Go alone." She swallowed hard. "Just me. I'll hunt them one by one, find them alone out in the swamp and kill them until they kill me."

He grunted noncommittally. "Are you sure that you don't want to stay here, live with me, help to keep your silly brother from pitching us headfirst into lunacy?"

She turned then, staring at him for the first time with impassioned eyes. "They *killed* me, Uncle! Not my body. My souls. I am not the young woman you knew. I am someone, some*thing* else. When I close my eyes, I see them, ripping pieces out of my friends, slinging their intestines around in the air. I see them throw a human liver into the air to watch it spatter when it hits the ground. I watch them urinate into Mist Finger's eye sockets over and over and over again. Those things fill my souls. Knowing that, do you really think I can just step out of here, marry some young man, and be the woman I once was?"

He pursed his lips, allowing the sting in her words to chill his souls. "No, Niece. Of all people, I understand." He paused, waiting, knowing that she was watching him, trying to read his pensive expression.

"But you don't agree with me," she said bitterly.

"I agree with your goal, yes."

"But?"

"I don't think you will accomplish much." He cast her a sidelong look. An old, often discarded plan surfacing between his souls. *Is she the one? Could she do it?*

"Why is that, Uncle?"

"Because in the end you may kill one or two, maybe even three or four before they find you and kill you. It has been tried before. Your actions are those of a mosquito. You draw only a little blood before they swat you and go on about their business."

He could see the hardening in her eyes, the distrust mingled with suspicion that he knew something she didn't. "What other way is there?"

If you tell her, if she accepts, you will be condemning her to death. The memory of the endless faces came back to haunt him, as if all those long-dead eyes were watching, waiting. Hatred stirred like a serpent in his breast.

She was expecting him to try and talk her out of it, so his answer caught her by surprise. "I don't know if you are strong enough, dedicated enough. I have waited, planned, and hoped, but until now no one has impressed me with their dedication to our people. None of the other clans would have permitted it, not with the risk to their young woman."

"What risk?"

"The risk entailed in truly harming our enemy. Oh, I don't mean killing some stray fisherman, or some woman out digging for ground potatoes. I mean striking into the heart of one of their clans. Wounding their pride, soul, and spirit."

"How would this be done?"

Is her life worth it? And even if she succeeds, will it make a difference in the end? He ignored her, allowing an expression of satisfaction to change the lines in his face as he imagined the consternation among the Sun People.

"Uncle?"

He drew a breath, letting her stew, then asked, "What was the name of the one who captured you?"

"White Bird."

"Yes, of the Owl Clan. He has just been made Speaker. I've heard that that foul beast Mud Stalker has offered two of his clan's women in marriage. Indeed, quite a name the young White Bird is making for himself."

"How do you know that?" Anhinga was up on one elbow, watching him now, a dark gleam in her eyes.

"Traders passing along the White Mud River have talked to some of our people who were out casting nets. Word gets around, and White Bird, it seems, is the source of a great many words." He smiled happily. "Owl Clan. He is the son of Elder Wing Heart. Quite a woman, that one. A most worthy adversary."

"How would you strike her?"

"In a way she would never suspect. Through cunning, patience, and misdirection." Yes, she had taken the bait the way a catfish snapped up a minnow.

"What would I have to do?"

"The hardest thing that any hunter must do, wait. Bide your time while opportunities pass before you. You would have to control your hatred, bury it deep like a coal in an ash pit. You would have to accept the man you hate the most, smile into his eyes, open your body to him. But, most difficult of all, you must earn his trust." He slapped his hands on his thighs. "And, that, I fear, is beyond you. Injured though you are at this moment, I don't know if you have the true dedication of the souls to really harm this White Bird and his clan."

"Then you do not know me very well, Uncle." She flashed him a defiant glance, hands knotted. "I Dream of seeing him bent down, in tears, blood running from wounds I have dealt him."

"It's a nice Dream." He shrugged. "But if you succeeded, they would kill you—kill you in a most unpleasant way. For that reason, I can't let you do this."

"I am already dead."

"Yes, for the moment. But if you stay here, I think you will heal in the end. Perhaps even smile again."

She looked away. "You don't know the things I saw." She swallowed hard. "Souls don't recover from that."

"I know what you saw." He shrugged. "I just don't know if you really hate him enough to go through with it in the end."

Her hand fastened on his arm, bruising in its intensity. "They took *everything* from me," she hissed. "My brother, my friends, my future. They made me an exile among my own people. I *hate*, Uncle. Deep down between my souls, the burning is there. Upon my honor, upon my souls, I *hate* like no one you've ever known."

"So you hate? Even the weak can hate. In the end it eats them like a liver fluke. From the inside. And ever so slowly." A pause. "If you want to *hurt* them for what they did to you, it would take something more. Something I'm not sure you have within you."

"What?"

"Strength." He was watching her eyes, searching for any hint of dismay or fear when he said, "If you would truly hurt him, go back. Marry him, Anhinga. Be his wife, earn his trust. And then, when the time is right, you may kill him and his mother, too."

Not even a flicker of doubt reflected when she said, "I can do that."

"Are you sure? Do you understand what I'm asking? You must deceive a man you are living with day and night. You must trick him into believing that you love him. Have you any idea how difficult that is?"

She was smiling now, eyes fixed on the distance in her souls. "Uncle, I am strong enough to do this thing. He will never know until it is too late. On the souls of my dead friends, I swear it."

The thing that horrified Mud Puppy the most was his brother's head. The lightning bolt had split the skull, popping it open like the husk surrounding a chinquapin seed. Both of White Bird's eyes protruded, pushed out from inside. No amount of pressing could return them to the sockets so the corpse just stared in a gray-filmed, crab-eyed amazement. The Serpent had managed to wipe the white foam from his lips and press the tongue back in. He had wound the head tight with a length of cord to keep the gaping mouth shut. A seared streak ran from under the jaw, along the side of the throat, across the right chest and stomach to follow the inside of the thigh down through the heel.

White Bird lay on his back, arms thrust out, legs stiff as logs. A faint gurgling could be heard from inside his gut. The way the fire-light from the central hearth flickered over the smooth and tight skin teased Mud Puppy's imagination. Unwilling to dwell on the horrifying corpse, Mud Puppy kept staring up at the sooty rafters, searching in vain for any sight of his brother's souls. They should be hovering up there, twirling around in the haze of smoke, watching, exploring what it meant to be freshly dead and talking with all the other relatives who had preceded him. Mud Puppy saw nothing in the haze that reminded him of White Bird's souls.

The Serpent rocked on his heels, chanting the familiar Death Song that reassured the Dead that they were still cherished members of the lineage and clan. In the rear, Wing Heart was racked in sobs. She lay on her bed, cramped on her side, prostrate in a way that Mud Puppy had never seen before. Water Petal sat beside her, holding one hand, her face streaked by tears. Outside, voices could be heard periodically as kinspeople, friends, and well-wishers dropped by to leave gifts of food, or express their shock and grief at the young Speaker's sudden death.

It can't be true! The words kept repeating in a Dream-like resonance inside Mud Puppy's head. But all he had to do was look at the body an arm's length from his nose, and there was the terrible reality. White Bird was dead. In one instant he was alive, levering soil from the ground, and in the next, his blasted body lay straight-limbed in death.

Mud Puppy swallowed hard. *I told him not to plant the seeds.*

He could sense the Serpent's wary hesitance to work on White Bird. Yes, Power lay all over the body like a glittering spiderweb, shimmering and bright one moment, invisible the next. It radiated like heat from glowing cooking clays.

His mother broke into another violent fit of sobbing, her body writhing on the bedding. Water Petal tried to soothe her, failing miserably.

"My son," his mother's voice rose in a reedy wail.

"Shshsh!" Water Petal smoothed Wing Heart's damp hair. "He's gone, Elder. It just happened. It's no one's fault."

But Mud Puppy knew that it was.

"He's all I had left!" the Elder moaned, her voice breaking as she choked. "*All . . . I had . . . left!*"

The wound in Mud Puppy's breast lay open and jagged. He had loved White Bird, had admired him as the most marvelous of big brothers. It was all right that his mother cried. He wished he could, too, but instead he just sat there, empty-gutted, unable to do more than stare at the ruined body in disbelief.

The Serpent turned, his eyes intent, knowing, as he studied Mud Puppy. That look by itself was more frightening than death.

The unbidden voice inside said, *You are the Speaker now!*

The Serpent smiled absently, as if he, too, had heard.

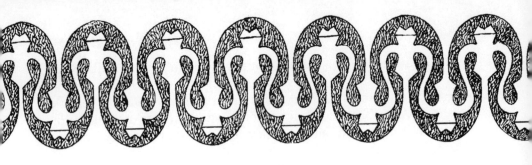

Eighteen

The fire burned hot and yellow, Mud Stalker adding branches anytime it seemed to slow. It was extravagant to burn a fire this hot and large, but it was a night to celebrate.

To Mud Stalker's right sat Red Finger, to his left, on the sleeping bench, Elder Back Scratch hunched, a shawl around her age-bowed shoulders. Young Pine Drop and her sister, Night Rain, sat across from him, their backs to the door as they glanced uneasily back and forth. They looked, and no doubt felt, out of place. Alas, given the status of their birth, the frail innocence of youth had been pulled back to reveal their future in clan leadership and responsibility.

"You are thinking you should be with your husband's body," Mud Stalker said as he fixed them one by one. "Well, he's over in Wing Heart's house. Let them care for him. I've taken the liberty of having White Bird's possessions sent there, with the offer that we will support whatever decision Wing Heart makes about the treatment and disposal of the body."

"Let her burn her house down." Red Finger jerked his head in a nod. "We just built the one Pine Drop and Night Rain are living in." He smiled. "And, it seems that we have to begin the search for new husbands. It isn't often that fortune casts as wide a net for us as it has this day."

"They have a husband lined up," Back Scratch said in her thin and reedy voice.

Red Finger stopped short, a puzzled look on his face. "Who? Surely you're not thinking . . ." He couldn't finish.

Mud Stalker suffered a moment of sadness as Pine Drop's eyes fastened on his. Yes, she understood.

She cried, "You don't really mean for us to marry that *boy*!"

"What?" Night Rain chimed in. "You mean, *Mud Puppy*!"

"That was the arrangement," Mud Stalker replied firmly. "Though we couldn't have guessed the rapidity with which the event might befall us."

"Why?" Red Finger demanded. "Tell me, what is the point of following through with this mad plan? Right here are two young women, in line to be Clan Elder. We could use them to create obligation with Deep Hunter or Cane Frog? Snakes, if you don't want to go there, if it has to be someone in Owl Clan, marry them into Moccasin Leaf's lineage. That would really cut the ground out from under Wing Heart."

"And strengthen another lineage in Owl Clan in the process," Mud Stalker reminded. "You are making the assumption that the enemy we know is worse than the one we don't."

"Mud Puppy is still a boy!" Pine Drop insisted. "Not just a boy— a *peculiar* one at that!"

"Do I have to?" Night Rain asked in a timid voice.

Mud Stalker steepled his hands, glanced at Back Scratch, and nodded. "Nieces, there is more at stake here than either of you knows. For three generations we have watched Owl Clan's authority and prestige grow. Wing Heart and her brother made a formidable team. Given the way young White Bird was developing, it made a great deal of sense to marry the two of you to him. It gave us a way of controlling him, using his talent for our advantage."

"Name a single advantage we would gain by marrying my two cousins, here, to that idiot, Mud Puppy!" Red Finger snorted, his jaw cocked.

"Cousin," Back Scratch said from her place on the bed, "we want Mud Puppy to become the new Speaker. The one thing we can count on for the future is that Wing Heart will do anything to maintain her position on the Council. To do that, she must remain the Owl Clan Elder. If Moccasin Leaf is able to remove her, she has many heirs. It will be a smooth transition. Imagine, if you will, that Wing Heart remains the Elder and, with our help, is able to name this half-wit, Mud Puppy, as Speaker. Now, put the two of them in the Council, say in a debate with Deep Hunter about the redistribution of disputed resources?"

Red Finger made a face. "That boy would be ludicrous."

"Exactly." Mud Stalker ran gentle fingers over the ridges of scar tissue on his forearm. "You see, Wing Heart made a bargain. We intend to honor it."

"At the price of our freedom," Pine Drop muttered, looking away angrily.

Mud Stalker raised an eyebrow. "Oh, come now. He's just a boy."

"I would rather have a man," Pine Drop retorted.

"There are plenty available," Back Scratch said reasonably. "It doesn't matter where you father a child. It still belongs to the clan. Just be discreet for the first year or so. After Wing Heart and the Owl Clan are broken down to size, a divorce will be an easy thing to negotiate. Better yet, it will add to Owl Clan's disgrace."

Pine Drop considered that. Night Rain looked horrified.

"In ten years, Pine Drop, when you finally become Clan Elder," Mud Stalker added, "it will be as the most prestigious Elder in the Council. Not, as it is now, with us in second place."

Night Rain might have been unconvinced, but Pine Drop nodded, saying, "Very well, but you're going to have to run that brat through the Men's House first. I'll not be made a laughingstock by taking a boy into my bed."

"That can be arranged." Red Finger seemed to have seen the logic. "And, who knows?" He fixed his eyes on Pine Drop. "He is young, and not very bright."

"That is supposed to make me feel better?" Pine Drop asked hesitantly.

"I was just thinking." Red Finger's pensive look did little to relieve her. "Could you make him love you? Pine Drop, do you and Night Rain see where I'm going with this? If you could seduce his souls as well as his body, he could grow dependent upon you. He might be induced to rely on your advice in matters of clan politics. It would take finesse and dedication on your part, but little Mud Puppy might just be young enough and dumb enough to grow into a real asset for us."

Pine Drop sat lost in thought, her expression one of distaste. "In other words, you want me to find a way to use him against his own clan."

"He's young, impressionable. You are older than he is, smarter. Handled correctly, an inexperienced boy can be twisted like a length of twine."

"Treat him well in your bed," Mud Stalker suggested. "The rushing of his loins might be your greatest ally."

Night Rain's silent expression tightened. She continued to sit with her hands in her lap, looking glum.

Back Scratch growled. "What's the matter with you young women? What makes you think that lying with a man has anything to do with your own pleasure? I know that a lot of these young people slip off and couple just because they *like* each other. It's a waste, that's what. Breeding is meant to be done for the benefit of the clan, not just so that you can feel pleasure burn through your hips." She smacked her lips in disgust, adding, "The only reason the Sky Beings made it feel good was to compensate for its being a person's duty, that's all."

Mud Stalker's eyebrow cocked as he studied his mother, but he said nothing.

Red Finger, however, blurted, "What is this, Back Scratch? Have the seasons dulled and blunted your memories? Have you completely forgotten all the trouble you caused as a young girl when you slipped away for three moons, supposedly to go Trade with the Ring Villages on the coast? Wasn't the man's name Black Legs?"

"Yes," Mud Stalker nodded, remembering. "Black Legs."

Back Scratch scowled at him. "You weren't even born then."

"No, but the stories persisted for years. I was only a boy, but I recall the opposition to naming you Clan Elder. People still recalled your transgressions, and how you returned pregnant with my older brother." He ignored his mother's hiss of irritation as he looked at Pine Drop and Night Rain. "The Elder may have forgotten what it is like to be young, with your body bursting with desire for a certain man. She is, however, correct with regard to your duty to our clan. You will marry Mud Puppy, and, as Cousin Red Finger points out, you must win him to us." He smiled. "Your elders understand the difficulties. We hope that you will understand the advantages to both yourselves and the clan in making this happen." He glanced back and forth, trying to read behind the young women's dark eyes. "If you must find relief in some other man's bed, come to me, and I will arrange it so that no one grows suspicious."

Pine Drop lowered her eyes. "Yes, Uncle."

He nodded to Red Finger and Back Scratch. "Now that that's settled, I suppose I had best make myself presentable and go deliver our sympathy and support to Wing Heart." As he rose, he turned his attention to the young women once more. "Remember, we are counting on you. That boy is the key to the Snapping Turtle Clan's future. With him, we can break Wing Heart and Owl Clan once and for all."

The afternoon sun sent shining bars of light through gaps in the milky white clouds as they drifted out of the southwest. Moist air hung heavily on the land, barely stirred by a lazy breeze. Moccasin Leaf helped Elder Wing Heart as they tackled the task of preparing a funeral feast. They were in the work area between the burnt-out ruins of Speaker Cloud Heron's house and the Elder's now-abandoned structure.

Moccasin Leaf couldn't make up her mind about Wing Heart. The Clan Elder hunched over a soapstone bowl filled with sticky dough while Moccasin Leaf used a stick to prod at a heating fire burning beside the empty earth oven.

Her son is dead. That would affect anyone. *Dead so quickly after her brother.* But did that explain the woman's complete listlessness?

Moccasin Leaf jabbed pointedly at the cooking clays as she carefully studied Wing Heart from under lowered brows. Wing Heart looked as if a great hollow gaped between her souls. She might have been a husk, her spirit flown away like cottonwood down in the breeze. She worked mechanically, as if to do anything else was too painful.

Dough clung to Wing Heart's fingers, white and sticky. She continued kneading the mixture of little barley, cattail root, dried squash, and smilax root. Earlier that day she had used the pestle and mortar—a fire-hollowed tree stump—to pound the ingredients into mush. The mashed roots had been transferred to the soapstone bowl she now bent over. Adding water and white shooting star blossoms for seasoning, she had reached the right consistency.

Wing Heart hadn't spoken a word all day. Moccasin Leaf shot a glance at the shadowed doorway. *Her son is dead. His bones are just there, on a rick of dry wood. Is this the end of her lineage at last?*

Wing Heart's automatic hands formed the final shape of the root-bread loaf.

"Is it ready?" Moccasin Leaf kept her voice light.

Wing Heart stared with empty eyes. She might not have heard.

Moccasin Leaf used a forked stick to stir the cooking clays. The size of green-husked walnuts, they glowed a dull red among the gray-white coals. A combination of shapes had been placed in the shallowbasined heating fire: Some were biconical, others square and pocked by round indentations made with cane ends. By mixing shapes and sizes of cooking clays, the earth oven's temperature and cooking time could be regulated and tailored to the kind of food being cooked.

"These clays are plenty hot." Moccasin Leaf waited for a reply that did not come. "Wrap your dough, Wing Heart."

The Clan Elder lifted a loaf of dough and placed it in the middle of a large green catalpa leaf. This she curled into a roll before picking up the next and woodenly continuing the process. It was eerie to watch her work that way.

Moccasin Leaf scooped a third of the cooking clays into the curve of a broken ceramic pot before dumping them into the excavated pit of the earth oven. Wing Heart knelt to one side as she finished wrapping the dough. The vacancy in her eyes never wavered as she went through the motions.

The oven had been dug arm deep into the ground and about the width of a forearm across. Moccasin Leaf quickly placed the rolled loaves side by side in the pit, jerking her hands back after each one. "Hot in there."

Wing Heart remained mute.

"Good." Moccasin Leaf was ready with another scoop of coals, which she deposited around the sides of the loaf, retreating as the heat came boiling out of the pit. She scooped the last of the clays onto the piece of broken pot and sifted them over the loaf. "Cover it."

Wing Heart laid a flat section of bark over the hole and sat back, a slight frown on her face.

"Elder, it is plain that your souls are aching. Can I help you?"

Of course it was hard on Wing Heart. This was the second such feast she had prepared for in the last five days. Nor did she risk so much as a glance at her gloom-shrouded house, where White Bird's body, or at least his bones, lay. The dull vacancy in the woman's face sent a shiver up Moccasin Leaf's spine.

"Elder, since I came here, you haven't spoken a word. It might help if you talked about it. Sometimes words can free the grief from where it is lodged between the souls."

That morning the Serpent and Bobcat—their faces streaked with charcoal—had come by with their sharp chert knives. White Bird's flesh had been cleanly removed from the bones and carted off in baskets. By now it had been carried outside the protection of the ridges and laid out at Owl Clan's little hollow in the forest. There, crows, feral dogs, and other carrion eaters would dispose of it. Only the bones remained in the house for White Bird's Dream Soul to watch over.

Wing Heart closed her eyes, and a faint smile graced her lips.

"Are you seeing him, Elder?" Moccasin Leaf asked. "White Bird is alive, his eyes sparkling and brown. I see him that way, too."

Wing Heart said nothing.

Moccasin Leaf shook her head. She deserved some sort of a response. "What are those Snapping Turtle women bringing?"

Wing Heart eyes opened and she stared absently at the ring of blackened ash where her brother's house had once stood. By tomorrow night, her house, too, would be nothing more than that. A second ring of ash. Tomorrow, witnessed by the entire town, she would raise her torch to that roof and incinerate her son.

Then what, Wing Heart? Where does the clan go from there? Did she dare broach the subject? Wing Heart was obviously wounded, her natural craftiness blunted by grief.

"We need to talk."

Silence.

"Despite your grief, someone must attend to the business of replacing the Speaker."

Wing Heart gave her a dull glare.

Moccasin Leaf's gaze slid away. "Half Thorn is ready to represent the clan. He has been preparing for the role of Speaker for years. But for Mud Puppy's coming initiation, he would be here, ready to discuss matters with you."

Wing Heart's eyes seemed to lose focus.

Moccasin Leaf stiffened. "Wing Heart, it is time that you began to place the needs of the clan above your own."

The Clan Elder's lips twitched.

"I think you are hurting, the loss of your brother and son, along with worry about your youngest, has clouded your abilities. It is with this in mind that I have come to offer my services. Perhaps you should take some time for yourself, allow your souls to heal before you resume your duties. You need not face the coming trials alone. We are ready to . . ." At the glittering intensity that suddenly burned in the older woman's eyes, her words went dry.

Wing Heart drew herself up, back stiff; she looked ready to lash out.

"Do not fight me over this, Elder," Moccasin Leaf crossed her arms. "You and your lineage have dominated this clan for three generations. You have done well for us."

Wing Heart's lips moved, her voice little more than an unintelligible mumble.

"Those days are over. You have no heir."

Wing Heart's glazed eyes wavered as she said, "The Speaker will deal with you. The Speaker . . ." The rest trailed away into babble.

"Give it up!" Moccasin Leaf stepped forward. "Half Thorn is the logical choice for the next Speaker. He has the age, maturity, and respect of the clan."

Wing Heart blinked, expression turning empty as she shook her head.

Moccasin Leaf smiled sourly. "Ah, I see. You will do anything to maintain your authority."

Her features sharpened as though she had just awakened. "My concerns are for the best interests of the clan."

"She lies." Wing Heart worked her hands, stepping forward. "We must deal with her, Speaker. This is intolerable."

Moccasin Leaf watched, seeing Wing Heart's souls begin to fray, her control shredding. *Snakes! What is she thinking?*

"Yes, Cloud Heron, I agree. Let's wipe that arrogant face clean of that nasty smug look," Wing Heart muttered. She had balled her fists, back arching, and taken another step forward.

A sudden panic flushed Moccasin Leaf. She swallowed, retreating a step. Panic spurred her as she read Wing Heart's breaking rage in those glittering black eyes.

Don't do this! a pleading voice called from down in the hollowness in Moccasin Leaf's breast. She lifted placating hands. But Wing Heart wouldn't stop, the threshold had been breached. In one more step she would . . .

"Good evening," a pleasant male voice interrupted. Wing Heart stopped short, trembling. Moccasin Leaf spun to find Mud Stalker standing beside Water Petal's house. His mangled arm was cradled in his good left. A smirk bent his lips as his face reflected amusement.

"How long have you been standing there?" Moccasin Leaf demanded tartly to cover her fear-shaken relief.

"Long enough to decide it would be prudent to announce my presence. Bloodshed is always a nasty business. It upsets my stomach, and I'm expecting a delightful feast in honor of a newly made man later tonight." He stepped forward, greased skin gleaming in the fading evening light. "Elder, I have come to collect your son, Mud Puppy. We are ready for his initiation." He nodded at the bark-covered pit, where the first threads of steam carried the odor of baking. "That smells exquisite."

"The boy is up on the Bird's Head with the Serpent." Wing Heart waved absently at the distant mound. She seemed to half stumble as she dropped to a sitting position. Her back against the ramada pole, Wing Heart's expression slowly grew blank, as if when the rage leaked away, it took her souls with it.

Moccasin Leaf stared in fascination. *What is happening to her?*

Mud Stalker, too, seemed amazed at Wing Heart's behavior. Unwilling to be caught gawking, he glanced toward the high mound. "Good. I'm sure the Serpent has prepared him for the ordeal much better than I could."

"And what do *you* care for an Owl Clan boy's initiation?" Moccasin Leaf demanded. "What is he to you?"

Mud Stalker's eyes were half-lidded, his smile neutral and pleasant. "He is about to marry my cousins."

She couldn't stop the shocked look. "You mean to go through with that?"

He studied Wing Heart thoughtfully, then replied, "Oh, yes. Snapping Turtle Clan's alliance with Owl Clan is still solid and irrevocable. Which, if you will excuse me, brings up the matter of Half Thorn's appropriateness as a Speaker."

"You have no business meddling in our clan's decisions." Moccasin Leaf wagged her finger back and forth in chastisement.

"Of course not." Mud Stalker yawned, stifling it with his good hand. "But I do want you to understand that *should* Half Thorn be nominated to the Council as Speaker, his confirmation would be heatedly disputed." A grizzled eyebrow lifted. "It would be unpleasant for him, especially since I believe that Eagle, Rattlesnake, and Frog Clans will vote with me. As to Alligator Clan, well, perhaps, Moccasin Leaf, with the appropriate incentive, you might manage to sway them to your side. Have anything in mind? I'd be happy to mention it to Deep Hunter and Elder Colored Paint, just to see if they'd be receptive. Call it a personal favor to you."

Moccasin Leaf stood frozen. In horror, she shot a look at Wing Heart, but the Clan Elder seemed oblivious.

Saluting with a finger, Mud Stalker said, "Good evening, Elder, and to you, too, Moccasin Leaf. I shall be looking forward to sharing that loaf with you after Mud Puppy's initiation." With that he turned and strode off down the ridge, his course set for the Bird's Head.

"You and he *planned* this? Did you do this to humiliate me?" Moccasin Leaf was shaking, her face working.

Wing Heart's tumbling expressions were her only reaction. She should have been angered, should have lashed out at Mud Stalker for intruding on Owl Clan business. But she had done nothing! They had to have planned this whole performance. The silent grief, the vacant looks, they were all an act, a way of laying Moccasin Leaf and Half Thorn low.

"You are a foul woman, Wing Heart. I came here to help you. For the good of the clan."

"Witch, witch, you're a witch!" Wing Heart began in a singsong voice, her head nodding in time. "Take a war club, break her head. Leave her body for the Dead. Witch, witch, you're a witch, throw her body in a ditch."

Cold fear traced its way down Moccasin Leaf's back as she stiffened her resolve. "I hope you know what you're doing. Because tonight you have made an enemy whom you will never vanquish." She stalked off, stiff-legged, in barely suppressed rage.

Wing Heart watched her go, then flinched as if touched with the whisper of wings in the still air above her. But when the old woman looked up, only the translucent skies of evening extended to infinity.

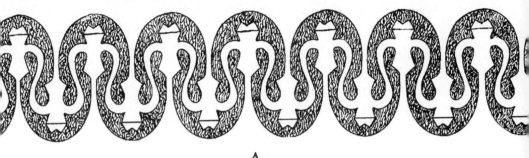

Nineteen

This was the event that boys most eagerly anticipated and desperately feared. Unlike most, who had time to prepare, the initiation into manhood was being thrust on Mud Puppy at a moment's notice. He lay on his back on the split-cane matting beside the great fire in the Men's House.

Normally, he would have been excited to see the interior. Until this moment, it had been forbidden to him. Upon being led within, he had the briefest glance of the colorful masks that hung on the walls, the atlatls, darts, and smooth skulls. The latter, trophies of hard-fought battles, watched him with empty black eyes and grinning brown teeth.

All of the Speakers and lineage heads had come to the Men's House for his initiation. His only relative, Yellow Spider, sat just to his right, a sober concern in his eyes as Mud Puppy had undergone the ritual lashing with palmetto whips. They beat him to drive the child from his body. Then his smarting skin was splashed with salt water to begin the healing.

After that, he had been ordered to lie down on the floor, his head facing the West—symbolic of the fact that one day he, too, would die. The sharp cane cut into his raw back as the Serpent began the process of tattooing his chest. He closed his eyes against the pain. His jaw ached and knotted, and his teeth hurt as he clamped them against the stinging fire that prickled his chest.

Don't be afraid. You cannot show fear. They can kill you if they think you are unworthy. He hadn't wanted to do this. His heart had been thumping like a shrunken drumhead as the Serpent and Mud Stalker led him here. It had taken all of his courage to keep from breaking and running. But for the surprise of the moment, he would have.

Around him the irregular chanting of the men kept time with the clacking of rhythm sticks and thumping of a hide-covered drum. They were all here: the leaders of the clans, prominent men, and lineage leaders. They had dressed in their finery, brightly colored feathers in their hair, faces painted in red, white, blue, yellow, and black. Many had slathered alligator or bear grease on their skin, the mixture containing crushed honeysuckle, redbud, or other flowers to scent their bodies.

The last image before he'd squeezed his eyes closed was of the Serpent bending over him, blotting out the sight of the soot-grimed thatch roof. The copper needle in the old man's hand had gleamed in the firelight. A smile had split the Serpent's flat face as he stared affectionately down at Mud Puppy.

Again and again the copper prick was twirled into Mud Puppy's skin, only to be followed by the old man's blood-caked fingertips as he dipped them in charcoal and rubbed the black color into the wounds.

Mud Puppy would not receive the intricate pattern of dots his brother had been given. He had achieved no accolades in war or Trade. No one sang of his great deeds during the hunt. Instead, only a line of dots running down from the notch between his collarbones to the end of his breastbone and simple arches over each breast were being tattooed into his skin: the marks of manhood.

"You must make no noise, no sound. You must not show the least sign of fear or pain. If you do, they will beat you with clubs and chase you out of the Men's House. You will live the rest of your life in shame. If you cry like a baby, they will be forced to kill you to cleanse the shame from inside the Men's House." The Serpent's words echoed in his head. *"But you do not worry me, Mud Puppy. This is nothing compared to the terrors of that night on the Bird's Head. After Dancing with the mushroom and walking hand in hand with the spirits, this will pass like a dream."*

A whimper rose unbidden in his throat; he swallowed hard to stifle it before it could be heard. No, he must not allow them to see any trace of pain or fear. But how? The pricking needle, the rubbing fingers, the line of fire crossing his chest was growing worse. Panic curled and flexed under his ribs. Within heartbeats, he would be screaming his fear and pain.

"*Talk to me!*" the voice came echoing from deep in his souls.

"Masked Owl?" he asked, hardly aware that he'd spoken aloud. The faintest break in the rhythmic chanting and clacking could be heard.

"Hush!" the Serpent muttered angrily.

The voice told him: "*Keep your eyes closed. Concentrate. I am here. Hovering above you, around you, my wings beating away the pain. Look with your souls. Do you see me?*"

Mud Puppy tried to see Masked Owl's familiar form, but a glowing blackness, a hovering dark shape, flew around him on midnight wings that traced rainbows through the air.

"Many Colored Crow?" Mud Puppy asked. "Is that you?"

"Hush!" the Serpent's voice chastised again.

"*Yes, I have come to watch you be made into a man. You are important to me, young friend. The future lies with you.*" A pause. "*Your brother is here. He says you look like a splayed worm, wiggling and jiggling.*"

At that, Mud Puppy laughed and spoke from his Dream, "That's like you, isn't it, White Bird? You always made me laugh when you teased me."

"*He says to tell you he misses you.*"

"And I miss you, Brother."

"*He asks, Do you remember the time you greased the log bridge across the gully?*"

"We thought Yellow Spider was supposed to come home that way, but it was Uncle Cloud Heron who appeared on the trail. He started across, carrying a sack of poison sumac cuttings to make fish poison out of." His uncle had slipped, and plunged headfirst into the sticky black mud. The subsequent rash had deviled him for weeks. Mud Puppy chuckled out loud, remembering his uncle's mad roars as he and White Bird cowered in the modest concealment of a cane patch and hoped they wouldn't be discovered.

From somewhere in the distance he heard the Serpent make a shushing sound.

"And the worst thing was, we did it to him again, not a year later," Mud Puppy added silently, then burst into giggles.

"Quit that!" the Serpent's voice intruded.

Mud Puppy blinked his eyes open, the last of the giggles dying on his lips. He realized that the room was silent, that the pain in his chest was returning. The Serpent had a puzzled look on his face.

"I was talking to Many Colored Crow," Mud Puppy blurted. In panic he realized that the men lining the walls were staring at him with uneasy brown eyes. "Did I do something wrong?" He tried not to wince at the returning pain.

"No one laughs," the Serpent muttered. "It is supposed to be a test of courage. To be taken seriously."

"I'm sorry." Mud Puppy glanced around nervously. "Forgive me."

He nodded for the Serpent to go ahead, and couldn't help but hear the soft whispering as the chanting began again. The words didn't carry the conviction this time, and Mud Puppy could feel the difference in the air: uncertainty, hesitation. He screwed up his face to mask the renewed pain as the Serpent twisted the needle in the seemingly endless process of making him a man.

Can't I do anything right? When he opened his eyes again, it was to see Mud Stalker staring hard at him from one side, something dangerous and provocative behind his eyes.

"*Beware,*" Many Colored Crow whispered to his souls. "*They will begin to fear you now.*"

Fear me? The notion took him off guard. Since when had anyone feared Mud Puppy?

"*You laughed during your initiation,*" Many Colored Crow reminded. "*They will remember that. And the fact that you talked to me.*"

A sudden fear ran through him.

"*From this night forward,*" Many Colored Crow whispered, "*you must live differently, Mud Puppy. Everything has changed. Hear my words: After tonight they will try to destroy you. Place your trust in your Spirit Helpers, in the animals, and in the plants. Look beyond the skin. See into the souls. You will not find allies in the usual places.*"

"Masked Owl said—"

"*Has he promised you the One? Promised you the Dance? Are you just another of his playthings like your brother, White Bird? A thing to be broken and discarded if you disappoint him?*"

"What?"

"*Let me show you what Masked Owl has in mind for you.*"

The vision came spinning out of the darkness behind his eyes. Death swirled around like a charcoal wind. The odor of putrefaction wafted past his nostrils, while coldness touched his skin. He could sense the huge black shape of a malignant bird hovering above, feel the cold strokes of the spirit bird's midnight wings.

Mud Puppy bolted into a sitting position, pointing up at the charred rafters. "*There!*"

"What?" The Serpent stumbled backward, clawed for balance, and craned his thin neck to peer up at the smoke-hazed ceiling of the Men's House. The clacking music died along with the chanting on everyone's lips. Heads craned, wide eyes fixed on the ceiling.

"A big black crow!" Mud Puppy blinked, his chest pulsing with agony. He could feel blood trickling down the sides of his ribs as he searched the ceiling. "Up there," he sputtered lamely. "Dark, and . . . smelling of death."

In the deepening silence, only the crackle of logs in the fire could be heard.

"Yes, I feel him up there." The Serpent drew a wary breath, letting it out as a hiss. "Leave here!" He pointed a finger at the dark roof. "This place is not for you. This boy is not for you! Go back! Back to the darkness of the West and your lair of corruption."

Mud Puppy could feel the rising tension in the room. He was acutely aware of the stares going from him, to the ceiling, to the Serpent, and back to the ceiling again.

Mud Stalker broke the silence, hardly masking his impatience. "I don't see anything."

"You wouldn't," the Serpent replied softly, his eyes still fixed above.

Mud Puppy cocked his head. "Did you hear that?"

The Serpent frowned. "What?"

"Giant wings beating the air," Mud Puppy told him. "Like the whistling a crow makes when it takes off fast."

The Serpent nodded, as if this made perfect sense.

"What is going on here?" Mud Stalker demanded, stepping forward. "Is this the way a man is made?"

"It is tonight." The Serpent shot him a hot glance. "Power is loose! It is shifting and curling, surrounding us—held back only by these four walls!" Silence filled the room. "Now, watch, you men. Study this boy! Your futures are borne upon his blood!"

The Serpent slipped a hand into the sack hanging from his waist thong and removed a sliver of milky gray chert. "This stone comes from the far north. There, the Earth Beings deposited their semen and it hardened, became this stone." He straddled Mud Puppy's legs, pushed him flat again, and squatted. In two quick motions, the old man slashed a deep cross on the middle of Mud Puppy's breastbone over his heart. "With it, I mark you."

Mud Puppy's souls twisted, and his lungs jumped and pulled at the bottom on his throat. Tears silvered the edges of his vision.

The Serpent raised the bloody flake of stone for all to see, and cried, "Know all, that this man, whom I today name Salamander, is marked with two crossing lines. The cross on his chest reminds us of the four directions. It is the place where things come together, an intersection between Power and the world. From now on, when you see this man, you will think of things coming together, crossing."

"This isn't right," Clay Fat muttered from his clan seat along the south wall.

"No, it isn't," Deep Hunter agreed. "This boy isn't acting right."

The Serpent stalked forward; his hard eyes challenged the Speakers. "It is *very* right. More right than you could know. What has happened here tonight isn't about you, or your scheming clans. This new man, this place where we live, is caught between warring Powers. I will tell you this thing once, knowing you will not understand or heed my warning. This man we have made tonight, Salamander, will have to fight for you all. He will have to do it alone, for most of you will betray him!"

Mud Puppy blinked against the tears and tried to understand the seemingly insane words the Serpent spoke. The slit skin oozed and pulsed in red—the flow of it down into his navel frightening and terrible. He barely registered the looks of uncertainty that passed from man to man, or comprehended how individuals were shifting warily, jaws working. The room roiled like water about to erupt into steam.

The Serpent pointed a gnarly blood-caked finger at Mud Puppy, and cried, "I give you Salamander, son of Wing Heart, of the Owl Clan! Nephew to the great Cloud Heron, brother to the late Speaker, White Bird. Greet him and praise him."

With that, the Serpent pitched the bloody flake into the fire and strode toward the doorway. He walked as though possessed of a terrible purpose; then his thin body vanished into the night beyond the Men's House.

Salamander. I am now called Salamander. That is my man's name.

Through the agony in his chest, Mud Puppy was aware of one or two muttered greetings. One by one, the men seemed to shuffle to their feet, easing away as if they were tendrils of smoke. He barely noticed, his blurring vision fixed on blood that had begun to mat and dry on his chest. The throbbing pain was growing worse, and he could do nothing about it but endure.

"I don't understand what happened here tonight," Mud Stalker said as he bent down and met Mud Puppy's gaze with hooded eyes. "But know that I am your friend, Salamander. Don't forget that. In the coming days you are going to be in need of a friend." He offered his good hand. "Come, let me help you up. Your mother and your late brother's wives have prepared a feast for you."

Yellow Spider appeared by his other elbow. "I don't know what you did, but it got everyone's attention." To Mud Stalker he added, "I'll take his other arm. Let's get him home."

Salamander's souls screamed in agony, but no sound passed his lips as Mud Stalker and Yellow Spider pulled him upright.

The room seemed to sway; and through the pain, an urge to throw up coiled in Salamander's stomach. He fought it, struggling to keep his balance despite the weakness in his knees. Mud Stalker's firm hand stabilized him.

"*They will fear you now,*" Many Colored Crow's voice called through the haze of pain and blood, "*. . . and people always seek to destroy what they fear.*"

Salamander lay on a cane mat in the midday shade behind Water Petal's house. The incisions on his chest burned and ached under the slathering of bear grease. Before rubbing it on, the Serpent had mixed it with a concoction of gumweed and pine resin. The latter, he said, promoted healing and kept the insects away.

So many things were wheeling through his head. From where he lay, he could see the smoking remains of his house. Or, rather, his old house. It had been torched the evening before, in full ceremony, and White Bird's bones had been incinerated along with everything that had been Mud Puppy's. Not only had his few possessions gone up in fire, but so had an entire lifetime. Nothing remained the same.

He kept stumbling over the inevitability of that, eyes focused on the smoking rubble. It was then that Hazel Fire and Jackdaw came trotting along the edge of the embankment, turned onto the ridge, and approached. Their bodies were lithe and lean in the midday sun, muscles flexing and sliding as they trotted forward. Their hair had been pinned to one side as was the manner of their people, and they carried atlatls and darts in their right hands. As they caught sight of Salamander, both waved and turned in his direction.

Salamander managed a smile, but the pain that accompanied the subsequent wave brought a grimace to his face. His chest skin might have been pulled apart given the way it felt.

"Greetings, Salamander," Hazel Fire called as he slowed and led Jackdaw into the cool shade. "It is our pleasure to greet you as a man."

"I am happy to receive you." Salamander smiled at them. "Could I get you something? There's water inside. I think some of the root bread is left." He gasped as he started to sit up.

Jackdaw waved him down. "Don't move, at least, not on our account." The Wolf Trader was frowning at the swollen scabs and pustulant tattoos. "We have come to bid you farewell."

"You are leaving?" Salamander asked. "I hope it's not because of White Bird. He wouldn't want you to go just because of what happened to him."

"It isn't just that," Hazel Fire said as he hunched down and leaned his back against the wall. "The water in the swamp is beginning to drop. People have been more than generous. We can't carry all that we've been given in Trade as it is."

"White Bird was our partner," Jackdaw added.

Hazel Fire gave Salamander a serious inspection. "He was more than that. He was married to my sister in my own village. That strengthens the tie between us. It is for that reason that we are leaving you all the goods we cannot carry. Some we have given to Yellow Spider. The rest are yours to dispose of as you will."

Salamander frowned. "This isn't necessary."

"You will need it," Jackdaw replied, squatting and resting his wrists on his knees. "You should hear the talk. People are saying all kinds of things about you, about your mother, and what Mud Stalker is planning."

"I don't want any part of it." Salamander looked away, a sadness in his breast.

"No, but it is being thrust upon you." Hazel Fire rubbed his back against the rough mud wattle, scratching between his shoulder blades. "We have learned a great many things while we have been here in your town. You were kind to us, Mud Puppy."

"Salamander," Jackdaw reminded. "They call him Salamander now."

"Your brother spoke to us of you." Hazel Fire studied the smoking ruins of Wing Heart's house. "But I don't think he understood who or what you are."

Salamander cocked an eyebrow as Hazel Fire pulled the little red owl from his pouch.

"This owl has brought me Dreams." He held it before his sober brown eyes, studying it thoughtfully. "I have thought about the day you talked to the alligator. You wear Power the way other men wear a cloak."

"I'm just me." But he wasn't sure he wanted to be himself any longer. Nothing led him to believe that things were going to get better. Many Colored Crow speaking to him at his initiation had frightened him. As of that moment, the Spirit World had taken on a threatening quality.

"Your people see you through slitted eyes." Hazel Fire turned the little polished owl in the light. "Sometimes it takes a stranger to look at a man with his eyes wide open. I speak for all of us when I tell you we are honored to know you."

"I had a Dream last night," Salamander said cautiously. "It concerned you."

"I would hear your Dream." Hazel Fire gave him a clear-eyed look.

"In it I saw you reach the mouth of a great river that fed in from the east. High bluffs rise on that eastern bank. Raiders lie in wait there. They have a camp on a stone outcrop that overlooks the Father Water. From there they can see who passes on the river."

"You saw this?" Jackdaw asked uneasily. "From the river?"

"No, I was riding on Masked Owl's wings. Circling high above. These raiders, they wear black stripes on their faces and do not honor the Power of Trade. In the Dream, you passed the mouth of that river at night and no harm came to you. Do you know this place?"

Hazel Fire nodded. "It sounds like the mouth of the Great Eastern River that feeds the Father Water. What if we were to pass during the day?"

"The raiders will sweep down on you. In loaded canoes, you will not be able to outrun them. On the open water, flooded as that place will be, you will make easy targets."

"Why do you tell us this thing?" Jackdaw asked, clearly uneasy.

"You are my friends." Salamander smiled. "You are good men. Kin to me through marriage. We are bound by the gift of that carved owl. I would have you return in safety to my brother's wife and his little daughter."

"You know that Lark had a girl?" Hazel Fire narrowed a skeptical eye.

"She has a birthmark, like a flower petal on her hip." He pointed to the fleshy swell of his own hip to mark the place. "If you pass that place I have told you of with great care, you may yet see that mark on my brother's daughter."

"I would dearly like to see that." Hazel Fire had turned his attention to the gleaming stone owl. "We will deliver those goods to your house, Mud Puppy."

"They call him Salamander now," Jackdaw reminded.

"Yes, yes." Hazel Fire shot Salamander a sidelong gaze as he raised the small carved owl in his fingers. "We live far away, my friend. I know not what I can ever do for you, but by the Power in this owl, I will do what I can to help you."

"I ask only for your Trade. That, and that you beware at the mouth of the Great Eastern River. They will be waiting for you there. It would pain my souls if they caught you."

"We hear your words, Salamander. And are warned." Hazel Fire gave him a wary scrutiny. "You are headed for great things, young friend."

He smiled sadly. "Greatness and tragedy seem to embrace like lovers."

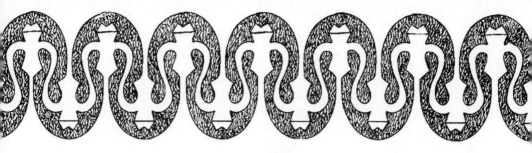

Twenty

Wreaths and streamers of rain cascaded from the low bank of afternoon clouds as Pine Drop, Night Rain, and Mud Stalker stood on the high embankment above the canoe landing. In silence they watched the Wolf Traders lean into their paddles, pushing their heavily laden canoes toward the channel that would take them east to the Father Water.

Yellow Spider accompanied them in his empty canoe, leading the way lest they get lost in the backswamps.

A number of people had come to wish the Traders off on their long journey homeward. The three Wolf canoes bulged with goods produced in Sun Town: woodwork, rope, netting, black drink, smoke-cured alligator meat, red snapper, black drum, smoked conch, and other delicacies from the gulf that were Traded through Sun Town via its extended clans.

"I wish it was Yellow Spider that we were going to marry," Night Rain whispered. "He's a handsome young man. He's been to the north and has prospects for a great future."

"That is precisely why Salamander is the one you must marry," Mud Stalker replied. "I could not have planned better myself. You should have seen the young fool. He had half the Men's House in a panic before his initiation was complete. Even the Serpent, who believes in the young fool, was driven away by the rantings."

"Your words don't inspire us with confidence," Pine Drop noted sourly.

"You don't need confidence," Mud Stalker added in a precise tone. "All you need is to think of your future, and the clan's."

"How long will we have to endure this?" Night Rain asked.

"Just until Owl Clan is discredited," Mud Stalker replied. "And, given the anger growing between Wing Heart and Moccasin Leaf, that may not be as long as I had originally thought."

"So when do we marry this half-wit?" Pine Drop had crossed her arms under her pointed breasts.

"Today, if you'd like." Mud Stalker turned to study his young kin. At the expression of dismay on their faces, he burst into laughter.

The forest rose tall and green. Interlocking branches heavy with the bright growth of spring leaves cast a perpetual gloom over the leaf-matted earth. Wraiths of mist, like ghost fingers, wove their way between moss-encrusted trunks whose thick girths were wrapped and wound with vines. Mushrooms poked colorful heads from the moldy soil and broke through the thick and spongy layer of leaf mat. Water dripped from above, pattering here and there. Occasional patches of heartleaf, mayapple, and native pipe lived in the gloom. Dead saplings, their battle for the light long lost, and rotting corpses of long-felled giants scattered the forest floor.

Salamander slipped silently through the trackless depths. The few sounds of his passing were immediately masked by the endless noises of living forest. Birds sang in a melodic cacophony. The chirring of insects and the chattering of the squirrels fought in direct competition with the rustle of the highest leaves. Occasional discarded flower petals came drifting down from the gum, ash, and maple as new seeds were born in swelling green pods.

Salamander stepped carefully, his bare feet rising and falling with the grace of a cat's. He tightened his grip on his atlatl where it rested in his right hand. He wasn't particularly good with the weapon, but only a fool wandered the forest unarmed. The danger posed by the occasional black bear or cougar, though slight, was not to be discounted; but nothing could make a young man feel more like an idiot than to watch a deer, raccoon, or porcupine walk out, present a perfect target, then fade away into the forest. Meat was forever at a premium.

He slowed, bending his head back to stare up at the high canopy. Sunlight filtered through layers of green, speckles of light but mere pinpricks that glittered in the heights. The branches were interwoven with vines of honeysuckle, cross and trumpet vine, fox grape, and greenbrier until they resembled webs. Filling his lungs, Salamander took in the scents of the forest, damp, sweet, and perfumed.

No one would find him here. Salamander allowed his souls to relax and enjoy the solitude of the forest. In the dense isolation of the endless trees, he had time to sort out the painful vortex of the last few weeks.

Masked Owl and Many Colored Crow? I am caught between warring Powers. The Serpent had as much as told him so when he incised that painful and deep cross in Salamander's chest. *Why did they choose me? What do they want of me? Why do they call on a mere boy?*

He still had trouble thinking of himself as a man. The name Salamander echoed oddly in his ears—but he still held hopes that one day the Earth Being might deign to become his Spirit Helper.

In the midst of horrific events young Mud Puppy had been plucked from obscurity by both the forces of Power and the dealings of the clans, and in one fell swoop thrust from a boy's preoccupations into the role of an authoritative man. All this while Spirit Power loomed ever larger in his life.

Why, for instance, had he been given the vision of the Swamp Panther raid? Why had he been told to free the captive girl? Why had Mud Stalker insisted on becoming his mentor—and worse, remained intent on seeing him married to his brother's widows? The sensation was similar to being held by the wrists and spun around so fast that his feet had flown off the ground. He was being spun faster and faster until the world was a blur and his arms were aching from the tug.

What if the Powers that held him suddenly let go? Would he fly off like a cast dart to land who knew where?

He swallowed hard, the fingers of his left hand prodding tenderly at the scabs on his chest. Where the wounds were swollen and inflamed, his touch produced yellow pus and a sting.

He took the faint trail down an embankment, crossed a sluggish creek, and climbed the other side. Figuring himself to be deep enough in the forest that no one would stumble upon him, he seated himself on a fallen beech tree, laid his weapons to one side, and removed a bit of red stone from his pouch. Using a chert flake he began the laborious process of carving the round body of another of his endless line of owls.

A thought startled him. Why owls? He had been carving them ever since he had been a child. Had it been happenstance that he had settled on the form, or was there more to it? Something he knew

down in his souls but had ignored on a higher level? He glanced up
at the green canopy again.

*How long have you been talking to me in my Dreams, Masked Owl?
Have I only now started to remember?*

No answer came to him, but he felt the short hairs on his neck
prickling. Yes, he had been having Dreams, hadn't he? Dreams he
couldn't quite remember during the waking moments.

Layers upon layers, deceit and guile, death and life, and him right
in the middle of it—without a clue as to why, or what he was supposed to do. A sick feeling ate at his stomach. Was he, too, destined
to be a pile of bones within a couple of weeks? Were his muscles,
skin, and organs to be stripped away by the Serpent's sharp chert
knife and carried out beyond the ridges for the scavengers?

He could imagine his bones: red, raw, and bloody, with bits of
tissue clinging to them. In the shadowed depths of the hut, they
looked dark where they rested on the broken branches and other
lengths of firewood. The thought amused him that his lineage within
Owl Clan was running out of houses to burn. Only Water Petal's
remained, and she would need it when the baby came.

The whirring of the forest almost swallowed the knock of wood
on wood. Salamander froze, his eyes searching the shadowed forest
around him.

There, the faintest trace of movement! He barely caught a
glimpse through the trees. Something moved on the trail he had just
come up. With cautious hands he retrieved his atlatl and fingered a
dart into the hook.

Bits of color and movement flickered between the boles, and then
she stepped into the clear. Young, a newly made woman's kirtle
swaying at her hips, she plodded steadily forward, eyes on the trail
before her. A tumpline crossed her forehead, the thick straps leading
to a heavy pack that centered on her hips just above the buttocks.
She poked at the ground with a walking stick in her right hand, her
left swinging in time to her gait. Long black hair had been braided
and curled at the side of her head, held in place with a striking blue
feather from a jay's tail. In the dim light, grease made her rounded
breasts shine, the brown nipples conelike. Her pretty face expressed
sadness and desperation.

"Spring Cypress?" Salamander asked softly.

She stopped short, eyes flashing this way and that until she dis-
cerned his form on the half-rotten log. "Mud Puppy?"

"It's Salamander now," he told her wearily. "They made me a
man." He indicated her kirtle. "And I see that you have just been
released from the Women's House."

Her lips wiggled as if words were running in her head that she refused to say. In the end, looking wary, she asked, "What are you doing out here?"

"Escaping."

A weight might have lifted from her, relief rising to be mimicked in a smile. "You, too? I'm so glad to hear that." She swung the heavy pack down and walked over to him, her shining eyes on his. "We could go together. Anywhere. I thought I'd go north. Follow the White Mud River up into the mountains. I don't know what we'd do there, but I'm sure we could find a valley, someplace out of the way where the hunting was good and enough plants grew that we could feed ourselves."

Salamander blinked hard, trying to fathom what she was saying. "You mean, you're running away? Leaving Sun Town? For good?"

Her mouth hung open for a moment, the words forgotten, then she blurted, "You said you were escaping!"

"I am. But just for the day. I needed to get away! My chest hurts, my brother and uncle are dead, and everyone wants to marry me off to those horrible Snapping Turtle women."

A sudden fear brightened her eyes. "I just told you where I was going."

Salamander sighed and returned to his work on the little red owl. He had the head mostly right. The two triangular ears, the round eyes and pinched beak were visible. From the neck down, however, the wings and protruding belly were owl-like only if the viewer had a good imagination.

"You'll tell!" Spring Cypress looked crestfallen. "It means I have to go somewhere else."

"People are going to be very concerned about you. What about Clay Fat and Graywood Snake? They are your relatives. If you just up and disappear, they'll be worried sick."

The way her probing brown eyes were watching him made him nervous. "Mud Puppy?"

"Salamander."

"Salamander? Would you come with me?"

"Why?"

"They want me to marry Copperhead."

"He's a cruel old man!"

"I don't want to marry *anyone*! I wanted to marry White Bird. I loved him!" Her fists were knotted, her pretty face strained as tears edged her eyes.

"Tell them no."

"I *can't*! My uncle, Clay Fat, has made some kind of agreement with Mud Stalker. The Elder, my grandmother, has agreed." She shook her head, staring down at the damp carpet of fallen leaves under her small brown feet. "My life is ruined, Mu—Salamander. First the Snapping Turtle Clan took White Bird from me, then the lightning made it final."

"You're not the only one who lost him."

She sniffed and squared her shoulders as she looked at him. "I couldn't stand it the night he was married."

"I saw you paddle off in your canoe."

She nodded. "I went away, out into the swamp. I just wanted to be alone. I stayed away all night, but the cramps started at dawn, so I came back. Announced myself, and Aunt Turtle Mist took me straightaway to the Women's House until my moon passed. That's where they told me that I would marry Copperhead. Tonight."

Salamander shifted uneasily, wondering what to say, what to do to help her. Snakes, a young man didn't just interfere with another clan's internal affairs. Worse, when he looked up at her, something deep in his souls was terribly aware of her slim body and the way her woman's kirtle hung slightly askew below the indent of her navel. Even when he looked away the eyes of his souls retraced her thin waist and shapely stomach. The curve of her firm breasts gleamed in the light.

"I'll do anything if you'll go with me." Her words were spoken softly, and he could sense her presence as she stepped to him. The faint odor of her carried on the warm moist air. His heart began to quicken.

"What?" He looked right up into her large brown eyes. He might have been paralyzed, pinned in place by the mixture of longing and desperation there.

"Anything." Her fingers were plucking at the knots that held her kirtle in place, and before Salamander could understand, the pale fabric loosened and slipped down the round curve of her hips. "I'm a woman, now. You are a man."

He caught the falling of his jaw in time to keep from gaping like an idiot, his gaze stopped short on the black triangle of her pubic hair. It glistened, cupped in that Y of soft brown flesh. He found himself unaccountably short of breath.

She began gently stroking the sides of his face, her fingertips dancing lightly on his skin. Had anything ever stoked such a fire within him before? Dream-like, she bent until her face was but a handbreadth from his. His souls were falling into her, drawn into that brown magical stare. Tremors ran down his arms and legs.

"Lie with me, Salamander." She was pulling him down onto the folds of the kirtle. An excitement, half fear, half anticipation had begun to pound with each beat of his heart. He shivered as her strong fingers pulled the restraining breechcloth away from his hardened penis. A gasp escaped his lips as she wrapped her fingers around his tingling shaft.

She was drawing him onto her as she lay back on the crumpled kirtle and the cushion of leaf mat. A flood of energy bore him along.

He would never know whether it was the sting in his abused chest or the pain deep within her eyes that stopped him. He winced as he pulled back and shook his head. "No."

She propped herself on her elbows, staring at him like he'd just lost every wit in his body. "What do you mean, no? Do you know how many men would give anything to lie with me?"

Salamander scrambled backward, awkwardly shoving his throbbing penis behind his breechcloth. "It's not that. I mean, you're beautiful."

Her expression collapsed, soft sobs causing her breasts to heave in a way that completely unsettled Salamander. "Then you'll tell on me?"

"No." In defeat he rose and walked in an aimless circle, shaking out his arms and hands the way a runner did when he needed to shed excess energy. "Go on, run away. I'll tell no one where you're going."

"Why?" Even wounded she remained suspicious.

"Because I wish I could go with you."

"Then why don't you?" she demanded. "That way I wouldn't have to go alone."

He closed his eyes, a terrible longing growing inside him. "I can't."

"Why?"

He looked at her, still achingly aware of her gorgeous body, so young and bursting with charms. She had been forever beyond him, the woman his brother would marry. "I cannot explain it. I just can't go with you, that's all."

"Afraid?" She cocked her head, those glistening dark eyes trying to read behind his souls.

He shrugged. "Maybe. Yes, that's it." But he dare not tell just what he was afraid of. "And besides, you don't want me, Cypress. Not really."

"Then why am I lying here on my back?" She spread her hands in frustration and sat up, irritation replaced with exhaustion. "I would have taken you, Mud—Salamander. I've never lain with a man before."

"You're not thinking well."

"And you are? They say that you giggled and saw things during your initiation. They say you're a half-wit. Given what just happened here, I'm not so sure they aren't right."

"You didn't want me just now."

"Then what did I want?" She was glaring at him.

"A dream, Spring Cypress. You were desperate for a dream. The trouble is, dreams don't come that easy."

She was frowning at him the way she might if his words made no sense to her. "So, what? Are you going back to tell Uncle Clay Fat that I'm running?"

He shook his head, an unexplained sadness rising to replace the desire his manhood had pumped through his body. "No. I'm giving you this." He bent down and picked up the partially carved owl from the moss-spotted log. "I wasn't finished with it yet, but you can tell what it is."

She took the stone figure and held it between thumb and forefinger as she inspected it. "An owl," she noted. "Yes, I can see that. What is it for?"

"For you." He tried to shrug off the confusion that clouded his ability to think. "Unfinished. Just like you are." He waved. "Go on, Spring Cypress. If anyone asks—which they won't—I'll tell them I haven't seen you since the night my brother was married."

She stood, reached down, and whipped her kirtle up with a fluid motion. He watched as she wrapped it about her hips and cinched the cords that held it in place. With slender hands she rearranged her hair, flicking bits of leaf from the glossy black braid before repinning it with the blue jay feather. "You're a strange one, Mud Puppy."

"Salamander."

A smile bent her full lips. "Salamander. Odd that they'd name you that."

"People underestimate salamanders."

She considered that as she walked back and picked up her pack. Before slinging it onto her back and fixing the tump line, she placed the little red owl carving into a pocket. "I've heard that some salamanders can change their colors."

"I've heard that, too."

She smiled wearily at him. "Good luck with your colors, Salamander. I thank you for this thing you're going to do for me. If you ever need me, I'll be in the mountains up in the northwest. When you find your way, come looking for me."

"I will."

He watched as she recovered her stick and started off again. She never turned, never looked back, just walked onward until her form was hidden by the endless trees.

"Watch over her, Masked Owl." He fought the terrible desire to pick up his weapons and run after her.

Maybe I just don't have that kind of courage.

The Serpent

*C*ourage?

Why is it that humans think bravery is either leaping into a fight or running away from everything that comforts them? The most courageous act a human being can perform is to truly love another person.

There are those who would have us believe that love is easy, that it comes childlike from our hearts and floods out as effortlessly as rain falls from the fingers of the Sky Beings.

That is just foolishness.

Love is standing guard all the time. It is becoming a world to yourself for another's sake, and learning to share its most intimate corners. There is nothing more courageous than that. And nothing more achingly beautiful.

But I am an old man. I have failed at truly loving another person so many times that I know the misery of cowardice.

This boy is just about to find out.

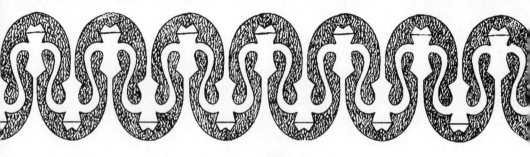

Twenty-one

Pine Drop watched the gentle rain fall and tried not to think about what was happening. People stood in a ring just across the borrow pit from her house. Most wore flat bark hats that shed the rain. In her damp hands she held the offerings of food and turned toward Salamander. His gaze was fixed on the people as though they were a writhing den of water moccasins instead of his kin and hers. A swamp rabbit caught in a snare might look like that. Panic bulged behind his round brown eyes as he took the wooden platter from her hands. He raised the plate that carried the first meal he would eat as a married man. "By accepting this meal . . . I tie my life . . . with that of Pine Drop . . . and . . . and . . ."

"Night Rain," Pine Drop growled.

"Night Rain," he agreed, "daughters of Sweet Root, who is the daughter of . . . of the great Clan Elder, Back Scratch. My clan is now their clan, their clan is now mine. I accept these women . . ."—he seemed to pause forever—". . . as my wives, to share with equally, to comfort and care for."

In the now-familiar ritual, Pine Drop and Night Rain held their hands demurely before their kirtles, and cried out in unison, "We accept this man, Salamander, of the Owl Clan, as our husband. In doing this, we bind ourselves to him and to his clan. Let it be known among all people that we are married."

"Let it be known!" Mud Stalker called from his place. He carried a war club for the occasion, and Pine Drop wasn't sure if it was for ceremony or to whack Salamander should he suddenly bolt from the proceedings.

"Let it be known!" Wing Heart mumbled absently from her place on the east. The Clan Elder's eyes were oddly glazed, her expression remote, as if lost in other memories. Something about her sent a shiver down Pine Drop's spine.

Salamander's cousin, Water Petal, stood to Wing Heart's right. The woman looked worried, her stare darting back and forth between Salamander and Wing Heart. She had worn a small hat against the rain. It barely shielded her face, let alone her protruding pregnant belly, which was now rain-streaked over her kirtle. The woman's time was close, her belly button protruding.

How long until I look like that? Pine Drop glanced sidelong at Salamander and used all of her will to keep from showing her disgust. Not only was he scrawny, but he still looked like the foolish boy he had been but a week ago. *Him? Sharing my bed? After the likes of Blue Feather—and even his brother? Never!* But she knew it was a lie.

"Let it be known!" the gathered people shouted. This time there was no smiling and slapping each other on the back. Despite the promise of food, people seemed to slip away like stringers of mist.

Wing Heart, her face still a mask, simply strode off, heading northward across the clan grounds for her own territory. To Pine Drop's surprise, it was the cousin, Water Petal, who leaned over to Salamander, and said, "If you need to talk, Cousin, come see me." And with that she gave him a sympathetic pat and started after Wing Heart, her gait more of a waddle to compensate for that enormous belly.

Pine Drop shot her uncle a hard look, but his expression urged caution in return.

"Come," Pine Drop said, as the last of the observers turned for their own dry homes or the protection of ramadas. "That food is getting soaked."

"Let it," Night Rain muttered, sharing her unease as her glance stole back and forth between Pine Drop and Mud Stalker. Salamander stood as if roots had grown out of his feet. She took the tray from his hands and ducked into the house she had shared with White Bird for only one night. Now the form of his little brother darkened the doorway. A moment later Night Rain ducked in and made irritated sounds as she wrung the water from her hair. "You'd think we could have waited until the sun came out."

"Uncle wanted this done," Pine Drop retorted as she seated herself behind the fire and dropped two pieces of wood into it. As the flames rose and cast yellow light over the interior, she studied her new husband. He was standing like a bulge on a pot, hands nervously twisting above his breechcloth.

"Sit." Pine Drop pointed to her right. "You, too, Night Rain. Come sit here beside me."

Night Rain at least did as she was told. Salamander seemed not to have heard, his eyes fixed on the fire. She caught his horrified look as he shot a glimpse at the pole beds behind her.

"Will you sit, *Husband!*" she chided, and slapped the floor to her right. "We have things to discuss."

He swallowed hard and lowered himself the way he might if a nest of red ants were near.

"What things?" he asked.

She could see his pulse jumping at the base of his thin neck. The oddly cut cross on his chest looked infected, swollen and angry.

"First, there are rules to be followed in this household." She took the tray from behind her and handed it to him. "Eat. Or do you want to mock the marriage ritual the way you mock everything else?"

"I don't mock everything."

"Oh?" she arched a brow, aware that Night Rain was watching silently, her lips twitching. "You didn't giggle during your initiation?"

"What happens in the Men's House is not to be spoken of to women." He looked sullen.

"Don't be a fool." She reached back for a buffalo-horn spoon and used it to scoop up some of the mashed squash. This she handed to Night Rain, indicating that she eat. "I suppose that men never hear the gossip from the Women's House, either."

Salamander said nothing, but did manage to at least plop a soggy bit of cattail-root bread into his mouth.

"As to the rules," Pine Drop continued, "they are as follows: First, you will not speak of the things that happen inside this house. Second, what you hear of Snapping Turtle Clan dealings are not to be shared with your relatives from Owl Clan. Third, neither I nor my sister will be made into fools. Do you understand?"

He shook his head, looking clearly uncomfortable.

"People are already talking out there." She gestured with her hand toward Sun Town. "Night Rain and I are laughingstocks. They are saying, 'Married to that half-wit, can you imagine?' Well, I won't have that. My sister and I will not be singled out for their pity or their ridicule."

Salamander swallowed his bit of bread.

"When you are asked about our marriage, you will simply answer that things are fine, do you understand?"

He nodded again.

"I want to remind you that you married into Snapping Turtle Clan. You have come here, to our territory, to live in *our* house. While you are here you will obey my instructions, is that clear? If not, well, it won't be a pleasant thing. Do you understand?"

What was it about his innocent face? He looked like a child with his hand caught in the stewpot. "Well, can you speak, except to spout nonsense?"

He nodded again.

Pine Drop rolled her eyes and glanced at Night Rain. Her sister looked absolutely miserable.

"One last rule, Salamander." She gave him a hard squint. "I understand that you have obligations to your clan. I don't expect you to sit around here, lazy as a bead on a necklace. Go off and do what you need to do. We would appreciate it if you could bring back some fish, game, or roots on occasion. It would make things look normal here. But you come home every night, do you understand?"

He frowned at her, obviously confused.

Snakes! Did she have to sound everything out for him? "One of us will always be here. So you come home. We would not like to find out that you were slipping off and spending the night at some other woman's house." She steepled her fingers and smiled. "Like I said, we will not be humiliated by you, so hear this, and remember it: If we find out that you've been slipping your hard little worm into some other woman, we'll use a serrated stone knife to cut it off. Are we understood?"

He gulped and nodded, looking as if he'd grown gills.

She sighed in resignation then. "Very well, Night Rain, hand me that cloth. Those wounds on his chest are oozing, and I will not have him dripping all over my breasts while we finish this marriage business."

At his increasing panic, she added, "You can carry out that part of your obligations, can't you?"

He was looking longingly at the door. Sweat, or was it old raindrops, beaded on his forehead.

The air was hot and muggy, one of those early-summer days when the sun burns down out of a white-hot cloudless sky. Heat rolled across the grassy plaza to the east of the Council ramada, where Salamander stood next to his mother. He didn't want to be here, listening to Mud Stalker singing his praises to the Council. He wished he were far away, deep in the swamp, floating with the alligators.

He stared thoughtfully out past the crowded people beyond the Council House. They had come to watch his appointment as Speaker for Owl Clan. The crowd was huge, many of them from distant camps who had come for the solstice ceremonies and heard the amazing news that a mere boy was being made Speaker for the influential Owl Clan. They hadn't come out of respect for him or his clan. They were here for the spectacle.

By turning his head he could catch occasional glimpses of the ball game practice through the press of spectators. The Northern Moiety team practiced pitching in their half of the plaza.

On the last day of the solstice ceremonies, after the masked processions, the Dances, and feasts, the ritual game would be played. To win, one side had to score four goals. A deerskin ball was flipped or batted back and forth between the players by means of a long stick, flattened on one end. The object was to fling the ball across the borrow pit and onto the first ridge of the opposing moiety.

The stakes were high. Clans, lineages, and families bet huge piles of food and possessions against the outcome. Losing could leave entire clans destitute. It was such a loss that had first led Frog Clan into their slow spiral of decay. During the last two years the Southern Moiety had achieved victory, and, given the looks of the Northern team's practice, it would happen again this year.

The games were the culmination of the annual summer solstice ceremony, which in turn was one of the most important observances of the year. People came from all of the dispersed camps as far away as the gulf coast. They brought canoe-loads of food and locally manufactured goods to be wagered on the great ball game. It was a time of gift giving, fulfilling obligations, feasting, and socializing. Marriages were brokered between widely scattered clanspeople, and news was dispensed.

Salamander thought of the influx of people who came to solstice like a wave that washed into Sun Town, swirled around in the ceremonies, then washed back out again, renewed and revitalized. It not only reminded the People who they were, but invigorated them with the knowledge that Sun Town was indeed the center of their world. So long as Sun Town remained, the People could return to their roots.

The crowd closed in, blocking his view of the players. The last glimpse had been of Yellow Spider sprinting up to battle with a young woman from Alligator Clan for possession of the ball. Across the distance Salamander thought he heard the clacking of their sticks as they struck and parried.

"Pay attention!" Water Petal hissed.

Salamander blinked, shook himself, and looked back to the open center of the Council House. There, under the brutal sun, Mud Stalker had his good hand raised. He was turning slowly, meeting the gaze of the Council members one by one as he looked at them.

Salamander followed his gaze around the circle, past Frog Clan, Alligator Clan, into his own eyes, and then beyond the entrance to Snapping Turtle Clan, where Pine Drop and Night Rain sat behind old Back Scratch, looking both hot and embarrassed. Then Thunder Tail from Eagle Clan and Clay Fat from Rattlesnake Clan rounded out the circle.

"We face an unusual circumstance," Mud Stalker stated matter-of-factly. "Young Salamander has my confidence. He is, after all, brother to the dead Speaker, White Bird. Nephew to Cloud Heron. He is the son of Clan Elder Wing Heart."

Salamander glanced up, but his mother, standing a step to his left, was staring off into the high distance. The slight frown on her forehead made Salamander follow her gaze up past the open roof and into the white sky. The only thing he could see were two far-off vultures wheeling around in circles in the hot air.

"I am happy to cast my vote to acknowledge Speaker Salamander to this Council." Mud Stalker balled his upraised hand into a fist. To Salamander it looked more like the expression of victory than anything else.

As if in a blur, he heard the voices of the Clan Elders and Speakers calling out in favor.

"Nay!" came the strident cry.

Salamander started, following all eyes as they turned to Deep Hunter. The Alligator Clan Speaker stepped out with his sister, Colored Paint.

It was Colored Paint who said, "Alligator Clan believes that the Council would be better served by more mature leadership. We want it stated on this occasion, that although we are outvoted, we believe the acceptance of a mere boy does not serve the Council well."

Mud Stalker glanced at Wing Heart, clearly expecting some answer from the Council's leader. She might have been sculpted of mud, as aware as a cooking clay as she gazed vacant-eyed at the sky.

"Cousin?" Water Petal called from behind. "Clan Elder, do you have a response?"

Wing Heart might have been deaf, lost in her thoughts.

With a slightly perplexed look, Mud Stalker turned, glaring at Deep Hunter. "Well, it is obvious that Clan Elder Wing Heart considers your objection so ludicrous that she needn't even acknowledge it."

Chuckles broke out. Salamander felt his ears redden with embarrassment. Deep Hunter was right. He shouldn't even be here. Why was this happening? What was Mud Stalker's purpose in insisting on his following in White Bird's footsteps when Alligator Clan's objections seemed eminently logical?

With renewed interest, Salamander studied the people in the circle. *They are laughing!* The notion came to him as he studied the smug faces of Mud Stalker and Back Scratch. Clay Fat and Graywood Snake looked uncomfortable, as if caught doing something embarrassing. Thunder Tail's expression was wooden, while Cane Frog's blind face exhibited a grin, as if she, too, sensed some sort of victory.

"The objection of Alligator Clan is noted," Mud Stalker replied with satisfaction. "The vote, however, is clear." His voice rang in the hot air. "*Speaker* Salamander, of the Owl Clan! Step forward and meet your Council!"

Water Petal's sharp jab sent him unsteadily forward, half-tottering on his feet. Mortification seared his souls as he forced his feet to carry him into the open. His tongue knotted at the back of this throat; he tried to keep his knees from trembling. As he looked up into Mud Stalker's gloating eyes, he couldn't find a single word to say.

"Speaker Salamander," Mud Stalker cried. "With your acceptance, this Council has finished its business. In honor of the occasion, will you do us the favor of dismissing the Council?"

Salamander froze for a moment, the only sensation that of his heart battering against his ribs. "Dismissed," he croaked.

Laughter broke out, adding to his misery. He shot a quick look over his shoulder, hearing Water Petal telling Wing Heart, "The Speaker dismissed the Council, Elder. It's over now. Salamander is now Speaker."

"Who?" Wing Heart asked faintly as she turned away.

Salamander didn't hear Water Petal's response.

"I feel like a fool," Salamander muttered.

"You did fine." Mud Stalker beamed down at him. "Just trust me, young man. I'll see you through this."

And then they came, each of the Elders and Speakers, each congratulating him. The hands, pats on the back, and smiling faces blurred as they crowded around him.

Only after the others stepped away did Deep Hunter and Colored Paint approach. Deep Hunter's face reeked of disgust as he leaned forward, voice low. "So, you are now Snapping Turtle Clan's tool? My old adversary planned that well, boy."

"I am Owl Clan," Salamander managed.

"Yes, well, we'll see, won't we?" Then Deep Hunter turned and stalked off, his muscular body betraying an unbending anger.

"We'll see," Colored Paint agreed, following her brother.

Thankful to be left alone, Salamander noticed that Mud Stalker seemed to be the center of attention as the remaining Council members wished him well.

Is that the plan? I am supposed to do as Mud Stalker wishes? Is that why he insisted on me?

The knowledge was sobering. Even more so when Mud Stalker turned to him, slapped him on the back, and said, "Come, Speaker Salamander. Your wives have made a great feast. We look forward to celebrating our good fortune!"

But when Salamander looked in Pine Drop and Night Rain's direction, they glared back at him as though he were some sort of carrion-eating bug.

I could have gone with Spring Cypress. I should have.

Mud Stalker's heavy hand propelled him forward toward his future.

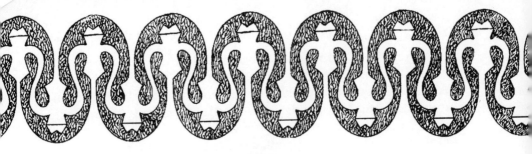

Twenty-two

Two days after the solstice ceremonies, he had followed the Serpent to the house where Clan Elder Graywood Snake had lived. The oval-shaped house had been built on the first ridge, just to the left of the low causeway leading up to the Bird's Head.

Graywood Snake had died suddenly. One moment she was hobbling across the plaza, the next, she cried out and fell over. Her souls had fled before she hit the ground. That had been last night.

Heat filled the house, heavy like a weight, and more stagnant, if possible, than the muggy afternoon beyond the door. In such hot weather a corpse had to be processed quickly, for in hot air corruption was drawn quickly to feed on a corpse. Salamander wasn't sure why that was. Something about corruption's ability to scent death? The Serpent had never given him a straight answer as to the reasons—which led Salamander to suspect that the old man didn't really know.

Salamander squinted in the dim light, his hands working with smooth strokes as he severed the thin muscles inside the old woman's thigh. He had to saw at the thick tendon that tied her thighbone to the mound of her pelvis. In the process, he tried not to touch the woman's deeply wrinkled vulva. It reminded him of a shriveled gourd husk, whiskered with mold. Worse, it reminded him of his wives'.

Beside him, the Serpent's raspy old voice rose and fell as he chanted the Death Song. The melody called to the Sky Beings and

Earth Beings, asking them to come and see, to be witness to the passing of the great Elder's souls. Next he Sang to reassure Graywood Snake that she was being cared for in the manner of her people, that her corpse was being treated with the proper respect.

The thick tendon parted, and Salamander was able to roll the leg back to expose the ball joint to his sharp stone knife. The Serpent turned his attention to the skin still left around the woman's hips. With practiced strokes he peeled away the old woman's vulva and severed the tissues inside to leave an arched hump of bone, raw and bloody. The bowels, vagina, and bladder that had once been cradled within had already been removed when they excised her organs.

Outside the door, Salamander could hear soft weeping as Speaker Clay Fat and his sister, Turtle Mist, mourned the death of their Elder.

What had been Graywood Snake's leg came free in Salamander's hand. He set it carefully to the side, picking bits of tissue from his fingers and wiping them on the inside of the wicker basket that held the old woman's flesh and organs.

"You have become practiced at this." The Serpent studied him with thoughtful eyes. His sagging face—like Salamander's—had been streaked with black charcoal stripes to appease the Dead. "You are already better than Bobcat. Have you given thought to following me?"

"No, Elder. That is Bobcat's place. He knows the songs. He did very well walking at your side for the summer solstice ceremonies."

"You could, you know. Follow in my footsteps, I mean."

"I have other responsibilities."

"You are no longer the child I once knew. You have aged in the last three moons since you were made a man and married."

"I have too much to worry about."

"Yes, I haven't heard a word from your Clan Elder at Council since you were accepted there." Then he resumed his chanting.

Salamander pinched his lips, frowning, his thoughts locked on Wing Heart's perplexing silence. She might have lost part of her souls, given the way she walked about, a listlessness in her eyes.

He picked up the Serpent's words and Sang in gentle accompaniment as he thought of his mother. He couldn't help but compare her to Graywood Snake. Unlike his mother, he had always liked Graywood Snake. Even after his near-unanimous nomination to the Council, she had treated him like a fellow rather than a jest, as the others had.

Salamander ran his blade down the inside of the leg, separating the thin skin. With careful strokes he severed the ligament and tendons in the round, peeling the muscle back from the bone. That done, he had placed the cool flesh in the basket; reverently, he severed the tendons at the kneecap and folded the leg bones double. He laid them with the arm and leg bones that already rested on the rick of wood. Dry and seasoned, the pyre would burn hot and completely, in defiance of the moisture that hung in the summer air outside.

"I will miss you, Elder," Salamander said as he cleaned the last bits of tissue from his knife and ritually passed it over the smoking coals in the fire pit. Not that the house needed a fire, given the melting heat of the day, but the smoke was required, not only for purification of the tools, but to keep evil spirits out and away, and to assist Graywood Snake's souls in their passage from this life to the next.

Sweat beaded on Salamander's forehead as he Sang the final verses of the Death Song. Then he and the Serpent carefully placed the naked bones of her torso atop the pyre, propping them in the cradle of her limbs so that they wouldn't roll off.

"Rest well, old friend." The Serpent patted the rounded globe of her skull with blood-encrusted hands. "You have always been a light in my life. Your fond wit and smile brought happiness to many of my days. I will see you someday soon."

Salamander watched the old man's gentle motions as he caressed the bones. "Does it bother you?"

"Hmm?" The Serpent turned, gaze absent. The skin seemed to hang like a wet rag from the flat planes of his charcoal-smeared face.

"She was your friend." Salamander gestured toward the bones. "We have just cut her into pieces. It seems like a violation."

Salamander hated it when the old man gave him that look of irritated consideration. "Her souls have left the body, Salamander. I am overjoyed to be the one to help her during her passing. Put yourself in her place. If your souls were hanging here in the air"—he pointed at the smoke-filled ceiling—"would you want some rude stranger, or an old and dear friend, seeing to the care of your body?"

"I'm not sure."

"Ah, that's because you have not considered death, my young friend. The living lose themselves in the pain of the moment. They are completely absorbed by their own sense of loss. They never think about how fragile the souls of the freshly dead are. Imagine yourself as having just died: You are lost, grieving, your body refuses to respond to your orders as it did when you were alive. Your loved ones are all around you, crying, pulling their hair. You try to help them, to calm them, but they are deaf to your entreaties. You can only watch their pain, unable to soothe it. Meanwhile, all around you, spirits are gathering, calling to you, trying to get your attention. Old friends, long dead, are crowding around and demand to speak with you. Other spirits are circling, knowing you are vulnerable, easily attacked. You must guard against them, but you are so confused, worried, and scared like you have never been before." He shook his head. "I think dying is much more frightening than being born."

"You think they are linked?"

"Yes," the old man replied. He looked at the basket made of split cane. "Can you carry that?"

"If you can Sing. I'm still learning the words." Salamander stepped over, crouched, and shifted the basket onto his back. Graywood Snake had been old and frail; she weighed almost nothing. He took the load and ducked out into the hot sunshine. Eyes slitted against the glare, he could see Clay Fat, his portly body streaked with perspiration, his round face stricken. Turtle Mist's features were drawn, her eyes sad.

They will be all right, won't they? Not like Mother. The aftereffects of death now scared him. His mother hadn't been the same since White Bird's death. Instead, she had turned into a walking husk, the seed that should have been within gone black and shriveled. He wondered if perhaps White Bird had been so frightened that he had clawed away part of Mother's souls as his own had been drawn into the realm of the Dead.

The basket leaked, and as he walked, Salamander felt wet drops of fluid spattering his legs. Their route took them southwest, proceeding through the gap that separated Rattlesnake Clan from Eagle Clan. One by one they passed the remaining ridges. From the rows of houses, people from Graywood Snake's clan watched with somber eyes, many singing and calling final wishes to their departed Elder.

"So, where are the souls?" Salamander asked.

"Hovering close to the bones, you know that." The Serpent paused in his Singing. "Why do you ask?"

"Because of the people," Salamander replied quietly, keeping his head down as was respectful toward the dead. "They call out to Graywood Snake, but what is left of her in the basket is soulless meat, correct?"

The Serpent grinned humorlessly. "That is the way of people, Salamander. The living see the Dead everywhere. It hurts nothing and makes the living feel better. Perhaps the Dead hear all of the calls. I don't know, and worse, I can't find out until I, myself, am dead."

They passed the last of the ridges with their mourners, and walked out onto the beaten grass beyond. To their right, the Bird's Head rose high and resolute into the yellow-hot air. The ramada at the top looked fuzzy and wavered in the humidity. Bright fabrics that had been tied to the sun poles hung limp and heavy.

As they walked toward the distant forest, insects chirred and whizzed around them, transparent wings glittering in the white light. Looking to the south, across undulating dimples of old pits, Salamander could see Dying Sun Mound, flat-topped and green at the end of the causeway. On this day a group of children and dogs chased across the low-walled expanse of the mound, flinging a leather-wrapped ball back and forth with sticks. Their shouts and barks barely carried in the heat.

Sweat broke free to stream down Salamander's body and mix with the juices that streaked his buttocks and legs. He batted at the growing number of big black flies that buzzed around, drawn by the odor of fresh wet flesh.

Their route took them past the southern end of the huge borrow pit. As they rounded the rim of the deep pit, Salamander could look down into the dark waters. Insects broke the surface, and a flight of ducks exploded from the green weeds that lined the shore, their wings whistling as they battered the air.

Salamander was wishing for a drink by the time they made the forest margin. Entering the shadows provided the slightest relief from the searing sun, but the hot wet air seemed to press in close.

The Serpent led the way along a narrow trail beaten into the leaf mat by the passing of tens of tens of tens of bare feet over the ages. They walked under the arching span of hickory and beech trees before stepping into a small clearing thick with old brush.

"Clay Fat needs to send someone to burn this brush next winter," the Serpent muttered.

Each of the clans had a spot like this, removed from the Sun Town by a short walk. Here, in a small clearing, the cuttings were disposed of.

Salamander glanced around, seeing the thick brush. Old branches, worn gray by weather, poked out of the clusters of palmetto, privet, and honeysuckle. Raspberries were forming, the fruits green and lush. They would produce a harvest that no one would come to collect. A thousand spiderwebs laced patches of white in the branches.

"They catch the flies and beetles," the Serpent said, noting his interest. "For some creatures, there is good hunting around the leftovers of the Dead."

A crow cawed above. Since the night of his initiation, he had grown more than a little leery of crows. Salamander looked up, seeing the black bird alight on the waving tip of a branch to watch with one beady eye. Only then did the white droppings that marred the leaves and branches catch his attention. No wonder the place looked so lush. Death fed life here, be it the carrion eaters or the plants. He swung the basket down, reaching in to help the Serpent remove slimy strips of muscle, skin, and viscera. These they draped around on the brush, easy at hand to the scavengers. More crows called in the treetops, eager for the coming feast.

Salamander batted at the flies as he laid the last of Graywood Snake's body onto the sagging branch of a privet bush. He realized the crunchy stuff under his feet was maggot casings.

"Evil spirits!" the Serpent cried to the open sky. "Stay here, and away from the souls of our departed friend. This is your place! Take what you will of what we leave here, and be content. Come no closer to Sun Town, or I shall have to do battle and destroy you."

Salamander swallowed hard. He never felt safe when they made these deposits. His Dreams, always uncertain to start with, were labored after he and the Serpent processed a body. That he involved himself in such doings irritated his wives to no end—perhaps explaining his willingness to help the Serpent with his grisly chores.

"Come, my friend." The Serpent turned and led the way back into the forest. "We have finished this portion of our duty. All that remains is to help Clay Fat fire the house tonight. I shall have Bobcat do most of the Singing. I think he is ready for that."

They walked in silence as they retraced their tracks. Breaking into the open again, the sight of the Bird's Head to the north and the children playing on Dying Sun Mound to the south reassured Salamander.

"Mud Stalker came to see me last night," the Serpent said offhandedly. "Knowing that Bobcat had been called to Ground Cherry Camp to attend a broken leg, he asked me to find another to help with the Elder's body."

Salamander shot him a glance. "He did?"

"It appears that some do not approve of your interest in acquiring the arts necessary to handle the dead."

"That is not their concern." Salamander swung the basket back and forth, slinging the loose gore from its stained bottom.

"You are not happy in your marriage," the Serpent stated.

"You have divined this on your own, have you?"

"Do not mock me. You have been married now for almost three

moons. And a Speaker for your clan for nearly as long. I can feel Power and trouble gathering around you."

"Mud Stalker is disappointed with me. I haven't always voted the way he would like. And Mother, I don't understand. She mostly just stands there, eyes lost on the distance. I have caught her talking to Cloud Heron's ghost when no one's around."

The Serpent sighed. "What about your Dreams?"

Salamander ground his teeth, then admitted, "They come sometimes. Many Colored Crow has come to me since the night of my initiation. Sometimes I fly with Masked Owl. He tells me things."

"Such as?"

"He tells me to watch out for certain people. He gives me glimpses of faraway lands. Sometimes he warns me of things."

"What things?"

Salamander shook his head. "I'm sorry, Elder. They are between Masked Owl and me."

Carefully, the Serpent said, "You are aware that Mud Stalker and your wives are plotting?"

"Oh, yes. Though why they insisted that I marry is beyond me. And why, for the sake of Snakes, did they appoint me to the Council? I just sit there. I'm an embarrassment. Look at me! But for the political necessity, I wouldn't be made a man yet. Who ever heard of a boy like me sitting in the Council?"

The Serpent slowed as he reached the deep borrow pit. With care he stepped over the edge. The slope was steep, but a narrow trail had been worn through the thick green grass and into the brown earth. A misstep meant a nasty tumble through the weeds and grass and into the stagnant water below. Salamander started as a snake slithered rapidly away. He could see the plants moving as the reptile wound along the slope. Wood snake? Or water moccasin?

At the bottom, the Serpent crouched on a thin strip of beach and splashed his hands into the water. Cleansing had to be done on the western side of Sun Town, every bit of blood, liquid, and tissue washed away. The borrow pit pond was the perfect place for these ablutions. With great care, the Serpent washed his hands, taking time to pick the dried blood from under his fingernails. "Bide your time, Salamander. You are meant to be a joke. It is the revenge Mud Stalker has planned for your mother and clan."

"It humiliates me," Salamander agreed as he stepped to one side and perched on the steep slope. He bent forward and dunked the basket into the water, seeing minnows, tadpoles, and insects swimming away. He sloshed it back and forth before hauling it out, ripping a handful of grass free and scrubbing the insides to remove the stains.

"And what does a salamander do when a raccoon is snorting and sniffing around a fallen log? Does he run out immediately in search of insects?"

"Of course not."

"There is a lesson in that." The Serpent rubbed at a blood spot on his forearm and looked up pointedly. "Do you know what it is?"

"I didn't want to be a member of the Council." Salamander tipped the basket to dump the red-stained water out. "I didn't ask for any of this."

"Sometimes the best people are those who didn't ask for the responsibility."

"Sometimes they aren't."

"Power chose you, Salamander. At each important event, it has settled around you like a blanket. Just as it did atop the Bird's Head and at your initiation." He paused, looking down at his hands again, inspecting them to make sure they were clean. "I won't be around to help you much longer."

"What are you talking about?" Salamander bent down and began washing his hands.

"I'm talking about the future. What is to come. You are so young, my friend. That is your strength and your weakness."

"That doesn't make sense."

"Listen to me!" the old man demanded. "Something is coming, something I cannot see over the horizon of time. I am an old man, and I will probably not live to see this thing happen. My friends are dying. Graywood Snake was younger than me. Elder Back Scratch is ailing and will die soon—leaving that witless Sweet Root as Clan Elder. Cane Frog will be lucky to survive another winter. Who can tell how many moons I have left? This, however, I know: Learn from your Spirit Helpers. Learn from the world. Do not seek fame, or revenge, or any other petty gratification. Do you hear me, Salamander? *Be who you are!* That is why Power chose you."

"Be who I am?" He glanced at the old man in puzzlement.

"Exactly. And be it smartly. You are caught between Masked Owl and Many Colored Crow because they saw something in your souls. Dreams are crossing here. Different paths to the future. Like those crossed lines I carved into your chest, you are the place between the North and the South, the East and the West. You lie between Masked Owl and Many Colored Crow. A battle is being waged, and you are the key."

"What battle? What are they fighting over?"

The Serpent shook his head slowly. "It is an old thing between them. They are brothers, you see. Masked Owl and Many Colored Crow. They take other forms at times, sometimes wolves, ravens, eagles, lions, bears, but one is always light, the other dark. Forever separate, forever bound, but never in agreement. They pull the world back and forth between them."

"And I am supposed to bring an end to this?"

"No. You are just supposed to help one side win for the time being."

"But how can I be part of this? I don't even have a Spirit Helper to advise me. Not even Salamander."

The Serpent made a face. "Are you *that* dull-witted?"

"How do you mean?"

"Many Colored Crow sits atop the Men's House during your initiation. Masked Owl takes you flying in your Dreams. Boy, just *what* do you think a Spirit Helper does, anyway?"

Salamander blinked, a cold shiver running down his back despite the dripping heat. *No wonder he laughed when I asked if Salamander would consider being my Spirit Helper.*

"That's right," the Serpent told him fondly. "Just be yourself, Salamander. That will save you. So long as you do not lose yourself, do not become like the others. If you forget who you are, become like them, you are going to be crushed like a caterpillar in a lizard's jaws."

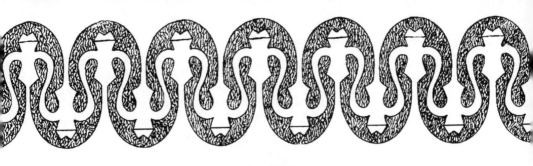

Twenty-three

Evening had settled on Sun Town the way it did in the days after the solstice—with great rapidity. Water Petal sat to one side of the ramada, her back propped against one of the support poles. Her infant, a son, suckled noisily at her left breast. As it worked the brown nipple, the baby's little fingers kept grasping and flexing, as if he didn't have enough to occupy him in the busy pursuit of filling his belly.

A low fire smoldered under the ramada's northern edge, that location receiving slightly more protection from the intermittent summer rains. Wing Heart tended it by adding another branch from the pile Salamander had brought in from the forest.

Lost in thought, Salamander studied the circular wicker framework of the new house that rose immediately to the west. Still unroofed, the walls looked like a huge round basket sticking out of the ground. Poles had been dug into the earth and saplings woven between them to harden as they dried. This in turn would eventually be smeared and plastered with clay and allowed to cure before brush was piled against the walls and set on fire to harden it. Only then would the pole rafters be put in place for the roof. Saplings, again, would be woven across them to provide a lattice to which shocks of grass thatch could be attached.

Salamander turned, studying the preoccupied look on his mother's face. *What is wrong with her?* Was this the woman he had known, and so often feared? Where once a cutting sharpness lay behind those dark eyes, now only emptiness remained.

Wing Heart had decided to rebuild on the location of Uncle Cloud Heron's house rather than her old one. Though she'd never said, Salamander suspected that she couldn't bear to build where she had burned her son's bones. It didn't make sense, but then, where Wing Heart was concerned a great many things didn't make sense anymore.

"Moccasin Leaf is continuing to spread her poison," Water Petal announced. "She is spreading the story among the lineages that Salamander, with the advantage of two wives, is unable to plant a child in either one."

"White Bird has only been married for three moons," Wing Heart answered absently.

Both Salamander and Water Petal flinched at the use of her dead son's name. Oblivious, she continued, "I'd been married for six before Black Lightning planted White Bird in my belly. And, if memory serves, Pine Drop's mother, Sweet Root, took nearly a year to catch." Wing Heart turned and settled herself at her loom. A half-finished kirtle hung there, the center decoration consisting of a bird woven out of the whitest hemp thread she could find. Her fingers rose like thin brown spiders to the warp and began plucking the threads.

Water Petal turned her attention to Salamander. "You are lying with them, aren't you?"

"Of course." Great joy that it was. He looked out at the night with a bitter feeling in his breast. In addition to the worry over his mother's frequent lapses and odd snatches of conversation with dead people, his nights with his wives bore down on him like rough sandstone on soft wood. The memory of Spring Cypress pulled at his souls like a tightening cord. He could feel his heart hammering, the blood running hot in his veins. Snakes, he had wanted her with a desire that had burned him. Why wasn't it that way with Pine Drop and Night Rain? Both women had bodies every bit as well shaped as Spring Cypress's.

"Salamander?" Water Petal's voice dropped. "How often do you mount your wives?"

He shifted uncomfortably. "When they tell me to." The admission felt like drawing a rose stem through an open wound.

"Snakes!" Water Petal cried, startling the baby, who spat out her nipple and gave a lusty bawl. She maneuvered his mouth back into place and resettled his fabric-wrapped body into a more comfortable position. "I suppose each time they *let* you exercise your rights as a husband, it is a week just before or just after they've been in the Women's House?"

He nodded, wishing they could talk about something else.

"Salamander," Water Petal's voice dropped, her eyes taking Wing Heart's measure as she asked, "is it fun? Do you enjoy coupling with them? Or have they turned it into work, a thing that must be endured?"

"Endured." He ground his teeth, taking his own suspicious glance at his mother. "It wasn't as if our marriage was something any of us looked forward to."

"Salamander, there is talk that you may not have heard. Moccasin Leaf overheard it in the Women's House. It seems that . . ." She winced as if her teeth hurt.

"That Pine Drop is bedding that Frog Clan man, Three Stomachs." He finished for her. "How did he get that name, anyway?"

"From the way he eats. What would fill three men barely lasts him until his next meal. But that's not the point. Is it true?"

He nodded. "I have seen them. One of the advantages to being invisible is that it's easy to pass unnoticed. They plan meetings any chance they get." He paused. "At least she enjoys coupling with him."

"Rot her crotch away," Water Petal hissed. "You know what she's doing by putting you off, don't you?"

"Yes, Cousin. She is avoiding having my child. Though why she would mate with Three Stomachs is beyond me. None of his children have lived. His wife, that Rattlesnake Clan woman, has borne him five stillborns."

"Of course," Water Petal noted, putting the pieces together. "If she does have a child by him, and it's stillborn, it reflects on you." She shook her head. "Do they hate us that much?"

"More, I'd say." Salamander reached out, fingering the polished wood in the ramada's support pole. "But do not concern yourself."

"Indeed?" Acid, like cactus juice, laced Water Petal's voice. "Do not concern myself about the woman who seeks to insult my cousin, not to mention the Speaker of my clan?"

"It is not time yet," Salamander told her. "She isn't conceiving any child by Three Stomachs."

"Snakes and Lightning, Salamander! It's his seed he's planting inside her slippery tube!"

"Please lower your voice." Salamander shot her a hard look. "Not everyone in Sun Town need be part of this discussion."

"And *how* do you *know* that his seed is not already growing in your wife's womb?"

"I have my ways." He watched his mother as he spoke, but Wing Heart seemed oblivious, a slight smile on her lips as she worked the loom. This world might have been but a shadow of the world she saw. "You must trust me, Cousin. She will not conceive, and she suffers as a result of her roaming."

For the first time, Water Petal's expression softened. "That makes me feel just a little better, Cousin. It gladdens my souls to hear that you are carving at least a little revenge off her slim body. Would you mind telling me how you're accomplishing this feat?"

"It is not revenge, Cousin. And, no, I will not tell you how I deal with her infidelity." He noticed a young man hurrying along the embankment toward their ridge. A slim fellow, Salamander couldn't place him in the gloom. Then he recognized that loose run: Little Needle. "Cousin, you must trust me about this."

"Thank the Sky Beings, I hope this is something that you're learning from the Serpent? People talk about that, too, you know. Many wonder what to think of you. It's not like you will step into his shoes when he dies. He has made it clear that Bobcat will. As to why you help him with the death rituals, well, it seems depressing to me."

"He needs me."

"So do other people, Salamander! Your mother, the Clan Elder, could use a little help on the house she's building. But for Yellow Spider, it's a wonder we've even raised the walls!"

He stood, stepping out from the ramada as Little Needle came jogging up, his breath rising and falling.

"Salamander?" the boy called.

"Greetings, Little Needle. What brings you at a run? Not more gossip about my wives, I hope." He glanced back, unable to read Water Petal's expression.

"No." Little Needle managed between puffing breaths. "But I'm glad you have heard these things about them. Especially Pine Drop. Did you know that she's been—"

"Yes, yes, go on." He clamped a hand on the boy's greased arm and dragged him into the shadows of the ramada. "What brings you here?"

"Jaguar Hide!" the boy cried. "You wouldn't believe it! I talked to my cousin, Bluefin, who was fishing in the south. He has a set of gill nets placed where the channels are draining out of the swamp. He went to check them, and who should be waiting but Jaguar Hide!

Bluefin thought he was dead! But then Jaguar Hide asked him his clan. And when he told him Owl Clan, Jaguar Hide asked him to carry a message to Elder Wing Heart."

"What message?" Water Petal stood and stepped forward. Salamander didn't need to see her quick glance at Wing Heart.

"Cousin," Wing Heart interrupted, surprising them all, "Speaker Cloud Heron and I will hear what Jaguar Hide says." She turned her head in the darkness, though how she could still work the loom baffled Salamander. "Tell me, Little Needle."

"Jaguar Hide wants to come here!" Little Needle had stopped bouncing from foot to foot, puzzled at the mention of the dead Speaker. "He wants to meet with you, declare a truce between our peoples. He wishes to know if you will speak in the Council and grant him safe passage to come and see you?"

Wing Heart had stopped weaving, her form a dark shadow in the gathering night. For a long moment she remained frozen, then said in her old familiar voice, "Yes, Little Needle. I will speak for him. Send word: Owl Clan guarantees his safety. Let him come and tell the Speaker and me what is on his mind."

"Don't do this, Elder." Water Petal turned to stare at Wing Heart's dark shape. "Whatever he is after, it is no good. And we have never been weaker."

"We are *Owl Clan*!" Wing Heart snapped. "No one challenges our authority. Let him come!"

Water Petal's sagging posture betrayed her defeat. No matter what, Wing Heart remained the Elder. Her word was final.

Salamander turned back to his friend. "Go. Tell Bluefin that the Elder will see Jaguar Hide. I take it that he has a way of getting the message to the Swamp Panthers without ending up skewered on a pole in their village?"

"He does. Jaguar Hide gave him instructions on how it was to be done."

"Then you had best get a good night's sleep," Salamander told him. "It will be a long trip through the channels tomorrow."

"Yes, Speaker." Little Needle turned, trotting away into the darkness to find his mother's house on the third ridge.

"What does Jaguar Hide want?" Water Petal repeated to herself.

"He will bring trouble," Wing Heart said from her loom. "I have no doubt of that. Don't worry, Cousin, it is nothing that the Cloud Heron and I can't handle."

Salamander could feel Water Petal's unease as she studied the Elder. White Bird, Cloud Heron, they cropped up in Wing Heart's conversation as if they had never died. Maybe this was just what his mother needed to bring back her old confident self. Was she still canny enough to deal with the terrible Swamp Panther warrior?

Masked Owl, why haven't you warned me about this in my Dreams?

Pine Drop followed a deep-forest trail through the gathering dusk; a heavy fabric sack hung over her shoulder and weighted her down with freshly picked bladderwort. The plant was her excuse to walk a half day's journey to the south and had taken her but a finger of time to collect. The rest of it she had spent satiating herself on Three Stomach's male member. In the beginning she had hesitated taking him as a lover. The man simply had no brain to go along with that magnificent body of his. The reason for his prodigious appetite was directly related to the fact that he had a lot of body to feed. Three Stomachs was big, muscular, hardy, and endowed with an incredible vitality. His male part was built like the rest of him: huge. The sight of his hardened organ had frightened her the first time, but to her delight, he was skilled enough to prepare her womanhood to accept it without discomfort.

She winced, placing a hand to her abdomen. While she would have liked to blame the cramps on Three Stomachs and the oversize root he slipped into her, the painful irritation had started earlier that week. And Night Rain, too, complained about it. The malady didn't affect her seriously, but was annoying, peaking about midway through her moon.

You should see the Serpent about it. Yes, she should, but the idea of discussing such a problem with someone who was close to her husband rankled. What if the old shaman went straight to Salamander to say, "Your wife is having female trouble the week before and after she is bedding her lover."

That assuredly wouldn't do. And, rot take it, why hadn't Three Stomach's seed planted in her womb? It was common knowledge, spoken of in the Women's House, that a woman took about midway in her cycle. Snakes knew, the man had pumped her full enough times in the passing moons. His own wife had conceived in the last moon. She and Three Stomachs were hoping that this sixth child would be the one who lived.

She followed the trail out from the canopy of trees south of her clan grounds and trudged toward the distant curve of Sun Town's ridges. In the gloom, she could see the lines of houses, some haloed by cooking fires.

"Greetings, Niece." Mud Stalker's voice startled her. He was sitting in the grass, his head and shoulders barely visible. "Sorry to frighten you."

"Uncle!" She took a breath to resettle her heartbeat. "I didn't expect to find you out here."

"Nor did anyone else." He grunted and climbed to his feet, then gestured toward home. "I had hoped that you would take this trail back. I need to talk to you. Several things have happened. First, I don't think you should see Three Stomachs again. At least, not as a lover. We are starting to hear talk."

"Let them talk." She matched her stride to his, the bag of bladderwort swinging from her shoulder. "I could care less if people know I'm dissatisfied with Salamander now, or later."

"Ah, yes, but I do care." He studied her in the darkness. "You are not pregnant, I take it?"

"I won't know for another half moon, Uncle. Let's see if I have to retreat to the Women's House, shall we?" She winced, slowing, a cramp tightening just below her navel.

"Are you all right?"

"Yes, Uncle." She made a face and forced herself to straighten. "It comes and goes. I'll be over it in a week or so."

"Here, let me take the bag." He reached for the sack. "What's in it?"

"Bladderwort. I'll look like a perfectly dutiful wife when I prepare it for our household." She glanced at him, walking with one hand pressed firmly against her abdomen. "So, tell me, Uncle, have you found a lover for Night Rain yet?"

"She must be handled a bit more judiciously." He had his head cocked, his strong left hand knotted around the sack of bladderwort. "Has she mentioned any young man besides Saw Back? Anyone that might have caught her eye?"

"No. And I have even suggested several. She's very young, Uncle. She thinks only as far as Saw Back."

"She's a woman, no younger than you were when you married Blue Feather."

"I loved him." She shook her head, relieved that the cramp was fading. "Give her time, Uncle. She is younger than I was at her age. She has always been unsure, and for the moment, she is confused and unhappy. Marriage hasn't been what she expected, and I think it will take a while for her resentment to pass. When it does, we can find a man to pair her with. Until then, forcing her to do so might cause us more harm than it will do good."

"We agree." He paused. "You can stop seeing Three Stomachs without regret? This thing between you, it hasn't gone to the heart yet, has it?"

She laughed at that. "No, Uncle. It hasn't gone to the heart. I don't mind locking hips with him, but I would hate to be married to him. I think he only has a single thought in a day, and not a very interesting one at that."

"Good. He shouldn't be much of a problem. He has had affairs before and never made a pest of himself afterward. If you gently tell him that you can't see him anymore, he should just shrug and walk away."

"Indeed, Uncle? You know a lot about him, then?"

Mud Stalker chuckled. "Let's just say that he has proven useful when it came to placing women in compromising positions. Depending upon the woman, and depending upon the nature of her indiscretion, a great deal of leverage can be acquired by the party who happens to 'stumble' over them in the act. Politics is partly flexibility, partly being smart, and partly leverage."

"I will remember that."

"Good." He made a smacking with his lips. "A runner went to Wing Heart tonight from Jaguar Hide asking for the Owl Clan's support in safe passage to Sun Town. What one of our kinsmen overheard at the canoe landing was that Jaguar Hide wants to make peace between our peoples. He evidently still thinks that Owl Clan is preeminent."

She already guessed where this was headed. "You want me to find out what this is really all about?"

"I do. And I want to know if it is to our advantage to let Owl Clan make this peace, or whether we can use this as an opportunity to cut yet another support out from under them."

"Such as?"

"Such as allowing Elder Wing Heart to promise safe passage, then ambushing Jaguar Hide on his way home." He made a gesture. "Not that we would have to do it, mind you. Deep Hunter would have more than a passing interest in bringing that Swamp Panther cutthroat to justice."

She nodded. "I see." A hesitation. "My husband and I don't talk, you know."

"That is another reason for interrupting your affair with Three Stomachs. At least until the whispers dry up. We don't want him to find out. If he does, he could become completely alienated, and, as much as I would love to humiliate him and Owl Clan, it is a bit soon for such a revelation."

She glanced at him. The notion of taking Three Stomachs to her bed had been bothersome in the beginning. What if she did conceive? And what if the child were stillborn? Given the man's incredible potency, she had convinced herself that it had been a combination of bad luck and his wife's infertility that had led to the five dead infants his wife had delivered, but what if it wasn't? That she hadn't caught in three moons was starting to worry her—as were the cramps during the weeks of her heightened fertility.

That thought having lodged between her souls, she cocked her jaw. Just how deep did Mud Stalker's hatred run? Deep enough to place his own kin at risk? She shook her head, unwilling even to consider that the uncle she had known and looked up to all of her life could even contemplate such a thing. No, he was acting in the clan's best interest—and in hers and her sister's.

Leadership depends on these kinds of things. The words lingered in her thoughts. *A leader cannot be like the rest of the people. More is demanded of him. To be a leader means giving up part of yourself for the rest of your clan.*

She had taken those adages into her souls as her infant body had taken her mother's milk. With the exception of a few times as an adolescent girl lost in daydreams, she had never questioned it. Now she found herself a confidante of the Speaker, her mother in line to be named clan Elder, and married to the Speaker of Owl Clan, dolt though her husband might be.

I am in the center of my clan's leadership.

"You have grown silent," her uncle noted.

"Thinking about what it means to be a leader, Uncle. About the things we have to do. Until now I have never really understood the words I have heard all of my life. About a leader's responsibility to her people."

"And now that you understand?"

"It is a terrible burden, Uncle."

"Yes?"

"One I will carry." She felt a tingle in her loins, and tensed against a cramp that didn't intensify. "I will see what I can learn from Salamander about Jaguar Hide's purposes in coming here."

"Good. I am so proud of you, Niece. So very proud." He made a gesture. "You should know, your grandmother is dying. She may not last the night."

"I should go to her."

"Yes," he replied. "And think of what her death will mean for your future."

The Serpent

We humans spend so much time working to shrink the miraculous to the size of our own pettiness that it's a wonder we manage to get anything else done.

Our lives are filled with miracles that we do not see. Every time a hawk shrieks or a bear roars, it is the visible breath of the Creator entering our world.

But we look and look away.

Each time a raindrop lands, our world is clothed in the glory of its greatest possibilities.

But we go inside our houses where we can't see it.

We are too preoccupied with who might be saying bad things about us to care that the wildflowers have bowed their heads in profound gratitude and the vines have spread their arms in prayer.

That is the challenge we face. It is only when we allow ourselves to experience the divine presence each moment that we live our lives to the fullest.

And that is the dilemma. It is a summons to wonder that most of us will turn our backs upon in favor of belittling someone else.

Are we really so terrified to look into the Creator's eyes?

What do we fear we will see?

The primary purpose of a miracle, after all, is not revelation. It is redemption.

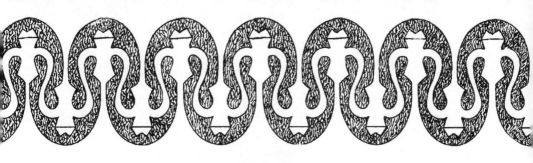

Twenty-four

The night after Back Scratch's funeral, Salamander blinked his eyes open and listened to the sounds. Birdsong had sent its first melodies through the darkness. Dawn couldn't be more than a hand's time from breaking over the eastern horizon. He reached out and lifted the deerhide, aware of Night Rain's sleeping form where she lay beside him. His second wife was snuggled against the wall, her back to him. She shifted, some sleep-ridden sound deep in her throat as he slipped from the covers into the cool air and resettled the deerhide over her shoulders.

The events of the previous night came tumbling out of his sleep-heavy souls. After Wing Heart had excused herself and gone to bed, he and Water Petal had sat up late, discussing the implications of Jaguar Hide coming to Owl Clan. Did it mean that he had heard of their weakness, or did he still come to them believing that he dealt with the most prestigious of Sun Town's clans? Assuming the former, did he have designs on Wing Heart, seeking to further damage her standing among the clans? Or would this be the challenge that would snap her out of her endless mourning for her brother and son?

Salamander stretched in the dark shadows and glanced at the door, a bare gray portal to the predawn outside. Moving in silence, he tied a cord around his waist and pulled his breechcloth into place.

Under his bed he found the wooden box that contained his herbs. The sweetgum wood had been decorated with an interlocking owl motif, the wings of one blending into the wings of another to encircle the box. Opening it, his fingers encountered a soft leather bag in one corner. This he lifted and loosened the drawstring. He took a pinch, sniffing to ensure he had the right mixture. A quick glance ensured that both women were hard asleep; he dropped a dash of the powder into the stewpot. Sniffing his fingers again, he confirmed the ingredients: wild ginger, licorice root, dogbane, milkweed, and rue. Both Pine Drop and Night Rain were destined for another day of female discomfort.

He wearily returned the herbs to his box before closing it and restoring it to its place under the bed. From the clay pot beside the box he scooped out a liberal handful of rendered bear grease laced with pine resin. This he smeared liberally over his arms, legs, face, and belly—protection against the hordes of stinging and biting insects.

Finished, he reached for his atlatl and darts. To his dismay, one of the long cane shafts caught on the deerhide hanging from Pine Drop's bedding.

"Huh?" she mumbled. "What's wrong?"

He could see her shifting, sitting up under the soft hide. "Nothing. I'm sorry. It's still early. Go back to sleep."

"Salamander?" she groaned. "Snakes, the sun's not even out yet."

"Shush, go back to sleep." He started for the door.

"Wait. Where are you going?"

"Out to greet the sun. And then hunting."

"Have a good hunt." She started to roll over, then stopped short as if suddenly thinking of something. "Wait. I'm coming with you."

He froze. "Why?"

"I'm your wife. Can't I come with you if I want to? You might be able to use some help."

He could feel his souls sinking. "I might be gone for most of the day."

"It's all right. Night Rain can do the chores. I brought us bladderwort from one of the bogs down south. She can boil it and drain it."

Fortunately, she couldn't see his face while he waited for her to stand, tie her kirtle around her waist, and grease herself.

"Drink some of that stew," he told her insistently. "If you don't, you'll be chewing sticks in two hands' time."

She crouched, lifting the ceramic pot and drinking deeply of the mixture. That, at least, brought him a little satisfaction.

"Wretched Snakes," she said as she replaced the bowl and wiped her lips. "The fire is stone dead, and that tastes like swamp muck."

"It's food," he reminded. "You'll need the strength." He wondered what he was going to eat. It wouldn't do to go begging breakfast from Water Petal as he'd been doing for the last couple of months while he laced his wives' food with the Serpent's potions. It might turn into a very long day for his stomach.

He led the way out into the morning. Moisture rode on the southern breeze, speckling his skin and filling his nostrils. In the darkness, he could see tufts of mist curling along the ridge. The line of domed houses seemed to solidify as if from fragments of dreams as he and Pine Drop walked along the earthen berm to the first gap. From there he crossed to the Southern Moiety commons and cut across for the ramp leading up the eastern side of the Bird's Head.

"Do you do this every morning?" she asked.

"Yes." It had become a ritual with him. The last place on Earth he wanted to be was in Pine Drop's house when his wives awakened. Having begun with such low expectations, their relationship had been deteriorating every since. It had been safe to assume that they wanted as much to do with him as he did with them.

He passed the Council House and started up the long ramp. It never ceased to amaze him that his ancestors had built such a triumph. He often tried to wrap his comprehension around the number of baskets of earth that had been dug, carried, and piled to create the Bird's Head. The sheer size of it filled his souls with awe.

He had taken to sprinting up the long climb and chafed now that Pine Drop was clambering along behind him. Still, he hurried as much as he could, hearing her breath begin to strain when not even halfway up.

"Is there some pressing hurry?" she called from behind.

"Normally I run up this."

"Well, go." She waved him on in the foggy grayness. "I'll see you at the top."

Thus freed, he ran, enjoying the pull in his muscles as he dashed to the top. He came to a halt just past the ramada and filled his hot lungs with the cool air. As he turned back to the east, he could see the faint graying of the horizon. The south wind pushed at him, a last faint filtering of stars visible through the heavy air as they began to fade in the east.

She emerged out of the mist below, thin and well formed, her movements female and sinuous as she climbed. Her hair, loose and long, swayed with each step. Were it anyone but Pine Drop, the moment would have been enchanting. As she neared, her image grew into Spring Cypress's. A fantasy that passed as she raised her face to his.

"Now what?" she asked, a tone of resentment barely hidden.

Salamander seated himself and dug into the moist soil with his fingers. "Now we wait."

"Just wait?" She turned, staring out at the graying world around them. Her breathing slowed as she paced back and forth.

He found the little stone owl he had been carving and the flake that he had buried beside it the morning before. Wiping the black clay from it, he resumed his carving.

"*That's* what you do up here? Just sit and carve?" She pointed at the stone image in his hands.

"Why don't you go back and sleep? This can't be pleasant for you."

He could make out her features now. She was a striking woman, her round face balanced with a thin nose and perfect cheeks. She comported herself with a proud bearing and quiet dignity. He could see her teetering on the verge of stomping off. At the last instant, apparently by force of will, she relented and plopped herself down beside him to stare out toward the eastern horizon. The light there had begun to yellow.

He asked, "Why are you doing this?"

She mulled over the words before she said, "I thought that, perhaps, we might try spending some time together." She was winding her gleaming black hair into tight ropes, only to flip them free and repeat the process. "If we are to live together, we must build some trust between us."

"All right." He shot her a wary look.

"Do you hate me?"

The question caught him by surprise. "No. I don't hate you. I just don't like you."

She stared out at the distance, arms crossed as she leaned forward. He could see her expression tensing, as if she were fighting a pain in her stomach. Returning his concentration to the little red owl, he carefully began the notch that would separate the figure's feet.

After several heartbeats, she said, "Just because we are married doesn't mean that we can't be friends."

"That wasn't the impression I had when I first moved into your house."

"I'm sorry."

Ask her if she is just friends with Three Stomachs. He resisted the impulse, thinking instead of how Salamander was when raccoon was sniffing around his log.

"Sacred Snakes," she whispered, and he looked up. A band of red had burned across the far northeastern horizon. Before them, Sun Town was wreathed in silvered mist, only the black tips of the rooftops protruding in curving rings.

"It's beautiful," she continued. "I had no idea."

"That's why I come here. For this one moment of the day, everything in the world is at peace, locked in beauty. In this instant, my souls Dance in joy and breathe the miracle of life."

The distant fire of morning had illuminated her eyes with an unearthly shine and cast her smooth face in orange. Her lips were parted, and she moved her hands from her belly to the spot between her breasts, as if to feel the beating of her heart.

". . . My souls can Dance in joy," she murmured absently, ". . . breathe the miracle of life."

"Watch this." He raised a hand, anticipating the moment as the sun cracked the horizon and shot a seething sea of red across the mist. It rolled toward them, flicking color from the fingers of mist that deepened as the filaments of dawn threaded in to illuminate Sun Town itself in a warm orange glow.

"Beautiful," she whispered, her face alight with joy.

Her expression stopped him. He had never seen her look this way. Monsters of the deep, she hadn't actually allowed the morning beauty to touch her souls, had she?

"On clear mornings"—he watched the glowing world of color— "you can watch the sun as it moves through the Sky. The turning of seasons is marked as Mother Sun makes her way north and then back south. If you pay close attention, you can see her pass each of the ridges."

"This is a thing the Serpent taught you?"

"Among others."

"And there is Power in this?"

"There is Power in many things. Humans just don't always understand them. Most of the time we refuse to hear the voices the world uses to speak to us. Listening for them isn't something that comes naturally to people."

She studied him, her face profiled in the red light. He had the sudden urge to reach up and trace the line of her forehead and straight nose. To follow the hollow onto her full lips and around her chin.

"Do you really hear those voices?" she asked in an oddly shy voice.

"Some of them." With reluctance, he had to remind himself that this was the same woman who had been in Three Stomach's arms yesterday. That, coupled with her sudden interest in sharing his day, brought wary reality back to roost between his souls.

"Well, come," he said, carefully replacing his owl in its hole and covering it up. "We ought to get on with our hunting. I was thinking of taking a canoe and loading it with fish traps. The water level has dropped enough that the channels are forming."

She looked uncharacteristically sad as she sighed and stood up. "Yes, I suppose so."

Wouldn't it be wonderful if we really could live like this, share not only moments of beauty but the heart, too? A bitter laugh formed in the back of his throat. Such things were not meant for him. He might as well consider walking across the surface of the water.

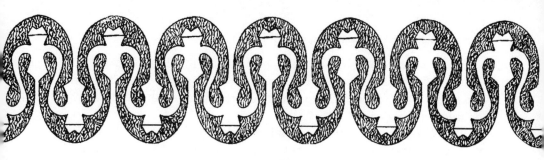

Twenty-five

Who is this man? Pine Drop turned her head, cheek resting on the flattened wood of the canoe bow. From that angle she could surreptitiously watch Salamander's face while at the same time keeping the blue heron in her sight.

A midday sun beat down, the air muggy and filled with insects who rose, fell, and circled on gleaming wings. Birdsong filled the backswamp forest, and the rich odor of wet earth, water, and plant life penetrated her nostrils.

Their canoe rested in a marshy shallow, partially lodged in a stand of swamp grass that obscured their outline. Herons were keen-eyed birds, among the most difficult to sneak up on. Nevertheless, by patience and stealth, Salamander had eased their canoe within a stone's easy pitch of the tall bird. Through the stems she could see it as it hunted the lily pad-filled shallows. The graceful heron took one sure step, then, several heartbeats later, another. Between each step, the heron stopped, serene, its head slightly cocked, an alert eye on the dark water.

"He is so precise," Salamander whispered. "No movement wasted."

This is a day of revelations. She considered both the heron and her husband anew. She had known herons ever since she was a child. Her people hunted them: their meat was prized; the bones were used for awls and flutes; and the feathers served as personal adornment at ceremonials and special occasions. Through all those years, she had never observed a living bird up close—let alone for any length of time. She had never peeked into another creature's life, never even considered that it might have a personality and unique characteristics.

The same way her husband, Salamander, did. Who *was* he? *What* was he? That morning in her presence, Salamander had transformed himself from a fool to a mystery. Clearly uncomfortable with her presence, he had been aloof, hesitant, and protective. After the miracle of the morning sunrise, they had walked down, loaded his canoe with fish traps, and paddled out into the channels to bait and set the traps. In the process, Salamander had stopped them under a low-hanging cypress to watch as one of the large yellow-and-black spiders spun a beautiful web between the branches.

At first she had chafed at the inactivity, baffled by the rapt expression on his face. It had finally occurred to her that for the first time, his guard was down. She was seeing him as he really was. The wonder she saw reflected in his face was the image of his true souls shining through. Then, in an effort to understand his fascination, she had really paid attention to what the spider was doing.

Strand by strand the spider enlarged the spiral of its web. Each action was like a carefully practiced Dance. The gossamer threads were spun and carefully set in place by a graceful manipulation of the legs.

"I've never realized how perfect their webs are," she had remarked. "Isn't that curious? In all of my life, I've never watched one being built."

"People are too busy," Salamander had remarked offhandedly. "We are in such a hurry to feed our bellies that we forget our souls."

"So tell me, what does a soul need for food?" she had asked somewhat sharply.

She had never seen his eyes like that. They looked ancient, knowing, like tunnels to the infinite. He said, "Beauty, peace, and tranquillity."

For a moment she mulled his words. "What about authority, prestige, and security?"

"Tell me something, Pine Drop. Are you happy with your life? Don't just answer for the sake of answering. Think about it. When you close your eyes at night do you take a deep sigh and say to yourself, 'Feel the joy in my souls. Thank the Sky Beings that I have had such a good day.' Then, do you look back over the wondrous things you saw and experienced that day?" He smiled shyly. "Tell me the truth."

She had searched his eyes, then lied. "Yes, I do."

A knowing smile had been his only answer before he turned back to watching the spider.

His question had unsettled her, as had his serene presence as they finished laying out fish traps. He had seen the heron, and drifted them silently into the marshy flats where they now watched the bird through a screen of grass. Pine Drop had taken the time to study him with the same scrutiny she applied to the wondrous heron.

"How do you answer that question, Salamander?" she whispered softly. "Do you go to sleep happy every night?"

He shrugged slightly where he lay beside her in the canoe. "Depends on the day. On a day like this, I will. If I have to spend the day involved in clan dealings, I won't."

"You're a Speaker. You have to deal with those things."

"Responsibility can kill the souls," he whispered.

"It can also fulfill them. It is what you make of it."

"The difference is where you find responsibility. Is it responsibility to yourself, to your lineage, your clan, or your people? That's the soul killer. Responsibility to self, however, fulfills."

"So, what are you doing today?"

"I am feeding my souls."

"And when people are looking up to you as Speaker?"

"My souls are dying." A pause and a gesture. "Watch."

The heron took a half step and froze. Balanced on one foot, it shot its head forward, the long yellow beak flashing into the water. It lifted its head in a sinuous motion, flipping the silver fish in the air and swallowing it. Only then did it gracefully insert its raised foot into the water.

"Isn't that remarkable?" Salamander's voice was reverent. "A person couldn't do that, not with that kind of balance. Did you see how the heron just seemed to flow. At the Creation, Heron must have done something wonderful."

"Why do you say that?"

"Because the Creator gifted Heron with so much grace and beauty."

"People generally don't think of herons that way."

"People usually don't receive the kind of gifts that you and I have just received."

"You think this is a gift, being able to spy on a heron this way?"

"Of course."

"Why?"

"Because my souls have been fed. How about yours? What will you tell yourself tonight when you lie down to go to sleep? Will you look back on today and smile as you remember the sunrise? What about the way the spider's legs moved so precisely to place each strand of web? Or the way the heron moved?"

She evaded giving an answer. "Does it bother you that people think you're a fool?"

"No one wants to be thought of as a fool. They just don't understand, that's all."

"Why don't you do something about it?"

"What? Change myself. Try to be White Bird? I can't be like him. He was who he was. I have to be who I am. Not only that, it's not worth it. I won't give up Power just so that people will like me."

"What do you mean, give up Power?"

She could see the reservation return, and he said nothing, eyes on the heron, who had stepped farther away.

"Is that why you spend so much time with the Serpent? He's teaching you the ways of Power?"

Salamander shrugged. She could sense that she was losing him again, so, after a pause, she said, "You are right. About souls, I mean, and what they need for food. When I go to sleep at night, I don't feel very good about myself." She felt nervous as she added, "I am usually too exhausted to think about anything but who did what to whom. I repeat conversations from earlier in the day and worry about what I should have said. Sometimes I repeat them over and over, as if I'm practicing conversations that are forever gone. That or I worry about all of the things I didn't get done or have to do the next day." She made a face. "So, no, by your standards I guess I don't go to bed happy."

"I'm sorry to hear that."

"Why should you be concerned about what I feel?"

"Because, like me, you are trapped. You didn't want this any more than I did."

"Would you change it?"

He turned then, a warmth in his eyes that made her heart skip. "Oh, indeed I would."

"But you are Speaker for your clan? You are Owl Clan's leader! People look up to you. You are one of the most important men in the world. There are only six Speakers, and you are one of them. Do you expect me to believe that you would give that up?"

"In a heartbeat."

"To do what?"

As he considered, she watched his gentle eyes, seeing the complexity, the turmoil behind them. Something about him sent a shiver through her, as if for the first time she could see the depth and breadth of his souls. No man had ever looked at her with such infinite patience and understanding. Snakes, he was three summers younger than she was, but that look sent a tingle through her souls. Did Power really possess him?

"I would ease other people's souls," he finally answered. "I want to learn all the hidden things. I want to know how a firefly glows without getting hot. How snakes move without feet. Why ants can carry things that are bigger than they are."

"And why bears don't have tails?"

"Yes!"

She laughed for the first time. "And how mushrooms can grow without roots?"

Frightened by their rising voices, the heron leaped into the air, flapping away on liquid wings.

"Mushrooms don't have roots? That's one I have never thought of," Salamander remarked thoughtfully.

"Hanging moss doesn't have roots either," she told him, smiling. "Why not? It's a plant, too."

"See! There are so many things. Everywhere you look there is a mystery hidden, and it's so wonderful. Why is it that some people never seem to grasp the wonder?" His expression saddened.

"What?"

"Mother never understood."

After an awkward pause, she said, "I think you have had a lot of nights when you didn't go to bed happy either, Salamander."

That shy smile slipped past his lips. "Perhaps not. But I have learned to live with it. I cherish the memories. Like today, just now, watching the heron. Talking with you like this. After a day of dealing with Mother, I take them out, share them."

"Share them? With whom?"

He just smiled wistfully.

"Do you hate her?"

"Who, Mother? No. I know who she is, who she had to be for the clan and the People. I understand what it meant to her. I don't think she can stand the pain anymore."

"Is she all right?"

"No. I'm worried about her."

"People are talking."

He nodded, obviously unwilling to discuss it.

Did she dare? Was this the right moment?

"What does Jaguar Hide want from Owl Clan?"

She saw the change in his eyes, felt the coolness as he straightened and picked up the paddle. "We'd better be getting back."

"Are you going to meet with him?"

"The Clan Elder will give him safe passage."

"For what? Why would he—"

"I have to be getting back. I'm sure that you have clan business to attend to."

At his abrupt tone, she nodded, sat up, and reached for her paddle. As they pushed the canoe out of the shallows, it was as though something delicate and precious had suddenly turned cold.

Mud Stalker sat in the ramada as the evening fire crackled and popped, thankful that one of the youngsters in his lineage had thought to bring a supply of wood. The day had been busy, his authority called upon to mend a rift between two brothers over a woman and to make a judgment in a case of fish stealing. In the first instance, he had forbade either brother to see the woman, a member of Rattlesnake Clan. Perhaps they would learn a valuable lesson in this: Kinsmen did not compete with each other. Acting in such a manner had been disrespectful of the clan.

In the second case, he had found against the thief, requiring him to forfeit his canoe and to deliver one basket of fish to the aggrieved family per moon for an entire cycle. That the thief had been from Snapping Turtle Clan, and the victim from Owl Clan, had made his day more than a little sour, but with two neutral witnesses from Alligator Clan observing the theft, he couldn't have found any other way.

The fire popped, and he slapped at the mosquitoes that came with the fall of night. Despite his greased skin, they seemed unusually bloodthirsty. They kept flying into his ears, somehow aware that the insides were vulnerable. The soft whining of their wings was about to drive him mad.

He had a length of cane before him—the shaft for a new atlatl dart. To compensate for his bad arm, he had the shaft pinched in the crook of his right leg and clamped in his worn teeth. Staring from the corner of his eye, he reached out with his left hand and carefully placed a stone point into the grooved end of the cane. This next was the delicate part. Careful not to jiggle the point loose, he retrieved a length of damp sinew from the bowl before him and carefully maneuvered a pretied loop around the point. When it was in the right place he pulled it snug. In the process, he barely noticed someone coming to take a seat opposite him. Whatever they wanted could wait.

Having immobilized the point, he wound the sinew round and round the shaft, pulling it tight enough to keep the point in place. As he came to the end of the sinew, he formed a complicated knot, bending and rolling the fine thread between his fingers. Switching his grip, he took the shaft in his left hand and used his teeth to yank the knot tight.

Satisfied, he studied his work in the light of the fire. The point lay straight, perfectly aligned. The thick wrap of sinew would dry and shrink, tightening into a hard, immovable hafting.

"It always amazes me to watch you do that," Pine Drop said by way of greeting. He lifted his new dart and balanced it in his good hand. She had seated herself across the fire from him. He tried to read her expression but couldn't decipher the complex frown that marred her young forehead.

"Where have you been all day? Night Rain was here, and there, and the other place looking for you. She wasn't entirely sure what you wanted done with that bladderwort. In the end, I think she boiled the whole sackful. It took every pot in the house." He cocked his head. "Is she feeling all right? Her stomach seemed to be bothering her."

"It's nothing," Pine Drop answered. She had her legs bent before her and was rubbing her hands along her smooth muscular shins. "I was out with Salamander all day."

"Ah. And?"

The preoccupied look deepened. "Nothing." Her expression betrayed puzzlement. "Such an odd man. We watched the dawn from the Bird's Head. Why have I never done that before?"

"I have no idea."

"After that we went fishing."

"That's good." He suddenly understood her thinking. Smart girl. Men liked to talk when they were fishing. For some reason, it directed their thoughts to important matters, unlike hunting, which might deepen a man's thoughts but had to be conducted in quiet and discipline.

"Is it?" she wondered. "We spent more than two hands' time watching a blue heron stalking the shallows. Another two hands' time was spent studying how a yellow spider spins its web."

"I assume that you talked during these things?"

She nodded absently. "About everything but his clan. We talked about patience and organization, and what humans refused to hear or learn. Thinking back, none of it made sense." Her lips bent with irritation. "Do you know that I've never watched a spider build a web from nothingness before? Or seen that a heron flips a minnow in the air to swallow it?"

"Fascinating, I'm sure. I don't suppose that Jaguar Hide came up in any of these conversations?"

"No." She gave him a flat look. "When I grew desperate, I even asked him straight out." She paused. "I think he was expecting that question. I'd swear that he gave me a faint smile after that, a sadness in his eyes. The only thing he would tell me was that Wing Heart was going to promise Jaguar Hide safe passage, and that beyond that it was clan business."

"That was it?"

She nodded, her fingers still moving up and down her thighs.

"You didn't press him?"

"Of course I did, Uncle. But his entire manner had changed. I might just as well have slapped him."

He ran his fingers along his new dart. "I don't suppose you took the opportunity to lie with your husband? That usually loosens a man's tongue."

Her eyes fixed on his, dark, penetrating; the effect left him unsettled. "It wouldn't have been right, Uncle."

"What's not *right* about it? You're his wife! Wives couple with husbands. It's what they do."

"After having been with Three Stomachs the day before?"

"You know why we're doing that."

The corners of her mouth tightened. "It wasn't that kind of day," she muttered. "Excuse me, Uncle. I was up with the dawn. I'm tired."

"Don't forget, with Back Scratch's death your mother is confirmed in the Council in three days. We need to prepare a feast for her, and we want you and your sister there for her confirmation. Dress in your finest." He paused, failing to understand her irritation. "And don't stop working on your husband. I'm sure you're smart enough to pry this information out of him."

"I doubt I'll see him anytime soon, Uncle. Not after today."

"What? Why not? He sleeps in your house, doesn't he?"

"That's about all he does." She rose gracefully, her parting glance upsetting his protest before she strode off toward her house on the third ridge.

He frowned as he fingered his new dart. Firelight danced in yellow waves along the cane shaft. *What just happened here? What did I miss?*

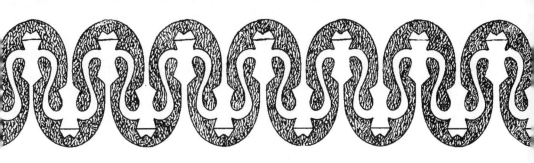

Twenty-six

The Council House was filled; the six clans occupied their respective sections along the edge of the ring. While a great fire was built in the center at night, on daytime occasions such as this, a smoldering log in the middle of the fire pit sufficed. The afternoon sun was slanting at an angle from the northwest. The shaft of light illuminated Mud Stalker and his sister Sweet Root, the newly appointed Clan Elder.

Wing Heart studied her new opponent and tried to concentrate. Sweet Root. This was Sweet Root. Elder Back Scratch was dead. Dead. Just like Graywood Snake. Just like White Bird. Cloud Heron . . . dead.

When? She blinked, confused.

The terrible ache in her souls continued to muddle her thoughts. As the meeting continued, she kept hearing Cloud Heron, his deep voice booming as he stepped out and addressed the Council. She could see him there in the slanting sunlight. Watched as he raised his hand and spoke so eloquently to the crowd. His voice, so clear and resonant, echoing in her souls.

Look at him! Isn't he magnificent? Has there ever been a Speaker as grand as Cloud Heron?

She tried desperately to focus her attention on Sweet Root, but tears tugged at the corners of her vision.

Sweet Root was speaking, her voice sounding far away. She remained a handsome woman, her hair still midnight black despite her age. She might have delivered eight children, two of whom had lived, but her body remained slim, only a thickening of her waist evidence of the seasons she had spent carrying children in her womb. She had been tattooed around her flattened breasts, down the midline of her belly, along the arch of her shoulders, and across her chin. Another pattern of concentric circles had been tattooed on her abdomen between the navel and pubis in an effort to increase her fertility; that pattern was now obscured by the dust gray kirtle she wore.

Wing Heart glanced about, looking for Cloud Heron. She had just seen him, addressing the Council. Not a moment before. He had to be here somewhere. *Where is he?*

Snapping Turtle Clan was well represented on this day, as was their right. Not only did Speaker Mud Stalker sit proudly as his sister was confirmed as Elder, but so did both of the woman's daughters, Pine Drop and Night Rain. The girls had dressed resplendently: Brightly colored headdresses made from painted bunting feathers perched atop their gleaming black hair, and yellow shawls of tanned young alligator hide hung from their shoulders. Each of their kirtles was tied immaculately at the waist.

Such beautiful girls. Very worthy of White Bird. She looked around, losing her thoughts. *Where is White Bird? He should be here for this.*

"*Dead,*" a voice echoed in her head.

"No, not dead," she snapped in irritation as she glanced around, seeking to identify the speaker. It was impossible. Absolutely impossible. He lived, yes, that's right. Something held him up. Something important.

"As my first act as Clan Elder," Sweet Root's raspy voice called, "I must ask this Council to consider the matter of Owl Clan's invitation to the Swamp Panther leader, Jaguar Hide."

Attention turned in Wing Heart's direction. In the eye of her soul, Cloud Heron was sitting behind her, his age-lined face somber as he steepled his fingers. She waited for him to speak.

Another memory drifted into focus, and she watched her son, White Bird, as he stood, alive, strong, straight, raising his hands to accept the cries of approbation that had risen from the gathered Elders, Speakers, and the crowd outside the confines of the Council.

Look at him, Cloud Heron! How proud he stands, his back straight, the sunlight beaming down on his head. Look at the smile, the ease with which he accepts leadership!

"Elder?" Water Petal said from behind.

"What?" Wing Heart blinked, her son vanished. She turned, but Cloud Heron was nowhere to be seen. Her souls staggered, only to remember her brother sinking into fever, his body wasting over the long moons. A nightmare image—a yellow tongue of fire—leaped from a torch to ignite the roof of the house that held his cleaned bones.

You are alone! Her souls shriveled at the knowledge.

"I was . . ." She blinked as she tried to find herself, to recall what was happening. Glancing around, she realized that everyone was waiting, waiting for her. "Cloud Heron, tell them," she muttered.

At the stunned expressions on Water Petal's and Moccasin Leaf's faces, she whirled around, searching. Where was Cloud Heron? She had just seen him, his hand up, voice ringing as he addressed the Council.

"Where did he go?" she wondered.

"Who, Elder?" Moccasin Leaf had a horrified look on her face.

"Tell them." Wing Heart looked into Water Petal's eyes, and waved at the Council. "Just . . . tell them." She tilted her head as she tried to understand what was happening. If Cloud Heron hadn't brought this up, who had? Surely this was something that Water Petal had mentioned. She must know. "Speak for me."

Water Petal swallowed hard and stepped forward. Moccasin Leaf's eyes might have been deer-bone stilettos, piercing her souls with hate and embarrassment. Seated on a palmetto mat, young Mud Puppy watched her with wide, frightened eyes. Mud Puppy? What was he doing here?

"Does this Council not deserve the Elder's respect?" Sweet Root demanded. "Does Wing Heart not speak for her clan when it comes to allowing an avowed enemy to step into our midst? I may be new here, but even as a freshly made Elder, it would appear that I have more respect for these proceedings than the revered Elder from Owl Clan."

"If the Council will hear my words," Water Petal stepped forward, a curious tremor in her voice.

"I, for one," Sweet Root immediately answered, "wish to hear from the Clan Elder."

"She's not well!" It was Mud Puppy's voice. He was on his feet, stepping out in front of Water Petal, his fists clenched at his sides. He wore a beautiful white mantle, one that shone in the afternoon sunlight.

Wing Heart turned, blinking hard. *Why is he here?* This was a place for Speakers recognized by the Council, not uninitiated boys. "Where is my brother? Where is Cloud Heron? Why isn't he here?" Fear bloomed within her like a lotus.

It was Water Petal who swung around on one heel, deftly catching

Wing Heart's elbow. "Come, Elder. Let's get you home. The Speaker can handle this." But fear lay in Water Petal's eyes.

"Yes," Wing Heart agreed, quick with relief. "The Speaker can handle this. Cloud Heron always knows what to do."

She was being led away as she heard Mud Puppy say, "The Elder meant no disrespect. If the Council will just be patient . . ." A roar of voices erupted in answer.

Cold shivers ran down Salamander's body as he shot a quick look over his shoulder. Water Petal was leading his mother away, one hand on her elbow. Even from this distance, he could see his mother's face—a stricken look etching her once-indomitable features.

He swallowed hard, turning his attention back to the jeering calls of the Council. His heart hammered at his ribs, fear bright in his veins. Behind him, Moccasin Leaf was hissing something in poisonous tones.

I can't speak to the Council! I'm not a Speaker! He nerved himself to step out into the open where a Speaker should stand. His skin had the hot nervous prickle of embarrassment. For a moment, he couldn't find words.

He glanced at Clay Fat, only to read disappointment in the appalled expression on his face. Turtle Mist, beside him, looked horrified. People shifted on their feet, clearly uncomfortable. Deep Hunter sat with his jaw cradled in his right hand, head tilted forward as he glared out with hard eyes. Stone Talon was shaking her head, tsking sounds coming from her toothless mouth. Three Moss, her hand on her mother's shoulder, gaped incredulously.

Cane Frog demanded, "What is happening? What do you see? Tell me, Daughter! Who is doing what?"

Salamander turned his pleading eyes to Mud Stalker, only to encounter a burning intensity, a hard smile on the man's thin lips. He stood behind Sweet Root, cradling his ruined right arm. Long white heron feathers had been inserted into bands on his upper arms so that they stuck out like snowy wings. Where she stood, a pace in front of him, Sweet Root might have been tasting something delicious, her eyes half-lidded and blissful.

"The Elder is sick!" Salamander cried. "Just leave her alone. Let her rest. She'll get better. She will."

He hated himself, embarrassment growing hotter with each beat of his heart. They could see the sweat breaking out on his face now. See his losing battle as his muscles began to tremble.

Sweet Root asked loudly, "Do I speak for the Council when I say that no 'sick' Clan Elder should be dealing with Jaguar Hide within the limits of Sun Town? What has Wing Heart done? Asked the leader of the dreaded Swamp Panthers to come here? A foreigner, allowed to walk unpurified into our midst? And bringing what with him? A black cloud of curses? Witchcraft? Will he unleash disease and misery among us?"

A roar of agreement went up, members of the Council nodding and bobbing their heads.

"Then we will meet him on the Turtle's Back!" Salamander shouted, hoping at least to mollify some of the sentiment against his mother. Snakes and lightning, what had happened to her?

"Why meet him at all?" Deep Hunter asked from where he sat.

"To find out what he wants," Salamander answered, his stomach curling and twisting inside him. He had fastened his eyes on Pine Drop and Night Rain. Their expressions jolted him: a mixture of pity, embarrassment, and loathing.

"Why did he send a runner to Wing Heart?" Mud Stalker demanded as he stepped forward to stand beside his sister. "What is his business with Owl Clan? Why didn't he ask to speak with the Council?"

"I don't know." Salamander tried to swallow the knot in his throat. Their eyes were boring through him, seeing his quaking souls. Why had Mud Stalker insisted he take his brother's place? Surely anyone could have known he wasn't supposed to be a Speaker.

"Perhaps," Mud Stalker said evenly, "there should be some representation from the Council at this meeting? What do you say?" He took another step forward, where he could meet the eyes of the others. "An old enemy comes, and we should allow him to meet only with Owl Clan? To broker what sort of deal? Something that leaves the rest of us out? Or something which, for our own safety, we should know about?"

"Alligator Clan agrees," Deep Hunter remarked. "We will send our delegates to this meeting to see for ourselves."

"As will Frog Clan," Elder Cane Frog called, her sightless eyes alone blind to Owl Clan's humiliation.

"Eagle Clan will be there, too," Stone Talon called. "Speaker Thunder Tail will represent our interests."

"So will Rattlesnake Clan," Clay Fat agreed, his voice less strident than the others.

"Owl Clan votes no," Salamander said in a futile and small voice. Atop everything else came the sting of defeat. He had just spoken for his clan for the first time, and been party to its worst defeat. "It is our business."

"Not anymore," Mud Stalker replied coolly.

When Salamander turned and walked back to his seat, Moccasin Leaf's face was livid, her jaw grinding as white rage mottled her features. Had she a club at hand, he didn't doubt that she would have crushed his skull on the spot.

The canoe slipped silently along the channel, its wake spreading in a long V over the brown water. A muggy heat hung in the still air, heavy and deadening on the lungs. Overhead branches of sweetgum, bald cypress, tupelo, and water oak wove into an impenetrable mat of green draped with vines, flowers, and hanging moss. On either side, ferns, brambles, and tangled vegetation carpeted the banks.

Turtles plopped off logs and dived for the depths as the canoe passed. Birdsong accompanied them, as did the whining of the insects. The smell of vegetation, mud, and stagnant water cloyed in the nostrils.

Anhinga dipped her paddle resolutely as she propelled them forward. She could feel her uncle's piercing stare as it ate into her back. The knowledge that he doubted her sent a flame of anger through her.

Anticipating her, he said, "Remember, this must be done slowly, thoughtfully, and with great skill."

"I *know,* Uncle."

"The gravest danger is time. It will lull you, soften your resolve. You will look around you and begin to see these people as not so different from us."

"You have told me this time and time again."

"I will tell you yet again," Jaguar Hide insisted. "Think, Anhinga! You are going to marry a man. You will live with him, day in and day out. You will look into his eyes, watch his smile. You will welcome his body into yours. His child will begin to grow within you. Do you understand what I'm saying?"

"Yes, Uncle. That by pretending to fall in love with him, I really will." She shook her hair, flipping her raven locks in a dark swirl. "Looking at my back, what do you see?"

"Outside of a healthy and attractive woman?" He hesitated. "The scars are healed."

"Yes, but you can still see them." She drove her paddle vigorously into the water. "And so can I. I can run my fingers over them, feel the ridges, and remember the pain. Those are the things I do when I am awake. I remember what each wound felt like when they inflicted it. Over and over, I see the bodies of my companions. See what they did to them. It is better when I am awake, Uncle. I can shut most of the memories out of my head. When I am asleep, the terror comes. The Dreams wrap around my souls, and I relive every moment, watching them be cut apart, their hearts, livers, and intestines ripped from inside their bodies. I see those animals squatting over ruined faces, defecating into bloody eye sockets. Unlike being awake, I cannot stop the Dreams, Uncle."

He paddled silently behind her for a moment. "The past cannot be killed, Anhinga, but it can be built anew. It is that which you must guard against. You will be tempted."

"I will be *strong*!" she insisted. "I have no life left. At the Panther's Bones, I had to look into eyes of Mist Finger's relatives, see Cooter's sister, wince as Right Talon's mother's eyes asked me, 'Why?' I had no answer for them, Uncle, only the ache in my heart that I was alive, and their sons and brothers were not."

"No one holds it against you."

"I do," she snapped. "And I'm the only one who matters."

After a long silence, he asked again, "Are you sure that you want to do this thing? It is fraught with danger."

"It isn't a matter of wanting, Uncle," she told him hollowly. "I must."

With a leaden heart, she continued to paddle doggedly toward her destiny. In her souls she was already delighting in the surprise as she drove a deer-bone stiletto into White Bird's heart. But before that, yes, she could be patient. She could wait for years if she had to. It would make the act all the more terrible for the witnesses.

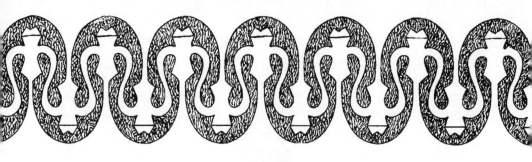

Twenty-seven

I felt like such a fool!" Salamander cried as he reached out from the bobbing canoe and grabbed at the duck-shaped wooden float. He caught it, pulling it toward him. Straightening in the canoe, he reeled in the cord that hauled the wicker fish trap to the surface.

He sat in the stern, Water Petal in the bow. The center of the narrow hull was cluttered with pointed wicker fish traps. Each was the length of a man's leg, two hands wide, cylindrical, with a funnel-shaped opening that allowed a fish to swim in, but not out.

Water Petal remained silent as Salamander grasped the wet staves and pulled the trap from the opaque brown water. A single buffalo fish flopped inside. He placed the trap across his lap and untied the door that allowed him to reach in. He caught the fish behind its gills and pulled it from the trap. Using a round rock, he bashed it in the head and dropped it, quivering, into a basket.

"I've never felt so worthless in my whole life." His thick fingers retied the cord after he closed the hinged trap door. "I couldn't think of anything to say. I was so embarrassed and shamed."

Water Petal picked up her paddle, propelling the canoe forward, steering with the blade. She glanced over her shoulder, checking to see that her son slept soundly in the moss-padded cradle. "Salamander, don't blame yourself. No one expected the Elder to react that way. She was like a ball of soil in a rainstorm. She just melted away."

"My brother wouldn't have made a fool of himself."

"Perhaps not, but he's dead, and you are the Speaker." She shook her head. "I'm not sure how this happened, but it has. Like it or not, you are the Speaker. Sick or not, your mother is the Elder. At least she is until Moccasin Leaf can marshal enough support from the clan to dismiss her."

"She has started on that," Salamander noted. "It will take her a while to get concurrence from the outlying camps. It's the middle of summer. People are off everywhere, hunting, collecting, making a living."

"I don't have much hope," Water Petal told him heavily. "As bad as it was on you, I watched any chance of succeeding Wing Heart vanish. Without her, our lineage is too weak."

Salamander's heart fell. She didn't hold it against him, did she? "Water Petal, I didn't do it on purpose."

She glanced back at him over the pile of fish traps and read his expression. "No, not you, Salamander. I don't blame you. By the Earth Monsters, I don't know how this happened so fast. It's as if Power just blew through like the south wind and left us broken and beaten."

"I am still Speaker." He considered that. "Moccasin Leaf might be able to have Mother removed, but as Speaker . . ."

She turned, expression thoughtful. "Finish that. What were you about to say?"

"Mud Stalker wanted me as Speaker. He saw more clearly than anyone. I would love to know how. He has wanted our clan to be disgraced for years. He brokered the marriage with White Bird and placed me right in line to succeed my brother if anything happened. It's as if he knew White Bird was going to die."

"Salamander, no one can foretell a lightning strike."

"No, but having seen the things I have, it makes me wonder."

"What? That Mud Stalker would have killed White Bird? Do you know what an awful chance he would have been taking? Murdering another clan's Speaker would destroy Sun Town, split the clans right down the middle! It would mean war . . . between us! At best he would be hunted down and murdered! His family and lineage cast into exile, or maybe even killed!"

Salamander stopped short, images reeling in his souls. "Blessed Owl," he whispered.

"Yes? What?"

"It's me!"

"What's you, Salamander?" She was focused on him now, the canoe drifting listlessly toward a lush green bank. As the spring flood had receded, it had left behind a braided web of channels like this one that crisscrossed the wide Father Water's floodplain.

"It's me that he's been counting on. He's been ahead of me all along. He is counting on me to be a failure."

Water Petal said nothing, her expression pinched.

Reading it, Salamander smiled sadly. "I know, Cousin. We're relatives: you, Yellow Spider, and me. Outside of Mother, we are the last of our lineage."

"It's not your fault, Salamander." Water Petal turned away, her hands slipping up and down the paddle as if agitated.

"It isn't time yet," Salamander said gently.

She turned, caught off guard. "Time for what?"

"To take back what is ours."

"I don't understand you."

"I'm not sure I do, either. Cousin, I am going to need an ally."

"Salamander, what are you talking about?"

"I'm not sure yet. But when I know, I'll tell you, all right?"

"You're starting to sound as crazy as your mother."

"Let's hope the rest of the clans think so." He smiled for the first time, pitching the fish trap atop the pile. "The next float is just up there. That's the last one that Pine Drop and I set. I say we cut up this crappie for bait and make another set in the next channel."

For the first time since he had caught his cricket the night White Bird returned from the north, he actually felt tendrils of hope.

Accompanied by six of the enemy's canoes, Jaguar Hide and Anhinga paddled ever closer to Sun Town. It had been a trial for Anhinga, meeting those canoes full of Sun People and traveling side by side with them. In the narrow channels, the enemy were so close that she could reach out with her paddle and tap them. They were propelled by muscular young men, their bodies greased and wearing their best. Colorful feathers were tucked into armbands, hair was done up in high buns and pinned with bone skewers. They wore layers of necklaces across their swelling chests that proclaimed Sun Town's immense wealth. Curiosity and danger reflected in their hard gazes as they paralleled her course.

To keep her nerve, she ignored their called questions, allowed Uncle to do the talking, and kept her back straight, eyes on the channel before her.

She considered it her first challenge, one that she had met, smiling, but remaining aloof enough to keep them at bay. She was, after all, Swamp Panther, the niece of the most noted warrior in the history of her people.

Two other canoes had shot ahead to carry word to Wing Heart that Jaguar Hide was nearing. In spite of her vow of self-control, Anhinga felt a quickening, a thrill and fear mixing within her. She was entering the camp of the enemy to take up a new and secret life.

"Easy," her uncle whispered behind her as they followed a winding channel past a stand of bald cypress, the boles knotted and thick where they rose from the still water. There lay Sun Town, dominating the high bluff across a sun-silvered lake. Dark soil was exposed on either side of the canoe landing, and up high she could see the Father Mound topped by the dreaded Men's House.

Once before she had been brought here to be carried up that slope, degraded and bound—and there, during that foul day, she had suffered while her life was destroyed.

"Are you all right?" Jaguar Hide asked gently. "You haven't taken a stroke in half a dozen heartbeats."

"I was just seeing the past, Uncle." She speared her paddle into the water, driving them forward. She watched as an incredible number of people began to spill down the bank, a host of them launching canoes. The slim craft pointed in their direction, sunlight flashing on paddles as they pushed their craft forward.

"Sobering, isn't it?" Jaguar Hide asked from behind. "That is a lesson, Anhinga. Look at their numbers. And you and your fellows thought to bloody their nose?"

"Does this have a point, Uncle?"

"It does. When you are setting out to harm a great beast, the only way you can deal it a mortal blow is to strike at its heart. Swiftly, without remorse or pity. You must drive your blade true and straight, lest it kill you before you can escape."

"I have already figured that out, Uncle."

One of the lead canoes had closed and was turning sideways, a tall man in the bow, his right arm oddly cradled. "Greetings, Jaguar Hide," the fellow called. "I am Mud Stalker, Speaker of the Snapping Turtle Clan. I am to direct you to the Turtle's Back." He pointed with a muscular left arm. "It is that hump of land there with the gum trees. We shall have our council there."

"Snapping Turtle Clan?" Jaguar Hide muttered. "What do they have to do with anything?"

"Beware, Uncle. A great many things may be happening that we are unaware of. Just get me to Owl Clan, and all will be made right in time."

In a loud voice, Jaguar Hide called, "Accompany us to that place. We have come in peace to see the great Elder, Wing Heart. It is time to bring an end to this senseless killing and raiding."

"Especially as it has cost you so dearly," Mud Stalker agreed in a jocular tone.

"I will drive a dart into his body myself," Anhinga swore under her breath.

"Careful, Niece." Jaguar Hide's smooth voice warned. "Patience is the straightest dart in a hunter's quiver."

When they landed at the small island, it was to encounter a mob. "Not quite what we had expected, is it?" Anhinga asked.

"No, indeed," he replied as he shipped his paddle and stepped out into the warm water. In one hand he retrieved a sack of smoked fish as an offering. In the other he carried his stone-headed ax. A tool equally useful in felling a tree or a man.

Anhinga nerved herself and reached for the sack that contained her personal possessions. The crowd parted, the way leading up to the shadowed base of the sweetgum tree. There a contingent stood, all dressed in finery, bodies greased, colorful feathers adorning their bodies.

"Courage," Jaguar Hide whispered as he passed.

"You, too," she shot back as she fell into step at his side. That short walk, surrounded on both sides by ranks of the enemy, every eye on her, was one of the most terrifying moments of her life. If this were a trap, they would be prisoners before either could react. Death was not nearly as frightening as the prospect of having her tendons cut and having to live the rest of her miserable life here as a slave.

By the time they reached the standing Elders, Anhinga was more than ready to run. Snakes and rot, could they see how scared she was? Even her tongue had stuck in her mouth. But for the grease on her skin, sweat would have beaded and gleamed as it ran.

"Greetings, Elders," Jaguar Hide cried smoothly as he came to a stop. In that instant, he was the noblest man Anhinga had ever seen. Not a sliver of fear was visible in his demeanor or expression. The sunlight played in his silver hair and danced on his broad shoulders. "I am Jaguar Hide. You know me."

"Indeed we do," the tall man, Mud Stalker, replied as he stepped through the crowd to stand beside a middle-aged woman. "We have come to hear what you want from us."

"Peace!" Jaguar Hide cried. "Nothing more, nothing less."

"Peace?" A chubby man asked. He had a moony face, his belly

like a giant smooth brown squash. What would have normally been pleasant eyes looked skeptical.

"Peace," Jaguar Hide answered. "In the last several cycles, we have had too many of our young people murdered."

"That is a strong word," a grizzled old woman stepped forward. "I am Elder Stone Talon, of the Eagle Clan. My son and several of my cousins were butchered by you and your sneaky warriors, and over what? A couple of flats of sandstone?"

Anhinga discovered that she couldn't swallow. Fear had gripped the bottom of her throat until breathing was hard. *Find yourself, curse you! If you can't face this, how are you going to stay here among them?*

"Butchered is precisely the word." Jaguar Hide lifted his arms, the ax held high. "Murdered, killed, slain, what does it matter what we call it? The effect is the same, be it in Sun Town or in the Panther's Bones! We wail and grieve for the lives and souls of our dead loved ones. How many generations have we done this? More than I can relate. Can any of you tell me when this started, how far back?"

A voice called, "It began just after the Creation when the Hero Twins began to battle each other. We have been fighting ever since." The speaker, what looked to be a mere boy, stepped to the fore. Thin, he might have been half-starved. His face was taut, as if he were frightened by speaking out in the presence of his Elders. He pinned Anhinga with large dark eyes that seemed to fill his bony face. "It goes back forever."

That voice! It touched Anhinga's souls. She noticed that the Elders had turned disapproving eyes on the skinny boy, distaste in the set of their lips.

"The boy is correct," Jaguar Hide agreed. "And I, for one, am ready to try something new."

"Why?" A muscular brown man, his face deeply lined by countless days in the sun, asked. "I am Deep Hunter, Speaker of the Alligator Clan, and I would know why Jaguar Hide, who fought so many battles and killed my brother, would come here asking for peace."

Anhinga watched her uncle's face, seeing the slight tic in the corner of his eye. Yes, he knew this Deep Hunter.

"Greetings, Speaker. It has been a long time since you and I faced each other."

"We could take that up where we left it." Deep Hunter's voice had dropped to a growl.

"We could, but it would make more sense if we didn't." Jaguar Hide fingered his ax and stared out from lowered brows. "I have grieved enough in one lifetime, and caused enough others to grieve, that I would find another way."

"Why?" the middle-aged woman beside Mud Stalker asked. "I have been told all of my life that you hate us. What has changed your mind?"

Jaguar Hide smiled, his voice firm. "Oh, I do hate you. Do not believe for a moment that anything we do here today will stop that."

Anhinga tightened as a ripple ran through the crowd.

Jaguar Hide let it hang for a moment before adding, "But I can still hate you without killing your young people. I can hate without hacking their dead bodies apart in a futile attempt to frighten their souls. I can hate you without having to bury one of my young men or women every other moon."

Uncle thrust a hard finger toward Deep Hunter. "*And so can you! You can hate us without killing us!*" A pause in the tense silence. "Who knows, perhaps as we are taken by other means of death, our young people might not hate as we have. Perhaps they will do things differently than we did."

"I still do not understand this," Mud Stalker said warily. "What do you have to gain by peace?"

"The lives of my young people." Jaguar Hide cocked his head. "And you, and your clans, have sandstone to gain, as well as your young people's lives."

"We can take your sandstone anyway," Deep Hunter growled.

"Yes, you can," Jaguar Hide agreed. "But at what price, old enemy? Your nephew? Your grandson?" He shook his head. "I am not here to trick you. I am here to offer you sandstone in return for leaving us alone. I am not fool enough to think that we will remake our world, or forget our hatred and live like brothers. I want to try this for a couple of summers, that is all. Who knows, it may be that we really *enjoy* hunting and killing each other and burning our children's bones in grief." His sad smile seemed to touch them more than the logic of his argument.

"How will this work?" the skinny boy asked before the others could.

That voice! Yes, she knew that voice. But from the darkness, hands fumbling at knots. The sweet words, "*I'm cutting you free,*" echoed in her memory. This forward youth, *he* had been the mysterious shadow in the night?

Uncle said, "From this moment, you will not raid our territory. In return we will allow one canoe per moon to come and take sandstone. If you wish to send two canoes for sandstone, the second must bring gifts for my people. That is all." Jaguar Hide crossed his arms.

"And how do we know you will keep your word?" Deep Hunter's jaw was cocked.

"I bring my niece, Anhinga. I will marry her to the son of Wing Heart, Elder of the Owl Clan. Wing Heart's reputation has traveled far and wide as the greatest among you. We believe that she, of all of you, will see the advantages to this agreement between our peoples."

The words caught the Sun People by complete surprise, but before the Elders could speak, the skinny boy cried, "Owl Clan accepts your offer, great Jaguar Hide."

The boy stepped boldly forward, and for an instant, Anhinga expected his mother to leap from wherever she had been hidden in the crowd to drag him back.

"No, you don't," Mud Stalker growled, narrowing an eye as he studied the boy.

"*Owl Clan* accepts!" the boy fired back, effectively silencing Mud Stalker. The tension between them couldn't be mistaken.

"Who *are* you, boy?" Jaguar Hide asked, obviously surprised.

"I am Salamander, son of Clan Elder Wing Heart and Speaker for the Owl Clan."

Laughter broke out, and Anhinga could only stare as a cold shiver, like a whisper of Power, coursed in her veins. Mud Stalker was glaring daggers at the boy.

"Where is Wing Heart?" Jaguar Hide demanded.

"The Elder is ill," the boy replied, his dark eyes fixed intently on Jaguar Hide. "I have offered to accept your conditions. Yes, or no, revered Elder? Will you marry your daughter to Wing Heart's son, or were your brave words something else?"

Anhinga turned, seeing her uncle's eyes glitter as he said, "I meant what I said! I came here seeking peace!" He looked as if he had just pulled his arm from a hole and found a water moccasin wrapped around it.

The boy took another step forward, offering his hand to Anhinga. "Then, as of this moment, I accept this woman for my wife."

"Salamander!" a young woman cried from the crowd. "What are you doing?"

He ignored her, his gaze burning through Anhinga's shock as he said, "Do you agree to take me as your husband?"

"Yes." Her reply came involuntarily.

Salamander glanced at Jaguar Hide. "I presume that you have

brought the traditional gifts of food. If you will distribute it to the assembled guests here, it will formalize the arrangement between us."

Anhinga stared at Salamander's extended hand, frozen in the moment.

The young woman from the crowd—a baby at her breast—elbowed her way forward, panic on her face. "Salamander, what did you just do?"

"Water Petal, I just cast myself adrift in the Dream," he replied with a weary smile. "I just wish I knew where it will carry me."

Anhinga placed a hand to her throat. She couldn't breathe. Chaos seemed to erupt as the stunned crowd realized what had just occurred. Everyone began talking at once, crowding around her and the skinny youth who took his place so naturally at her side.

Blessed Panther, what have I done to myself?

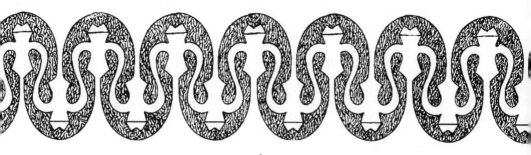

Twenty-eight

Shouts of disbelief drowned the questions being called by others. Aware that he had trapped himself, but unsure how, Jaguar Hide reached into the sack of smoked fish and began handing it out. The boy, first in line, stared into his eyes, taking an oily chunk and thrusting it into his mouth as if in defiance.

Those eyes! Jaguar Hide shook his head. He had seen eyes like that, but never before in a child's face. A child's? The boy—the young man—was Speaker for Owl Clan? Had that been a joke? It was only later, in the milling swelter of people, that he had learned about White Bird's death and the dissolution of Elder Wing Heart's souls.

White Bird died over three moons ago! Elder Wing Heart discredited and soul sick? Why haven't we heard? The question shifted back and forth between his souls.

At times the remoteness of their swamp, safe as it was, left them far removed from the activities of other peoples. Nor, obviously, would the young Owl Clan man he had contacted have admitted to these scandalous happenings within his clan.

Jaguar Hide returned his attention to the present, listening as he handed out gifts of smoked fish. He kept an eye on his niece, watching her as she stood, half in shock, at the youth's side.

"How can Salamander just up and marry her?" a woman was asking her companion. "He didn't even ask his clan!"

"He's the Speaker, that's how."

"But his mother, she should have been consulted," another declared hotly.

"Who? Wing Heart? She's lost her souls: all she does is sit at her loom and Dream of the past."

"You think Wing Heart retains enough of her wits to tell him no?" another asked.

"I'll tell you what," a man insisted, "when Mud Stalker insisted that Salamander follow his brother, he dealt a deathblow to Owl Clan."

So it went, people passing him, collecting pieces of the rapidly vanishing fish, and through it all, he had no time to discuss this unsettling turn of affairs with Anhinga. She looked as if her own souls were floating, white-faced, back stiff, while the skinny man-boy who stood beside her accepted the well-wishing of individuals.

"So, you have your peace," the gruff voice interrupted Jaguar Hide's reeling thoughts.

He centered himself on the threat hidden in that deep voice. Turning, he met Deep Hunter's narrow stare with his own. "We have *our* peace. You and me, old enemy."

Deep Hunter shot a look over his broad shoulder to where Anhinga and Salamander stood in the center of a knot of people. "It didn't quite turn out the way you expected, did it?"

How could he know? Old reflexes from countless Council sessions and clan meetings came to his rescue. "You tell me. Is that boy really the Owl Clan Speaker?"

Deep Hunter nodded, amusement in his eyes. "He is indeed, confirmed by the Council after his brother was stuck dead by the Sky Beings."

"Then, being only somewhat familiar with your laws, his action carries a great weight with your Council."

Deep Hunter sensed the trap. "It does, but his decision to marry your niece does not bind the Council. We will discuss this peace of yours. We can still dismiss it out of hand."

Jaguar Hide handed the last piece of fish to Deep Hunter before folding up the bag. "I understand that. But Owl Clan is bound, isn't it? If the other clans should decide not to accept my offer of peace, it would appear that Owl Clan will have a singular and unlimited source of sandstone. And—excuse me if I'm unsure of your ways— that would grant them a great deal of status, wouldn't it?"

"Status, prestige, authority, it comes and goes like the wind, old enemy. Look at how Owl Clan has fallen, from the top to the bottom, and just within a few moons."

"They could rise again, just as quickly, I would assume. And yet another clan could fall like a dropped stone. A lesson I would well remember, Speaker." Jaguar Hide grinned wickedly. "If this could happen to the great Wing Heart, I'd say none of you is truly safe. Wouldn't you?"

"You didn't come here seeking peace." Deep Hunter's eyes were probing.

"Ah, old enemy, but I did." He gestured at his niece, looking like a surprised deer suddenly surrounded by a ring of hunters with nocked darts. "Let's you and I see what the future brings, hmm?" Somewhere deep down between his souls, a voice cackled in raucous laughter. No matter the way of it, his weapon was planted. From here on, he must hope that Anhinga was as tough and single-minded as he believed her to be.

"Welcome to the future, Deep Hunter."

Night Rain ran as she had never run, breath pulling at her throat as she sprinted full tilt across the plaza to her clan grounds, passed the first two ridges, and rounded the borrow pit. She charged along the row of houses, her kirtle flapping, her young breasts bouncing. She leaped a barking dog that rushed out to intercept her. The cur continued growling and snapping at her ankles. Ripping a stick from a firewood pile outside her cousin's house, she paused long enough to smack the dog along the side of its head before charging headlong past the last house and into her yard.

"Sister! *He's married!*"

"What?" Pine Drop asked, poking her head through the door. Ground smilax root covered her hands in a paste.

"Salamander! He's married!" She was gasping, one hand to her burning throat.

"Well of course he is, you silly toad. To us!" Pine Drop had an irritated look on her face.

"Yes, to us! And to this Swamp Panther woman!" She pointed to somewhere behind her. "It just happened! Out there . . . on the Turtle's Back. I told you you should have come!"

"What on earth are you talking about?"

"Jaguar Hide! The Swamp Panther! The meeting he wanted with Owl Clan? It was to make a peace. This Anhinga is part of it."

"Who is Anhinga?"

"His new wife! Salamander married Jaguar Hide's niece to seal the agreement! It just happened!"

Pine Drop looked confused. "He wouldn't have married this quickly. He'd need time to discuss it with his clan. This must be some sort of joke."

"No, I swear, Sister, Salamander just took this woman for his wife. It happened so quickly no one could do anything about it. It even caught Mother and Uncle by surprise."

"So, what are we going to do about it?"

That question caught Night Rain flat-footed. "I don't have any idea."

"What did Uncle say?"

"He told Salamander no. And then Salamander defied him in front of everyone. Uncle is fuming."

"What did he say to you?"

"He said to come and tell you. Right away!"

Pine Drop's brow lined, puzzlement mixed with disbelief. "Well, he's certainly *not* bringing her here!"

Night Rain's gasping had slowed to deep breathing. "Sister, this isn't good, is it?"

"I don't know," Pine Drop said softly, her gaze growing absent. "Maybe I just need time to think, that's all."

The sun had dipped below the high embankment of Sun Town to cast a blue-green shadow across Morning Lake. Puffs of cloud gleamed as they continued their endless march north from the gulf.

People slowly trickled away, taking to their canoes to paddle back to the landing. Salamander paused for a moment to gather his thoughts. The afternoon had passed like one of the whirlwinds that ripped out of late-summer thunderheads.

Several clumps of young men stood in furtive groups by the shore, talking over the day's events as they studied their canoes and shot curious glances back at Jaguar Hide. Salamander couldn't help notice the stacked atlatls and darts lying inside those narrow hulls. Something about the way they waited, the way they stood, quickened his souls.

Jaguar Hide stood to one side, his head bowed as he studied the charcoal-stained dirt at his feet. His face was a deeply lined mask, the thoughts hidden, almost brooding. If Salamander could read the set of his shoulders, a terrible nagging worry lay within the man.

Salamander glanced at his new wife. Jaguar Hide had every reason to be worried, most likely about his current situation. His life was under the protection of a broken and impotent clan. Anhinga, however, looked absolutely miserable and terrified, as if she were once again some sort of captive.

"Do not be frightened," he said as he turned to her. "I think this was meant to be."

Her eyes were partially hidden by the fall of her long black hair. She stood with her arms crossed under her breasts, the nipples like darts pointed at his souls. "Who are you?" Her voice was laced with frustration.

"I am Salamander, Speaker for the Owl Clan, as you have heard over and over this day."

"*Who* are you?" she repeated more vehemently. "Why did you step out today? You're no Speaker. The Sun People only choose old men for Speakers."

"This time they chose me. It happens, but very rarely."

"Why you?"

"Because my brother was killed. He was struck by lightning. I was made Speaker in his place."

"That makes no sense." Her beautiful face trembled as if she were fighting sudden tears.

"It wasn't supposed to." He narrowed an eye. "They made me Speaker in order to discredit my clan."

"It worked."

He smiled. "Yes. For the moment. Come, we must talk with your uncle." But she didn't move as Salamander walked over to where Jaguar Hide stood lost in his musings. "Elder? Are you staying the night on the island?"

"I think not." He lifted his head to scan the sky. "It will be dark in a couple of fingers' time. That will be good enough." His smile turned predatory. "Were I to stay here, boy, I'm not sure my souls would find my body alive in the morning. There are men here who wouldn't trouble themselves over a silly little agreement made between you and me. And, as I have discovered, the great Wing Heart's authority is a thing of the past, so I doubt she could protect me." He shook his head, eyes taking in the waiting youths. "No, better that I take my leave as dark is falling. By the time a pursuer catches up, I will have vanished into the channels like the fog."

"As you wish, Elder."

The old warrior studied him as if he were a piece of meat. "Are you a fool, or a joke, boy?"

"I am Speaker for the Owl Clan." He couldn't help meeting that gaze. "I am supposed to be a joke. The spirits will decide who laughs longest."

"I see." He turned his attention to Anhinga. "I will be going. Take care of my niece. If you don't, I will hear about it; when I do, it will take you a long, long time to die."

The way he said it made Salamander's blood chill. This man had been raiding from the swamps when Salamander's mother was but a suckling. It took no stretch of imagination to believe the stories about the number of men Jaguar Hide had killed.

The Swamp Panther Elder turned and walked toward the shore. He bent over the canoe, laying out what Salamander determined were sandstone slabs. Then, without a word, he pushed the canoe out, jumping lithely into it. The craft didn't even rock as the old warrior settled in the stern, picked up his paddle, and pulled the canoe around.

"Wait!" The cry strangled in Anhinga's throat as she rushed up, staring in disbelief, a slim hand to her throat. In a louder voice, she called, "Uncle?"

He raised a hand to her, but didn't look back as he stroked vigorously for the channels. The young men, clustered as they were, were caught by surprise. Salamander could see them, talking in hushed tones before they raced for their canoes.

"Let him go," Salamander called. "No matter what your orders, it is only right! He came according to his word: Owl Clan has guaranteed him safe conduct."

"He killed my father!" Saw Back, of the Alligator Clan, cried passionately.

"Animal," Anhinga hissed under her breath.

"And your clan has killed more than one of his kin in return," Salamander replied as he blocked their way to the canoes. "I said let him go."

"Who are you to give someone in Alligator Clan an order?"

"I am Owl Clan's Speaker. I stand in the Council and know its wishes! If you push this thing, it will be between your clan and mine. Do you want to come and explain that to the Council?" Salamander crossed his arms.

Saw Back picked up a pointed paddle engraved with alligators and stepped up to Salamander. "You're the smallest whelp in the litter, Mud Puppy. I don't care that you were made some Speaker! You're barely off the nipple yourself, and you want to give *me* orders?" He smiled as he gripped the paddle. "Move out of my way!"

"Go ahead. Strike me, Saw Back. Do it right and break a couple of bones. Better yet, kill me." Salamander took a step forward, aware that the youths were watching, waiting, a keen anticipation in their eyes. "Deep Hunter will be so pleased when he has to defend his clansman in the Council. You see, it's not just me, but the very notion of a warrior striking a Speaker. It sets a precedent that the Council can't allow, no matter what they think of me."

Saw Back stared at Anhinga, taking in her perfect body. "I think after I smack some manners into you, I'll break your wife in for you."

Salamander took another step forward, crowding him. "No, you won't."

"Why?"

"Because your mother will be crying as she burns your bones."

That brought laughter from the youths. They were crowding around now, that hunter's gleam in their eyes. They were primed to fight, to kill.

Saw Back had to take a step back to tap his chest. "You'd kill me? Here are my souls, Mud Puppy, come and take them."

"I am Salamander," he replied calmly. "As long as you do not defy the Council, I won't take your souls. But if you push this thing, I will. Not tonight, but sometime when—"

"He's getting away!" Needs Two, another of the Alligator Clan hunters called as he looked over his shoulder. Jaguar Hide's rapidly moving canoe was halfway to the channel.

Anhinga backed away. From the edge of his vision, Salamander watched her pick up one of the pointed paddles. The way she held it assured him she hadn't considered using it in the water.

A handful of young warriors eased off to one side and bent to shove one of the canoes out.

"I said, *leave him alone!*" Salamander pointed a finger at them. "As a member of the Council, I *order* you."

Saw Back made a face. "You couldn't—"

"*Fool!*" Salamander shouted into his face. "The Council could care less what *I* order, but as a Speaker, it would make an exception. Would Deep Hunter want it whispered around that a Speaker can be disobeyed? This isn't about *me,* Saw Back!"

"He's almost to the channels!" Needs Two cried as he hopped from foot to foot, unwilling to take action on his own.

"Well?" Salamander cried, walking between them, his hands waving. "What is it? Are you going to attack me? Are you going to throw a burning ember into the tinder of clan relations? Why don't you run and ask Deep Hunter if he wants a fight with Owl Clan? That wasn't in the orders, was it? No, just go kill Jaguar Hide! But Owl Clan has made a bargain since that order was given." He thrust a finger at Anhinga. "You would kill my wife's uncle! I would have to seek retribution!"

They looked confused, half of them fingering their darts as they glanced out to where Jaguar Hide's canoe slipped into the channel, vanishing behind the bald cypresses.

Salamander gave a frustrated sigh, hoping that fear sweat hadn't broken out on his hot face. "All right, get off the island. I have things to attend to with the Serpent. This woman must be cleansed." He made shooing signs with his hands. "Stop pestering me, and think about your actions before you go against the Council."

"I'll leave in my own good time," Saw Back insisted.

"Hey," Sour Mouth, another of the Alligator Clan youths called. "Come on! He's made it into the channels!"

Salamander smiled as they turned, trotting for their canoes.

"Why didn't you fight them?" Anhinga asked. The paddle was clutched in her hands, ready to be swung at the nearest foe. Her eyes were on the two canoes lancing out into the lake, hot in pursuit of her uncle.

"We couldn't have won." Salamander shrugged. "All we needed to do was give Jaguar Hide time to get off the lake. He's in the channels now. In a finger's time, it will be dark. Long before Saw Back and his warriors could possibly catch up." He paused. "Sometimes the best way to win is by not starting a fight in the first place."

She gave him the same disbelieving look she'd been giving him all day. "How did this happen to me?"

"I cut you free one night and started it all," he reminded.

"But why did you offer to marry me? It wasn't your place."

"Because, I think *he* wanted me to."

"Who? Who wanted you to?"

He turned again, looking at her. She stood half a head taller than he did, her body a slim silhouette against the darkening sky. Her long legs, the curve of her hips under the kirtle, and her round pointed breasts were softly bathed by the twilight.

"Has anyone ever told you that you are the most beautiful woman in the world?"

She just stared at him in wonder.

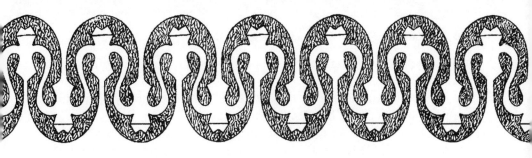

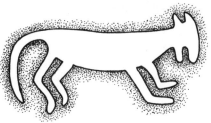

Twenty-nine

Does it make any sense that your people could drag me right up to the front of your Men's House the last time I was here, but this time I have to be cleansed?" Anhinga demanded, her hands clenched in her lap as she stared at Salamander's lean form across the fire.

"I have never thought of it that way," he answered, a puzzled frown on his forehead.

The fire burned before a low hut made of woven palmetto leaves. It stood beneath the sweetgum, having sheltered countless travelers and Traders. This, Anhinga had learned, was to be her bridal home during the cleansing of her souls.

Around them a halo of insects insisted on swirling, most of them to be eventually sucked into the flames. In the night sky, a thin sliver of Father Moon shone between the clouds and cast patterns of silver across the blackness.

"I could have brought all kinds of evil into Sun Town. Believe me, for all the terrible things I wished on your people, they should have died of a terrible wasting disease, their muscles turning to pus, their skin becoming a mass of boils." She glared her hatred at him.

His large dark eyes seemed to swell, and her souls stumbled. What was it about him? His people considered him some sort of comic fool, but when she looked into those eyes, it was as if they drew her souls down into their brown depths. He made her skin shiver with a curious excitement that she couldn't understand. Was it because she was destined to kill him? Is that what made him such a novelty?

"If you hate us so, why are you here?" he asked softly. The fire popped, sparks rising between them.

"My uncle wants peace." She could see he didn't believe her so she countered, "Why, in Panther's name, did you cut me loose that night? I was your brother's property."

He took a deep breath. "For the same reason that you came back. We are tied by Power. You and I."

She bit off a bitter smile before it could touch her lips. *Yes, bound by Power! It has brought me here to destroy you, fool!* Aloud she said, "You took a great risk setting me free."

"Yes." He shrugged, looking curiously vulnerable as he eyed the fire. "The vision isn't clear yet, but you should know that you're not the only one trying to destroy me."

By Panther, does he hear my thoughts?

"I don't know where Masked Owl is taking us, or how it is supposed to end. All I have is my wits, but everyone else has theirs, too." His smile went crooked. "However, until they destroy me, I shall do my best to care for you. I don't understand the balance of it, but for all that White Bird would have done to hurt you and demean you, I shall do everything the opposite."

She frowned, unable to see the sense in that, but willing to accept its oddity given the alternatives. "I still don't understand why you spoke out. You could have let the others find a husband for me. Perhaps Deep Hunter, or that Mud Stalker."

"I told you." His eyes had become passive again. "We are tied. When I recognized you, I knew that was why he asked me to free you. So that you could come back. You came here to marry White Bird, the man who captured you and hurt you. You were meant for me. I realized that in a flash of understanding."

"But I still have to undergo this cleansing?"

He nodded. "It would be most unpleasant if you didn't."

"It was *most* unpleasant the *last* time I was here."

For a long time, he said nothing, just stared into the fire.

"I heard that you are already married."

His smile might have been a ghost. "Yes, to two women in Snapping Turtle Clan. Pine Drop and Night Rain."

"So, I am a *third* wife?"

He steepled his fingers, brow lining. "This will be difficult. Among my people, a man goes to live with his wife, in her territory."

"Among mine, too. So, what is my territory? This little heap of mud in the middle of a lake?"

"For the next six days it is." He seemed oblivious to her anger. "After that I will build you a house in Owl Clan territory. I know just the spot. You will appreciate it, my brother's bones were burned there."

Owl Clan territory? Good, things were beginning to look up. It would place her in the middle of the enemy, in a position where one day she could drive the terrible dagger of revenge into their hearts.

"I will work the rest out with my other wives." He mused, seeing it all in his souls. "Which will be interesting in its own right."

"They will not resent me? Try to make me miserable for taking you away from them for part of the time?"

Amusement, like faint and distant lightning, flickered in his face. "I could be wrong, but I doubt it. Like you, they were not particularly pleased to marry me—especially after my mother's souls began to loosen. I imagine that the nights I spend with you will relieve them. Perhaps, after you come to discover your situation, you may be just as grateful for them."

She took a deep breath against the tightening she felt in her chest. Tonight she should be bedding her enemy, taking the first step on the long passage to final revenge on Owl Clan. Instead, she was here, removed from Sun Town by their silly fears of spiritual infection, talking to this unusual boy. The top of his head only came to her chin. Unlike Mist Finger or the others of her suitors, he was mostly thin bones. Hardly the ideal of the young warrior-hunter that had filled her fantasies.

Wait until he's asleep, steal a canoe, and head south.

"And do what?" she asked aloud, eyes fixed on the fire. He seemed not to hear as she imagined her uncle's face, saw the expression of disappointment in his eyes. It had been bad enough during the months that she healed in the Panther's Bones, living amidst Mist Finger's, Right Talon's, Cooter's, Spider Fire's, and Slit Nose's families. What made her think that after this second failure, it would be any easier?

Armed with the stony beating of her heart, she stood. He was watching her as she stepped around the fire and reached her hand out to him. When he took it, a curious tingle ran through her. His eyes seemed to grow as she pulled him to his feet. For a long moment she looked down into his fascinating eyes, seeing the growing desire.

She held his hand as she walked to the small shelter, ducked inside, and loosened the knots that held her kirtle. The fabric slipped smoothly over her hips to settle beside the moss-covered bed.

He had frozen, mouth parted, his eyes fixed on her body where the fire cast its feeble light. The vein in his neck was pulsing, his chest rising and falling. When she untied the knot that held his breechcloth, it fell away to reveal him, taut and ready.

Her own heartbeat had begun to pound, a warm sensation spinning itself inside her hips. She lay back on the bedding, watching him with a building anticipation. The faint firelight played across his thin body as he lowered himself, his skin sliding warmly across hers.

Instinctively, she wrapped her arms around him and felt the life burning brightly within him. Her breasts tightened as his chest met hers. She was leading him to her, thrilled as his penis slid inside her.

She was thinking about how she was going to kill him when the liquid waves of ecstasy burst through her pelvis. She gasped, taken completely by surprise. Nothing in the naive experimentation of youth had prepared her for the likes of this.

Moments later, he, too, shivered and tensed, a strained sound choking in his throat. Then his arms cupped her shoulders and he buried his face in her hair.

Atop the thick thatch of the Women's House, the rain sounded like a continuous whisper rather than a drumming. The runoff beat a staccato as it spattered into pools of water that in turn dribbled off to the sides of the Mother Mound. The building was large, filled with baskets and pots that contained the ceremonial items provided by each clan for its women. Each moon, when a woman's cycle came full, she came here, to attend to herself through the menstrual period.

The time she spent in seclusion with her sisters provided a respite from the never-ending trials of life. She had time for reflection, attention to the spirits, and a break from the normal routine of running a household. Children, husbands, and relatives could not constantly pester or demand her attention. Here, surrounded by women, she could catch up on gossip, hear news of other clans, build friendships, and strengthen ties with friends and acquaintances. The walls of clan politics tended to soften. Negotiations took place, and problems could be solved in a more relaxed environment, woman to woman, without the pressures of others bearing down.

Night Rain had put off leaving for the Women's House until the last moment when she discovered herself spotting. Like her sister, she had suffered intermittent cramps for the last several moons. Even the swelling and tenderness in her breasts wasn't an indicator. She should have known, however, from the moods, and the fact that her cycle had begun to coincide with her sister's.

She removed her bark rain hat as she stepped into the low doorway. The building, large and rectangular, was oriented north–south atop the low mound. The doorway opened to the west, while on the east, two large windows were situated so that the first rays of the morning sun shot light into the two rooms, one for the Northern Moiety, the other, hers, for the Southern.

She nodded to the clusters of women who sat in clan areas along the walls. They were working at tasks, making beads, others twining cord. Some ground pieces of hematite against slabs of Swamp Panther sandstone in the endless process of crafting net sinkers. They nodded, smiling and waving as Night Rain crossed the room. She rounded the small central fire and located Pine Drop where she sat on a furry buffalo hide, the hair flattened from long use. She lowered herself onto the space her sister opened for her and placed her sack of provisions and her rain hat to one side.

"I thought you'd be following close behind me." Pine Drop smiled. "I take it you left a stew for Salamander?"

Night Rain snorted. "Why? He's still over building a house for that wild Swamp Panther woman. I swear, I hope she chokes on the Serpent's cleansing. I don't trust her. She's evil. And why, Sister, do you care if he eats or not? He and that barbarian are the talk of Sun Town! *We* are mentioned by everyone! You should hear the things they're saying. That somehow it was *our* fault. That we couldn't conceive, that you were off with Three Stomachs, that we hurt his feelings so much he had to go to a barbarian for companionship! People are laughing at us and not just him!"

Pine Drop stopped short, a pale look washing across her face. She had been grinding ocher on a sandstone tablet. Beside her sat a small pot of grease with which to mix the bright red color. "I should never have listened to Uncle."

Night Rain cocked her head. "What's wrong with you? For nearly half a moon, you've been different. Something's changed."

"Nothing has changed."

"Yes, it has. You haven't spoken a single word to Three Stomachs. What did he do to you?"

Pine Drop widened her eyes expressively. "As you can see, Sister, he did nothing to me. I should be happily at home, delighted with the notion that my moon was late, assured that I was pregnant. Yet, here I am, taking my share of absorbent from the pot, trying to figure out why I'm barren."

"You're not barren. It just hasn't taken is all." Night Rain resettled herself, reaching into the sack she had brought. From it she took root cakes, dried fish, and smoked deer meat to put into the stone bowl her lineage left for storage. She slipped out of her shawl and massaged her breasts, wincing at the ache. "Snakes, why has my moon come to be so miserable?"

Pine Drop stared at the smoking fire pit in the center of the room. A flame flickered in halfhearted effort as it slowly chewed at the bottom of a blackened log. "I don't know. I just wonder, is all."

Night Rain perked up at that. "Yes?"

Her sister shook her head. "I never had these problems, the unending cramps, I mean, until I started coupling with Three Stomachs. It's as if . . ."

"What? Snakes! Don't drag this out. Tell me."

Pine Drop tilted her head, asking in a whisper, "Do you think we're being punished?"

"By whom?" Night Rain leaned forward, searching her sister's face. *What does she know? What does she suspect? She is more intimate with Mother and Uncle's plans. Have they told her something?*

"Power," Pine Drop answered, a hand covering her mouth. "Spirits. Something."

"Why would you think that?"

She shook her head as though baffled. "It's just a feeling."

"A feeling?" Night Rain shifted, glancing covertly around the room. "What happened the day that you and Salamander were gone? Remember? The day you left me the bladderwort?"

Pine Drop smiled slightly, then her perplexed look returned. "It was . . ."—she seemed to be searching for the right word—". . . fun."

"Fun? A day with Salamander?"

Pine Drop raised her hands and dropped them. "You can't understand."

"That's drilling the bead in the center. You're right, I *don't* understand. I think he's about as much fun as a lump of mud. He hasn't so much as broken a smile since we've been married. He's a dupe, Pine Drop. People laugh at us behind their hands. I can't wait until Uncle says the time is right to divorce him. I just thank the Sky Beings he hasn't crawled into my bed for nearly a moon."

Pine Drop's lips pinched. After a long pause, she said, "How does it make you feel now that he's spending his time with that Swamp

Panther and not us? I mean, doesn't it bother you that he prefers the companionship of some wild barbarian to ours?"

"Eats Wood says it's the same woman White Bird captured during the raid at Ground Cherry Camp. The one who escaped so mysteriously in the night. Remember? She took Red Finger's canoe? He says it's a Swamp Panther plot, that she came here to do something terrible to us in revenge for what we did to her and her friends."

"Eats Wood is an idiot."

"Well, so is our husband."

"Is he?" Pine Drop wondered. "I've heard Uncle and Mother talking about it. About this marriage. They want to believe like Eats Wood, that it is some terrible plot hatched by Owl Clan with the Swamp Panthers to hurt the clans, but they are both worried they might be wrong."

"How so?"

She shook her head. "Think about it. Wing Heart has lost her souls. Any action Water Petal would take is instantly challenged by Moccasin Leaf. The fight between the lineages has paralyzed Owl Clan. Salamander is the Speaker, but everyone thinks he's a fool."

"He is."

Pine Drop ignored her. "Nevertheless, this *fool* now has an alliance with the Swamp Panthers, and Owl Clan receives a canoe load of sandstone every moon." She gestured around, pointing.

At every location at least one, and generally several pieces, of sandstone were lying on the packed clay floor amidst pieces of wood, leather, and stone. The material was essential to Sun Town. The finishing of most stone tools and all woodwork depended on the abrasive quality of the sandstone. Anything that needed to be smoothed or fitted had to be ground, and Swamp Panther sandstone was the perfect abrasive. She opened her other hand, showing Night Rain the piece of sandstone she had been grinding the ocher on.

"Sandstone will not return them to authority," Night Rain declared. "Snapping Turtle Clan now occupies that position."

"We're not on top yet. Thunder Tail has been given leadership of the Council. But for us the vote would have been unanimous."

"Give Uncle several more moons, and we'll be on top. Just wait and see."

Pine Drop asked, "Did you know that Deep Hunter detailed men to kill Jaguar Hide? Our husband managed to delay them. Somehow he kept Saw Back's party on the Turtle's Back just long enough so that Jaguar Hide escaped into the channels. Salamander baited them, confused them, and the Swamp Panther got away. Deep

Hunter was furious. He stalked back and forth in a rage for a whole day. He still can't understand how he was thwarted, but he exiled Saw Back to Yellow Mud Camp for four moons."

"Delayed how?" Night Rain was curious for the first time. "Saw Back is a really a handsome man. He's Alligator Clan, and, well, you know, I've been thinking that after we're through with Salamander, he'd make a fine husband."

Pine Drop gave her a sober look. "You'd better hope he can placate his Speaker. That, or, assuming we are ever 'through' with Salamander, you had better plan on enjoying your life in Yellow Mud Camp."

"Having a man like him to share my bed, I could stand the climate over there. I'm surprised that he didn't just ignore Salamander. Everyone else does."

"Perhaps, but Salamander talked Saw Back out of fulfilling his Speaker's orders. And Deep Hunter blames Saw Back, not Salamander." She seemed to retreat again, lost in her thoughts.

"You've been preoccupied ever since he married that barbarian." Night Rain shook her head. "It's not a disaster! It frees us! Think, Sister. Why does he need us? He's got her, a barbarian, for a wife. That makes him more of a freak than he already is. I think we should ask Mother and Uncle to get us a divorce."

Pine Drop was nodding absently. "Perhaps." A pause. "What could he see in her?"

Night Rain stood and walked to the large ceramic pot that held the mixture of cattail down and hanging moss. At just the mention of sharing a bed with Saw Back, her flow increased.

When she returned, Pine Drop was still looking confused.

"Sister, who cares what he sees in her?"

Pine Drop airily replied, "I just wonder, that's all."

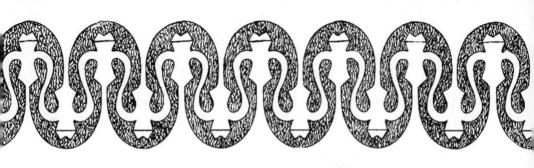

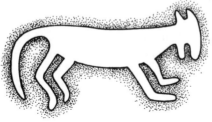

Thirty

Anhinga stepped out of the canoe and planted her feet firmly on Sun Town's muddy landing. Above her on the high bluff she could see the hated Men's House. The old Serpent stepped out of the canoe behind her, helped by Salamander. He was studying her, eyes prying at her souls, perhaps sensing the danger she brought to his people.

Anhinga walked warily behind her husband. Husband? The word still startled her. Of course she had known she was coming here to marry the man she was going to kill. Knowing and anticipating, seeing how it would be in the soul's eye, was one thing. In that vision she was smiling as she stepped into White Bird's arms, every essence of her being fixed on his painful death. He had been a tough and cunning warrior. A hero worthy of Anhinga's wrath.

Now, six days after she had first laid eyes on him, she walked behind a skinny boy possessed of pain-haunted eyes. His hair was mussed, and she could see most every bone in his body. He walked with an ungainly amble, his souls off somewhere distant, lost in Dreams.

Where, Anhinga, is the glory in murdering this simple boy? He has neither craft nor cunning, and shows all the wariness of a rotten stump.

Patience. She would wait. Besides, the ordeal of having undergone that flat-faced Serpent's "cleansing" made the souls cry out for someone to kill. Miserable though she had been, she was Anhinga, niece of Jaguar Hide. The last thing she would allow these foolish Sun People to see was any hint of weakness.

The old Serpent watched her, his brown eyes like keen shining stones behind those folds of sagging skin. He might have been a fish eagle perched on a low branch, trying to peer below the surface of her skin for a glimpse of her souls. She had given him nothing, bearing the sweats, purges, chants, and smokings as if they were but a pleasant relaxation. By Panther Above, she *would* kill someone for that!

She fought a grim smile as she remembered the last time she had staggered down this very slope; the darkness had been complete, her body and souls filled with pain and horror. This boy had been with her then, too. Where she had left this place broken, shattered with grief, an escaped slave in the night, she came back in triumph as the wife of a Clan Speaker, walking head upright toward the small knot of people who had come to watch.

Salamander called greetings to some, nodding to others as they passed. One by one, Anhinga met their eyes, seeing one or two faces she thought familiar. And, yes, there was that one! The pus-sucking chigger who had twisted her nipple. She willed her face into a bark-solid mask, avoiding his narrowing eyes. Did he recognize her? Cleaned as she was, dressed in a finery of feathers and finely woven cloth?

Then they were atop the bluff and turning northward. She had seen this place through pain-blurred eyes, but now, from a different perspective, it took her breath. How huge! The immensity of Sun Town hadn't registered when, as a captive, she lay blinking against a headache, bound and trussed, watching her friends being butchered. Now she saw the incredible height of the huge Bird's Head to the west, the span of the house-topped ridges that arched around her like the jaws of an immense monster. The entire place was open, mantled in green.

And the sky! She looked up in awe. She came from a forest people. She had never seen so much of the sky! Mother Sun beamed down on her, hot and bright. The sensation stunned her, left her feeling exposed, alone, and vulnerable. Never before had she been less than a stone's throw from trees. Even at the Panther's Bones, when she stood on the high Sun Mound, it was but an island among the trees.

Unnerved for the first time, she swallowed hard.

"It is something, yes?" the old Serpent asked from where he followed her.

"I hadn't realized. The size of it!"

"The world crosses here," Salamander said, turning his thoughtful eyes to hers and smiling shyly. One by one he pointed out the clan grounds. "And this building"—he stabbed a finger at the rectangular building that topped a mound overlooking Morning Lake—"is the Women's House. Where you will have to go when your moon comes full." Uncomfortable, he asked, "Uh, is that anytime soon?"

"Perhaps," she replied offhandedly, her attention on the place. That would be unbearable, sitting in there for four days surrounded by hostile strangers, avoiding their prying questions, enduring their presence. "I might just go to the forest, if you don't mind."

Salamander gave her a short nod. "If you would be more comfortable. Up ahead are the Owl Clan grounds. There, that first ridge, is where my lineage lives. I am building your house there, next to Mother's. It is a good location. From the front door you can see straight out across the lake to the east. Every morning the sun shines right through the doorway."

"There was no house there?"

"There was. My brother was burned in it after lightning killed him. It happened right there." He indicated a place on the edge of the borrow pit. Several wispy goosefoot plants stood on the spot, the trilobed leaves insect-chewed. "He was planting that goosefoot when he died. We don't touch it." He gave her a serious look. "It is not for us, do you understand? It belongs to the Sky Beings."

After dark I shall be sure to urinate upon the spot. "Who am I to question the Sky Beings?" she asked.

He led her around the borrow pit to the toe of the ridge. It was a stunning location. The view was the finest she had ever seen. At her feet the bluff dropped away to the shores of the lake, a moderate-sized body of water. Two canoes were trolling a net behind them, or so she assumed given that the occupants were paddling mightily, their bows pointed outward, and each trailed a rope into the water. Beyond them an endless vista of sweetgum, tupelo, bald cypress, and water oak stretched in a vast forest that merged into the distant horizon.

Looking northward, she counted out the five ridges to a low bank of trees. "What is there, beyond the sixth ridge?"

"A deep gully," Salamander told her. "Beyond that a wide trail runs to the north, to the Star Mound. There, at the summer solstice, we thank Mother Sun for returning to us again and bringing the world to life. For the rest of the year it is a guardian against the Dark Powers."

She nodded, thinking how similar their beliefs were to her own.

At the Panther's Bones, her people retreated to the high rise at the north end of the village to conduct their summer solstice ceremonies.

"Our house will be there." He pointed, a hesitation in his voice.

She looked behind her, seeing a collection of building material beside a burned circle. Charred posts still protruded from the ground. Grass had grown around the black outline where the heat from the burning house hadn't killed the roots.

"My brother's bones were burned there." Salamander looked even more frail.

Good! May his souls watch as I couple with his brother. May he scream his warnings from the Spirit World onto deaf ears. May he wail as I avenge my people upon his family.

She could feel the Serpent's piercing gaze boring into her back. She realized that a grim smile had come to her lips. Salamander was watching her, brown eyes large. "It was the way of Power," he said simply. "Everything is."

To cover herself, she said, "It will make a wonderful house, husband. The sooner we finish, the better. Who is that?" She pointed to the elderly woman who sat under a ramada not ten paces beyond, her body bent over a loom.

"That is Elder Wing Heart, my mother."

She heard the worry in his voice. "You say her souls are loose?" Before he could answer, she added, "I would meet your mother. Your family is now mine, husband. Introduce me."

Reluctantly, he led her forward. A wooden pestle and mortar stood halfway between the house locations. Charcoal and old cooking clays were scattered about, as were bits of stone: flakes and crumbled sandstone, the latter looted from her own lands, no doubt. She cataloged the belongings under the ramada: cordage and fibers, several soapstone bowls, bark plates, a ceramic pot half-full of cloudy water, and an array of bone needles and combs.

The woman held her attention; she looked used up, wrung out, and discarded by life. Despite the drawn lines in her face, she still carried a regal air. She would have been attractive once, could be again if her eyes weren't lost and roving. She still sat erect, her strong fingers caressing the fibers with a lover's touch.

"Mother?" Salamander asked softly as he bent down beside her. She seemed oblivious to his presence, her head tilting back and forth, smiles rising and falling on her lips. Her expression kept changing, as if she were having silent conversations inside her head. "I have come to introduce you to Anhinga. The niece of Jaguar Hide. Elder, we have a new daughter for you."

Wing Heart continued her weaving. Her son's words might have been the droning of insects for all the attention she paid.

"Mother?" Salamander touched her shoulder, looked unhappily back at Anhinga. "I want you to meet my wife."

"Yes, yes, White Bird. Go tell your uncle. And don't let that idiot little brother of yours miss supper tonight. He's probably off looking under logs or something. Now, go on, and don't bother me. The Speaker and I have things to do. Plans to make before the next Council."

Snakes! This was Elder Wing Heart? By the evil mist, how could she have come to this?

"It's all right," Anhinga said softly. "There will be times in the future when her souls are closer." She smiled at him, allaying his discomfort and reaching out to take his hand. "Our life together is just beginning. I am sure there are tens of tens of things to do." She glanced cautiously at the old man. What did he suspect? "We have a house to build, and it must be a grand one, worthy of a Clan Speaker. Let us start there." She led the way back past the pestle and mortar and surveyed the charred circle. "This must be cleared."

Patience. Her uncle was right. The Serpent kept watching her as though she were a copperhead loose in a children's play area.

She ignored the old man and his seeing souls. Her first concern was to lull Salamander. She smiled at him, taking his hand in hers. "We shall build a grand house here, and when it is finished, we shall make a great feast for just the two of us. When we are full, we will lie on a thick buffalo blanket and you shall fill me in the light of a happy fire."

He smiled at that, as if seeing a fantasy in his souls. "I would like that."

A memory flashed . . . a human liver, rising high into that wide-open sky above Sun Town. It flipped and jiggled as it rose, sunlight flashing on the wet, gleaming surface. For a brief instant it stopped, hanging magically before beginning its rush to the Earth. She remembered the sound so clearly: a hard splat! In a crystal image she saw the tongues, pink and fast between white teeth as the camp dogs licked up the pieces.

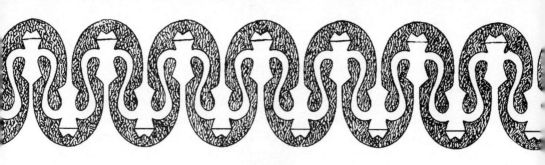

Thirty-one

A large turtle, a slider, lay on its back in the center of the coals. Its head and legs had been lashed tightly with green vines so they didn't protrude and burn. The flesh steamed, hissing and sending aroma around the activity area between the houses. Salamander's nostrils kept catching hints of it on the wind. He glanced back from his precarious position atop the thatching of his new roof. The house they had built on the location of his old one was almost completed.

Elder Wing Heart sat under the ramada, preoccupied with her incessant weaving. Her nimble fingers plucked at the warp and weft stretched between the peeled poles. This fabric, nearly complete, was a series of white birds on a brown background. One of the most beautiful pieces Salamander had ever seen. Even Anhinga had stopped short, gasping at its beauty.

The sky was overcast, gray with a thick bank of clouds that threatened even more rain. It cut the muggy heat that made a man's bones want to wilt. The teasing wind, rising and falling, carried the warm moist scent of the forest, grass, and trees while it promised moisture.

Salamander had never built a house before, and but for Water Petal's advice and guidance, he'd have made a bad affair of it. Together, the three of them—he, Anhinga, and Water Petal—had excavated the foundation holes, planted the uprights, woven the lattice, and plastered the walls.

They had retrieved longer poles and wrist-thick lengths of cane from the floodplain forest, their quest taking them a day's paddle down the winding channels while they searched for just the right sizes of bald cypress. Power laced the wood, making it more resistant to rot than other kinds. Sweating under the sun, they had stepped the largest of them for roof supports. The rest they muscled up, setting them on the wall and interior supports as rafters. Slim cane stringers had been laid crosswise and tied in place with peels of freshly stripped bark. Vines had been interwoven to form a lattice both to support the thatch and to allow it to be fastened tightly.

Thatch, as Salamander found out, wasn't as easy as it seemed. After the backbreaking labor of cutting the grass and bundling it, care had to be taken to pack the sheaves and tie them. Placing the bundles was as much art as it was hard labor.

Salamander used a length of cord—material provided by Water Petal's husband, Darter—to pull the last bundle tight. "Watch your hand. Here it comes," he called as he slipped the bone needle through the thatch.

"Got it," Water Petal called as she grabbed the needle tip inside and pulled it through.

Salamander watched the cord pull tight, compressing the sheaf, and could imagine her knotting it and cutting it with a stone flake. He turned, perched like a big bird at the peak of the roof. "How does it look?"

Anhinga had her hands placed on her hips, her head cocked as she studied the final product. "It is a house, husband. At last, it is a house."

He grinned, enjoying the harsh accent that came with her speech. Their languages were mutually intelligible, most of the words the same, but sometimes the usage led to incomprehension, and sometimes mirth. He'd been shocked when she referred to his penis as "your slug." She had been stopped short in confusion when she found out his people called a vulva "a canoe."

Water Petal ducked out of the interior and looked up, satisfaction on her face. "We are finished."

"Tonight we shall conduct the proper ceremonies to bless it." Salamander turned himself on the wooden ladder they had manufactured—two poles lashed together with thick rope—and balanced carefully, his toes seeking a purchase as he backed down. Water Petal and Anhinga reached up to steady him as he clambered down the last steps.

He helped them lower the ladder and looked up at the dull green thatch. Freshly cut grass couldn't be used; moist, it would rot and disintegrate. The cuttings had to be seasoned, dried to just the right consistency before being bundled.

"I feel better seeing a house there," Water Petal told them with a sigh. "It reminds me of better days." She turned to look at her baby where it lay in wrap of moss-lined fabric.

"How is he?" Anhinga asked, pointing at the child.

"Still asleep, thank the Sky Beings," she answered. "He cried all night. I dabbed a bit of nightshade paste on my finger and touched it to his tongue before coming over here."

Anhinga narrowed one of her eyes. "That must be done with care." She was inspecting the little baby.

"He has to sleep," Water Petal answered, turning back. "Perhaps it will keep his bowels quiet. For the last couple of days milk goes in and moments later, water comes out. I've wiped his bottom until it's raw."

To Salamander's eyes, his little cousin didn't look healthy; the delicate skin around the infant's face had shrunk and taken on a dark cast. The baby fat had disappeared from sticklike arms.

"My best thoughts are for him," Anhinga said.

Salamander watched the interplay between the two women. Anhinga and Water Petal had reached some sort of uneasy coexistence. Not friends, not enemies, but during the hard days since the completion of Anhinga's cleansing, a careful toleration had developed as they had labored together to build Anhinga's house.

Looking toward the ramada, Salamander could see his mother, oblivious, her hands working the shuttle as she talked to herself. He dared not step closer, or he would hear her carrying on a conversation with her dead brother. He wondered if she could hear his Dream Soul talking in reply. If so, what was his dead uncle saying? Why didn't he send her souls back to her?

Instead, he inspected the turtle. It's once-yellow belly had mottled. The black spots that marked the scoots were now blotched with ash. "He's about cooked. Every new house must have turtle for the first meal."

"Why?" Anhinga asked.

Salamander was admiring the way her long black hair hung over her round breast, to be teased aside by the wind. "Among our people it is said that Turtle's Power is imparted to the new house. Wherever Turtle goes, his house protects him, keeps him from harm."

She frowned. "My people eat snails as a feast when a new house is occupied. For the same reasons. Snail always has a house, no matter where he travels." She pointed. "Your turtle there, his house didn't keep him safe from your fire."

Water Petal's lips twitched with irritation. Salamander, however, smiled, replying, "And I'll bet your snails' shells don't save them from your boiling pot, either."

"I have sassafras and cedar root," Water Petal told him as she hid her expression by inspecting the cuts on her hands. "I'll bring them tonight for the first fire."

"Why?" Anhinga asked.

"Cedar smoke cleanses," Salamander told her. "And my people believe that sassafras-root smoke brings good luck. For the same reason, we must not reenter the house until we have made necklaces of flowers, so that all the thoughts and words that people share inside will be sweet."

Anhinga studied him through sultry brown eyes, the look barely masking the turbulence within her. His souls thrilled. Not only was she the most beautiful woman he had ever seen, but the danger communicated by her large dark eyes drew him like a spell.

"What is it with you two?" Water Petal asked, sensing the tension between them. "I swear, when you look at each other it's like rubbing fox fur on a winter day. The very air crackles and sparks."

"It is the Power between us, Cousin." Salamander turned toward Water Petal. "Anhinga and I are tied by a curious bond." The secrets of their relationship would be beyond her, and he dared not try to explain about what happened under their blankets. His aunt might be young and adventurous herself, but somehow, Salamander doubted that anyone could comprehend the intensity of his matings with Anhinga.

"It must be something." Water Petal sighed, reaching down to scoop up her sleeping baby. "You've turned the clan on its ear with this marriage. I swear, Moccasin Leaf begins to foam at the mouth if I pass within a stone's throw of her."

"She is what she is, Cousin."

Water Petal turned, eyes flashing. "So you say, but I believe that she has found the votes to remove Wing Heart as Elder."

Salamander's smile tightened. "All things in their time. You must trust me. That's all."

"And wait until they remove you, too?" Water Petal's voice tightened. "We're the last of our lineage, Salamander."

"What we are is never as important as who we are. We must wait and be smart."

But for the baby in her arms, she would have thrown her hands up in despair. "You exasperate me, Salamander." Then a slow smile crossed her lips. "But what else can I do? You're family." She turned. "I'll see you this evening."

"Thank you for your help, Cousin."

A final wave was all he got as she disappeared between the houses on her way home.

Anhinga had watched the exchange silently, her arms crossed under her high breasts. "Is it not enough that you are Speaker?"

"She had thought to follow my mother."

Anhinga glanced sidelong at Wing Heart. "I have heard the stories. Your mother was once a great leader. Even Uncle respected her."

He frowned. "Perhaps she will be yet again. It is up to her souls to decide whether they will return or not. Not even the Serpent has been able to help her."

She turned those probing eyes on him again, her expression still guarded. The breeze was toying with her long black hair, dancing it around her slim shoulders with their faded scars. "What about Masked Owl?"

He stopped short, startled. "What do you know about Masked Owl?"

"You talk to him in your sleep."

"I do?"

"Not everyone talks to a Sky Being when they sleep." A suspicious look crossed her face. "Does he say anything about me?"

"Sometimes." He bent and began to work on the knots that held his two-pole ladder together. The rope would be reused, the poles cut into firewood when they dried.

"What?" she asked, stepping to the other end of the ladder and using an awl to loosen the knots.

Did he dare tell her? She was giving him that look, the slightly arrogant and dangerous one. "He said that you came here to kill me."

She stopped short, fingers frozen, eyes widening. Then, smoothly, coolly, she smiled, flashing her teeth at him. "I will not kill you anytime soon." A pause. "Unless your heart stops tonight when we share that new bed in there." She jerked her head toward the house, shining black hair flowing with the motion.

It was, he thought, a most challenging affirmation of his suspicions.

Night's soft dark cloak still covered the skies as Pine Drop climbed the last several steps to the rounded summit of the Bird's Head. Her lungs were pulling, her muscles warm from the climb. She turned back to stare out at the charcoal east. Silence, as deep as the night itself, met her ears. She had left early, desperate to be at this place first. Would he come? She seated herself and clutched her jay-feather cloak about her shoulders.

Darkness smothered her.

Then the stillness stirred. She could feel Power gathering. Her skin reacted as it would to the faintest touch of flower petals. The air grew heavy, pressing down from above. She would have sworn she felt giant wings passing silently above. Her heart tripped, hammering at her chest. Every nerve in her body demanded that she rise and charge headlong down the steep incline that led to the open plazas below.

She closed her eyes and forced herself to sit. With all of her will she remained motionless, taking deep breaths of the night. It might indeed be late summer, but she drew the jay-feather cloak more tightly about her shoulders. The breeze that skipped out of the southwest chilled her to the very bones. It ruffled the bright blue feathers, teased at locks that had come loose from her head, and prickled the hair on her arms. Born of the chill or the spirits that hovered around her, a shiver tightened her spine.

Snakes! Where is he? Or had this been a fool's errand? *One fool for another,* her souls answered. Only an idiot would come here to this place on the edge of darkness and death. She swallowed hard. An idiot, or a man of Power.

He had sat on this very spot that morning. Curious, she tested the soil, finding a loose spot. Her questing fingers parted the dirt, feeling around until, yes, right there. She picked up the irregular stone. No bigger than a large pebble, it lay cool on her palm. Rubbing the clinging dirt away, her fingertips traced the recognizable shape of a little potbellied owl. The same one he had been working on that day, or another? How many of these had he crafted?

Pine Drop pursed her lips. There were so many things she didn't know about her husband. With the exception of one magical day, they had never talked. Never spoken as a woman did with her husband.

You never made the effort.

Was it her fault that he had married the barbarian? The morning after she had left the Woman's House, she had passed that way, seen the new house he had built Anhinga on the location of his mother's old one. Just the sight of that building had stung something in her souls.

Spiders and scorpions, why? What did it matter? Why did she care what Salamander did, or who he did it with, so long as it did not reflect on her, or her clan? It was an arranged marriage only, the interminable result of an attempt to align her clan with his. Or, it had been until Wing Heart's souls had fled. Now it was a political relic. Owl Clan was effectively emasculated. She, herself, had done her part in their undoing. She had helped to lower her husband's prestige by her dalliance with Three Stomachs.

It had been her duty to her clan, ordered by her mother and her uncle, not some wild impulse generated from her loins. She had done as her elders wished, and done it well. She had enjoyed coupling with Three Stomachs; he had conjured sensations she had never experienced with a man.

Then why don't you feel happy about it?

Memories of Salamander's face haunted her. She remembered the expression he had worn every night when he entered their house. He might have strapped on a mask so that no one could read the thoughts behind it. With it, he had seemed impervious to her viper's tongue, and oblivious to her disgust when he climbed into her bed to perform his husband's function for her clan.

It takes two to lie together with pleasure. She had at least had a husband to teach her the ways. Embarrassed, she remembered her first fumbling attempts at coupling and how Blue Feather had patiently shown her the body's secrets. From the awkward manner Salamander had come to her, it had been his first time with a woman. He had been rudely jerked from boyhood and placed in his dead brother's bed, to sire children on his wives. Wives who took every opportunity to mock and belittle him. One day he had been playing with toys, the next he was Speaker. Then he had been thrust forward in the Council to explain his mother's very public spiritual disintegration to a hostile audience that wanted nothing more than his and his clan's destruction.

That was the same young man who had brought her here to see a marvel. In a face that should have reflected revulsion at her mere presence, he had instead displayed delight as a heron hunted the shallows and a spider built a web. She recalled the happiness on his face as they paddled the canoe load of fish traps out into the channel, baiting and dropping them into the still waters.

When did I ever see magic? It wasn't a prerequisite for being Mud Stalker's niece.

For a few hands of time, she had been free. That notion surprised and saddened her. In an entire lifetime she had never enjoyed happiness like she had out paddling around with Salamander. At the height of it, she had ruined everything with a carefully crafted question when she tried to trick him into betraying his clan.

She reached down, patting her stomach below the navel. The cramps were gone. After this last period, she felt better than she had in moons. Had it been guilt over spearing herself on Three Stomach's giant member?

By the Sky Beings, I'm tired of all this. Perhaps this morning she could begin to put things right. A future might not exist for her and Salamander. She was, after all, Snapping Turtle Clan, and no matter that she might now disapprove of what her mother and uncle had asked her to do, she was nevertheless in line to one day become Clan Elder. If the clan leadership ended her marriage with Salamander, as they soon would, it did not mean that Salamander should have to hate her for the rest of his life.

If this were handled right, they might be able to make some agreement between them, a way to balance the competing needs of their clans with an understanding of each other. Surely a woman who might someday become Clan Elder could manage that.

Was it her imagination, or was the eastern horizon now gray? Yes, indeed it was. It would be soon, or not at all.

His form was a murky shadow among shadows as it passed the ramada. She could hear the soft whisper of his feet on the packed clay.

She took a deep breath, closing her eyes and rehearsing the things she wanted to say.

"Masked Owl?" he asked plaintively. "When you came to me last night, you told me to climb the Bird's Head at dawn."

Pine Drop started, staring around in the darkness. Was there someone else up here? Or was he talking to the Sky Being?

Salamander called, "Can we go flying again?"

She could see him now, his thin form barely outlined in the building gray. His skinny arms were raised, his head tilted up at the fading stars in the night sky. Her skin began to prickle as if bobcat fur were being rubbed across it. She swallowed hard, heart racing. Snakes and lightning, he *was* talking to the Sky Being!

"Is Water Petal's baby going to die?" he asked and cocked his head, listening. He must have heard an answer because he said, "I'm sorry, too. It will bruise her souls. Haven't my people suffered enough?"

He nodded, his eyes still fixed on the sky. "Yes, I understand. I just hurt for her, that's all."

Another pause. The light had grown enough that she could see his face: rapturous, and, unless her eyes tricked her, glowing of an unearthly light. His eyes were pools of spinning darkness. She could feel her souls knotting and twining around themselves, frightened, frozen in place. Pus and blood, she wasn't supposed to be seeing this!

Her mouth had gone dry; her muscles tensed, ready to leap to her feet. Frantic fingers wound into the blue feathers, crushing them, pulling some loose. Where she had cherished them for the beauty and warmth they provided, now she was thankful that their dark coloring helped to hide her shivering form.

"When they arrive I shall take very good care of them," Salamander said quietly. "Yes, I know." A pause. "In time, Masked Owl." He closed his eyes. "Just for the moment, can we Dance with the One. Just until the sun breaks the horizon? Take me on your wings, fly me up into the sky one more time."

In moments, the light would be bright enough that he couldn't help but see her when he opened his eyes. Pine Drop screwed a bit of courage from her terrified souls. Glancing up to be sure his eyes were still closed, she slipped over the rounded summit of the Bird's Head. Obscured by the brow of the great mound, she hurried away, placing each foot with care lest she slip on the dew-slick grass.

She sprinted down the final incline on the mound's southern shoulder and reached the level grass. Only then did she realize that the little stone owl was still clasped in her sweaty palm.

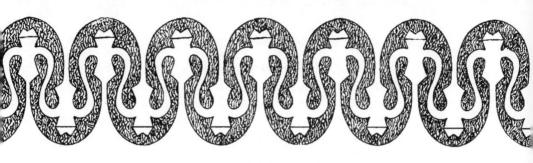

Thirty-two

The wind had changed, blowing down from the north and bringing uncharacteristically cold air with it. Bits of branches, flower petals, nearly ripe seedpods, and occasional leaves torn from distant trees went flying past.

Salamander walked with his back hunched against the blow as he tried to sort his churning emotions. The session in the Council that day had been particularly bitter. Moccasin Leaf had been given recognition and had asked if the Council would recognize a new Elder should Owl Clan present one. The vote had been unanimous: yes. When it came to Owl Clan's vote, he had stood and quietly added his yes to the vote.

Now his stomach ached at the memory. *Was it disrespectful? Did I betray Mother?* He had no answers, nothing that would help this feeling. The vacancy had to be filled, and it would not be with Water Petal. Not enough support existed for her among Owl Clan's lineages. Moccasin Leaf had done her job well. People were ready for a change.

Then, during other discussions, had come the periodic gibes and barbs concerning people who married barbarians. About their lack of respect, about their shiftlessness. He had watched Pine Drop's expression as the remarks were made. His wife had sat calmly in the rear of the Snapping Turtle delegation, her face reflecting nothing. She had refused to meet his eyes, even once.

So now he walked past the Southern Moiety's pole, its top decorated by streamers of colored cloth, feathers, and painted bones that dangled from leather thongs. He walked down the gap separating Alligator Clan from Snapping Turtle. Only a blind man would have been unaware of Elder Stone Talon as she sat at her ramada on the first ridge. She might have skewered him with a dart, so piercing was her glare.

He climbed onto the third ridge, walking eastward past the line of houses. When people spoke to him, he answered politely. He could almost taste their curiosity as they watched him pass; and he dared not look back as he approached his wives' house for fear that they were following in a parade to see what happened.

Salamander hadn't been here since Anhinga's arrival. For most of the time, both Pine Drop and Night Rain had been in the Women's House. Since then, well, he had been putting this off.

He rounded the last house. Night Rain was crouched under the ramada, grabbing up spilled cordage where the loom had been blown flat by the restless wind. She had laid a stone on a small ceramic jar full of red feathers, probably from a cardinal, that she had been weaving into the warp and weft.

"Can I help you with that?" Salamander asked, bending over beside her.

She shot him a scathing look. "No."

He nodded, backing away. This was going to be as bad as he had imagined. "Where is Pine Drop?"

"Inside. She took the stew in before it blew full of dirt. As if you'd care."

He took a deep breath and walked to the door as Pine Drop called, "Night Rain? Who is it?"

"Our *husband*, Sister. Evidently his barbarian camp bitch has given him time to come collect his things."

Salamander ground his teeth, a sinking in his chest.

"Come in, Husband." Pine Drop's face appeared in the doorway. "If you don't, you'll be blown away. Oh, would you mind helping Night Rain with the loom? Another gust like that last one, and she'll be blown clear down to the Panther's Bones." At that she smiled. "And, fortunately for us, you're probably the only man here with the ties to get her back without bloodshed."

The tone in her voice shocked him. Apparently it flattened Night Rain, for she made no other comment as he helped her maneuver the loom through the doorway while the wind tried to rip it away.

Inside he peered around in the gloom. To his surprise his belongings were just as he'd left them. Truth be told, he had expected to find them piled outside the door and reeking of dog piss.

Pine Drop resettled herself behind the fire. Newly kindled, the first flames were licking up around the sides of her carved soapstone bowl.

"It's still warm, but if you'll wait it will be hot soon." She looked up at him and smiled. "Please, be seated, Salamander. We have a lot to hear about."

He opened his mouth, but words stuck in the bottom of his throat. Still mute, he seated himself, aware that Night Rain, too, was gaping.

"Sister?" Pine Drop asked. "Could you pour some of that raspberry juice from the gourd for our husband?"

"N-No!" Night Rain sputtered. "He can drink toad urine for all I care!"

To Salamander's complete surprise, Pine Drop reached out and slapped her sister hard across the cheek. "You will do as I say, Sister. Pour our husband some of that raspberry juice. *Now!*"

"No, it's all right," Salamander managed to blurt. "I didn't want to be any trouble."

Night Rain was speechless, her eyes wide, fingers to her cheek. She gaped in disbelief at first her sister, then Salamander.

"It is no trouble, Salamander," Pine Drop said. "It is only your due as our husband. And before I forget, thank you for the baskets of fish you had your kinsman, Bluefin, deliver to us. We really appreciated them."

"I would have brought them myself," he said through a tight throat. "I was busy. Every waking hour . . ." How did he finish that?

"It took me more than a half moon to build this house," she replied reasonably. "You and your kin did it quickly."

Night Rain unsteadily reached for the gourd hanging on the peg by the door and handed it to Salamander. She was still stunned as she said, "You hit me!"

Pine Drop shot her a glance as she used a stone knife to slice sections of lotus root into the stew. "And I'll do it again if I ever hear you use that tone of voice with me."

"What has gotten into you?" Night Rain demanded hotly.

Pine Drop fixed her with a hard stare. "Responsibility, Sister. My lack of it, and yours."

"What?" Night Rain's face twisted.

"Very well, let's discuss this. Has our husband failed in any of his responsibilities to us?"

"He married that barbarian bitch!" Night Rain thrust a finger at Salamander.

"Our husband is Speaker for his clan." Pine Drop sat back on her haunches, hands on her brown thighs. "The Swamp Panthers came to Owl Clan, offering a daughter to them in return for an agreement to stop raiding. It was not our business what he did. Since that time, our husband has had to find lodging for his new wife." She lifted a wry eyebrow. "Or did you intend to welcome her here?"

Night Rain's mouth opened and closed as if she were a fish.

"That's what I thought," Pine Drop finished, then looked at Salamander. "You have behaved as an honorable man should." She lowered her eyes. "We, on the other hand, have not."

"I don't understand." To cover his discomfort, he sipped the thick raspberry juice. Sweet and delicious it helped to snap him out of his confusion.

Pine Drop met his eyes with an honesty he had never seen there before. "Salamander, we have behaved badly. You are our husband, and for as long as this marriage lasts, we are your wives. You have fulfilled your responsibilities to us without flaw. From this day forward, we will fulfill ours. Isn't that right, Night Rain?"

"What?"

Pine Drop might have been stone. "I am the first wife, Sister. When it comes to this marriage, I have the right to expect obedience from you—something I have been lax in. You do not have to like Salamander, but you will treat him with respect. It is the way of our ancestors. You don't have to like it, you must only obey. If you have a problem with this, we will go out behind the house and settle it once and for all. Do you understand?"

Night Rain nodded in a daze.

"There, good. Let us start fresh, then." Pine Drop smiled when she looked back at Salamander. He had managed to keep his jaw from falling.

"Now," she began brightly, "what are your plans for tonight? Can you spend it with us, or must you go back to Anhinga?"

He tried to bring his racing thoughts together. "I told her I might not be back until morning."

"Good." Her eyes reflected concern when she said, "I want you to know, I have never seen the courage that I saw today when you voted with the Council on Moccasin Leaf's motion."

His voice turned hoarse. "Afterward I heard people whispering that I had shown disrespect for Mother."

"Did you?" Pine Drop asked.

"No. She cannot lead. She is ill. I, alone, am responsible for my clan. As much as I hated to do it, it was the right thing," he said woodenly, the wound in his souls opening.

She reached over and placed her hand on his. "Sometimes the right thing is hard to do, isn't it?"

He nodded, jarred by the sincerity he saw in her eyes. Snakes! Who was this new Pine Drop?

"I have to get air," Night Rain said, bursting for the door.

"Give her time," Pine Drop told him as he watched his young wife flee. "She still has a lot to learn."

"We all do," he murmured warily.

Anhinga watched the evening fall. The shadows cast by the rows of houses lengthened, the dome of the sky deepening in color. A trio of buzzards circled in a high spiral overhead, mocked by a single surly crow who dived and harassed them. Children's voices rose and fell as they engaged in a stickball game on the grassy Northern Moiety flat just across the borrow pit. Even the smoke from the evening fires seemed lazy as it rose into the quiet air.

Anhinga rubbed her arms, smearing the grease that kept mosquitoes from her skin. Casting an uneasy glance down the row of houses, she could see Water Petal's and sense the worry there. The little baby's fever had burned hotter, cooking life out of that thin and fragile flesh. She had seen it among her own people. It would be soon now.

Here I am. Alone in the camp of the enemy. She made a face and walked from her house, past the pestle and mortar, to the ramada where Wing Heart sat at her loom.

Anhinga cocked her head, watching the old woman's nimble fingers as they slipped thread back and forth through the warp.

"Hello, Elder," Anhinga called.

Wing Heart seemed oblivious.

Anhinga stepped over and seated herself on the cane matting. She snugged her knees inside her arms and studied the old woman's visage. Fleeting expressions seemed to shift like leaf shadows in a breeze. They rippled across the texture of the old woman's face, slipping among the wrinkles and hiding at the corners of her mouth. Her dark eyes, like midnight droplets, sparkled and danced, animated by some clinging remnant of her souls.

"My uncle always feared you," Anhinga ventured. "Do you remember him? Jaguar Hide? Does that name conjure any spark in your memory, old woman?"

The bony brown fingers never skipped, the vacant eyes never flickered.

Anhinga frowned and reached down. Salamander's adze lay forgotten on the cane matting. Anhinga picked it up, staring thoughtfully at the tool. The handle was the length of her forearm, and had been crafted out of the Y of a branch. The angle of the Y held a thin slate celt that had been set into the wood and bound by wraps of what looked like deer sinew. She tested the edge with her fingertip. Recently sharpened.

"Does it worry you to be here alone with me?" She studied Wing Heart from the corner of her eye.

Nothing.

"Your people killed my brother."

Wing Heart's eyes remained focused on a far horizon.

"Your son killed the man I would have married."

Wing Heart's lips twitched, and unexpectedly she said, "No, Cloud Heron. I don't think you should marry Back Scratch." Her head dipped, as if hearing a reply. "Surely not."

Anhinga glanced around, seeing no one the old woman could be talking to. "What happened to you?"

"Thumper's a good man. Hard to believe he's kin to young Mud Stalker."

The adze balanced well in Anhinga's hand. She glanced around again, seeing that no one was close. In the shadows, it would be so easy. She could rise, drive the sharp stone head of the adze right through the Clan Elder's head. The body wouldn't be found until morning. She would be long gone, having struck the Sun People a terrible blow.

"I have hopes, Brother." Wing Heart smiled at that, her face lighting with joy.

Uncle's words came back. *"Wing Heart? She is the greatest of them. She and Cloud Heron remade Sun Town. Oh, to be sure, they had started on the ridges and high mounds several lifetimes ago, but those two, they dominated the Council. What may have never been finished has been done in two tens of years under their leadership. Never forget: None is as crafty as Wing Heart."*

"You don't look so crafty now," Anhinga noted. Instinctively she reached out, brushing a mosquito from the old woman's shoulder where Water Petal had missed greasing her. "Panther's bones, you can't even take care of yourself."

The gray head bobbed in the twilight. "White Bird will return, Brother. I can feel it in my bones. With the spring. That's when we'll see him." When she smiled, a thin drop of saliva tricked from the corner of her mouth.

"He's dead, Elder." She pointed at the spot across the borrow pit. "He died there, remember?"

Was that a reaction? The old woman's smile dimmed; pain glistened in her eyes.

Anhinga lowered her gaze, a heaviness on her souls. The smooth handle of the adze had warmed in her hand. She absently rubbed her thumb along the grain, then laid it to one side. What honor came from tormenting the tormented?

"Elder, you are drooling," she murmured as she reached for a bit of fabric and wiped at the corner of the old woman's mouth. "There, that's better."

She rose, stepping over to where the grease pot sat. "If you will allow me, you need a bit more grease or the mosquitoes are going to eat you alive."

W hat is going on?" Mud Stalker demanded as he matched step with Pine Drop. She was carrying a grass-stem basket full of chinquapins. Midday sunlight peeked through low wads of clouds that scudded out of the southwest on a never-ceasing passage of the white-blue sky.

"Going on?" Her self-possessed look caught him off guard.

He tried to balance Night Rain's hysterical ravings against this calm young woman. "Night Rain came to me. She's upset. She says that you've either lost your souls like Wing Heart, or you've been witched. Which is it?"

"If it has anything to do with my souls, Uncle, it's that I found them." She gave him a smile too old for her age. She looked more mature than he remembered. The petty tightness at the corner of her mouth was gone. Her smooth brown cheeks seemed to have more color, and a serenity lay behind those dark brown eyes.

"I don't suppose you'd like to elaborate on that?" He cradled his ruined arm, fingers stroking the scars.

"Uncle, let me ask you a question."

"Go ahead."

"Do you expect me to be ready to step in as Clan Elder someday?"

"It is the natural order of things. The Sky Beings willing, I'll be long gone before your mother is, but yes, I fully expect our lineage to maintain its control. You are the logical one to follow your mother in the Council."

"I thought you'd say that."

"Oh, don't be ridiculous! You knew that full well. That's why I devote so much time to you." He realized he was scowling, too cagey a politician not to know that this was going somewhere he wasn't going to like.

"I have to learn to be an Elder," she told him. "I have to be worthy. To do that, I have to learn to think, to feel, and to lead. Do you agree?"

"Of course." Had he just stepped full under the deadfall?

"I was hoping you thought that way, because I want you to know that I will do my best for the clan. I need your advice in all things, as I need Mother's, but from here on, I am making my own decisions."

"You've always made your own decisions."

"No, Uncle. In the past I did as you said, as Elder Back Scratch said, and after her, as Mother said. But something has happened. I realized what I was becoming: Someone who only does the bidding of others, who can only follow orders, cannot give them."

"So, what does this have to do with Night Rain and Salamander? We are almost at the point where we can rid you of him. Once we replace Wing Heart with Moccasin Leaf, it will be time to castrate the little tadpole. A statement of divorce will do that as effectively as—"

"No, Uncle."

"What?"

"I don't want a divorce."

Mud Stalker grabbed her arm, pulling her to a stop. She stared at him over the basket rim. He searched her eyes, seeing a stubborn resolution there. "You will divorce him when *I* say so."

"The clan may not arrange a marriage without the consent of the parties. Nor can it break a marriage unless the husband and wife agree. I disagree."

"Night Rain doesn't. She thinks you've been chewing jimsonweed. I'm not sure that she's wrong. What is this crazy talk? Why are you defying me? I am your uncle, your clan's Speaker."

"Do you want my advice?"

"Given what you've said so far, probably not."

"Then hear it anyway. I think Night Rain should stay in the marriage."

Mud Stalker released her arm, shook himself, and asked, "Very well, Niece, since you've discovered all of these magical things, why?"

"Because she needs the discipline."

"I'm not terribly impressed with yours at the moment."

"Not discipline to the clan, Uncle. Discipline with life, with responsibility. She's ready to run off to exile with Saw Back. You know, the Alligator Clan youth?"

"The one your husband got into trouble?" Mud Stalker nodded. "The one who was supposed to see to Jaguar Hide's death but let him get away?"

"He's not the sort we would want Night Rain to be married to. He's dumber than a cooking clay—and not nearly so durable."

"Obviously, considering it was Salamander who outsmarted him." Mud Stalker rubbed his jaw, seeing the logic of her words.

"And another thing, Uncle. We have been blinded by our own preconceptions."

He raised an eyebrow. "We have?"

"Why do you think Salamander is a stupid fool?"

"Because he is! Snakes, girl, four moons ago he was a weird little boy lost in games and silliness. Even his soul-scattered mother considered him to be an idiot and a failure. It took everything I had to maneuver her into marrying you to White Bird, and even more to ensure that addle-brained nit would follow his brother! By the Earth Monsters, who'd have thought that a bolt of lightning would deliver him to us like solstice supper?"

Her enigmatic smile cooled his enthusiasm as she said, "Watch him, Uncle. He is more than he seems."

"You would advise me? About that fool boy we put on the Council? He's a laughingstock!"

"For the sake of my clan, yes, I would advise you."

"But you won't divorce him?"

"No, Uncle. Not until he gives me a reason to."

He hated the resolve filling her large brown eyes. Rot it, there had to be some way of talking sense into the girl. "Well, so be it." An idea came to him. "After this last session in the Women's House, it is apparent that Three Stomachs hasn't been able to—"

"No, Uncle."

"You're right, Three Stomachs is out, but"—he narrowed his eyes—"have you thought about Speaker Deep Hunter? True he's a little old, but for the moment he absolutely *hates* Salamander for aiding Jaguar Hide's escape."

"No, Uncle."

"Deep Hunter is a Speaker, Niece. From a powerful clan. A man of real authority. Your coupling with him will balance some of the obligation we have to him. Not only that, but if this works out, if he can sire an heir, it might be a reasonable mating."

"No, Uncle."

"Well, it's probably early to talk about marriage. I can tell you, however, that he has had his eye on you. I watch these things. Red Finger is going hunting with him in the next couple of days. I'll have him delicately broach the subject. Trust me, Deep Hunter will oblige. And afterward, well, it will make him a little more amenable to our position in the Council."

"*No*, Uncle." She cocked her head, meeting his stare with defiance. "I am married. That's the tip of the snake's tail. The end. Find someone else." With that she walked away, her feet swishing through the tall green grass.

Mud Stalker frowned, trying to grasp where the problem was. Snakes, she wasn't really enamored of that skinny little idiot, was she?

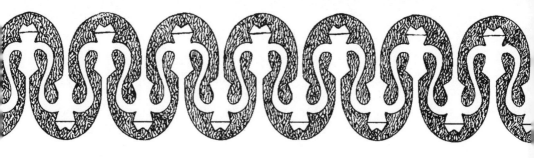

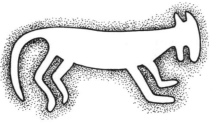

Thirty-three

Anhinga cursed and rested the heavy wooden pestle on her shoulder as she studied her thumb. The long dark sliver had run under the skin where it folded at the joint. She used her teeth to pull it, turned her head, and spat it out. The pestle had been made of a long pole, taller than she was. The bottom had been sanded round to match the hollow burned into the stump.

She glanced over her shoulder at the old woman seated at her loom. From the first glow of dawn to sunset's last light she sat there, humming, talking to the dead, and weaving the most beautiful fabrics Anhinga had ever seen.

She had approached Wing Heart several times since that first night, cautiously seating herself and remarking about the weather, the taste of the stew, or the beauty of her weavings. Each time she might have been a leaf blown in by the wind for all the notice the old woman gave her. Sometimes she wiped up drool. Since the death of Water Petal's baby, Anhinga had found Wing Heart's kirtle fouled. She couldn't stand the thought of the soulless Elder squatting in her own waste. Irritated by her compassion, Anhinga had sponged the woman clean before walking down to wash the fabrics in the borrow pit.

I came here to kill her. Now I'm caring for her infirmities. Anhinga slammed the pestle into the mortar, flattening more of the ground nuts into paste. As she worked, images kept swimming out of her memory. If she closed her eyes she could smell the fires of home.

That blue smoke hung low in the trees surrounding the Panther's Bones. She could imagine the earthy scent of the swamp clinging in her nose with a blossom's intensity.

She could see Striped Dart, seated before a fire, his legs akimbo. He had that preoccupied look on his face, his smooth black hair pulled back into a tight curl and pinned to the side of his head. In the fantasy, her brother looked up at her and smiled.

Panther's blood! They'd had some times. She could see him again as he had been as a boy. How they'd played, she, Striped Dart, and Bowfin! Tag, hide-and-seek, ball games, and play war. She remembered splashing in the waters of Water Eagle Lake when they'd traveled east to the bluffs. The sun shone on their naked brown skin as they frolicked and dived in the murky depths.

Her mother's and father's faces formed as they had been then, young and in love, happy with their family. That had been so long ago, those golden summers, lost with the passage of time like water down the rivers of her homeland. Bowfin was dead. When she conjured her mother's face it was to see the lines of grief as she wailed over Bowfin's body.

Other memories rose to fill her. Firelight flickered as Mist Finger stood before her. She was on her stomach, propped on her elbows, her knees and toes digging into the soft black dirt. Her breasts had barely begun to bud, his shoulders only beginning to widen.

"I will be a great warrior!" he had said as he strutted back and forth before the fire, his walk an exaggerated mimicry of a great blue heron's.

"You'll be a lazy fisherman," Cooter had replied where he lay on his side, the firelight flashing yellow on his belly. "Me, I'm just going to make canoes."

"Canoes?" Anhinga had cried. "When you could be a great warrior and have pretty young maidens like me sing your praises?"

"I like making canoes," he had said simply. "It's an art to make a good one."

"I'll let the maidens sing *my* praises," Mist Finger had declared. "But, just for you, old friend, I'll use one of your canoes to carry them off into the swamp when I choose the right one."

They had all laughed at that. Now, over so much time, it echoed hollowly in her ears.

I miss them. She bent down, setting the pestle aside, and scraped the paste from the mortar bottom, placing it in a ceramic bowl. She studied the vessel for a moment. One thing was sure, Sun Town potters made better bowls than her people did.

That led her to remember Webfinger, the young potter at the

Panther's Bones. She wasn't a known beauty, her face round but pleasant. Anhinga had spent hours sitting at her feet, watching those quick fingers as they worked. Through her magic a lump of mud was turned into a thin-walled hollow by means of pinching, scraping, and pressing with her palms and the wooden anvil.

Home! What I'd give to be there now.

"Excuse me?" A female voice caught her by surprise. Anhinga straightened, picking paste from her fingers.

The woman was young, comely, her breasts still firm, the lines of her belly unspoiled by the growth of a child. She wore a tan-and-black kirtle tied with a married woman's knot. Her gleaming black hair was tastefully parted down the middle and pinned on the sides of her head. A basket hung from the crook of her right arm. Her face caught Anhinga's attention; it had a regal bearing. Something in those eyes made her alert. She didn't need to see the strings of beads, the tufts of exotic northern furs woven into her hair to know that this was a woman used to authority.

"Yes?" Anhinga instinctively rested her hands on the pestle. The solace of the stout wood reassured her. Not all of Sun Town's people could be counted on to be happy with her presence here.

"I have come to see you." The accented voice carried no hint of malice or anger.

"Assuming that your eyes work, you have succeeded. I am Anhinga. Daughter of Yellow Dye, who was daughter of Red Walnut, of the Sunrise Clan."

The young woman nodded, every manner correct and polite. "I am Pine Drop, daughter of Elder Sweet Root who is the daughter of Back Scratch, of the Bluejay lineage of the Snapping Turtle Clan." She smiled soberly. "I am also first wife to Salamander, Speaker for the Owl Clan."

Anhinga started. Salamander had told her that his other wives could have cared less about her, as they had apparently cared so little about him. Yet here was this self-assured woman standing before her, bearing a basket.

"Is my husband available?" Pine Drop asked, her eyes straying first to the humming Wing Heart and then to the partially visible doorway of Anhinga's new house.

"He has gone," she replied carefully. By the Panther's blood, she hadn't come here to check up on Salamander, had she? "He is at his cousin's. Water Petal, do you know her? Her infant is dead."

The woman nodded, her eyes still taking Anhinga's measure. "Yes. I have just heard. I have come offering my clan's sympathy to my husband and his relatives." She indicated the basket. "Food for the family. Smoked raccoon, some boiled crawfish, and smilax-root bread."

"I wouldn't have thought you would care." The words just came out, surprising Anhinga of their volition. "Forgive me, that was not my right to say." Rot it, Pine Drop might be straight out of the pampered Sun Town elite, but that was no reason for rudeness. *And why do I care what she does or how she treats Salamander?*

Pine Drop lowered her eyes, smiling ironically. "If you know Water Petal, you have heard some terrible things about me."

Anhinga said nothing, guarding her suddenly impetuous tongue.

"I'm afraid most of them are true," the woman replied, raising her eyes again.

"You admit to lying with another man?" Anhinga asked, curious to see how far she could go. "Just like that?"

A slightly raised eyebrow was the only reaction she elicited. "Among other things." A pause. "I owe you no explanations."

"He said he wishes to spend the next few nights with you." Anhinga fingered the pestle, wondering why the woman's presence bothered her so. She had known from the beginning that he was married, not just to this woman, but her sister also. Multiple wives were nothing exceptional. Her uncle had *five,* but why did she feel so possessive about Salamander in the presence of this woman?

"My sister and I will be looking forward to his company." She hesitated. "I may be out of place, but if you need anything, come and see me. I was remiss not to have come to you sooner." Her smile seemed honest, warm. "You are alone among a strange people, your souls must be longing for home."

Blood and spit! Is it that obvious? "Thank you for your kind invitation. I shall discuss it with Salamander. If he approves, I may come and see you."

"And the Women's House?" Pine Drop asked. "Have you made arrangements?"

Anhinga jerked her head to the east. "I would prefer to seclude myself in the swamp. It would be better for all."

Pine Drop's expression tightened. "Out there? Alone?"

Anhinga laughed. "What man is going to bother me in that condition? Do you think he would want to be close to a woman during her bleeding? And besides, I am Swamp Panther. To me it is more like home."

Pine Drop seemed to accept that. "As you wish, however, should you need, my clan would offer you space."

Anhinga's heart actually lightened. "Thank you, again. You are very kind."

"I am keeping you from your work." Pine Drop indicated the pestle and mortar. "I shall take this to Water Petal." She glanced uneasily at Wing Heart again, and added, "Do come to see me, even if it is just to visit."

"I will," Anhinga promised. And she would. Here was yet another opportunity opening before her. "It was nice of you to come here."

Pine Drop nodded and went on her way.

Anhinga watched the woman walk past Wing Heart's house and follow the ridge down to Water Petal's household with its grief and shattered dreams.

Anhinga placed more ground nuts into the mortar and began smacking the pestle home. The sound make a rhythmic *thump-tump thump-tump*.

The invitation to the Women's House had been unexpected, and something that, had the roles been opposite, she wouldn't have thought of had Pine Drop been at the Panther's Bones.

Anhinga frowned, removing the pestle. She placed a hand to her abdomen, trying to count the days. Her last menses had been just before leaving the Panther's Bones, had delayed it, in fact.

You still have time. But soon. Very soon. She couldn't be pregnant, not only wasn't it time, but her stomach felt fine in the mornings. Whether she passed her moon or not, she had to get away. The four days to pass her bleeding would give her time for something she had just begun to plan.

The Serpent

We are all frightened of the Stranger.

Probably because the Stranger is not nearly as far away as we think. She can come upon us suddenly, after an act of cruelty, the death of a loved one, or stumbling over an unknown dog in the forest. For no apparent reason, we cross some hidden border and the stranger is born. In a heartbeat, we do not even recognize ourselves.

Our own fear with a face—that's who the Stranger is.

And that is what makes her so very dangerous.

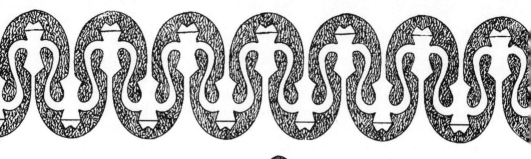

Thirty-four

In the two moons since Salamander's marriage to the Swamp Panther, Night Rain's irritation had grown. Late summer light slanted through the trees. From where she lay in the hunting blind, Night Rain could look up and see sunshine reflecting from the glossy green leaves of the magnolia. Great white flowers, the last of the summer, still whispered their scent into the sultry air. To either side sassafras trees stood like resolute sentinels. The lobed leaves undulated on the late-afternoon breeze.

Deep Hunter stirred and shifted on the thin deer hide they lay upon. He propped himself on one arm, his appreciative dark eyes tracing the length of Night Rain's young body. She could see the pattern her body had made on his; the grease had been smeared on his chest, belly, and thighs. His penis lay limp, the scrotum that had been so taut moments ago had descended, lax in the heat.

She sighed, the warm tingling still fading from her loins. Snakes! So that was what it was all about? No wonder people made such a fuss about coupling. A glow of satisfaction still traced fingers of delight through her hips.

"You are so beautiful," he whispered.

She smiled as she studied the lines in his face. He might have been her grandfather, but his gnarly old body had surprised her. She hadn't understood that coupling could proceed slowly, gently, like a long leisurely soak in a warm pond. Her previous experience with Salamander had reminded her of the rapid way camp dogs joined, then faced away while locked, as if longing to be somewhere else.

"How do you feel?" he asked.

"Good." She stretched, dreamy, aware that his eyes were fixed on her supple body. "I didn't know it could be like that."

"You have only had boys." He yawned, smiling satisfaction. "And it pleases me that your Salamander is no better with his women than he is with his politics. Have you given any thought about what you will do when he's broken and dismissed from the Council?"

"This will be soon?"

"No, not for a while. Maybe next summer. A great many people want Owl Clan broken, not merely wounded."

She remembered her uncle's admonitions: "*Give him nothing but your body, Night Rain. This isn't some dazzle-headed youth, but a skilled Speaker, crafty in the ways of intrigue. Say nothing that will give him any advantage.*"

She told him offhand, "I don't care. Just so long as he is out of my bed and gone for good. I have been told that if things are handled correctly, an alliance with Alligator Clan might be considered." She lifted an eyebrow. "Currently you only have one wife."

He chuckled. "Yes, and she is possessive. Trust me, you wouldn't want to move into her house with me. We have been together for a great many turnings of the seasons. She has her own ways of doing things, and I daresay, the pot would boil over within the first hand of time. I wouldn't want your tender flesh scalded by those waters."

Despite the warnings from her uncle, she said, "You have others from your lineage. Let's see, there's Saw Back."

"Yes, you'd think he was born of Owl Clan instead of mine." His expression soured. "You would be interested in a stone-headed boy like that? I still can't understand how anyone could fail in such an easy assignment. All he had to do was follow that murdering weasel into one of the channels and kill him! Jaguar Hide was alone, vulnerable. The added benefit was Owl Clan's abortive protection! It was a way of striking two birds with one cast of the bola."

Startled by his outburst, she placed a hand protectively on her breast. "But he was tricked!"

Deep Hunter's eyes narrowed, expression changing as he studied her. "Is this another one of his pathetic games? Did he put you up to this, little temptress? Are you playing with me? Hmm?"

The afternoon's warm delight had turned cold in her bones. Her uncle's warnings were spinning about in her head like bees. "No, I swear!"

She tried to recover her shaken confidence, smiling in what she hoped was a coquettish way. His continued silence, the chert-hard look in his eyes, indicated he was anything but fooled.

"You swear?" he finally said. "Really? That reassures me, little wren. So, did your uncle know that you were working for Saw Back when he mentioned this little tryst? Is he going to be happy when he discovers that you and Saw Back manipulated him like a leaf on the wind?"

"No!"

"And does your mother, the Clan Elder, know that you are using her position for your own scheming?"

"No!" Her desperation was growing.

"I think I shall have to extend Saw Back's banishment for trying to trick me like this."

She felt herself crumple inside, closing her eyes as she whispered, "No. It's no scheme, I swear it."

"Ah, swearing again? When I have caught you in the middle of a lie?"

"I'm not lying," she declared, on the point of tears.

"Indeed you are," he added smoothly, a glint in his eyes. "Either you are scheming with Saw Back, or you are scheming with me. If you weren't in some sort of scheme, you would be home, tending your household and your duty to your clan."

"This *is* my duty to my clan!"

"Then supposing we accept your desperate protestations and believe that you are not here for Saw Back's benefit. That would mean that Mud Stalker had an ulterior motive when he mentioned that I might meet you here. I wonder what that could be? Hmm? Care to share it with me?"

"I don't know," she pleaded, rising, frantic to escape as his hand clamped on her wrist.

"No, stay. I'm not finished yet." He nodded in triumph, a slow smile spreading on his lips. "You have made a mess of your seduction, my little wren. I have caught you in a botched attempt to wiggle your canoe around Alligator Clan's internal business." Satisfaction gleamed behind his veiled brown eyes. "What a story this will make in the Men's House. Every lip will be telling of how Night Rain will part her legs for those who can do her a favor. The young men are going to be snickering and offering favors every time you walk past."

"Dear Sky Beings," she cried, bolting up. "You wouldn't!"

He continued watching her, spiderlike in his intensity. "Wouldn't what? Make you a laughingstock? It would depend. You know, don't you, that you are already suspect in most people's eyes. You're married to that idiot Speaker. What would a little push do to you? Send you right over the canoe's side, that's what. I suppose I should tell you, the water is deep and cold."

"Why?" she cried, hearing fear in her voice. "I am the daughter of Sweet Root, the Elder of—"

"I *know* who are," he snapped. "That's what makes you even more vulnerable. Don't tell me you hadn't figured that out on your own." He raised one hand in a calming motion. "But it doesn't have to work that way, you know."

She swallowed hard, her thoughts scattered like a flock of frightened bobwhite. She could feel the tangling of his web around her.

"Let us say that what happened here today could stay between the two of us," he mused, releasing his hold on her wrist. "There is no reason to destroy you, Night Rain. It would be unnecessarily cruel. All that talk, people laughing every time you passed. You've seen other women like that, living in constant shame, afraid to be seen in public. I can only imagine what the whisperings would be like in the Women's House."

Her breath shortened. It would be horrible. She was an Elder's daughter. Her uncle was the Clan Speaker. All of Sun Town would delight in tearing her down like an old ramada.

"What do you want?" she asked with a shallow voice.

"Oh, let's play this charade for a while." His smile broadened, rearranging the lines in his old face. "I rather enjoy teaching you the arts of your body." He ran his fingers down her side, along the curve of her hip and over the top of her thigh. "But don't think I would be ungrateful for your cooperation. Quite the contrary, actually." He studied her, seeing right through the front she put up, reading her souls. "What do you really want, Night Rain? Tell me the truth. I will know if you are lying."

She swallowed hard, thoroughly defeated. "I want to be somebody. Not a *second* wife to an idiot. Not a younger sister to Pine Drop. Everyone knows that Pine Drop is going to be Clan Elder someday. Snakes, she already acts like she is! You should see her. The way she orders me around. She treats me like a slave taken in war rather than a sister."

His knowing eyes had narrowed, watching her the way a hawk did a swamp cottontail. "Ah, honesty at last." He twisted a long lock of her hair around his finger. "Nothing is beyond attaining, Night Rain. Not if you ally yourself with the right accomplices. What you become, who you become, depends on you, on what you are willing to do to make your dreams come true."

She bit her lip, saying nothing.

He made a calming gesture. "You must understand, these things take time. They take compromise and dedication. Sometimes you must make difficult choices, decisions that place you in uncomfortable positions with your clan, and even your lineage." He shrugged. "You are here, coupling with me. That proves that those decisions are not difficult for you."

"You want me to work against my clan?"

He studied her, expression neutral. "Would you be Clan Elder one day? All you need tell me is a simple yes, or no."

Her heart sank in her chest. "Do I have any choice?"

"Oh, there is always a choice, little wren. I can tell that you enjoyed coupling with me. I can teach you more ways of kindling that fire within your hips. And, as an added benefit, I might be persuaded to send for Saw Back. If you are good, I might even allow the two of you to dally here in secret occasionally." His eyes narrowed. "I am told that Saw Back has come to absolutely hate your husband. He blames him for his misfortunes."

Night Rain's heart was pounding. Deep Hunter noticed, reaching out to place his fingers against the pulse in her neck. "Relax, little wren. In life there is punishment and reward. If you help me, I will see that everything you want comes to you." He paused, searching her eyes. "Clan Elder?"

Mistrusting, Night Rain stared at him. "You could really do that?"

He nodded, so assured of himself that she couldn't help but believe him. "Of course. But only with the right accomplice." He leaned back, drawing her down beside him. "Tell me, Night Rain, are you that accomplice? Can you become my ally, knowing that with a little discretion, you can have everything?"

Her souls were trembling, but she hesitated. In that instant the memory of Pine Drop slapping her in front of Salamander flashed before her. She spoke almost without volition. "Yes, Speaker."

"Good," he whispered, bending close to brush his lips across hers. "Now, let me show you some new ways to throw tinder on a man's fire."

Water dripped in a line of rings as Green Crane, Trader of the Wash'ta People, lifted his paddle for another bite in the murky brown swamp. He had begun to question the wisdom of this journey southward to find the People of the Sun.

The canoe he and Always Fat paddled, slipped forward, powered by their muscular strokes as he glanced uneasily around him. Everywhere he looked, an endless pattern of green masked the trees. Through the few breaks in the foliage he could glimpse a dim world of black tree trunks wound with vines. The forest seemed to stretch on forever.

Ahead of them, the channel narrowed, ending in a verdant mat of reeds, duckweed, and flowering vines that swarmed over the fallen carcass of a bald cypress. The rotting trunk lay square across the passage, blocking any travel. The baleful eyes of a medium-sized alligator glared out at them from the scummy green surface. Turtles wearing forest-dark shells slipped from the protruding branches where they had been sunning themselves.

Green Crane shipped his paddle and looked back at his skinny companion. "We are lost."

"Good!" Always Fat made a face. His name was a jest. Always Fat looked like a walking skeleton. His ribs made a cage of his chest. Stringy arms held the paddle, and his knees looked like knobs in the middle of thick cane stalks. Mild resignation filled his long face. "I'm so glad you don't leave me baffled with hidden meanings. It pleases me that you can be so blunt when all I'd like to hear is something hopeful. Like, 'It must just be around the next bend.' "

Green Crane rubbed the back of his muscular neck as the canoe drifted forward. He and Always Fat were opposites, as well as inseparable companions. They had been planning this journey for a whole turning of the seasons, content to leave it hovering at the edge of imagination until Spring Cypress had arrived in their little village. Green Crane had been smitten at the sight of her. His attraction had only grown as he came to know her.

She was an enigma: A woman from Sun Town, that's all she would say. In the days it had taken to woo her, he had learned little more about her. He knew that she had come to his bed as a virgin, that she had left Sun Town of her own will over a broken love, and little else. One of the other Traders in his village thought he might have seen her before, and that she might have been Rattlesnake Clan; but he couldn't be sure of it, nor would Spring Cypress confirm the story. She had just smiled sadly, and told him, "That life is dead."

Green Crane, however, wished to start a life of his own, one in which she figured not only as his lover, but as his wife. Among his Wash'ta people, a woman came to a man's clan with a dowry. Spring Cypress had arrived with nothing but a fabric bag slung over her back and her incredible beauty. Before his clan would allow him to marry, a payment had to be made. Her subsequent status within both clan and village would be dictated by the value of that payment.

The hide-covered load behind him consisted of an entire turning of the seasons' worth of Trading, dickering, hunting, and collecting. The bulk of the goods were from buffalo: finely tanned winter hides, smoked and dried meat, carved and polished horn implements. In addition, they carried lumps of silvery galena for ornamentation, different mineral pigments, raw hematite, and large quartz crystals, all of which brought a premium at Sun Town.

"*I shall ensure that you come to me as no woman has come to this clan in living memory,*" he had promised.

In that brief moment, her eyes had shone and she had thrown her arms around his neck, hugging her slim body to his. "*I cannot go with you, Green Crane. I cannot step into that place again. Not as I am now, a failure and a fugitive. My clan could reclaim me, hold me. I will not be their prisoner again.*"

So he had come here, paddling down the White Mud River from his Wash'ta Mountain homelands. But somehow, along the way, he had become lost in the winding channels that led into narrow distributaries, dead ends, and ever-circling swamps of cypress and tupleo.

"How do people live in this mess?" Always Fat wondered.

"They must know the ways like we do the valleys of our home. I've heard of flatlanders getting lost, not being able to tell one valley from another."

"Mountains make sense," Always Fat reminded. "They have ups and downs. This place just has around and around."

Green Crane shook his head. He pointed a finger at the tiny patch of open sky over their heads. "Up!" He turned his finger toward the calm water. "Down!"

Always Fat pointed a finger over his shoulder. "Back."

They turned the canoe around and began paddling the way they had come.

After a hand of time they had retraced their way to the branch they had last taken. There, the canoe bobbing, Green Crane bent over, his hand cupping water as he slaked his thirst. "Tastes like tree roots and mud," he muttered.

"It could be worse." Always Fat pointed at the yellow lotus flowers in the shallows. "At least there's always something to eat here. Out in the western plains you can die of thirst and starve to death."

Green Crane glanced up at the sky, seeing the angle of the sun. By the Striking Eagle, had another day gone? "Well, from the sun, that way is west." He pointed.

"Hǫoraw! Saved." Always Fat lifted a mocking eyebrow. "Which way is Sun Town? For that matter, which way is anything?"

Green Crane considered the webwork of waterways around him. The hanging moss draping the low branches reminded him of green buffalo beards. Gaudy birds chattered and sang as they flew past. Two anhingas perched on a protruding log, unconcerned by a human presence as they sunned their wet wings in the afternoon.

"I don't think we could retrace our path even if we tried." Always Fat tapped his fingertips on his paddle. "So, we take the little channel, there."

"Why would that little channel take us through when the wide one we just tried wouldn't?"

"Because it's a way we haven't tried yet," Always Fat reminded. "If it turns bad, we'll come back and try something else."

Green Crane smiled as he shrugged, lifted his paddle, and drove them into the narrow channel. Many of his friends didn't appreciate Always Fat. But in the turnings of the seasons that they had passed together, Green Crane had come to value his companion's ever-present good humor. What a gift the gods had given him. No matter what the trial, Always Fat could only see the bright side.

The trees closed in, arching over their heads as they guided their slim canoe between the narrowing banks. Light dimmed; the canopy overhead turned opaque. Green Crane ducked vines, batting away spiderwebs. "Are you sure about this?"

"No. But our canoe isn't stuck in the mud yet."

Tufts of leaves began brushing his elbows as he used the point of his paddle to push them along. The forest sounds tightened, bearing down on him. Gods, this was getting narrower.

He ducked a low branch, its bark scaly with moss and algae. What he thought was a vine turned out to be a green snake that slithered away within inches of his eyes. He caught his breath, placing a hand to his heart.

"You all right?" Always Fat whispered.

"What if that had been a water moccasin?"

"We would have apologized when it bent its fangs on your tough hide."

At the sound of their voices, a dark shadow shifted in the Y of a tree. The panther cast a yellow-eyed glance their way, then leaped to the packed leaf mat, vanishing like a silent shadow into the gloom.

"Gods, that was a big cat!" Green Crane felt for his atlatl and darts. The fine white chert points had been chipped to an edge sharp enough to cut, but would he have time to prepare before some swamp monster plucked him from the canoe?

Always Fat swatted something off his head. "A centipede," he muttered. "I swear it dropped right on top of me."

"Precious Striking Eagle, just get me through this and I'll stay home, love my wife, and treasure my children."

"You haven't got a wife," Always Fat reminded. "Just the promise of a wife. Until you pay for her, you can't have children. You can't pay until you trade all this stuff with the Sun People for exotic goods we can't get at home."

"Must you be so cursedly pragmatic." He craned his neck, gaze following the winding vegetation up into the murky heights of the trees. Had there ever been a sky up there?

"I think it's a little brighter up ahead." Even as he spoke the watercourse widened. Within moments they were pushing the pointed bow of their canoe through a tangle of marsh ferns and out into the light.

"Pumpkin soup!" Always Fat cried. "Now where are we?"

Green Crane noted the shadows. "That way is west."

"Which way is Sun Town?"

"I have no idea."

"We could figure out where up and down are again."

"You think that would help?"

"Did it help last time? Wait. Who's this?"

Green Crane turned his head seeing a low-slung dugout canoe heading his way. The center was heaped with long pointed baskets that he recognized as fish traps. A skinny youth sat in the rear, his hair parted in the middle. His greased skin caught the light as he paddled steadily toward them.

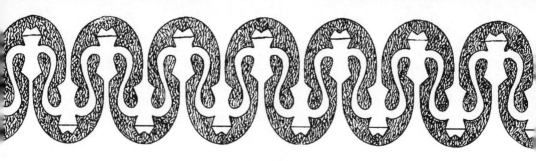

Thirty-five

Hello!" Green Crane called in Trade pidgin as he carefully stood in the bow and waved.

The youth raised an arm, apparently unconcerned as he paddled closer.

"Trusting sort," Always Fat noted. "Maybe strangers pop out of the hidden channel all the time."

"We are Wash'ta," Green Crane called. "Come to make Trade." He dare not say more until he found who the youth was, where he was, and if he were friendly. Green Crane could almost sense Always Fat's fingers as they surreptitiously rearranged his atlatl and a dart for quick utilization.

The youth dragged his paddle like a rudder to steer as his canoe glided toward them. He turned large brown eyes on Green Crane and nodded. Thin and reedy, he looked little more than a boy. A smudged white breechcloth was wadded around his waist, at his feet lay a pile of fish. An atlatl and darts rested close at hand. "I had hoped to find you."

That set Green Crane back. "You did? You knew we were lost?"

The youth cocked his head, those odd eyes seeming to enlarge. "Did you see an owl watching you?"

"We saw many things," Always Fat answered. "Alligators, snakes, and one very big panther." He jerked his thumb back at the bruised ferns they had just passed between. "Was that one of your spirits?"

"That might have been one of my wife's," the youth replied, an ironic smile on his lips.

"Where is your wife now?" Green Crane asked. What terrible thing had he led them into? He and Always Fat were lost in the swamp. Witches could capture them, devour their souls, and no one would ever find their remains in the maze of this terrible place.

"She has gone back to her people. I am to think she is in the middle of her moon. It is all right. She is lonely and homesick and needs time to plot with Jaguar Hide."

Green Crane shook his head, unable to quite grasp the meaning behind the words.

The youth stood then, balancing in the rear of the dugout. "I am Salamander, Speaker for the Owl Clan, son of Wing Heart."

"Of Sun Town!" Green Crane cried, his worry evaporating. "We made it!"

"We came to Trade," Always Fat repeated.

"I was told to seek out Owl Clan," Green Crane added, taking the skinny kid's measure. "Do you know a boy named Mud Puppy?"

The wry smile had a mocking quality. "I knew him very well."

"Knew? As in the past?" Green Crane felt a sinking in his breast. "My Trade pidgin isn't very good. You mean he's . . . what? Dead?"

"He was *called* Mud Puppy," the youth said, "now is he known as Salamander."

"But you said you were Salamander." Always Fat shifted in the back of the canoe.

"I was Mud Puppy before I was made a man."

Green Crane slapped his sides. "We have come to find you! To show you this." He fished in his belt pouch to retrieve a little red stone owl.

At sight of it, Salamander's face brightened. "How is she?"

"Safe. Spring Cypress said to give this little owl to you when I saw you. To tell you it bore her safely to my people. Being safe, she would return the owl with great thanks. She thought you might need it to keep your own luck strong."

He made a pushing-away gesture with his hands. "It was a gift— not just for her journey, but for all of her life. She is my friend forever. Return it to her with my love and my fondest wishes for her health and happiness."

"You said you are Speaker?" Always Fat had his paddle balanced across his knees. "As in the Council?"

Salamander nodded sadly.

"But you are a . . . a . . ."

"A boy?" he supplied. "I'm afraid my body has not caught up

with the age that this last turning of the seasons has branded into my souls."

"Can you show us the way to Sun Town?"

"It would please me to do so."

"How far?"

Salamander glanced at the slanting sun. "We shall be there sometime after nightfall. You shall have to stay on the Turtle's Back until you are cleansed. Are you familiar with our ways?"

"We have heard of this." Green Crane reseated himself and collected his paddle. "We have only come to Trade. Not visit. Once we have done that, then we can return to our people. You need not bother with a cleansing."

They had not followed Salamander for even a hand's time when the youth looked across at them, asking, "Is Spring Cypress happy?"

"She is. Or rather she will be once we return with our Trade."

"She is to be his wife." Always Fat pointed at Green Crane. "He has fallen in love with her and makes this journey to acquire wealth to pay for her."

Salamander studied him thoughtfully across the short distance separating the canoes. "Are you worthy of her?"

Green Crane shifted. What was this youth to her? Who was he? An old interest of hers? "I would hope that I am."

"Do not hope," Salamander said soberly. "You must always *be* worthy. There is a difference, a matter of commitment that you would make when dedicating yourself to such a woman as Spring Cypress."

"Did you once hold hopes of marrying her?" Always Fat asked the question Green Crane couldn't.

Dreamy eyes covered Salamander's smile. "She was beyond my aspirations. She will have to tell you the story when she thinks it proper. Let us just say that she and I share a special bond between our souls. We had a single precious moment together that filled us both with courage. She left rather than spend her life in misery." He shot a measuring look at Green Crane again, as though he were weighing his souls.

"I think," Green Crane mused in a voice only Always Fat could hear, "that he is more than just a green youth with a title."

"Indeed he may be."

In a louder voice, Green Crane asked, "Can you help us conduct our Trade, Salamander? Say, for the sake of Spring Cypress? Our success benefits her."

Salamander barely seemed to hear, as if lost in his thoughts, but then said, "I am happy to advise you. By that Owl you carry and the Spirit Helper who watches over you, I will make you a most favorable Trade. Just what did you bring, and what do you need?"

Green Cane knotted a fist in victory. He could already imagine Spring Cypress's smile when he returned with a canoe loaded to the gunwales with finery.

The knoll protruded from the swamp like a floating monster's back. Anhinga sat cross-legged on the dark soil, her eyes on the lofty green depths of the cypress forest. The canoe she had used to come here was pulled up on the muddy bank. A fire smoked beside her, the blue wreath rising pungently from the damp wood. Mosquitoes hummed in a column, stymied by the crushed gumweed she had mixed into grease and slathered over her skin.

As she waited, she absently wound her finger around and around a long black lock of hair. Her other hand pressed against her abdomen. She was late, that was all. It happened to women who were worried, working hard, or under pressure in strange circumstances. Had anyone been more anxious than she married to a stranger in a strange land filled with enemies?

You're all right. You haven't had the morning sickness. You don't feel different. But how did a woman feel? She made a face. Surely Salamander couldn't have planted a child that quickly.

What is it about him? He wasn't what she had had in mind when it came to a husband. Her thoughts immediately went to Mist Finger, recalling his smile, the rolling muscles in his shoulders and arms. A man should look like that, have that brave glint in his eyes.

So why, she wondered, did skinny Salamander absorb so much of her? Her first surprise had come when they had consummated the marriage. That sudden and magical explosion in her loins had taken her by complete surprise; and better yet, he shot lightning through her each time they coupled. But his lure on her interest was more than that. His large brown eyes had a Power she didn't understand. He seemed to see past her skin, down into her souls. Most perplexing, he always smiled when she lied to him, as though reassuring her.

He can't know that I am going to kill him. It was impossible—unless his Spirit Helper had told him. She and Jaguar Hide were the only ones who knew the plan. Not even Striped Dart had been informed. They couldn't trust her brother to keep his silence. What, then, caused Salamander to give her that knowing look, the one that reminded her of a parent one step ahead of his errant child?

She lifted her lip, irritated at the very thought. Salamander? A step ahead of her? Everyone in Sun Town thought him a fool—with the possible exception of Pine Drop.

A fish jumped in the water beyond her camp. The thickened boles of bald cypress, tupelo, and overcup oak protruded from the still waters. Strands of hanging moss drooped, lacy and gray-green; here and there thick patches of mistletoe had knotted and strangled their host's branches. The first fernlike needles were beginning to brown on the cypresses. A dry crispness hung in the air, a precursor of the winter to come.

Through the trilling of the songbirds and the hissing of the insects, she heard the hollow thunk of a paddle against wood. Movement caught her eye as Jaguar Hide paddled through the maze of waterlogged roots and protruding knees.

When he met her gaze across the distance, he smiled and raised a hand in greeting.

She rose gracefully to her feet and stepped down to the water's edge. He slid his canoe in beside hers as she offered him her hand, helping him to his feet. He groaned and made a face as his legs straightened. "Age," he growled. "Used to be I could live in a canoe."

"Hello, Uncle." She threw her arms around him, hugging his hard body against hers. "I see that you escaped the nasty Sun People. But I still haven't forgiven you for just paddling off like that."

He held her at arm's length, inspecting her from the parted crown of her head to her brown toes. "I came as soon as I got your message. What are you doing here?"

"They think I'm off to spend my moon in solitude."

Sudden fear leaped behind his eyes.

"Don't worry, Uncle, I passed that on the way here," she lied. "I wouldn't expose your souls to woman's blood."

"I would hope not." He grabbed a sack from the canoe and led her over to the fire. With a careful glance he studied her small camp. His gaze fixed on the tall, delicately leafed plants that grew on the far side of the small island. "What is that? Water hemlock?"

"It is indeed. People don't come here because the death plant grows here. Some think it taints the surrounding waters. We can meet here in private." She indicated a ceramic bowl resting in her canoe. "I bring water with me."

"Very well, you have exceeded all of my hopes. Tell me everything!" he cried, lowering himself beside the fire. "You are married, yes? To Salamander? You didn't kill him yet, did you? And what of

Sun Town? What have you learned? What can we do to harm them? What is the truth about Wing Heart? Has she really lost her souls?"

"One thing at a time, Uncle!" She threw up her arms in mock surrender. She related her time in Sun Town, telling of building the house, Wing Heart's condition, and the collapse of Owl Clan.

"Tell me about this boy, Salamander. Is he really a Speaker?"

"He is. But most think him a young fool."

"From your tone, I take it that you don't?"

"I am not sure, Uncle. But fool or not, there are forces gathering to act against him. He has no allies except for his cousin, Water Petal, and she's ignored by everyone. There is a move afoot to replace him. They have already replaced Wing Heart. She is nothing more than a husk of a woman, like a pod stripped of its seeds."

"They have treated you well?"

She shrugged. "I am not one of their people. I am tolerated. Uncle, I can kill them anytime—with impunity—and escape in the night. I am unguarded. Not trusted, but not a prisoner, either. I think I should strike. I can be home before the next moon."

"I would prefer that you wait," he told her. "The time is not right. Not yet. Will it bother you to stay for several more moons?"

"Why?"

"Anhinga, think about this very carefully. You can learn about them, discover who their leaders are. Not just the ones now, but the ones who will lead in the future. You can come to know them as none of our people ever will, discover their strengths and their weaknesses. Do you see how such knowledge could be used to our advantage?"

She considered the passion in his eyes. Could she do that? Go back for a long period? She felt a tearing in her souls. "You ask: Would it bother me? A little. It is not pleasant, but not unbearable. The worst part is the loneliness. I miss friends. Family."

"You can come here. Meet me. At this place. Every time the moon is full. Sometimes I will bring your mother, or your brother. Any of your friends." He smiled. "Just as long as they don't learn what we are really about."

"In the end I am still going to kill them."

He nodded. "Yes, but I think we need to reconsider given what you've told me. What good would it do to simply kill Wing Heart and Salamander? No one would notice that they were gone." He steepled his fingers, thinking. "Which clan is dominant?"

"No one is sure. Thunder Tail, of the Eagle Clan, has been voted leader of the Council. Snapping Turtle is gaining in prestige. Alligator Clan is fighting them." She smiled. "When Salamander delayed Saw Back's warriors and allowed you to escape, it infuriated Speaker Deep Hunter."

"He did that?"

"Most cleverly, Uncle. If for no other reason, we owe him for that."

"You are growing fond of him?"

"No, Uncle. I remember your warning. I constantly guard against forming any attachment to these strangers. I need only remember Bowfin, remember them butchering my friends, and my heart hardens."

"Good." He frowned, staring down at the soil. "In that case Salamander's action on my part has earned him a quick death, out of respect."

She took a deep breath. "I do not wish to, Uncle, but I will go back. I will wiggle my way into their confidence and learn what I can about them."

"Trust me, Niece,"—he smiled grimly—"it will make them that much easier to destroy."

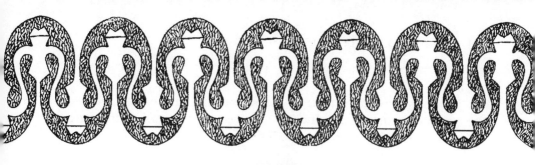

Thirty-six

From the heights atop the canoe landing, Salamander watched Green Crane's slim canoe as it paddled northward across the calm waters of Morning Lake. The wake, in the form of shallow Vs, trailed behind the long dugout; the surface looked pocked where their paddles had swirled the water. He gave one final wave as the two Wash'ta Traders looked back. Each waved in turn.

"It is good," he told himself. "Masked Owl, see to their safe return."

"*If you ever need anything,*" Green Crane had said as he took Salamander's arm in a firm grip, "*send for the stone owl. I will come.*"

"Make her a good husband," he had answered, before giving both Green Crane and Always Fat sturdy hugs.

Now he watched as they nosed their craft into the narrow channel that led north along the floodplain.

"So," Pine Drop's familiar voice said from behind him. "They are off."

Salamander nodded. "Indeed they are. I wish them safety and a speedy journey."

"I sincerely hope they don't get lost again." She stepped up beside him, tangles of her black hair curling around her shoulders as the breeze played with it. Her thoughtful brown eyes followed the Traders' canoe as it disappeared behind the willows.

"I think I explained the channels correctly."

She glanced at him, a question in her eyes. "Was it worth it? You almost stripped your clan for the meat and hides you received in return."

"Oh, yes, it was worth it." In his imagination he watched the canoe winding its way northward. "I have heard the talk. Others are saying that I make as poor a Trader as I do a Speaker."

"Do you, Salamander?"

"Would you believe me if I said there was more to this than the textiles, beads, carvings, medicine plants, and dyes?"

For a moment she hesitated, then said, "I think I would, Salamander." Her attention turned to his face as she said, "I think there is more to you than most people think." Her gaze went to the canoe landing. "Anhinga has still not returned?"

"No. It is but five days."

To his surprise, Pine Drop reached out and linked her arm in his. "Do you think she's coming back, Salamander?"

"Oh, yes. She doesn't want to, but she will. She can't stay away."

Pine Drop shook her head. "I don't like it. I mean the idea that she just goes out into the swamp for her moon. Anything could be happening out there."

He gave her a sidelong inspection. "Are you worried about her?"

"No, husband. I'm worried about you. Deep Hunter and some of the others might not be the only ones who are bitter about the past. I think you can wager that Jaguar Hide isn't acting in your best interests."

How much did he dare tell her? "No, he has his own plans."

"And Anhinga? There is talk. Eats Wood swears she is the same woman your brother captured in the Ground Cherry Camp raid."

"She is."

"What?" Pine Drop cried, using his arm to turn him so that she could stare into his eyes. Did all the women in his life have to be taller than he?

"We are bound, she and I. It is a thing I cannot explain. Something that no one but I can understand."

"You and Masked Owl!"

He started, instantly regretting it as she read his expression.

Her voice dropped. "Is he real, Salamander? Does Masked Owl really come to you?"

He swallowed hard, knowing it made him look nervous, unable to help it. He bargained for time. "What do you think?"

She shook her head, a fragility in her eyes. "I don't know. I just don't know. Tell me, please. Tell me that it's just an act, a thing you do to keep your enemies off-balance."

That brought a wistful smile to his lips. "Pine Drop, why is it easier to believe that I'm making this up than it is to know that I converse with Masked Owl?"

She sank white teeth into her lower lip, searching his eyes, then said, "Spirit Power scares me, husband. I don't know what it wants from you, or from me. I just have a feeling, is all. And you, you're vulnerable, Salamander. You have a great number of enemies. Don't you understand, they are waiting to destroy you."

He reached out, running the backs of his fingers along her smooth cheek. "All but you and Water Petal. What has happened to you, Pine Drop? What do you see in me that the others don't?"

Her expression pinched. "I don't want you hurt. It is important that you understand that. I don't know what I can do to protect you. I have my duties to my clan, and I will attend to them, no matter what."

"I am forewarned, and I thank you for that. I wouldn't expect you to act against the wishes of your clan. Whatever you must do, I will understand. You must not worry about me. I will take care of myself."

She sighed wearily, shaking her head. "That doesn't make it any easier."

"It should." He turned his eyes back to the northern end of the lake, where the Traders had disappeared. "When the time comes, Wife, we must follow our hearts. Remember that I said that. Things are happening. Power is gathering."

She tightened her grip on his arm. "Come home with me, husband. The Snakes know where Night Rain is off to, but maybe she'll stay gone for the night. I would like to have you to myself for a time. Just you and me together for as long as we can keep the world away."

He let her lead him south past the Men's House, hardly aware of the grim stares that Eats Wood and Red Finger gave him as he passed. He held his wife's hand, and wished he were someone else, someone that Power and circumstance hadn't called upon. Later, in Pine Drop's arms, he forgot even that.

The canoe bearing Yellow Spider and Bluefin arrived in late morning. Mud Stalker matched his stride with Deep Hunter's as they descended the trodden soil of the canoe landing. Squinting into the hot sunlight, he could see a small crowd already gathering. People were slapping Yellow Spider on the back, asking questions.

"Did you have trouble?"

"None," Bluefin replied, a grin breaking his normally placid face.

"Did you see any Swamp Panthers?"

"A canoe with two men," Yellow Spider replied. "We called out that we came for sandstone under Jaguar Hide's peace. They said nothing, just nodded, but they watched us the entire time. Seeing what we did, and that we did nothing more than collect sandstone."

One of the Eagle Clan men spoke. "I would be obliged for a piece of that. In fact, that piece right there on top. I'm sanding beads for a necklace."

"We are pleased to present it to you," Yellow Spider remarked with a smile as he handed over the thick piece of sandstone.

"What is this?" Clay Fat asked as he strode up to stand beside Mud Stalker and Deep Hunter.

"The first canoe load of Swamp Panther sandstone," Deep Hunter answered.

"Then it is true?" Clay Fat asked, one eyebrow raised.

"So it would seem." Mud Stalker cradled his ruined arm.

"What does it mean?" Clay Fat asked.

"Nothing!" Deep Hunter's lip curled. "An occasional canoeful of sandstone isn't going to bring Owl Clan back to prominence."

"But we must keep an eye on them," Mud Stalker mused.

"Why?" Clay Fat asked. "Wing Heart is crazy. That boy sure isn't any Speaker."

"Indeed he is not," Deep Hunter agreed. He glanced up, meeting Mud Stalker's eyes and nodding. "We must watch this Trade with the Swamp Panthers. If it becomes too popular, we must take steps to stop it."

Mud Stalker fingered the scars on his right elbow. "You and I may not agree about many things, Speaker, but we do about this."

Clay Fat looked uneasy. "It is Owl Clan's business."

"Not if we make it ours, old friend." Mud Stalker replied. "I still haven't forgotten your obligation to my clan, Clay Fat. We prepared quite a feast. Copperhead turned down several *very profitable* offers in order to save himself for Spring Cypress." He paused, letting Clay Fat squirm.

"All it would take would be a raid. A party of warriors sent into the Swamp Panthers' lands. This Trade would end as quickly as it began."

Clay Fat swallowed hard. "You would have to have Council approval. This is Owl Clan's business. You cannot do this alone."

Mud Stalker considered the situation. Deep Hunter would act immediately given the slightest encouragement. But would that necessarily be good for Snapping Turtle Clan's position among the people?

"I must agree, reluctantly, with Clay Fat." Mud Stalker watched Deep Hunter's expression harden and smiled to himself. "However," he soothed, "if this sandstone becomes too irksome, Deep Hunter, I might be prevailed upon to support you."

"Indeed?" Deep Hunter muttered, sensing a trap.

"All things in time, my old friend." With that Mud Stalker turned on his heel and strode off.

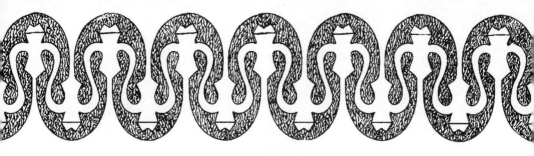

Thirty-seven

The fire popped and cracked, curls of thin white smoke rising from the dry wood. Pine Drop had built the rick in a hollow square, placing the cooking clays in the middle, where they would absorb the heat. The arrangement had to be made correctly so that the specially formed cooking clays heated to a white-hot glow in the center of the fire.

Normally water lotus was gathered for the great solstice feast, but the harvest had been so good this turning of the seasons that she had extra. It wouldn't keep in the midsummer heat, so she had mashed the remaining roots in the mortar to form a sweet paste. One by one she had formed the cone-shaped cooking clays, indenting the convex side to resemble the lotus's seedpods.

During the process, she sang the Harvest Song that recounted the origins of the lotus. In the beginning Mother Sun and Father Moon had both shared the Sky with equal duration and brightness. There was no night, no summer or winter, for when one dropped behind the horizon, the other waited until the first reemerged.

And then one day Father Moon glanced down and saw a beautiful woman bathing in a pond. She was the daughter of a great Clan Elder. His light shone in her long black hair and on her soft bronzed skin. He had never seen such a beauty before, and resolved to have her.

That night, when Mother Sun slipped behind the western edge of the world, Father Moon eased down from the Sky. He took the form of a young man and found the pretty young woman. She had never seen such a handsome man before, and lay with him.

Meanwhile, the night Sky had gone dark. The animals that normally were awake, bats, raccoons, flying squirrels, and crickets were all running around, bumping into things, saying, "Where is Father Moon? What is happening?"

But Father Moon was busy locking hips with the pretty young woman. He was so involved that he forgot the time. Thus it was that Mother Sun peeked over the eastern horizon to find the world in darkness, and the animals of the night running around in panic.

"Where is Father Moon?" she asked, concerned that some terrible thing might have happened to her mate.

"He is lying with a beautiful woman," opossum said. "He has left us in darkness so that he can lock hips with her."

Mother Sun sent her rays over the earth, and sure enough, there was Father Moon, lying with the pretty young woman. Rage burned in Mother Sun's heart, and in anger she fled to the south. She kept going and going, going so far that the world was plunged into darkness.

Horrified, Father Moon rose into the Sky, calling for Mother Sun to come back to him. But she refused, heading ever southward.

Father Moon chased after her, following her south across the Sky. As his light waned, Winter came roaring down from the north, cloaking the land in snow and ice. Plants died, turned different colors, and lost their leaves. Animals burrowed into the ground, desperate to save themselves from the freezing weather and the endless darkness. Birds, desperate for Mother Sun, flew south, many disappearing out in the gulf; where they ended up, no one knows.

In the end, it was Bird Man who, seeing his world dying, flew south after the birds. There he found Mother Sun sulking at the edge of the sea, where it joined the Sky. He told her of the cold, of the dying trees, and how the animals had burrowed into the earth. He told how Father Moon was so lonely that he had hidden his face in sorrow.

"If you do not come back, the world is going to die!"

Mother Sun listened, and realized that no matter how mad she was at Father Moon, she couldn't let the rest of the world die. So it was she came back to the Sky, and the plants came alive, and people and animals were warm again. Seeing how grateful the creatures were, she shot beams of light onto the water, and a beautiful flower grew there. To this day the yellow lotus grows, its flower reflecting the face of Mother Sun. It is her promise to the world that she will always return to light the Sky.

Mother Sun never forgave Father Moon. That is why she forever moves across the Sky, always avoiding him. Father Moon still hides his face in shame and never glows as brightly as he did before the night he betrayed his mate.

Among the animals, bear, raccoon, the bats, the bees, and so many other creatures still hibernate when Mother Sun goes south with each cycle. In return, Mother Sun marks her return to the high summer Sky with the blooming of the yellow lotus. When the people harvest it for the solstice ceremony, its roots are sweet, and its flower resembles the face of Mother Sun so that people never forget her gift of life to them.

As she Sang the song, Pine Drop took damp lotus leaves from a stone bowl and wrapped balls of dough in the leaves. These she laid to one side on palmetto matting.

Her heating fire had burned down to coals, the central cluster of lotus-shaped cooking clays having taken on a white glow. She used a stick to scrape half of them onto a thin wooden platter and gingerly lowered into the earth oven. As she poured them, she had to jerk her hand back from the searing heat.

"Hey, Cousin!"

She glanced up, seeing Eats Wood as he strode down the ridge. Sunlight shone on his muscular chest. His lightly greased skin reflected the light; his tattoos stood out as dark blue designs on his brown skin. Several necklaces of stone and bone beads hung around his neck, and he wore a green-dyed breechcloth. A mocking smile curled his round face, and his hair had been parted down the middle and cut short to bob just above his shoulders.

"Greetings, Cousin." She shot him a polite smile and bent down to lay the first of her wrapped lotus-root breads onto the cooking clays.

To her irritation, Eats Wood knelt beside her, asking, "Can I help?"

"No. Just a moment." She artfully laid the rest of the wraps onto the cooking clays. She couldn't help but wonder what he wanted as she scraped the last of the cooking clays from the fire and shook them from the smoldering plate into the earth oven. She had never liked Eats Wood. He let his penis dominate any good sense he might have had. The parallels between Father Moon and Cousin Eats Wood couldn't have been more clear. When she had placed the bark lid on the earth oven to seal in the steaming heat, she looked up.

"I just came to see how you were doing," Eats Wood began. He gestured around at the ramada, then at her house. "Do you need anything? Can I bring you anything? Firewood? Some palmetto for that place where the wind shredded your ramada roof?"

She picked little bits of dough from her slim brown fingers. "I appreciate your offer, but I suspect that you didn't come here because you were worried about my firewood supply."

He settled back on his butt, rubbed his sun-browned shin, and looked around at the near houses. His expression had a slightly pained look as if he were trying to find the right words.

"Is it about your mother?" she asked. Eats Wood still lived at home. He had been notoriously hard to marry off. Despite the size of Sun Town, Eats Wood's reputation preceded him. Few in the other clans considered him a likely candidate for marriage—even though Snapping Turtle Clan's influence had grown like a north wind at winter solstice.

"She is fine, but thank you for asking." He pressed his lips together, studying her with narrowed brown eyes. "It is said that you will very likely become our Clan Elder someday."

"That day—if it comes, Eats Wood—is a long way off."

"It is said that you had a chance to divorce Speaker Salamander."

"Any woman has a chance to divorce, Cousin. That's a little fact that I hope you keep in your head when and if you do marry." She arched a challenging eyebrow.

He grinned sheepishly. "Yes, I know." Then he sobered. "Why do you stay with him?"

"I have my reasons, Cousin. Among them, because of who he is."

"He is a Speaker in name only. You could have—"

"I wasn't referring to his title."

"Most people think he is a fool, Cousin."

She considered him frankly and lowered her voice. "They are wrong, Eats Wood. I may be speaking to emptiness, but I want you to listen to me. Do not underestimate Salamander. I tell you that as a kinsman."

His round brown eyes didn't register any comprehension. "He's got that Swamp Panther woman for a wife. You could have anyone else you wanted."

"He has his reasons for marrying her."

"She was here before. She is the one his brother caught down at Ground Cherry Camp."

"So?"

"Cousin, look what we did to her and her friends!" He leaned close. "You are part of his household, don't you hear things about her? About what she's after here?"

"You mean, does my husband trust her?"

"Yes."

"Not completely."

"She goes away every moon."

"Of course she does. Think it through, Eats Wood. Would you want her here during her moon? Hmm? Bleeding where any man, yourself included, might step in it? No, I suspect you would have her gone, far away, where her woman's blood won't make you ill."

"What's wrong with the Women's House? She can go there for her moon with all the rest."

"Put yourself in her place. Would you want to be shut up in the men's Society House in the middle of the Panther's Bones? Would you want to be surrounded by their suspicious warriors for days? Would you want to hear them snicker at your expense?"

He stared suspiciously at her. "I'll bet she meets with her Swamp Panther kin, what will you bet?"

"She has no friends here. If I were in her position, I would want to see kin, too."

He seemed perplexed. "You don't seem at all worried."

"I will worry when I have reason to." She gave him a sidelong look. "But why are you so interested in her?"

He spread his hands, trying to look casual.

"Uh-huh," she answered. "One of these days, Cousin, you are going to be like Father Moon. Some woman will possess your thoughts and lead you into a mess you can't find your way out of."

"She's dangerous," he muttered uncomfortably. "You just watch, Cousin. She's going to get you into trouble before she's done here."

Wind howled in the thatch, poking cold fingers through the gap where the roof overhung the walls. It made a soft whistle as it blew around the house. Gusts shook the structure, cracking the wattle and daub. This wasn't a night to be out.

Salamander lay awake under the snug buffalo robe and stared up at the darkness. Anhinga cuddled next to him, her warm rump pressed against the angle of his hip and thigh. Cold air played patterns across his face, tickling loose strands of Anhinga's hair against his cheeks.

Turning his head, he could hear the soft rattle as leaves blew past. From the flapping sounds, the palmetto matting that roofed his mother's ramada was shredding and would have to be replaced.

His house shivered under a particularly hard blast. In his bones he could feel the storm's strength as it blew down from the north.

He blinked, wishing he could sleep with Anhinga's soundness. Instead, images flashed through his mind. Bits of the Dream that had awakened him replayed over and over. He had been flying, sailing across the sky on Owl wings. A black shadow had blotted the sun, and talons had ripped painfully through his back. In that instant he was falling, the ground spiraling as though rising to meet him.

Breath had frozen in his lungs, his throat locked. His stomach had lurched, weightless, falling, plummeting like a carved piece of hematite. The air rushing past had become the roar of the winter wind outside his house before he plunged headfirst into Sun Town's earthen plaza. At the last instant he had jerked awake.

"What?" Anhinga had murmured, shifting on their narrow bed.

"Nothing. A Dream. Sleep." He had patted her shoulder as she slipped her arm from across his chest and rolled onto her side facing the wall.

But he had lain there, awake, his heart pounding, the terrible image of falling still tingling in his blood, muscles, and bone. The sight of that green ground had been so real! The spreading arches of the clan grounds, the buildings casting shadows, couldn't have been imagined. Even the pathways, beaten into the grass by countless bare feet, could be seen spreading out like veins.

With great care, he slipped out from under the heavy robe. Chill washed his sweat-clammy skin as he tied his breechcloth on and found a feather cloak to wrap around him. Moving the palmetto-mat door to one side, he stepped out into the gale.

Wind whipped his hair, half blinding him. Bits of sand and debris shot pinpricks into his skin. Turning, he pulled the cloak tight and walked straight into the teeth of the storm until he reached the third ridge. Counting houses, he hunched his way to the Serpent's.

He huddled against the south wall, in the lee of the blast, and called, "Elder? It is Salamander. Are you awake?"

"I am now," the reedy voice called. "Come."

Salamander ducked into the wind, wrestled the wicker door aside, and replaced it behind him as he stepped into the cold darkness of the Serpent's house. Here, at least, the gale was moderated to a gentler movement of air.

Wood clattered as the old man threw it atop the gleaming red-eyed coals in the central fire pit. Helped by the cool breeze, flames immediately leaped up. Their flickering yellow light showed the Serpent, sitting naked on his bed, his flesh hanging in wrinkled folds, his flat face puffy with sleep. Gray hair stuck out like winter grass in all directions.

"What is it? Salamander? What brings you here? You are not ill are you?"

"No, Serpent. It was a Dream," he explained as the old man seated himself and pulled his elkhide blanket around his shoulders. The fire shot yellow light, and Salamander glanced about the interior. The clay walls had been engraved with designs of interlocking owls, sitting foxes, panthers, and snakes. Above the old man's bed a great bird had been carved into the daub, its wings and feet outspread, the beaked head turned sideways.

Bags of herbs hung from every rafter, their sides sooty from countless fires. A line of wooden and leather masks were propped along one bench, ritual faces that the Serpent adopted for healings and ceremonials. A pouch that Salamander knew contained stone sucking tubes, feather wands, and diamondback rattles rested by the old man's swollen feet.

Other ceramic jars and small soapstone bowls held bits of mushrooms, dried nightshade, jimsonweed, gumweed, snakemaster root, dried hemp leaves, and other medicine plants. One big bowl was filled with bear fat as a base to mix his potions.

The old man listened to Salamander's recounting of the Dream, nodding. As he spoke, Salamander realized that the old Serpent's flesh seemed to be even thinner on his bones than it had been.

"Many Colored Crow is gaining in Power," the Serpent said after Salamander finished. He ran a hand over his flat face, the action rearranging his wrinkles.

"What does it mean? Falling like that?" Salamander extended his hands to the fire and shivered at the warmth.

"It is a sign." The Serpent pulled his elkhide close as another gust of wind shivered his house. "You are supposed to be frightened. Many Colored Crow is telling you that if you give up, go away, you will not have to be destroyed."

Salamander studied his hands, black silhouettes against the flame. "I have started to relax, Elder. As fall came to the land and the leaves changed, my world began to take form."

"And Anhinga?"

"She carries my child, but leaves with every full moon to pretend to pass her woman's bleeding in seclusion. She uses that time to plot with Jaguar Hide."

"That is very dangerous."

He bowed his head. "I know."

"Why do you not throw her out? You know she bears you no goodwill."

"Masked Owl whispers that I will need her."

"To achieve your death?"

Salamander shrugged. "I am not certain, but maybe. If I must die, Elder, to serve Masked Owl, and if Anhinga is to be the manner of it, then I accept that."

"I, too, am dying."

Salamander looked up, startled. "What?"

The old man pointed to his gaunt stomach. "I have a pain inside that only gets worse with the passing of the moon. Something evil is growing in my gut. When I squat to defecate, what comes out is half blood. It gets worse with the passing of days."

A sinking sensation left Salamander shaken. "No, not you, my old friend. I need you! Without you, I am alone. You must take something! Do something. Surely some licorice root, or . . ."

The old man was shaking his head. "I'm afraid the something to which you refer has already been done. It is some spirit, some evil that is eating me. When I press, I can feel it. A hardness so painful it brings tears to my eyes. Probably something I picked up from someone I cleansed. Maybe I wasn't careful enough with their vomit."

"How long has this bothered you?"

"A moon. Maybe more."

For what seemed an eternity, they sat in silence.

The Serpent asked, "What of your other wives?"

"Pine Drop missed her moon. She seems satisfied."

"Indeed. I noticed that you haven't come for more dogbane. Nor have I heard that she has been carrying on like a camp bitch anymore."

"It was Mud Stalker and Sweet Root who put her up to it."

"Umm. And Night Rain?"

"I would feed her plenty of dogbane if I could. The problem is that I can't just put a pinch into the communal food bowl without harming Pine Drop as well."

"There is talk. Deep Hunter has recalled Saw Back from Yellow Mud Camp. It is said that he did it to favor your youngest wife. Have you heard?"

"That Night Rain is coupling with him? Yes." Salamander rubbed his hands together. "Pine Drop disapproves, but says nothing. That tells me that Night Rain has Mud Stalker's approval to lock hips with Deep Hunter and his kin." His lips tightened. "My young Night Rain has been learning new tricks. When she does share her bed with me, she isn't the same limp bundle of cloth I first married."

"Deep Hunter and Mud Stalker make a strong alliance." The Serpent bowed his head. "Moccasin Leaf seems to relish her new position as Clan Elder. I am sorry I could not bring your mother's souls back. I fear they are too tied to the souls of the Dead."

"Sometimes, Elder, we cannot win every battle. I do not understand why Power has left her demented. Perhaps it is part of the balance, part of the price I must pay." Salamander sat back, some of the warmth returning to his body. "My enemies will not act yet. They are waiting, slowly turning their attention to each other."

"Why do you not act against them?"

"Masked Owl once told me that my salvation lay in the things I knew, in being who I was. I watch, Elder. I study. It is for a reason that you named me Salamander."

"But if the fox or eagle should catch you . . ."

"The ways of Power are not without risk, Elder." Salamander smiled. "Since we last talked, I have watched the leaves turn and fall. The clans have returned from most of the distant camps, their bags full of acorns, walnuts, beechnuts, hazelnuts, goosefoot seeds, squash, knotweed seeds, and chinquapins. Canoe loads of fish have been dried and smoked, and the hunters have taken ducks, geese, pigeons, herons, and cranes. Deer are plentiful, and Trade has been good from the prairies, so buffalo and elk meat are plentiful. For the moment, bellies are full, and the clans are eyeing each other, trying to determine who has incurred the greatest obligation."

"The winter solstice ceremonies are barely a moon away." The Serpent rubbed his callused hands, a dullness to his eyes. "Have you given any more thought to following me?"

"Yes. My answer is the same. Bobcat must follow you—and for many reasons. I do not know the Songs, Elder. I barely know enough of the plants and rituals. I couldn't follow you if I wanted to. I must serve Power in another way."

"As your Spirit Helper deems."

Salamander nodded, smiling. "You once asked me a question, Elder. You asked why the Great Mystery ripped the Earth from the Sky."

"Ah, yes. I remember. Have you found the answer?"

"I think so. It was because before the Creation, everything was One. Everything was the same."

"Ah!" The old man's face lit with joy, the wrinkles on his face stretching. "What was wrong with that?"

"Being One is being nothing, Elder. The world wasn't really Created until Sky and Earth were separated."

"Why is that, Salamander?"

"If you are One, you cannot see. Cannot hear. The only sensation is of yourself. There is no 'Other.' The world had to be divided in order to see itself, in order to become itself. In the One, there is no beginning or end, no me or you. Only when we are separate can we inspect each other and learn the complexity and beauty of the universe. That was the lesson you were trying to teach me that night atop the Bird's Head. That is why Sun Town is so important. It is here that all things come back together. North and South. East and West. Sky and Earth."

Smiling gently, the old man nodded.

The fire popped and crackled, sending sparks toward the roof. Then the old man reached into a rabbit-hide sack and withdrew a small figurine. "Do you know what this is?" He handed it to Salamander.

The piece was smaller than his knotted fist, formed into the shape of a corpulent woman's seated torso, breasts and buttocks pronounced, arms and legs but nubbins. The head depicted the center-parted hair of a married woman, her eyes and happy mouth mere slits. The nose had been pinched out of the face, almost beaklike.

"No." Salamander turned it in the light. "I've never seen a charm like this before."

The Serpent reached into his bag, retrieving yet another one, similar to the first, and handing it over. "Men usually don't see these. Women ask for them. Take them. Bury one under Anhinga's bed when she is not present. Bury the other under Pine Drop's."

"What do they do?" Salamander studied the two figurines in his hands.

"Any evil or illness that comes to sneak up your wife's sheath to infect the infant will be fooled and will invade the clay charm instead." He pointed his finger. "Now listen. This part is important. When your children are born, the charms must be dug up. This must be done immediately. When the afterbirth is passed, it must be rubbed over the charm to cleanse it. Then, and only then, you must bring the charm back here, to this house, and snap the head off."

"Why?"

"The afterbirth feeds the evil, tricks it into thinking it is living in the baby. When you snap off the neck, you trap it inside the charm. It must be buried here because it came from here," the old man said. "From this earth, here, outside of this house. The Power must be returned to the place from which it came. Bury the pieces of the charm, Salamander, put them back where they came from. If you do not, the Earth Mother will become angry. The evil will fly back, angry at being deceived, and kill your child. Do you understand?"

"Yes, Elder."

The Serpent closed his eyes, and breath caught in his frail chest. His expression twisted, neck bending as he tenderly placed his hands against his left side.

"Elder?"

A moment later, he blinked, and tears appeared at the corners of his eyes. "I need to lie down now, Salamander. Forgive me. I cannot think when it hurts like this."

"Can I do anything for you?"

The old man nodded. "There, in the bowl with the fox on the side. That paste, it is made with ground jimsonweed seeds. Take that stick, there. That's it. Dab just a little on the end. Thank you."

The old man leaned back, taking the stick in trembling hands as he touched it to the tip of his tongue. "Things will be better now. Yes, better."

Salamander placed the pale elkhide robe over the old man's bony body, ensuring it was tucked tightly. "Sleep, Elder. I'm sorry I bothered you."

"No. It's fine." He smiled wearily. "You will be the greatest of them, Salamander. If they don't kill you first. Many Colored Crow is a Powerful enemy, but he will not take you himself."

"Like he took my brother?"

The old man's eyes flashed open, brown, penetrating, as if the pain had vanished in an instant. "What makes you think that? Your brother wasn't killed by Many Colored Crow."

"Then who? Who else could control the lightning?"

"Any of the Sky Beings," the Serpent told him, voice low, as if he were sorry he'd said anything. "Now, go away. Let me sleep. Nothing else eases the pain."

The Serpent

A Dreamer's first ascent into the Spirit World on the wings of a Spirit Helper is like a return to the womb, to a safe place filled with an awareness of the beginnings of who we are. It is a miracle of silence and beauty. A miracle that is swiftly gobbled up when we plant our feet on dirt again.

That is the heart of the Dreamer's struggle—not learning to soar, but learning to walk after you've soared.

Walking on solid ground, as though you've never sailed through blinding sunlight, is the most difficult thing any Dreamer ever does.

It is the fork in the trail.

The decision.

It may be the instant of rebirth, the moment when a man or woman is born into the Spirit World and sprouts his own glistening wings.

Or it may be the instant of accepting less, and the beginning of life-long regret. Dreamers call this the "little death."

I cannot hope to convey to you how terrible it is. The "little death" is like a serpent forever coiling and uncoiling inside you, forever striking, biting, and filling you with poison.

I had heard of the "little death." Somewhere along the way, every Dreamer does, but no one told me that it was everlasting. Perhaps they didn't have the courage.

I'm not sure I do either.

How can I tell this haunted boy that from the moment I decided my earthly duties to the People were more important than wings, I've never stopped dying?

Should I tell him? Would he even listen?

I wouldn't have. The People were everything to me.

But he is stronger than I was.

He sees more clearly.

I pray with all my soul that he is brave enough to "abandon" his duties and fly away. . . .

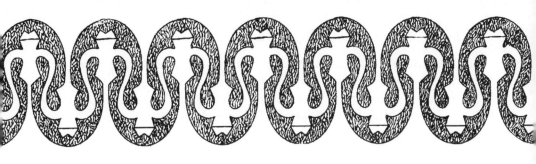

Thirty-eight

A thick belt of clouds gave the winter day a dull cast. From the north blew a bitter wind that sucked a man's heat from his bones and sent it whimpering away toward the gulf. Mud Stalker led the way as Speaker Thunder Tail and the other hunters followed a winding trail. The way led through the depths of the forest a half day's journey north of Sun Town. The four younger men carried packs, atlatls, and darts. Their bodies were cloaked in deerskin, elkhide, and buffalo hide, giving them a thick and burly appearance as they trailed along behind the elders.

Mud Stalker squinted into the gray light. In the vacuum left by Wing Heart's insanity, Snapping Turtle Clan had grown in influence among the clans and in the Council. To his irritation leadership of the Council had gone to Thunder Tail, but that, too, would change as the seasons passed.

Now it was time to solidify his clan's position. Despite the overture of reaching out with Night Rain, Deep Hunter was playing his own games, seeking to limit Mud Stalker's growing influence. That was to be expected. In time, he would deal with Deep Hunter.

Thunder Tail was another problem. As leader of the Council, he was still uncommitted when it came to a firm alliance with Snapping Turtle Clan. Mud Stalker would need the Eagle Clan Speaker's goodwill before he moved on Salamander and the remnant of Owl Clan. Today he would begin the process; he would play on Thunder Tail's one weakness: a bear hunt.

Mud Stalker glanced up at the trees, naked and black in their winter bones. Great vines wove up the trunks, stretching from one forest giant to another. Some were as thick as a man's leg.

"There," Mud Stalker pointed as he sighted the dead tree. The Eagle Clan hunters, Bitten Legs and Spread Thorn, pulled up grinning. The trunk was huge. Four men would have to stretch, fingertip to fingertip, to reach around the base. Rot had eaten the heart out of the dead forest giant. Then some past gale had cracked it, sheared off the top two-thirds, and sent it crashing down through the forest. Punky wood, cloaked in leaves, vines, and rising saplings marked the fallen remains.

The remaining trunk, barkless and gray from weather, stood five times the height of a tall man. At the top, jagged wood thrust up around the hollow center like stone knives.

Mud Stalker nodded, using his good arm to motion Eats Wood and Water Stinger forward. His two young kinsmen trotted ahead, each slinging a pack from his shoulder as he approached the trunk.

"He's there?" Thunder Tail asked as he fingered his finely carved atlatl. "You're sure?"

"He's there. You can see the sign." Mud Stalker stepped close, pointing to the weathered wood. Deep scars had been driven into the grain, bits and splinters crushed as if under a weight. "Those are not woodpecker holes."

"From the size and spread, I'd say he's a pretty good-size boar." Thunder Tail placed his hand over the pattern of scars. A slow smile was spreading across his broad face. "A sow wouldn't have this big a paw."

Mud Stalker bent his head back, staring up at the jagged top. "I think it's a boar, too. Too bad it's not a sow. She'd have a cub by now. I wouldn't mind taking a cub. The meat is delectable."

"A boar will do just fine."

Of all of life's treats, Thunder Tail loved bear hunting the most. He had a fascination with the animals. Their meat, hides, organs, and fat were prized throughout Sun Town. Unlike most hunters who took bears only when the opportunity arose, Thunder Tail spent full hands of time in the study of bears. He had been known to lose himself for days stalking a bruin. Not one was brought back to Sun Town but that he didn't go to see it, to measure the paws against his hand, to inspect the teeth and feel its muscles. His house was stuffed with skulls, bear bones, hides, claws, and other trophies he had taken over the turnings of the seasons.

When Water Stinger had come with news that he'd found a winter "bear tree," Mud Stalker had been jubilant. It gave him the perfect lure to draw the Speaker out of Sun Town. Mud Stalker had Thunder Tail alone for the entire day—and in a very good mood, as his smile indicated.

"By the Snakes! He's a big one if these claw marks are any indication." Thunder Tail slapped a callused hand against the wood and grinned, his eyes shining as he shared a happy conspiratorial glance with Mud Stalker.

"I hope you find him worth your while," Mud Stalker said with a casual shrug. He and Sweet Root had begun planning the moment they had learned of the bear tree. Though they had an uneasy alliance for the moment, Deep Hunter's Alligator Clan would eventually challenge Mud Stalker's growing influence. Thunder Tail's Eagle Clan was now the unpredictable element—the clan could vote either way in Council.

"*I have worked all of my life to achieve this!*" Mud Stalker had declared to Sweet Root, his good hand clenched into a hard fist. "*I am going to leave nothing to chance. Those I cannot cow, like Thunder Tail and Clay Fat, I will seduce!*"

Sweet Root had nodded, smiling her encouragement. Night Rain, sitting to one side, had given him a curious look as she plucked feathers from a duck.

"*Green Beetle remains unmarried,*" Sweet Root had reminded. "*Eats Wood needs a wife. No one else wants him. Given his attitude toward women, he doesn't make himself particularly attractive.*"

Night Rain had said, "*I wouldn't want him for a husband, and neither would anyone else I know. If you will recall, we were warned as girls never to be alone with him. Remember? You didn't even trust him alone near his own kin.*"

Sweet Root had shaken her head. "*He talks too much about that Swamp Panther woman. He's obsessed with her.*"

"*We need to bring Thunder Tail under our influence,*" Mud Stalker had insisted. "*I will have a talk with Eats Wood before we take Thunder Tail to the bear tree. If we can sway the Speaker to our perspective, Deep Hunter will have nowhere to go.*"

"*Eats Wood isn't the sort of man to pin many hopes on,*" Sweet Root reminded.

That might be true, but the young man was the closest unmarried male relative he had. Next was Water Stinger, a distant cousin whose family spent most of the turning of the seasons two days' journey to the east over at Yellow Mud Camp. So, here he was, with two eligible young hunters for Thunder Tail to inspect. At Mud Stalker's insistence, Eats Wood had been on his best behavior and doing a creditable job of entertaining Thunder Tail. To his relief,

Eats Wood hadn't made a single rude comment about either Salamander or his barbarian wife.

From their packs, Eats Wood and Water Stinger had taken a fire drill, tinder, and kindling. On the other side of the tree, Bitten Legs and Spread Thorn had likewise laid their atlatls and darts to one side, producing their own fire-making kits. While Eats Wood and Spread Thorn twirled the spindle in a hardwood block, Water Stinger and Bitten Legs dragged up old branches.

In moments, puffy gray smoke rose and was blown to flame in the tinder. Mud Stalker stepped back, cradling his maimed arm as the hunters added wood, spreading the fire around the tree bottom. He enjoyed the expression on Thunder Tail's face, reading the Speaker's growing excitement.

Winter bear hunting was always exciting. Bears tended to hibernate in standing dead trees like this one. The hollow centers, soft with rotten wood, made warm nests, protected from the worst of the weather. Setting fire to the bottom of the tree awakened the bear, causing the groggy animal to emerge at the top. There, clinging to the wood as smoke billowed past, he was an easy target.

Yellow tongues of flame licked up around the wood, popping and crackling.

"We need more wood," Mud Stalker called. "Eats Wood, go drag in some of those big branches." He pointed to the wreckage left by the fallen treetop. "We want this fire a lot hotter."

"He's a good young man." Thunder Tail watched Eats Wood as he trotted off with Bitten Legs for more fuel.

"It is high time he was married. His mother, my cousin, is loath to turn him loose. He keeps her in birds, fish, and meat. When he marries, she loses that surplus. The excess in her household keeps the rest of the lineage obligated." He said it offhandedly, watching Thunder Tail's expression from the corner of his eye.

"Hmm, a young man like that is quite an asset." Thunder Tail answered, his eyes on the top of the bear tree. Smoke was curling upward along the wood.

"You have a young woman, don't you? The one who finds pearls."

"Green Beetle." Thunder Tail squinted up at the treetop as he fingered his atlatl and darts. One by one he fitted them to the spur in the back of the atlatl, testing their balance in anticipation of a cast. "The bear won't know what's happening for some time yet. The heat is still too far away, and the smoke going up the outside isn't being drawn in with this wind blowing."

"Green Beetle, that's right," Mud Stalker mused. "She's an attractive thing. I'd have thought you'd have married her by now."

"I have."

The simple pronouncement stopped Mud Stalker short. "You have?"

"Yes. It's odd that you should mention her. Deep Hunter and Stone Talon came to see my mother and me last night. To our surprise they made us a very good offer. Needs Two will marry Green Beetle."

"He will?" Mud Stalker fought to keep his voice conversational. "You got good terms?"

"Green Beetle's lineage is allowed access to those smilax-root grounds over by the sassafras grove. You know the ones I mean?"

"I do." Mud Stalker felt his heart sink. Deep Hunter guarded those grounds jealously.

"I am very fond of Green Beetle," Thunder Tail continued, apparently oblivious. He only had eyes for the treetop. "I almost married her to White Bird, you know. Good thing that I didn't. Look what happened there."

Mud Stalker studied the man through slitted eyes. "You were an old lover of Wing Heart's, weren't you?"

"Yes. It's a shame. She used be as sharp as a chert blade." Thunder Tail shot him a measuring glance, his dark eyes veiling the thoughts in his mind. "Curious, isn't it, old friend, that even the strongest of us can lose our souls?"

"Yes. Curious indeed." Mud Stalker stepped back, fingers running along the scars on his arm. How on earth had Deep Hunter managed to pull the catch out of his nets like this?

Enjoy your bear hunt, Speaker.

Anhinga wedged a thick branch between two closely spaced trees and threw her weight against it. She flinched at the crack as the dry wood gave. It took a well-placed kick to knock the piece loose. The process of bending over to retrieve it proved laborious. She no longer even attempted to hide the swelling of her belly. She puffed against the cold and placed the short lengths of firewood in her irregular stack. Satisfied, she bound them with a braided leather thong.

The desperate need to escape had been brewing like black drink within her. Using their need of firewood as an excuse, she had come here, deep in the forest west of Sun Town. She needed time to think. Her souls had gone to war with each other.

Salamander lay at the bottom of it. He knew she was pregnant—so obvious had it become—but indulged her in her need to get away. He hadn't said a word about her absences each moon.

She glanced up at the sky, trying to decide what sort of man he really was. Clouds rolled out of the northwest, keeping the chill in the air. During the night, fog had settled over the land. A light mist had fallen, adding to the chill. By morning everything had been sheathed in ice.

She resettled her fox-hide cloak against the cold. A gift from Pine Drop, it was nicely done. Tanned to soft perfection and sewn with care, the rich red fur gleamed in the light. She began knotting a leather strap to create a yoke to be used for a tumpline.

Bending down, she positioned the cord on her forehead and wrapped several lengths of furry rabbit hide around it for a cushion. She grabbed up her ax, positioned the load, and straightened. The wrap of rabbit hide pressed into her forehead as she balanced the load on her hips and leaned forward. Straightening her legs, she stood.

Looking down she could barely see over her belly.

Three moons had passed since that day his gaze had fixed on her swollen belly. She had said, "I'm pregnant."

"You have been for many moons." He had just looked at her with those fathomless brown eyes, and said, "It's all right, Anhinga. Go to them. The four or five days you spend away harms nothing. But perhaps, as the child comes to term, you might not travel so far? I think your uncle would understand."

The words had struck fear into her in a way that no threat, no angry denunciation could have. Deep in her heart she had the distinct feeling that Salamander knew her every plan. Why, then, hadn't he taken some action against her?

Logic might have led her to believe that the sandstone was worth it to him, but her worried souls knew better. No, he was playing some complex and terrible game, betting on her. How? To do what? Thinking that she wouldn't go through with her plan to kill the father of her child?

Then you are wrong, husband. When Uncle tells me the time is right, I shall strike the Sun People in a way that will shiver their hearts for ages!

She need only remember that terrible day she had watched her friends butchered, their bodies cut to pieces and fed to the dogs. That nightmare lived and ached in her souls.

Knowing that he knew had changed something in their relationship. Salamander continued to treat her with respect and kindness. He had stopped coupling with her, fearful of damaging the child, and that, oddly, concerned her. Pine Drop was several moons behind her and just beginning to show. A worry had begun to form down in Anhinga's souls. Was he going to spend all of his nights at his first wife's house now that he could only couple with Night Rain? Not that she was any kind of a faultless wife.

Why do you care what they say about her? You are going to kill them in the end anyway!

It took all of her concentration to remember her uncle's warning. *"You cannot see them as people, Anhinga. That is the single greatest threat to your success."*

Some subtle reflex caused her to look up. There, perched on a high branch, a huge barred owl stared down at her. She almost missed a step. The bird's penetrating stare ate clear through her, probing like shafts of dark light. The round head bobbed slightly, accenting the facial disks. He might have been peering at her through a mask.

Unease crept up her spine. She hadn't known they could grow so big. Despite the bird's size, it triggered a memory. With its white-spotted red feathers puffed against the cold, she couldn't help but think of Salamander's carvings, of the potbellied owls he made.

"I have nothing to do with you," she called over her shoulder as she hurried away. A prickling of danger rode lightly on her nerves. She could almost feel Power crackling along the ice-shrouded branches. Hear it throbbing in the winter depths of the forest. Only after passing beyond the bird's sight did she slow down again.

Sighing with relief, she picked her way with care, watching her deerhide moccasins crush the frosted grass underfoot. Overhead, bare black branches webbed the sky. The ground, covered with ice-coated leaves, required all of her concentration. Her moccasins, while warm, made each step a tricky proposition. The smooth soles had no grip on ice-slick leaves.

She picked her way past gray vines that hung from the trees, seeking the trail she knew led the way back, past the hunter's blind. Rounding the thick bole of a beech tree, she stopped short. A naked man stood in the trail, steam rising from a fresh puddle of urine.

As their eyes met, she recognized him: Saw Back. The youth who had been sent to kill her uncle. The one Salamander had tricked on the Turtle's Back. He was holding his dripping penis, naked but for a necklace made of two sections of a human jawbone. Naked? A curious state considering the breath whitening before the young man's mouth. They stared at each other in disbelief.

"Saw Back? Are you coming back?" a familiar female voice asked from the low hunter's blind at the side of the trail.

"It's you!" Saw Back cried, finding his voice. "What are you doing here, you barbarian bitch? Come to spy on me?"

"Anhinga?" A face appeared in the blind's shadowed doorway, "Here?"

"Night Rain?" Anhinga asked. She saw the hatred rising in Saw Back's eyes. "Slipping out to part your legs for just any camp dog?"

"Camp dog?" Saw Back cried, stepping forward, his dark skin prickling against the cold. "You call me a camp dog? You're nothing but a murdering barbarian weasel. They sent me away because of you! You *and* that skinny joke of a Speaker."

Anhinga ducked out of the tumpline, letting the firewood bundle drop with a clatter. She groped for her ax handle, quartering as she backed away, keeping it out of his sight behind her kirtle. If this turned nasty, her only hope lay in his belief that she was defenseless.

"It's me she's spying on!" Night Rain declared as she scuttled out of the blind. Her mussed black hair fell around her bare shoulders in tangles. Cold had hardened the nipples on her round breasts and coaxed a faint mist from the damp tuft of her pubic hair.

"I spy on no one," Anhinga answered hotly. "You can part your legs for every flea-infested cur in camp for all I care, fool."

"Fool? You're calling me a fool?" Night Rain thrust out a slim finger. "At least I find satisfaction with a real man."

"Look at my tattoos, barbarian bitch!" Saw Back thumped his chest. "I am a *warrior*! Not like that child who shares your bed." He stepped closer, a dangerous gleam in his eyes as he lifted the jawbone necklace. "These I made from the Swamp Panther slime I drove a dart through at Ground Cherry Camp!"

Her vision swam for a moment. Which of her friends was it? Cooter? Spider Fire? Slit Nose? From the way the bone had been ground, she couldn't be sure. The teeth gleamed whitely in the gray light.

"I could add yours," he told her, tapping the polished bone. "I could tie them under right here so they would hang under your dead kinsman's."

"You are a sneaking cur." She could feel the danger settling around her like haze, see it in his sharpened eyes, in the tensing of his muscles.

Through gritted teeth, he said, "I am a warrior. My Spirit Helpers have brought you to me." He danced a half step toward her. "My ancestors are watching, crying for your blood, and now you have stepped into my hands. After I am done with you, no one is going to find your body."

By the Panther's bones, he is going to kill me! The revelation blew through her like a winter wind.

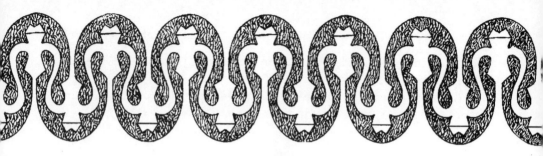

Thirty-nine

Saw Back?" Night Rain called, unsure for the first time. "If anyone finds out . . ."

"They won't," he called over his shoulder. "We'll hide her body until after dark. Bury it in the hollow under a deadfall. Once covered with leaves, she'll be rot before spring: meanwhile, her souls will wail in the lonely depths of darkness."

Anhinga swallowed hard. A vision of Spider Fire's face lingered in her memory. Somehow she knew that's whose jaw he wore.

"I thought about this the entire time I was exiled, bitch." He crouched, ready to spring. "I dreamed of my fingers choking the life from your skinny neck." He bared his teeth and leaped.

Anhinga's reaction was instinctive. She swung her ax up from behind her. To his credit, he was quick, twisting away in midair. The sharpened ax, freshly ground that morning on a slab of Panther sandstone, sliced neatly along his ribs. The impact, pain, and surprise sent him reeling, feet slipping on leaves to dump him full on his butt.

He sat there for a moment, stunned, reaching down to run fingers through the blood that began leaking out of his side.

"You witch!" Night Rain cried. "You've *killed* him!"

Anhinga stepped back just as Saw Back bunched his feet under him and leaped for her. She could have killed him. Perhaps should have. At the last instant she turned the ax and caught him full on the side of the head with the flat. The snapping smack was loud on the still air, the handle stung her hands.

The blow sent him sprawling into the frozen leaves. He lay there, gasping, fingers clenching spasmodically in the leaf mat. A look of surprise filled his face, eyes wide and glassy, mouth gaping like a dark round hole. As she watched, the damaged skin on his freshly dented cheek reddened.

Kill him! Kill him now! She hesitated, swallowed hard, and tightened her grip on the ax.

Something in Night Rain's horrified expression stopped her. If she killed him, she would be forced to flee—all of the moons she had spent here gone like smoke.

Think! How do you get out of this? Everything was changed. Her position was in peril. All because stupid Night Rain had to warm her canoe with Saw Back's worm? She stalked up to her co-wife. The young woman watched her with wide eyes, jaw hanging. Anhinga reached, twisted a fistful of Night Rain's hair, and yanked.

Night Rain came squealing as Anhinga dragged her to the tied bundle of wood. Night Rain reached out, scratching with her hands, trying to kick Anhinga. To quell her, Anhinga thumped her between the shoulders with the ax handle.

Night Rain shrieked and dropped flat beside the tied firewood. "I'll kill you! I swear! My uncle will rip your throat out!"

"Perhaps." *Panther's blood! What have you gotten yourself into here?* She had just gone for firewood, wanting time alone in the forest to think, and here she'd twisted herself into the middle of one of the Sun People's political messes.

Anhinga glanced at Saw Back; he was moaning as he tried to sit up. He had one hand to his face; blood from where the binding on the ax head had broken the skin was leaking red behind his fingers. When he pulled his hand back to look, she could still see the dent in his cheek. Had she broken the bone?

You can't explain this, Anhinga. Who's going to believe that he was going to kill you? She fingered the ax. *Or you can kill them both, hide the bodies like they were going to do with yours.*

No, that was too risky. No one might have cared if Anhinga had disappeared, but people would come looking for these two. She needed a reason, something people would believe. That, or she had best smack them both in the brains and run for all she was worth, hoping to make it south before the bodies were discovered.

And be a failure again? You'll be letting yourself, Uncle, and all of your dead friends down again. Think! You're smarter than this!

Night Rain was blubbering and shivering, her naked body squirming as she cast a frightened glance over her shoulder. "What are you going to do with me?"

"Since it's all your fault"—Anhinga smiled as she figured a way out of her mess—"I'm taking you home."

"Saw Back!" she squalled. "Kill her! Kill her now!"

One glance showed her that Saw Back had problems of his own. He couldn't seem to get to his feet.

"Pick up that wood!" Anhinga gestured with the ax.

"My kirtle and cloak . . ." Night Rain glanced back at the blind.

"If you can rut naked in this weather, you can work naked!"

"You want me to walk back naked? I'll freeze!"

"The cold didn't seem to bother you before I showed up." Anhinga accented her order by whistling the ax head past Night Rain's ear. "*Move!*"

Night Rain scuttled on her hands and knees, gaping as she passed Saw Back. Blood washed his sliced side in a crimson sheet. He was dazed, eyes half-lidded at the pain in his head. Was it imagination, or were his pupils two different sizes now?

"*Pick it up!*" Anhinga ordered, pointing at the stack of wood with her ax.

Night Rain broke into sobs, her limbs shaking as she fumbled for the cord. "Why are you *doing* this? What do *I* mean to you?"

You're my excuse, you silly, stupid bitch. Anhinga fingered the sharp edge of her ax. It was greenstone—a fine piece traded down from somewhere far upriver. "By rutting around with scum like him, you disgrace yourself, your sister, your husband, and me."

Night Rain wailed, "Saw Back? Help!" But her lover had just bent double to throw up on his thighs.

"By the Panther's blood," Anhinga whispered, "if you don't pick that up, I'm going to kill you both!" She took one more menacing step toward Night Rain, her face contorting.

Night Rain nearly toppled as she swung the load up, clawing to set the tumpline on her forehead. The rabbithide cushion had slipped so that the cord ate into the young woman's forehead.

"It hurts!" Night Rain pleaded.

Anhinga slapped the ax handle across Night Rain's buttocks, leaving a red welt. Night Rain screamed.

"To hear you, I'd think someone was burning a bobcat to death."

Night Rain tottered forward, shoulders jerking with each of her sobs. "You just wait! Wait until you get hurt sometime! I'll laugh while you scream."

Anhinga fingered the scars on her shoulders, remembering, hating. "You are worthless, Night Rain. A whimpering little child. By Panther's bones, why did he ever marry a wretch like you."

She turned, reaching down. Her fingers knotted around the necklace at Saw Back's throat. She threw her weight against it and jerked. Saw Back flopped backward and clawed at his throat. The cord parted with a snap. Stepping away from him, she inspected the two halves of human jawbone that had been polished, drilled, and strung with beads.

It is only a small justice, my friend. I cannot kill him now. Not yet.

She glanced over her shoulder. Saw Back just sat there, naked and cold in the leaves, looking bloody and sick.

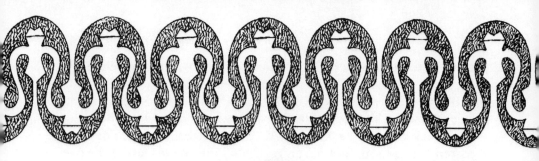

Forty

The following morning, Pine Drop waved off the calls as she hurried across the southern half of the plaza. By the Sky Beings, it was the talk of every tongue!

"Pine Drop?" Eats Wood called. "Have you heard?" Her cousin came trotting toward her, breaking away from a group of his friends.

"Yes, yes." Of all the people to have to talk to, Eats Wood wasn't her favorite. Something had always been wrong with him, and she suspected that someday, as he grew older and bolder, he would finally submit to his desire for a young girl. It would fall upon her uncle to slip up behind him and cleave his head in two. The clans dealt out justice like that, taking responsibility for their own.

"What is going to happen?" Eats Wood demanded. "Elder Sweet Root has called the Council into session. She is going to demand that Swamp Panther woman pay for the insult she has paid us!"

"We don't know the details yet."

"What details! Yesterday that camp bitch drove *your* sister naked through camp! Made her work like a stinking slave! And Deep Hunter is as mad as a teased cottonmouth about Saw Back! His head is broken and swollen! You should see him. He can't stand up without weaving and falling. He may die."

"That is Alligator Clan's concern." Pine Drop frowned. "What no one has asked is what Night Rain was doing out there with him. Why were they both naked, Cousin?"

Eats Wood grinned in a manner that roiled Pine Drop's stomach.

"Why do you think? I would have enjoyed seeing what happened out there." He turned away. "But for now, I have to find my weapons. If this turns as ugly as I hope it will, we might have to back Uncle with darts as well as words."

With that he was running, headed for his mother's house on the fourth ridge.

Weapons? She hurried forward, joining the stream of people headed toward the Council House. Tiny flakes of snow whirled past as Pine Drop pulled her blue jay-feather cloak tight about her. Snakes! This couldn't come to fighting, could it? Generations had passed since the last time blood had been spilled between the clans. Of all the People's nightmares, that was the worst. If clans began fighting with each other, they would rend the world in two.

Blessed Sky Beings, say it isn't so.

She didn't see him as he stepped up to match her pace. One of the curious things about Salamander was that he could be invisible if he wanted to. Overlooked, and unnoticed. She had often thought that a curious ability of his, and one that she often wished were her own. Now, however, he was the last person she wanted to see.

"I would ask a favor of you?" he began, voice muted.

"What would that be?" She couldn't keep the hostile tone from her voice.

"There is more to what happened than you know."

"What if they were out there locking hips? What of it, Salamander? Was that reason for that Swamp witch to humiliate my sister? Did she have to drive her infant-naked through the middle of Sun Town like a barbarian slave? Was that reason to half kill Saw Back?"

"No," he answered steadily, and placed a hand on her elbow, stopping her so that he could stare into her eyes. What she saw reflected there made her pause. What was it about him? That look penetrated her souls, carrying a terrible warning with it. What Power possessed him at moments like this?

"Pine Drop, you must hold your uncle back. Do you understand? If he pushes this thing, I will not be able to control it. One thing will lead to another, and there will be no way back for us. *There is more here than you know.*"

The words seemed to grow, shivering her souls. "What? What more?"

He glanced at the throng heading for the Council House, ignoring curious looks of the passersby. "I don't have time right now. I was just lucky to have found you first. We have to go. Please, you must trust me. We can't allow this to get out of hand, or our worst nightmares will become real."

He let go, a terrible fear brimming in his eyes. That look, more than anything, frightened her.

"You must trust me," he insisted as he hurried off. "Will you?"

She nodded halfheartedly, seeing relief flooding in his eyes. Then he was gone, trotting for the Council House on his thin legs.

What had she just done? What had she committed herself to?

Mud Stalker gripped his stone-headed hammer, tightening his hold until his fingers ached. Through slitted eyes he glared across the Council lodge at Salamander. The young Speaker was bundled in a warm buffalo robe. Occasional snowflakes drifted past. Wind seemed insolently to finger the thick brown hair, waving it this way and that as the cold gray day pressed down. Curse him, he had been trading one buffalo hide after another—spoils from his Trade with those Wash'ta fools who had piled all of their wealth on Owl Clan last fall. In the winter day's chill, Mud Stalker could feel everyone's envy of Salamander's buffalohide cape.

Sweet Root had arrived, a double wrap of fabric around her shoulders. Pine Drop appeared, looking worried. She wore her blue jay-feather cape pulled tightly against the chill. As she stood beside the Clan Elder, her thoughtful eyes turned to Mud Stalker. What was that measuring look? In the confusion of the Council being called, he had yet to speak to her and find out what she knew of Night Rain's humiliation. Something in her expression bothered him. Distress about her little sister, no doubt.

Thunder Tail was there, resplendent in his new bearskin—the only person who didn't cast a covetous gaze at Salamander. He wore the glossy black pelt over his shoulder, the fur gleaming. The very sight of it made Mud Stalker's stomach twist. It seemed that embarrassment dogged him at every turn these days.

He shot a hard glance at Deep Hunter. The Alligator Clan Speaker looked as if he were about to burst like a squashed chinquapin. His expression was a hard mask, and behind him, Saw Back looked ill. The side of the young warrior's crushed face had mottled into blue-black under an angry mass of swollen scab.

Cane Frog entered Frog Clan's part of the Council circle, her thick-veined hand resting on Three Moss's shoulder.

Clay Fat and Turtle Mist were the last to take their places.

No sooner had Thunder Tail stepped out from under the awning than Deep Hunter strode out into the center by the charcoal-blackened fire pit, and shouted, "You all know why we are here by now! The Swamp Panther woman, Anhinga, has attacked a member of my clan. A young man of my lineage! She has maimed him! Crushed the side of his face! Alligator Clan demands that this matter be taken up by the Council!"

"If you will wait your turn," Thunder Tail called, "I will recognize you. You may think you are the leader of the Council, Deep Hunter, but that honor has not yet been bestowed upon you."

Deep Hunter's hands knotted as the muscles in his arms bulged. The expression on his face brought a latent smile to Mud Stalker's lips. Despite his own rage, he could enjoy Deep Hunter's rebuke.

"Very well," Thunder Tail said with simple dignity. "Speaker Deep Hunter has brought a matter of some gravity before the Council. It seems that an altercation has resulted in one of his kinsmen receiving a serious and crippling injury."

Mud Stalker hadn't made a step to second Deep Hunter's call when Salamander leaped forward, his buffalo robe flapping. Behind him, Moccasin Leaf was a half heartbeat too slow as she tried to grab him back.

The entire Council waited in hushed silence as Salamander strode up to Deep Hunter, his small frame dwarfed by the burly Speaker. "Do you wish to pursue this, Speaker?"

"By the Snakes, I do, boy!" Deep Hunter's arm muscles bulged, his face reddening. "You hand that Swamp Panther viper over to me!"

"You may not have my wife." Salamander said it calmly, as if he were discussing a basket of prized stone blanks. His very demeanor, so thoroughly in possession of himself, left Deep Hunter off-balance.

"She attacked my warrior!"

Salamander crossed his arms, lowering his voice. Mud Stalker heard him say, "Are you sure you want to open this jar of ants, Speaker? Before it is done, we may all be bitten."

Mud Stalker stepped out into the circle. "Open it we shall! The Swamp Panther woman has made allegations! She has sullied the name of my niece. Worse, she humiliated her! Drove her naked through the middle of Sun Town like a slave!"

Salamander shot him a level glance, then looked back at Deep Hunter, saying, "This is an internal matter within my household. I will deal with my wives in my own way."

"You can't deal with anything!" Deep Hunter bellowed.

"Uncle?" the soft voice caught Mud Stalker by surprise, as did the firm hand that grasped his elbow and subtly dragged him back.

Pine Drop leaned her head close, whispering, "Do not push this, or we will all regret it."

Sweet Root stepped forward, a stunned look on her face as she in turn began pulling on Pine Drop's arm.

"Please," Pine Drop urged. "Step back, or this will burn out of control like hot sparks in a dry forest."

"You would do this?" He couldn't believe the determination in her eyes as she nodded yes.

"Trust me, Uncle. Trust Salamander. There is more at stake than you know. My husband will snuff this fire before our clan is burned."

"*Him?*" Mud Stalker jerked his head back at Salamander. From the corner of his eye he could see Salamander lean close to Deep Hunter, speaking in a low, earnest voice. Even as near as he was, he couldn't make out the words.

Deep Hunter stood like a lightning-riven oak, trembling while his expression blackened. Salamander had evidently finished, for he simply stared up at Deep Hunter with calm brown eyes.

"What did he say?" Clay Fat cried. "We can't hear! Repeat what you said, Salamander."

"Speak up!" Cane Frog shouted. "This is the Council! Not some Men's House! Either we all hear, or no one speaks!"

"Speak up!" Thunder Tail and Stone Talon called in chorus. The Clan Elder leaned forward on her crutches, her toothless jaw stuck out in irritation.

"It is your decision," Salamander said loudly enough for everyone to hear. "I could repeat myself in a voice loud enough for the rest to hear."

To Mud Stalker's surprise, Deep Hunter shot him an evaluative look, hesitated, then shook his head. He stepped back, hands still balled into fists. The muscles in his arms knotted and writhed. Before he turned on his heel and stalked back to his place, he muttered, "Alligator Clan retracts its statement. This matter is up to Salamander."

"What?" Mud Stalker cried in amazement. He started forward again, only to have Pine Drop take his bad arm in a tight grip.

"Leave it, Uncle," she insisted. "It is between Salamander, me, and Night Rain. Our time will come later, when it will not make fools of us in front of everyone. More is at stake here than you know."

"How dare you?" Sweet Root exploded, struggling to keep her voice down so the others didn't hear.

"Be smart," Pine Drop whispered through gritted teeth before she let go of Mud Stalker's arm. "Figure it out yourself. I just did." Then she turned, striding purposefully out of the Council House, pushing her way through the people who had come to watch.

That, more than anything, sank through Mud Stalker's anger. He stopped short, meeting Sweet Root's eyes, seeing nothing there but baffled frustration.

Suddenly unsure, Mud Stalker stepped out into the circle, catching Salamander before he could step from the ring. "Just tell me, Speaker. What did your barbarian do out there in the forest?"

Salamander stopped short, glancing back at Saw Back, before meeting Mud Stalker's eyes. "Exactly what she had to, Speaker. Nothing more, nothing less."

As Salamander walked past the stunned Moccasin Leaf and stepped out of the Council House, people parted to let him pass. Mud Stalker ground his teeth, his mind racing. He narrowed his eye as he shot a hard look at Deep Hunter. What bit of information could Salamander have used to back Deep Hunter down? What did they have in common?

Night Rain! She's at the bottom of this!

As the Council broke up, he stood in the gray center of the circle, thinking. Deep Hunter's game, he could understand. There were ways of dealing with the Speaker. But what about Salamander? Just what sort of game was he playing? Why did he care if Night Rain and Deep Hunter were dragged through the mud? What difference would it make to him if Alligator and Snapping Turtle Clans tore each other apart?

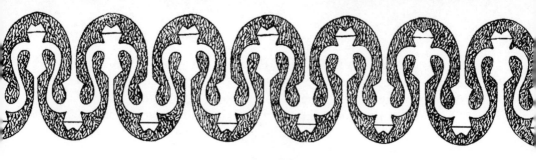

Forty-one

Salamander kneaded his temples in a futile attempt to soothe his pounding headache. The idea of sneaking over to the Serpent's for some jimsonweed paste, or perhaps for a couple of puffs on the old man's pipe, was so tempting.

Now, with the Council mollified, or at least held at bay, he considered his more immediate problem. He looked at his wives, together for the first time. They sat in his house, equidistant from each other, eyes hard, brown, and fiery. Their feet rested on the burned bones of his ancestors. That thought seemed to stick sideways inside him. Was White Bird's Dream Soul watching him even now? Was he shaking his head in pity, or just laughing outright? A man with three wives deserved anything they dished out for him.

Anhinga sat defiantly, muscular arms crossed over her rounding belly, her chin high. Pine Drop shifted back and forth, fists knotting and opening as if she'd like to wrap them around Anhinga's smooth throat. Night Rain glared miserably up from the floor, a fabric wrap around her waist. Her face was swollen from tears, and a red welt marked her forehead where the tumpline had bruised it.

"The whole of Sun Town is talking about what happened!" Pine Drop cried.

"Good! Perhaps we will finally get some respect!" Anhinga shot back.

Salamander raised his arms. "Stop it!" Pain blasted through his head, reflecting on his face.

In the sudden silence, only the cracking of the fire could be heard. Then his mother's voice asked from outside, "Is everything all right in there? Do I need to send the Speaker to deal with this?"

He winced, wishing he could press the ache out of his skull. "He's here, Mother. He's already dealing with it."

"All right. Be sure and send your uncle home when he's finished. I have a stew cooking. Acorns and raccoon mixed with squash. His favorite."

"Yes, Mother." Salamander closed his eyes, fists knotting. "Snakes, if it's not one thing, it's another!"

"Husband?" He heard the first change in the timbre in Anhinga's voice. By Masked Owl, was that concern replacing the anger? "What would you have had me do? Let Saw Back break my neck and leave me under a log?"

"You did what you had to," Salamander replied, making up his mind.

Pine Drop pointed a hard finger. "Very well, Husband, I see where this is going. You just remember, I did as you asked me to today. Against my judgment I held my uncle back during the Council. You asked for a favor, and I trusted you enough to grant it—at no little risk to myself. But I'm not finished with Anhinga. She didn't have to humiliate my sister. She could have let her sneak back to camp, dressed, and with some self-respect."

"Then it would have been her word against mine!" Anhinga cried, thumping her chest between her breasts. "She and that slithering serpent she had locked hips with could have said anything about me! Who would the Sun People have believed then, first wife? Who? Night Rain? Or the barbarian bitch?"

"Enough!" Salamander cried, his souls aching in time to his head. "Night Rain, do you understand how dangerous the game is that you are playing?"

"Husband, you can't—"

He silenced Pine Drop with a slash of his hand. "She has betrayed you, too, Wife. Not just your position as first wife, but your position as the next Clan Elder." He saw the struggle inside as Pine Drop juggled the information. She was caught between loyalty and what Night Rain had done to them all.

"She is young," Salamander added in a gentle voice. "People make mistakes when they are young. We have controlled the damage."

"You *forgive* her?" Anhinga asked in disbelief.

"This stops here." Salamander squinted against the throbbing. "This is not a matter for the clans, or the Council, or the Clan Elders to work out. We barely kept our world from exploding like a mud-tempered pot out there. But for Deep Hunter's guilt, and Pine Drop's intervention, we would have Snapping Turtle and Alligator Clans at each other's throats. If it had come to blows, if some of the hotheaded young warriors had started to fight . . . Well, you know how close we just came to the abyss."

Anhinga's cunning eyes narrowed.

"Don't even think it." Salamander turned on her. "You are part of this. Start that fire, and you will not only scorch the Sun People, but the Swamp Panthers, too. Warfare between the clans will burn its way through the Panther's Bones as surely as you broke Saw Back's head." He held her eyes. "You know I'm right."

Anhinga shrugged and turned away. Pine Drop's eyes hardened in response.

Salamander reached down and tilted Night Rain's tear-puffy face up. "Do you understand? If Deep Hunter wasn't as smart as he is, he would have forced me to tell everyone. Would you have wanted that? Wanted your uncle and mother to know you were plotting against them?"

Pine Drop's expression slacked with understanding. "Snakes, then it's true?"

"Answer me," Salamander insisted.

"No." Night Rain's voice sounded small.

He ignored Pine Drop, holding Night Rain's gaze. "He was playing with you like a toy on a cord. You are meaningless to him. A tool to be used. No more than a stone dart point. Once you lost your edge, he would have discarded you."

"No!" Night Rain blurted hotly. "He would make me Clan Elder!" Realizing what she had just admitted, she stared aghast at Pine Drop.

"I don't believe what I'm hearing." Pine Drop shook her head.

"You could only be Clan Elder if Alligator Clan could dominate Snapping Turtle Clan," Salamander replied gently. "Think, Night Rain. They have been trying to get rid of me as Speaker for moons now, but I still speak for my clan. It isn't as easy as Deep Hunter led you to believe. The clans won't allow outsiders to meddle in their business."

"Who cares about Owl Clan? It's broken," Night Rain shot back.

"Night Rain, Saw Back tried to kill Anhinga. That's true, isn't it?" Salamander asked.

Pine Drop looked sick to her stomach as she settled back on the bedding.

Night Rain tucked her arms into her lap and leaned forward. "He didn't even have a weapon! He didn't see her ax. The camp bitch hid it behind her."

He turned to Anhinga. "Couldn't you have just walked away, ignored them?"

"Maybe you could have done something like that." Then, sensing his distress, she added in a softer voice. "He mocked me with the bones of my dead friends. He would have come after me. I could see it in his eyes."

He nodded, wondering what he would have done. Walked away probably to bide his time. It just wasn't in Anhinga's souls to react that way. He raised his eyes. "Pine Drop?"

"She is my sister." The words were wooden, pained.

"She's my wife." He lowered himself to the bench, using fingertips to massage his temples. "I remember an evening in your house when you cautioned her about behaving with responsibility. Since then she has given Deep Hunter and his warriors both her body and your clan's private dealings. I would imagine she heard a great many things discussed at Elder Sweet Root's fire."

"This is how a wife behaves? She *humiliates* us!" Anhinga cried.

"That is enough!" Salamander shot her a cautionary look. "Indignation is like sassafras root, Anhinga. Use too much of it, and the pot turns bitter." He rubbed his hands together. "The question remains: What should we do about this?"

"I *hate* you," Night Rain managed through clenched teeth. "All of you!"

Pine Drop's lips hardened. "You hate me, too?"

Night Rain nodded, lip twitching. "No one shamed you when you were bedding Three Stomachs."

Pine Drop paled.

Anhinga lifted an eyebrow. "Ah, now we see how deeply the rot runs."

"Enough!" Salamander avoided Pine Drop's stricken eyes. "What is past cannot be undone. I know of no one in this room who has not made mistakes." Going from Anhinga, to Pine Drop, to Night Rain, he met their eyes. "So let us start anew tonight. We have all done terrible things to each other, and to ourselves."

"I have to tell Speaker Mud Stalker," Pine Drop said listlessly. "This goes beyond this household. It's clan business."

"No!" Night Rain cried, looking stricken. "You can't tell the Speaker. He'll beat me! Cast me out! Send me off into exile!"

"You *betrayed* us!" Pine Drop cried. "Betrayed *me*!"

"Uncle arranged it! Just like he did with you and Three Stomachs!" Night Rain began to leak tears again.

"But I didn't tell him clan secrets while I . . ." Pine Drop winced, shaking her head. "By the Sky Beings, never mind. Our husband is right, what's done is done and can't be undone."

"There is a way for us to solve this, Night Rain," Salamander spoke wearily.

"I hope leeches drink your blood," she mumbled.

"Sister!" Pine Drop warned. "I will not hear you speak that way."

"You and your ways," Night Rain muttered. "You make me sick! So proper and correct. Over what? Him? He's a fool, Sister. You're married to a fool, carrying *his* fool child! You're a laughingstock!" She glanced up at Salamander. "And you? Are you a warrior? I see no tattoos. You are a coward. You send your barbarian bitch to do your fighting for you!"

Pine Drop paled, a hand against one of the support poles. Anhinga smiled like a fox over a nest of hatchlings. At a word, she'd have been happy to help Pine Drop thrash Night Rain into pulp.

"Your sister is a fool?" Salamander managed a bitter smile. "Strong words, Night Rain, for a woman who was marched naked through the middle of town after being routed away from her lover. Do not talk to me of fools."

"What did he promise you?" Pine Drop asked. "What did Deep Hunter say would be yours?"

"He told her that you would never be Clan Elder," Salamander supplied for her. "That's what Deep Hunter promised her. That, and Saw Back, and prestige, and status, and who knows what else. She's not as smart as you are, Wife."

"Indeed?" Night Rain asked smugly. "We'll see who's smart in the end."

"If you were," Pine Drop said wearily, "you would know Deep Hunter is through with you. Disgraced and embarrassed, you can't serve him. Uncle is suspicious now—if he hasn't already figured it out like I told him. So is Mother. They will never speak freely in your presence. You'll be watched like a mouse in a jar. Despite the pleas of our husband, I am still tempted to tell Uncle and Mother the extent of what you've done. If I do, you *will* be destroyed, Sister."

For the first time fear glazed Night Rain's eyes.

"There is a way out, Night Rain," Salamander said carefully.

"What?" Pine Drop demanded. "Hold this over her so that she can become Owl Clan's pawn?"

"No. I would not do that. She is my wife, as you are. As Anhinga is." He paused. "Night Rain, everyone in Sun Town has heard about you. From the moment you walk out of this house, every eye is going to be on you. There are probably thirty people within a stone's throw of this house right now, their ears pricked like a dog's to hear the row."

"I could step outside," Anhinga suggested, and tapped her ax. "I'll bet they'd scurry away like wood rats in a cane patch."

"Night Rain," Salamander continued, "if we forget what you've done, will you act like a proper wife?"

"Just forget?" Pine Drop asked in wonder. "Like you just said, every tongue is going to be wagging! And it's clear that she's been working with Deep Hunter!"

Salamander nodded soberly. "If she can see this thing through, learn from her shame, I would suggest that you not tell your Clan Elder, or your Speaker, about her transgressions."

Anhinga interjected, "You will be considered a fool, Salamander. People will look at you and whisper behind their hands, saying, 'Look, there's Speaker Salamander! He took his wife back after his barbarian brought her home still steaming with another man's sweat!' "

"They will, Salamander," Pine Drop agreed.

He shrugged. "I am used to it. Night Rain isn't." He took a deep breath. "Let us be honest, Wives. A great many forces are building against me. Alliances are being made in dark places, all seeking eventually to destroy me. We must ensure that the rest of you can go home and restart your lives."

Night Rain looked as if sunshine had penetrated a cloud. Pine Drop and Anhinga both looked uncomfortable. He closed his eyes for a moment, wishing the headache would pass. When he reopened them, his little world hadn't changed.

Pine Drop relented. "Night Rain, do you think you can do this? Act like a wife should to Salamander?"

She nodded.

"What if Saw Back planted a child in her?" Anhinga asked, shooting a hard glare at Night Rain.

Salamander shrugged. "That is Snapping Turtle Clan's concern, not mine. Like your people, the child belongs to the mother's clan."

Pine Drop filled her lungs and exhaled a roomful of tension. "Very well, Sister, let's take you home and clean you up."

"No." Salamander gave a brief shake of his head. "We all sleep here tonight."

All eyes turned to him, expressions ranging from Anhinga's arched eyebrow to Night Rain's sudden horror.

He pointed at the door. "A small crowd is loitering out there in the cold. It would do them good to wait, to watch the fire's glow grow dim around the roof. Some can't wait to rush back to their clans with fresh gossip."

"Very well, for tonight," Pine Drop agreed.

"And periodically after that," Salamander amended. "If we are to survive this, we must do so together. From now on we are going to be a household."

"Yes, yes, we are agreed." Pine Drop looked at her sister, then at the crackling fire, and added with a wary chuckle, "Fortunately, someone carried in a good supply of firewood."

Anhinga smiled ironically at Night Rain.

Salamander's own smile was false, a mask to relieve his wives. His thoughts turned to Saw Back. The side of his face was crushed. He would be clawing at the walls for revenge.

Water trickled in the close darkness to explode into hissing, spitting founts of steam. Bobcat retracted the thin-walled stone bowl. The hot rocks sizzled, and invisible rolls of wet heat rose around Salamander's body. He opened his mouth, gasping, feeling the steam eat at the insides of his nostrils and his throat.

"Is that better?" Bobcat asked, his form barely visible in the red glow of the hot stones.

"Better," Salamander agreed. He used his fingers to slick sweat from his forehead, eyebrows, and nose.

The close darkness inside the sweat lodge cupped around him like hands, the rounded roof close over his head. It pressed the stinging heat into his skin, threading it through his muscles, blending it with the blood in his veins.

"You need to be cleansed every so often, Speaker." Bobcat shifted in the darkness. "Water can only wash the outside of your skin, but steaming cleanses not only the whole of the body, but the souls as well. It maintains a purity of the blood, a balance of the organs. These things go back to the beginning of the world, to a time when First Woman used fire and water to cleanse herself."

"First Woman?" Salamander smiled, feeling water dripping from his chin to spatter on the folds of his stomach. The tops of his thighs prickled, his sides burned, and only by rubbing his hands along the outsides of his arms could he stand the steam's bite.

"So many stories are told about her," Bobcat replied. "One of the things I have learned, talking to the Traders who come from all over the world, is that they have stories about the Hero Twins, and about First Woman. About how she was there at the Creation."

"I know little about her."

Bobcat rubbed the sweat from his arms. "It is said that she lives in a cave at the center of the world. It is said that her essence is released in steam. That she was the first to teach the values of hot water to the People. She was the First Dreamer, the one who taught Wolf Dreamer the way to the One."

"Do you believe that?" Salamander asked, thinking about all the stories he had heard about First Woman. "Do you really think she lives in a cave at the center of the Earth, and that a huge tree grows out of the cave's mouth?"

Bobcat shrugged. "I don't know, my friend. She is reclusive. Few Dreamers, Serpents, or Soul Flyers see her. It is said that while the brothers and the lesser Spirit Helpers often interact in the world of men, she prefers her cave, her Dreams slipping in and out of the One, while she mourns a long-lost love. It is said that even the Hero Twins and Sky Beings defer to her. That she is the heartbeat of the One."

"She must be very Powerful."

"I would not want to be the individual who disturbed her Dreams, I'll tell you." Bobcat shivered.

After a moment, Salamander asked, "How is the Serpent?"

"Not well. I do not know what to do for him. I have had him here, day after day. In an effort to prolong his life I have been feeding him a diet of snake meat."

"Snake meat?"

"Have you ever seen a snake that died from old age, Salamander? Snakes live forever, or until something eats them, be it a man, an eagle, a raccoon, or a weasel. Power lies in their meat."

"But it isn't helping?"

"No, my friend." Bobcat sounded weary.

"I cannot prove this, but I think that men like the Serpent hear Dream Souls, Bobcat. I think the Dead talk to them, call to them, and the Dream Soul begins to long to talk back. Think about it. So many of the Serpent's friends are dead. Perhaps he longs to join them."

"Perhaps. But I do not think so in his case. Have you felt the lump in his belly?"

"No."

"It is something evil, some vicious spirit that is growing inside him, eating away at his life."

"You're sure you can't kill it?"

"No, and neither can he. Snakes know, we've tried everything."

"I am sorry to hear that. He has always been good to me."

Bobcat was silent for a time. "The Serpent picks few people for his close association. He is fond of you."

"As I am of him."

"I know. It is a rare thing for him to show that kind of affection: therefore, I will have you know that I extend my own friendship, no matter what the future brings."

Salamander smiled wistfully as droplets of sweat tickled on his face. "You may wish to reconsider, Bobcat. I am caught between Masked Owl and Many Colored Crow. I don't understand my destiny yet, but I fear it will not be pleasant. Those who stand close to me should fear the lightning."

"As your brother did?"

"As my brother should have."

Salamander stared sadly at the faint glow of the hot rocks. They lay like giant red eggs in the shallow pit—cobbles imported from the source of the White Mud River. A hot fire of white ash had been burned around them for several hands of time. The heat rolling off the stones curled his skin when he reached out.

"You should know that Deep Hunter is enraged." Bobcat's voice caressed the darkness. "His nephew's face is ruined. I have done what I can for Saw Back. He will be marked for the rest of his life, and his sight is blurry in the left eye."

"You should not tell me these things. When you become the Serpent, you must favor no one."

"I have learned something from the Serpent that you have not. I must favor those who are favored by Power," he replied. "I know the responsibilities of the Serpent. I will not abuse them, Speaker. Not for you, or for anyone. But being the Serpent doesn't mean that I can't help those I think work for the common good."

Salamander steepled his fingers. "Do you think that of me?"

"I do."

"I am not so sure, Bobcat. Trouble is brewing around me like a pot of black drink. Sometimes I think it would be best if I simply left, went down to the Owl Clan holdings at Twin Circles on the gulf, or over to Yellow Mud Camp, or one of the outlying camps, and lived out my life."

"You can't, Salamander. You have responsibilities." Bobcat trickled another finger of water onto the rocks. Steam popped and billowed, the cloud suffocating in the close confines of the lodge.

Salamander leaned his head back, mouth open, and let the steam drive needles into his flesh. His skin might have been blistering, splitting from the muscle beneath. He coughed when he inhaled, and the damp fire stung his throat.

"Someone wants to kill your wife," Bobcat said softly.

"I know."

"He says she is a witch, come to kill us all. He says she was the prisoner White Bird brought back from the Swamp Panther raid at Ground Cherry Camp."

"She was."

"He says that malevolent spirits freed her in the middle of the night."

"No malevolent spirits freed her. It wasn't magic, or anything nearly as frightening," Salamander said wearily. "I did, Bobcat. I cut her loose that night."

"Why?" An incredulous tone filled the young man's voice.

"Masked Owl told me to. He came to me in a Dream, when we were flying, and told me she would be important."

"Then she's not dangerous?"

"Oh, no, Bobcat, she is *very* dangerous. Perhaps the most dangerous person in Sun Town."

"If that is so, why do you keep her? Why don't you cast her out, send her back to the Swamp Panthers and let them suck on her poison?"

"I don't know."

"That's a crazy answer."

"Perhaps, but she's part of Masked Owl's plan. I just don't know what it is yet."

"Be very, very careful. She made a great many enemies when she wounded Saw Back." Bobcat hesitated. "I don't know how to tell you this, but I have heard that someone is following her. I have not heard who, but word is that she is stalked every time she leaves Sun Town."

Salamander took a deep breath. "I shall be careful, Bobcat. Not only is she part of Masked Owl's plan, but she carries my child within her. She is my wife. I will take care of her."

"Even if she destroys you in the process?"

"I think I will have warning before she does."

"You *think*? That doesn't sound very promising."

"No." He smiled. "I suppose not."

"Beware, Speaker Salamander. Your enemies are growing stronger by the heartbeat."

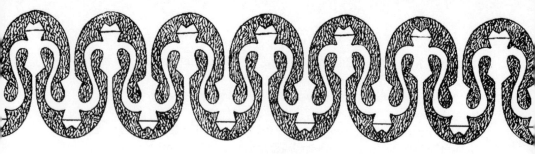

Forty-two

Night Rain squatted to relieve herself at the edge of the borrow ditch below her sister's house. The night was still, cold. Only the distant barking of one of the camp dogs broke the silence. Smoke hung low; its odor tickled her nostrils. When she looked up it was to see a white ghosting of stars across the night sky. Father Moon still hid in shame below the horizon, and Bird Man's path across the sky glowed with an eerie luminescence.

As she started to stand, a hand reached out from behind to grab her. That touch brought a squeal from her frightened lungs.

"*Hush!*" the familiar voice ordered. "What's going on?"

"Uncle?" her voice failed, breath short in her panicked lungs. Mud Stalker wheeled her around to face him, his crushing grip hurting her elbow.

"What is your game, Niece? Who are you playing against whom? Deep Hunter against Salamander? Deep Hunter against me? What's your sister's role in this? What were you doing out there with Saw Back? Rutting, like everyone says? That I don't doubt! But why didn't you tell me?"

"Uncle, please!" She squirmed away from the pain.

"You tell me, woman. You start at the beginning, and you tell me."

"Uncle, honestly, I didn't do anything . . ." His hard slap sent her stumbling. She slipped, falling backward into her damp urine.

"Don't lie to me!"

She caught her breath, swallowed hard, and cast a desperate glance at the dark shape of her house up on the ridgetop. Pine Drop would be asleep, ignorant of her plight. Not that it would matter, not even Pine Drop would interfere with their uncle over clan business.

"Please don't hurt me."

"I'll beat you until your souls cling to your body by a thread!"

He drew back a foot, as if to kick her. She scrambled back, hands and feet sliding in the mud. "I swear, I did nothing against the clan. I just wanted Saw Back! You know that! You know I've always been in love with him!"

Mud Stalker loomed over her. "Deep Hunter knew I was going to offer Eats Wood for Green Beetle. He beat me to it, offered Thunder Tail his cousin, Needs Two, and access to a root ground before I could take the Speaker out to that bear tree. I couldn't figure it out. But after the Council meeting, and what Pine Drop did, I finally understand. You were there, you heard me discuss it that night with your mother."

"I *didn't*, I swear!" She was suddenly thankful for the darkness. He couldn't see her face, couldn't read the lie in her expression.

"Why did Salamander take you back? Why didn't he just throw you out like the punky worm-riddled piece of wood you are?"

"I don't know! You'd have to ask him. He's . . . he's . . ."

"What?"

"Odd, Uncle. Strange. He hears things, has Dreams." She lurched backward like a crawfish on land as he stepped nearer. "I don't know what possesses his souls to make him do the things he does."

"What does the barbarian hold over him? Is she a witch? Does she control his souls?"

"I don't think so. She's just mean. She hates us. You heard Eats Wood; he says she's the one White Bird caught. You've seen those scars on her skin? We did that to her when she was a prisoner."

"Why did you betray me to Deep Hunter?" His voice sounded tired now, wounded.

"Uncle, I didn't. You have to believe me."

"I shouldn't have trusted you. You were too young, not smart enough. I see that now. Snakes! What was I to do? Don't you understand, woman? We're almost at the top! We've worked all of our lives to see our clan become preeminent. The gains we have made can disappear from beneath us like water from a puddle, and you let a little pleasure in your canoe, and the promises of a crafty lizard like Deep Hunter, turn you against your own family!"

"Uncle, I swear!"

She squatted there, her butt in the mud, waiting as his dark body hulked against the stars. The silence grew interminable.

When he finally broke it, he asked, "What part did Salamander play in all this? What did he do to get Pine Drop to support him in the Council?"

"He asked her to trust him," she whispered, unable to see what it would hurt. "That it would explode like a chert nodule in a fire if she didn't."

She could see him, a dark blot against the sky as he fingered the scars on his maimed arm.

"Salamander was trying to keep our clan from fighting with Alligator Clan." There, would that mollify him?

"Why? What difference does it make to him?"

"We're his wives." She swallowed hard, trying to find the right answer. "He cares for us. For me."

The kick caught her by surprise. His foot slammed into her ribs, rolling her. She yelped at the pain, frightened by the hollow thump.

"You're *stupid*, Night Rain! No one cares for a woman like you." Mud Stalker turned his head and spat. "Least of all your skinny, witless husband." A pause. "No, this is something else. Some plotting he must be doing at the behest of that Panther witch who wraps him around her bony fingers."

"Uncle, I—"

"Shut up! I'm thinking, trying to understand."

"Please, Uncle, I didn't do *anything*!"

"You betrayed me. You and Pine Drop. But don't think I haven't learned, Niece. Indeed, I have learned a great deal about you—and your husband. I've underestimated him. I won't do that again."

She could feel his gaze as he studied her. She wanted to shrink, to shrivel up and burrow into the waste-tainted mud.

"In the future when I come to you, you will tell me the truth, Night Rain. And someday, to make up for this humiliation to Snapping Turtle Clan, to your lineage, and me, I am going to ask you for something. When I do, you are going to do as I say, or I am going to break your head with a stone-headed hammer. Do you understand?"

"Yes, Uncle." Her voice came as a hoarse whisper.

"In the meantime, stay out of my sight."

He turned, walking wearily away—head down, shoulders bowed. He plodded up past her house and headed east on the ridge.

She closed her eyes and sagged into the stinking mud.

Branches, like gray fuzz, softened the distant border between the forest and sky as if one faded into the other. The morning was cold, silent but for the calls of the winter birds. Not even the ducks stirred when Anhinga's canoe slipped silently down the channel.

Her breath puffed whitely. Despite the cold she paddled with her cloak thrown back over her shoulders; her muscles provided enough warmth. On the still water the cold seemed thicker, sticky, ready to sap a body's heat. She glanced at the canebrakes, tawny and gray. The banks were brown, the trees black, their fringe of branches lonely and longing for spring.

"You shouldn't be taking this trip," Pine Drop had warned the night before.

As if I need advice from her! Anhinga made a face, feeling the cold in her cheeks. The bulge of her belly made sitting in the canoe awkward, but she needed time away. Besides which, her brother, Striped Dart, would be coming to meet her this time. Half a cycle had passed since she had seen him last. He would be bursting with news about people at the Panther's Bones. She, in turn, had so much to tell him about the Sun People, and Night Rain, about smacking Saw Back, and the ruckus she had stirred in the Council as a result.

Thinking about Saw Back brought a shudder to her. The side of his face looked horrible. In the weeks since the incident, he had healed, but her ax had peeled a long scar that ran from beside his navel to just under his left nipple. The thin arch of bone ahead of his ear had been crushed. Had she not turned the ax at the last moment the blow would surely have penetrated his skull.

When he, or any of his clan, looked at her now, it was with a simmering hatred.

He attacked me. That memory clung to her like summer cobwebs. The incident filled her thoughts, recurring in her Dreams.

By the Panther's bones, that had been a close one. But for her quick wits, it could have turned out worse than it had. Oddly, she rather enjoyed having put Night Rain in her place. Over the long term, however, she had a hunch that her actions that morning would come to haunt her.

Overhead a V of geese crossed above the web of branches. The swish of their wings and the lonely honking were the only sounds outside of the water gurgling around her paddle.

She glanced up at the banks—just enough higher that each tangle of dormant honeysuckle or nightshade could conceal a crouching warrior. She could imagine Saw Back's smile of anticipation as her slim canoe coasted within range. He would feel the joy of revenge in his breast as he rose, sighted, and drove a dart through her body.

He will kill my baby. Her mouth went dry. Panther! Why hadn't that thought occurred to her? It wasn't just her anymore. If anything, the baby was even more of a temptation to Saw Back. He could kill her and Salamander's child in one stroke. He could wreak his retribution on her while repaying Salamander for his trickery in allowing Jaguar Hide to escape: two for one.

A stick cracked in the forest. A squirrel dropping a nut? Or the weighty step of a man's foot?

The silence pressed down upon her. As the canoe coasted she pulled her atlatl and darts closer to hand. Next she slipped her ax through the belt of her kirtle.

Ghostly fingers of breeze stirred the quiet air. She whirled, rocking the canoe. The channel behind her lay empty, her wake spreading toward the banks. In the cold winter sun the water had a silver sheen. She couldn't see far, the channel twisted and looped, choked with cypress, tupelo, and water oak. The trees watched her, silent, as if their ancient souls were waiting.

Eyes, a thousand of them! She glanced around, looking up in the branches where brown-tinted hanging moss drooped wearily. Her quickened imagination saw faces leering out from the patterns of dry vegetation.

Swallowing, she picked up the paddle and drove her canoe forward. *Hurry! Just leave this place behind. If he is after you, outrun him. Paddle like you have never paddled before.* The canoe flew ahead.

He could be just behind her, and knowing these passages, he could beach his canoe, cut across a narrow neck of land, and ambush her from any patch of tangled brush.

Flee, you have no other choice. She couldn't go back, not and take the chance of running headlong into him.

She tightened her hands on the paddle handle. *You're being silly, Anhinga. You have no proof that he's behind you. No proof that he's after you at all.*

She was just jittery. Her imagination was teasing her. The strain had begun to make itself felt in her shoulders and arms.

I would be out hunting, if I were he.

She couldn't help but remember that she herself, smarting from injustice, had brought a war party north to avenge Bowfin's death. Perhaps Saw Back wasn't as impetuous as she, but could she take the chance? How many eyes had been watching that morning as Salamander saw her off from the landing?

Paddle! A new surge of fear drove her onward. They would know she would have taken this channel south. It was the most direct way through the bottomlands paralleling Sun Town's high silt bluff. If she made it to the rendezvous alive, she could always take another route home. It might be longer, out of the way, but a hunter wouldn't know when or where to expect her.

If I go home. That thought caught her by surprise. She didn't have to go back. Not after the affair with Saw Back. Uncle wouldn't expect her to and neither would Striped Dart. They would rather have her safe, especially carrying her clan's child.

She shot a quick look over her shoulder again. Nothing. Her wake was undisturbed by so much as a fish jumping.

Salamander would approve of her caution. In the gray dawn of the canoe landing she had seen the worry in her husband's eyes.

"I have to go," she had told him simply. "They will be waiting for me. If I don't show up, they will worry. It might lead them to foolishness. We both know how dangerous it would be if they came here looking for me. Only Owl Clan is bound by your word of peace."

He had nodded, a terrible reluctance reflected in the set of his mouth. "I need you to come back to me."

Impulsively she had reached out and drawn him to her in a desperate hug. She had held his thin body against hers, her swollen belly pressing the hollow of his. Then she had turned, grateful for his help as she awkwardly pushed the canoe into the cold water and climbed in.

I hugged him. Panther's blood, why? It isn't as if I really care for him. He's the enemy. No matter that he severed my bonds one night.

Was it her imagination, or had something about Salamander changed over the moons? Men, she had heard, acted differently after they planted a child and could see it growing in their wives. Or was it that she had fought for him, for his honor, that day when she surprised Saw Back and Night Rain?

You didn't mean to, she argued with herself. *It was expedient to shame Night Rain that way. If you'd killed them both, you would have been finished in Sun Town.*

She no longer went out alone to gather firewood, or collect nuts, or check the snares. Somehow, Pine Drop, Salamander, or Water Petal always seemed to be ready to accompany her.

Night Rain had surprised them all, demurely taking her place like a proper wife. Anhinga suspected that she buried herself in household activities to avoid facing people. Laughter still broke out at the sight of her, and occasional calls followed her around Sun Town, asking if she needed to borrow any clothing. The teasing would eventually die off like fall grass; Night Rain need only wait it out.

He is a better man than I would be in his place, she concluded. Indeed, she'd have thrown the little witch out. Salamander, however, had acted as if nothing had happened, welcoming Night Rain into his house and his bed with great dignity.

How many nights had Anhinga lain in her bed, hearing their whispered conversation? Something was being forged between them, although Night Rain still shot her looks that bordered on the murderous.

At the end of the next strait, Anhinga glanced back, barely catching movement behind a distant cypress knee. She blinked hard to clear her eyes and stared. What was that dark blot behind the old roots? A man, or a shadow? Her canoe almost drifted into the bank before she straightened it.

Imagination, or trick of the light? She dared not take the chance, and drove her paddle into the water with renewed fury.

She shot out of the narrow channel and into one of the wide, shallow swamps. Her flying canoe sailed into the maze of trees as she followed her way south. A lightning-blasted cypress marked the entrance to the far channel, and gratefully she cast a final glance over her shoulders. Nothing. No. Wait. Movement, there, back in the trees! But was it a man, or an animal? Before she could determine, her canoe coasted into the channel, the banks obscuring her view.

Desperate again, panting, she drove herself onward. A red smear caught her eye as she shifted her grip on the paddle. When had her palm blistered and broken? Compared to the ache in her forearms and shoulders, it was nothing.

Time collapsed into fear, pain, and exhaustion as she raced her canoe down the winding passage. A hand of time later she emerged into a familiar swamp and marked her progress. Known landmarks, fallen trees, stumps, and oddly shaped cypress knees guided her through the brackish shallows.

She cried out with relief as she drove her narrow craft onto the muddy shore of the little island. For long moments she could only sit there and gasp for breath. Her arms barely supported her as she tried to get up. She propped herself on the gunwales and struggled against the bulk of her swollen abdomen.

Coming within a hair of capsizing herself into the muddy shallows, she stepped into the water, staggered sideways, and caught her balance.

As her legs came alive, she turned and looked back at the silent swamp. Nothing moved, not even birds, usually ever-present in the winter moons. The water reflected the sky's dull gray sheen, motionless, heavy.

Slogging out of the water she rolled her arms, wincing. Tomorrow would be agony. Bending over her girth, she pushed the canoe higher up the bank and grabbed the sack of supplies she had brought. The drinking bowl that she normally filled before arriving here was empty, forgotten in the frantic flight.

She collected her atlatl and darts, tapping her ax with reassured fingers. Let him come. Here, on dry land, she could vanquish any fool who paddled a canoe up to the island.

Walking through knee-high dry grass, she stepped into the beaten campsite she had shared over the moons with her relatives. A few damp pieces of wood lay on the wet ground. Looking around, it appeared that no one had been here since she and Uncle had left.

"You need dry wood. This won't do to make a fire." She kicked the wet wood and started off through the grass in search of old flood-deposited flotsam. She stopped and inspected a large branch. Thick as a man's thigh, it had fallen from a water oak. Partially protected by the overhanging branches, the wood felt moderately dry to her touch. She looked around at the brown grass and weeds. Hip high, they masked her movements. The island slept, dormant and silent.

She laid her atlatl and darts to one side and worked her tired fingers, feeling the joints ache. It would take two hands to drag this back. The smaller branches would make kindling, and she could talk Striped Dart into hacking up the rest when he arrived.

She bent, got a grip, and heaved. The branch moved, and like some ungainly turtle, she dragged it one pull at a time toward her camp. With each tug, she took a moment to rise and peer out at the swamp. No movement marred the surface. No sound intruded on the normal noises.

As she bent once again and pulled, she caught a blur at the corner of her eye. Something struck her from behind, knocked her forward over the branch. The hard wood smashed her chin and left breast.

For a terrified instant her thoughts scrambled, then she rolled onto her back, staring up in disbelief. For a moment she could not place his face. "You?"

She was gasping, her heart pounding as Eats Wood grinned down at her. "Hello, bitch. Snakes, it's been a long time that I have been waiting to do this."

"What are you doing here?" She remembered him, remembered his fingers twisting her left nipple as he carried her from the canoe landing up to the Men's House. His leer brought back all the terrible memories of that day.

"It took me a while to work out your trail. I learned a little more every time you left. Never followed you all the way. Just a bit at a time. And what should I find? You, bending your head with Jaguar Hide, planning ways to hurt us all."

"He is my uncle!" She managed to brace her elbows under her. Eats Wood held a stone-headed ax in one gnarled fist. He swung it back and forth, each swing promising pain.

"He is our enemy." He smiled down at her. "You made good time today. Jaguar Hide shouldn't be arriving here for at least another hand of time."

"What are you going to do?" Her atlatl lay back at the tree, her ax, however, was pinned under her hip. Had he seen it hanging from her kirtle?

"What I wanted to do the first time I saw you." He tilted his head to the side, eyes half-lidded. "I'll bet you don't remember me."

"I remember you," she spat. "You and your grasping hands."

"I'm going to grasp you again," he told her. "I'll consider it a warm-up before your uncle gets here. He'll see the canoe, be expecting you. I might even be done with you and have a fire going before he gets here. Jaguar Hide's head will be on Deep Hunter's hearth by nightfall. A gift from my clan to his. He will be obliged to me and to Snapping Turtle Clan. I suppose you know, a great many good things come to a hunter who has a Speaker obliged to him."

"I'm carrying a child!"

"Not after today," he told her offhandedly. "I haven't decided yet whether I'll cut it out of you, or just leave it to rot in your body."

"Salamander is married to your kinswomen!"

"No one will know what happens here. Besides, the Speaker and Clan Elder will be making other arrangements for Pine Drop and Night Rain. They're too valuable to waste on your silly Salamander. So, are we going to do this easily, or am I going to have to soften you up a little? Conscious or knocked dumb, it won't matter to me."

With one hand he pulled the knot loose that held his breechcloth. The fabric fell away from his erect penis.

"Do as you will," she murmured, trying to sound broken, wondering how she could turn to lay her fingers on the ax.

"Toss it away." He wiggled his club. "The ax you are wearing. I'm not the fool Saw Back was. Toss it to one side, or the first blow I land will be right in the middle of that big belly of yours."

She bit her lip, a sinking sensation folding around her hammering heart. With half-numb fingers she pulled the ax free, giving it a weak-hearted toss. Was it still close enough?

"Prepare to die, you stinking barbarian bitch." He leered at her, dropped to his knees, and slapped her legs apart. He was reaching for the hem of her kirtle when movement flashed in the corner of Anhinga's vision.

She barely recognized Salamander as he rose behind Eats Wood and swung a stone-headed ax down onto the crown of the man's head. Bone snapped. A violent shiver shot through Eats Wood's body. His eyes popped in surprise. A spasmodic jerk of his legs drove his face into the crushed grass between Anhinga's tense thighs.

She gaped, speechless, glancing back and forth between her husband and the jerking body. Blood, bright and red, welled from the oblong hole in Eats Wood's head. His hair soaked it up like a vibrating brush as his twitching worsened. A gasping rattle came from his throat.

"Are you all right?" Salamander stepped over the man's body.

"I . . ." Words were dead inside her. She could only nod, her eyes fixed on Eats Wood's quivering body. She almost collapsed again when Salamander pulled her to her feet. She shrank against him, burying her face in the hollow of his shoulder and bursting into tears.

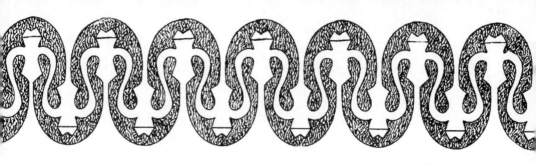

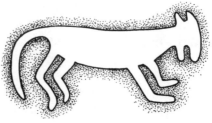

Forty-three

Spots of blue broke the overcast of gray winter clouds. The island, normally her refuge against the world, now felt oppressive, dangerous. Anhinga's souls kept flashing images of the assault. The leering expression on Eats Wood's face hung behind her eyes. She could glance over her shoulder to see the tree. Beneath those branches, Eats Wood's body was growing cold, his empty eyes turning gray.

His angry and frightened souls are rising, staring at me from among those naked branches. A shiver traced down her muscles, as if he were reaching out for her with ghostly fingers.

She didn't feel better. Not even Striped Dart's arrival, a half hand of time ago, reassured her. Salamander sat close beside her. He kept reaching out, patting her in reassurance. When she looked into his eyes, though, she could see the disquiet he tried so hard to hide.

Panther's blood! Why am I still scared? After all I've been through, I shouldn't be shaken by anything!

"Anhinga?" Salamander asked as he leaned forward, searching her face.

"I thought it would be Saw Back," she whispered.

The fire popped, blue smoke rising from the fire pit that separated her from Striped Dart. Her brother looked anything but happy; the deep grooves of worry might have been carved into his forehead. She could tell he didn't approve of the situation. His expression darkened at Salamander's solicitation, as if he begrudged this stranger's intimacy with his sister.

Salamander made a face as he scrubbed Eats Wood's blood from his ax. He kept shooting curious glances at Striped Dart.

In the moons since Anhinga had seen him last, Striped Dart, too, had changed. She didn't remember this long-boned young man, his hair coiled tightly on top of his head. He wore a new puma hide; the gray-brown pelt hung over his shoulders with white belly fur gleaming in the gray light. He had a triangular face, attractive, much like hers but with harder, masculine lines. A stifled anger burned behind his brown eyes and reflected in the set of his jaw. He held an ax in his hand and slapped it against his callused palm.

"I thought I saw movement behind me." Anhinga closed her eyes and hugged her bulging belly protectively.

"I didn't want to get too close," Salamander told her. "It was difficult, racing after you, then having to slow down and wait for you to get out of sight."

"Why didn't you call to me?"

He made a dismissive gesture. "If you had been safe, I would have turned around and left." He inspected his ax, picking at bits of dark red in the binding. "You didn't ask me to come here, Anhinga. This is your time with your own people."

She stared. *Why would you do that? Surely you know I come here to plot against you!* Aloud she said, "I don't understand."

His dark brown eyes seemed to see right through her. Another shiver ran down her spine as he said, "You must be free to follow your heart, Wife. Wherever that takes you. Whatever the price."

By the Sky Beings, what did he mean by that?

"She could have been killed," Striped Dart's accented voice interrupted. "This is too dangerous."

"What do we do, Brother-in-law?" Salamander asked. "If you come farther north, someone—like Eats Wood—will take the opportunity to kill you."

Anhinga glanced back at the oak, feeling the presence of the corpse lying there in the blood-soaked grass. *Snakes! What is Pine Drop going to say? Eats Wood is her cousin.*

Striped Dart finally said, "If she will not come home with me to the Panther's Bones, she is safer staying in Sun Town until the child is born." He looked up at Salamander and smiled. "It would seem that you are more than capable of protecting her."

"When she's not battering her enemies herself," Salamander replied. She could tell from his expression that he didn't feel the levity he projected.

"I was told that you were a fool." Thick muscles slid under

Striped Dart's smooth brown skin. "But my uncle, he sees things differently than I do."

"Many people call me a fool," Salamander replied.

"But you're not, are you?" Striped Dart asked.

Salamander's lips twitched. "Can any of us truly know that he is not a fool, Brother-in-law? I doubt myself all the time."

Anhinga blinked, as if seeing her husband anew. He seemed so controlled, possessed of a calm sadness. He had just killed his first man—one of his own, someone he knew, not a stranger. He sat across from an enemy, yet he might have been comfortably at his mother's fire rather than deep in Swamp Panther territory with the corpse of Pine Drop's cousin weighing on his souls.

Striped Dart's eyes narrowed. "I did not approve of Anhinga going north. I did not approve of this 'peace' of his. Our sandstone is ours, given to us by the Creator at the beginning of the world." Striped Dart shot Salamander a steely look, daring him to disagree.

"You speak truthfully, Striped Dart. I cannot second-guess the Creator's reasons for placing things where he did when he made the world." Salamander stood and slashed his ax through the air to fling the water off, then walked over to lower himself beside Anhinga. He took her hand, rubbing his fingers across her soft brown skin. The touch soothed her as he added, "In Sun Town, we have a need for sandstone."

Striped Dart said bitterly. "Along with your thefts, your people killed my brother—and countless others over the turnings of the seasons!"

"We were wrong." His dark brown eyes seemed to suck up her souls. She felt a tingle run through her as he said, "For that I apologize." He turned his attention to her brother. "Looking back, Striped Dart, one cannot say who started this or who is more wronged. The sandstone is yours. For now Jaguar Hide has offered us safe passage to take one canoe load each moon."

Anhinga took a deep breath, relieved at the cool air pumping into her oddly starved lungs. *Salamander saved my life. This is the second time. I owe him for that.* But how did she balance that against her vow to strike back in the names of Bowfin and her friends? Just being here, in the presence of her brother, rubbed the wound raw again.

Striped Dart was giving Salamander a hot look. "I tell you now— do not come for sandstone again, *Brother-in-law*. My people will kill yours." He made a dismissive gesture. "It is *our* sandstone. Why should we allow you to have it just because you promise not to kill us while you help yourselves?"

"We have a peace," Salamander reminded, "but for one, I do not wish to send my kinsmen where they are not wanted." He steepled his fingers, thinking. "Jaguar Hide told me that we could have one canoe load per moon, but that if we wanted to take two, we would have to send a load of gifts." He glanced at Striped Dart. "You are right, Brother-in-law, it is not equitable."

What are you saying? Anhinga wondered. *That sandstone is one of the few things Owl Clan has left to barter with for obligation!*

Striped Dart opened his mouth, but the hot retort died on his tongue. "I'm right?"

Salamander nodded. "Of course you are. We are getting many things for nothing. I have a beautiful wife, a canoe load of sandstone each moon, and peace. You, my friend, just have the peace from one clan. Mine. It is not fair."

"What are you saying?" Anhinga snapped.

"I'm saying we should renegotiate." Salamander spread his hands wide. "Striped Dart, what if we sent a load of gifts with each trip? What would your people like?"

"Fabrics," Anhinga said quickly. "No one makes fabrics like Sun Town. And dyes. You make the most beautiful dyes. Smoked meat, like the buffalo and elk you have Traded for. My people don't get such luxuries."

"Stone?" Salamander asked, indicating the sharp greenstone celt hafted onto his ax.

"No. We have plenty of our own," Striped Dart answered. "Trading rocks for rocks sounds silly. But these other things?" He looked genuinely interested. "You would do that when you didn't have to?"

"I would, Brother-in-law. I would simply because it is right. And we have to consider safety." Salamander jerked his head toward where Eats Wood lay out in the weeds. "Someday soon, someone like Eats Wood, from one of the other Sun Town clans, will come to raid and steal sandstone. He will come to break the peace, not because he hates the Swamp Panthers, but because it is a way to hurt my clan."

Anhinga asked, "So what will you do? Kill him, too?"

"No, Wife. I will try to be smarter than my enemies." Salamander's brows lowered. "I will only send a canoe on the full moon, Striped Dart. I will always send someone you know: Yellow Spider, Bluefin, one of my kinsmen. If you see a canoe with strangers in it, be wary. My advice would be to avoid it."

"Why? It is our territory. Why should we put up with raiders?"

Salamander let that strange brown gaze of his bore into Striped Dart. To Anhinga's amazement, her brother squirmed, then lowered his eyes.

Salamander spoke in a respectful tone. "The decision is yours, Brother-in-law. I cannot tell you whether or not to attack them, but I would have you consider that so long as this peace lasts between you and me, it is a thorn in the side of the other Sun Town clans. If we break it, they will have won . . . and you won't get fine fabrics and exotic foods in return for your stone."

Anhinga shook her head. "Striped Dart, you can't make this agreement. It is up to Uncle. He is our Elder! When he hears, he'll be furious! He already distrusts you."

"He and I think differently, Sister." Striped Dart had pursed his lips. "I had to beg to get this chance to see you alone. He has the winter solstice to plan for, or he would be here, telling me 'no.' I'm not a child any more than you are. One day, I will be Elder. I want to be a good one."

"We need not tell Jaguar Hide," Salamander said easily. "If there is trouble over the Trade, simply say that Anhinga has talked me into sending it as a 'gift' to my wife's people. Such things are done." His expression went solemn again. "Like you, I am planning not just for this moon, but for many moons in the future."

Striped Dart smiled, reaching out with a strong hand. "Done." Then his smile slipped. "We have one other thing to settle between us. The child."

"Yes?"

"It is ours. A member of my clan. I want my nephew to be raised as a Panther, not as a Sun person. He is to learn our ways, and I am to teach him."

"And if it's a girl?" Anhinga asked.

"Then she is to be raised by Mother."

"Our child will be raised by me!" Anhinga told him sharply. "I will see to its needs." What was she saying? She wasn't going to be in Sun Town for much longer. All she needed was Jaguar Hide's order to act, and she would impliment the plan she had in mind. Immediately she would take a canoe, head for home, and her clan would raise the child.

"You are going to teach my nephew to hunt?" Striped Dart cried. "How to fish and stalk enemies?"

Salamander raised his hands. "This is a matter between the two of you. But know this, Striped Dart, if anything should happen to Anhinga, I will bring you the child as soon as I safely can."

"Why?"

"Because it will be your kin, Striped Dart."

Striped Dart looked confused, as if he fished for thoughts in his head. He asked, "Do you fear me? Is that why you do this?"

Salamander shook his head. "You do not scare me. No, just the opposite. I think that you and I could become great friends in spite of what our peoples have done to each other in the past."

A crooked grin crossed Striped Dart's lips. "You are *not* what I expected." He paused. "I think you should keep my sister safe until the child is born."

"No!" Anhinga started to say. "I have . . ." Her voice trailed off as both men gave her an inquiring stare. To say more was to give away everything. "Very well, tell Uncle I will come after the child is born." Somehow she had been outmaneuvered, placed in a position she didn't want to be in.

Salamander said, "I will send word with the sandstone boat when she will be coming to meet you again. And perhaps I shall send an escort, trusted warriors who will deliver her safely, then stand off. This place"—he gestured around—"is too well known now."

"We think alike." Striped Dart's eyes were hooded. "I didn't agree with Uncle's plan in the beginning. You, Speaker, have shown me that it is good."

"If I can be of service, Striped Dart, if a problem should develop, send word with the stone shipment. Give me a time, and I will meet you here, or send a known representative if I cannot come."

Salamander stood. "I will leave you now. You probably have family matters to discuss."

"You're leaving?" Anhinga cried as she struggled to her feet. "Now?"

"I must get back." He jerked a nod toward the body. "There are things I have to deal with."

Worry tightened in her breast. He couldn't just up and leave her. Not on this island, not with Eats Wood's souls lingering about. "What will you tell Pine Drop and Night Rain?"

"Nothing, Anhinga. I am going to load his body into my canoe. Somewhere, out there"—he indicated the swamp—"he might slip off the side. That's all."

"You can't just ignore it." She thumped her breast in emphasis. "You killed to protect your family! Your child and your honor!"

"Do you think I should announce myself at the Men's House and demand a warrior's tattoos?" He smiled sadly, reaching out and running his fingertips along her cheeks. "This must remain our secret."

"He *attacked* me!"

"Put yourself in Pine Drop and Night Rain's position. I have killed their kinsman. You know the pressure Mud Stalker and Sweet Root are already putting on them. No matter what, Anhinga, I will spare them."

She could only stare in disbelief. He did everything for others. Did he do nothing for himself?

"Wait!" Anhinga turned, looking at Striped Dart. "I am going back with my husband. Brother, take the body, dump it on the way home. Someplace where no Sun Person can stumble across it. That way no bloodstains will be on our canoes when we get back to Sun Town."

"And his canoe?" Salamander pointed to the craft they'd found hidden in the grass.

"Take it, Striped Dart. But you must promise me that you will destroy it." She walked up to him as he rose to his feet. "Do you understand why that is so important to me?"

He nodded. "No one must recognize anything of his in the future. He will just have vanished." A grim smile played on his lips. "Perhaps some large cat was out hunting?"

"You must tell no tales!" she reminded, shaking a finger in his face. "Not one, nothing about what happened here today."

Striped Dart offered his hand to Salamander again. "You have my silence, Speaker, and my sister's respect. A rare combination." A veiled look crossed his eyes. "I look forward to dealing with you in the future."

Salamander reached into his belt pouch. "A token," he offered. "My Spirit Helper. If you ever need anything, send me this carving of Masked Owl."

Striped Dart studied the little potbellied owl he held between thumb and forefinger. "It looks as pregnant as my sister."

"Come, Husband." Anhinga studied the brooding sky. The patches of blue had vanished, and the clouds had taken on a heaviness. "I think it will rain, and in this weather that will be most uncomfortable."

The Serpent

I *am coming to the end of words.*

I breathe slowly. I feel the way I am lying on the floor. I see the un-changing inner stillness that lives in my heart and, like a deer dying in the forest, I find myself absorbed by it. My attention focuses solely on these final moments. My chest rises and falls. My heartbeat pulses in my ears. The voices around me are faint, but pleasing. I thank the ancestors that I am not alone.

There is only one thing I have done in my life that I am truly proud of. I have tried to be a teacher.

I think some of my students actually heard me, though the gods know, listening is not easy. The greatest danger for the Student is thinking he has heard everything perfectly. It takes a long time to understand that the wisest words are not rolls of thunder. They don't strike at the heart like lightning. They are whispers, softly spoken into the ear, easily ignored by the spiritually intoxicated.

Oh, I am old, but I remember that intoxication, that heady rush of certainty. Even now, just thinking about it, I'm a little tipsy.

That's why wisdom sneaks by. We're tipsy. We can feel revelation surging in our veins. Who has time for whispers when the whole world is a divine shout?

Unfortunately, shouts are just air. Genuine spiritual awareness is hard work. It's like quarrying stone beneath a blazing sun, day after day. A man gets tired.

So very tired.

It is just easier to sit down, smile, and think great thoughts in the shade.

The truth, you see, is that revelation isn't fun. Revelation is pain.

I close my eyes.

My vision is growing dim.

I hear voices calling to me from far away. I think I recognize my mother's voice.

I force myself to listen.

I listen for a long, long time.

And finally . . . I swear to you, I do hear the whispers.

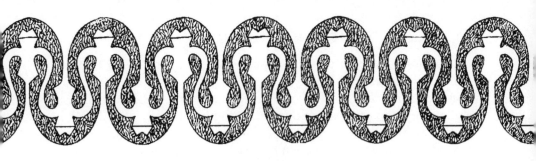

Forty-four

In the Serpent's central fire pit, flames flickered and cast their warm light. Smoke rose, pooling around the rafters and the sacked herbs hanging from the roof.

In the wavering yellow glow, Bobcat sat on his haunches, forearms propped on his knees. A worried look filled his moon-shaped face with its odd, beaklike nose. His mild brown eyes communicated his concern as he looked at the Serpent.

Salamander tried to breathe in shallow gasps. The stench of feces, clotted blood, and closing death permeated the air. Even now, after having been smothered with it for days, it clung in his nostrils.

Death was everywhere. It filled his dreams, creeping out of the corners of his souls. It showed him Eats Wood's face as it rotted in some secret location. In his dreams, he watched the flesh turn brown, soften, and slip from the skull. In off moments, he felt the cracking of bone through the handle as he drove his ax through the top of Eats Wood's head. His souls flinched as the corpse twitched in his memory.

He hadn't expected killing to be like that. Not after the way the warriors spoke. He had found no glory in the murder of Eats Wood. Instead, he was plagued by an aching hollowness, the lingering nightmares, loss, and the bruise of regret.

Now Death lurked here, Dancing with the firelight, slipping among the shadows. It hovered with the smoke in the rafters, clinging to the sooty cane poles as it peered down at the dying Serpent with liquid black eyes.

My friend is dying. Who am I going to talk to now? Salamander's souls ached in anticipation of the coming loneliness.

The Serpent lay on his back, faceup, mouth gaping. Rasping air passed back and forth between his dry lips. His body was little more than bones with a thin leathery skin sagging off them. Only his belly, just left of the navel, was swollen. Scabs showed where Bobcat had punctured the skin, using a stone sucking tube to try and draw out the evil. When Salamander touched the lump, he discovered it was hard, like a rock.

"He said that it entered him sometime ago," Salamander replied wearily. "How could it beat him? He is the strongest of us."

"Sometimes evil is the strongest of all." Bobcat laced his fingers together.

They waited.

The Serpent muttered, half of the words garbled, but now and then a name would come out: that of someone long dead. Or a snatch of conversation, one-sided, as the Serpent babbled to someone only his frantically jerking eyes could see. At other times his limbs moved. He might have been walking in some distant time or place.

"He's talking to the Dead," Bobcat said. "It won't be long now, Salamander."

"Then they are all around us." He looked up at the cloudy smoke, hearing the rain pattering in puddles as it trickled off the roof. Ghosts? All around? Who were they? Was his uncle there? Did White Bird circle in the hazy smoke, looking down at Salamander?

Hello, Brother! Hello, Uncle. Are you there? His souls ached to speak with them again.

Bobcat reached into a bowl of filthy water and squeezed out a red-brown–stained cloth. The stench strengthened in the air. Raising the Serpent's stick of a leg, he wiped at the man's fouled anus and cleaned the slight dribble of urine from his thigh. Finished, Bobcat dropped the cloth back in the water.

"Wolf Dream," the old man gasped suddenly, his eyes flickering. He began to mumble:

> *"Raise the infants to the god in the sky.*
> *Earth, hey, Earth, from it spread,*
> *Raise the Underworld of the Dead."*

A rattle sounded in his throat before he added:

"Flight of the bird, so big so loud.
Calls the lightning from the cloud."

"What is he saying?" Bobcat watched the old man as his mouth opened and closed, the tongue moving pink and silent behind his toothless gums.

Salamander leaned forward. "Serpent, are you saying that Masked Owl calls the lightning?" Coldness ran through him. "Did Masked Owl kill my brother?"

"Yes . . . coming . . . for the seeds . . ."

"The goosefoot seeds?"

The old man's eyes flickered weakly from side to side, the muscles spasming this way and that. "Not time . . ."

"Not time for what?" Salamander asked.

"We don't understand, Elder," Bobcat cried. "What are you trying to tell us?"

Muscles tensed in the Serpent's legs, his limbs pumping weakly then going still. His fingers nibbled, like a dog after a louse.

"Take . . . care, Salamander . . . between the gods." The Serpent shuddered, a croaking in his throat. "To see . . . mushrooms . . ."

The eyes rolled back, whites showing a tracery of blood vessels as the old man's shallow breathing came in weak gasps.

"Mushrooms?" Bobcat turned uneasy eyes on Salamander. "You have journeyed?"

"I rode the clouds with Masked Owl," Salamander replied absently, his souls locked on the Serpent's revelation. "My Spirit Helper? He killed my brother?"

Bobcat had a sick look on his face. "You should be the next Serpent, Salamander. The Elder always favored you."

"You know I cannot, Bobcat. Nothing has changed since the last time we had this conversation. I don't know the Songs, the ceremonies, or the rites. Power wants something different from me." He looked across at the young man, seeing the uncertainty in his eyes, the fear of the future falling so rapidly toward them. "You are the Serpent."

"But this thing between you and Masked Owl? You ride the sky with his wings? You are touched, Salamander. Power has woven itself through your life. You are part of things I cannot comprehend."

"Nor can I. However, I can tell you from my souls, you *must* be the Serpent. For all I know, I may be dead soon."

"Dead?"

Salamander rubbed his face wearily. "When one is caught between warring Powers, one can't count on digesting supper, let alone savoring its taste."

"What do you know?"

Salamander shook his head. "I can feel Death, sense it stalking me. In bits and fragments of Dreams, I am dead, Bobcat. It is coming so quickly—and I have only recently discovered what it means to be alive."

"You look frightened. I'm not used to that in you."

"I just don't know, Bobcat. That is the part that is driving me crazy! What am I supposed to do? What does Power want with me? Why *me*, of all the people to chose from?"

"If the Serpent knows, he's taking the answer with him to the Land of the Dead." Bobcat reached for the smelly cloth and cleaned the old man's anus again.

"The Land of the Dead," Salamander mused, his eyes straying to the lines of pots, stone bowls, and bags with their carefully tended herbs. Reaching over he lifted a thin bit of dried plant from one of the stone bowls, and stared at it with worried eyes.

"You're not thinking of going after him, are you?" Bobcat asked as he recognized the dried mushroom cap.

"I need answers, Bobcat."

"Are you willing to take the risk of losing your souls to get them?"

The Serpent whispered, ". . . *Sing, Sun God, blood rises . . . stingers . . . in the sky . . .* "

Stingers in the sky? The words rolled around Salamander's soul as he fingered the desiccated mushroom cap. *Do the answers lie there? Is that what you are trying to tell me, Serpent?*

A softening of the rattle in the Serpent's lungs was accompanied by a relaxation of his arms and legs.

The old man died.

Rain slanted at an angle. Bobcat's breath fogged as he pranced around the Serpent's house and shook his painted-turtle rattle. He Sang in the old tongue. In better weather he would have carried a torch with him, but the constant drizzle and intermittent rain hadn't let up for days. Clouds hung low overhead, heavy and dark with moisture.

Clan Elders and Speakers were gathered in the front of the crowd, breath misting as they stamped their cold feet in the mud. Cane Frog, Thunder Tail, Sweet Root, Clay Fat: they were all here, clustered around Pine Drop and Salamander to mourn the passing of the Serpent.

Pine Drop's heart ached at the expression on her husband's face. How did he deal with the terrible load that Power had placed upon his shoulders? She had come, hearing that Salamander and Bobcat had finished with the ceremonial preparation of the dead Serpent's corpse. When she had walked up to Salamander, she might have discovered another person inhabiting her husband's body.

Pine Drop shivered and reached out to take Salamander's hand. What was wrong with him? She had never seen him look so odd. He seemed hardly to be aware of the weather, of her, or the people around him. He was wet and clammy, his fabric cloak soaked. Rain dripped from the back of his square bark hat. He looked slack, unresponsive. Unshed tears pooled within his souls. When his eyes met hers, they had a liquid quality that unnerved her.

"Go free, Serpent!" Bobcat called as he ended the Song. Then he ducked into the doorway.

Because of Salamander's prestige as Speaker, he and Pine Drop stood in the front of the crowd and could see inside the low doorway. Bobcat lit a pine-tar torch from the central fire. In the flickering light, the Serpent's carefully stripped bones gleamed where they rested on a wooden rick inside.

Bobcat raised the torch, holding it high so that it ignited the soot-stained interior thatch. For long moments, nothing seemed to happen, then blue smoke began welling out of the gaps between the roof and walls.

Bobcat ducked out, coughing, as thick smoke bellowed from the doorway behind him. He gasped mouthfuls of the cold clear air and sniffed before turning back to watch.

The fuel load overcame the saturated thatch, and a spear of yellow fire leaped up from the dark roof to challenge the sky. Steam hissed and popped. A huge plume rose as a low roar built, and sparks gyrated upward in the white-gray column.

"Good-bye to you, too, old friend." Salamander might have been answering an unheard speaker. He leaned his head back and let the rain pelt his face. "Yes, I hear you just fine. Your words are clear, Serpent. Look at you flying! Take him, Masked Owl. Bless his souls and fly with him to the One."

She glanced around uneasily and squeezed Salamander's hand. "Shhh! People are listening." *Snakes! What is he hearing?* Pine Drop considered the words, wondering what the One was. Then her husband shivered, and she could see pimpled flesh on his thin arms. The welling heat from the burning structure barely seemed to dent the cold.

Clay Fat stood just to their right, his round stomach dwarfing her pregnant belly. He was watching Salamander, puzzlement on his face.

"We'll miss him," Pine Drop said, trying to act as if nothing had happened.

"There won't be another like him anytime soon," Clay Fat replied, then looked up at the spiraling white plume that carried the Serpent's souls to freedom.

"A Serpent is a Serpent," Cane Frog muttered, her unseeing white eye blinking as she reached a hand out to feel the heat.

"Mother!" Three Moss hissed. "Keep your voice down!"

Pine Drop arched a slim eyebrow. *And they think Salamander is an idiot?*

"They think many things, Wife. It is a clutter. Hear them? Like a thousand birds." Salamander turned those eerie wounded eyes on hers.

Surely her thoughts hadn't sent that painful sliver into his souls?

Salamander tilted his head back to stare into the leaden sky. He didn't seem to mind the rain pattering on his open eyes. "One man's idiocy is another's Dream." A pause. "They have never seen the world from above."

Was anyone else hearing this? She looked past Salamander to where Mud Stalker stood with his mangled arm wrapped in warm fox hide. Uncle wore a conical hat that shed rain in all directions. His prune-sour expression reflected distaste at the event, the weather, and life in general. Everyone's spirits were down, as waterlogged as everything else in their world during the endless winter rain.

Deep Hunter and Thunder Tail stood next in line. It seemed like everywhere Thunder Tail went, Deep Hunter showed up.

He is being wooed. That knowledge sobered her. Too many things were changing. Even Mud Stalker and Deep Hunter—who had been lifelong rivals, barely sharing a civil word—stood together like brothers.

"They are hardly brothers, Wife," Salamander said absently, his dreamy eyes on the rising smoke and steam.

Snakes! I never spoke!

Salamander's tongue stumbled over the words. "You Dreamed it."

A sudden fear tightened around her souls as her eyes darted warily around. Her heart began to race, a fear, colder than the rain, tickling her skin.

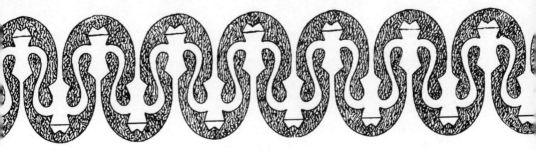

Forty-five

With a whoosh, one-half of the Serpent's roof let go. People stepped back as sparks and bits of burning thatch began sprinkling down from the sky.

"Come," Pine Drop said, tightening her grip on Salamander's hand. "You are cold, Husband. You have been up caring for the Serpent for a night and a day without sleep. You have done your duty."

"He's here. See him flying? Right here around us." Salamander raised his other hand, his finger pointing up into the rain. "Go in peace, my old friend."

Pine Drop jerked him hard enough to pull him off-balance. It took all of her strength to keep him from falling into the mud. People were watching, curiosity in their somber black eyes.

"What's wrong with you?" Pine Drop demanded as she tried to lead him away with some semblance of dignity.

"He was the only one who . . ." He caught himself, pinching his mouth closed.

"Who could understand?" she asked. "Is that what you were trying to say?"

He clamped his jaws, his huge glazed eyes looking back at the flames. Thunder! What was he seeing? Surely nothing of this world.

"Nothing of this world," he whispered.

She tugged insistently on his arm, desperate to get him away as fast as his ill-balanced tottering feet would carry him. By force of will she overpowered his reluctance to leave.

"Salamander, I would talk to you." She kept glancing around, trying to hide her fear, telling herself it was nothing. He was tired. That was all. Grief left him dazed, his souls crying for his lost teacher and friend.

Snakes help them if anyone heard his disjointed rambling!

"You have done enough! Come home. Anhinga and Night Rain have fixed something special."

"There is no hurry. The buffalo tongue hasn't baked all the way through yet." He might have been talking to a shadow. "I just have to make sure that he knows . . ."

"He knows, Husband. You and Bobcat made sure." She nearly jerked him off his feet again, aware of the stare that Clay Fat and Three Moss gave them. The latter had already leaned to whisper into Cane Frog's ear. When the old woman died, would Three Moss continue leaning over to whisper, even if only the empty air heard?

"It is her way," Salamander said simply.

The roar inside the Serpent's house was dying as Pine Drop pulled him down the ridge, their feet slopping in the silt. As they passed, rain dribbled from house roofs to patter into ring-shaped puddles around the walls. Wet dogs lay in the scant shelter of the overhang before the house doors, looking cold, miserable, and starved.

"He told me so many things," Salamander said half to himself. "He opened my eyes to the One."

"The One?" He seemed to be half out of his head. Snakes, his souls weren't coming loose like his mother's, were they?

"The One," he whispered in assent. "The Dance. The place where Dreams cross." He smiled sadly. "What I would give! Oh, Pine Drop, I don't want to die. If I could only rise and fly away from all this. Just spread my wings . . . and fly!"

"I think your souls are loose enough already." She tightened her grip on his hand. She had to tug to keep him moving as they passed the head of the second ridge. His house huddled in the rain before them, faint threads of smoke lost in the downpour. She had kindled a fire there, just in case the rain stiffened. As it had.

She led him to the door and set it aside, ducked into the dark interior with him, and reset the cane door behind them. In the gloom she stepped over to the woodpile. Placing several lengths on the glowing coals, she made the awkward descent around her pregnant belly to blow the embers to life. As the flames licked the logs with yellow light, she looked up. His eyes were large and hollow, his expression vacant. Water dripped off him to spatter on the ash-stained floor in little round star bursts.

She grunted as she stood up. He seemed oblivious, so she took the rain hat off his head. "You are soaked clear through, Salamander."

"His souls were loose," he said in that oddly detached voice. "He didn't know who we were. One minute he was fighting evil spirits, the next he was grinning, curing people long dead. He was talking to the Dream Souls of the Dead. I never really understood. They're here, right in the air around us."

She took the wet cloak from his shoulders, shocked by its sodden weight, and laid it next to the fire to dry. She plucked the knot loose on his breechcloth and pulled the wet fabric from between his legs. Setting it aside, she positioned him over the fire, where the warm heat and smoke rose along his shivering naked body. Trickles of water ran down his skin, reflecting like silver veins in the firelight. Droplets beaded silver in his pubic hair.

"Stand there while I find you dry things." She waddled around to his bed and retrieved his buffalo hide. Wrapping it across his shoulders, she made sure the edges were well clear of the flames and backed onto the bench. Stripping off her own cloak, she realized she was as wet as he.

"Snakes, it feels good to be alone with you again." She glanced at him. "What is happening to you? Salamander? Please, tell me."

"You said Anhinga and Night Rain were expecting us?" At least that thought was lucid. Maybe his belly was eating through his grief.

"They are at my house. We thought it better. The food is there." *And I have you alone for the first time in weeks.*

"They do not expect us yet. Night Rain has just stepped outside. She can see the smoke plume through the rain."

"How do you know that? You can't see through walls—let alone that far across the plaza."

"She doesn't think we're coming yet. She's ducking inside, telling Anhinga we will be longer."

"Salamander, you are frightening me! It's as if you can hear my thoughts. Talk to me. Are you well?" *Just tell me that the spirits haven't taken possession of your souls!*

The corners of his lips curled, threads of smoke rising from the confines of the tentlike buffalo hide. "I am the only one in possession of my souls. They bind me like rawhide. They suffocate me. It is so hard to breathe."

"What?" She placed a hand to her breast, searching his eyes for an answer.

"My souls are cages, like fish traps. I can't get free of them."

"I don't understand."

"You've never flown," he whispered sadly, and closed his eyes.

"Flown?" she asked. "How did you fly?"

"Masked Owl comes. He shows me the way." His eyes were still closed, expression turning blissful. "Why can't I ever do it on my own? Why can't I break the cages that surround my souls?"

"Because you'll die," she cried.

"Death is release." He smiled. "I never understood until the Serpent told me."

"You really did talk to his souls?"

"It isn't like speaking, Pine Drop. It's different. Dreaming. I Dreamed him. I Dreamed them all. Saw into their souls."

"What do you mean, Dreamed them all? The other Speakers? The Clan Elders?"

"They are so bitter. Their souls taste like green walnut rind. They leave a yellow cast within me."

She nodded. "So many hands are raised against you, and I never hear a cross word, never see your temper flash. And sometimes, like today, you are gone somewhere, flying on Masked Owl's wings, I think."

She saw his smile growing. Her words had touched him.

"Salamander? They are drawing the net around you. You know that, don't you?"

He gave the barest nod.

"You can't just let them trap you."

"I am who I am." He was talking to emptiness again, eyes still closed. "I learn, watch, and absorb the lessons. I am Salamander, the one never seen. I have Danced with the mushrooms. I am floating."

"Mushrooms?" she asked, heart tapping hard against her breastbone. "What mushrooms?"

"I see your soul, Pine Drop. I see our daughter's life, glowing like an ember inside you."

You really are scaring me.

"I'm sorry. You have no reason to fear me."

Are you a mystic, or an idiot?

"You must understand: I am caught between Masked Owl and Many Colored Crow. The Serpent told me the night he died. Masked Owl killed White Bird."

"What?" She was suddenly oblivious to the water that ran down her forearms from the soggy fabric.

"He was warned, but his pride wouldn't let him stop. The goosefoot seeds, they would have changed this place. Changed us as a people. Masked Owl doesn't think it's time. So he killed White Bird."

"What are you talking about?"

"The Brothers, the Hero Twins. Born of Light, Born of Dark. Wolf Dreamer, Raven Hunter: the Two who make One."

"You see this in the Dream?"

"Yes."

"You're a Serpent?"

"No. I am the place where Dreams cross." His smile seemed to cast a glow into the gloomy interior.

"But . . . but Masked Owl. He is your Spirit Helper," she stammered, trying to understand. "And he *killed* your brother?"

"It is a battle for the souls of men. Just like the one being fought here. Between the clans. Power sways and rises, like mating copperheads, twining and spinning, Dancing, and pulling apart. Look at it! So very beautiful—and so deadly! We are all part of the One, forever split apart, lonely, yet united. I see now. I begin to understand."

He spread his arms wide. The buffalo robe unfolded like huge wings.

She gasped at the sight of his naked body. Lit from below, his thighs, the tip of his penis, his bony rib cage, and his jaw glowed orange. Shadows were cast across the hollows of his hips, over the twin arcs of his breasts. His eyes were hidden in blackness atop his lighted cheeks, his brow golden under a dark forehead. A man of fire and shadow, he stood before her, and she felt Power swelling within him.

"Salamander?" she asked timidly.

"Summer," he said suddenly. "I have until the solstice. They will move then."

"How can you fight them?" She shook her head. "Salamander, they are suspicious of me, but even I know that every clan is being turned against you. Deep Hunter is rabid, especially after Anhinga wounded and scarred Saw Back." She clenched her teeth. "The Speaker, my uncle, suspects you of murdering Eats Wood. The young man has disappeared, and no one knows where."

She was watching his face, searching for any reaction as she asked, "Did you have words with him? Did he threaten you?"

"I said nothing to him."

She heaved a sigh. "Snakes, I was worried."

His head tilted, the birdlike image ever sharper. "You may have to choose: Light, or Dark. You may have to Dream with us."

She closed her eyes, souls dulling. *Blessed Sky Beings, what am I involved in here?* "Don't ask me to go against my clan, Salamander. Don't put me in that position."

"Would you chose the clan," he asked, "or the People?"

"I am nothing without the clan. Kinship is who we are. Without it, we are lost. Nothing. Faceless and nameless."

"Nothingness is all there is," he told her sadly. "It is the One. You can only understand when you Dance with it. The clans, this struggle to dominate, it is all empty, Pine Drop. In the end, it is as bitter as a green nightshade stem. Illusion, spinning around us like a waterspout."

"So you will just let them destroy you?"

"You stand at the center of the world, Pine Drop. When the time comes, you will reach out and pick a direction."

"What are you talking about?"

"The navel," he answered. "The place where life starts, and peoples are born. Something special is happening here. See it growing? Carried by the Trade, borne by the bonds we form. The future flows from within our ridges. Like that infant in your womb, Pine Drop, we have made the future. Sun Town is the starting point. The clans don't understand. They are bound, circumscribed by their mighty mounds."

"Is that bad?" she felt herself lost, adrift in the peculiar ideas spinning out of his Dream.

"When the time comes, you can reach out to them. Accept their canoes, and make the future."

"I can reach out to whom? What are you talking about?"

"I can Dream the future, Pine Drop. *You* have to *live* it!"

Blessed Owl, tell me he is not insane!

As the words formed in her souls, he threw back his head and laughed.

Sick! So very sick! Salamander curled on his side, eyes closed against the violence in his aching head. He kept one arm on his stomach, feeling the painful knots that had tied themselves in his guts. Between breaths, they pulled tight, only to twist and then loosen. The watery tickle of vomit hung behind his palate.

"Salamander?" Anhinga's voice came from far away. He barely felt her cool hand on his sweat-ridden forehead. "I went for help."

Anhinga? Where had she come from? Where was he? Floating. Floating above a dark pool of death.

"How are you feeling?" Pine Drop asked, also from a distance.

"Can't . . . Dance . . ." he whispered, and in his fractured souls, the images of what he had experienced tried to form. Like bent and distorted memories, they wavered and refused to coalesce. As if part of his souls could just reach out. There. In the red-black haze beyond his consciousness.

"Drink this." The thick rim of a ceramic cup was placed to his lips.

He opened his eyes to slits. The misery of white light burned the backs of his eyeballs, searing his thoughts into charred meat. Cool liquid rolled around his tongue, only to make him gag as he tasted the bitterness. Nevertheless, he drank, each swallow knotted agony, until the cup was pulled away. He let his eyelids slide closed, accepting small relief in the hot acid darkness.

I am sick. Dying. The mushrooms are going to kill me, I wasn't strong enough. Help me! Help! By all the Beings in the Sky and Earth, Help me!

His calls echoed away like thunder over a distant and dark land.

He felt himself turning, ever so slowly as his body slipped away. His souls had begun to float, carried on the waves of fever, spasms, and chill. A burning sensation, like half-dead embers, lay heavily on his gut.

A dull glow—like a forest burning in the distance shone crimson in the darkness.

Dying.

The glow continued to grow, filling the horizons of his consciousness.

Help!

"Help you with what?" a crone's reedy voice asked.

Why are the mushrooms killing me this time?

"Because they want you to die."

He focused the eye of his Dream Soul, and saw her—a shadow behind the red glow.

Who are you?

"I have been called differently by different Dreamers. In the beginning I was 'Spirit Woman' to some. 'Witch' to others. Wolf Dreamer knew me by the name of old Heron. Other names have come and gone through the passing of ages."

What are you doing here?

"I heard you call, boy. It happens, with the ones who have Power."

I called you?

"Not by name," she told him.

He could see her now. She didn't look like the old woman her voice suggested, but beautiful, with gleaming black eyes that danced with internal light. Sharp cheekbones made soft angles over her full mouth and delicate chin. Hair, in a raven wealth, tumbled from her head and pooled around her shoulders before spilling down to her waist. Her high breasts and narrow waist were partially hidden by a white bearhide that she draped around her naked flanks.

You are beautiful!

"Not as beautiful as Broken Branch was." She smiled, and he felt his souls soaring. "I can appear as I please. For the moment, it pleases me to appear as I was, before I tripped over love and fell facefirst into the Dream."

Are you one of the Sky Beings?

"Older." She stepped closer in a fluid grace. "I was there at the beginning. I have been here since, tied to Power. I came before First Woman, before First Man. I was there before Runs In Light Dreamed the Wolf. I have Sung the Sacred Bundles, and watched the world change. I have seen the final Dance of the mammoth, mastodon, sloth, and short-faced bear. I have loved and cursed the People, and tricked and beguiled the Dreamers as they came and went. I have Danced between the Hero Twins." She smiled, and the radiance of it melted his heart. "As you now Dance between them."

You mean Masked Owl and Many Colored Crow?

"They, too, have had many names." She cocked her head, exposing her perfect throat. "Who are you, boy?"

Salamander.

"You are aptly named." Her dark gaze sharpened like obsidian. "Powerful, boy. The golden haze of the mushrooms surrounds you. Dangerous things, mushrooms. They live off Death, grow out of rot and corruption. They are rebirth, Salamander. Treat them with respect. Never toy with them. The most Powerful Dreaming of all comes of Dancing with the mushrooms. Unless you become the One, they will kill you."

Sick. So sick. Pain is tying knots in my body. My bones and muscles ache. My souls . . . they are floating up into Death.

"Why did you wish to Dance with brother mushroom? What were you trying to do, Salamander?"

I wanted to Dream. To fly on Masked Owl's wings. I wanted a vision! To see the channels of the future. I must know why Masked Owl gave me such gifts—and killed my brother. Why did Many Colored Crow warn me? What does Power want of *me? How can I do what is right when I don't know what Power wants?*

She was so close now, he could almost reach out and touch her. He had never seen skin so beautiful, soft, and sleek. Her perfect round breasts rose and fell behind the white bear's hide. "Do you ask for yourself, for your own gain? Is it glory you seek? Fame? Authority or prestige?"

I just need to understand, Heron! That is all. I want to know what to do. What is right. For everyone.

"My poor young Dreamer, are you truly so naive? People are good and evil at the same time, in the same breath, in a single heartbeat. Justice for one is injustice for another."

Would you help me?

"What would you give for my help?" She gave him a predatory stare.

Fear stabbed through him. *Whatever you asked.*

"Would you give your life? Would you let me destroy you? What if I say I will help, and let brother mushroom take you here, now? Alone? Will you give me your souls here, in the darkness?"

How did he answer that? How could he do the right thing if he were dead? How could he make things better if he didn't understand? How could he find the One?

"Ah, the One? That is a different matter entirely." She laughed, the sound so musical his souls ached at the beauty. "You are not even close to finding the One, Salamander. You have a long, long way to go." Her expression saddened. "And no one among your people to teach you. Like me, you must find it on your own."

Grief stung him.

Heron's gleaming eyes ate through his souls, turning him inside out, seeing into the corners, behind his thoughts. Fear paralyzed him, and he cried out. In that instant, he felt himself vanishing, burning away under the heat of her blazing dark eyes.

She's eating me! She is devouring my souls. Terror, horrible engulfing terror, filled him as she violated every corner of his souls, eviscerated his memories and thoughts, and inspected his most private fantasies. Bit by bit she tore pieces out of him the way a fisherman plucked guts from a catfish's belly.

It seemed an eternity before she backed away, leaving him whimpering and weak like a wounded puppy. Her chin was down, brow furrowed. This time her eyes didn't violate him, but simply watched in a passive stare.

After an eternity she said, "You are an unusual young man, Salamander." She paused. "You would have made a great Dreamer."

I won't be a Dreamer? Nothing had prepared him for the sense of loss that washed atop his fear.

She smiled then, an expression of pity on her perfect lips. "Nothing comes without a price."

A feeling of despair washed through him. How did he chose between Dreaming and helping his people? How did he know what was right. *It would be easier to let brother mushroom kill me.*

"It would." Her smile challenged him. "Is that your choice?"

No. I will live.

"Once upon a time, I, too, followed the path you have taken. Brother mushroom can show you a great many things, but unless you are trained, it is illusion. Not to be taken lightly."

I know.

"I will help you Dance with brother mushroom's Power. We will have to do this together, you, and I, and brother mushroom."

Thank you!

"Do not thank me, Salamander. My help will rouse jealousies. Wolf Dreamer and Raven Hunter rarely join forces, but my interference could be enough to ally them against you."

Who?

"You know them as Masked Owl and Many Colored Crow. They are the Hero Twins, the brothers of Light and Dark. Terrible things happen when opposites are crossed."

She reached out, her slim fingers tracing his cheek. Waves of cool relief washed through him. Had he ever felt such pleasure?

"You cannot escape brother mushroom by yourself, Salamander." She stepped closer, her ethereal body a hand's breadth from his. Her dark eyes sucked at his souls. "You do not know the way to the One. I will have to Dance it with you. In the process, you can see the channels of the future. I warn you now, it will come at a price, young Salamander. Will you pay it?"

Yes.

He was aware of the white bearhide as she wrapped it around them, pulling his souls against hers, locking them together. He opened his mouth to cry out.

And then . . . ecstasy!

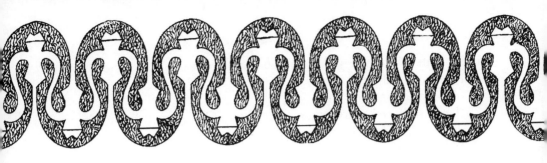

Forty-six

Secrets! The whole world was filled with secrets! Night Rain
fumed, but it did little good. She kept her own secrets, while the
secrets of others remained hidden from her. She didn't want to be
here, out in the cold gray day, pinned in place by her uncle. Alone,
she had to bear that hard penetrating look in his eyes.

Mud Stalker clamped a hand on her shoulder. "You must have
heard something about Eats Wood?"

"I can tell you honestly that I have never heard my husband or
Anhinga mention Eats Wood. Not once."

Uncle's gaze pricked at her souls like a copper needle. "He vanished the last time that barbarian bitch left Sun Town, Niece." His
eyes narrowed. "You and I, I thought we had a special relationship.
Especially after our last little talk."

Like a fish in a weir, she could feel bars rising to catch her. "I
would hope that we do, Uncle."

He shook his head, glancing around at the blustery brown day.
"I raised you better. Think, woman, what could you possibly owe
that barbarian bitch? And after what she did to you? The way she
humiliated you?"

Night Rain bit her lip.

"What are you hiding?" Mud Stalker shifted, leaning back.
"Don't trifle with me, woman. I've been at this game for so long I
can smell deception."

"I swear to you on my souls that I haven't heard a single word about Eats Wood from anyone! Salamander hasn't mentioned him. Neither has Anhinga!"

"And your sister?"

"I can only tell you that she doesn't think Salamander had anything to do with his disappearance."

"What does Deep Hunter say?"

"I haven't seen him since I went home to my husband."

"And Saw Back?"

"I haven't seen him either, and I don't want to."

He watched her through narrowed eyes. "For the right reasons I could be tempted to support a divorce. Owl Clan couldn't deny us—and that silly Moccasin Leaf would agree to fly off to the moon if I asked her to. She is desperate to curry our favor."

"No, Uncle."

"What?"

She glared at him. "I will stay with Salamander." Assuming she could figure out who this new Salamander was. During his illness, something had changed. When he looked at her now, it was with a longing that melted her souls. She could feel it, a sensation of Power that spun around him. It was as if he could touch a winter-dry stem, and it would burst into bloom.

Uncle, his eyes narrowed, might have heard her thoughts the way Pine Drop claimed that Salamander had heard hers. "What is it, Night Rain? Snakes and poison! I'm your uncle. You can tell me. What hold does he and that cunning barbarian witch have on you and Pine Drop? Is it witchcraft? Some spell he's cast on the two of you?"

"He is my husband," she replied softly. "I can't . . . well you wouldn't understand." Snakes! How did she explain to her hard-eyed uncle that no matter what happened in their bed, but for Salamander's goodwill she'd be a laughingstock throughout Sun Town? That in his arms, she was safe from the guffaws and jokes?

Mud Stalker studied her thoughtfully. "I saw him the day of the old Serpent's cleansing. He was hearing things, talking to the air. His eyes were vacant, as hollow as the Land of the Dead. Pine Drop was so frightened she dragged him away—and then he was out of sight for days, rumor said he was sick."

"He was." Night Rain swallowed hard. "He ate mushrooms. Something he found at the Serpent's after cleaning the bones. It did something to him."

"I see. Are you sure it wasn't poison? Something a witch would be involved in?"

"Salamander? A witch? No, Uncle, he's no witch." *But what is he?* That question had begun to preoccupy so many of her thoughts.

"You are protecting him! Why? What has he done to you?"

"Nothing!"

He grunted, lips pressed in thin anger.

"I have told you the truth." She could feel sweat beginning to warm her armpits, and the flush that rose in her face.

"Yes," he hissed. "I see. The truth." He paused, as if an idea had been born in his head. "A witch would have many ways to bend people to his will. And, what if . . ."

"What if what?" she demanded, a feeling of unease creeping through her.

Mud Stalker's smile took on a predatory look. "If I asked you to make a choice, would you choose to serve your clan, or Salamander?"

"The clan," she insisted doggedly.

He chuckled then, a coldness in his eyes. "Remember this day, Niece. I will hold you to your words."

She breathed a sigh of relief when he stalked off. But what had been behind that last hard look?

Salamander sat with his back to the clay-daubed wall and watched his mother as she worked at her loom. Her hair, once so dark and perfectly kept, now reminded him of dirty cottonwood seed, wind-blown and tumbled. Her face had sagged. He thought the tissue that had once held it to the bone had grown tired and no longer cared.

A yellow fire popped in the central hearth, sending sparks to dance up toward the rafters. Above him the packed thatch slumbered under a blanket of soot. Bags and netting hung from the high poles, preserving the last of the pecans and acorns against the coming of spring. The other bags he remembered from fall had disappeared over the winter.

His mother's bed, on the west side of the house, was unkempt, as if she'd just thrown the buffalo robe to one side and gone about her work.

"I have come to understand something," Salamander said. "About you. I began to understand the night I watched the Serpent's souls rising. With the help of the mushrooms, I could hear his souls."

His mother slapped at her ear as if pestered by a mosquito.

"I think you tried so hard to talk to Uncle Cloud Heron that your Dream Soul slipped into the realm of the Dead. When White Bird died, he took the last of your world with him. I understand why you would want to send your souls after White Bird and Cloud Heron." He paused. "I have seen the different paths of the future, Mother. I have to make some terrible choices. It would be so easy just to let go."

She tilted her head, her fingers using the shuttle to pass more of the white thread through the warp. If he listened intently, he could hear the soft hum of the Lotus Gathering Song coming from deep in her throat.

"I want you to know that I don't blame you." He looked down at his thin hands. "Since I Danced the One with brother mushroom and old Heron, I have been haunted by what is coming. There is a very good chance that I will lose everything: my wives, my children, my family and clan. How am I supposed to choose between my life and a Dream?"

She plucked a knot out of the weave, part of a pattern of interwoven flowers and swooping eagles.

"I caught a faint glimpse of myself in the future. Old, wise, and surrounded by my children and grandchildren. At that moment, I knew complete contentment. I was surrounded by love the way a person is bathed with golden morning sunshine in the spring. I had this knowledge that I had lived my life to the fullest. My souls were bursting, and my wives were smiling their love at me. It was so wonderful!"

He smiled at the glorious ache of happiness.

Wing Heart mouthed words, lips moving silently.

"Another part of the vision let me share the One. Old Heron Danced me through it. You cannot imagine! Mother, it is bliss. Like flying while weighing nothing. The purity of that brief instant makes a part of my souls crave it with a hunger you can't conceive." He shook his head. "No words will describe the silent thunder of its beauty. How can I give that up?"

She began to hum louder. He could see the thin muscles in her neck and imagine the brittle bones under that sagging skin.

"Another fragment of the vision showed me Sun Town, tens of tens of tens of years from now. All that was left was unbroken forest. The People were scattered, living in little villages among the trees. We no longer built our giant earthworks, no longer built monuments to the Creator and the Sky Beings. The Trade was dead. Each tiny band feared its neighbors. They lived in isolation." He shook his head. "They had lost their souls, Mother. Had lost that inner strength that told them who they were. I felt such emptiness."

He watched Mother's long fingers. Never had anyone seen such fabrics as those that came off of Wing Heart's loom after she lost her souls. The weave, so tightly packed, could hold water. The intricate designs she wove into the warp and weft were magical. The creatures she created looked real. Even the texture of feathers could be seen in the pattern of threads she used to make her birds. Veins filled the leaves and flowers. With a fingertip, one could trace the texture of bark on the stems she wove.

"I caught another flash of the future. Of all the bits and pieces of visions, this is in many ways the hardest to explain. The people were so different. They lived for one ruler, crushing all others under their feet for his glory. Imagine what the clans would be like if instead of obligation, they used force to achieve their ends. What makes that future enticing is the size of the cities, the splendor of the high mounds and great buildings. I see canoes so huge they carry tens of tens, and cross the oceans to the ends of the world. We could be so great." He shook his head. "Imagine your great-grandchildren raising mounds in the distant lands. Imagine them speaking your name in barbarian languages."

Wing Heart smiled despite her empty eyes. Her lips must have felt something the rest of her body did not.

"I don't understand how the visions are linked together yet. The choices I make will influence those futures. To make one come true, I must give up something else. I just don't know how it all fits together." He leaned his head back, an emptiness in his breast. "I can see the coming trial. I know what they have in store for me. I have seen it, Mother. When I flew with Masked Owl, I caught glimpses, but only those that Masked Owl wanted me to see. When Heron and I Danced with brother mushroom, I saw the whole future unfolding like a magnolia flower in the morning."

She chuckled under her breath, hearing something in her imagination. The twitching of her lips slowed, humor in her eyes before it faded to blankness.

"I understand why you made the choice you did. I wish I could choose the past, too. It would be so easy." Salamander frowned down at his hands. "I could tell Heron that I wanted to Dance the One. She could take me away from all of this. How does a lone man make that decision? How can Power expect me to choose misery over paradise?"

Wing Heart gave him no answer.

"Oh, Mother, how I envy you."

Mud Stalker lay with his back pressed into the rounded stern of the canoe and peered out through the screen of cane and grass that had been tied around their craft. He fingered the hard knot of his bola with his good left hand. The weapon lay on his flat stomach. The bola was a series of three leather thongs the length of a man's arm, each tied with a round stone at the end. When thrown, it rotated through the air like a three-legged spider to ensnare whatever it encountered.

In the bow, Clay Fat lay with his bulk wedged between the gunwales. The Rattlesnake Clan Speaker made the bow float considerably lower in the muddy shallows than Mud Stalker's stern.

On the strengthening southern winds, the migratory fowl were riding their way northward toward spring. Sun Town lay at the southern end of the great flyway. This was just the beginning of the great migration. For days the flocks would blacken the sky, Vs of birds winging northward. From it the people harvested any number of ducks, geese, coots, cormorants, herons, and other species.

Mud Stalker's clan had used this old choked channel for many turnings of the seasons. Last night he and his kin had strung nets along three sides of the narrow cove. The netting was stretched from tree to tree, and propped on posts to overhang the brackish water.

The open end that emptied onto a sluggish channel had two screened blinds at the entrance: One that he and Clay Fat rested behind, and the other, opposite them, where Red Finger and Thumper waited, their canoe obscured with a similar willow, grass, and cane blind.

In the middle of the trap, duck decoys made of feathers, wood, and bundled reeds floated in a fair imitation of a flock.

Mud Stalker's party had been here, waiting for more than a hand of time. Two flocks had gone winging past, neither falling for the bait.

Red Finger clicked a warning that brought Mud Stalker alert.

He heard the rasping of wings before he spotted the ducks—mallards all—flying up the main channel. Immediately Thumper began his quacking and chattering. Of all the hunters in Snapping

Turtle Clan, none was as talented when it came to calling ducks.

To Mud Stalker's delight, the flock turned, wheeled overhead, and came swooping in to land just past the decoys.

"Be ready!" Mud Stalker whispered as he loosened the cord that held their blind up. He would have to drop the blind, grab the knot of his bola, straighten, and cast as if in one motion.

"Ready!" Clay Fat said in a breathy exhale.

In heartbeats the ducks would detect the ruse. Mud Stalker, as hunt leader, watched the ducks as they splashed to a halt behind the decoys. Paddling, they turned to inspect the decoys. They couldn't have been more perfectly placed in the trap.

Thumper was continuing his calling, making the sounds ducks made by blowing air past his cheeks, onto the back of his hand, and clicking his tongue.

"Now!" Mud Stalker called, letting the blind fall and sitting upright. As he rose he grasped the center of his bola, whirling it around his head. The taut thongs hissed as they tore through the air.

The ducks began to bolt, reaching out with their wings as they turned away from the falling blinds.

Mud Stalker made his cast. From long practice, the whirling stones, bound by their leather thongs, sailed out, neatly wrapping around the nearest mallard, fouling her wings.

Clay Fat, too, cast—then capsized their canoe as he floundered out into the knee-deep water.

Mud Stalker clawed for balance, then closed his eyes as cold murky water rolled over him. He thrashed, twisted his way upright, and managed to get his feet under him. As he shot up out of the water, he flipped his head to clear his vision.

Clay Fat was howling, sloshing like a giant buffalo through the water. Mud churned in his wake. Across from them, Red Finger and Thumper were likewise charging forward, waving their arms and howling.

Retreat cut off, the panicked ducks flapped and paddled, taking off straight into the overhanging nets. As they entangled themselves, the net was pulled loose, dropping down over the frightened birds.

"YoooYaaah!" Clay Fat yelled, splashing from foot to foot in the waist-deep water. Mud Stalker ran his hand over his wet face. Next time the big oaf could wait in a blind onshore. He looked back at the capsized canoe, the gunwales just breaking water, then waded over and grabbed up his bola-entangled duck. He grasped the duck by the head, whirling it around and around until he broke the bird's neck. Then he unwound the leather thongs from the wings.

Ahead of them, the mallards thrashed in the net. In a line, the men waded forward, taking the ends of the netting and gathering it in.

"Where's your canoe?" Thumper asked as he floated his up to the catch.

"Underwater." Mud Stalker jabbed a thumb over his shoulder.

"There's a lot of me to get out of a canoe in a hurry," Clay Fat said with a wide grin. "It was faster just to turn it over."

"And drown me in the process," Mud Stalker growled, but he could see Clay Fat's delight. The Rattlesnake Clan Speaker was happy. Against that, a dunking in the water hardly mattered.

One by one they retrieved the terrified ducks from the netting, breaking their necks and tossing their spasming carcasses into Thumper's canoe. In the end, they had trapped three tens and eight, a nice morning's work. The feathered mound in the middle of Thumper's canoe gleamed cream, brown, and greenish blue in the light. In the pile of ruffled wings he could see orange-webbed feet, yellow bills agape, and the green-headed males, their eyes dimming and half-lidded in death.

Feathers from the spring molt drifted in the calm air and dotted the roiled water.

"Come," Clay Fat called to Mud Stalker as Thumper and Red Finger began drawing in the net, neatly folding it between them. "Let us right your canoe. They can take the catch, we'll carry the net."

"If you don't sink us again."

It took but a moment to lift one end, shipping the water out. The knuckle's worth that sloshed in the bottom didn't seem to bother Clay Fat as he carefully climbed aboard. Their paddles were recovered from where they floated under the crushed blind.

Slipping over the stern, Mud Stalker seated himself and tucked his paddle under his right arm, using his left awkwardly to maneuver the craft around. They paddled up to where Red Finger and Thumper waited. The two men carefully lifted the wet net and settled it amidships.

"Don't lose Clay Fat's ducks on the way back to Sun Town," Mud Stalker warned. "The Speaker will sink your canoe next time."

That brought a round of good-humored laughter from everyone.

"Are you sure you want to give me all of those ducks?" Clay Fat asked, as they paddled out to the main channel.

"You seemed to take the greatest pleasure in the hunt. I still have ducks from last fall. Snakes, my sister keeps insisting on boiling one every ten days. I'm tired of duck meat."

"But these are fresh. Not dried and covered with soot. They won't taste like smoke and mold."

Mud Stalker laughed, making his irregular strokes with his paddle. "Enjoy them. It is a gift from Snapping Turtle Clan to you, Speaker."

"We are obligated."

"Can I ask you a question?"

"Of course."

"Clay Fat, were you and Wing Heart ever lovers?"

"No." A cautious pause. "Why do you ask?"

He jerked his head back, indicating Thumper's canoe where it followed a couple of lengths behind them. "My cousin back there was married to her for a while. In a fit, one night, she divorced him. I think she was mad at me and took it out on Thumper. It hurt him more than he ever admits. I think he really loved her."

"We were never lovers." Clay Fat sounded sad.

"Just . . . what? Friends?"

"Yes. I always admired her. I enjoyed just sitting, talking to her. Some of those times were the best in my life. I can remember the dark sparkle in her eyes, the way her throat looked when she laughed. In all of my Dreams I would never have thought she'd have lost her souls like she did. She was so strong. I thought she was the smartest Clan Elder I'd ever met."

"From your voice, I can tell you liked her." He made a face. "She and I fought like weasels."

"She always enjoyed beating you."

"I'm sure. That's why, in the end, I let her win."

"Indeed?" Clay Fat's tone was neutral.

"What do you mean, 'indeed'? How could any of us have stood against White Bird? The youth would have made one of the greatest Speakers ever."

"He didn't last very long if you will recall."

"You needn't remind me. I grouse every time I remember that I married my favorite nieces to him. Who would have thought they would have gone to that skinny little scorpion?"

"I'm not sure I'd use that word to describe him."

"How well do you know Salamander?"

"I saw him a lot at Wing Heart's."

"Was he always into sorcery?"

Clay Fat was silent.

"My nieces are married to him. They haven't been the same since they went to his bed."

After a while longer, Clay Fat asked, "Don't you think sorcery is a harsh word? Are you sure it isn't just jealousy? Perhaps they like him?"

"Do you think my girls would like that Swamp Panther bitch, too? No, I tell you, there's something going on there. I tried to get Night Rain to tell me the other night. She insists on hiding something." Mud Stalker paused, then cast his gaming pieces. "Tell me, what did you hear him say the other day at the Serpent's cleansing?"

"He was talking to his dead friend." But Clay Fat didn't sound too certain.

"Did you see how quickly Pine Drop dragged him away? Did you see the expression on his face? The way his eyes looked? That wasn't a man in grief, my friend."

"Now that you mention it, he looked almost euphoric. As if he were seeing something wonderful instead of the freeing of a dead Serpent's souls."

"What did he ever get from the Serpent, anyway?"

"The old man liked him."

"They processed bodies together. Salamander spent a great deal of time with the old man. I'm not sure he wasn't learning other things."

"Such as?"

"Poisons. The dark uses of Power. Is Salamander truly an idiot, or is that just what we are supposed to think?"

Silence.

"I want you to remember that, Clay Fat. I want you to keep an open mind. You owe me nothing for the ducks but your promise that you will keep an eye on Salamander. And consider him anew."

"I will, Speaker. But what are you really thinking? That Salamander is a sorcerer?"

"Do you remember the night of his initiation? He talked to spirits! He laughed, Speaker. When has any young man laughed? And do you remember how the Serpent stalked off into the night? Had you ever seen him do that before? I hadn't. Let me add one last thing: Salamander's enemies never seem to last long."

"I don't understand."

"His uncle, Cloud Heron, lingered in death for many moons. Curious, wasn't it, that he didn't die until White Bird had returned from the north?"

"You can't blame that on Salamander."

"Who stood between him and the Speakership?"

"White Bird."

"He is dead."

"Salamander can't throw lightning, Speaker."

"What did Wing Heart think of her youngest son? Did she like him? Was she proud of him?"

"No." Clay Fat didn't sound so sure of himself anymore.

"And what happened to your old friend, Wing Heart? What kind of person can drive his own mother's souls away?"

"I can't believe that Salamander is a witch! He doesn't look like one, doesn't act like one. He's not that smart."

"Perhaps he isn't," Mud Stalker said offhandedly, knowing full well the seed had been planted. "What about his Swamp Panther wife? Eats Wood had been spying on Anhinga. He came to me, telling me that he suspected she was here to harm us. Do you remember that she went away every moon, even when her belly was swollen with Salamander's child?"

"Yes."

"She was meeting with Jaguar Hide. Eats Wood was sure."

"Did he ever see her meet with him?"

"He did. From a distance. The thing is, the last time he left to spy on her, he never came back. I have no proof, but, as I said before, I just want you to think about these things. Especially about what happens to people who are close to Salamander."

"You have two nieces married to him. What do they say?" Clay Fat's voice had taken on a pensive tone.

"They say nothing, Speaker. If you were married to a witch, to someone who could drive his own mother's souls away, would you say anything?"

A deep frown lined Clay Fat's forehead.

"Oh, forget it. It's probably nothing." Mud Stalker smiled.

Pine Drop rinsed her cloth in a bowlful of water before she bent over and sponged Anhinga's brow. Outside a wind whispered and moaned, driven by a spring storm. Had she ever known such a wet winter and spring? No sooner did one storm blow itself out than another rolled in.

Anhinga lay on a bison hide that padded the dirt floor. To her side the fire crackled and popped, its flame illuminating the inside of Salamander's house. Over the winter, soot had blacked the roof and laid velvet fingers on the hanging bags of squash, smoked fish, jerked venison, and the desiccated carcasses of geese, ducks, and turkeys that hung from the rafters.

Anhinga gasped as another contraction tightened in her belly. Pine Drop smiled down at her in reassurance and took one of her hands, squeezing it. She glanced at Water Petal. Steady as a stone,

Salamander's cousin had seen them through the long watch.

"Aiiahhh!" the cry broke through Anhinga's clenched teeth. Her pretty face contorted; water beaded on her skin before trickling down the lines of pain.

"You must push now," Water Petal said as she squatted between Anhinga's bent knees.

Night Rain watched from the side, a wad of dried hanging moss in her hands ready to soak up fluids. She had sponged up the Swamp Panther woman's water several hands of time ago.

Pine Drop continued to hold Anhinga's hand, squeezing firmly. "Don't fight it. When the time is right, when your womb is ready, the little one will come."

Anhinga's expression relaxed, and she gasped for air. "By the Panther's bones, nothing prepared me for this."

"It is a first child," Water Petal reminded. "Your body has never done this before. That infant has to push your hipbones apart."

"Crack them in two, you mean." Anhinga gasped as another contraction tightened inside of her.

"Push," Pine Drop told her. "Push."

The realization that she herself was only two moons from this same ordeal brought a trickle of fear into Pine Drop's guts. She absently reached down with her free hand to feel the swell of her pregnancy.

"I'm . . . ah . . ." Anhinga didn't finish but gasped a full breath, chest swelling, her heavy breasts taut as she bit down hard and grimaced with the effort.

Water Petal looked up, met Pine Drop's eyes, and said, "It is soon. She is opening."

"By Panther's blood!" Anhinga gasped, her head flopping weakly to the side as she gulped breath. "My insides are tearing apart!"

"If they were, I would be seeing a lot of blood," Water Petal answered matter-of-factly. She patted one of Anhinga's brown knees, her critical eyes monitoring.

"And there isn't?" Anhinga asked.

"A bit. Watery. Just what's normal."

The next contraction brought Anhinga's head up. Strong thigh muscles slid under her smooth brown skin as she strained. Her hand tightened on Pine Drop's in a grip the likes of which would slip the skin from her finger bones.

"Aaiiiahhh!" she cried. Her legs were trembling.

Pine Drop saw the change, the difference in the swell of Anhinga's belly as the infant moved lower.

"Soon, now." Water Petal smiled. "The tissue down here is swollen. Night Rain, be ready to hand me that moss."

Anhinga's jaw worked like a beached fish's. She kept blinking against the sweat as Pine Drop wiped her brow with the damp cloth.

"Deep breath. Push!" Water Petal ordered, as Anhinga contorted with another contraction. "Hold it! Keep pushing!"

Pine Drop bent to one side in time to see Anhinga's red vaginal lips peel out and part as the blood-streaked globe appeared. "Push!" she cried. "The head's almost out!"

"Araghhh!" Anhinga gasped a lungful of air, curled up, and tightened her muscles. Her eyes were wide, staring, as the mound of her belly deflated.

Water Petal smiled in delight as the infant slid into her hands. Pine Drop could only stare at the wet thing, splotched in red, its unsightly blue color picking the odd memory of fish guts from her memory.

Night Rain thrust handfuls of hanging moss out, looking oddly cowed by the sight of the squirming infant, slick with fluid, its thick umbilical trailing back into Anhinga's vagina.

With practiced hands, Water Petal wiped the mouth clean. She turned the infant facedown, lifting the hips and massaging the lungs. Fluid dribbled from the mouth, and Pine Drop watched the baby take its first breath. It coughed, expelled more fluid, then drew its lungs full and squalled.

"A girl," Water Petal told the exhausted Anhinga. "Your lineage has an heir."

Anhinga lay panting, her hands knotted into fists. She had fixed her eyes on something beyond the dark roof. A weak shudder ran through her.

Water Petal used a white chert flake to sever the umbilical. She tied it off with callused fingers. Mindless of the infant's squalls, she continued to wipe the now-pinking flesh dry. "There, there, little one. You are safe among us. We want you to know that you are welcome here, and we hope that good souls come to fill your body."

Pine Drop sat back, one hand on her belly. "I pray that it will be that easy for me."

"Easy?" Anhinga rasped. "My guts are pulled in two."

It was Night Rain who said, "I don't know about the rest of you, but I don't think I'm going to let Salamander's manhood ride in my canoe again. It isn't worth it. I can find my pleasure in some other way than with a man."

"You'll take Salamander back to your bed." Water Petal chuckled dryly. "Having been through this, I can tell you that the body forgets the pain, remembering only the pleasure." She arched an eyebrow. "Night Rain? Could you go find Salamander? He's atop the Bird's Head, praying. Tell him he has a daughter, and that his wife is healthy, too."

"I'll be right back." Night Rain ducked out the door into the windy evening.

Pine Drop sighed, smiling down at Anhinga. "How do you feel? The afterbirth still has to come out."

"In its own time." Anhinga raised her arms to take the tiny infant to her breast. As the little pink mouth found the nipple, Anhinga closed her eyes. "By the Panther's blood, that feels good."

"Is she sucking?" Water Petal asked. "Are you making milk?"

Anhinga nodded, and Pine Drop noticed the wetness around the baby's mouth. "She's doing fine."

Water Petal grinned. "Well, women, that's that. No complications. We're off to a good start." She reached up, massaging her own breast. "It brings a tenderness to me."

"You will have more children," Pine Drop said evenly. "We pray for you."

Anhinga's breathing turned shallow. She blinked, tears hidden behind her eyes as she said, "Thank you. Thank you all for staying with me."

"We are a household," Pine Drop said, speaking for all of them. "You would have been there for us."

"If I survive this"—a faint smile crossed her lips—"I'll look forward to watching your expression as I repeat all the things you told me."

Pine Drop laughed as she handed Water Petal the damp rag to clean her hands. *So, somehow, in the face of looming disaster, we have become a household. What a delight it would be if forces were not gathering to destroy us all.*

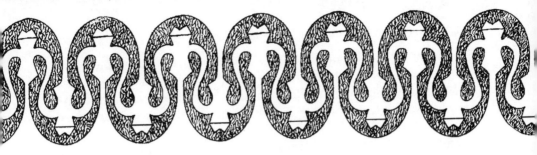

Forty-seven

Salamander crouched in the darkness, his bone stiletto driving into the dark soil. He laid it to the side and used his fingers to pull the loosened earth from the hole. In his other hand he held the baked silt effigy recovered from under Anhinga's bed. The hard part had been wiping the fetish with the afterbirth. It had taken all of his wits to accomplish that before Water Petal took it out beyond the rings for a proper burial.

He looked up at the night sky, so incredibly clear on this moonless equinox night. The stars wove patterns of white across the blackness. Bird Man's trail looked like fog running from north to south.

"Are you watching, old friend?" Salamander stared up into the darkness. "My wife's baby was born healthy. I am here, as you told me to be. I remember what you instructed me to do."

He reached down and grasped the little figurine around the head with one hand and the body with the other. Twisting, he snapped the neck cleanly. Then, laying the pieces in the hole, he covered them with the dark earth. "Thank you, Elder. I ask your souls to look over us, to watch out for this little infant girl who has joined our lives. Anhinga has enemies here who would harm her and her child. Guard us from all manner of evil."

He picked up his stiletto and stood in the darkened ring of the Serpent's burnt house. His old friend's flat face smiled at him from the firelit warmth of his memories. Did he feel that warm soul drifting around him now?

Bobcat's cleansing on the Turtle's Back was almost complete. He would come here with the full moon and begin construction of a new Serpent's house on the foundation of the old one. It had always been thus, one Serpent after another living on this spot on the third ridge in the center of Owl Clan's territory.

In that instant he could feel Power washing around him. Unseen eyes peered at him out of the darkness. Just how many of those little figurines were lying buried around here? How many of the Dead pressed around him, stroking his skin with their fingers? The thought of it brought a shiver to his cool flesh, and he turned his steps for home.

A couple of dogs barked at him, but no one would be out this late at night. He walked alone, accompanied only by the Dream Souls of the Dead.

He ducked into his doorway and crossed to Anhinga's bed before lifting the buffalo hide and slipping next to his wife's warm body.

"What was that?" Anhinga asked, catching him by surprise.

"What was what?"

She shifted, and he could feel her eyes with the same intensity that he had those of the ghosts. "That thing you dug up from under my bed?"

He took a deep breath. "I thought you were asleep."

"The infant was sucking. I watched you dig something out from under the bed."

"A charm," he told her. "Something the Serpent gave me before he died to ensure that your pregnancy was healthy. Now that you and the little girl are all right, I had to care for it properly."

"That is all it was?"

He could hear suspicion in her voice and slipped his cold arm around her, careful not to disturb the infant sleeping between them. "It was enough. You and the baby are fine."

"Are you witching me?"

"Why would I be witching you?"

"To make me like you."

He laughed. "Too bad I didn't think of that earlier. I might have tried it. Instead, you have only me, as I am, with no witching."

She shifted again, snuggling the infant into the hollow of her hips. "Why did you follow me to the island that day, Salamander? What am I to you? Why did you care if I was safe? Is it just the sandstone?"

"You are my wife."

"Is it that easy for you, Salamander? No questions about what truly lies in my souls?"

"I know who you are." He smiled sadly in the darkness. "And I know that in the end, you will do what you must."

She lay silent in the darkness, and after a moment, he heard soft sobbing.

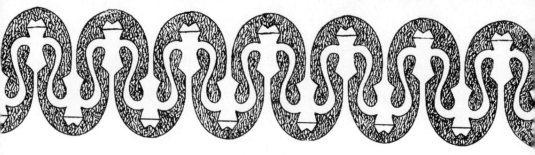

Forty-eight

Pine Drop climbed the long slope, stopping on occasion to catch her breath. She was tired of pregnancy. Tired of the discomfort, of having to rise every so often in the night to waddle out and urinate. The shifting of her daughter—for she assumed Salamander had been right about that—disrupted what little sleep she managed.

Above her the Bird's Head loomed out of the graying dawn. The last of the stars were fading. A warm misty breeze blew up from the south, carrying with it the scent of greening grass, the perfume of dogwood, redbud, elder, and locust blossoms.

Spring had warmed the land, stirring the life that had lain dormant in memory of Mother Sun's flight to the south. As she climbed she could hear the high piping of one of the last flocks of blue herons heading northward on the gulf wind.

The grass, thick and lush, fed by the winter rains, curled around her feet when she wandered off the path. A vole rustled away from her passage.

When she looked up, she could see the ramada, and there, on the palmetto-thatched poles of the cane roof, she made out the solitary shape of an owl. In the twilight, it watched her, huge, the largest barred owl she had ever seen. Black eyes studied her from within the twin circles of the facial disks.

She froze, a prickle running through her as their eyes met. Her souls began to tingle. She could swear that she could not only feel her own heartbeat, but that of her daughter deep in her womb.

Time seemed to swoon, silvering and shifting around her like vision through clear moving water.

She sensed rather than saw the owl spread its wings. The giant bird drifted down, silent, its wings enlarging until they filled the sky. To the last moment she stared into the liquid depths of those huge brown eyes, and then, as if with a snap, the owl was gone. Vanished.

She spun on her feet, staring behind her—and saw nothing. The clear gray air was empty.

Snakes! Where did it go? How could such a big bird have just disappeared into the air? Her throat had tightened, her mouth become dry. She could feel her blood, bursting through her with each pounding of her heart.

Resuming the climb took every resource and all of the courage she could muster. She laid a hand on one of the ramada poles, panting for breath, and looked up at the great mound's peak.

She could see him sitting there, legs crossed on the summit, his head back, eyes closed. His hands rested, palms up, on his bent knees. Morning dew had settled on his black hair, turning it silver.

The expression on his face stopped her. He had a beatific look, a lax smile on his lips. He might have been savoring some taste, perhaps a sweet squash flavored with honeysuckle that lay so delicately on the tongue.

Filling her lungs, she forced her weary legs up the last slope and lowered herself quietly to sit beside him. Every muscle in her body vibrated like a stretched cord. An electric sensation, like that from rubbed fur, crackled along her nerves.

She swallowed hard and studied him. *What sort of man are you, Husband? Does Power flow through you like sap, or is it a madness?*

Salamander seemed oblivious, so locked away in his visions that nothing else existed in the world.

She waited, turning her eyes to the eastern horizon and the reddening beyond the distant tree line. The bulge of the sun slowly emerged from behind the forest's bulk. She sighed, unconsciously reaching out for Mother Sun's light, as if she could grab hold of those first glorious rays and scrub the darkness from her souls.

"It is glorious, isn't it?" Salamander barely spoke above a whisper.

She spared him a glance. His eyes remained closed, the blissful look on his face.

"Yes." She took a breath to still her souls. "Look how far north it has moved since the solstice. We are forest people, Husband. Knowing that Mother Sun moves across the sky is one thing, actually seeing it makes the stories about her come true."

He remained as calm as a rock, unmoving, his hands still on his knees as though supporting something in the air.

"I saw Masked Owl," she told him nervously. "I think I sacred him away."

"You did not scare him."

She shifted, pulling her kirtle around so that it didn't chafe her pendulous belly. "Does he always come when you call him?"

"No. He came to see me. He is worried."

"About what?"

"About my new Spirit Helper. She has changed the balance between Masked Owl and Many Colored Crow. The future is no longer certain, Pine Drop. They don't know what I am going to choose."

"I don't understand. What do you mean, choose?"

His smile was sad. "Nothing comes without a price."

She ground her teeth for a moment, then asked, "Husband? I must ask you something. It is very important to me."

"I am not a witch. Masked Owl is not evil. I seek to harm no one."

A flood of relief washed through her. "Then you have heard the talk?"

"No. You are the first to mention it to me."

She flinched, unsettled. "You are becoming ever more strange, Salamander. Power is growing in you, and it frightens me."

"You are a wise woman."

"I don't feel very wise these days, Husband. Things are happening. A trap is being built for you, and I can sense the cords that run to the deadfall trigger. I can feel people tugging on them. If they pull the trigger loose, the weight is going to fall and crush you."

"I Dance on such a thin edge," he whispered. Sunlight flooded his face, washing his delicate skin in red. He looked so young and fragile. "I'm scared, Pine Drop. If I slip and fall, it will be into a horrible nightmare. The worst thing is, it isn't just me. It is you and Night Rain and Anhinga and Water Petal. One misstep on my part can destroy you all."

She clenched her fists. "The clans are moving against you."

"Wife, it would be so sweet if my only concern was the clans. Masked Owl would have me believe that the One and the Dance are all that matter. The One is so Powerful. It calls to me. It would be so easy to give in. To find happiness like Mother did. The only thing that calls me back is you, Pine Drop. My wives and my daughters. They need me. The People need me."

"Of course we do."

A great sadness filled his voice. "Wolf Dreamer said that a man couldn't love and Dream. I want to do both. If only I could tear myself in two, send my Dream Soul to spin with the One, and my Life Soul to embrace you and watch my daughters grow."

"Half the time I have no idea what you are saying."

He smiled sadly. "Someday you will. You are the future."

"Forget that for a moment *and listen to me!*" She took a breath. "Uncle is working in secret, building an alliance to have you declared a witch." There, she'd done it. Betrayed her clan as surely as Night Rain had done. A sick feeling stirred in her gut.

"They can't destroy what they do not comprehend."

"They can smack you in the back of the head with an ax," she declared. "If the Council decides to brand you as a witch, they won't give you any warning. They will act by surprise, and you won't know until you feel your skull split open."

For a long time he sat there, eyes flickering under the closed lids. "Why do you care, Pine Drop?"

She looked down miserably where she picked at her fingers. "I have come to love you."

"There is no greater gift and no greater curse."

"Curse? What do you mean?"

"You draw me back from the edge."

She squinted in disbelief. "You really want to fall off that edge you were talking about?"

"More than anything you can imagine, Wife." A faint smile bent his lips. "But for you, all of you, I would be drawn like a bee to a pitcher plant. I would lick desperately at the sweetness as I fell into the depths."

"By the Sky Beings, why?"

"Because the other way would be too painful."

"What are you talking about?"

"I'm talking about what I will have to give up for the future, Pine Drop. I just don't know if I am strong enough to see it through. I am so tempted to choose a long and happy life."

"Then choose it! Help me stop this witchcraft story before it starts."

He smiled, as if amused by her worry.

"I need to know something, Salamander. Did Anhinga kill my cousin, Eats Wood?" There, she had asked. Now, waiting for his reply, her souls twisted in anticipation. In response, he just sat there, legs crossed, eyes closed, holding his hands palm up. "Salamander?"

"No, she did not." He raised his hands, inspecting them intently as he worked his fingers back and forth. He blinked, clenched his fists, and stiffened his back as if stung.

"Salamander? Did you kill him?"

"I think it would have taken someone with a warrior's courage to kill your cousin." He shot her an innocent smile. "I've been meaning to give you something."

She frowned, unsure what had just happened between them.

He reached into the tuck of his breechcloth and pulled out a sinew-wrapped square. With careful fingers he unwound the thread, revealing two pieces of flat bark. This he handed to her.

The wood felt warm to her fingers, as though they had been baking in the sun. She separated the pieces finding five blue jay feathers that had been resting there, perfectly pressed by the soft bark.

"What?" she asked, lifting the delicate feathers.

"You left them the morning you took the little carved owl. I am returning them. You didn't have to leave anything in payment. That owl was for you. I just hadn't finished it yet. I would rather see those feathers sewn into the bare patch on your cloak."

Tears caught her by surprise and blurred her vision with silver. "What is happening to you, Husband? What are you becoming?"

"The future."

Pine Drop's daughter had been born in the middle of the night while a misty spring rain fell. They had run low on wood, having to send Night Rain to borrow from one of her cousins. Anhinga wrung out a cloth as she cleaned the blood-streaked infant. Curious, wasn't it, that caring for a newborn could become such second nature in so short a time?

She glanced at her own daughter, asleep in a cane-framed cradleboard. The child's wispy black hair was visible above the cloth bundle, her skull like a delicate gourd. Looking closer, Anhinga could see that her eyes were closed, the tiny mouth open to expose pink gums and a curl of tongue.

"It was easier this time," Night Rain said as she held Pine Drop's hand.

"Easier for you," Pine Drop answered wearily as she lay gulping air like a dying fish. Sweat beaded on her brown skin, pooling in the stretch marks around her navel.

"I thought it was enjoyable," Anhinga said, eyes flashing. "I enjoyed repeating those things you told me."

"Next time," Pine Drop mumbled, "you can deliver your own child."

Night Rain used hanging moss to wipe up the last of the blood from the matting that lay between Pine Drop's legs. She pressed it into a bundle, and before Anhinga could draw breath to stop her, tossed the moss into the smoldering fire. Flames licked around it before climbing through the moss. The wet blood and tissue steamed and hissed as it burned. The air filled with a pungent odor.

"I would have burned it outside," Anhinga said, scrunching her nose.

"I didn't think of that," Night Rain replied sheepishly.

Anhinga finished her cleaning before dropping to her knees beside Pine Drop. The newborn hung on Pine Drop's right breast. The woman's tired arms cradled the infant. Anhinga watched from half-lowered eyes as the tiny mouth worked the nipple.

She thought it curious that Salamander had arrived bearing a fiber-tempered bowl and offered to carry the afterbirth out beyond the clan grounds for burial. Shifting, she noticed the turned earth under Pine Drop's bed, as if something had been recently dug from there. A slow smile crossed her lips.

"Snakes," Pine Drop whispered. "I could sleep for a solid moon."

Anhinga sighed, throwing her head back and feeling her dark hair falling down her back. Panther's blood, she was tired. "I, too, am ready to fall over. If you need me, you'll find me at Salamander's. Sleeping."

"I can call on kin," Night Rain told her. "Thank you, Anhinga. We didn't think it would take so long."

"Mine did," she replied as she reached for her daughter. Wrapping the fabric to protect the baby's face from mosquitoes, she took a last look around, nodded, and ducked out into the night.

The faintest of breezes played with the heavy night air. She could feel the promise of summer's coming warmth. A cloudless sky was painted with stars, while a sliver of moon hung just above the eastern horizon. A whippoorwill called plaintively from beyond the house-topped ridges. Crickets and frogs added their voices to the night. Woodsmoke hung in the air, mixing with the cloying odor of rotting trash and the tang of human waste.

She tucked her daughter close to her shoulder and walked down the ridge before turning north along the edge of the bluff. The ridges here, she was told, had been built atop an old gully. One the Sun

People had filled before plotting out the Snapping Turtle Clan ground.

Below her the tree-filled bottom land south of the lake lay in dark shadow. She could smell cooler air, the pungent scent of the swamp carrying to her position.

She passed the edge of the ridges and glanced uneasily at the dark houses. The last one belonged to Mud Stalker. She stopped, staring at it.

A wicker door blocked the entrance. She cocked her head, stretching down with her free hand to reach into her pouch. Her fingers caressed the stone-tipped knife that lay there. Salamander had sharpened it, using an antler tip to pressure flake an edge keen enough to slice hair.

It would be so easy. She need only slip that doorway aside, step in, and one quick slash would leave his throat severed from side to side. Before he could fully call his souls to wakefulness, he would be choking on his bubbling blood, tasting it as it rushed up in his mouth and nostrils.

She snorted to herself and hurried on. Pus and blood, what was happening to her? Uncle hadn't been right, had he? She wasn't beginning to see these people as her own?

Disgusted with herself, she strode purposefully on her way, passing the head of the narrow ditch that drained Snapping Turtle Clan when she stopped short. Her path had taken her to the plaza where the Men's House stood on its double-humped mound.

She stared at the structure, its thatched roof inky against the sky. The carvings atop the ridgepole guarded the building—black silhouettes against the night.

She swallowed hard, taking careful steps to the pole where she had been tied. Reaching down, she touched the grass-covered earth. The dirt was cool, damp on her fingertips.

She tucked her chin, smelling her baby daughter's delicate scent as it rose from the cradleboard. How many things had changed since she had been bound and helpless here?

In the eye of her soul, she relived that terrible day. Remembered how they had cut Cooter's liver out of his body. How they had laughed as they bent down to defecate into Mist Finger's empty eye sockets. Once again the camp dogs slung silver drool as they snapped up bits of raw flesh cut from her friends. She could see the stripped rib cage, all that was left of who? Slit Nose? Spider Fire?

So much hatred. So much death.

What brought me here?

A fist tightened around her heart. Was that the price she had paid by waiting for so long? That her memories would begin to weaken, that the pain of that day, the humiliation to their spirits and memories, would begin to fade?

She could feel Bowfin and her dead friends, watching her from the darkness, their eyes burning as they studied her. She could sense their frustration and swelling anger.

Will you act? The words seemed to linger on the night.

She steeled herself and stood. To her surprise her fingers hurt, and something firm filled her palm. She opened her hand, wondering when she had clawed the soil from ground.

He sat in the doorway of the Men's House, his form obscured by the deep shadow. He had barely seen her coming as she walked across the plaza. Hadn't recognized her until she stopped at the pole and bent down to feel the ground.

Now he watched as she hurried away, her gait halfway between a run and a walk.

Saw Back reached up and fingered the side of his crushed face. It would have been so easy. He could have sneaked up on the balls of his feet. She'd have never known he was there until the snapping of her skull as he drove his ax through it.

"Someday, woman."

It would not be in the darkness. Not in the quiet night. No, he wanted her to know he was going to kill her. He wanted to look into her eyes, see her fear, as he choked the life out of her body.

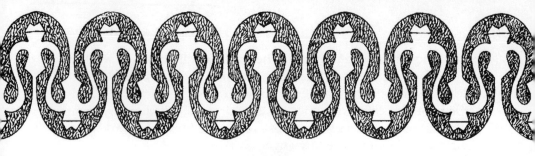

Forty-nine

Salamander had spent the last week since the birth of Pine Drop's daughter alternating back and forth between his two houses. On this night he lay in Night Rain's arms. Their coupling had been like an intimate dance that led to a pulsing ecstasy that Night Rain shared as she absorbed his seed. Wrapped in each other's arms they had fallen into an exhausted sleep.

Salamander didn't hear the rasp of black feathers in the night. Above the house, midnight spirit wings enfolded his Dream Soul in downy softness.

The Dream, so vivid, captivated him: He was climbing the Bird's Head. The day was one of those that came in late spring: bright, sunny, with a scattering of clouds in a light blue sky. Humidity had softened the air, its moist touch on the verdant growth.

Grass waved at his feet as Salamander climbed. Around him, the world seemed to glow with an emerald heartbeat. He could feel the earth, alive, breathing. Even the air seemed to swell in his nose and lungs.

His climb was effortless. He almost floated upward—a leaf borne upon the breeze.

At the top, a lone figure made a dark silhouette against the sky.

Salamander squinted against the glorious light, trying to identify the person. But no, not a person at all. Rather, it looked more bird-like, or was that just a black-feathered cape that hung from the figure's shoulders? The head, when it turned, was indeed a giant bird's. A straight black beak protruded, shining like polished jet.

Salamander slowed, suddenly uncertain.

"Come, my friend!" the being called, waving a feather-laced arm. "It is time that we finally talked."

Salamander trod the last couple of body lengths, studying the apparition. Long black feathers hung down from a cloak that covered the man's arms. From behind a raven's mask, two sharp brown eyes could be seen. A short tunic made of snakeskin ran down between the man's legs to end in a rattlesnake's tail.

"Bird Man?" Salamander gasped.

"I have come to see you, Salamander. Come to see who and what you are. There are things you have not been told. It wasn't easy to reach you as it is. Masked Owl guards you well."

"Why? What is he afraid of?"

"He fears that you might find all the pieces of your scattered visions. He fears that when you fit them together, you may choose a different path than the one he has been so carefully planning for you."

"I don't want to be in the middle of this!"

Bird Man extended a feathered finger to indicate the cross-shaped scar on his chest. "You have been marked with it, young Dreamer. Whatever you wished, Power has found itself at the center of those intersecting lines over your heart. Do you feel it?"

When Salamander lifted his fingers he detected the throbbing under the hard knot of scar tissue. Looking down, he could see a yellow glow at the center of his breastbone.

"Yes, there," the gentle voice told him. "What an unlikely sort of hero you are. I can understand Masked Owl's interest in you. He always seems drawn to the odd ones, to the deformed, or the naive."

"I don't understand."

"Neither do I. He seems taken with that silly notion of looking for strength in weakness. You are his type, but what I really don't understand is how you could have managed to involve the old woman. Mostly she huddles in her cave like an infant wrapped tight in the womb. She seems content to watch from afar."

"What old woman? Do you mean one of the Clan Elders? Cane Frog, or . . ."

"No, young fool. I mean old Heron. For some reason—and it's beyond me—she has taken a liking to you. It upsets things, you know. Any hint of predictability vanished the moment she saved you from dying from your stupidity."

"Stupidity?"

"Taking those mushrooms you found in the Serpent's lodge.

That first time the old man gave you just a taste. Only enough to allow your souls to drift up and glance the Spirit World. The second time, you ate too much. I thought all of our problems were over—and by your own hand, too."

"Problems?"

"What did the old woman promise you? That you would become a great Dreamer? Is that what you intend to do? Just when everyone needs you the most, you are going to bundle yourself into a canoe, paddle off to some secluded isle, and Dream for the rest of your life?"

Salamander frowned. "The One calls to me."

"It calls to everyone," Bird Man said irritably. "Just because it has a certain lure, you're set to abandon all of your responsibilities to your wives, your children, Water Petal and Yellow Spider, your lineage, and Owl Clan. How noble of you. You will spend the rest of your life eating bugs and leaves, trying to escape yourself in an attempt to find nothingness."

"But to Dance with the One—"

"Means disappointing people who love you and depend on you."

"Then why is it there?"

"An accident of the Creation. You answered your Serpent's question, didn't you? When the sky was separated from the land it was to create duality, otherness. Opposites, if you will. Do you really think a young man like you can Dream them back together? What you feel, fool, is the hole that was left, and it's trying to pull you in."

"It is?"

Bird Man cocked his head. "Think about it, Salamander. I remember my idiot brother trying to tell me once, long ago, that I was unschooled, but that I could still find a way to the Dream." His lips quirked behind the mask. "Now, having been part of the Spirit World for so long, I can tell you that the One isn't all that there is."

"It's not?"

Bird Man spread his feather-clad arm to take in the huge vista of Sun Town. "Look down there, Salamander. Do you realize the majesty of this place? Nothing else like it exists in our world. It is from here that the vision will spread. You and your brother have spurred it. Hazel Fire and his companions have taken the bait! So, too, have so many of the others. You have set fire to their imaginations, like blowing on a dying coal. Even Striped Dart is beguiled. Your impulses are correct, Salamander. You can grasp the future!"

"As my brother did with his seeds?"

"Yes, my friend." A thoughtful brown eye studied him. "I could do nothing to save him."

"Masked Owl killed him." Salamander frowned. "I don't understand it. White Bird would have made a brilliant Speaker, the greatest ever."

"You are wrong."

"I am?"

"You could make an even greater Speaker, Salamander." Those piercing brown eyes were taking his measure. "That is one of the things Masked Owl doesn't want you to know. As Speaker you can change the People forever. You can start them on a path of greatness that will rival anything in the world."

Bird Man smiled at Salamander's surprise, and said, "Salamander, you have been agonizing over your visions of the future. You caught glimpses, but not a full picture. You saw the grand ruler, high above the river. Do you remember?"

"Yes."

With a swirl of his feathers, Bird Man outlined a burning circle against the sky. Within its ring Salamander could see pointed pyramids of stone, people beyond count laboring in fertile fields alongside a winding brown river. Giant stone buildings stood above the sun-baked shores. Square stone spears thrust into the sky like giant awls.

"They are already building marvels over there," Bird Man whispered.

"Where is that?" Salamander gasped, trying to understand the scale of the buildings and pyramids. Was it his imagination, or did they dwarf Sun Town?

"In another world, my friend. Far to the east, across a huge ocean of water." Bird Man shrugged.

"We could do that? Here?" Salamander marveled. "We don't have the stone!"

Bird Man laughed again. "Just because you live on a low ridge of windblown silt, do not worry about stone. I can teach you to think in grander terms. I can help you to break the petty politics of the clans. Smash them once and for all. You can begin the process of molding the People into a new direction. You can do it the same way you shape your little red owls. It won't be easy, it won't be painless. But *you* could do it! You could sit atop this mound and control this entire river! Generations of your descendants will speak your name with awe as they rule from on high."

Salamander shook his head in disbelief, thunderstruck by the images that formed within Bird Man's fiery circle: Scenes of people in huge canoes that crested tremendous ocean waves. Cities of stone and wood. A literal flood of people tending fields where plants grew. Others, warriors bedecked with plumes of colored feathers, marched in thick rows and carried weapons of shining silver metal.

"It is illusion!" Salamander cried.

"A possible future," Bird Man corrected. "A shining vision of what could be. Provided, of course, that you have the courage and commitment to see it come true. That, or we can fulfill my brother's vision. You could turn the People into nothing more than scattered bands of Dreamers, lost in the mystical, empty-eyed and wandering the forests, ever tied to the One."

"I could make that kind of difference?"

Bird Man smiled in a beguiling way. "Somehow, my young friend, it has come down to you. Sun Town, at this time and place, can change the future of the People. Choose one way, and you, and this place, will be remembered forever. Choose another, and you, and the greatness that is Sun Town, will vanish from the People's memory."

"I would have to give up the One?"

"It would seem a small sacrifice, Salamander. In return you get to live your life, watch your children grow. You saw yourself in old age, surrounded by your wives and basking in contentment from having *served* your people. In doing so, new earthworks will rise. Trade will expand from ocean to ocean. In your lifetime you will see cities founded across your world. *You* will make the Dream live."

"And if I choose Masked Owl's way?"

"Mud Stalker and Deep Hunter will destroy the magic of Sun Town. The clans will be at war within a turning of the seasons." Bird Man flashed his feathered arm in a circle, and Sun Town appeared. Houses were blackened and burned. Wreckage lay scattered about. Among the weeds and seedling trees growing along the ridges lay the rotting bodies of dead people. "Masked Owl didn't show you that, did he?"

Salamander stared at the half-rotted corpses. "Mud Stalker and Deep Hunter will cause this?"

"Along with the allies they convince to side with them. Despite public appearances, in their hearts they hate each other. They will do anything to place their respective clans in the void left by Wing Heart's madness. In their rush to rid themselves of you, they will set in motion the seeds of their destruction. Lies will lead to betrayal and murder. Yours first, and then Thunder Tail's, and Clay Fat's and Half Thorn's. They have already forgotten their obligations.

Honor will be next. Their actions will split the People down the middle. You and I, however, can prevent this."

"This is the result of my choice?"

"You must choose the future, Salamander." He added softly, "Choose well."

With that, Bird Man spread his arms and leaped into the sunlit sky. His cloaked arms flattened, becoming black wings that shone in the sunlight. With each changing position they blazed in blue, red, orange, and green.

Salamander jerked upright in his bed, stunned. "*Many Colored Crow!*"

Night Rain cried, "Ouch! You smacked me with your elbow!"

Salamander blinked in the darkness of Pine Drop's house. A faint glow marked the fire pit. Coals still smoldered among the branches of green wood they had left to smudge the mosquitoes.

"A Dream," he murmured. "A Dream unlike any other."

"What are you talking about?" Night Rain repositioned herself, one hand on his shoulder.

"The future, Night Rain. Giant cities like Sun Town up and down the river. Warriors beyond count, marching in lines. Huge canoes that can cross oceans of salt water."

"You saw this?" she asked.

"That, and war between the clans. Sun Town deserted and burned. Many Colored Crow showed me. He was dressed as Bird Man. He said I could save Sun Town. All I had to do was choose it."

"You will do this thing, won't you?" Night Rain's voice pinched with excitement.

"I don't know."

"What do you mean, you don't know? You could be the greatest Speaker ever! You would have Many Colored Crow as a Spirit Helper! No one could stand against you."

Then Heron's words echoed in his memory. "*Everything comes at a price.*"

The day had turned out clear but humid. Sunlight touched the leaves with a green that almost wounded the eyes. Brightly colored birds flitted among the trees. Thick curls of vines bloomed, the colored flowers at odds with the tiny green blossoms on the tupelo.

"I just can't believe Deep Hunter and Mud Stalker would start a war between the clans! Would they really stoop to murdering their rivals?" Salamander cried as he helped Anhinga bait and drop one of the fish traps into the current. He played out the thin cord that tied it to a wooden float with its identifying owl carved in the weathered wood.

Their canoe sat in the middle of one of the winding channels, riding on smooth chocolate waters. The spring flood was marching across the bottoms, carrying silt and water into the backswamps. With it came fish, eager to feed in the newly created shallows, to breed and lay their eggs. Life was coming to the bottomland swamp.

In the rear of the canoe, Water Petal watched him with uneasy eyes. "There are stories of witchcraft circulating about you, Cousin. If they will lie to get you murdered, why not someone else?" When she used the paddle to drive them forward, smooth muscles made her greased skin shine.

"He is no witch!" Anhinga declared, then glanced suspiciously at Salamander. "Are you?"

"No."

"Did you bury one of those little statues under Pine Drop's bed?" Anhinga was watching him with hard eyes. "I saw where the dirt had been disturbed."

"Yes."

"Did you dispose of it?" She glanced thoughtfully back at her baby where it rode in the cane cradleboard.

"I did. Just as the Serpent told me to."

"What is this?" Water Petal asked.

"I wanted my wives to have healthy deliveries. Relax, Cousin. It was the Serpent's charm, not something from the dark side of Power."

"You worry me," Water Petal told him.

He chuckled uncomfortably. "You have no idea what worry is. One night I Dream and I fly with Masked Owl, knowing he drove a lightning bolt through White Bird. The next, it is Many Colored Crow who comes to talk to me in my sleep. Each wants me to choose his way." He dared not mention Heron. She was the most enigmatic of all. "I just don't know what the right choice is. Everything is coming together here, and I am right in the middle of it."

"That is an understatement." Water Petal sent them deeper into the channel, her face marked with unhappiness.

Salamander took the moment to study Anhinga. She, too, looked uneasy. A tension lay behind her pretty face; something smoldered behind her eyes. With the sunlight glistening in her raven black hair, she looked dangerous yet vulnerable. An irresistible combination. He stifled the sudden urge to reach out and run his fingers down her muscular thigh. Since giving birth, both she and Pine Drop seemed oblivious to his sexual desires. Water Petal had told him that would pass with time.

"I feel trapped," he said. "Whatever decision I make, I will offend one or the other."

"I'd keep an eye on the clans, Cousin," Water Petal retorted. "Within a moon, they will act to remove you from the Council. You know that threat is coming. What about the ones that are being planned in secret? Who can tell when someone might call you a witch and use that excuse to sneak up behind you and smack your skull in two!"

He gave her a wry smile. "I should be worried about a simple smack from behind when a lightning bolt might explode my head the way it did White Bird's? Somehow, upsetting Masked Owl or Many Colored Crow is a little different than worrying about Mud Stalker and Deep Hunter."

"You could leave," Anhinga told him. Her dark eyes burned. "You don't have to stay here. You could come with me. We could go to the Panther's Bones, and you could leave these people who do not appreciate you."

He reached out and took her hand, beguiled by her desperation. "I thank you for that, Wife. Your offer means more to me than I can ever tell you. As much as I would like to have that freedom, it wouldn't solve my trouble here."

"It would take you away from Sun People who want to murder you!"

"Masked Owl could drop a tree on me down at the Panther's Bones just as well as he could here. Spirit Helpers aren't bound by human territories."

"As you described it, Many Colored Crow would make us great," Water Petal said thoughtfully. "Our clan would become preeminent. No one could challenge us. Imagine that, Salamander. Owl Clan would be forever. Everyone else would be obliged to us. The uncertainty would be gone. We would lead the Council."

"At a price, Cousin." He reached for another piece of bait and dropped it into the next fish trap. "Power doesn't promise these things freely. You speak of obligation? What would we owe Many

Colored Crow?" He shook his head. "The Hero Twins are just like us—like our clans. If you just choose one, the balance will be ruined. The harmony that we have tried so hard to maintain will be broken."

Anhinga was weighing his words, a frown on her smooth face as she played out the cord while the trap sank in the murky water.

"Did we do so badly?" Water Petal asked. "Has Thunder Tail been a better leader in the Council than Wing Heart? What of Mud Stalker if he is chosen for the leadership? Would Deep Hunter have been better than Cloud Heron over the turnings of the seasons? Or, Snakes help us, Cane Frog? Could she have done the things your mother and uncle did? Our lineage has been good for Sun Town, Salamander. Look at the building we have done! The ridges are finished. People live in constant protection from the forces of the North and West. We are Trading with peoples we have never heard of before. Life is good."

He nodded, unable to argue with her. "That might have been luck."

"Luck?" Water Petal asked.

Anhinga raised a questioning eyebrow.

"What if Mother hadn't been chosen to follow Grandmother? What if Moccasin Leaf had been chosen Clan Elder instead? Would life still be good?"

Water Petal's eyes hardened.

"This talk is helpful, but it doesn't dig down under the guts where the real question lies." He dropped a square of fish meat into the next trap and with Anhinga's help, lowered it over the side. The marker float bobbed in the current as Water Petal steered them down the channel.

"And just what do you think lies under the guts?" Anhinga asked.

"Doing what is right," he answered. "Not just for us, not just for Sun Town, but for everyone."

"Right? By the Panther's blood, what is right?" Anhinga's frown deepened. "What is right for Sun Town will not be right for my people. Even your own clans have different ideas about what is right."

"That, Anhinga, is my problem," he told her. "How I can choose what is best for everyone?"

Water Petal cocked her head. "Salamander, why should you have to?"

"What?"

"Why should *you* have to do this? Why not someone else? Why did Power choose *you*?"

He shook his head sadly. "I don't know, Cousin. All I can tell you is that if I don't choose correctly, I just know something bad is going to happen."

A shaft of ocher light bored through the Dream, as though barely penetrating a midnight gloom. Anhinga stood passively—partially hidden. She could barely discern the grim surroundings. Darkness swirled at the edges, as if smoke choked the air and devoured the reddish light that illuminated the place. Dark shadows, beings of some sort, flickered and twisted at the sides of her vision. She could barely make them out—only that they were whip-thin, quick, and dangerous. In the center, the bloody light bathed five somber young men.

Mist Finger stood at the head of the group. His arms were raised high, like a bird preparing to leap into flight. Behind him Cooter, Spider Fire, Right Talon, and Slit Nose followed his lead, lifting their arms at angles. About them, the eerie figures detached from the darkness, lunged, struck, and withdrew. The attackers were menacing, vaguely human, thin as whips, and so incredibly fast. They struck with blurred movement, and each touch of their sharp arms sliced skin on one of the youths. Each feint, each stroke, came with the rapidity of a snake's lightning tongue.

Anhinga watched in horror as her friends' bodies writhed in pain. Their faces twisted in terror. Why didn't they run? Why didn't they act to protect themselves? She found her voice, calling out, "Mist Finger?"

He turned terror-bright eyes on hers, his face contorted, the black hole of his mouth open in agony. "Dead," she heard him say.

"Get away!" she cried. "All of you, flee! Run! Escape!"

Yet they stood, arms lifted, heads rolling as they flinched from each blow given them by the darting wraiths. Their bodies shone red as blood slicked their quivering skin in sheets. Each gaping cut hung open, and beneath the cleanly sliced skin she could see exposed muscles straining and jumping like knotted ropes.

The darting manlike shadows continued their dance, flitting, slashing with pointed hands. Anhinga stifled a cry as patches of skin began to hang, draping like soggy cloth. Her friends opened their mouths and shrieked—but she heard only silence.

"*Run!*" she pleaded, clasping her hands in front of her as she sank to her knees. "In Panther's name, run!"

Cold stone ate into her knees as tears streaked down her cheeks.

The shadowy apparitions ducked, whirled, and lanced out with greater frenzy.

Anhinga saw sections of muscle sliced away, bloody bone exposed here, entrails dropping out of gut cavities there. And still the screams her ears could not hear shattered her souls.

Bit by bit their guts came tumbling out, falling past their savaged crotches to puddle in a slippery mess at their feet. It didn't end as bits of their bodies were flayed away. It didn't even end when only crimson skeletons stood teetering in the gaudy light, bits of sinew hanging like web from the brutalized bone.

The darting wraiths continued to collect in the smoky shadows only to strike repeatedly. Now each flashing stab of arm or leg neatly severed a bone from the wavering remains.

One last strike snapped Mist Finger's blood-matted skull from his neck, sending it tumbling down. Like a gourd, it spattered into the steaming viscera, and rolled down to rock on its side no more than an arm's length before Anhinga's face.

Wide-eyed, she stared into that grisly visage. Where once Mist Finger's dark brown eyes had rested, now raw hollows rimmed with torn tissue gaped. Blood caked the skull's teeth as it gave her a thin grin.

"What can I do, Mist Finger?" she wailed, sagging further toward the cold stone floor.

The voice, lonely, as dismembered as the corpse before her, hissed, *"Kill them, Anhinga. Kill them for all of us. It is time! Send our souls some relief. Make them pay . . . for us!"*

Jerking awake, she bolted upright, surprised at the vividness of the Dream. Cool air washed over her sweat-slick skin. Her daughter was crying in the darkness, disturbed by her thrashing.

A Dream! Blessed Panther, only a Dream. She closed her eyes, seeing that blood-smeared skull staring back from her memory. So real, as if Mist Finger's Dream Soul had been wrapped around hers.

She rubbed a nervous hand over her damp face. Tangles of hair clung to her clammy cheeks.

"It is time, Anhinga," she whispered to herself. "It is time to do what you came here to do."

She reached out, feeling the bed where Salamander usually lay. Empty. He was at Pine Drop's on this night.

Her fingers caressed his bedding, tracing the memory of his face. She could see his worried eyes, sense the tension in the set of his lips. If she tried, she could imagine the beating of his heart.

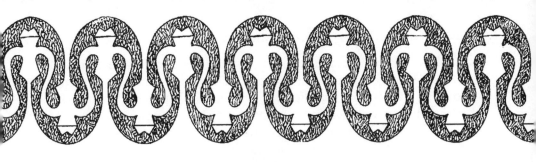

Fifty

I think you should be fasting," Bobcat said to Salamander as he leaned forward and lit the end of his stone pipe with a twig from the fire. The mixture of sumac, sweetgum, and wild cherry leaves left an acrid tang in the air.

The Serpent's house was new; but the poles, saplings, and vines that supported the roof already had stained to a dark amber color. The place smelled new, having yet to develop that characteristic smoke-flavored stuffiness of an old house. The plaster hadn't been smudged by greased bodies.

Bobcat leaned back, puffing contentedly, and raised his eyebrows as he studied Salamander. "I don't know what more to tell you, my friend. Perhaps if the old Serpent had lived? Who knows? He might have known what you could do to prepare yourself."

Salamander squirmed as he leaned forward on the pole bench. He propped his elbows on his knees and blew through his fingers before saying, "Fasting would do little good."

"Purification always helps when it comes to the ways of Power."

"In my case, I don't need to find a vision. It seems like every time I close my eyes some Spirit Helper is chasing down my Dream Soul to impart advice. Masked Owl wants to lead me away to bliss as I Dance with the One. Many Colored Crow will give me the authority and prestige to save Sun Town from clan violence. He will make us great. That is the choice that looms before me. Enlightenment or fame and glory."

"Given my calling, Salamander, I would have to choose enlightenment. I can only imagine what the One must be like." Bobcat shook his head. "Truly, friend. I wonder sometimes if I am not fooling myself and everyone around me by becoming the Serpent."

"You know how to Sing the cures. You know the plants, Bobcat, and how to conjure their spirits to heal. I've been thrilled at the sound of your voice as you Sing the ceremonies." Salamander paused. "I think being the Serpent is more than losing your souls in the search for the One. Many Colored Crow is right about that. You have a duty here, to do your best for the People." He chuckled hollowly. "That is the trap, my friend. Do you save yourself? Or do you save others?"

"How can you save others if you do not save yourself first?" Bobcat asked.

"For that, I have no answer." Salamander rubbed his face. "But if you fall into the One, you will not want to leave it. I've touched it, felt its caress at the edges of my soul. It's . . ."

"Yes?"

"More wonderful than I can ever tell you."

Bobcat frowned at the wistful tone in Salamander's voice. He puffed and exhaled a cloud of blue, thoughtful brown eyes watching the smoke rise. "I would give anything to have even that. Why don't you just give in to the Dream? Let the rest of us sort this out on our own."

"I have obligations."

"Ah, yes, obligations."

"They are what make us the Sun People, Bobcat. Obligations and responsibilities are what separate us from the animals." Salamander pulled his hands back, studying the lines in his palms. "Snakes, I recall Mother giving me that lecture the night she sent me up the Bird's Head. What I would give to be that simple boy again."

"You could go away, Salamander. Take your wives and travel off to the Twin Circles Camp on the gulf. Or perhaps over to Yellow Mud Camp. We have camps and villages throughout the land for five days' journey in any direction."

"That might solve my problems here, but what about Many Colored Crow's vision? Do you really think Deep Hunter and Mud Stalker could end up fighting? Could they really cause a war?"

Bobcat nodded seriously. "Yes, my friend. I believe it. They are driven men who see an opportunity. Owl Clan's very success has led them to desperation."

"If I choose one, how does the other react? If I choose Many

Colored Crow, is my head split by a lightning bolt the next day?"

"If you leave, you are no longer at the center. Maybe they will lose interest in you."

"And maybe they will torment me and my wives for having disappointed them!"

"Well, you never can tell about Spirit Helpers."

"Thanks."

"I don't feel like I'm doing you much good."

"What would the Serpent have said?" Salamander mused. "What do you think he would have told me to do?"

Bobcat squinted one eye as he inspected the sooty end of his tubular stone pipe. "I think he would have told you to listen to your souls and to follow their bidding."

"My souls are full of questions and troubles, Serpent. They have no answers." Salamander rubbed his hands together as he watched the smoking fire pit. The pattern in the coals eluded him. "I know things about the future. I have seen Sun Town burned and abandoned. I have seen it strong and invincible. I have seen myself dead in one vision, and old and joyous in another."

"You have?"

Salamander nodded. "I've heard voices whispering on the future's wind as it blows to the past. I've caught flashes of things. Things I don't understand. Tens of tens of canoes paddling to Sun Town in some visions. And great evil like a foul cloud settling onto us in others."

"Is this some evil I can fight?"

"No, my friend. Not unless you have a salve for the souls of men."

"In that realm, I am lost, Salamander."

"So am I."

The day was mild, the hazy sky filled with occasional patches of white cloud that sailed northward on the endless breeze. Salamander sat at the edge of the ramada, drilling holes in bison bone while Wing Heart sat at her loom, humming and talking to the ghosts, her gray head nodding back and forth.

In the northern half of the plaza, the moiety's solstice team practiced pitching. They used sticks as long as a person's leg, flattened at the far end to cup and sling a deerhide ball. Made up of young men and a few women from the Northern clans, the team would defend the moiety at the conclusion of the summer solstice ceremonies. In the game the teams represented the struggle of the Powers of the North and South. It was thought that the winning side would be favored by luck and the Spirit Beings during the coming turning of the seasons.

If only it could be so easy. Salamander watched the sleek bodies, greased and streaked with sweat. Yellow Spider ran in the fore, gracefully dipping his stick, flipping the ball up, and while still hanging in the air, batting it with the flat to send it flying forward.

But no game would settle Salamander's dilemma. He rubbed his hands together and picked up his bow drill. With the device, he could drill holes in beads with dispatch. The hardwood drill stem was pointed by a red chert perforator, essentially a stone needle crafted from a flake. He would twist the stem around his small bowstring, place the tip into the dimple in the end of the bead, and, using a wooden block to guide the stem, saw the bow back and forth to spin the drill. A drop of saliva eased the tip as it cut through the soft bone in the bison scapula.

Drilling the hole was only the start of the process. Short sections of cane, essentially hollow tubes of different diameters, lay ready for use. Beside them on the palmetto matting sat two bowls, one filled with sand, the other with water. Sun Town, lying as it did on fine silt, had no sand deposits. Sand, like so many things, was imported from afar. Salamander's had been sifted through fabric to obtain the correct grit, and then shipped in by canoe. He had Traded some of the buffalo hide for it that he had in turn obtained from Green Crane and Always Fat the summer before.

Once he had finished the line of holes, he removed his drill and selected one of the sections of cane, studying the size of the hole it would bore. He wet the end, dipped it in the bowl of sand, and fitted it to his bow. In the bead-making process, this final step was the most important. It took great concentration to start the cut so that the sand-tipped cane would grind a precisely round groove around the center hole in the bead. If he were not perfect, the bead would be off-center.

Salamander didn't realize his tongue hung out the side of his mouth as he fitted the cane over the first of the holes in the bison scapula.

"Have you ever thought of drilling the hole afterward?" Mud Stalker asked, his shadow blotting the sunlight.

Salamander looked up. "It's harder to hold a small bead and drill the center than it is to do it this way." He cocked his head. "We always make beads this way. Even when we're making them of stone."

Mud Stalker smiled, the lines in his face deepening. "Yes, but you like to do things differently than most people, Speaker." Knees crackled as he squatted, his ruined arm cradled in his lap. A faint smile bent his sun-creased lips as he looked at Wing Heart. The old woman's fingers plucked at the fabric on her loom. He raised his voice. "Good Morning, Wing Heart!"

Salamander's mother remained oblivious, her lips moving as she talked soundlessly to her lost souls.

"Can I be of help, Speaker?" Salamander asked.

Mud Stalker turned flinty eyes on him. "I thought perhaps we could have a little discussion, you and I."

"Speak." Salamander eyed his drill, positioned it just so, and began rotating the sand-encrusted cane. To his satisfaction it didn't slip to one side or the other.

"I made you."

"What?"

"I made you what you are, Salamander. Without me you would have had nothing. On White Bird's death, the Speakership would have gone to Half Thorn."

"I suppose."

"Good. I'm glad that you have enough sense to understand that." His eyes hardened. "You are in a great deal of danger, Salamander."

He couldn't stop the faint smile. "If only you knew, Speaker. But I think you are more worried about Pine Drop and Night Rain than any predicament I might find myself in."

"I would like you to divorce my nieces."

Salamander sawed back and forth on the bow as the drill ate its way through the bone. Only when the sand-tipped cane cut a clean round hole through the bone, did he look up. "Have you discussed this with Pine Drop?"

Mud Stalker's gaze hardened. "She has decided that she will stay with you. I am hoping that you—obliged as you are to me—will be a little smarter than she is." His smile widened. "I would not like anything to happen to you."

Salamander carefully positioned his drill over the next of the holes. Using his block to bear down, he rotated the tip carefully to create a guide. "Speaker, let us make one thing clear, shall we?"

"Indeed, Salamander."

"I admit that you had a hand in making me Speaker. You were responsible for my initiation at the Men's House, and for all of that, odd as it may sound, I thank you."

"Why would that sound odd?"

"Because each of the things you did for me was for your own

personal gain. You wanted me as Owl Clan Speaker precisely so that you could destroy me. Through me, you could strike at Mother and at Owl Clan. Given that fact, I have no obligation to you. That is the thing I would like made clear."

Mud Stalker reached up with his left hand to stroke his chin. "Others might not see it that way, Salamander."

"But I do, Mud Stalker. So does Pine Drop." He smiled. "Night Rain is pregnant."

"She hasn't missed her moon yet!"

Salamander enjoyed the rasping sound of his drill as it ground through the bone. "Shall we dispense with the rest of our pleasantries? Stated as briefly as possible: I owe you nothing. You and I have no obligation between us. In fact, if memory serves, Snapping Turtle Clan still has obligations to Owl Clan in return for the many gifts that my brother, White Bird, bestowed upon you when he returned from the north." With his chin, Salamander indicated the copper turtle hanging on Mud Stalker's necklace.

The Speaker's eyes narrowed to slits. "Do not attempt to remind me of my obligations."

"It is the food that nourishes the clans, Speaker." Salamander shot him a measuring glance. "Without obligation, we are nothing. Harmony disappears, and we end up at each other's throats. Depending on what happens, will you remember that in your dealings with Deep Hunter?"

"I have the ability destroy you."

"By branding me a witch?"

Mud Stalker made a forgiving gesture. "All right, perhaps you are not obligated to me. I grant you that, but if you work with me, help me to unseat Thunder Tail and put Sweet Root in his place, I might be persuaded to save your life. Allow you to remain married to Pine Drop, at least."

Salamander chuckled softly. "As if that was my only worry? Oh, Speaker, if you only knew the choices that lie before me."

"Then I take it we cannot come to an accommodation?"

"Not this way, Speaker."

"This is your last chance."

"You railed when Night Rain acted in concert with Deep Hunter. Don't you think it difficult to blame her when you would use me, meddle with my clan's affairs?"

He didn't answer that, only saying. "I must destroy you, then."

"It is what you have wished from the beginning."

Mud Stalker jerked a nod, his eyes on the ballplayers across the barrow pit. "They're going to lose, you know. And so will you."

Salamander said nothing as the Speaker stood, shot a piteous look at Wing Heart, and walked around the borrow pit before heading south to his clan grounds.

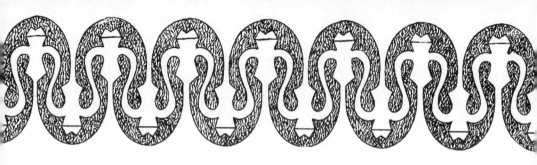

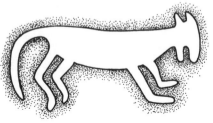

Fifty-one

Anhinga filled her lungs with the damp odor of the swamp. Her canoe drifted the final lengths to slide onto the muddy beach of the island. She could see the blue haze of smoke from the fire. The tall figure of Jaguar Hide reassured her. Her uncle stood with his hands on his hips, his gray hair spilling around his muscular shoulders. A keen wariness lay behind his eyes.

Lifting herself above the gunwales, Anhinga swung out of the canoe and pushed it up onto the bank. From within she lifted the cradleboard that held her sleeping daughter. The infant was wrapped against the mosquitoes and flies, her face greased, while beads of pinesap added further discouragement to the pests.

"Niece! Let me see my heir!" Jaguar Hide came striding down the slope, his arms out.

She charged up to him, a desperate sense of relief bursting her breast. Her daughter began to cry, jounced as she was by Anhinga's run.

After a crushing hug, she handed the cradleboard over to Jaguar Hide. He inspected the little round face. The baby girl had her eyes closed, her mouth open as she squalled her displeasure to the world.

"Yes, that's it, my little joy, you tell the world that you are here. Bellow your presence out like the thunder itself so all may know that Jaguar Hide's lineage goes on."

"She needs changing and feeding," Anhinga said, unwilling to take her daughter back from the fawning Jaguar Hide.

"At this age, they usually do." Jaguar Hide was smiling, wiggling his finger like a worm in front of a catfish. "Here, little one, open your eyes. Yes, that's it. Let me look inside you. Are you there yet, my little niece? Have souls fastened themselves to your little body?"

"We don't know yet," Anhinga replied. "She is still so young. The Sun People don't believe that the Dream Soul fastens itself to a body until a child speaks. They claim that is the first actual proof that a soul is there."

"That's silly drivel," Jaguar Hide insisted as he played with the crying infant. "You've been among them too long. The Life Soul comes with the first breath. That's when the infant sucks it in." To the little girl, he asked, "How could you live otherwise?"

Anhinga reached out and half wrestled the cradleboard from her uncle. "I take it that we are safe?"

His smile faded, and he nodded. "I got your message. Warriors are out and about. There will be no surprises. What has happened? We haven't talked for moons."

"Striped Dart didn't tell you?"

Jaguar Hide shook his head, frowning. "Tell me what?"

Anhinga walked up to the fire, glancing uneasily toward the place where Eats Wood had been killed. Was his ghost still lurking here, prowling among the patches of hanging moss?

"Salamander killed a man who followed me. We swore Striped Dart to secrecy. Apparently, Uncle, my brother has taken such responsibilities to his heart."

"A man followed you? And Striped Dart didn't tell me? I'll pull his arms out of his sockets!"

"No, you will not. He gave Salamander and me his word."

Jaguar Hide narrowed his eyes. "You had better start at the beginning."

She related the story as she unwrapped the baby from the cradleboard and changed the fouled moss with fresh. Then she raised her daughter to her nipple. "But for Salamander's timely arrival, I would have been dead and Striped Dart ambushed," she finished.

Jaguar Hide frowned pensively at the fire. "I should have thought of guards in the beginning."

"We were being clever, remember? The fewer the people who knew, the better?"

"And this time?" He shrugged. "How do we know that you will not be ambushed when you return?"

"Yellow Spider will meet me. He has gone for sandstone at the quarry."

"I have been wondering about the fabrics that were left there.

Striped Dart said little about them, only that he had bartered with the stone boat."

"I am starting to think he will make a good leader, Uncle."

"Bah! He's soft. Willing to take the easy way for less when the hard path will give him more."

"Is that so bad?" She studied the little mouth working so desperately at her breast.

She looked up at his silence, startled to find his expression hard, an unforgiving glint in his eyes. "Are you giving up on me, Niece? Is that what you are trying to tell me? That now that you have a husband who fought for you, and planted that child within you, that your heart has lost the fire of revenge?"

She gave him a grim smile. "No, Uncle. I came here to tell you that the time has come to strike."

He settled back, exhaling as he closed his eyes. "I cannot tell you how I worried. First Striped Dart returns, obviously bearing secrets. Then moons pass without word from you, and finally, when you do come, it is with the warning that we must be guarded here. What was I supposed to think?"

"Perhaps you should have thought less and looked deeper into my heart."

"So, you want to strike now? Why?"

"We are running out of time. The clans are gathering against Salamander." She frowned at that, surprised it hurt to admit that in front of her uncle.

"You fear for your life if they move against him?"

She shrugged. "It's not that. I will have warning enough to get away. He's a good man, that's all. And the odd thing is, he's a Powerful one. Uncle, he knows what is coming, but does nothing to avoid it."

"How is that?"

"He knows that the clans are poised to strike him down, but he goes about his life searching for the proper actions to save not himself, but everyone else."

"Sounds like the ways of a fool, if you ask me."

She gave him a bitter smile. "Never think him a fool, Uncle."

"A man with Power against him—not to mention so many people—isn't smart."

"My husband is a very smart man, Uncle." She gave him a half-lidded stare. "Smart in ways that I don't think you can understand, but we're straying from my reason for meeting you." She met his eyes. "The Dead have been coming to me, pleading with me. I have to act, Uncle, or they will lose their patience with me."

"How do you intend to do this?"

She gestured over her shoulder. "Do you remember the hemlock that grows on the far side of the island?"

A slow smile spread on his lips. "Ah, and then?"

"The next time I paddle south, Uncle, will be for the last time."

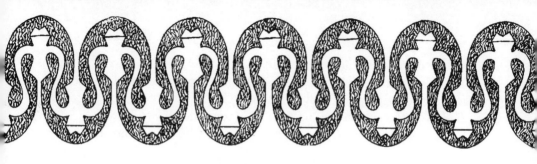

Fifty-two

Firelight illuminated the interior of the Men's House; it flashed on the masks and danced over cane walls decorated with the hanging trophies, war clubs, sets of antlers, and grinning human skulls. Beyond the east-facing windows, the night was black, veiled with thick clouds that promised rain. But for the crackle of the fire, only the sounds of the night insects broke the silence.

Mud Stalker reached for a section of broken oak and tossed it into the fire. Sparks crackled and whirled, dancing in the air. He stroked his chin, dark eyes watching the licking flames.

"Speaker?" Water Stinger called from the door. "Speaker Deep Hunter is coming."

"Is he alone?"

"Yes, Speaker."

"Please see that we are not bothered. And make doubly sure that no one is lurking around the windows or pressing their ears to the walls."

Water Stinger's lips twitched. "Yes, Speaker, I understand."

"Also . . ."

"Yes, Speaker?"

"Stick your fingers in your ears. You don't need to hear this either."

Water Stinger smiled, nodding. "Yes, Speaker. I understand." He ducked out the door and into the night. Several heartbeats later Mud Stalker heard soft voices, then Deep Hunter stepped in.

The Speaker wore a bobcat pelt over his shoulder; a dark brown breechcloth with interlocked alligators on the flap hung down the front. He raised an eyebrow as he stopped short and studied Mud Stalker. Then his eyes made a quick survey of the room, a question reflected in the set of his mouth.

"There is no one else here. Thank you for coming." Mud Stalker gestured at the mat across the fire from him.

"Just the two of us?" Deep Hunter asked. "In the middle of the night?"

"Just the two of us. My young hunter will ensure that we are not interrupted and can speak our minds without having it carried to every hungry ear and flapping set of jaws among the clans."

Deep Hunter shrugged and walked across to ease himself down onto the matting. His bones cracked as he settled himself and removed the bobcat hide from around his shoulders. With careful fingers he folded it and laid it neatly to one side.

Mud Stalker indicated a small steaming bowl that rested at the side of the fire. "I have provided us with fresh black drink."

Deep Hunter's hard eyes never wavered. "If I drink any of that, I won't sleep. It's already late."

"So? Do you have a busy day tomorrow?"

A faint smile curled Deep Hunter's lips. "No, I suppose not." He lifted the bowl, tilting it to sip at the hot liquid. When he set it down Mud Stalker reached out with his good hand and grasped it, lifting it to his lips to drink some of the dark bitter liquid. It almost scalded his tongue.

"You brewed it strong."

Mud Stalker set the bowl down and wiped his lips. "Something about black drink. It makes the thoughts clearer and races the blood."

Deep Hunter's eyes had narrowed. "I would assume, however, that you didn't call me here in the middle of the night just to share a pleasant drink and make a little companionable conversation."

"We have a problem."

Deep Hunter cocked his head. "We have a lot of problems, you and I."

"What are we going to do about Owl Clan?"

"What are *we* going to do? Why should anything my clan decides interest you?"

"Because no matter what is between us, you and I must work together on this."

"Why?"

"I think you know. You are waiting, planning on striking at Jaguar

Hide. You would have done it sooner, but Owl Clan has an agreement with the old rascal. If you take action on your own, it could cause a stir in the Council. Thunder Tail, Cane Frog, Clay Fat, and Salamander could vote to condemn Alligator Clan. I might be tempted to side with them against you."

"You are assuming that the Council would take an interest in the Swamp Panthers' response to a 'peaceful Trading expedition' that went wrong." He smiled warily. "You just can't tell about those people down there."

"That might work. And again, it might not. Someone could make the plausible argument that your warriors took that action as a provocation. That you were jealous of Owl Clan's domination of the sandstone Trade." Mud Stalker massaged the elbow on his ruined arm. "Or, Snakes take us, worse, that it was personally motivated, a backhanded way to repay Anhinga for what she did to young Saw Back."

After a pause, Deep Hunter asked, "What did you have in mind?"

"There might be a way that you could attain your ends, and I might attain mine."

"Your ends and mine have nothing in common." Deep Hunter's smoldering eyes took Mud Stalker's measure, his jaw muscles tight.

Mud Stalker made a pacifying gesture. "Let us lay our gaming pieces in the open. You and I have been adversaries for a long time. I know how you used Night Rain against me. Perhaps I deserved that. I shouldn't have placed such a naive young girl in that position in the first place." He chuckled at himself. "Knowing where we stand with each other, I propose that we work together."

"Why should we?"

"Because I think young Salamander has too much of his mother and uncle in him. If he has done the things he has as a fresh-made man, what will he be like in another ten summers?"

Deep Hunter digested that for a moment, his expression pensive. "We thought him pretty foolish for the way he stripped his clan for Trade with those Wash'ta Traders. But look how well he did this last winter, giving out those hides. Who would have thought the weather was going to be so miserable?"

"Even a fool pulls in a full net on occasion, but this is something more."

"I would hesitate to mention that it was your insistence that put him in such a position of authority to start with." He gave Mud Stalker an ironic smile. "Let me guess. When White Bird was killed, you thought luck had dropped control of Owl Clan into your lap, didn't you?"

Mud Stalker shrugged. "I wanted to see Wing Heart's authority compromised."

"What prompted you? Everyone thought you were crazy when you married those girls to that boy."

Mud Stalker chewed his lip, hesitating.

"You said we should speak freely."

"A Dream," Mud Stalker admitted. "A Power Dream. Now I cannot be sure if it was for good or evil."

"Which, I suppose, is the real reason you brought me here. What did you want to offer me?"

"An alliance. At least until we can fix our current problem. You have Thunder Tail's obligation. Cunningly done, I might add, through information provided by Night Rain. I have influence with Clay Fat. Rattlesnake Clan is obliged to me for the moment."

"What are you planning?"

Mud Stalker lifted the bowl and sipped black drink. Handing it to Deep Hunter, he said, "Salamander doesn't behave the way a young man of his age should, don't you agree?"

Deep Hunter drank, wiped his lips, and shrugged. "How should he behave?"

"A normal young man doesn't work with the Dead. He doesn't spend every morning atop the Bird's Head where he can look out into the Land of the Dead. He doesn't ally himself with Jaguar Hide for purposes that we can only guess at. And, most of all, have you noticed how those who stand in his way have been removed?"

"What?"

"You saw him when the Serpent's house was burned."

Deep Hunter gave a thoughtful nod. "Do you have any real proof that he's a witch?"

"We need only the accusation. People will do the rest. He has only a handful of allies."

"If I support the accusation of witchcraft, what do I get in return?"

"Warriors from Snapping Turtle Clan, and perhaps even Rattlesnake Clan, will accompany yours on the raid against the Swamp Panthers. We will break Owl Clan's peace and destroy their access to sandstone. Who knows, if we use Anhinga as bait, perhaps you might finally manage to lure Jaguar Hide into your reach. Whether you do or not, with Snapping Turtle Clan involved, no one in the Council will vote against you."

Deep Hunter sat silently, lost in thought. Then he nodded. "I agree, as long as I can kill Jaguar Hide, and Saw Back gets Anhinga—at least for a while."

"I think we can arrange that."

"What about afterward?"

"Owl Clan is discredited for as long as either of us is alive. Then you and I can go our separate ways. There will be no remaining obligation as we seek to replace Thunder Tail."

"If Salamander is declared a witch?" Deep Hunter asked, apparently satisfied. "What then?"

"A witch who belongs to Owl Clan becomes their problem, not ours. I have spoken to Half Thorn. He will be happy to attend to it. After all, he has everything to gain."

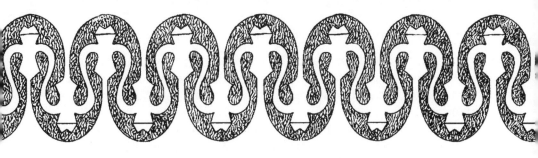

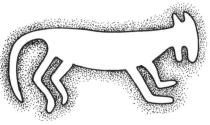

Fifty-three

In the light of a half-moon, Anhinga drove her canoe onto the muddy landing below Sun Town. Her stealthy arrival frightened a raccoon that searched in and among the beached canoes for bits of fish guts or other edibles left by the fishermen. The beast hurried away in its rolling waddle, lucky to have escaped. Raccoon had a succulent and sweet meat.

The night pressed warmly against the land, a blessing after the cold and drizzly winter. The presence of the raccoon made it doubtful that anyone was close enough to witness her return. For a long moment, Anhinga remained still and listened to the sounds of the night: Insect wings whirred around her head. Frogs croaked. Somewhere in the distance a bull alligator roared.

Nothing moved along the line of canoes; many had been flipped over to keep water from collecting inside. The vessels reminded her of a school of sleeping fish.

She carefully stood, stepped out of the canoe, and dragged her slim boat onto the muddy bank. She bent and slung the loop of her daughter's cradleboard onto her shoulder. Then she reached for the fabric-wrapped bundle that lay in the bow. She handled it with great care. As she started up the slope she made doubly sure that her daughter's cradleboard hung as far as possible from the fabric bundle. She dare not even let them touch.

She slowed as she neared the top of the slope, hearing music coming from the Men's House. The clacking rhythm of hardwood sticks, rattles, and the thump of drums almost covered the sound of bare feet shuffling on cane matting. A heron-bone flute piped a delicate melody. Male voices rose and fell as they sang in accompaniment.

Light reflected in soft yellow from the building's roof openings. The east-facing window made a glowing square in the dark wall. Figures darted back and forth inside. She could see that they wore masks. Some had deer antlers, others birdlike heads. Still others looked to be redheaded woodpecker, alligator, and dragonfly, all totems of war.

Let them Sing and Dance while they can.

War, like the dancers, wore many different masks.

A grim smile crossed her lips. Women weren't supposed to see any part of the men's secret rituals. She considered that as she turned her steps north toward the house she and Salamander had built. The mysteries of the Men's House had always intrigued her. They had more fun than the women did, the latter sitting around weaving baskets, making pigments, and gossiping while they changed absorbent and passed their moons.

I should have been born a man. But no, had she been, she would never have had the opportunity that now presented itself. A Swamp Panther warrior would never have been allowed—as she had—to walk freely among the Sun People.

What is it about them that they do not consider a woman to be dangerous? Arrogance? Stupidity? Or just a lack of respect for her and her kind? Certainly their Clan Elders, also female, should have had the intelligence and resources to appreciate the threat she posed.

Then she recalled her uncle's insistence that she bide her time, endure the passing seasons among the Sun People. How she had hated the wait. How smart her uncle had been; she now passed where she would, hardly garnering a second glance. She would have been faceless but for her reputation for breaking Saw Back's face.

Thinking back, she didn't regret it. Of course, she would have been faceless, even more invisible than she was now. Over the moons, however, that act had brought her a curious sort of recognition. People made way for her, sometimes giving her a curt nod. Not friendly, just respectful. She decided she liked that, liked it a lot.

One day soon, she would be returning home. She would see that same look in the eyes of her people. If she managed to do this thing, if it unfolded the way she planned, it would stun the Sun People to the roots of their souls. Indeed, her descendants would speak her name with awe for generations.

All it would take was courage, and the hope that she didn't get caught before she could remove herself well beyond the Sun People's wrath.

As she walked past it, the Women's House was silent and dark, although the faint smell of cooking cattail and smoke hung on the heavy air. A lone dog stood up in the doorway, shook, and growled at her. She made a soft cooing noise and the cur trotted down the incline of the Mother Mound, its tail wagging. The animal appeared happy that she hadn't thrown an old cooking clay at it.

"How are you tonight?" she asked softly.

If she could trust her night-veiled eyes, the dog was a young bitch. She bounced and whined as she followed along behind. Like most dogs in Sun Town, she didn't receive kind words very often.

"Shsht! Don't do that!" She raised the bundle high as the dog grabbed it with its teeth and tugged. "That's poison! Not for you to be playing with!"

The bitch whined again, and backed off at the harsh tone. Tail wagging expectantly, she stared up at Anhinga in the faint light of the half-moon.

"Go on!" She waved her away. "Go back to whoever was feeding you back there. You don't want any part of me."

Cowed, the bitch dropped behind, trailing by a short distance.

Anhinga walked past the borrow pit to her dark house. Swallowing hard, she removed the door and ducked inside. On stealthy feet she crossed to Salamander's bed, feeling his empty buffalo robe.

Good. He's at Pine Drop's.

She carefully laid her sleeping daughter on the bench, felt for the small ceramic pot she knew was by the bed leg, and walked back to the square of light that marked the doorway. There she found her fire-hardened digging stick where she had left it. With the pot in one hand, and the digging stick and her bundle in the other, she stepped out into the night. Haze softened the half-moon's face, dimming the brighter stars. From Wing Heart's house Anhinga could hear the burr of the woman's snoring.

Anhinga laid the pot and fabric bundle on the ground. Pressing her breastbone against the end of the digging stick, she drove the sharp point into the soft earth and levered it up. It took her less than two fingers of time to dig a hole large enough to take the pot. Using only her fingertips, she placed the fabric bundle inside the pot and then capped it with a wooden plate that lay beside Wing Heart's loom. Lowering the pot into the hole, she scooped earth over it. The excess dirt she scattered around here and there. Finally, she laid a section of cane matting over the hump of earth and pressed it down to hide her handiwork.

In that instant, the image of Salamander's face flashed between her souls. Panther's blood, this was going to hurt him so. Only at that thought did her souls ache.

The crow caught Red Finger's attention when it swooped down out of the overhanging forest and clutched a lock of his graying hair in its feet.

Shocked and surprised, Red Finger ducked, then yipped at the pain as the gleaming bird pulled the length of hair out by the roots.

In anger, he almost capsized his canoe as he scrambled for his atlatl and darts. He sent a long dart flying after the bird, clawing for balance as his canoe wobbled with the force of his release.

The crow dodged artfully to one side, the dart sailing between the branches of a tupelo before arcing down to cut cleanly into the water.

Red Finger rubbed the top of his head, glaring at the circling crow.

"What do you want?"

The bird answered with a raucous call and dived at him again. Red Finger flattened himself into the bottom of his rocking craft and glanced up warily.

The crow had landed on a low-hanging branch. It stared at him with a curious brown eye, opened its mouth, and flicked a sharp-tipped tongue at him.

"Insolent bird." Red Finger carefully braced himself; easing his atlatl back as he fitted another dart into the nock. In a sinuous movement his arm went back. The cast was liquid, fast, and accurate.

To his amazement, the crow bobbed down, flattening itself on the branch as the dart hissed within a feather's breadth of its shining back.

Caaaawwwww! The sound echoed through the swamp as the crow mocked him and bounced to yet another branch. There, it flapped its wings, teasing him.

Red Finger muttered under his breath and picked up his paddle. The cursed bird had to have been someone's pet. A fledgling stolen from the nest, raised and trained by some swamp hunter.

As he closed, the bird flipped off the branch and sailed farther into the swamp. Red Finger paddled after it, stopping on occasion to reach up and finger the raw place on his scalp.

For a hand of time he followed the pesky bird. Each time his interest waned, the crow dived at him, snatching at his hair, raising his ire to the boiling point again.

Thus it was that by the middle of the day, he found himself deep within Swamp Panther territory.

The crow circled him, fluttering just out of reach. Red Finger used his atlatl to flail at it, hoping to smack the miserable pest from the sky. It avoided his wild blows with uncanny ease.

"What do you want of me?" he declared, half in anger, half in wary suspicion. Snakes! This wasn't a spirit bird, was it? Or, blood and pus, worse, it wasn't some creature trained by the Swamp Panthers to lure unwitting hunters into their territory where they could be ambushed and killed?

With that thought, he lifted his paddle, prepared to leave the accursed bird to its own devices, when he saw it wing to a cypress knee. Sunlight shone on its sleek black feathers. It studied him with an intelligent brown eye.

The crow bobbed its head, pointing its beak toward the brackish water.

"What do you *want* of me?" Red Finger glanced around, wary of a Swamp Panther ambush. Every direction he looked, he could only see the swamp, the surface of the water marred here and there by the normal rings left by water bugs, fish, and bubbles. Insects fluttered around him, songbirds filled the spring-flush leaves with song.

Red Finger cocked his head as the crow plucked a white stone from the top of the cypress knee and dropped it into the water with a plop.

A stone? Out here? Atop a cypress knee?

He paddled forward, an eerie fear climbing his spine. No, this was no trained pet, but something else. He wasn't a man used to Power, but he could feel it swelling around him.

As the bow of his canoe slipped past the knee, the crow gave him a loud squawk, leaped into the air, and flapped through a ragged hole in the canopy above. Rays of vibrant color, reds, blues, and greens flashed off its wings.

Red Finger scratched his cheek in confusion. Then, bending over the side of his canoe, he looked down into the water. There, several hands below the surface, he could see a small round white stone. It was resting in what looked like a sunken canoe.

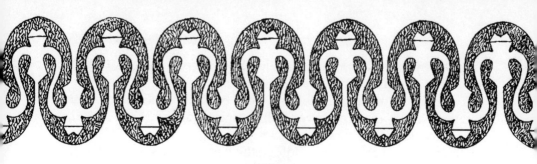

Fifty-four

Salamander trotted down from the Bird's Head after his sunrise devotions. He felt a lingering sense of foreboding, partly from his disturbing Dreams the night before, partly from Night Rain's violent bout of morning sickness. Whereas neither Pine Drop nor Anhinga had been bothered much, Night Rain's first experience of pregnancy was proving to be downright miserable.

"Must be a boy," Pine Drop said as she cuddled her suckling daughter to her breast.

"That or a monster," Night Rain had insisted as she wiped her mouth and cast suspicious eyes on Salamander.

He had raised his hands in defense, and said, "I would have asked Power for another daughter. I'm in deep enough trouble with your uncle as it is. Knowing that I had produced another heir for his lineage might make him smile a bit more kindly when I'm around."

The round red-yellow sun seemed to drift off the horizon and higher into the morning sky. The light made Salamander squint as he rounded the first ridge, where Cane Frog's house stood. The old Clan Elder hadn't emerged yet to greet the morning with her sight-less eyes. Nor had Three Moss come to check on her mother and see to her needs.

He cast a cautious glance at the round Council House as he passed, knowing that soon, no doubt just before the solstice cele-bration, he was going to face expulsion. The topic of his witchcraft was now on every lip, some people even speaking openly of it.

How does a person prove he is not a witch?

How could he blame them? Last spring he had been considered an odd boy, even despised by his mother. Within a turning of the seasons his popular brother was dead, Salamander was Clan Speaker, with three wives, two houses, and an unheard of alliance with the Swamp Panthers. People knew that he was tied up in the ways of Power, that he spent a great deal of time with the Serpent. He had helped prepare the bodies of the dead. Each morning found him alone at the top of the Bird's Head when normal young men were waking up in their wives' arms. If witchcraft didn't explain that, what did?

With those thoughts lodged in his head, he was surprised by a sudden prickling of unease. He stopped short, collecting his thoughts. He came this way every morning, following the trail that was beaten into the grass where people rounded the eastern end of the borrow ditch before climbing Owl Clan's first ridge.

The dog lay on its side in the weeds at the water's edge. From the way the vegetation was bruised, it was apparent that the animal had thrashed as it died. Even the earth was torn up where it had clawed frantically in its last moments.

Salamander stepped over and bent down. The animal, a bitch, was young. Her expanded nipples and fat sides indicated that she was just days shy of a litter. Her lips were pulled back, exposing foam-flecked teeth and gums. Even in death, terror reflected from her wide brown eyes, the pupils gray. Feces had been squirted onto the matted weeds behind her.

"What happened to you?" Salamander asked, his heart softening. He grabbed a foot, pulling the stiff animal over. She hadn't died that long ago. Not even the flies had found her yet.

Salamander made a face, feeling the presentiment that tingled along his soul.

"Why are you trying to warn me, little mother?" he asked gently. "What do you wish to tell me?"

He closed his eyes, trying to hear the dead dog's Dream Soul. With an aching longing, he listened, and heard nothing.

Some people said dogs didn't have Dream Souls, but he didn't believe it. Too many times he had seen the sleeping animals, their eyes twitching, their feet jerking, as they made muffled woofs. If they weren't Dreaming, running in the Dream world, what were they doing?

"I am sorry, little mother, but I will beware. Thank you for trying to tell me, even if I'm too stupid to hear."

He lifted the animal, feeling how stiff the body was, as if wooden beneath the thin hair. With great care he bore the carcass to the drop-off overlooking Morning Lake and laid it over the edge. The dead dog slid down along the steep embankment and lodged in some stalks of marsh elder that clung there.

Depressed, he turned his steps for home. Wing Heart sat at her loom despite the early hour. Water Petal—hunched at the side of the ramada—was graining a deerhide on a polished post set in the ground.

To Salamander's surprise, a third person sat in the morning sun just outside the ramada. It took a moment for the silver hair, the thick shoulders, and lined face to register. Thunder Tail wore one of his bear necklaces, which consisted of claws strung to either side of twin mandibles. A sleek cloak of black bearskin was draped over one shoulder.

Salamander walked past his house and over to the ramada. "Good morning, Council Leader. What brings you here?"

"Good morning to you, too, Speaker Salamander." Thunder Tail's serious face reflected the gravity of his visit. "I came to see Elder Wing Heart. It has been a while since I have had the pleasure of her company."

"She is no longer an Elder."

"She will always be an Elder to me, Salamander." Thunder Tail smiled precisely.

Salamander could see that his mother was oblivious to her guest. Her fingers continued to work the threads, arms rising and falling with a supple grace. Those vacant eyes saw nothing of this world but the fabric before her. Her head continued to move loosely as she dwelt on conversations no one else could hear.

"We thank you for your concern, Speaker. She didn't say anything to you, did she?"

Thunder Tail shook his head, pensive brown eyes on Salamander.

"I am sorry you didn't reach her. We remain hopeful. Water Petal and I keep believing that some familiar face will draw her back long enough that her souls would remember this world."

Thunder Tail gestured for Salamander to sit, then wrapped his thick arms around his knees. "I was a good friend of your mother's. She and I . . ."

"Yes, I know. You were lovers. She always spoke of you with great respect and admiration, Speaker. I'm sure that she is proud that you followed her into the leadership of the Council."

Thunder Tail studied him for a long moment. "You speak very well for such a young man, Salamander."

"I had good teachers." He indicated his mother. "I spent my childhood listening to her and Uncle Cloud Heron. Something of their skill must have rubbed off."

He hesitated. "I didn't just come to see Wing Heart."

"You are concerned about the talk of witchcraft," Salamander filled in. "Mud Stalker and Deep Hunter are going to introduce that claim at the next Council meeting, aren't they?"

"Are you so complacent that you do not understand the threat, young Salamander?"

"It isn't a matter of complacency, Speaker. I face the perennial problem of those accused of witchcraft: belief. No matter what I state in my defense, people will believe what they will believe. I am not a witch. I wish no one—even my enemies—ill. The more strident my voice is as I cry out my innocence, the more assured others will be that I am guilty of using Power for my own gain."

"And what gain is that, Salamander?"

He gestured around. "If I had that kind of Power, Speaker, I would return my mother's souls to this world. Owl Clan and the People have more need of her wits and knowledge here than do the souls in the Spirit World."

"Are you sure of that?"

"Yes, Speaker Thunder Tail. The Spirit World is already well served—it has my uncle and brother."

"Your mother never spoke very highly of you."

"Let us say that I wasn't what she expected in a son."

"But you ended up as Owl Clan's Speaker."

Salamander smiled wryly. "I think we both know how that happened. But, since it did, I will do my best for my clan, Speaker. I was unprepared for this. I can only hope that as time passes, I will do a better job."

"And the witchcraft?"

"Were I a good witch, my clan would be preeminent. I would be basking in the reflected fear and respect of my fellows. I would be plotting with Mud Stalker and Deep Hunter to replace you as leader of the Council. I would be surrounding myself with copper, stone, and exotic hides from the far reaches of our Trade. I think I would be busy destroying my enemies, making them die horrible deaths." A smile crossed his lips. "I ask you, do my enemies tremble at my name?"

"No, Speaker Salamander, they do not." Thunder Tail fingered the soft bearhide on his shoulder as he thought. His eyes kept straying to Wing Heart, and Salamander could see the hurt.

"She loved you," he said softly. "More than all the others."

Thunder Tail looked uncomfortable as he returned his attention to Salamander. "I don't know what good it will do in the end, Salamander, but for one, I don't think you are a witch. There is, however, something about you that worries me. When I am around you, I can feel it, a tension in the air, as if you are headed for some terrible fate."

"With all of my souls, Council Leader, I hope not. But I give you my word, I will do everything within my ability to keep from hurting the People."

"What of your barbarian wife? People would accuse her of witchcraft, too."

"Assuming that I knew how to recognize a witch, I've never seen it in her."

"And when she goes away?"

"She meets with her family."

"Does she plot against us?"

"Of course. We killed her brother and her friends."

"But you don't think she's dangerous?"

"Speaker, never, under any circumstances, believe that she isn't dangerous."

"Then why do you live with her? Surely not just for the sandstone."

Salamander chuckled softly, shaking his head. "It is a complicated thing to explain. I love her. She is my wife, and I enjoy the time I spend with her. Can you understand that? She does things for me, excites my souls when I look into her eyes."

"What of your other wives?"

"They are the same. Each one is different, each has her own qualities."

"But you can trust Pine Drop and Night Rain. You know they won't cut your throat in the middle of the night."

Salamander felt the prickle of warning again. "Speaker? Whatever made you say that? I can anticipate the threat Anhinga poses. She came to us as an enemy. It is those we trust the most who will drive the dagger deepest into our hearts."

Thunder Tail nodded in agreement, and a fist tightened around Salamander's souls.

Night Rain slipped as she followed her cousin, Water Stinger, down the path south of Sun Town. The trail was slick with mud from an afternoon rain shower. Water Stinger had appeared at her house as she patiently drilled stone beads while seated in the ramada's shade. The young warrior had been winded from a long run, and asked for her and Pine Drop.

"Sister is gone. You just missed her. She has taken a basket and gone to collect the first goosefoot greens."

"Then you come!" Water Stinger had insisted, practically dragging her after him as he headed south the way he had come. "It's important. Uncle wants you there."

So they hurried, taking a deeply worn path that led south along the steep embankment overlooking the bottomlands. The way wound through trees that gave periodic glimpses of the cane bottoms where the channel was obscured by the spring flood. Water gleamed silver as sunlight was reflected through the vegetation. The whole world had taken on a blinding green, and the smell of blossoms carried on the air.

"What is it?" Night Rain placed a hand on her belly, wondering what a run like this would do to her queasy stomach.

"Uncle will tell you."

"Where are we going?"

"The landing just below Raspberry Camp."

She knew the place: the first camp south of Sun Town where the south channel looped back against a break in the high terrace. Not more than a half hand's run away, people often camped there when they came from the outlying settlements. Close enough to allow easy access to Sun Town, it was far enough away to avoid the noise and confusion. Not all of the Sun People liked the bustling of Sun Town. She had relatives—people in her own lineage—who lived in the outlying camps, preferring the solitude of the swamps and forest to the city of ridges.

For her turn, Night Rain couldn't stand the slow pace of life in the camps and outlying settlements. After several days, the monotony, the limited companionship, and boredom set in. She swore she would pull her hair out if she couldn't return to Sun Town with its constant activity, games, feasts, and visiting.

Water Stinger surprised her when he directed her off the beaten route just outside of Raspberry Camp. Following a faint trail in the grass, he led her over the sloping embankment and down the steep incline. The way wound around roots of walnut, oak, and sweetgum. A spongy leaf mat muffled their steps as the path leveled into a brushy bottom.

Pushing through the willows and cane, Water Stinger led her into a small clearing. There the willows had been pushed flat and several canoes dragged up onto the crushed vegetation.

To one side, Red Finger had his arms crossed. Uncle and Mother stood over a mud-stained canoe, faces grim in the morning light. Sweet Root's face reflected anger, grief, and frustration. Uncle just seemed to brood as he fingered the elbow of his ruined arm. Of them all, Red Finger had a look of satisfaction.

"What is this?" Night Rain asked as she stepped forward to stare down at the canoe. At first she didn't recognize what she saw: A large yellow gourd with holes in it, bits of sticks and . . . "Snakes!" She placed a hand over her pounding heart. "Who is it?"

"Do you recognize the canoe?" Uncle asked softly.

She studied the craft, seeing the familiar lines. "It looks like Eats Wood's." She swallowed hard, leaning forward, fingers pressed to her breastbone. What she had first taken as sticks and a gourd were long bones and a skull. What might have been collapsed willow stays from a fish trap could only be the remains of a rib cage.

Looking more closely she could see that the body had been laid out, supine, the arms and legs straight. Muddy water had yellowed the remains. Waterlogged brown fabric about the waist had been a breechcloth. She could see the familiar turtle motif woven into the cloth. Eats Wood's mother was quite a weaver. While Night Rain couldn't be absolutely positive, she was pretty sure that that cloth had come from the old woman's loom.

"Where did you find him?" The fingers at her breast had closed into a knotted fist.

"Deep in the Swamp Panther's territory." Red Finger shifted. "Believe it or not, a crow led me to him."

"A crow?"

"But for the bird, no one would have ever found Eats Wood. His killers sank the canoe with his body in it. Once it was submerged, they wedged it under the roots of a cypress, where it wouldn't come loose." Red Finger shook his head.

"We were meant to find him," Uncle said as he massaged the scar tissue on his arm. "Your crow was a messenger. Power leading us to justice."

"You think the Swamp Panthers did this?" Night Rain asked incredulously. "Why would they hide the body?"

"They wouldn't," Sweet Root answered. "This isn't war, silly child."

"I don't understand." She was shaking her head, staring at the oblong hole in the top of Eats Wood's round skull.

Mud Stalker leaned forward, his hard brown eyes burning into hers. "We're talking *murder*!"

Murder? "Why would the Swamp Panthers murder Eats Wood?"

"They didn't," Sweet Root hissed. "If they had killed him, they would have taken his body to the Panther's Bones and strewn the pieces around like the animals they are."

"Think, Night Rain!" Uncle leaned closer, his eyes boring through her. "Who travels to the Swamp Panthers every moon? Who would have had a reason to hide the body instead of abusing it? Who would have done anything to *avoid* having to face us with our kinsman's death?"

"Snakes, you think Anhinga did this?"

"She's very good with an ax," Sweet Root reminded. "If you will recall, daughter."

Night Rain stared wide-eyed at the oblong hole in the top of Eats Wood's skull. "You think Eats Wood would have let her drive an ax into his head? He knew what happened to Saw Back. I heard him say he'd never be that stupid."

"Look at him, Cousin. Look hard, then you tell me what you think." Red Finger crossed his arms.

"There is a way to prove what we suspect," Uncle replied stiffly. "That is, assuming you still have any loyalty to your clan." He pinned her with his eyes. "How is it with you, Night Rain? Are you still Snapping Turtle Clan, or are you someone else? Someone who betrays her blood and kin. Someone without relatives?"

Her throat tightened, and she wished she were anywhere but here, looking down on these pitiful remains. "How can we be sure? I mean, how can we know that Anhinga did this? Only bones are left."

Red Finger bent down, picking up the globe of the skull. Muddy water drained from the big hole where the spine had been. It spattered off the damp wood and pattered onto her bare legs. She cringed at the feel of it on her warm skin.

Mud Stalker frowned, pained, as he studied the skull. "It doesn't take long for the crawfish, minnows, and bugs to clean up a body, does it?" He indicated the oblong wound in the top. "Here, Night Rain. This will tell us."

"How?"

"I want you to bring me Anhinga's ax." Mud Stalker gave her a blunt stare. "You can do that, can't you? Borrow it? Sometime when she isn't looking?"

"I . . . Uncle, don't ask me to do this."

"You *owe* us!" Mud Stalker thrust his face into hers. "*We are your kin!*"

She stepped back, desperate to get away from him.

"Or do you serve someone besides your own flesh and blood?" Sweet Root asked. "Is it Deep Hunter? Salamander? Or perhaps that witch, Anhinga?"

"Have you forgotten your ancestors?" Red Finger asked, a sneer on his lips. "Would you rather serve strangers than your clan? Would you leave your cousin's, Eats Wood's, souls to wail over the injustice of his murder while you laugh with his killers?"

Night Rain couldn't catch her breath. She glanced from face to face. Water Stinger had stood to the rear, his expression brooding and angry.

"Do this thing," Uncle added in a softer tone, "and all will be forgiven between us. You and I will begin again on a new footing . . . as if the problem with Deep Hunter, and your betrayal, never happened." He paused. "Night Rain, do you understand the opportunity we are giving you?"

She bit her lip and nodded, feeling her heart thudding in her chest. "Yes, Uncle."

"Good." Mud Stalker took a deep breath, stepping back to look down into the canoe. "In the meantime, I think we should tell Pine Drop. Have her—"

"No," Night Rain whispered. "Don't tell her yet. Salamander will find out. She will demand an answer from him. Anhinga will find out, and her ax will be gone long before I can get to it."

"What makes you think Night Rain can manage this?" Sweet Root asked Uncle in a caustic voice. "She couldn't even manage a meeting with her young lover without getting wound up in another's snare."

"I can *do* this!" Night Rain stamped her foot. "If it means fixing the damage I have done, I can." She took a breath of the muggy air and waved at a pesky fly that came to buzz around her ear. "I will get Anhinga's ax. No one will know. Not even Pine Drop."

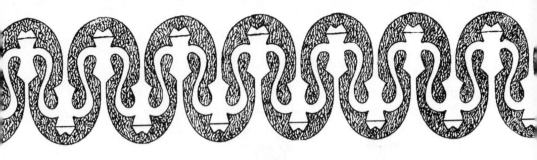

Fifty-five

Salamander saw morning come from his perch atop the Bird's Head. As he watched Sun Town in the hazy yellow light, he saw it as Many Colored Crow had shown him in the vision: abandoned, burned, and littered with rotting corpses and wreckage. That scene had filled his nightmares, now it intruded into his waking thoughts.

The full moon hanging over the western horizon had depressed him further. When it came full again, it would coincide with the summer solstice. If his vision was correct, he had that long to find a solution. The tendrils of his souls could feel the strands of Power pulling tight.

After breakfast with Anhinga he walked to the canoe landing where Yellow Spider worked on a new canoe. The sky that day had a hazy white cast, and the sun's heat beat down unmercifully. On Morning Lake the milky brown waters shot beams of light from sluggish waves. They lapped at the muddy shore in irregular and weak splashes.

Salamander squinted his eyes at the acrid smoke that boiled out of the hollow cypress log. Yellow Spider had towed it in from the heart of the swamp several days ago. He had had his eye on this particular bald cypress for several turnings of the seasons. The trunk was straight, fine-grained, and just the right diameter for a good Trade canoe. Last summer, after his return from upriver, he had ringed the tree by cutting through the bark. After killing it, he had allowed the wood to cure over the long fall and winter.

Now the partially formed hull had been muscled up onto the beach, and the laborious process of burning out the interior had begun.

Salamander waved at a shining black fly that tried to suck sweat from his forehead. He watched as the pest rose, buzzing in a lazy circle—and was in turn snatched from the air by a long green dragonfly.

"Sometimes things do work out for the best," he called after the departing dragonfly.

"What was that?" Yellow Spider asked as he added kindling to a pile of coals in the hollow. Flames crackled as blue smoke rose in a smudge.

"Occasionally good comes of the right timing." Salamander changed the grip on his adze and began chipping at the charcoal inside the cavity. Making a canoe was an art that involved moving fire constantly up and down the interior of the boat. The burn had to be hot enough to char the wood, but not so hot as to split the grain. Easy at first when the log was thick, it became a great deal trickier when the hull began to thin.

For two days Salamander and Yellow Spider had been at the chore while Bluefin made the Trade run for Swamp Panther sandstone. He chipped charcoal loose and flicked it back into the fire to be completely consumed. All in all, though slow, it was a great deal easier than hacking hard cypress wood out by hand.

Yellow Spider bent to his work, satisfied the fire was burning as he wished. For a time nothing but the hollow *thunk, thunk* of their adzes disturbed the morning. That, and more flies, drawn by their sweat.

Yellow Spider straightened and ran a hand over his damp forehead. "Did you know that Moccasin Leaf has been talking to people in the lineages?"

"She is saying that it is time that I was replaced as Speaker," Salamander replied flatly. "There is talk that I am not worthy of being Speaker. That I have been dabbling in witchcraft."

Yellow Spider nodded. "People are uneasy, Salamander. Some think you had something to do with your mother losing her souls. Others think you and Anhinga have forged some kind of destructive alliance, that you are plotting with her to harm the People." He shook his head. "I don't understand it. I've never seen you act like a witch."

"I frighten them."

Yellow Spider stopped short and stared. "I thought they just didn't like you."

"It's not that. I'm something they can't understand. They can feel the Power that has wound around me. It whispers to their souls, but they can't quite hear the words. They can feel the struggle about to be unleashed."

"What struggle?"

"For the future of the People. I am supposed to choose."

Yellow Spider's soft brown eyes looked puzzled. "I don't understand. No one wants you to choose anything."

"Masked Owl does, and so does Many Colored Crow."

"So, choose one. Why should that be so difficult? People align themselves with Spirit Helpers all the time. I should be so lucky to have Power interested in me."

Salamander could only stare at his cousin. "You don't have the faintest idea what you are saying."

Yellow Spider waved at the noxious blue smoke that curled around him and tapped his chest. "I'd ask for prestige, a beautiful wife, and long happy days filled with friends."

Salamander smiled sadly. "Then Many Colored Crow should have gone to you instead of me. He has offered me those things."

"So, why don't you take them?"

"Because if I do, Masked Owl will probably drill a hole through me with a bolt of lighting."

Yellow Spider squinted one eye. "You're right. Choose Masked Owl instead."

"If I do, all of this"—he gestured a big circle to include Sun Town—"will be gone by next summer solstice. Deep Hunter and Mud Stalker will turn the clans against each other, Cousin. Those of our people who are not killed outright will flee into the forests. The Dream that is Sun Town will die."

"You're right. Better that it's only you who gets drilled by lightning." Yellow Bird tried to make a joke of it but failed. "Sorry, Cousin."

Salamander took a deep breath. "When you boil the fat off the alligator, what you have left is a choice between my souls and the greater good. I could go off and Dream the One, my souls in bliss. Or I could become the greatest leader our people has ever known. Whichever way I choose, it will be at another's expense. Masked Owl said that if I choose Many Colored Crow's way, uncounted people will end up as slaves. If I choose Masked Owl's way, Many Colored Crow has shown me the destruction of our people."

Yellow Spider parked himself on the unfinished gunwale upwind from the fire. He flicked his adze as he asked, "I don't understand this. Why you?"

Salamander shrugged. "I don't think they planned it this way. Lines of Power have come together in a way that leaves Masked Owl and Many Colored Crow trapped in two possible futures. For them it is one or the other. Because of the way the lines of Power came together, they just happened to cross on me."

"Like the lines on your chest?"

Salamander nodded, feeling the muscles in his back knot as he chipped at the charcoal. "Cousin, I want you to promise me something."

"Anything, Salamander."

"I have something in mind. Maybe it's a way out of this."

Yellow Spider glanced up, his face sooty from the fire. "Such as?"

"I can't tell you. You'll just have to wait and see."

"Salamander, maybe if you shared this idea of yours with someone, it might help."

He smiled wanly. "You will just have to trust me, Cousin."

"I'm not sure I understand what—"

"I need you to promise that you will support what I'm about to do. I am going to ask you to do certain things for me. They will need to be done quickly and just as I say. I want you to tell me right now that you won't argue or make trouble for me."

"What you're saying doesn't make any sense."

"Neither will the instructions I give you. But believe me, it's the only way out."

"What is?"

"If this doesn't work, if the clans turn on each other, I want you to promise me something more."

"Of course."

"When it looks like fighting is going to break out, I want you to take some kinsmen and capture Pine Drop and Night Rain and my children. Take them far away. North to the Wolf People, or up to Spring Cypress among the Wash'ta, I don't care."

"What about Anhinga?"

"Send her south right away if anything happens to me. Saw Back and Deep Hunter will move on her immediately. You might have to bind and gag her, but get her out first thing. Deliver her to Jaguar Hide in person if you have to."

"And hope I get back alive," Yellow Spider muttered.

"He will let you go for keeping his niece safe."

"Then I take it you are going to choose Masked Owl?"

"I have something else in mind."

"What?"

"The price I have to pay," Salamander said pointedly.

"The way you're speaking is scaring me, Cousin."

"Not half as much as it scares me."

Pine Drop cried out, her body jerking her awake. She sat up, feeling for her daughter. The baby cried in the darkness as Pine Drop lifted her to a nipple and struggled to catch her breath.

"Are you all right?" Night Rain asked from her bed across the room.

Pine Drop blinked in the darkness, smelling the charcoal scent from the smoldering fire pit. "A Dream. By the Sky Beings, I've never had a Dream that vivid."

"What was it about?" Night Rain shuffled under her deerhide. Pine Drop heard her yawn.

"I was on the Bird's Head. Way up at the top. It was morning, the sun rising behind my right shoulder as I looked off into the West."

"The Land of the Dead?"

"Yes. The sky was lavender and pink, so wonderfully colorful, and someone was standing in the distance. Huge, as if rising out of the forest and towering over it. In spite of the light, he was shadowy, vague. Looking through the light was like looking through mist. I couldn't make out the face at first, and then I recognized him."

"Who?" Sleep filled Night Rain's voice.

"Salamander." Pine Drop shivered, remembering the sight.

"In the Land of the Dead?"

Pine Drop nodded in the darkness. "He was looking at me with such longing. I could see the sadness in his eyes. He reached out with one hand, but as soon as I started to reach back, he shook his head and lowered his arm."

"You mean, if you would have taken his hand you would have been pulled into the Land of the Dead?"

"Yes. He wouldn't let me. Snakes! I wanted to, Night Rain. I wanted to like I've never wanted anything before."

"Wanted to be dead?"

"Yes, maybe. Pus and blood, I don't know. I just wanted to be with him."

"It's just a Dream, Sister. Go back to sleep."

"I can't." She paused, eyes searching the darkness. "I don't know how it happened?"

"How he died you mean?"

"That, too, but no. I mean I don't understand how I came to love him so much. Remember when we were married? How horrified we were?"

"And how nasty we were to him."

"I would go back and change that if I could."

From the darkness, Night Rain said softly, "Me too."

"I never expected to fall in love with him." She shook her head. "What is it about him? He's not even a single turning of the seasons past boyhood, but he seems so much older. Why did Masked Owl choose him?"

"You really think that Salamander talks to Masked Owl, don't you?"

"Night Rain, I've seen things that I haven't told you about. I wasn't supposed to see him with Masked Owl, but I have."

"You were spying?"

"No. It's not that. I don't know how to explain it, but I know that Salamander is in great danger. I just don't know what to do about it. Night Rain, what if something happens to him? I've lost two husbands already. As much as I loved Blue Feather, I have come to love Salamander more. He is greater than any of us know. The Power that fills him frightens me at the same time it thrills me. When I look into his eyes, there is something there, some patient caring that makes my souls yearn."

"I'm happy for you, Sister."

"I'm scared, Night Rain. Scared that something is going to take him away from me. I can feel it."

"Well, walk over to Salamander's and crawl into bed with him and Anhinga. At least you'll sleep."

"In the Dream, he was trying to tell me something. Why would he be in the Land of the Dead? That makes no sense."

After a long silence, Night Rain said, "Our husband isn't very popular these days."

Pine Drop asked sharply, "What do you know?"

"The same thing you do, Pine Drop. That something terrible is coming."

"Is Uncle behind it?"

"Uncle is behind a lot of things, but no. Everything is going to be all right. Either go to Salamander's or go back to sleep, Sister."

Pine Drop laid her head back against the wall and cuddled her daughter. Night Rain had never been any good at hiding things.

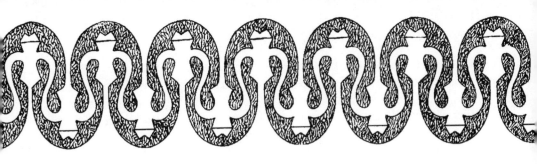

Fifty-six

Mud Stalker seated himself across the fire from Cane Frog and Three Moss. He studied the old woman in the flickering yellow light. Not for the first time, he wondered what it was like to have darkness for a constant companion. The old woman's remaining white eye stared off into the night beyond the ramada; the empty pit of her other eye was a grime-rimmed hole. He had never had the courage to ask her what her souls saw. Did they only replay visions from the past, or did they make new images woven out of past and future, a sort of skewed pattern like a blind weaver might conjure?

Three Moss sat on the fabric blanket she shared with her mother and measured Mud Stalker with her flat brown eyes. She was intent on his expression as if she might decipher the real purpose of his visit to their ramada—and unfortunately there was nothing wrong with her vision. Three Moss wore a fabric shawl over her shoulders, her skin greased against the mosquitoes that hovered in the air around them.

"What have you come to ask us for?" Cane Frog asked bluntly. She extended a hand, feeling for the warmth cast by the fire. "Can you see him, Daughter? Is the firelight good enough?"

"Yes, Mother." Three Moss reached out and placed her hand on her mother's bare shoulder.

"It has been a long time, Elder," Mud Stalker began in a non-committal voice. "I thought it was high time that we visited, got caught up on things. I hear that the crawfish harvest has been ex-

ceptional this spring. I saw the latest catch down at the canoe landing this afternoon. Three Stomachs and Copper Toad brought it
in. And then earlier this evening I could smell the aroma as they
were boiled. I thought about sneaking in like a naughty child and
spooning some out of the boiling pot when no one was looking."
Frog Clan had a shallow lake in one of their holdings that reliably
produced more crawfish than any other place known in the region.

"Yes, it has been good. We would be happy to provide you with
some, Speaker." Cane Frog rubbed her wrinkled hand down the
top of her leathery thigh. "It will be my pleasure to send a youngster
over with a couple of bags full when the boiling is finished. We
seasoned them with honeysuckle blossoms and some of those mus-
tard leaves. It gives them a sweet and tangy taste."

"Snapping Turtle Clan will be obligated. For your fine gift we
would reciprocate and send you a sack of hematite net sinkers. Some
of my young men have just finished shaping a batch. We have a few
more than we can use. It has been rumored that some of your fishermen are having trouble anchoring their nets. I saw some of Copper Toad's. He has ordinary rocks tied on with string."

"Ah." She smiled. "Yes. It has been mentioned that you Traded
quite a bit of squash last winter for raw hematite to make net sinkers
out of. Something about that deal Salamander made with those
Wash'ta Traders last fall. People thought him a fool for stripping
his clan of all their finery. Then, while his clan wove and crafted
beautiful replacements through the winter, that same fool was judiciously giving away hides, stone, and dried buffalo meat to the
needy. When people weren't approaching him for some of that Panther sandstone, that is."

"Yes, well, Speaker Salamander seems to have uncommonly
good fortune." Mud Stalker smiled flatly at Three Moss to hide his
delight that Cane Frog had brought up the very subject he wished
to pursue.

"Good fortune? Is that what they call it?" Three Moss asked, the
faintest hint of amusement curling her lips. "Many would like to say
that Owl Clan has lost most of its prestige. At least, we hear that
among the Speakers and Clan Elders and from those who are versed
in the intrigues of the Men's House."

"And the Women's House, too, no doubt," Mud Stalker returned
in a gracious voice.

"No doubt," Three Moss agreed, her round face betraying nothing. "So we find it curious that while the leadership speaks of Owl
Clan's doom, people in the clans keep slipping over there for a piece
of that Panther sandstone, or a buffalo robe, or a bit of tool stone

from the far north. All the while, I keep tallying the amount of obligation that my clan has incurred to that young man. In another few turnings of the seasons or so, I'm afraid half of my clan grounds will be owed to Owl Clan."

Mud Stalker tried to read her expression. Was Three Moss for or against Owl Clan? He couldn't be sure.

Cane Frog surprised him when she said, "Quite the Speaker, isn't he?"

"Your pardon, Elder?" Mud Stalker asked.

"Salamander," she replied. "Let me guess, old friend. You didn't expect this, did you?"

"Expect what?"

"His success." Three Moss made no bones about it. "The amount of obligation he seems to accumulate."

"I can only be pleased with Speaker Salamander's success. His abilities reflect on my nieces."

Cane Frog erupted in a rasping laugh. "Indeed. A good reflection indeed. This time last summer, as I recall, my Three Stomachs and your Pine Drop were polishing the spear. A fine reflection indeed. In a more public display, people still wonder why he took Night Rain back after that fiasco last winter." She smacked her lips. "Touchy bit of business, that. Had tempers been allowed to flare, it could have become very nasty."

"Yes, well, responsible heads prevailed. Pine Drop, in particular, stands out in my memory. She counseled patience and restraint that day." Mud Stalker inclined his head pleasantly to Three Moss. The woman still had her hand on her mother's shoulder. Something about the way her fingers moved on the old woman's skin caught Mud Stalker's attention. Then, in a flash, he thought he understood. Did the younger woman signal to her mother? Was that why they always touched during the Council sessions?

"It was more than Pine Drop." Cane Frog sucked her lips back over toothless gums, and added, "Although I think she will make a very competent Clan Elder when she comes of age. Very competent indeed."

"Our lineage thanks you for your confidence in her. We are obliged."

"I think you are even more obliged to young Salamander for his eloquence that day, Speaker." Cane Frog tapped her right ear. "These have grown sharper since my eyes went away. They hear more than most people know. Your Salamander did more than his share in keeping the lid on an overflowing pot."

"Some would say he did almost too well," Mud Stalker replied offhand.

"Indeed?" Three Moss asked. "You *wanted* an ugly brawl with Alligator Clan to break out?"

He made a face at the incredulous tone in her voice. "Not at all, Elder. I am glad that the situation was resolved in a peaceful manner that satisfied all parties."

"Then what did you mean?" Three Moss asked.

"I mean it's curious, isn't it, that anyone's misfortune seems to end up as Salamander's advantage?" Mud Stalker tried to read Cane Frog's reaction in the firelight. The old woman's face might have been a mask.

After several heartbeats Cane Frog asked, "What do you want, Speaker? Talk to us in words that do not balance on the tongue like a magician's trick."

Mud Stalker fingered his scarred elbow and considered his next words. "Some people have begun to worry about Salamander's continued good fortune. Even my nieces cannot understand how he always seems to come out ahead. It is unnatural."

"We have heard the whisperings of witchcraft," Three Moss said. "We are still unsure what to make of it. Is it really witchcraft, or just the jealousy of others? What proof do you have?"

"Just look at his life over the last turning of the seasons. Think about everyone who stood in his way. Some, like his brother, have been killed, others, like his mother, have had their wits blunted. His barbarian wife walks freely among us, wielding her ax while she slips away to spoon poison about us into her uncle's thirsty ear. A suspicious young warrior follows her out into the swamp and disappears. People who oppose Salamander find themselves in very deep water."

"Ah, like his Clan Elder, Moccasin Leaf? Do you consider her elevation in Wing Heart's place a coup for young Salamander? Or do I recall a certain Speaker promoting her acceptance by the Council?" She didn't let him answer, stating, "Young Salamander is most unassuming for a witch."

"He seems innocuous, but when one looks past his misdirection and attempts at humility, they will find Salamander gathering ever more prestige and authority, especially, as you have noted, with the common people."

"So," Cane Frog cut straight to the hunt. "First, you placed him at the top, and now you want to remove him. Why, Speaker? Is it because he is better than you thought he'd be?"

"Oh, go ahead," Three Moss chimed in. "Speak to us with a clear tongue. There is no one to hear. Your words will be carried in silence between our souls."

"It's not a matter of me," he hedged. "Nor is it a matter of what my clan wants."

"Indeed?" Cane Frog asked. "And who else might it be?"

"All of us," he said pointedly, eyes making the challenge to Three Moss. "We have had Owl Clan's leadership for too many generations. On the whole, I admit, Sun Town has prospered. Owl Clan, in particular, has prospered mightily. My clan wasn't alone when it came to giving up certain resources because of obligation."

"You are referring to those lotus ponds that I ceded to Cloud Heron the time of the bad drought?" Cane Frog asked in irritation.

"That is but an example."

"How, Speaker, do you think you can badger Salamander into returning them? By simply accusing him of being a witch? Do you think he will surrender Owl Clan's assets just to make the charge go away?"

"I am not that simple." Mud Stalker watched the fingers move on the old woman's shoulders. When he smiled, Three Moss tapped with an index finger. He shrugged, as if absently, and watched the thumb and little finger move. Fascinating!

"Then how would a complicated man make such a thing happen?" Cane Frog was interested now, sensing for the first time, that some advantage might be in the wind for her and her clan.

"I don't just want to accuse Salamander of witchcraft, Elder, I want to convict him of it." Mud Stalker smiled again, seeing the first finger tap.

"Killing Salamander as a witch will not bring my root grounds back!" Cane Frog reminded shortly. "Nor will it cancel my clan's increasing obligation to Owl Clan."

"Moccasin Leaf would see Half Thorn take Salamander's place as Speaker for Owl Clan," Mud Stalker said firmly.

Cane Frog's wrinkles deepened as she made a sour face. "I've made cooking clays that were smarter than Half Thorn."

"That's just the point." Mud Stalker leaned back, a satisfied grin on his face.

"How would this be done? Would you deal with Salamander? Or did you have someone else in mind?"

"If he is declared to be a witch, he would be Owl Clan's problem. I happen to know that, odious as the duty would be, it would befall the Clan Elder to ensure that justice was done. I would imagine that someone like Half Thorn would use that opportunity to demonstrate his leadership abilities."

Cane Frog's expression seemed to sharpen, her lips pulling back and forth over her gums. Finally, she said, "If we were to support you in this, we would need a guarantee. Some assurance that our root grounds would be returned."

"Let me see what I can do. As I said, Moccasin Leaf would have a great deal of obligation to anyone who assisted her." Mud Stalker stood, seeing Three Moss's fingers rippling. "We may be dealing with an entirely new alignment of clans by the time the summer solstice feast is over."

"Just so Frog Clan isn't on the bottom," Cane Frog reminded. "If we are to be part of this, Speaker, we had better come out of it with renewed prestige."

"Give me your vote against Salamander, and you will, Clan Elder. I have great things in mind for the future of the People."

The backswamp slowly drained away during those last days as Mother Sun crept ever so slowly toward solstice. Each summer at this time shallow pools formed where fish thrashed, fed, and often became stranded. Knowing the lay of the low contours, a fisherman with a properly set net could drag the shallows, effectively sweeping up the bounty.

Salamander squinted as he stepped into a patch of sun between the shade of two sweetgum trees. In the knee-deep water, mud squished between his toes. The midday heat seemed to weight the humid air. Insects flitted past on silver wings, while birds and locusts called from the trees. He bent at the waist, struggling against the sodden weight of the net.

"Hot today," Pine Drop called from across the small pond. "I could almost wish for some of that miserable cold from last winter." She was struggling step by step, leaning as she pulled at the ropes that controlled the net.

Salamander watched her. Toned muscles slid under her smooth brown skin. He could see the strength in her arms and the swell of her thighs as she sloshed through the muddy brown water. Her broad shoulders tensed under the weight of the wet netting. Droplets of water mixed with perspiration as she bent her back, using her round hips for leverage. The top and bottom ropes had to be pulled correctly to create a pocket for the fish. Pine Drop held each rope in a knotted fist.

She glanced across at him, seeing the expression on his face, frowning. "What's the matter?"

"Nothing."

"Why are you looking at me that way?"

"You are so beautiful. I was just trying to understand, that's all."

"Understand what?" She seemed completely confused.

"How I could have been so lucky to have had you for a wife. I spend a lot of time watching you."

"I know. Sometimes it's disturbing. That look in your eyes, I mean. As if you're about to melt."

"You do that to me. If I have to melt for anyone, I would want to melt for you."

She smiled then—shy, but happy. Her teeth gleamed in contrast to her lustrous black hair. "Do you want to pull on this net instead of wasting the day staring at me like I'm a lost Dream?"

"You are a Dream." He leaned into the net, dragging it onward through the shallowing water and onto the muddy flats. As more of the netting was pulled from the water it grew heavier. He could feel the weight of the fish, their struggles carrying as vibrations in the netting. They thrashed in the shallows, hampered by the cords that bound them. He could see heads, tails, and fins protruding from the boil.

"Together now," he called. "Pull! Pull! Pull!"

With each gasp, they threw their bodies against the sagging net, dragging the catch onto the mud. In the process the netting twisted neatly, trapping the fish in the folds.

Lungs heaving Salamander laid his end down. Fish were writhing, gasping, slapping against each other. He could see catfish, bowfin, gar, bass, suckers, and buffalo fish in the mix.

"Good catch!" Pine Drop said between gasps as she walked over to stand beside him.

"I thought so when I married you," he said.

Her gleaming brown eyes reflected amusement. "What is it with you today? Do you want something?"

He saw delight shining behind a flawed mask of female cynicism. "I just want you. And my girls. I want everything to stay just as it is today and never change. I want to love you, and hold you, and watch my daughters grow. I want it so badly that it makes my souls ache."

She reached out, drawing him into her arms. He sighed at the heat of her wet body. Her breasts were against his. Damp strands of her hair clung to the side of his face. His arms around her, he reveled in her breathing, then detected her heartbeat as his ear pressed against her neck.

"You have me, Salamander. For as long as you want me."

"I have asked for too much."

"That's nonsense. I am staying with you. It is our decision and no one else's."

"I just wish the decision was ours."

She pushed him back far enough to stare into his eyes. "The clans cannot make us do what we do not wish to."

He reached up to finger a damp lock of her hair away from her eyes. "I do not worry about the clans."

"Then who?"

"Masked Owl."

He could see her doubt. "Salamander, why? I mean, I know you have visions. I know about you and Power, but this worries me. Why would Masked Owl harm you?"

"Because I cannot do as he asks."

"Why not?"

"If I follow the path to the One, I will lose you. I will lose everything. Like Wolf Dreamer, I will fall into the Dream and everything else will become meaningless."

"I don't understand."

He raised a sympathetic eyebrow. "I don't think anyone wants to be a Dreamer. The cost is so high."

"Why can't you stay just the way you are?"

"Because black clouds are gathering—among the spirits as well as among the clans. It is all coming together, Pine Drop."

A frown pinched her forehead as she nodded. "I know. Uncle is up to something. I think he's going to accuse you of witchcraft. I think he's been making deals."

"He thinks Snapping Turtle Clan will finally become preeminent." Salamander ran his finger down the side of her cheek. "It isn't going to happen that way, Pine Drop."

"How do you know?"

"I've seen that part of the future." He could see doubt firming her expression, and added, "You must trust me on this."

"Trust you?" Irritation tugged at the corners of her mouth.

"Have you done so poorly on those occasions when I asked you to trust me?"

"Snakes, no. But it leaves me wondering how someone as young as you can always be right. You're three summers younger than I! Where did you learn all this?"

"In the Spirit World," he replied uneasily. "The things I've seen—"

"You're not using those mushrooms again, are you?" Warning flashed in her eyes.

"No. Not recently. I don't have to. Bird Man showed me things."

"Bird Man? *The* Bird Man?"

"Before I choose one way or another, however, I have to go see someone in the Spirit World."

"You're not making sense!"

He let himself look into her eyes, seeing her souls as they tried to comprehend him. "She is older than the Hero Twins. She saved my life that time."

"The old woman you talked about?"

"Yes."

She shook herself, stepping away, looking at the fish as they gasped and flopped in the net. "I don't understand this, Salamander. I just don't want to lose you. I've come to love you. Do you understand? I'm afraid!"

"So am I."

"Well, let's stop it! Let's find a way to save you."

He hesitated before testing the idea on her. "Would you give it all up?"

"What?" The question had taken her by surprise.

"All of it," he insisted. "Could you give up Sun Town? Give up being Clan Elder someday? Your position in the leadership? Your clan? Would you just go away with me? Knowing that we could live the rest of our lives in peace? Raise our daughter?"

She gave him a blank look. "Just leave? Everything?"

He nodded.

"The clan *is* everything, Salamander. It's who we are. What we are. The clan is our blood and bones, our heart and lungs and souls. It is the air we breathe and the food we eat. It is our warmth and protection. Everything, the whole world, is determined by the clan. What we own, where we go, who we marry. The clan gives us our place in the world."

"Yes, it does."

"So, you're asking, could I give up the whole world?" He could see the confusion behind her expression.

"That's right. Can you give up everything for nothing."

She slowly shook her head. "I don't think I understand you. I don't think you can give up the world, Salamander. To do what? Just go off and live at the edge of the Earth? Be alone?"

"Totally."

"In other words, you're asking if I could give up being a person."

"It's a hard question, isn't it?" The answer—the one he had expected—was in her eyes. He smiled reassuringly at her and indicated the fish. "Come on, we'd better stun the ones that haven't died yet and lug them to the canoe. The thing about a big catch like this is that work is just starting."

But a great sadness lay between his souls. If Pine Drop, the bravest person he knew, couldn't even comprehend the question, how could he find the courage actually to do what she thought unimaginable?

Fifty-seven

Night Rain tried for all the world to look normal. Belted at her waist, she wore a fabric kirtle with a prominent turtle design on the front. A square bark hat perched on her head with two long brown pelican feathers stuck into her hair above her ears. A single round ceramic pot hung from the net bag over her shoulders.

Ceramic vessels were light, easily made, and reliable containers. For a people who practically lived in canoes, they served many purposes. Placed in a fire, they could be used to boil liquids and cook soups. By preheating cooking clays, they could become a portable oven for the baking of foodstuffs, and when traveling, fire could be built inside, and the pot changed into a portable heat stove. Finally, when collections of nutmeats, dried seeds, and other foodstuffs were stored, pots could be sealed so that rodents and insects couldn't gain access. Generally it was for the latter purposes that people carried ceramic vessels. The trouble with boiling water inside them was that given their poor firing, the food often acquired grit and tasted muddy as the inside of the pot began to flake away.

So it was that Night Rain approached the Owl Clan ridges from the north, her ceramic pot bouncing just above her buttocks.

She kept her head down, trying for all the world to appear as just another young woman at her daily tasks. She watched the ground ahead of her and cast surreptitious glances from the corner of her eye. After climbing out of the deep drainage that bounded the northern side of the Owl Clan grounds, she threaded her way along the path past the ridges. To her left, under the embankment, Morning Lake looked silver in the afternoon light. To the right, the ridgelines of houses cast shadows in curving ranks. Smoke drifted skyward from tens of tens of fires as meals were being prepared in anticipation of the solstice.

People were everywhere, many having arrived from outlying camps and settlements for the solstice celebration. Most had moved in with relatives, bearing sacks full of dried, smoked, and cured fish, meat, and plant foods. Most of these would be succulent meals by the time the ceremonies started.

Night Rain passed the second ridge and turned onto the first. She walked right up to Salamander's door and leaned her head in.

"Hello? Anhinga? Are you here?"

Silence.

Night Rain ducked inside and squatted by the smoking fire pit. She laid her ceramic bowl to one side and slipped it out of the netting. Only then did she take a moment for her eyes to adjust to the dim interior.

She rose and stepped to the wall where the tools lay. There, propped against the wall, were two stone-headed hoes, Salamander's ax and adze, several hardened digging sticks, an assortment of bow drills for fire starting and drilling holes in stone, bone, and wood, and finally, yes, Anhinga's ax.

Night Rain reached out, her fingers tracing the smooth wood of the handle. She grasped it, her gaze running the handle's length with its carved panther design. She studied the sharp greenstone head set into a notch in the wood and wound tightly with deer sinew. The freshly ground edge was sharp where she pressed her finger against it. Sharp enough to cut. How well Night Rain remembered the blood streaming down Saw Back's side in a slick sheet.

Could this be the weapon that knocked a hole into Eats Wood's head? She tried to remember the wound in the top of that mud-browned skull. Oblong, sinister. Just like this ax.

Night Rain made a face as she remembered this very handle slapping her cold buttocks as Anhinga drove her home under a load of firewood and humiliation.

What a child I was. The moons since that horrible event seemed to have run together, to have woven themselves into something else. Her life up to that day in the forest might have belonged to a different person—some child she no longer knew.

"But I still belong to my clan," she whispered, grasping the ax. She turned and hesitated—Salamander's face forming between her souls.

What if Anhinga *had* killed Eats Wood?

Night Rain reached out and encircled the ax head with her thumb and forefinger. Did the cool stone seem to vibrate? Was it alive, harboring some sort of soul?

Eats Wood was a maggot.

The often-uttered cautions slipped out of her memory: "*I don't want you girls alone with him! Do you understand?*" She could imagine mother bending down, pointing a stern finger in her face. "*That boy is not to be trusted! Not even with kin! Snakes, not even the horror of incest would worry his souls if it meant the opportunity to stick himself into pretty girls like you.*"

Night Rain's expression hardened as she remembered the way Eats Wood used to look at her. Something in those eager brown eyes had chilled her souls.

If Anhinga is proven to be the killer, she'll be banished at best. At worst, Uncle would manage to have her killed.

And Salamander? What would that do to him? How many times had Night Rain wondered at the love in his eyes as he watched Anhinga? Snakes, it would wound his souls if anything happened to her.

Night Rain bit her lip, considered, and carefully replaced the ax. The reason why would plague her souls afterward, but at that moment of decision, she grabbed up Salamander's ax instead. She slipped the handle into the kirtle's belt and turned back to the fire.

With a stick she scraped some embers into the pot before she tucked it back into the net bag. "I just stopped for some hot coals to take back. It was just quicker than building a fire at home," she would say if anyone asked.

With a final glance, she ducked out the door, and, casually as possible, started across the plaza for her uncle's.

Mud Stalker smiled as he bent down in the dusk and lifted the skull from the mud-caked canoe. Behind him, beyond the screen of thick cane and willows, he could hear talking as people passed up the channel in a canoe. Still more arrivals headed for Sun Town and the solstice celebrations. Their voices carried anticipation as they neared their goal.

Sweet Root and Night Rain stood across from him. His sister's eyes gleamed, while Night Rain's looked disconnected, lost in a tangle of conflict. Conflict over what? This was her chance to even the score and pay that barbarian witch back for the humiliation of that long-ago day in the forest. She should be happy to see her junior wife proven guilty of murder.

"Does it fit?" Sweet Root asked, leaning forward in the dusk to see better. She batted at the humming column of mosquitoes with an irritated arm.

"Just a moment." Mud Stalker turned the skull, feeling the cold bone in his hand. How did a human head become so light? He paused, staring into the empty eye sockets, seeing the Y-shaped holes at the back. Even if he could do it by a wish, he wouldn't will Eats Wood's eyes back into those orbits. The young man had been a disappointment from the days of his birth, and truth to tell, Mud Stalker had always accepted that someday Snapping Turtle Clan would have to pay for the boy's indiscretions.

"Better this way," he whispered softly to the grinning skull. "You are now serving your clan as you never would have in life."

"The ax," Sweet Root reminded as she lifted it from where it had rested on the canoe gunwale. "Does it fit the hole?"

Mud Stalker turned the skull until it faced her.

She lowered the sharp edge to the oblong wound. The ax made a partial fit. The length was right, but something about the width didn't work.

"Close," Sweet Root noted.

Mud Stalker frowned. "I don't know. The edges aren't quite right. This isn't anything I could take to the Council." He glanced to the side, seeing relief on Night Rain's face. What was this? She was truly relieved to discover that that Swamp Panther camp bitch hadn't killed Eats Wood? Why?

Unwilling to give up, Mud Stalker gestured with his head and when Sweet Root removed the ax, he turned the skull around. He would try everything just be sure that he hadn't missed some . . . Sweet Root neatly dropped the edge of the ax into the hole in the top of Eats Wood's head.

"Perfect," Sweet Root whispered, her eyes widening.

"I'll be," Mud Stalker breathed. "She *did* kill him. But she sneaked up and hit him from behind."

This time when he shot a glance at Night Rain, it was to find her expression betraying shock, astonishment, and disbelief.

F eeling weary to her bones, smelling of fish, and with every muscle aching, Pine Drop plodded to her doorway. A faint glow of sunset still shone in the northwestern sky. The night smelled of smoke, cooking food, and voices carried in the air. She could hear laughter, cheerful banter, and the soft murmuring of conversations. In any direction fires sparkled and illuminated thatch-roofed houses, ramada roofs, and countless people. So many people come in from the hinterlands. So many fires. The smoky air over Sun Town had taken on a reddish cast. Normally, she admired the sight.

She shifted her daughter with one hand and used the other to ease the tumpline from her forehead as she lowered the basket of fish that rode in the hollow of her back. Straightening, she winced and made a face at the stiffness in her back muscles.

Her house and ramada were dark, seemingly deserted. She walked to the fire pit on the north side of the ramada and bent down, her sleeping daughter cradled on her lap. With a stick she stirred the coals, finding a few gleaming red eyes in the heavy hardwood ash. From the tinder pile she placed some twigs on coals, shifted her daughter, and blew carefully until flames flickered.

Bit by bit she built up the fire until it cast a cheery yellow light to illuminate the insides of the ramada and the big wooden pestle and mortar.

For a long moment she sat, tired, and stared into the fire. How did a person give up being who they were? How could she just walk away from her world?

"Was he talking outside of his souls?" she asked her sleeping daughter. "What are we without our homes? Without our families, lineages, and clans?"

Her baby's face was a round golden brown globe in the firelight. Silky strands of black hair had escaped the fabric wrap. Her tiny mouth hung open under the smooth button of her nose. The tightly closed eyes reflected an innocent peace.

Had he been serious about just going away? What would that solve? The people who depended on him would just have to find someone else to depend on. Owl Clan would continue its decline, and Snapping Turtle Clan would continue to grow in prestige.

"Hello, Sister," Night Rain greeted from the night as she appeared from behind the house.

"Where have you been?"

"Uncle and Mother had some things for me to do," Night Rain said with a hollow voice.

Even weary as Pine Drop was, she looked up as Night Rain squatted at the fire across from her. Her sister's face reminded her of one of the Earth Monster masks the men wore on ceremonial occasions.

It was something about the set of the mouth, the emptiness in the eyes.

"What's wrong?"

"There will be a Council meeting called tomorrow." Night Rain reached a stick from the woodpile and inserted the end into the flames. As it caught fire, she lifted it, watching the fire eat at the wood before it went out and smoked. Night Rain inserted the smoking end into the flames again to relight.

"You don't always look like you're sick to your stomach when the Council is called."

"Uncle orders that we both be there."

"Blood and pus, I've got a canoe load of fish to dry." She jerked her head toward the basket. "That's part of it. I thought I'd get them split tonight and partially dried before the flies got to them." She worked her hands, feeling the muscles in her forearms, hot and cramped. "But all I want to do is sleep."

"You should know something."

"I should know many things." She rubbed her tired eyes, aware of how her hand smelled of fish. "I should know who I am."

"What?"

"Who am I, Night Rain? What am I?"

"What brought this about?"

"A question that Salamander asked me today." She studied her sister, seeing the sick worry in her face. "Could you give up being you? Could you just walk down to the canoe landing and paddle away from here? Maybe go and live somewhere in the forest without any clan or family? Could you just go away, Night Rain, and never see your mother, your uncle, or any of your friends? Could you stop being you?"

"No! No one could! That sounds completely witless. We are who we are: Sun People, Snapping Turtle Clan."

Pine Drop nodded. "I thought so, too."

Night Rain's expression had tightened. "Is Salamander thinking about running away?"

Pine Drop shrugged. "I don't know. I don't think so. It was just a question he asked . . . like so many of the other questions he asks. What is it about him? He can look you in the eyes, that gaze all soft and concerned, and ask you a simple question. It upsets your souls so that everything that you are is turned upside down and spilled out."

Night Rain's chuckle held a bitter irony. "I don't know, Sister. I don't know what to think of him." She paused. "He knew I was pregnant before I did. How could he know that?"

"How can he do a lot of the things he does? The man is a mystery!" She took a breath. "Night Rain, I have come to love him like I never thought I could love a man. When he's not around, I am obsessed with thoughts about him. I keep things to show him, just waiting to see his smile."

Night Rain nodded distantly. "I recall the day when we first married White Bird, and how horrified we were at the thought of ending up married to Salamander."

"After he asked that question today we were working on the fish, gutting them, packing them in the canoe, and the next thing I knew, we were touching. And the next we were on the grass. I will never forget that coupling. It was as if he was trying to make it last forever. In the end, when his loins let loose in mine, I would have sworn my body had exploded into beams of sunlight."

"And then?"

"And then, after I finally returned to my body and caught my breath, the baby was crying."

Night Rain smiled, teasing the fire with her burning stick. "Keep that memory, Sister. Hold it close to your souls like a precious stone."

"I will." She glanced at Night Rain, reading her troubled eyes. "What happened to you today?"

"I got out of bed. I shouldn't have."

"You get out of bed every day. Why should this one be different?"

Night Rain's shoulders jerked. "You are right about Salamander. Things happen to him. It's odd how coincidences are. Just after I got out of bed this morning, I saw Saw Back. Everything goes back to him and Anhinga's ax. It makes me wonder if I'm not just Power's tool."

"I have enough worries about Power. Don't you get involved in it, too."

"It's too late. I already am." She jabbed the burning stick angrily at the fire. "Somehow we ended up talking about Salamander. Saw Back hates him. Hates me. Not only for being there that day, for witnessing what Anhinga did to him, but because I went back to Salamander."

"He's your husband, what does Saw Back think wives do?"

"He knows that Uncle would have let me divorce. He knows that Salamander kept him from taking his revenge out on Anhinga by defusing that Council meeting. But the irony this morning was that he made such a big thing about Salamander being nothing more than a boy promoted beyond his means."

"Salamander's age baffles us all," Pine Drop agreed.

"Saw Back called him a coward, said that he'd faint if he ever had to really fight another warrior for his life. That he couldn't kill a beetle with a pestle."

"Salamander isn't a warrior," Pine Drop agreed.

Night Rain gave her a hooded look. "Isn't he?"

"What are you talking about?"

"Red Finger found Eats Wood's body. He was in his canoe, sunk under some roots down in the Swamp Panther country. Salamander's ax fits the hole in Eats Wood's head. Our husband killed our cousin, Sister. That's why Uncle has called the Council meeting for tomorrow. He is going to accuse Salamander of murder and witchcraft."

"We have to go. Warn him."

"No, Sister. Uncle and Mother both have ordered us to stay here. At this house, until tomorrow when the Council convenes."

"Rot eat them, Salamander is our husband. I'm going to warn him!" Pine Drop stood on aching legs, swinging her daughter up to her hip.

From the darkness, Water Stinger stepped out, calling, "Pine Drop, I am here on both the Elder's and Speaker's orders to see that you stay home tonight."

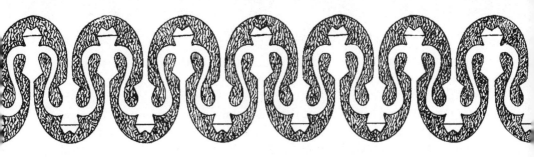

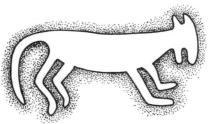

Fifty-eight

Over the past turning of the seasons, Anhinga had become used to Sun Town and its marvels. She had never expected to be awed by the place again, but this was her first experience with the summer solstice ceremonies.

She sat in the shadows of the ramada and watched the tens of tens of tens of fires winking around the span of Sun Town. A thousand yellow eyes flickered and filled the air with the scent of smoke. The reddish tint they cast into the hazy sky amazed her. Sun Town was shining its own light into the night. She could imagine the Sky Beings circling, looking down, and gasping with delight as night and day blurred.

Wing Heart sat at her loom, humming to herself as she worked the threads and continued her endless weaving. How she produced perfect fabric in the faint reflection of firelight never ceased to amaze Anhinga.

People passed in a constant stream, most of them strangers, clan members from outlying camps and distant settlements, many of them from as far away as the gulf, two tens of days distant by canoe. They came bearing gifts: feathers, meat, and bones from pelicans; or plumage from rosy spoonbills, red egret, and purple gallinue; fish like black drum, red snapper, barracuda, and even one odd flat specimen that had both eyes on one side of its head. Some came with the smoked crab, conch, and whelk meat, and some came to Trade tanned sharkskin. Other canoes arrived filled with dried yaupon leaves for making black drink, and others with items like stingray spines to be used as needles and awls.

Trade flourished everywhere. She had seen no less than five marriages brokered between the different clans. No sooner had she gone back to work before another greeting was called between old friends who hadn't seen each other for seasons. Until this day, she would never have believed so many people lived in the whole world! The numbers of the Sun People left her dumbfounded.

And I thought I could fight them? That by the six of us raiding them, we would pay them back for Bowfin's death?

What a fool she had been, and how wise her uncle was. Old weathered Jaguar Hide had truly understood. And now, so did she, in a way she wasn't sure that even her uncle could.

She nodded, remembering his wisdom in sending her back to stay. He had said something about learning their ways, not just for the moment, but for the future when she returned to the Panther's Bones for good. Yes, she knew them now. Knew their strengths and weaknesses. Most of all, she knew that the Swamp Panthers could never challenge such immense strength.

So how did her people prevail against so many?

She recognized Salamander before she could make out his features. It was the way he walked, the set of his shoulders, his movements. He had grown so familiar to her, become part of her in a most unsettling way. Panther's blood, wouldn't it be so much simpler if he just left with her? She could make a place for him among her people. He could be happy with her. They could live out the rest of their lives together, raise their children, and love each other until they grew old, knotty, and decrepit.

"Greetings, Husband." She rose, seeing that he labored under a burden. "What have you brought?"

"We made a good catch. Filled the canoe," he told her, fatigue riding his voice.

She caught the odor of fish as she walked up to him and helped him to lower a full basket to the ground. "What has been done with them?"

"We gutted them. They need to be smoked and dried. I don't know how long they will last, especially given the number of people who have come for the ceremonials."

"Husband, most of them arrived in canoes gunwale full of food. I've never seen so much to eat, or so many mouths to feed."

He bent over to hug her, and she felt the trembling in his muscles. When she wrapped her arms around him, it surprised her to find his body hot from exertion. She pressed him to her and sighed. "You feel good, Husband."

"So do you. I could keep you like this for days."

"Promise?"

"Yes, but it will make attending the solstice activities a bit awkward. People will point at us and talk."

"They talk anyway. Look! There goes Speaker Salamander and his barbarian wife. We are already the center of attention. You should have been here today."

"How is our daughter?"

"Fine. She slept, ate, and messed, and slept and ate and messed, all day long. I made three trips for firewood, figuring that as things get busy we won't have much time. It's a long way to go, and believe me, everything close has already been scavenged for the fires. Even the big trees that fell last winter are being chopped up."

"Thank you," he whispered. "I don't know what I'd do without you."

"Poor man, you would have to make do with only two wives!"

He chuckled at that and patted her shoulders as she broke away. She strained to lift the basket of fish and waddled to the ramada. Throwing more wood on the fire, she started laying the fish out on the split-cane matting.

"What's cooking?" Salamander indicated the two earth ovens.

"Lotus root," she lied heartily. "What would people say if the Owl Clan Speaker ate anything else for the solstice?"

"They'd say that he was deranged." He lifted his arms, smiling in the firelight. "But they say that anyway."

"As I started to tell you, a stream of people have been here. They come in bits and dribbles, wanting to speak to you. Most of them want to get a look at me, to see the famous barbarian wife. Others want to see you, to see if it's true that the clan has such a young Speaker." She made a face. "And many come to see your mother. Mostly the older ones, the ones who knew her when she and Cloud Heron were laying the opposition low. They look, shake their heads, and drift off to Moccasin Leaf's to discuss marriages, bickering between the lineages, and grievances with other clans." She pointed to the glow of a huge bonfire two ridges away. "Half Thorn is busy strutting back and forth like a mating pigeon. You could go look; he has all of his feathers preened."

"I'll pass," he muttered, a heaviness in his voice.

She watched him from the corner of her eye. "What is wrong, Salamander?"

"I want you to promise me something."

"Of course."

"If things begin to go badly, I want you to dress in Owl Clan clothing. Something Mother made, and take our daughter. I want you to get into a canoe and paddle south to your family."

"What are you talking about?"

"I'm talking about your safety. It is summer solstice. Canoes full of strangers are everywhere. If you're dressed as Owl Clan, no one will notice. You are just one of many. By the time you are in Swamp Panther country, you'll be safe."

She cocked her head. "What do you know, Husband?"

"I know that you are in great danger." Pain reflected in his smile. "I've done a terrible thing, Anhinga."

"What?" she asked, her gaze darting to the earth oven where the water-hemlock root roasted in a bedding of yellow lotus.

"I've been selfish. Kept you and my little girl here with me. I knew better. I should have sent you south during the past moon."

"You're being silly," she answered uncertainly. "We're a family, remember? We decided that night after the affair with Night Rain and Saw Back."

"He's yet another worry. You must leave in secret," Salamander warned. "And make three times sure that no one sees you leave, especially Saw Back. You, of all people, know how dangerous he can be. This time, I won't be there to save you."

She stopped short, the cold carcass of a bass in her hands. "What do you mean? Tell me, Husband. What do you know? What has Masked Owl told you?" She felt her heart skip with fear, and not over the poisoned roots she was cooking.

He sank down, his back against one of the ramada poles, his head tilted as he stared up at the palmetto roofing. "Sometime soon now, I am going to have to do something very difficult. I have no reason to believe that what I am planning will work. You have heard the witchcraft stories?"

"Of course. Half of Sun Town thinks I'm a sorceress. The other half thinks you are a witch. Let them stew. No one wants to make a witch mad. It has repercussions. Like Dancing on the Bird's Head during a lightning storm. You never know when the next bolt might blast you dead."

"I wish you wouldn't use that analogy." He glanced nervously at Wing Heart's shadow where she worked the dimly lit loom.

"Sorry."

"It's not a joke," he answered. "That's why I need you to promise. If I tell you to, you must leave. If I fail, they will come to kill you. Do you understand what that means?"

She nodded, sobered, memories of being bound to the pole at the Men's House still fresh in her nightmares. "Yes, Husband, I do."

"Then you will go if I ask? You will save yourself and our daughter?"

She nodded, meeting his eyes. They reminded her of dark pools of misery. "I will not let them cut me apart, urinate inside my chest, and feed bits of my body to the dogs."

He sighed then, body limp with relief.

Hope rose in her heart as she softly said, "You could come with me. They don't need you here, Salamander. You do so much for these people who despise you, who call you a witch and a fool. They think you are a joke, a spineless boy parading as a Speaker."

"Sometimes I think that, too," he answered.

"You are not, you know." She smiled, laid out the last of the fish, and reached out to grasp his hand. "You have the respect of my clan. Of my brother and my uncle. I *love* you, Salamander. I, for one, don't want to live without you."

His smile was wary. "I thought you came here to kill me."

She hesitated. What did she say? How did she handle this? "I did. I have no love for the Sun People. I never will. You know what they did to me—did to my friends. But I have a great love for you." She swallowed hard, and added, "I wish I had never had our daughter."

"Why?" He looked truly hurt.

"Because then I could stay and fight at your side," she said proudly. "If Half Thorn came for you, he would find two warriors ready to defend you rather than one."

"Warrior?" He stared off into the distance, no doubt remembering the blow that dispatched Eats Wood.

"Warrior," she affirmed. "Come with me, warrior. In time we can work something out, some means whereby we can see Pine Drop and Night Rain."

"We?" he asked with mild curiosity.

She shrugged, as if it were nothing. "Well, somehow, over the moons, I have come to like them a little. It wouldn't displease me to see them periodically."

"Your secret is safe with me."

She gave him a slow smile, hoping against hope. "Will you come away with me?"

"Funny, isn't it? I asked that same question of Pine Drop. Not meaning quite the same thing, but with the same result. She, too, said no."

"I don't understand."

"It would be so easy, and at the same time, so hard. We could all escape the pain, Anhinga. All we have to do is give up our responsibilities. Why is that so hard? Why is it easier to stay and die than it is simply to stop being ourselves to become someone else?"

She stared at him, frowning, hearing the importance of his words but not quite understanding the weight of the ramifications.

He pointed at Wing Heart. "Isn't that what Mother did? She gave up. Her souls left her body so that they didn't have to face the pain and disappointment. Pine Drop won't stop being who she is to run off with me. I won't stop being who I am to run off with you." A faint smile bent his lips. "You won't stop being who you are to stay here with me."

I won't stop being who I am? What is he talking about? And then her gaze slipped to the covered earth ovens with their simmering cache of hemlock-laced yellow lotus root. She felt a tingle race across her skin. Panther's blood! He couldn't know, could he? If he did, why didn't he stop her? Challenge her over it?

She could feel his knowing stare burning through her skin as she avoided his gaze. *It's your nerves. If he knew, he'd never allow you to get away with this!*

She took a breath, trying to think of what to say, but her response was cut off when Yellow Spider appeared out of the night, saying, "Salamander? There is news. Mud Stalker and Deep Hunter are calling the Council to session tomorrow morning."

"I see."

Anhinga saw the slow spread of misery in his expression.

"It's serious," Yellow Spider added, his muscles bunching under his smooth brown skin. "I have contacts, people who are obliged from the Trade White Bird and I brought down river. They are going to accuse you of witchcraft tomorrow."

"I have been anticipating that." Salamander's fists opened and closed. "Cousin, no matter what, I want you to remember your promise to me that day at the canoe landing. Will you do as I ask, not as your heart demands?"

What was this? Anhinga turned her eyes on Yellow Spider. He was fidgeting, rocking his weight from foot to foot. A faint nod was his only answer.

"Good," Salamander said with a sigh.

"What are you going to do?" Anhinga asked.

Salamander's lips twitched. "I am going to try to save myself and the clans," he answered. "As we were just discussing, sometimes in order to save yourself, you must give up everything. Timing will be the most important thing." With that, he pushed himself to his feet, looking completely haggard.

"What are you going to do?" Yellow Spider demanded.

"For the moment"—silver fish scales glittered on Salamander's hand as he rubbed his face—"I am going to see Speaker Thunder Tail. After that I have a stop to make at the Serpent's. Then, if I can, I am going to try and get a full night's sleep."

Wing Heart's voice caught them by surprise. "If there is any trouble, you be sure to alert Speaker Cloud Heron. He'll handle it."

"Yes, Mother." Salamander sounded like his souls were bleeding. "I will do that first thing."

"I'm coming with you," Yellow Spider said, and for the first time, Anhinga noticed the ax hanging from his hand.

"Me too!" Anhinga cried. She hadn't made two steps before Salamander's hand caught her elbow.

"No, please," he said gently. "If you would help me, be here when I return. I won't be able to sleep tonight unless you are here to hold me."

The fear in his voice paralyzed her. She stood rooted as her husband and his kinsman walked off into the night.

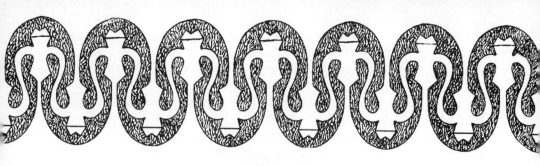

Fifty-nine

Dew gave the world a grayish tint in the pale light of dawn. Salamander prodded the smoking fire with a stick as he looked out past the pestle and mortar to the plaza. The grass had been beaten flat by the Northern Moiety players as they prepared for the game, now only three days away. Fingers of silky mist wound around the Women's House where it perched atop the Mother Mound. They drifted over the plaza and slipped between the houses like ghostly serpents on the prowl. The Bird's Head was sheathed in gray, a Spirit figure dominating the west.

He could feel the last tendrils of the Dream, like the dawn mist, slowly fading away. The vision had been so clear. He could still see the images old Heron had shown him of the coming day.

He had used the smallest sliver of mushroom. It had been enough to open the doors of his Dreams. He had reached Heron, Danced with her, and she had let him see.

Salamander poked at a coal and sniffed at the mint tea that steamed in a stone bowl at the fire's edge. In the growing light he could make out the latest of his mother's fabrics, a white, red, and purple design that sported a red potbellied owl with huge eye disks in the center.

Salamander stared into the round black eyes she had woven into the fabric. Was he still seeing through the fast-shrinking tunnel brother mushroom had opened, or was the creature really alive?

"So, we have come to it, haven't we?"

The weaving remained mute.

"Today I shall make my decision. You and Many Colored Crow must wait to see which of you I choose. Or will you take that chance? What if you just killed me? Would another be more compliant to your wishes than I am?"

The owl's large eyes pried at him, trying to see into his souls.

Salamander stepped over and inspected the fabric. He ran his fingertips over it, feeling the softness. Mother had used carefully separated flax fibers. As far as Salamander could tell, she had finished last night before retreating to her bed. Using a sharp stone flake, he cut the threads and lifted the fabric from the loom. After one last admiration, he draped it over his shoulders, then resettled himself at the fire to keep track of his tea.

His eyesight blurred with bits of the vision old Heron had granted him. The day's events unfolded like a lotus flower. He saw Pine Drop, her eyes blazing righteously as she faced the Council. Saw Back stood guard in the darkness, his souls wreathed in hate and anger. Anhinga pointed at two ceramic pots decorated with interlocking owls. Mud Stalker smiled at him in triumph. He saw the craftiness in Deep Hunter's eyes. Half Thorn gleefully clapped his hands, crying, "I win! I am to be Speaker!"

Salamander blinked hard to fracture the vision. He glanced back at his house, satisfied that Anhinga still slept soundly. After completing his errands the night before and tucking his daughter in, he had taken her to his bed. For a hand of time they had alternately held each other and coupled until she had fallen into a deep and exhausted sleep.

It was afterward that he had lifted the thin bit of mushroom to his lips and begun calling for old Heron.

The mint leaves swirled slowly in the hot water, the fresh tang flavoring the very air. In the growing light Salamander could see that the water had turned amber. Satisfied, he used an old rag to wrap his hand and moved the stone bowl to one side. Then he opened the little pouch and sprinkled a powder into the steaming liquid, making sure to keep his nose upwind of the rising steam.

He had realized that the tea was necessary to his plans when he noticed the missing ax and fitted it to the vision. Its spot in the collection of tools was ominously vacant. Coupled with the silence, he could guess at the reasons for Pine Drop's absence.

"It will be better this way," he told the morning, and glanced eastward. A glowing iridescent rose light surrounded by a softening lavender filled the northeast beyond the mist-shrouded trees across Morning Lake. Brother mushroom tugged playfully at his souls, smearing the colors in the sky.

Salamander smiled, imagining the view from the Bird's Head. It was going to be a glorious morning. He wondered how many of the people in Sun Town would take the time to enjoy it.

Mud Stalker smiled and stretched as he sat up on his bed. He could hear the murmur of voices outside, and the angle of light through the door told him that Mother Sun was nearly two hands high above the horizon.

"Is it morning?" Three Moss asked as she rolled onto her side and slitted her sleep-heavy eyes.

"It is." Mud Stalker bent his head back, feeling the bones in his neck crackle and the muscles pull.

Three Moss stretched before she threw back the elkhide, wiggled past him, and stood. The nipples on her full breasts looked like burnished copper. The width of her hips compensated for her thick waist, and the gleaming black wealth of pubic hair reminded him of bear fur.

"Would you like to eat with Mother and me before the Council meeting?" Three Moss watched him as she caught up her loose hair and pulled it back into a shock behind her head. She smiled as his gaze fixed on her taut breasts. "I would think you hadn't been with a woman for moons, Speaker. Had you forgotten what a woman's body is like?"

He chuckled. "I had indeed. Moons, yes. It's been even longer than that."

"I enjoyed myself," she told him evenly, eyes measuring. "Myself, I would have no objection to sharing a bed with you every so often."

"And your husband?" He raised an eyebrow.

"He is a hunter who prefers the swamp—and I think he spends a great many nights in beds that aren't warmed by my body."

"I see."

"For now, just consider the advantages that might be of benefit to your clan. After today, I would expect Snapping Turtle Clan to have a great deal of prestige. Frog Clan, with my influence, might be a solid ally for you, Speaker. I can't wait to tell Mother that Moccasin Leaf has agreed to return our root grounds. It will make her most happy. Almost as happy as I was several times last night."

He nodded. "I, too, enjoyed last night. At my age, and for as little practice as I have had in the last turning of the seasons, it was a delightful reminder that I'm not decrepit."

She laughed at that. "No, indeed you are not."

"But I will pass on breakfast. Give my regards to the Clan Elder. I have some things to see to before the Council meets. This is too important to allow anything to go amiss."

She nodded as she found her kirtle, wadded on the floor where it had been hastily discarded the night before. Her eyes held his as she slipped it on. "Why do men always give a woman that look when she dresses?"

"Because deep in our souls we see it as an ending rather than a beginning," he replied. "Endings are always laced with regret while beginnings are sprinkled with hope."

She stopped at the door, one hand on the cane-pole frame. "This is just the beginning, you know. After Owl Clan, you still have to unseat Thunder Tail. Deep Hunter will be thinking the same thing."

He nodded. "I have plans for him."

She smiled. "Will I see you tonight?"

He stood, making a face as his bones complained. With his good hand he recovered his breechcloth and belt. "If all goes as I hope, I was thinking of feasting the Council tonight. Invitations have already gone to the Clan Elders. Had you not been otherwise occupied last night, you would have heard."

"I see." A smile. "And after the feast, what? Politics with the Speakers?"

"Some. But after that, perhaps I would be interested in discussing some things with a Clan Elder's daughter."

"Yes, well, after last night it will be interesting to see just how long you can still paddle in my canoe, Speaker."

"Let's hope I'm not *that* decrepit."

And then she was gone.

He stood for a moment, frowning down at the smoldering embers in the fire pit. Cane Frog was old. How many seasons did she have left anyway? Was it worth a marriage to Three Moss? Or would his interests be better served with a different alliance? Perhaps one of Deep Hunter's nieces? True, they were all currently married, but, as he had come to understand so well, things could happen to a husband. Only this time, no crow was going to lead any hunter to the body.

Each time Pine Drop shot a glance in Water Stinger's direction, she fumed. How dare her mother and uncle treat her like a common captive? By blood and pus, she was their daughter! A woman married to a Speaker, one who had provided her lineage and clan with an heir! Yet here she was, treated like an errant child, who, if she pushed the issue, would end up in public humiliation when her kinsman physically prohibited her from leaving her house.

Her fire popped and crackled in the bright morning light as she continued the chore of smoking the last of yesterday's catch of fish.

It was but two days to the beginning of the solstice ceremonies. Sun Town had become a hive. People kept passing and calling solstice greetings to her. Some she knew, others were strangers. She played the game, keeping her voice light as she called polite responses. Reading their expressions, she realized that no one but her seemed aware that something sinister and brooding was being hatched. That gave her pause.

Night Rain ducked out of the house wearing a white kirtle belted at the waist. Her thick hair was parted, appropriate to her married status and pulled back over her shoulders. She had inserted long white heron feathers at an angle over her ears. As attractive as she looked, a single glance at her eyes would have been sufficient to discourage anyone from approaching her.

She walked over and crouched beside Pine Drop—so close that their thighs were touching. "We're still captive!"

"Water Stinger insists on watching my every move." Pine Drop reached over and tucked the cloth around her baby's face where the infant slept in the cradleboard. "I threw a cooking clay at him when he insisted on following me down to the borrow pit. I *don't* need my cousin peering up my rear as I squat."

"He is under Uncle's orders." Night Rain made a face. "But I'll take a cooking clay with me next time."

"I got my revenge when I changed Tadpole after her feeding."

"Tadpole?"

"It seemed more fitting for a little girl than Mud Puppy. Not only is she Salamander's child, but each time Uncle hears the name, it's going to drive him wild."

"When did you decide this?"

"Last night. She's old enough for a name, Night Rain. It's been three moons since she was born. If her souls haven't settled into her body, they never will. I think it's safe to name her now."

Night Rain ground her teeth as she studied Water Stinger. The young warrior leaned insolently against the house wall ten paces distant, face expressionless, arms crossed as he watched them.

"Why do you think Salamander killed Eats Wood?" Night Rain asked bluntly.

"*If* he killed Eats Wood—and we still don't know for a fact that he did—I would wager a moon's food that he had a good reason. Snakes! I wish I could just talk to him!"

"Did he ever flatly deny it?"

Pine Drop had been considering just that. "Now that you mention it, no. Thinking back, he very cleverly evaded the question. I need to talk to him."

"Uncle doesn't trust us when it comes to Salamander."

"You were there. Did the ax really fit the wound?"

"Perfectly." Night Rain shook her head. "I can't believe I did this to him. If I'd taken Anhinga's ax like Uncle wanted, it wouldn't have fit. The shapes are different. I looked at them very closely."

Pine Drop studied her sister. "I still don't understand why you did that."

Night Rain's shoulders rose and fell. "I don't either. Isn't it silly? I just want everything to be like it was. I want us to be a family. You, me, Anhinga, and Salamander. I should hate them, but somehow I don't. How did that happen?"

"You were happy," Pine Drop said. "We all were. Salamander made it happen."

"I didn't want to see him hurt." Night Rain lowered her head and squeezed her eyes shut. "I always do the wrong thing! I always hurt the people I love. What's the *matter* with me?"

"Do you follow your clan, or your heart?" Pine Drop asked absently. "That's partly what Salamander meant yesterday." She took a breath, coming to a decision. "All right, are you up to stopping this silliness?"

Night Rain wiped at tears that dampened her eyes. "What did you have in mind?"

"A way to save us, if you don't mind lying a little. It is sure to enrage Mother and Uncle. It may have terrible consequences for us. Uncle might even cast us out of Sun Town for it."

Night Rain was looking half-sick. "Why don't you tell me what you're thinking before I have to decide."

"I killed Eats Wood."

"*What?*"

"Uncle wants us at that Council meeting. He wants us to see Salamander charged with murder as well as with witchcraft. We are to be witnesses to his disgrace and humiliation. That way we will be docile nieces the next time he needs to marry us off for the clan's benefit."

"You mean to say that in Council? That *you* killed Eats Wood?"

Pine Drop peered coolly into her sister's shocked eyes. "Think about it. A clan is responsible for the behavior of its own. Eats Wood was a walking spineless leech. A wiggling bloodsucker who would have eventually glutted his appetite on some young woman. He was trouble waiting to happen. We agree on that, right?"

"Yes."

"Well, our story is that he came on me in the forest just after Tadpole was born. He wanted to taste my milk, wanted to slide into my canoe as he watched my naked baby's body."

"That's *disgusting!*"

"As disgusting as a man can get," Pine Drop agreed. "I had Salamander's ax that day. I had taken it from his house while I was on the way to gather firewood." Her lips quirked. "Our family has a history of getting into trouble when we're after firewood."

"Not funny."

"When I finally realized that Eats Wood wasn't just making crude jokes I was so upset and distressed that I crashed the ax through his head."

"From behind. That's the only way the ax fits."

"From behind," Pine Drop agreed, fitting that new fact into her story. "Let's see. He turned toward Tadpole, who was on the ground in her cradleboard, and I struck."

"So, how did he end up in a canoe under a root down in the Jaguar Hide's swamp."

"Because I asked Salamander to help me dispose of the body. You, Salamander, and I carried him to the canoe landing one night, and Salamander took him away. You and I had no idea where, and we didn't ask."

Night Rain looked horrified. "You would do this? Say this?"

"And you will say that it is the truth."

"Why?"

Pine Drop smiled. "Because, like you, I want to be happy again. I want to spend the rest of my life with the man I love."

"You might be giving up the chance to be Clan Elder."

"You can take my place. Most of the blame will be mine."

Night Rain gaped. "You would actually do that?"

Pine Drop nodded. "I know my husband. Whatever he did, it was done to protect someone, to keep them from harm. No matter what, Night Rain, he will not be given a fair chance in the Council. You and I both know that."

Night Rain nervously chewed her lip, her brow lined. "Uncle will know it's a lie. He will wonder why I didn't say something, do something, when I brought him the ax. Snakes! He still thinks it belongs to Anhinga."

"It was an easy mistake to make," Pine Drop said simply. "You were upset at having to steal Anhinga's ax. You ducked into Salamander's house, grabbed the first ax you found, and ran. Uncle may not believe it, but the Council will."

"Snakes, I'm already feeling scared," Night Rain muttered. "I've never done anything like this before."

"If we don't save him, Night Rain, we will hate ourselves for the rest of our lives. Do you want to live with that?"

"No, Sister. I'm with you all the way."

"Hello the camp!" a pleasant male voice called.

They turned to see Yellow Spider walking up with a drinking gourd cupped in his hands. "Salamander sends his greetings! He made tea this morning, and since there was extra, he wanted you to have this."

Water Stinger stepped forward, a keen expression on his face.

Pine Drop jumped to her feet, hurrying to meet Yellow Spider before Water Stinger could come close. She smiled into Yellow Spider's strained face and took the gourd. In a loud voice, she declared, "Thank you, Yellow Spider." In a hushed rush, she whispered. "You must tell Salamander to trust me today like I once trusted him!" With her eyes, she burned emphasis into each of her words.

"He told you to remember him fondly as you share it." Yellow Spider replied bluffly, playing his part with difficulty. The faint wink and slightest jerk of his head in acknowledgment filled her with relief.

"Would you care to join us?"

Water Stinger was now too close for subterfuge.

"I have things to do." Yellow Spider touched his forehead in respect. "But thank you for your kind offer."

"Give our husband our regards," Night Rain called in a too-shrill voice. "We will see him soon."

Yellow Spider managed a quick glance at Water Stinger, read the man's aggressive posture, and nodded before he turned on his heel and strode away.

He sent us a gourd full of tea? What is this all about? Pine Drop evaded Water Stinger's eyes and retreated to the ramada where she squatted beside Night Rain. Lifting the gourd, she sloshed the liquid and sniffed. The soothing aroma of mint filled her nose.

"He sent us tea," she said as she studied the gourd container. "Isn't that just Salamander's way? The whole world is about to fall on him with claws and fangs, and he sends us tea."

Night Rain took the gourd and drank. "It's good, too. Try some."

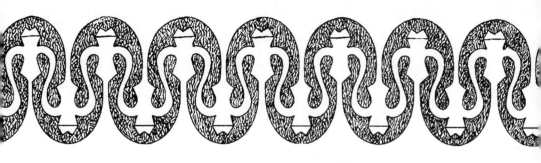

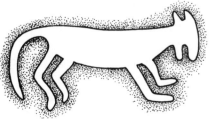

Sixty

Anhinga was wrapping clean moss around the baby's bottom when Salamander ducked through the door. He stepped over and smiled down at his daughter. Anhinga tied the thongs that bound the little girl in the fabric wrap.

"She's beautiful, isn't she?" Salamander said with longing.

"She has her mother's looks and her father's souls," Anhinga replied, and straightened. She lifted an eyebrow at the roll of clothing in his hands.

"For you." He extended them. "If you would put this on before you leave, anyone who sees you, even from a distance, will believe you to be a member of Owl Clan."

She read the tension he tried so hard to hide. "It has really come to that?"

Hating to, he gave her a short nod.

"You and I, Husband, are not like the others. We know that life is neither fair nor predictable." She ran her fingers along his face as she stared into his eyes. "Perhaps Power places us where we are for specific reasons, as your Masked Owl would have you believe. I will go the moment Yellow Spider assures me that Saw Back is otherwise occupied."

"Thank you," he said unsteadily.

"You made me promise," she recalled. "And now I will make you promise something."

"What is that?"

"Come to me." She bent down and kissed him gently on the lips. "You are the bravest man I know. If you live through this, I will be waiting for you at the Panther's Bones."

"I promise. If I live, I will come to you," he whispered. "Never forget my love for you."

From outside, Yellow Spider's worried voice called, "Salamander?"

"It is time." He turned reluctantly, then looked back, haunted eyes pleading with hers.

"Go, my husband," she told him simply. "Or come with me now, and we will leave this all behind us."

"We are who we are," he whispered, and ducked out the door.

For a long moment, Anhinga's heart seemed to sink right through her body and into the muddy earth. She closed her eyes, feeling the hammering of loneliness closing around her.

How long she stood, she couldn't say. Then a voice penetrated her benumbed souls. "Salamander?"

Her frantic thoughts searched and placed a name with the voice. "Little Needle? Is that you?"

A round and youthful face appeared in the doorway. "Has Salamander gone to the Council?"

"He has." Anhinga smiled at the boy. "But he asked me if I saw you, to ask you for a favor. He would like you to do something for him."

"He's Clan Speaker," Little Needle answered. "He can just order it."

"That's not Salamander," she told him warmly, "and you know it."

Little Needle smiled with an apparent wistfulness. "I know."

Anhinga pointed to the two large ceramic pots resting on cane matting beside the door. "Do you see those pots? The ones with the owl designs on the side? They need to be delivered, Little Needle. One needs to be placed at Speaker Deep Hunter's fire, and the other set inside Mud Stalker's doorway. You are *not* to do two things. First, you are not to sneak a taste! Do you understand?"

At the boy's solemn nod, she added, "And you are *not* to mention this to anyone! Not to the Speakers, and certainly not to Moccasin Leaf. Salamander wants to tell the Speakers of this special gift in his own way. Do you understand why that might be?"

Little Needle, big-eyed, jerked another nod.

"Good. Salamander thinks very highly of you, you know."

"I know." His voice sounded small.

"If you could place those pots without being seen, it would make the surprise even bigger. Could you do that?"

"I think so."

"Good." She smiled at him, thought for a heartbeat, and reached for the little red chert owl that Salamander had been carving. Finished, but for the polishing, the little potbellied figure was cool in her hand. "In return for your service, I want you to have this. It's to remember Salamander by."

Little Needle studied the little owl she dropped into his hand, and tears welled in his eyes. "Thank you, Anhinga. I'll do it." He swallowed a sob. "For him. No one will see me, I promise."

A terrible battle raged in Mud Stalker's souls as he surveyed the huge crowd that had gathered around the Council House. He wanted to pace back and forth irritably, to release the rampant energy that powered his bones and muscles. But he dare not. He had waited all of his life for this moment, planned of it, Dreamed of it. If Snapping Turtle Clan was to be ascendant, he must show himself and Sweet Root as controlled, steady, confident, and worthy of leadership.

His souls screamed to be about this last great task. He nodded to people as he met their eyes, keeping his face calm and possessed. He kept his bad arm cradled, struggling to project the countenance of a serene Speaker faced with a difficult task. The mighty weight of the clans was poised, watching, waiting with him.

Where are Pine Drop and Night Rain? The question ate at him as he looked at Sweet Root. His sister stood to one side, her back resting against one of the poles. She had a sour look on her face, her darting eyes betraying her growing anxiety.

Mud Stalker turned, looking across at Owl Clan's contingent. Moccasin Leaf's face was pinched, her eyes glittering. Beside her, Half Thorn had a stupid smile on his lips. He was greased, dressed in a fine white breechcloth with a purple-dyed cape over his shoulders. He had stuck so many white heron feathers into his hair that he looked like a bristly flower.

That is the man I am going to make Speaker of Owl Clan. Not even the elevation of Salamander had filled him with such disgust. *Ah, Wing Heart, if only your souls had stayed around to see this. But, perhaps it is better that they have fled. As great as you were, it is better that you have escaped the humiliation.*

At Alligator Clan's spot, Deep Hunter fretted. He reminded Mud Stalker of a male dog standing over a pile of scraps. He was anxious to growl and show his teeth, but he was unsure whom to snap at. Colored Paint was talking in low tones to Sour Mouth and Saw Back in the shaded rear where the rest of the lineage leaders were gathered.

Mud Stalker centered his attention on the young warrior with the misshapen face. Saw Back's eyes might have been hot stones. He kept smiling in that lopsided manner he had adopted, and his gaze kept turning to Owl Clan, as if in anticipation of his enemy's arrival.

In Frog Clan's spot, Three Moss was leaning to speak into her mother's ear, her hand on the old woman's bare shoulder. It would speak volumes through the silent movement of fingers against the old woman's skin on this day.

Clay Fat looked miserable, as if he'd eaten something for breakfast that disagreed with him. Clan Elder Turtle Mist's head was tilted his way, her mouth moving as she spoke in obvious irritation. Clay Fat was the only unknown. He might vote either way. Not that it mattered, with Cane Frog in hand Mud Stalker had his majority.

Eagle Clan's Thunder Tail sat beside Stone Talon, a brooding darkness behind his stiff face. He seemed not to see or hear anything but the plodding thoughts slipping between his souls.

Enjoy yourself today, Leader, it will not be many moons from now before I take your place.

A stir in the crowd was the only warning before Salamander pushed through the throng and walked into the eastern entrance. A sudden hush fell on the Council House as all eyes turned toward him.

Salamander seemed unreasonably calm, as if he had no idea what lay in store for him. He wore a simple brown breechcloth while a spectacularly dyed fabric draped from his shoulders. Wing Heart's work, most definitely. Mud Stalker could almost feel the owl's eyes staring back from the design.

To Mud Stalker's surprise, Salamander called some sort of greeting to Saw Back. The latter just glared in return.

A half heartbeat later, Salamander nodded to Yellow Spider, and the warrior slipped away through the crowd.

What was *that* all about?

It was then that Water Stinger appeared at his elbow. "Speaker?"

"Yes, what is it? Where are Pine Drop and Night Rain?"

"Sick, Speaker."

Mud Stalker blinked, trying to absorb the information. "What do you mean, sick?"

Water Stinger looked truly mystified. "They were fine until a half hand of time ago. Then, all of a sudden, Night Rain threw up. A moment later, so did Pine Drop. I put them in their beds, but they are not well. Their eyes are all wrong, their pupils have grown large. The worst thing is, Speaker, they are delirious, talking to people who are not there."

"What?"

"I think it is some kind of fever, but their bodies are not hot, and they aren't sweating. It's just the opposite. They feel cool to the touch, breathing slowly. You would think they were more corpses than alive."

"Attention! Your attention, please! I think we are all here," Thunder Tail called as he stepped out into the open by the smoldering central fire. "This Council has been called to deal with a most serious matter."

Mud Stalker pushed Water Stinger away in irritation, trying to recapture the string of his thoughts. "We'll have to do without them. Go, Cousin. Be ready for my signal." He stepped forward, waiting to be acknowledged by the Leader.

Thunder Tail raised his voice, trying to be heard by as many as possible. "It has been alleged by some that Speaker Salamander of Owl Clan has been involved in witchcraft, his spells and attacks having been leveled against not only his own relatives, but others as well."

A ripple of conversation rolled through the crowd. Mud Stalker tried to keep the smile of satisfaction from his lips.

"That is not the only charge." Thunder Tail looked from face to face around the Council. "Speaker Salamander's third wife, the woman known as Anhinga, is believed to have murdered a young man named Eats Wood, a member of the Snapping Turtle Clan."

Another eruption of conversation followed.

"These are serious charges!" Thunder Tail gave Mud Stalker a hard stare. "Who makes these charges?"

Mud Stalker and Sweet Root stepped forward, crying in unison, "We do!"

Deep Hunter also stepped out, not to be left behind, and cried, "Alligator Clan makes these charges."

"As does Frog Clan!" Cane Frog's reedy voice barely carried across the circle.

To everyone but Mud Stalker's surprise, Moccasin Leaf strode out, and cried, "So does Owl Clan!"

All eyes turned to Clay Fat, who stood uncomfortably and stepped out from under the palmetto-and-cane roofing to squint in the sun. "Rattlesnake Clan is unsure. We would hear the evidence."

Mud Stalker had been hoping for just that request. He raised his hand high over his head, the signal to Water Stinger. "Snapping Turtle Clan will address the murder of our young warrior first." Give them a brutally murdered corpse to start with, and the less substantive charges would follow of their own accord.

A buzz of voices and a stirring of the crowd preceded the six strong young men who came forward at a trot. Between them they bore Eats Wood's mud-caked canoe. Red Finger came striding along behind, a cardinal-feather cloak over one shoulder, his creamy white breechcloth swinging with each step. Sunlight glistened on his gray hair.

The canoe was borne through the eastern entrance and laid carefully on the ground at Mud Stalker's feet.

Mud Stalker glanced around the Council. "I would have this Council recognize my cousin, Red Finger. It was he who found Eats Wood's canoe."

As Red Finger recounted his story about the pesky crow, Mud Stalker's souls delighted at the expressions he saw in the audience. People were truly captivated and awed.

Red Finger finished and produced the little round white stone. He held it between thumb and forefinger as he turned so that all could see it.

Mud Stalker cried, "What are we to learn from this? Power wanted Eats Wood's murderer found!"

He glared hard at Salamander, expecting to see some reaction: embarrassment, guilt, confusion, something. The young Speaker just stood as if listening to a discussion of the weather.

Mud Stalker gestured with his left hand. "When my kinsmen returned with the canoe and Eats Wood's bones, we were at a loss. Why would this have happened? Who would have hidden his canoe and his body in the Swamp Panther lands? Why there?" He turned his head, directing everyone with his hard stare.

Salamander waited with his head cocked, paying attention, but unconcerned.

"Following the trail to its logical end," Mud Stalker continued as he stepped carefully back and forth behind the canoe, "we sent my niece, Night Rain, to obtain the Swamp Panther woman's ax."

He bent down and picked it up from the bones within the canoe.

Sweet Root lifted Eats Wood's skull, saying, "If you will look, you can see the fatal wound. Here." Her brown finger pointed to the oblong hole in the round dome of the skull. "Not only was Eats

Wood murdered by this ax, but if you will notice, he had to have been struck down from behind!"

Mud Stalker aligned the ax just so, while Sweet Root placed the skull so that all could see the perfect fit. At Clay Fat's scowl, Mud Stalker said, "Oh, don't worry. You will all have plenty of time to see how well this fits."

Clay Fat shook his head. "You might have used Anhinga's ax *after* you found the skull. This proves nothing!"

"Look at the mud in the wound!" Sweet Root cried. "If you crush a dirty skull, the bone breaks cleanly and has a different color. You know that." She pointed at Saw Back. "It's not as if we don't know this woman's handiwork with an ax!"

"Agreed! *Agreed!*" Deep Hunter cried. "We would have dealt with this once before, but for certain interference with this Council."

Again, all eyes turned to Salamander. His expression was thoughtful, his eyes almost dreamy, as if he had seen this all before.

Clay Fat muttered under his breath and shot a worried look at Salamander.

"Does the Speaker for Owl Clan have *anything* to say about this?" Thunder Tail asked gravely.

In his preoccupied manner, Salamander stepped forward. He paused for a moment, studied the ax in Mud Stalker's hand. The way he smiled it might have been a private joke. In a firm voice, he said, "That is not Anhinga's ax."

Mud Stalker realized he was staring—dumbfounded as the rest. "What? Night Rain herself took this ax from your house!"

"That is not Anhinga's ax," Salamander repeated. "If you are familiar with her ax, it has a series of panthers carved into the handle in an interlocking design."

"Then whose ax is it?" Deep Hunter demanded.

"It is my ax," Salamander said casually. "For reasons of her own, Night Rain took my ax from the house that day."

"Anhinga killed Eats Wood with your ax?" Mud Stalker wondered.

Salamander smiled as if in benevolence to a simple fool. "Anhinga killed no one, Speaker."

"Wait!" cried Clay Fat as he stepped out, one hand up. "Yes, that ax fits the hole in the skull. But, let us keep in mind, there are many axes! Axes, by their nature, are all roughly the same size. What if we tried fitting every ax in Sun Town to that wound? How many matches would we have? Tens of tens? More? This proves nothing!"

"It proves *everything!*" Mud Stalker thundered back.

"Speakers, please!" Salamander stepped forward, his hands up. "Let me speak."

Thunder Tail jerked a nod. "The Owl Clan Speaker has the right to speak."

Salamander threw a fond smile in Clay Fat's direction. "I thank you for your open mind, Speaker Clay Fat. It is refreshing to find yet another individual who thinks in terms of the People before he thinks of his own personal gain. For that, I am truly obliged in my souls."

"Who killed Eats Wood?" Mud Stalker shouted.

"Hush!" Thunder Tail ordered.

Salamander turned, his head cocked. In the open circle he didn't look like much—just a short skinny young man with large dreamy eyes and a knowing expression. "For reasons which need not concern this Council, I killed Eats Wood, Speaker."

Mud Stalker stopped short. "Why?"

"As I said, my reasons do not concern this Council. Further, I take full responsibility for my actions. Speaker Mud Stalker, I will see you later to discuss a mutual settlement for Eats Wood's death." He looked at Thunder Tail. "May I continue and address the other more serious charge of witchcraft?"

"You may," Thunder Tail said with a wary gravity.

Salamander walked around the fire pit in slow steps, expression pinched, as though searching for the right words.

When he finally looked up, he said, "Speakers, Elders, there are those among you who will be anxious, sit here in Council for hours telling stories about the reasons for my brother's death, about my mother's curious soul loss, about my dealings with Jaguar Hide, and so many other things. If we go through with this, you will hear how I sit atop the Bird's Head every morning to watch the sun rise. You will hear that I helped the Serpent with the care and preparation of the dead. Depending on how far some people are willing to go in pursuit of my destruction, there may be even wilder stories to be told." He looked at them, one by one, and added, "I don't care."

"What do you mean, you don't care?" Deep Hunter asked irritably.

"What I said, Speaker." Salamander turned to face him. "I don't care." A pause. "Let us speak honestly, shall we? This Council meeting is really about who will replace Owl Clan in the leadership. Removing me and placing Half Thorn in the Speaker's position will benefit both Snapping Turtle Clan and Alligator Clan. I have heard that Moccasin Leaf will return Frog Clan's root grounds in return for her vote to convict me of witchcraft." He faced Cane Frog, saying, "I congratulate you in getting your root grounds back, Elder."

Mud Stalker barely noticed Three Moss's fingers playing on the old woman's shoulder.

"What are you saying?" Clay Fat asked. "That declaring you a witch is part of a deal?"

"I am saying that I quit," Salamander replied. "If this is allowed to ferment, it will spoil. What we do here today will affect the future. If I act one way, I can destroy the clans. If I act another, Mud Stalker and Deep Hunter will be at war within a turning of the seasons. We are that close to disaster! So, I will choose a third way. I will just give up the Speakership."

"What?" Thunder Tail asked, looking confused.

"Last night when I asked you to allow me to speak uninterrupted, Leader, it was to give me the chance to tell my enemies that they win. Rather than fight them in a destructive and divisive battle that, innocent or not, I cannot win, I will give up everything. It is my only defense, Speaker."

"Defense how?" Clay Fat asked. "It sounds more like a confession!"

"Agreed!" Deep Hunter growled.

Salamander made a calming gesture. "A *real* witch is interested only in harming others, in accruing wealth, prestige, and authority. A witch wants admiration, respect, and status more than he wants life. That, or he wants revenge."

"Revenge for what?" Thunder Tail asked.

"That is a very good question, Speaker." Salamander stopped to stare down at Eats Wood's bones. "Revenge for what was done to my brother? How does one get revenge on lightning? Masked Owl killed him to keep him from planting those goosefoot seeds and changing the People. Revenge for my mother's soul loss? Do you take revenge on a woman because she can't stand her grief? Or perhaps I might want revenge for having been made a Speaker?" He gave Mud Stalker a thin smile. "Indeed, there might be some merit in that." A pause. "No, not even for being thrust into this position. I certainly wouldn't want revenge for having to live with my three beautiful wives."

"Then why are you casting spells?" Sweet Root asked.

"*I have cast no spells!*" Salamander spread his arms wide in a gesture of innocence. "Clan Elder, you have committed yourself to this course of action. Deals have been concluded. Promises made. You and the others have invested so much in this that though I am *not* a witch, you must declare me one. A fine predicament you find yourselves in. How do you declare Speaker Salamander to be a witch when he isn't?"

He held up a hand, stifling Sweet Root's outburst, and cried, "To solve this problem and release you from the trap you laid for yourselves, I will leave Sun Town forever. As soon as I settle my obligation to Snapping Turtle Clan, I will be gone. It saves you the odious chore of having Half Thorn murder me. It keeps peace between my lineage and his. It ensures that there will be no whispers through the coming seasons that you murdered an innocent man."

"Why?" Deep Hunter asked. "It means you will lose everything."

Salamander's eyes expanded like dark pools. "Yes, Speaker. I lose everything. I willfully and freely lose so that, unhindered, you may pursue your schemes in search of prestige and authority."

"You can't just let them win!" Clay Fat protested.

"Old friend of my mother's," Salamander said warmly, "I can, and I must. I have seen the future, and I know the price I must pay to save it. I ask you to vote to recognize Half Thorn as Speaker of Owl Clan until this Council is called tomorrow."

"*Salamander!*" Water Petal cried in disbelief, pushing past the stunned Moccasin Leaf. "What are you doing?"

He smiled at her. "Saving us all, Cousin. When Masked Owl called on me to make one choice, and Many Colored Crow called on me to make another, I could accede to neither."

"What are you talking about?" Mud Stalker asked as he stepped forward and spun Salamander around.

The youth's eyes might have been watching him from a midnight eternity. "There will be no cities of stone built by the People. But we will not be Dreamers locked away in the One, either. The Brothers will continue to squabble, but they will do so at another place, in another time."

"What is he saying?" Sweet Root demanded.

"*Hear* this!" Salamander cried, breaking away. "*Remember* these words! Tomorrow, when this Council meets, I ask you to recognize the voices of reason. Our strength has always been found in harmony among the clans. Your responsibility is simple! Just do what is right for the People." With a sad smile, he added, "May the rest of your solstice celebration be filled with joy."

In a lower voice, he said, "Speaker Mud Stalker, I will join you for your feast tonight if that is all right. We can discuss Eats Wood and what is a proper settlement for his death."

Mud Stalker was still gaping as Salamander touched his forehead in respect and walked out the western exit. The crowd parted for him like a wave as he passed.

"What did he just do?" Deep Hunter asked.

"I haven't the faintest idea," Cane Frog answered.

"What about Eats Wood?" Sweet Root demanded.

Thunder Tail gave her scathing look, and said, "That is between you and Salamander. It is no longer the business of this Council."

"I win!" Half Thorn clapped his hands gleefully. "I am to be Speaker!"

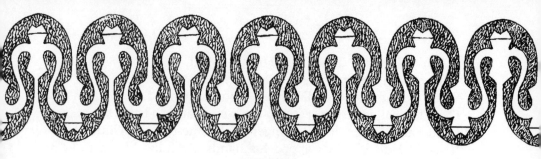

Sixty-one

When Salamander arrived that evening, the inside of Pine Drop's house was lit by faint flickers of fire from the central hearth. Someone had been coming to check on both women; the baby had been freshly changed, and, he assumed, fed by a wet nurse. Where he crouched at the bedside, Salamander could hold each of his wives' hands. The chill in their flesh cooled his hot palms.

He took that moment to study their faces, knowing how they were locked in the Dream. They were both so beautiful. How had he ever been so lucky to have been the subject of their smiles? He would carry the feel of their warm bodies against his even after his souls finally journeyed to the Land of the Dead.

"Relax," he whispered. "Don't be frightened. You are Dreaming. I used a potion of morning glory in the tea and covered it with the taste of mint. I knew what you would try to do. I couldn't let you claim to have killed Eats Wood. It would have ruined both of you. Your clan would never forget, never forgive. In the end, it would have cost you everything. I couldn't allow that. Not when I love you both so much."

He thought he saw a faint frown on Pine Drop's brow. "I give you my Dream for the People. Take it and make it yours. You shall become a great Clan Elder. I have seen these things come true."

Night Rain's lips twitched when he turned to her.

"You shall become the greatest of them all, Night Rain. Your sons will take the Trade across the whole world. Generations will speak your name with respect."

Night Rain sighed from deep in her Dreams.

"Take good care of my sons when they are born. I wish that I could stay and watch them grow. I wish that so much that my souls ache with the longing. But I have to finish my affairs with your uncle."

He smiled down at them, their soft skin under his fingers. "I have to leave now. In the meantime, I want you to fly. Just relax. Set yourselves free. Open your wings and drift into the air. Soon, we shall all be flying together."

Did he see a faint smile on their lips?

His daughter lay in her cradleboard, dark eyes watching him. The infant's arms were free, and she reached out with chubby hands, grasping for Salamander.

"I shall miss you, too, little one," he replied softly. "I just came to tell all of you that leaving you behind is the hardest thing I will ever do."

He bent, touching his lips to Night Rain's, then Pine Drop's. Finally, he stood, stepped over to his daughter, and traced his fingers along the softness of her rounded cheeks. "Live long and well, little one. When you feel a warm caress in your Dreams, it will be me."

Then he ducked out into the night, walking in the shadows at the edge of the borrow pit, smelling the rank water. He kept his head down, aware of the fires and the crowds of people moving back and forth between the houses.

"*For everything there is a price.*" Heron's words rang in his souls.

They would live because of him, because of what he was about to do. When solstice came next summer, Sun Town would be alive, vibrant, and children would be playing and laughing here. His wives would be smiling, and his children would not know fear, hunger, and grief.

As he had known they would be, several young warriors were posted around Mud Stalker's house to keep off the curious on this most important night.

"It is Salamander," he said to Water Stinger. "I have come to make a settlement with Speaker Mud Stalker."

Saw Back, a looming shadow in the darkness, said, "I want you to know, I personally am going to be dealing with you later tonight. Following that, I am hunting down that Swamp Panther bitch to pay her back. And, the day after solstice, the clans are going south to raid. Owl Clan will no longer control the sandstone. We have a debt to settle with Jaguar Hide."

Salamander told him. "What you do after this night is no longer my affair. My business here is with the Speakers and Elders."

"Pass," Water Stinger told him coldly. "I, too, will be waiting to deal with you. And, while you are in there, know that I was Eats Wood's friend."

"Yes, he has found a great many friends in death, hasn't he?" Salamander felt the man bristle in the darkness as he passed.

Without ceremony, he ducked through Mud Stalker's door to find the interior well lit by the central hearth. Mud Stalker and Sweet Root sat at the back. Cane Frog and Three Moss to the right, while Deep Hunter, Colored Paint, Moccasin Leaf, and Half Thorn were to the left. All of them looked up as Salamander settled himself at the last open space between them.

"We expected you to have run by now," Mud Stalker greeted jovially.

Food had just been set out. Two large ceramic pots were filled with baked lotus roots. A steatite bowl rested at the side of the fire, black drink steaming its invitation. The bark platters and gourd cups that were being passed back and forth had stopped short at his arrival.

"Good evening," Salamander greeted, nodding from one to the next. "Please, do not let me interrupt. Continue with your feast."

Mud Stalker scooped up some of the root paste. "What did you do to yourself today, Salamander?"

"What I had to, Speaker. Just as I have since the moment you made me Speaker."

"You are Speaker no longer," Half Thorn remarked arrogantly.

"No. I am nothing now."

"Did you really kill Eats Wood?" Mud Stalker demanded. "Or was that a trick to save your barbarian bitch?"

"I could not let him cut my unborn daughter from Anhinga's raped and murdered body, Speaker." Salamander hesitated, seeing the design on the clay-tempered pot beside the fire. The interlocking owls couldn't be mistaken. There, beside it, stood its twin. He smiled, feeling the last pieces of the future falling into place.

"Where is Anhinga?" Deep Hunter demanded. "We went looking for her today. No one has seen her."

"She is far to the south." His gaze remained fixed on the two pots. "After tonight, the ghosts that plague her will be laid to rest."

"What is this about?" Cane Frog asked, her single white eye on Salamander. "Why did you just give up that way?"

Salamander watched Moccasin Leaf scooping the thick root paste from the pot and piling it on her wooden plate. "I had a vision after the Serpent's cleansing last winter. Brother mushroom is not to be treated lightly. Some of you will remember when I was so sick? I fell so deeply into the tunnel I couldn't find my way back. There, in the Dream, I was dying."

"I don't understand," Half Thorn muttered.

"You never will," Salamander replied. "A Spirit Helper came to me, Danced with me. She showed me bits and pieces of the future. Seeing is tricky. A great many things may change. People make decisions that alter the way events may unfold."

"Now we are to believe that you are a seer?" Sweet Root asked derisively as she scooped some of the paste into her mouth.

"We have already discussed belief once today, Clan Elder. You may believe what you wish."

"So"—Deep Hunter waved a taunting hand—"tell me of this future you saw."

"There were so many futures," Salamander said carefully. "Different visions of what might be. That is one of the lures of the One. When you Dance, you see different futures as you spin about. But, to get back to your request, we could have followed Many Colored Crow's vision and made Sun Town influential beyond your most exotic imaginings. It would have happened under a great leader who bound our entire world together through Trade and war. Sun Town would have grown to cover a huge area. Other towns would have been built up and down the length and width of the river—as far as canoes can travel."

"A great leader?" Mud Stalker asked. "Just one?"

"All that authority," Salamander agreed, "all placed in one person who passed it on to his heir."

Mud Stalker was smiling grimly, seeing himself in that place.

"What about this other future?" Cane Frog asked.

"Other futures," Salamander corrected. "In some, my decision would have driven the clans into open warfare. Within moons, bodies would lie among the houses, and in the ensuing battles, the clans would be split, dispersing, raiding each other until Sun Town is only a memory. A no-man's-land where we kill each other on sight."

"Never," Colored Paint muttered under her breath. "Stop trying to frighten us."

"Alligator Clan would win anyway," Deep Hunter cried, smacking a hand to his thigh. He dipped a handful of pasty root from one of the jars and sucked it from his fingers, heedless of the hot stares of the others.

"What future did you choose?" Three Moss asked, glancing meaningfully at Mud Stalker.

"I chose a third way. I stopped at the Serpent's last night and obtained a bit of mushroom. Just enough to open the tunnel. Old Heron answered my call, and we Dreamed. Peculiar, isn't it? So many lines of Power, so many paths to the future ran through me. With one decision I would have been the greatest Speaker ever, uniting the People under Owl Clan. With another, I could have Danced and Dreamed the One. This place, and our People, would have evaporated in a few turnings of the seasons. They hadn't counted on my finding a third way."

"You?" Deep Hunter laughed. "The greatest Speaker ever?"

Salamander ignored him. "Tomorrow a new Council will be chosen. The lesson that we have taught them will survive for another five or ten generations, and then, as Morning Lake fills with mud, and the beliefs that we learned here spread, the people will slowly move away. In the end, Sun Town will be left to the forest, and the center of our world will move to other places, other peoples. Clans, peoples, and leaders will rise and fall. The meaning of our earthworks will change. Great Dreamers will carry the words of Masked Owl and Many Colored Crow across the land. Old Heron will sit in her cave, and watch the Tree of Life grow as she Dreams the One."

"So," Mud Stalker asked, "tell me, *Seer*, which clan will be preeminent in the next turning of the seasons?"

"Until Thunder Tail dies, Eagle Clan will be preeminent. Following that Clay Fat will lead the Council until his death. Only then, after many turnings of seasons, will he be followed by Clan Elder Pine Drop."

Both Mud Stalker and Deep Hunter erupted into guffaws, slapping their legs, as they eyed each like kestrels over a grasshopper.

Of them all, only Cane Frog, perhaps seeing more through her blind eye, remained serious. "Why, Salamander? Why would any of us in this room vote Clay Fat into the leadership?"

"You won't. Tomorrow you will all be dead." Salamander smiled ironically. "That is the lesson that we will teach this day. Harmony between the clans must be maintained. Fortunately, there are young leaders ready to fill our positions."

"Our positions?" Half Thorn asked. "I am already Speaker in yours."

"Yes." Salamander nodded pleasantly. "Enjoy it while you can." He indicated the pot before him. "May I share your bounty, Speaker?"

"By all means." Mud Stalker gestured with his good hand before he scooped more from the pot. "You know, Salamander, that despite your announcement today, we can't just let you go. It isn't just the matter of Eats Wood, but, as we were discussing before your arrival, we cannot allow you just to wander about."

"We would be uncomfortable," Deep Hunter added, "knowing that you were out there, talking to people, giving them ideas."

"We are afraid you might find allies," Cane Frog explained. "Bring them back to challenge the authority of the clans."

Moccasin Leaf gave him a humorless smile. "We are sorry, Salamander, but you are too dangerous. Of course, the people, Water Petal, and Yellow Spider, will think that you left in secret. Water Stinger and Saw Back will make sure that no one discovers your body."

He nodded, feeling a stone-heaviness in his heart. "Well, I shall hope that this last meal will be as good as it looks."

Mud Stalker smiled past hard eyes. "It is excellent! A solstice gift. I found it here upon my return. And then Deep Hunter brings a pot just like the first. Yellow lotus, our traditional feast, but seasoned heavily with mint, honeysuckle, and some strange tang that I cannot identify."

"Water hemlock," Salamander supplied with a numbness in his souls.

"Hemlock? The poison?" Moccasin Leaf cried, then burst into peals of laughter. "I see, you made a joke, Salamander. A grand joke indeed."

"Yes. A joke worthy of Masked Owl himself," he answered, and used his fingers to dip into the rich mixture of roots Anhinga had baked. Before the first debilitating cramps, he would make sure that he took an ample serving out to share with Saw Back and Water Stinger.

A hard day's paddle to the south, Anhinga bent over a handful of flickering fire that guttered in the ceramic pot she carried. Moths continued fluttering out of the darkness to circle her fire until the heat and flames engulfed them.

"He will be coming to us, little one," she told the infant at her breast.

Anhinga smiled at the thought. "You should know, Daughter, that Salamander is the most cunning of all men. He will come to us. You will see. His enemies will not defeat him in the end."

She turned her head, looking back in the direction of Sun Town, imagining the countless fires, the masses of people preparing for the celebration.

And there, among them, Deep Hunter and Mud Stalker would be feasting. Bowfin, Mist Finger, and the rest would finally allow her to Dream in peace.

Anhinga ran a finger along her daughter's cheek, an empty sadness deep in her breast. The elation she had expected didn't rise to bubble and froth between her souls. She had struck the Sun People, obtained her revenge. It left her hollow.

"As the endless seasons pass, little one, it shall be my secret." Anhinga looked out at the black night. "If they accuse me, I shall deny it. It is the price I shall pay for success."

She did not see the looming shadow of the great barred owl who sat in the tree above her, watching, guarding, and mourning.

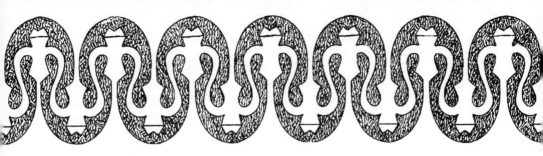

Epilogue

Pine Drop was having one of those aggravating days. They happened sometimes. A full turning of the seasons had passed since she had set fire to both her mother's and uncle's houses. A full cycle since Mother Sun had fled south and come back north—since the day she had watched fire consume Salamander's house and bones. That day after solstice had been marked by so many funereal fires. Bobcat, responsible for the ceremonies, as well as the preparation of the dead, had been sorely pressed to manage it all.

Had it been that long since she had held Salamander? Felt the hammering of his heart against hers? The hollow wound in her souls felt as painful as if it had been yesterday. But life went on.

As on this troublesome day.

That morning she had caught Tadpole splashing her hands in the large hide bag where the acorns were leaching. Pine Drop had looked just in time to make a desperate dash and pull the child back as she bent down to drink a mouthful of the poison-laden water.

Little Mud Puppy, three moons old now, had been squalling from his cradleboard like a wounded bobcat every time she turned around. Feed him as she might, the tiny infant burped, went to sleep for a couple of fingers' time and woke up squalling again.

Water Petal had been by to see if anyone had seen Wing Heart. The old woman had taken to rambling aimlessly around Sun Town. Where once she only talked to Cloud Heron and White Bird, now she was heard muttering to Salamander, too. That latter was particularly upsetting for both Pine Drop and Night Rain.

That morning a canoe load of Swamp Panthers had arrived from the Panther's Bones. Anhinga and Striped Dart had sent requests for certain fabrics in Trade for the once-a-moon shipment of sandstone. It might have originally been Owl Clan's Trade, but Anhinga preferred to deal with Pine Drop because of their former relationship. And, fulfilling what had become a ritual between them, Anhinga had sent Night Rain another bundle of firewood as a gift. When the canoe left, it carried a stone-headed ax from Night Rain in return.

Pine Drop had been interrupted no less than five and ten times that morning to settle petty little squabbles between the lineages, and one major one that involved Frog Clan.

"Pine Drop?" Night Rain's urgent voice called from outside.

"What now?" she cried, exasperated.

"Come quick!" Night Rain stuck her face in the doorway. "Canoes! Tens of tens!"

"Whose?" Pine Drop asked, a hand to her aching back as she straightened. Wisps of loose hair tickled her face.

"Barbarians! Traders! With bulging canoes! They have entered Morning Lake and headed for the Turtle's Back before even announcing themselves!"

"Where is our husband?"

Night Rain gave a faint shrug. "Headed for the canoe landing, no doubt. You'll find him there—along with everyone else in Sun Town. I just asked Little Egret to keep track of my son. She will probably watch your children, too." And then she was gone.

Pine Drop ducked out into the mottled sunshine created by a cloud-dotted sky. Little Egret sat next to a cradleboard under the ramada; Night Rain's baby boy gurgled and cooed from its restraint. "Cousin, could you watch my children? I must see to the Traders."

"Yes, Clan Elder," the girl replied.

Pine Drop fought the urge to run—that being inconsistent with her status. She joined the flow of excited people, fending off questions, as they passed the ridges, rounded the Men's House, and walked down to the canoe landing.

Recognizing her, people touched their foreheads and stepped back, allowing her to pick her way through the beached canoes to the waterfront. Council Leader Clay Fat had beaten her there, and was staring out from under the flat of his hand.

"Who are they?" Pine Drop asked—and fought to keep her jaw from dropping. So *many* canoes! It took her three tries to count them all. Three tens and four! All filled with oddly dressed strangers who wore their hair in buns. Sun Town had never seen such a thing.

"What is this?" Yellow Spider asked, elbowing his way to her side.

"Traders? Barbarians."

"Does anyone recognize them?" Water Petal asked as she pushed next to Yellow Spider.

"I do," Yellow Spider said warmly. "I see old friends out there. Come, let's take a canoe and greet them."

"Take a canoe out to the Turtle's Back?" Water Petal shot him a worried look.

"The water's too deep to wade. But you could swim out if you were determined not to take a canoe." Yellow Spider turned, searching the faces around them. "Little Needle! Go and find the Serpent, we have a cleansing to attend to." He smiled at Pine Drop. "Help me push this canoe out."

She looked at him askance as Night Rain slipped through the pack to join them.

The fact that they took Sour Mouth's canoe—because it was the closest—gave Pine Drop a feeling of satisfaction. The man had a bobwhite's brains when it came to sense.

I am not prepared for this. I look like I've been processing food all day long. "Quick," she asked, "do I have smears all over my face?"

"You're beautiful," Yellow Spider called from behind her."

"Don't give her airs," Night Rain shot back. "She's hard enough to deal with as it is."

Nevertheless, Pine Drop took a moment to reach over the side and scoop up a handful of water to sponge her face with. She smoothed her hair and wished she'd taken the time to grab a cloak.

Yellow Spider's sure strokes guided their canoe across the intervening water and onto the bank just down from the rows of Trade canoes on the beach. Pine Drop stepped out, helping to drag their craft ashore. Then she took her place at Yellow Spider's side as they walked toward the gathered strangers. A smaller group stood off to one side, dressed differently; a tall young woman spoke to two men in low tones.

A big fellow stepped out from the big group. Muscles packed his sweat-gleaming skin. In guttural pidgin, he called, "Yellow Spider! By the Wolf, it's good to see you again!"

"Hazel Fire! My kinsman!" Yellow Spider burst out, and charged forward, clapping the man in a violent embrace.

"Wolf People! Yes! That *is* Hazel Fire!" Water Petal cried before hurrying forward. "And there is Gray Fox, and I'd know Two Wolves anywhere."

Pine Drop waited her turn and, Night Rain at her side, was introduced to a great many young men with odd-sounding names.

"And these people," Hazel Fire added, pointing, "met us on the river. They, too, were coming to bring Trade."

Pine Drop turned her attention to the party at one side. Indeed, they were dressed differently, wearing carefully tailored hide tunics designed with quillwork. Pine Drop stepped forward, calling, "Welcome to Sun Town."

"It's good to be home," the young woman replied. Tall, attractive, she stood beside a muscular man and surveyed the crowd onshore. Her gaze had centered on Clay Fat, a frown lining her forehead. "My husband and I have come to Trade with Speaker Salamander, of the Owl Clan. Is he here?"

"You don't speak like a barbarian," Pine Drop observed. Why was she so familiar?

The attractive woman turned her gaze back from Clay Fat, her eyes measuring. "I would hope not, Pine Drop."

"Spring Cypress?" It took her a moment to place the face.

"The same, but I am of the Wash'ta now. You may have met my husband, Green Crane." She pointed behind her, "And back there is Always Fat, returned for more Trade."

"You are married to Green Crane?"

"She is, and with great status, thanks to Salamander," Green Crane told her in Trade pidgin. "We have canoes full of Trade to give to Salamander."

"As do we," Hazel Fire called. "I swear, we have stripped our country for you. Stone, furs, medicines, copper, dried meats, exotics from the far north, stone hoe blades, points, siltstone, you name it! It is all Salamander's."

"Salamander's?" Night Rain asked, hiding a stricken expression. "Why?"

Hazel Fire extended his hand. A small carved stone owl was pinched between his thumb and forefinger. "When we left here, two summers ago, he saw into the future and gave us a warning. We heeded his words. And used our warriors"—Hazel Fire made a slashing motion—"to open the river. Our Trade will flow freely now."

Yellow Spider shot Pine Drop a quick look, and said, "My cousin, Salamander, is dead. An accident at last summer's solstice ceremonies. Water hemlock, we think. Someone wasn't careful when they were harvesting lotus root. I am Speaker for Owl Clan now. Water Petal is Clan Elder. In Salamander's name, we bid you welcome."

Hazel Fire seemed stunned. Spring Cypress and Green Crane,

too, might have just been slapped, given their expressions. Spring Cypress looked down at her palm. Pine Drop could see the small red stone owl resting there.

She stepped forward, souls whirling as she reached up to touch the little stone owl that hung from her necklace. "I am Clan Elder Pine Drop, of Snapping Turtle Clan. In Salamander's name, we bid you welcome. Before my sister and I married Speaker Yellow Spider, Salamander was our husband." A pause. "*My* husband."

"How?" Hazel Fire demanded. "Power filled him! He spoke with the animals! How can someone who can see the future be killed by such a simple thing?"

"Because of the little stone owl you bear, you will hear what I have never told to a living soul. He died to save the People." She had their attention now. "That night I was sick, my souls floating outside of my body. The Serpent had come, listened to my heart, looked into my eyes, and felt how cold my skin had become. He told people that I was dying. My souls saw a great many things that night. I spoke with Many Colored Crow and Masked Owl. They told me what Salamander had done and why."

Hazel Fire shifted, shooting a nervous glance at Yellow Spider, then back at her.

"I flew that night," she told them. "Across from me in the sky, I could see Night Rain, sailing through the air on owl wings. Then out of the clouds, I heard Salamander's voice say, 'It is all right, my wives. I have fixed everything. I am going now.' At the sound of his voice, I knew he was dead. The last thing I heard was the echo of First Woman's voice, calling him to her cave."

She smiled, feeling the tendrils of Salamander's Dream spinning through time to this place. "I felt his touch that night, as did Night Rain. And in that instant I understood. From that moment on, I spoke with Salamander's voice. So, hear him, when I bid you welcome to Sun Town, the center of the world. You are part of his Dream, and we are obliged by your presence."

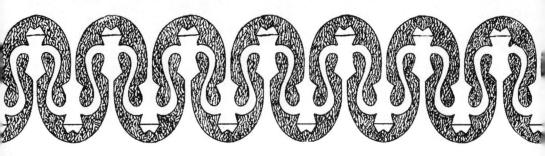

Bibliography

Alden, Peter
1999 *National Audubon Society Field Guild to the Southeastern States*. Alfred A. Knopf. New York, New York.

Amos, William H., and Stephen H. Amos
1985 *The Audubon Society Nature Guides Atlantic & Gulf Coasts*. Alfred A. Knopf. New York, New York.

Brecher, K. S., and W. G. Haag
1980 "The Poverty Point Octagon: World's Largest Prehistoric Solstice Marker?" *Bulletin of the American Astronomical Society*. 12:886.

Brian, Jeffrey P.
1988 *Tunica Archaeology*. Papers of the Peabody Museum of Archaeology and Ethnology No. 78. Harvard University Press. Cambridge, Massachusetts.

Brown, Calvin S.
1992 *Archaeology of Mississippi*. Reprint of 1926 edition. University Press of Mississippi. Jackson, Mississippi.

Bruseth J. E.
1980 "Intrasite Structure at the Clairborne Site." *Louisiana Archaeology*. 6:283–318.

Byrd, Kathleen M.
  1991 *The Poverty Point Culture: Local Manifestations, Subsistence Practices, and Trade Networks.* Geoscience and Man 29. Louisiana State University Press. Baton Rouge, Louisiana.

Coffey, Timothy
  1993 *The History and Folklore of North American Wildflowers.* Facts on File. New York, New York.

Connaway, John M., Samuel O. McGahey, and Clarence Webb
  1977 *Teoc Creek, a Poverty Point Site in Carroll County, Mississippi.* Archaeological Report No. 3. Mississippi Department of Archives and History. Jackson, Mississippi.

Duncan, Wilbur H. and Marion B. Duncan
  1988 *Trees of the Southeastern United States.* University of Georgia Press. Athens, Georgia.

Fagan, Brian M.
  2000 *Ancient North America,* 3rd ed. Thames and Hudson. New York, New York.

Foster, Steven, and James A. Duke
  1990 *Eastern/Central Medicinal Plants.* Peterson Field Guides. Houghton Mifflin Company. Boston, Massachusetts.

Fritz, Gayle J.
  1997 "A Three-Thousand-Year-Old Cache of Crop Seeds from Marble Bluff, Arkansas." In *People, Plants, and Landscapes: Studies in Paleoethnobotany,* edited by Kristen J. Gremillion, pp. 42–62. University of Alabama Press. Tuscaloosa, Alabama.

Gibson, John L.
  1980 "Speculations on the Origin and Development of Poverty Point Culture." *Louisiana Archaeology.* 6:319–348.

  1987 "The Poverty Point Earthworks Reconsidered." *Mississippi Archaeology.* 22(2):14–31.

  1991 "Catahoula—An Amphibious Poverty Point Manifestation in Eastern Louisiana." In *The Poverty Point Culture: Local Manifestations, Subsistence Practices, and Trade Networks,* edited by Kathleen M. Byrd, pp. 61–88. Geoscience and Man No. 29. Louisiana State University Press. Baton Rouge, Louisiana.

  1996 "Religion of the Rings: Poverty Point Iconography and Ceremonialism." In *Mounds, Embankments, and Ceremonialism in the Midsouth,* edited by R. C. Mainfort and R. Walling, pp. 1–6.

Arkansas Archaeological Survey Research Series No. 46. Arkansas Archaeological Survey. Fayetteville, Arkansas.

1998 "Broken Circles, Owl Monsters, and Black Earth Midden: Separating Sacred and Secular at Poverty Point." In *Ancient Earthen Enclosures of the Eastern Woodlands*, edited by R. C. Mainfort and L. P. Sullivan. University Press of Florida. Gainesville, Florida.

1999 *Poverty Point: A Terminal Archaic Culture in the Lower Mississippi Valley.* 2nd ed. Anthropological Study 7. Department of Culture, Recreation, and Tourism. Louisiana Archaeological Survey and Antiquities Commission. Baton Rouge, Louisiana.

2000 *The Ancient Mounds of Poverty Point: Place of Rings.* University Press of Florida. Gainesville, Florida.

Gibson, J. L., and J. W. Saunders
1993 "The Death of the South Sixth Ridge at Poverty Point: What Can We Still Do?" *SAA Bulletin.* 11(5):7–9.

Haag, W. G.
1990 "Excavations at the Poverty Point Site: 1972–1975." *Louisiana Archaeology.* 13:1–36.

Hillman, M. M.
1990 "1985 Test Excavations of the 'Dock' Area of Poverty Point." *Louisiana Archaeology.* 13:1–33.

Hirth, K. G.
1978 "Interregional Trade and the Formation of Prehistoric Gateway Communities." *American Antiquity.* 43(1):35–45.

Hudson, Charles
1976 *The Southeastern Indians.* University of Tennessee Press. Knoxville, Tennessee.

1979 *Black Drink: A Native American Tea.* University of Georgia Press. Athens, Georgia.

Jackson, H. E.
1991a "Bottomland Resources and Exploitation Strategies During the Poverty Point Period: Implications of the Archaeological Record from the J. W. Copes Site." In *The Poverty Point Culture: Local Manifestations, Subsistence Practices, and Trade Networks*, edited by Kathleen M. Byrd, pp. 131–158. Geoscience and Man 29. Louisiana State University Press. Baton Rouge, Louisiana.

1991b "The Trade Fair in Hunter-Gatherer Interactions: The Role of Intersocietal Trade in the Evolution of Poverty Point Culture." In *Between Bands and States,* edited by S. A. Greg, pp. 265–286. Occasional Papers 9. Center for Archaeological Investigations, Southern Illinois University at Carbondale. Carbondale, Illinois.

Kidder, Tristram.
2002 "Mapping Poverty Point." *American Antiquity.* 67:89–101.

Lazarus, W. C.
1958 "A Poverty Point Complex in Florida." *Florida Anthropologist.* 6(1):23–32.

Mainfort, Robert C., and L. P. Sullivan
1998 *Ancient Earthen Enclosures of the Eastern Woodlands.* University Press of Florida. Gainesville, Florida.

McEwan, Bonnie G.
2000 *Indians of the Greater Southeast.* University Press of Florida. Gainesville, Florida.

Morgan, William N.
1999 *Precolumbian Architecture in Eastern North America.* University Press of Florida. Gainesville, Florida.

Neuman, R. W., and N. W. Hawkins
1987 *Louisiana Prehistory.* Department of Culture, Recreation, and Tourism. Louisiana Archaeological Survey and Antiquities Commission. Anthropological Study 6, 2nd ed., revised. Baton Rouge, Louisiana.

Pearson, James L.
2002 *Shamanism and the Ancient Mind.* Altamira Press. Walnut Creek, California.

Penman, John T.
1980 *Archaeological Survey in Mississippi, 1974–1975.* Archaeological Report No. 2. Mississippi Department of Archives and History. Jackson, Mississippi.

Purrington, R. D.
1983 "Superimposed Solar Alignments at Poverty Point." *American Antiquity.* 48:157–161.

Purrington, R. D., and C. A. Child, Jr.
1989 "Poverty Point Revisited: Further Consideration of Astro-

nomical Alignments." *Journal of the History of Astronomy.* 13: 49–60.

Sassaman, Kenneth E.
1993 *Early Pottery in the Southeast.* University of Alabama Press. Tuscaloosa, Alabama.

Schlotz, Sandra C.
1975 *Prehistoric Plies: A Structural and Comparative Analysis of Cordage, Netting, Basketry, and Fabric from Ozark Bluff Shelters.* Arkansas Archaeological Survey No. 6. Arkansas Archaeological Survey. Fayetteville, Arkansas.

Smith, Brent W.
1974 "A Preliminary Identification of Faunal Remains from the Clairborne Site." *Mississippi Archaeology.* 9:1–7.

1976 "The Late Archaic-Poverty Point Steatite Trade Network in the Lower Mississippi Valley." *Louisiana Archaeological Society Newsletter.* 3:6–10.

1981 "The Late Archaic-Poverty Point Steatite Trade Network in the Lower Mississippi Valley: Some Preliminary Observations." *Florida Anthropologist.* 34:120–125.

Smith, Bruce D.
1992 *Rivers of Change: Essays on Early Agriculture in Eastern North America.* Smithsonian Institution Press. Washington, D.C.

Swanton, John R.
1979 *The Indians of the Southeastern United States.* Reprint of the 1946 Bureau of American Ethnography Bulletin No. 137. Smithsonian Institution Press. Washington, D.C.

1998 *Indian Tribes of the Lower Mississippi Valley and Adjacent Coast of the Gulf of Mexico.* Dover reprint of 1911 edition. Dover Publications. Mineola, New York.

2001 *Source Material for the Social and Ceremonial Life of the Choctaw Indians.* University of Alabama Press. Tuscaloosa, Alabama.

Thomas, Cyrus
1985 *Report on the Mound Expeditions of the Bureau of Ethnography.* Reprint of the 1894 Bureau of American Ethnography No. 12. Smithsonian Institution Press. Washington, D.C.

Thomas, Prentice M., and L. J. Campbell
1978 *The Peripheries of Poverty Point.* New World Research Report

of Investigation No. 12. New World Research. Pollack, Louisiana.

Tiamat, Uni M.
1994 *Herbal Abortion Handbook*. Sage-femme! Press. Peoria, Illinois.

Vogel, Virgil H.
1970 *American Indian Medicine*. University of Oklahoma Press. Norman, Oklahoma.

Webb, Clarence H.
1968 "The Extent and Content of Poverty Point Culture." *American Antiquity*. 33:297–321.

Webb, Clarence H., and J. L. Gibson
1982 "Studies of the Microflint Industry at the Poverty Point Site." In *Traces of Prehistory: Papers in Honor of William G. Haag*, edited by F. H. West and R. W. Neuman, pp. 85–101. Geoscience and Man 22. School of Geoscience. Louisiana State University Press. Baton Rouge, Louisiana.

1970 "Intrasite Distribution of Artifacts at the Poverty Point Site, with Special Reference to Women's and Men's Activities." *Southeastern Archaeological Conference Bulletin*. 12:21–34.

1982 *The Poverty Point Culture*. Geoscience and Man 17. 2nd ed., revised. Geoscience Publications, Department of Geography and Anthropology. Louisiana State University Press. Baton Rouge, Louisiana.

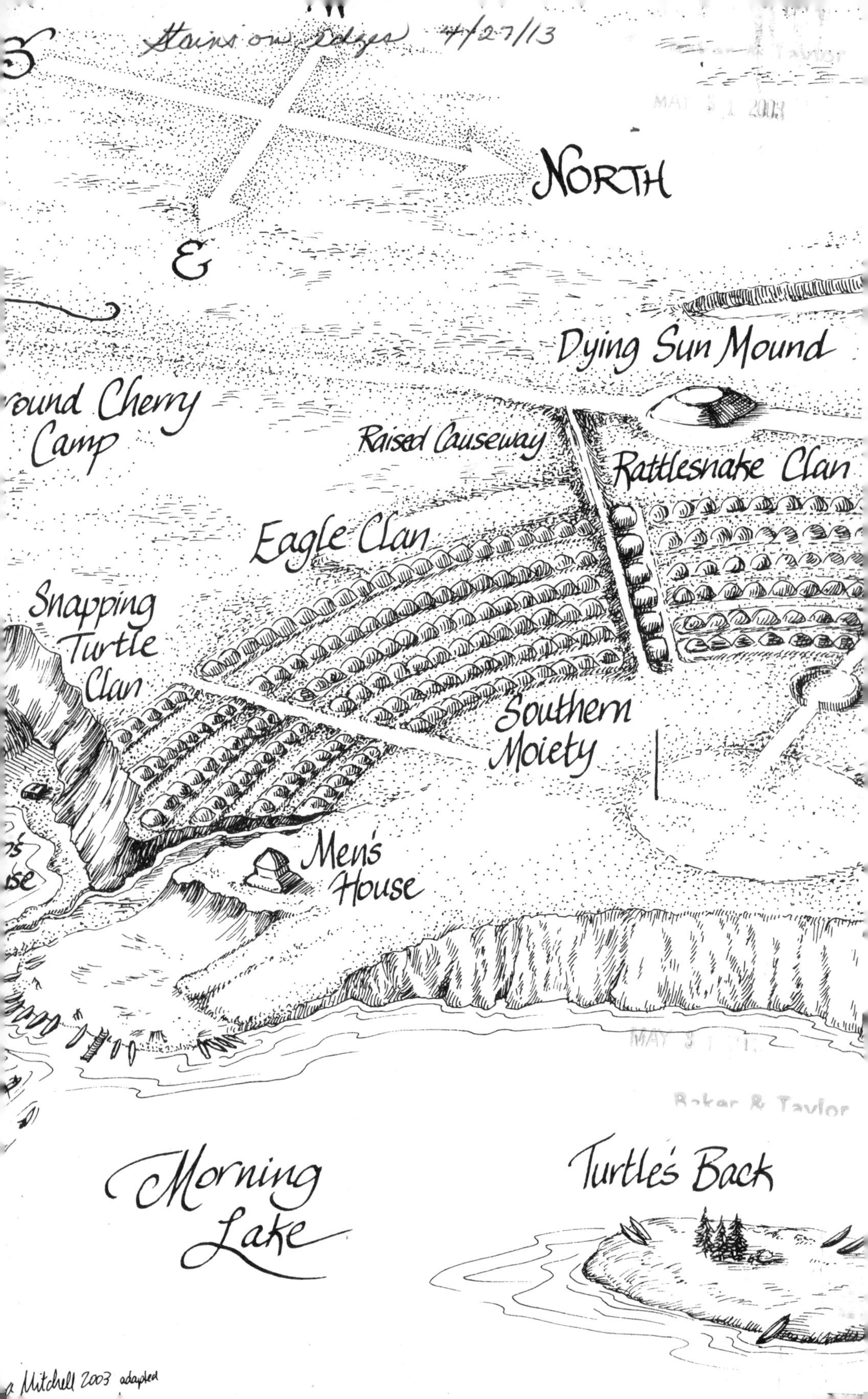

Stairs on Edges 4/27/13

S

NORTH

E

Dying Sun Mound

ound Cherry
Camp

Raised Causeway

Rattlesnake Clan

Eagle Clan

Snapping
Turtle
Clan

Southern
Moiety

Men's
House

Morning
Lake

Turtle's Back

a Mitchell 2003 adapted